W9-BMR-642

MEDICUS

MEDICUS

A Novel of the Roman Empire

RUTH DOWNIE

BLOOMSBURY

Copyright © 2006 by Ruth Downie

All rights reserved. No part of this book may be used or reproduced in any manner whatsoever without written permission from the publisher except in the case of brief quotations embodied in critical articles or reviews. For information address Bloomsbury USA, 175 Fifth Avenue, New York, NY 10010.

Published by Bloomsbury USA, New York
Distributed to the trade by Macmillan

All papers used by Bloomsbury USA are natural, recyclable products made from wood grown in well-managed forests. The manufacturing processes conform to the environmental regulations of the country of origin.

THE LIBRARY OF CONGRESS HAS CATALOGED THE HARDCOVER EDITION AS FOLLOWS:

Downie, Ruth, 1955–
Medicus : a novel of the Roman Empire / Ruth Downie.—1st U.S. ed.
p. cm.
ISBN-13: 978-1-59691-231-1 (alk. paper) (hardcover)
ISBN-10: 1-59691-231-6 (alk. paper) (hardcover)
1. Rome—History—Empire, 30 B.C.–476 A.D.—Fiction. I. Title.

PR6104.O94M44 2006
823'.92—dc22
2006013179

Originally published in the United Kingdom in 2006 by Michael Joseph, a division of Penguin Group UK
First published in the United States by Bloomsbury USA in 2006
This paperback edition published in 2008

Paperback ISBN-10: 1-59691-427-0
ISBN-13: 978-1-59691-427-8

1 3 5 7 9 10 8 6 4 2

Typeset by Westchester Book Group
Printed in the United States of America by Quebecor World Fairfield

To Andy, with love

MEDICUS

A NOVEL

IN WHICH our hero will be . . .

baffled by
- Tilla, a slave
- Merula, a bar owner
- Quintus Antonius Vindex, a recruit
- a family of native Britons

alarmed by
- Bassus, Merula's security guard
- Stichus, another of Merula's security guards
- a woman with chins
- Secundus, a builder
- Elegantina, a lady wrestler

assaulted by
- a soup bowl
- a senior centurion
- a trowel
- a fire

amused by
Rutilia the Elder
Rutilia the Younger, her sister

followed by
a dog
Albanus, a clerk
a barber's son

surrounded by
the Twentieth Legion, Valiant and Victorious
patients
women
mice

tempted by
Chloe, one of Merula's girls

sworn at by
Daphne, another of Merula's girls

avoided by
a barber's mother-in-law

harangued by
(in his memory) Claudia, his ex-wife
(in person) a signaler's girlfriend
(in letters) Lucius, his brother

annoyed by
Valens, a colleague
Claudius Innocens, a businessman
Priscus, an administrator
a civilian liaison officer
Justinus the whistler
a brothel-keeper on the Dock road

ignored by
his stepmother
his half sisters

informed by
a mortuary assistant's assistant
Decimus, a hospital porter
a barber
a barber's wife
Lucco, Merula's kitchen slave
Lucius Curtius Silvanus, a slave trader

mothered by
Cassia, his sister-in-law
Centurion Rutilius's wife

moved to sympathy by
Saufeia, one of Merula's girls
Asellina, one of Merula's girls
the signaler
Phryne, a slave
Tadius, a house slave

and ruled by
the Emperor Trajan
the Emperor Hadrian

O diva . . .
serves iturum Caesarem in ultimos
orbis Britannos.

Oh Goddess,
safeguard Caesar as he sets off for the remotest
regions of the Earth—Britain.
—Horace

1

SOMEONE HAD WASHED the mud off the body, but as Gaius Petreius Ruso unwrapped the sheet, there was still a distinct smell of river water. The assistant wrinkled his nose as he approached with the record tablet and the measuring stick he had been sent to fetch.

"So," said Ruso, flipping the tablet open. "What's the usual procedure here for unidentified bodies?"

The man hesitated. "I don't know, sir. The mortuary assistant's on leave."

"So who are you?"

"The assistant's assistant, sir." The man was staring at the corpse.

"But you have attended a postmortem before?"

Without taking his eyes off the body, the man shook his head. "Are they all like that, sir?"

Ruso, who had started work before it was light, stifled a yawn. "Not where I come from."

The description should come first. Facts before speculation. Except that in this case much of the description was speculation as well.

Female, aged . . . He spent some time frowning over that one. Finally he settled on *approximately* 18–25 *years. Average weight. Height . . . five feet one inch.* At least that was fairly accurate. *Hair: red, scant.* That too, although it might not be very helpful if no one had ever seen her before without a wig. *Clothing: none found.* So no help there, then.

Three teeth missing, but not in places that were obvious. Someone would need to know her very well indeed to give a positive identification from that.

Ruso glanced up. "Did you go over to HQ for me?"

"I told them we'd got a body and you'd send the details over later, sir."

"Did you ask about missing persons?"

"Yes, sir. There aren't any."

"Hm." This did not bode well. Ruso continued working his way down the body, making notes as he went. Moments later his search was rewarded. "Ah. Good!"

"Sir?"

Ruso pointed to what he had found. "If somebody turns up looking for her in a month's time," he explained, "we'll be able to tell them who we buried." He recorded *Strawberry birthmark approximately half an inch long on inside of upper right thigh, eight inches above the knee,* and sketched the shape.

When he had completed the description, Ruso scratched one ear and gazed down at the pale figure laid out on the table. He was better acquainted than he wished to be with the dead, but this one was difficult. The water had interfered with all the signals he had learned to look for. There was no settling of the blood to indicate the position in which the body had been left, presumably because it had rolled over on the current. The limbs were flexible, so that meant . . . what? Men who died in the stress of battle often froze and then relaxed again much faster than was normal. So if the woman had been frightened or struggling . . . On the other hand, how would the aftermath of death be affected by cold water? He scratched his ear again and yawned, trying to think what he could usefully write on the report that would not cause more distress and confusion to the relatives.

Finally he settled on *Time of death: uncertain, estimated at least 2 days before discovery* and gave his reasons.

He glanced up at the assistant's assistant again. "Can you write legibly?"

"Yes, sir."

He handed the tablet and stylus across the body.

"Place of death," he dictated, then corrected himself. "No, put *Location of body.*"

The man laid the tablet on the end of the table, hunched over it, and repeated, *"Location . . . of . . . body"* as he scraped with awkward but determined obedience.

"Found five hundred paces downstream from the pier, in marshes on the north bank," said Ruso, wishing he had carried on writing himself.

"F . . . found . . . five hundred . . ." muttered the man, suddenly breaking off in midsentence to look up and say, "She could have drowned a long way upstream and come down the river, sir. But then, she might have gone in farther along and come up on the tide."

"Pardon?" Ruso blinked, taken aback by this sudden display of initiative.

Moments later it was apparent that although this soldier knew nothing about hospital administration and very little about writing, he had devoted his spare time to learning everything there was to know about the local fishing. The assistant's assistant's detailed description of all possible points of waterborne departure that could end in an arrival in the marshes on the north bank of the River Dee left Ruso baffled, but one thing was clear. In a land where coastlines shifted in and out and rivers flowed backward twice a day, anything that floated could end up a very long way from where it fell into the water.

"Point of entry into water unknown," he dictated.

The man paused. "I didn't get the bit before that, sir." Ruso repeated the location of the body. The man wiped a scrape of wax off the end of the stylus with his forefinger, flicked it away, and began to write.

There was a bird chirping in the hospital garden and a murmur of voices. Ruso glanced out the window. On the far side of the herb beds an amputee practiced with his crutches while orderlies hovered at each elbow, ready to catch him. A soft breeze wafted in, fluttering the lamps that had been placed on slender black stands around the table, burning for the soul of the unknown figure laid out beneath them.

The lamps lurched wildly as the door was flung open. The assistant's assistant looked up and said, "It's not her, Decimus," but the intruder still hurried to the table to look for himself.

Ruso frowned. "Who are you?"

The man clasped both hands together and continued staring at the body.

"Have you lost someone?"

The man swallowed. "No. Not like this, no, sir."

"Then you'd better leave, hadn't you?"

The man backed toward the door. "Right away, sir. Sorry to interrupt, sir. My mistake."

Ruso followed him across the room and barred the door before turning to the assistant. "Is there a missing person that HQ doesn't know about?"

The man shook his head. "Take no notice of Decimus, sir. He's just one of the porters. He's looking for his girlfriend."

"In the mortuary?"

"She ran off with a sailor, sir. Months ago."

"Why look in here, then?"

The man shrugged. "I don't know, sir. Perhaps he's hoping she's come back."

Ruso, not sure if this was an attempt at humor, tried to look the man in the eye, but the attention of the assistant's assistant remained firmly on the writing tablet.

Ruso looked down at the body. "Write, *Cause of death*."

The stylus began to scratch again. "Cause of . . ."

"We'll start from the head down."

"We will start . . ."

"No, don't write that."

"Sir?"

"Just write *Cause of death*. Nothing else yet."

He frowned at the girl's head. The fishermen who brought the body in had sworn that they had done nothing to it, but Ruso was at a loss to explain the girl's hair. At first he had thought she was simply unfortunate. Now, on closer examination, he realized the patchy baldness was not natural. He ran one finger across the bristly scalp.

"Is this some sort of a punishment, do you think?"

"Perhaps she cut it off to sell it, sir," suggested the orderly.

"This isn't cut, this is practically shaved."

"Lice, sir?" suggested the orderly, suddenly sounding hopeful. "Maybe she went down to the river to wash out the lice and drowned."

Ruso took a deep breath of fresh air before bending down and holding the lamp closer to the body.

"She didn't drown," he said, lifting the girl's chin with the tip of one finger. "Look."

2

RUSO WAS STILL pondering the body in the mortuary as he walked out of the east gate of the fort. He was barely aware of his progress until he was abruptly recalled to his surroundings by a shout of "Get up!" from farther up the street. A man with a large belly was glaring at a grimy figure lying across the pavement just past the fruit stall. A woman with a shopping basket put down the pear she was examining and turned to see what was going on.

The man repeated the order to "Get up!" The woman stared down at the figure and began to babble in some British dialect. The only word Ruso could make out was "water."

"Burn some feathers under her nose," suggested the stallholder, bending down to retrieve a couple of apples that had tumbled off the edge of his display.

Ruso veered into the street to avoid the commotion and narrowly missed a pile of animal droppings. He frowned. He must try and concentrate on what he was doing. He had come out for a walk because he was unable to sleep. Now that he was walking, he was having trouble staying awake.

At the open shutters of Merula's he ordered the large cup of good wine he had been promising himself for days. When it came it was nothing like the Falernian it was supposed to resemble. He scowled into its clear depths. At that price and in this place, he supposed it was as good as could be expected. In other words, not very good at all.

The doorman watched as he drained the wine without bothering to add any water, and asked him if he would like to meet a pretty girl.

"Not before I've been to the baths," Ruso grunted. "Are you still serving those oysters?"

"Not today, sir."

"Good."

"I'm sorry, sir . . . ?"

"So you should be."

Ruso wondered whether to explain that a dish of Merula's marinated oysters was the indirect cause of his present unkempt state and uncertain temper. He decided not to bother.

Yesterday, strapping a poultice around the foot of a groom trampled by his horse, he had composed an imaginary notice for the hospital entrance.

"To all members of XX Legion Valeria Victrix. While the chief medic is on leave, this hospital has three officers. The administrative officer has gone shopping in Viroconium and taken his keys with him. One doctor has severe food poisoning. The other is doing his best, despite having no idea what's going on because he has no time to attend morning briefings. Until reinforcements arrive, nonurgent cases and injuries resulting from drunkenness, stupidity, or arguments with drill instructors *will not be treated*."

Before the sun had fully risen today he had been presented with a seized back, a dislocated elbow, three teeth in the hand of a man who wanted them replaced, and the body. When he pointed out that the body was beyond his help, he was told that they didn't know what else to do with it.

Mercifully Valens—a paler and thinner version of the Valens who had eaten the oysters—had reported for duty this afternoon. Peering at Ruso, he'd announced, "You look worse than I do. Go and get some rest." Ruso, who had been desperate to sleep for the past three days, suddenly found himself unable to settle down.

A group of youths with army haircuts was sauntering across the street toward Merula's. As they entered Ruso murmured, "Don't touch the seafood." He was gone before they could reply.

Passing the bakery, he realized that he couldn't remember the last time he had eaten. He bought a honey cake and crumbled it against the roof of his mouth as he walked along.

Ahead of him, a chorus of excited voices rose in the street. He recognized the fat man, still shouting orders in a thick Gallic accent. The female who had collapsed had now attracted a sizeable crowd. They seemed to be carrying her to the fountain. Ruso tossed the last fragments of cake to a passing dog and strode on in the direction of the amphitheater. It was nothing to do with him. He was not, at this moment, a doctor. He was a private citizen in need of some bath oil.

He took a deep breath before diving into the perfumed dusk of the oil shop. He had placed his flask on the counter and was naming what he wanted when the shopkeeper's attention was caught by something behind him. The man snatched up a heavy stick and leaped out from behind the counter, yelling, "Clear off!" The dog that had finished Ruso's cake shot out from behind a stack of jars and scuttled off down the street.

The shopkeeper replaced the stick under the counter. "Somebody ought to do something about those dogs."

"Are they dangerous?"

"Only when they bite. Now, what was it you were after?"

Outside, half a dozen pairs of hands were dragging a limp body along the pavement to where the fountain, a large and ugly stone fish, was spewing water into a long rectangular tank.

The shopkeeper glanced up from the jug he was pouring. "Something's going on over there."

Ruso heard a splash as he said, "A woman fainted in the street."

"Oh." The man twisted the stopper into the flask and wiped the side with a cloth. Ruso handed over a sestertius. As the man counted out the change, more people began crowding around the fountain. Voices drifted across the street.

"Get up, you lazy whore!"

"Give her another dunk!"

"If you burn some feathers—"

"Stand her up!"

"Lie her down!"

"Lie her down? She does nothing but lie down!"

Ruso dropped the coins into his purse and emerged into the fresh air. He was not going to offer to help. He had been caught like that before. Poor people, like stray dogs, bred huge litters they couldn't look after and latched on to you with the slightest sign of encouragement. As soon as the whisper went around that some doctor was treating people for free, every case of rotten teeth and rheumatism within a thousand feet would be rounded up and thrust under his nose for inspection. He would be lucky to get away before nightfall.

A voice whispered in his memory—a voice he hadn't heard for almost two years now—a voice accusing him of being cold-hearted and arrogant. He silenced it, as he usually did, by recalling other voices. The Tribune's praise of his "commendable single-mindedness" (of course Valens had to ruin it later by explaining, "He meant you're boring"). Or the officer's wife who had smiled at him over her sprained ankle and said, "You're really quite sweet, Petreius Ruso, aren't you?" That memory would have been more comforting, though, if she hadn't been caught in the bed of the chief centurion a week later and been sent back to Rome in disgrace.

Raising his fingers to sniff the smear of perfumed oil, Gaius Petreius Ruso headed back the way he had come.

The sharp crack of a hand on flesh rang down the street.

"On your feet! Move!"

A pause.

"Throw some more water on her."

A splash. A cry of, "Hey, mind my new shoes!"

Laughter.

Ruso pursed his lips. He should have stayed up at the fort. He could have helped himself to some of Valens's oil and used the hospital baths. Now he would sit in the steam room wondering what had happened to the wretched woman, even though he wasn't responsible for it.

"Wake up, gorgeous!"

More laughter.

If he managed to revive her, those comedians would take the credit.

"Turn her over!"

If he didn't, he would get the blame.

There was a sudden gasp from around the fountain. Someone cried, "Ugh! Look at that!"

A child was pawing at her mother's arm, demanding, "What is it? I can't see! Tell me what it is!"

Ruso hesitated, came to a halt, and promised himself it would only be a quick look.

The military belt was an accessory with magical powers. Several of the onlookers disappeared as soon as it approached. The rest parted to let its wearer through, and Ruso found himself staring down at his second unfortunate female today. This one was a skinny figure lying in a puddle by the fountain. She was still breathing, but she was a mess. The rough gray tunic that covered her was the same color as the bruise under one eye. Blood was oozing from her lower lip and forming a thin red line in the water that still trickled down her face. Her hair was matted and mud-colored. She could have been any age between fifteen and thirty.

"We're giving this girl some water, sir," explained someone with an impressive grasp of understatement.

"She's fainted," added someone else.

"She always faints when there's work to be done," grumbled the man who had been shouting at her. He bent as far down as his belly would allow and yelled in the girl's ear, "Get up!"

"She can't hear you," remarked Ruso evenly. His gaze took in the copper slave band around the girl's upper right arm. Below the elbow, the arm vanished into a swathe of grimy rags. The pale hand emerging at the other end was what had silenced the crowd. It was sticking out at a grotesque and impossible angle. Ruso frowned, unconsciously fingering his own forearm. "What happened to her arm?"

"It wasn't us!" assured a voice in the crowd. "We was only trying to help!"

The grumbler turned his head to one side and spat. "Silly bitch fell down the steps."

"Fell down the steps, *sir,*" corrected Ruso, restraining an urge to seize the man by the ear.

"Yes, sir. Didn't look where she was going, sir."

"It should have been set right away."

"Yes, sir."

"Get it done."

"On my way now, sir."

The girl groaned. The man grabbed her good arm and hauled her to her feet. She fell against him. Caught off balance, he struggled to stay upright.

Ruso was uncomfortably aware that he was now at the center of this entertainment. Whatever he did, he must not admit to being a doctor. Nor did he intend to waste his afternoon being soaked and muddied by dragging a sick slave around.

"You there!" He pointed to a greasy-haired youth who was lolling against a wall trying to dislodge something from his ear with his forefinger. "Yes, you! Give him a hand."

The youth withdrew the finger, opened his mouth to argue, then thought better of it. He slid a reluctant hand under the girl's good arm. He and the girl's owner began to drag the limp body along the pavement.

Ruso scowled at the crowd, which began to disperse.

"The fort's the other way!" he shouted after the owner.

No reply.

He overtook them, blocking the path. The trio paused. The girl slumped lower.

"She needs to go to the fort hospital. Now."

"Yes, sir," agreed the owner. "But the thing is, sir . . ."

The thing was that he was short of cash. The girl's last owner had driven away with a cartload of his best-quality woolens and palmed a slave off on him who was lazy and useless. Now she had gone and broken her arm and he couldn't even sell her. A harder man would have thrown her out into the street, but everyone knew Claudius Innocens was a man too soft for his own good. He knew the hospital at the fort had an excellent reputation—"Get on with it!" prompted Ruso—but it was too expensive for a poor trader. He had heard there was a good healer on the Bridge road. He was going there now.

"I just have to do a little business on the way, sir," he added. "So I can pay for the treatment."

Ruso had only been stationed in Deva for four days, but already he knew that the local healer wouldn't be able to do anything with that arm. He said nothing. It was not his problem. He had only come out for a drink and a flask of bath oil. The girl's face was horribly pale: she probably didn't have long left anyway. The healer would have henbane, or mandrake. Perhaps some imported poppy juice.

Ruso glanced around to make sure no one was looking, then undid his purse and placed two sestertii into the hand of Claudius Innocens. "Take her there now," he ordered. "Buy her a dose of something for the pain."

"You're a kindhearted man, sir!" Innocens's jowls bulged outward in a smile that failed to affect his eyes. "Not a lot of gentlemen would see a poor man in need and—"

"See to it!" snapped Ruso, and walked away, checking that his oil flask was still tied to his belt and had not been subtly removed by someone in the crowd. He was not feeling like a kindhearted man. He was a man who was deeply exasperated. He was a man who needed a good night's sleep. And before that, he needed a trip to the baths.

In a few minutes, stretched out on a warm couch with a soft towel beneath him, he would forget the merchant's slimy gratitude and the grisly shape of his slave girl's arm. He would forget the screams of the recruit this morning as his arm was put back into its socket. Distracted by the splash of the cold plunge and the murmur of gossip, his thoughts would drift away from the puzzle of that unknown woman lying in the mortuary. The perfumed oil would clear the stench of decay from his nostrils. The masseur's practiced hands would pummel away the tension of problems, which, when he thought about them logically, all belonged to other people.

There was no sign of the young soldiers at the tables in Merula's. The doorman pretended not to recognize Ruso. He must have overheard the warning about the food.

An elderly slave was limping past the place where the girl had collapsed. The stink of the two buckets swaying on the pole over his shoulders was unmistakable. The man stopped to scrape up the pile of dung Ruso had almost trodden in earlier.

Half the world, decided Ruso, raising his fingers to his nose again, spent its waking hours engaged in cleaning up the mess made by the other half. That girl's owner, like whoever had dumped that corpse in the river, had been a mess maker. Not fit to be in charge of a dead dog. That disgusting bandage had been on her arm for days.

Ruso stopped so suddenly that a child running along behind him collided with the back of his legs, tumbled full-length on the paving stones, and, refusing his offer of help, ran off howling for his mother.

That girl hadn't fallen down any steps. She had raised her arm to shield herself from the blows that had blackened her eye. The wool trader would pocket the money and leave town, and before long another unclaimed body would be found floating down the river. Gaius Petreius Ruso had just been swindled out of two sestertii.

It did not take long to find the unattractive trio again. The wet trail led away from the fountain and down a side street, weaving unsteadily around the legs of scaffolding poles. The scrape and slop of shovels mixing mortar announced yet another row of new shops. Ruso strode around the far side of the building site, entered the street from the opposite end, picked his way down past a burned-out building awaiting demolition, and came face-to-face with the shuffling threesome.

"The Bridge road is the other way!" he shouted over a sudden burst of hammering, stabbing his forefinger in the direction from which they had just come.

The girl opened her eyes and looked at him.

She couldn't see him, of course. It was an illusion. The eyes were blank; like the eyes of a sleepwalker. For the first time Ruso noticed the delicate shape of her nose, the tiny dimple in an earlobe where jewelry had once hung. And those eyes. The color of—what were they the color of? Like . . . like the clear deep waters of . . . Ruso's tired mind groped for a description that didn't sound like the work of a bad poet, and failed to find one.

The merchant was still talking. The youth was examining the toe straps of his sandals. Only Ruso seemed to be interested in the girl.

"If you don't get help for her soon, this slave is going to die."

He realized it was a mistake as soon as he had said it. The trader bent forward and dragged down the girl's lower eyelid with a dirty thumb. Then he forced her jaw open and peered into her mouth. He was clearly not a man to waste two sestertii on dying livestock.

"It's not the state of her teeth you need to worry about."

Innocens turned and looked at him curiously. "You wouldn't be a medical man yourself, by any chance, sir?"

Ruso glanced up, wishing he believed in the sort of theatrical gods who swooped down from the heavens at difficult moments and set humanity to rights. But the gods, if they were watching, were hiding in the gray British clouds beyond the scaffolding poles, leaving him to his fate. And then, as if inspired by something beyond himself, Ruso had an idea.

"You said she isn't worth anything."

Innocens paused. "Well, not the way she is, sir. After she's been cleaned up—"

"I'll take her off your hands."

"She's a good strong girl, sir. She'll perk up in a day or two. I'll knock a bit off the price for that arm."

"What price? You told me she was lazy and useless."

"Useless at cleaning, sir, but an excellent cook. And what's more . . ."—Innocens raised his free arm to steady the girl as he leaned forward in a haze of fish sauce and bellowed over more hammering—"just the thing for a healthy young man like yourself, sir! Ripe as a peach and never been touched!"

"I'm not interested in touching her!" shouted Ruso, just as the noise stopped.

Someone sniggered. Ruso looked up. A couple of men were leaning down over the scaffolding. One of them said something to the other and they both laughed. The youth holding the girl glanced up and grinned.

It would be all over the fort by morning.

You know that new doctor up at the hospital? The one that's been telling the boys to stay out of whorehouses?

What about him?

Hangs around back streets. Tries to buy women.

Innocens was smiling again. Ruso suppressed an urge to grab him by the neck and shake him.

"What would you like to offer, sir?"

Ruso hesitated. "I'll give you fifty denarii," he muttered.

Innocens's jowls collapsed in disappointment. He shrugged the shoulder not being used to prop up his merchandise. "I wish I could, sir. I can hardly afford to feed her. But the debt I took her for was four thousand."

It was a ridiculous lie. Even if it wasn't, Ruso didn't have four thousand denarii. He didn't even have four hundred. It had been an expensive summer.

"Fifty's more than she's worth, and you know it," he insisted. "Look at her."

"Fifty-five!" offered a voice from the scaffolding.

"What?" put in his companion. "You heard the man, she's a virgin. Fifty-six!"

Innocens scowled at them. "One thousand and she's yours, sir."

"Fifty or nothing."

The trader shook his head, unable to believe that any fool would offer all his money at the first bid. Ruso, remembering with a jolt that payday was still three weeks away, was barely able to believe it himself. He should have put some water in that wine.

"Two hundred, sir. I can't go below two hundred. You'll ruin me."

"Go on!" urged the chorus from the scaffolding. "Two hundred for this lovely lady!"

Ruso looked up at the workmen. "Buy her yourselves if you like. I only came out for a bottle of bath oil."

At that moment the girl's body jerked. A feeble cough emerged from her lips. Her eyelids drifted shut. A slow silver drool emerged from her mouth and came to rest in shining bubbles on the sodden wool of her tunic. Claudius Innocens cleared his throat.

"Will that fifty be cash, then, sir?"

3

WHAT ARE YOU doing in here?"

Ruso opened one eye and wondered briefly why he was being addressed by a giant inkwell. Opening the other eye to find himself in fading light and surrounded by shelves, he realized he must have fallen asleep in the records office. He hauled himself upright on the stool and yawned. "Catching up on some notes. How are you feeling?"

Valens grinned. "Better than that thing in Room Twelve. It looks as if it's just crawled out of the sewer. What is it?"

Ruso reached for the writing tablet before Valens could make out: *Female, history unknown, fracture to lower right arm, pale, dry cough, weak, no fever. Note: Launder bedding, treat with fleabane.* He snapped it shut and slid it into the Current Patients box.

"That thing is a sick slave with a broken arm."

"Whose?"

"Her own."

"Very funny. Whose slave?"

Ruso scratched his ear. "Couldn't say, really." He had entertained a faint hope that his purchase might be claimed by the lovesick porter and taken off his hands, but the man had not recognized her.

"I leave you on your own for a couple of days," said Valens, "and you fill the place with expiring females."

"A couple of fishermen found the other one already expired. The town council clerk wouldn't let them dump her outside his office and they couldn't think what else to do with her."

Valens shrugged. "Of course. We're the army, we'll deal with everything. If somebody doesn't identify her soon, I suppose we'll have to bury her too. So who said her friend could die in one of our beds?"

"She isn't dying," argued Ruso, seizing the chance to side step the question of who had brought her in.

"That's not what I heard. She on your list?"

He nodded.

"No hope for her, then." Valens glanced out into the corridor, pushed the door shut, and lowered his voice. "Five says she'll be dead by sunrise."

Ruso pondered this for a moment. Payday seemed farther away now than when he had foolishly offered all his remaining cash for a slave he didn't want. If he could just keep her alive until tomorrow, he would salvage some of his dignity and come out of it with money in his purse.

"She isn't dying," he repeated with more confidence than he felt. "Five says she's alive when they blow first watch."

"If she were a dog, you'd knock her on the head now."

"Well she isn't, and I shan't. So push off and find some patients of your own to annoy."

The hollow cheeks of the patient in Room Twelve looked distinctly yellow against the white of the blanket that had been draped over her. The injured arm, secured across her chest in a crisp linen sling, rose and fell gently with each breath. The drugged drink had done its work. She was asleep. Her doctor placed a cup of barley water on the table beside the bed and went to the shrine of Aesculapius.

The hospital entrance hall was empty save for a smell of fresh paint and roses. Aesculapius leaned on his stick and looked out from his niche with a quiet dignity that somehow transcended the inscription WET PAINT chalked underneath him. The god of healing needed more maintenance than most of his colleagues: The touch of his eager supplicants tended to damage his paint. Today the faithful had left a bunch of white roses and a couple of apples at his feet, hoping to be saved from their ailments. Or, more likely, from their doctor.

Usually Ruso spared the deity no more than a passing nod. Now he paused to stand in front of the niche and murmur a promise of two and a half denarii should the girl in Room Twelve survive until morning.

Having thus enlisted extra help for the cost of only half his winnings, and with nothing to pay if the god failed to perform, Ruso headed back to Room Twelve to see what more could be done to improve his chance of winning this unexpected and probably illegal wager.

4

"ARE YOU—SURE he's—dead?" asked Ruso, the words punctuated by grunts as he struggled to maneuver his end of the stretcher through the door.

"Positive, sir," said the surgical orderly, deftly kicking the door shut behind him. "The man who told me heard it from someone who got it from one of the kitchen staff in the legate's house. It'll be announced at parade this morning."

"How do the kitchen staff know?"

"The dispatch rider popped by for something to eat while the legate read through the message, sir."

Ruso suppressed a smile. "I suppose you know the cause of death?"

"Not sure yet, sir. All we know is, he had a funny turn on the way back from sorting the Parthians out."

They lowered the stretcher onto the table. "Do we know who's taken over?" asked Ruso, sliding out one of the carrying poles.

"The army are backing Publius Aelius Hadrianus, sir." The orderly slid out the other pole and stacked them both in the corner. "I'm told he's a very generous man when it comes to bonuses. Double the going rate is what I hear."

"Does anybody know what the going rate is?" asked Ruso. "Half the army wasn't even born when Trajan took over, let alone on the payroll."

"Hard to say, sir," said the orderly, "but in nineteen years it's bound to have gone up, isn't it?" He bent over the table. "Just lie on your left, now." As they rolled the girl first to one side of the table and then the other, slipping the stretcher sheet out from beneath her, he observed, "Nothing of her, is there?"

When they had settled the girl, the man hurried out to refill the water bucket, complaining that someone else should have refilled it the previous night. "You can tell Priscus isn't here."

Ruso waited, hearing distant voices. The clump of boots on floorboards in the corridors. The usual clatter from the kitchen. Window shutters crashing open to let in the new day. A day the anonymous girl in the mortuary would never see. Ruso, who did not like to inquire too deeply into matters of religion, wondered vaguely if she and Trajan would meet each other on the voyage into the shadowy world of the departed. He eyed the girl lying on the table in front of him. It might have been kinder to let her join them.

Laid out under a crumpled linen gown that smelled faintly of lavender, she looked smaller than she'd appeared to him yesterday. And younger. He wondered how old she was. She must have a name, a tribe, a language. The trader had been yelling at her in Latin but the words she had mumbled as the poppy juice carried her into oblivion sounded British.

That was the only time he had heard her speak. When he had put his head around the door of Room Twelve just after dawn and said, " 'Morning! Did you sleep well?"—She was alive! He must go and tell Valens—she had looked at him with those eyes that were the color of—well, whatever it was—as if she did not understand the question.

The eyes were open again now. The pupils had been shrunk to small black dots by the medicine he had given her. She was staring up at the dust motes floating in the sunshine that streamed in from the high windows. She showed no curiosity about where she was.

She did not seem to have grasped the purpose of the gleaming instruments laid out on the cloth beside the empty water basin. She was not alarmed by the rolls of bandages stacked on the shelves, nor did she seem to be wondering what so many empty bowls might be there to catch.

Ruso was pleased with himself. Deciding the right amount of poppy juice to administer had been a tricky business. The borrowed works he had hurriedly consulted last night had implied that in all respects that would matter this morning, women were the same as men, only smaller. In Ruso's experience, however, there was much about women that was dangerously unpredictable, and one of the attractions of army life was that he was no longer expected to live with one.

"Everything all right, sir?" The orderly was back, splashing clean water into the basin.

Ruso nodded. "I think she's about ready."

The orderly began to buckle a leather strap across the girl's legs. She lifted her head slightly.

"Nothing to worry about," said the orderly, who was a practiced liar.

The girl's head fell back. She closed her eyes and appeared to be drifting off to sleep.

The door opened. Valens's head appeared, then retreated. "Sorry! Didn't know you were in here."

Ruso called after him, "What about that five denarii?"

Valens reappeared, glanced at the body on the operating table, and grinned. "You must have cheated."

"I could do with some help."

"I'm supposed to be doing rounds. What have you got?"

As the girl continued to doze while the orderly strapped her down, Ruso jerked a thumb toward the bandaged arm lying on top of the linen sheet. "Compound fracture of radius and ulna about halfway down. Probably three or four days old. I redressed what I could last night but it was too dark to operate."

"I like a challenge," said Valens, and closed the door behind him. "Have you heard? Trajan's dead."

"I know," said Ruso, who had private reasons to mourn the emperor's passing. "Sounds as though it's going to be Hadrian."

Ruso began to remove the bandaging he had put on last night. The girl's body jerked as she tried to raise herself. The orderly gripped her shoulders and held her down.

On the other side of the table, Valens stroked her good hand, leaned over, and said gently, "We're going to see to your arm. We'll be very quick."

Ruso wished he had remembered to say that himself.

They began to soak the rag that had been stuffed into the wound.

"I met him once," mused Ruso.

"Hadrian?"

"Trajan. In Antioch."

"I suppose he'll be the Divine Trajan soon."

"No doubt," agreed Ruso. At least, none that he was foolish enough to express in public.

"May he rest among the gods," added Valens.

"Among the gods indeed, sir," echoed the orderly.

Ruso left a brief silence that could have been respect or rebellion, then murmured, "Water."

The orderly refilled the jug.

"Think Hadrian'll try and take the North back?" asked Valens.

"Why not?" Ruso said. "He'll be wanting to make an impression. Britannia's big enough to count, but remote enough not to matter."

"He'll have to send more legions if he's serious about it. We're spread pretty thin here."

"He might not go for it. He's Trajan's man. He might just carry on the Divine Trajan's policies." Ruso glanced at the orderly. "No doubt the kitchen staff will let us know. Here it comes . . ." He lifted off the rag and dropped it into the wastebasket.

Both men leaned forward to peer at the swollen and blood-caked mess that had once been an arm.

Valens brought one hand down over his own elbow with a chopping motion and raised his eyebrows in question.

Ruso shook his head. "It looks clean. The wrist's intact."

Valens strolled around the table, looking at the injury from a different angle. "I wouldn't," he murmured. "You'll only make a worse mess and end up taking it off anyway."

"It might work. If you broke your arm—"

"I'd pray I didn't get some would-be hero like you."

"I think we should try."

There was a pause.

"She's my patient," added Ruso.

Valens shrugged. "Fine. She's your patient. So, do we know how much Hadrian values his loyal troops?"

"He'll be doubling the usual bonus, apparently."

"How much is that?"

"Not a clue."

As they began to clean the wound, the girl gasped. Her face twisted into a grimace of pain.

"Try and lie still," said the orderly, tightening his grip and glancing to check that all the straps were fastened.

"We'll be very quick," promised Ruso, wishing he could make patients believe it the way Valens did.

"My friend's famous for being quick," added Valens. "Ask all the girls." He glanced at Ruso. "What's she called?"

"I don't know."

"Ruso, only you could round up two women and not know the names of either of them."

"Next time," said Ruso, "I'll tell them my friend would like to be introduced." He picked out a stray thread of rag with the tweezers. The girl gave a low moan.

"Shush now," said the orderly.

Ruso hoped she wouldn't be a whimperer. Whimperers were worse than screamers. Screamers made him cross, which made him work faster. The sound of a whimperer trying to be brave was a distraction.

The girl didn't whimper. She clenched her teeth and didn't make another sound.

There was a rap at the door.

"What?" snapped Ruso. A very young soldier appeared, swallowed, and announced, "Urgent message for Gaius Petreius Ruso."

"That's me."

"Sir, there's a man at the east gatehouse. He says you promised to pay fifty-four denarii first thing this morning."

"It was fifty," said Ruso, not looking up. "And I'm busy."

The youth did not reply. He was staring at the operating table.

"Tell him I'll be down later," said Ruso.

The youth swallowed again. "He said to tell you the extra is the tax and the cost of drawing up the documents, sir."

Ruso nodded toward the mangled mass of the girl's arm. "If you don't get out right away, I shall do this to you too."

The youth fled.

Ruso aimed the tweezers at the wastebasket, missed, and said, "I think that's clean."

Valens laid a hand on the girl's forehead. "We like this arm so much, young woman, we're going to put it back together for you."

The orderly leaned down until his face was almost touching the girl's. "Breathe deeply now," he ordered. "Ready? In, out—In, out . . ."

Ruso had rehearsed his speech all the way down to the gatehouse, but when he got there he found his time had been wasted. Instead of the wool trader, the guards presented him with an elderly slave with no teeth who made it clear that if he failed to return to his master with the right money, his life would not be worth living. Ruso, who had neither the time nor the inclination to get in line at the tax office, paid up. He also sent a message to say that if Claudius Innocens ever showed his face in Deva again he would be instantly arrested, but he doubted the slave would have the courage to deliver it.

The clerk of the Aesculapian Thanksgiving Fund gave him a receipt for the two and a half denarii that Valens had borrowed from someone who had borrowed them from someone else who had very possibly borrowed them from the Aesculapian Thanksgiving Fund in the first place.

Ruso went to thank the god personally. Standing in front of the statue, he fingered the two receipts tucked into his belt. One said that in gratitude and fulfillment of a vow, Gaius Petreius Ruso had paid the Aesculapian Thanksgiving Fund two and a half denarii. The other confirmed Gaius Petreius Ruso as the new owner of an injured and sickly girl with indescribable eyes and a name that seemed to be a series of spelling mistakes.

Ruso gazed up at the statue of the god who had answered his prayer. For the first time he noticed that the painter had not just performed the usual touch-up over the rough spots. The god had been completely re-painted. Ruso stood to take a closer look, and as he gazed into the brown eyes of Aesculapius he had the distinct impression that the god of healing was looking back at him, and laughing.

5

RUSO LAY ON the borrowed bed and stared into the gloom that hid the cracks in the ceiling plaster, reflecting that Socrates was a wise man. Surveying the goods on a market stall, the great one was said to have remarked, "What a lot of things a man doesn't need!"

What a lot of things a man doesn't need. That thought had comforted Ruso over the last few months. The more you own, he had told himself, the more you have to worry about. Possessions are a burden.

The kind of possessions which needed to be regularly fed were a double burden. They were only worth having if they earned their keep by doing the laundry, or barking at burglars, or catching mice, or carrying you somewhere, or chirping in a way that your ex-wife used to find entertaining. It was a pity Socrates hadn't thought to add, *Which is why I never shop after drinking on an empty stomach.*

"As far as I'm concerned," Valens had said, carefully lowering the lid back onto the beer barrel so as not to tip the stack of dirty dishes that had been there when Ruso moved in, "If there's no one waiting for the room and you're not using much staff time to nurse her, you can leave her there."

Ruso took the dripping cup of beer and wondered whether to clear up the dishes, or whether to wait and see how long it would be before Valens did. "She'll need proper nursing for a few days."

"Fair enough. But the other one's got to be out of the mortuary tomorrow, claimed or not." Valens tossed a broken fishing rod into the corner to clear himself space on the couch. As he sat down, three puppies scuttled out from underneath. The puppies were a legacy from the previous occupant, whose lone and portly terrier bitch Valens had agreed to look after while the man was temporarily assigned elsewhere. "Gods, I'll be glad when Marius gets back to pick this stuff up. It's not all my mess in here, you know."

Ruso, who had shared quarters with Valens before, made no comment. The offer of free accommodation had been too good to turn down, but he had known there would be a price to pay.

"To tell you the truth," said Valens, "I thought you'd be bringing a servant or two. You used to have lots."

"Claudia had lots."

"Ah." Valens squinted into his own beer, rescued something with a forefinger, and flicked it over his shoulder. A rush of inquisitive puppies followed its course.

"How long have you been a beer drinker?"

"I'm not. Some native gave it to me as a thank-you for treating one of his children."

Ruso frowned into his drink. "Are you sure he was grateful?"

"Smells like goat's piss, I know. But you'll get used to it."

Ruso tried another mouthful and wondered how long getting used to it would take. He said, "Can't the legion give us somebody to help keep the place straight?"

Valens winced. "If you want some squinty-eyed misery who makes a ridiculous fuss about a little bit of a mess."

Ruso deduced that this had already been tried. "What about a private arrangement? It wouldn't cost much between us."

"The servants here aren't much better than the beer, I'm afraid. The first one we tried had a bad back. The next one kept sitting on the floor and crying and we didn't have the heart to beat her, so we sold her. At a loss, of course. Then we tried hiring a local girl, but Marius saw her kick the dog, so she had to go." Valens leaned back and indicated the size of the room with a sweep of his arm. The motion sent beer slopping over the side of his cup. "This isn't a big house, is it?" He transferred the beer to the other hand and wiped his wet fingers on the couch. "It can't be much work. I mean, we don't even use that end room." The beer slopped again, indicating the direction of the corner room, which had been abandoned as impossibly damp and was now growing several fine blooms of strange-smelling mold. "There's only the two of us to cook for," he continued, "and half the time we eat at the hospital. Can your girl cook?"

"At the moment she can't even stand up."

"No matter. We don't want one in a splint anyway. We want some nice healthy lass who's handy with dogs and cleaning."

"And wants a challenge," observed Ruso, glancing through the open door into the earthquake zone that was Valens's bedroom. "Where would we put this healthy lass?"

"In the kitchen, I suppose. When your furniture turns up, she could have the mattress off that bed you're using."

Ruso did not reply.

"We could always get rid of her later if your girl shows promise," Valens added.

"I won't be keeping her. I'll start looking for a buyer as soon as she can be moved."

"You'll just have to hope Priscus doesn't come back in the meantime."

Ruso frowned. "Doesn't anybody know when he's coming?"

"Doubt it. He likes to take people by surprise. He thinks it keeps them on their toes. He's not keen on private patients unless they pay well. By the way, that other dog isn't yours too, is it?"

Ruso said, "What other dog?"

"I didn't think it was. I'll tell them to get rid of it."

Other dog?

Ruso yawned. The girl in the mortuary was not his problem, but if he didn't get the live one out of the hospital soon, not only would he get off on the wrong foot with Chief Administrative Officer Priscus, but he would be saddled with every other passing stray for whom no one else wanted to take responsibility.

Somewhere beyond the ill-fitting shutters of his bedroom window, a trumpet sounded the change of watch. He rolled over, wriggled to avoid the lump that always seemed directly under his shoulder no matter how many times he turned the mattress or shook the straw around, and closed his eyes. He was just dropping off to sleep when he heard a knock on his door and Valens asking if he was awake.

"No."

"Are you busy in the morning?"

"Yes."

"Too bad. Somebody's going to have to go down to Merula's."

"Uh. Send an orderly."

"It ought to be somebody official, and I'm on duty."

"Can't it wait?"

"No. One of the men's identified that body."

6

THE SHUTTERS HAD been pushed back to let in the autumn sunshine. Beyond them, Merula's was almost empty. Benches were upturned on the tables. A boy of eight or nine was shoveling ash out of the grate under the hot drinks counter. A young woman with lank hair tucked behind her ears was sweeping sawdust into a gray pile with limp strokes of a broom. A buxom girl was barefoot on a stool, displaying a dainty silver chain around one ankle as she reached above a lamp bracket to wipe at the smudges on the wall. Ruso looked at the girl with the ankle bracelet. He thought of the discolored figure stretched out on the mortuary table. He wished he hadn't.

A door opened somewhere at the back of the bar and a third girl, this one heavily pregnant, emerged carrying a jar of oil. From somewhere in the shadows a gruff voice said, " 'Morning, Daphne."

Daphne came to an instant halt on the far side of one of the tables. Ruso had the impression she was holding her breath as the taller of Merula's two doormen stepped up close behind her.

"Just got out of bed, have we?" inquired the doorman. The pregnant girl flinched as he leaned around to peer into her face.

From the doorway Ruso noticed the cloth dangling unheeded in the hand of the girl standing on the stool, who had turned to watch the encounter. The lank-haired one shuffled away to sweep under the stairs.

The doorman was shaking his head despairingly. "Daphne, Daphne, what am I always telling you about conversation? When a gentleman says hello, you say hello back. Good morning, Daphne."

If Daphne made any reply, it was covered by the screech of the shovel being slid into the fireplace.

"Very nice. Now come here."

He seated himself behind her on the table, placed his hands on her shoulders, and pulled her back toward him until she was standing trapped between his knees with the oil jar propped awkwardly against her swollen belly. "You ought to be more careful," he said, his large fingers retying her loose braid with a surprisingly deft touch. "You could have lost that ribbon. Couldn't you?"

She did not answer.

He gave her a rough shove forward. "Run along, then. The mistress don't want to see you standing around chatting."

As Daphne approached Ruso, her face was expressionless. She stood on tiptoe to fill the lamp on the bracket by the shutters. When she had finished, she wiped first her nose and then the neck of the jar with a cloth, and made her way back to the kitchen with the sway-backed walk of a woman working to counterbalance a heavy weight.

Ruso stepped forward onto the red tiles, avoiding a pile of sawdust. A broad figure emerged from behind the shutters to block his path. He recognized the fading ginger hair.

"We're closed," said the man in a tone that suggested he too remembered Ruso's last visit, and not fondly.

"Is the manageress in?"

The solid shoulders rose just enough to indicate that the man's job was to know nothing, see nothing, and be as unhelpful as possible, and he was intending to do it to the best of his ability.

Ruso looked him in the eye. He was saying "Would you like me to repeat the question?" when he heard another voice behind him.

"Who wants to know?"

He turned. The doormen had positioned themselves so that he was caught between them. "Gaius Petreius Ruso," he said to the second man, who seemed to be in charge. "Medicus with the Twentieth."

The man folded his arms. "Whatever it is," he said, "it didn't come from here. All our girls are clean. You ought to check down by the docks."

The man's bearing would have said *ex-legionary* even without the telltale scar where the scarf had failed to keep the armor from chafing his neck. Ruso said, "What's your name, soldier?"

The man assessed him awhile longer, then said, "Bassus. He's Stichus."

"Bassus. I'm here from the hospital to see your mistress on an official matter. It's confidential and it's urgent. So if you don't know where she is, you'd be wise to find out."

The crease between the doorman's eyebrows deepened. "Why didn't you say so?" He turned. "Lucco!"

The boy paused with the shovel in one hand and a brush in the other.

"Go and tell the mistress there's an officer to see her. Chloe, get the officer a seat."

Ruso said, "I'll stand," but the girl with the ankle chain had already stepped down from the stool. She heaved a bench off one of the corner tables and swung it over to land on the tiles with a clatter. "Take a seat, sir," she said, gesturing toward it as if he might not know what it was for. "What would you like to drink?"

Ruso declined. In the circumstances, it hardly seemed appropriate.

Bassus went back to whatever he was doing behind the counter. Stichus seated himself in a corner with the air of a man who had spent long years honing the skill of waiting for action.

Ruso's gaze ran along the loops of gold braid that had been painted at waist height along the deep red of the wall beside him. Similar loops ran along the adjacent wall. A large tassel blossomed in the corner, probably inspired by the painter's discovery that the two braids—which must have been started at opposite ends of the walls—weren't quite going to meet up.

The boy, Lucco, reappeared at the foot of the stairs, and assured him—with more optimism than accuracy, as it turned out—that the mistress would not be long. The girls went back to cleaning.

Merula evidently took just as long as other women to get ready. Ruso was pondering why, when seated at a bar table, the average soldier felt compelled to carve his initials into it, when a female voice from the top of the stairs snapped, "Chloe!"

The girl with the ankle chain looked up in alarm.

"Don't rub so hard, you stupid girl! You'll take all the paint off!"

The figure sweeping down the stairs was, Ruso assumed, Merula.

Ruso had no idea what the silky material in her tunic was called, but he knew it was expensive because his wife had needed something like it for a dinner party once and then had managed to lean across a brazier and burn a hole in it. Merula looked like a woman who would be more careful. The fabric was draped to make the most of an elegant figure. Her hair, which could almost have been naturally black, was pinned back, leaving little tendrils of curls framing her face. As she reached the foot of the stairs, Ruso observed that her eyelids were dark, her lips red, and her cheeks subtly pink. It was well done. Only the lines that ran between nose and mouth suggested that Merula would not look quite as good in broad daylight.

The lines deepened around something approaching a smile when she greeted him.

"Gaius Petreius Ruso," he announced, standing. "Medicus with the Twentieth."

"Gaius Petreius. Ah yes, the new doctor. Did my girls offer you a drink?"

He nodded. "Is there somewhere we could talk in private?"

Merula clapped her hands and called, "Out!"

Instantly the girls stopped what they were doing. Chloe threw the cloth down and beckoned Lucco to follow her into the kitchen.

Merula said, "Thank you, boys."

Bassus and Stichus glanced at each other, then retreated to stand guard outside.

"Now, Doctor." Merula seated herself opposite him. "What can I do for you?"

Ruso scratched his ear. There were good reasons why he was now facing the task of breaking bad news to this woman. Principal among them was that Valens was busy with morning clinic and the duty civilian liaison officer, whose job this surely was, was already late for a meeting. "You know the sort of thing," the man had explained from the back of his horse, swinging one leg forward so the groom could tighten the girth. "Just show them we take it very seriously, but whatever you do, don't promise we'll do anything about it."

Ruso cleared his throat again, reminded himself that the woman wasn't a relative, and began. "I'm afraid I have bad news."

Merula stared at him for a moment, then lowered her head and shaded her eyes with one manicured hand.

"It's about—"

She said, "Saufeia."

"Yes."

"I was afraid of this." The woman sighed. "No matter how many times you try to tell these girls, some of them just don't listen." She looked up. "What happened to her?"

"Her body was found in the river the day before yesterday and brought into the hospital. She was identified late last night."

"She had only been with us for ten days," said Merula, inadvertently explaining why none of the hospital staff, many of whom would be intimately acquainted with the local tavern girls, had recognized her. "Did she drown?"

"There were, uh . . ." Ruso hesitated. "There was some bruising around the throat," he said, "and her neck was broken."

"I see." Merula paused, then shook her head. "Poor, silly Saufeia."

Poor silly Saufeia, who had ended up naked and muddy and practically bald, unmourned until a gawker who shouldn't have been in the mortuary at all recognized the birthmark on her thigh.

"Was there any family?"

Merula shook her head.

"I don't suppose you have any idea who might have—?"

"Who might have taken advantage of a girl looking for business with no protection? Outside an army base?"

There was no need to answer.

Merula glanced through the open shutters to where one of the doormen was leaning against the wall of the bakery opposite, eating. "The boys will blame themselves, but they can't watch them day and night." A bitter smile twisted the red lips. "After we realized she'd gone, the girls were hoping she'd run off with a customer. It does happen."

"You didn't report her as a runaway?"

"We were busy. I suppose we might have passed her name on to a slave hunter sooner or later, but to be honest, I doubt she would have been worth the recovery fee. She wasn't really suitable for this kind of work."

"When did you last see her?"

"Five days ago. Early in the evening. She must have sneaked out when nobody was looking."

Ruso said, "She appears to have died quite soon after that."

Merula understood. "I will make the funeral arrangements as quickly as possible."

Relieved, Ruso got to his feet. He acknowledged the woman's thanks with a nod. Her composure had made a difficult task much easier than it might have been.

The girls emerged from the kitchen with a promptness that could only mean they had been listening behind the door. Ruso was passing Stichus in the doorway when a voice called, "Sir?"

He turned. Chloe, with the lank-haired girl hovering behind her, said, "You don't know who did it, do you, sir?"

Ruso shook his head. "I don't," he said. "But if you remember anything suspicious, you should go to the fort right away and ask for the duty civilian liaison officer."

7

SHE RAN FOR the door. The fat one got there first. She dodged behind a stack of barrels. He came after her. She tried to scramble out. The barrels were crashing down and rolling across the floor. She tried to leap free but her feet slipped in something wet. The smell of beer mingled with the stink of the fat one's breath as he loomed above her, raising the crowbar, his mouth twisted with the shouting. She tried to shield herself. The crowbar swung down. She heard the crack. Felt herself jolt with the blow.

She was in the white room again. The familiar pain was pulsing through her arm, but instead of her own bones looking back at her, the arm was hidden inside a thick bandage and strapped across her chest.

So. She was still in this world.

The door was opening. She closed her eyes. A hand was laid on her forehead. In the ugly sounds of Latin the man announced that it was not a fever.

"She's having bad dreams," he said, apparently talking to someone else. She pretended to be asleep, trying not to flinch as the bandages were tweaked and tidied while two men talked about postoperative fevers and swelling and things she did not understand.

Bad dreams.

She must have called out. She hoped she had not spoken in Latin. She tried to remember, but her mind had been traveling to strange places, fleeing from the pain and the bitter medicine the man kept making her drink. He had told her she was safe from the fat one, but what did he know? When the medicine gave her sleep, the fat one returned.

There were other dreams too. A man dressed in green who held her down and whispered in her ear while wolves tore at her arm. Voices echoing behind closed doors. Birds singing. The sun with four corners—

No. She must try to think clearly. *The sun has no corners. The white room has a square window in the outside wall. I am in a white bed. A tall thin table stands beside the bed. A black cup and a jug are on the table. Behind the door is a stool.* The man who brought the medicine had pulled a stool beside the bed and had sat down to ask, *"Quid nomen tibi est?"* as if he were talking to a small child.

When she had failed to answer, he repeated the question. She had continued to stare at his dark eyes, at his unshaven chin, as if she could not understand what he was saying. His Greek was easier to ignore because she genuinely did not understand it. She did not recognize his third attempt at all until, reciting it in her mind after he had given up and left, she began to suspect that it could be a mangled version of her own tongue, impossible to grasp unless you had first heard him ask in Latin: What is your name?

She had not heard her real name spoken since she had been captured. For two winters she had been "girl" at best, the Northerners at first deliberately refusing to honor her with the use of her name and later, she supposed, forgetting what it was. When the other slaves had asked what to call her, she had invented something. She had spoken to them—to everyone—as little as possible. But Romans were full of questions.

How old are you? Where do you come from? Do you understand what I'm saying? Does it hurt when I do that? Do you need to pass water? Did you really fall down the stairs? Do you know a girl with red hair? They seemed to have lost interest in the girl with red hair now. But they persisted with the other questions. *Quid nomen tibi est?*

She was not about to offer her name up to a stranger. It was almost the only thing she possessed that nobody had stolen.

A voice was asking, "How much poppy are you giving her?"

The left side of the bed heaved as the blanket was tucked in. "No more until nightfall." She felt herself being rolled the other way as he tucked in the opposite side. "I want her awake enough to eat."

8

RUSO WAS CONSIDERING trying a different poultice on an infected thumb that he didn't much like the look of when Valens knocked on the door to announce that the *Sirius* was coming in to dock on the midday tide.

The *Sirius*! After three months, Ruso and his possessions were about to be reunited. The last time he had seen them was when he had left Africa, fully expecting to return to his comfortable rooms after his leave. Instead, he was sharing condemned lodgings at the opposite end of the empire with the untidiest medic in the army.

He said, "I'll get down to the docks when I've finished ward rounds."

"I'll go down now," Valens offered. "To make sure they don't drop anything."

Several patients later, Ruso finally escaped from the hospital. As he nodded to Aesculapius on the way out, he thought he heard the patter of claws on floorboards. He turned to see something brown and hairy and just above knee height vanishing around the corner of the front entrance. When he got outside, there was no sign of it.

There was no time to investigate. He hurried along the Via Praetoria to the cashier's office, where the chief clerk beckoned him past the line and into the office to tell him that the donation to the Aesculapian Fund was very generous.

"Donation?" Ruso frowned, wondering if the man was being sarcastic about his two and half denarii.

"From the owner of Merula's bar, sir. In gratitude for the hospital's services to the deceased."

Ruso remembered. The grim-faced Bassus had arrived early this morning with a cart to carry away the body of poor silly Saufeia. Afterward he had mentioned making some sort of contribution to the hospital fund and Ruso had told him to go to the cashier's office. "Do you know where that is?"

"Know it?" Bassus had snorted. "I built it."

Ruso, encouraged by the size of the gift Bassus had delivered and the clerks' apparent belief that he was the cause of it, increased the size of the loan he had come to request. No doubt the clerks would talk, but with luck the rumors of his cash problems would not travel too far before they were brought to a halt by Hadrian's promised double bonus. As the trumpet was blaring the change of watch, he emerged from the west gate of the fort with an advance in his purse that was enough to redeem his possessions many times over.

On the way to the docks he passed a couple of bars that made Merula's look like a high-class establishment for country gentlemen. Glancing at a rusty cage hung outside a door, he saw a bird with scraggly feathers and a vicious-looking beak. He thought of Claudia's singing bird: the pampered pet released by a hired slave girl in a misguided fit of kindness. The next morning a noisy bunch of squabbling sparrows had been shooed away to reveal the little songster bedraggled and lifeless on the pavement. Claudia's fury had been vented on Ruso, since he had sent the slave back to her owner with a demand for compensation before Claudia had a chance to punish her.

Saufeia, it seemed, had understood no more about the dangers of freedom than the hapless songbird. She must have been very naïve indeed to abandon the protection of Merula's graceless but efficient "boys" to take her chances on the narrow streets of a military port like Deva. It struck him that whoever was charged with tracking down the culprit was going to have a difficult job. She would have been a target not only for vicious customers, but for the owners of businesses who did not want the competition.

Between the baths and the riverside warehouses, one of those businesses was displaying its merchandise. White shoulders and big earrings and fat ankles gleamed in the late September sunshine. Other establishments relied upon lurid paintings beside an open street door, but perhaps the owner of the fat-ankled and big-earringed couldn't afford a painter. Either that, or he believed the valiantly grinning females sprawled across the bench outside his crumbling walls were genuinely tempting. Ruso wondered how long a man would have to be at sea before he would agree.

His mood lifted as he approached the wharf, passing an altar to Neptune and a couple of surprisingly elegant houses probably built by traders wanting to enjoy the sight of the sea god safely delivering their latest cargoes. Ahead of him, a light breeze was lifting the broad river into a glitter around the silhouettes of fat-bellied merchant ships and a scatter of fishing boats. A slender trireme was moored at the distant end of the wooden jetty. Ruso paused to watch as a fishing boat, which had turned in from the main course of the river, dropped its sail and began to row in under the stern of the trireme. The shriek of gulls rose above faint shouts of orders and a chant of *One! Two! Three!* from a team shifting something heavy.

A man who had seen little of the world might think this was a beautiful view. A man who had never stood by a sea that was translucent, under a sky so brilliantly blue it hurt the eyes, would probably think this was a grand place to be.

Scanning the painted merchant ships tied up along the jetty, Ruso wondered which had brought the remains of his belongings, and how many years it would be before he could load them up again and have them sent to a posting back in civilization. The bars and the whorehouses would be the same wherever soldiers were stationed, but they didn't have to be set in a chilly place where gray sloppy waves retreated twice a day to leave the land and river separated by glutinous brown mud flats. No wonder the hospital was stocking up on cough mixture for the winter. Unfortunately the nature of the Britons was such that the army wouldn't let him prescribe a mass transfer of the legion to a healthier climate.

Valens's letters had made Britannia sound entertaining. The islands, apparently, were bursting with six-foot warrior women and droopy-mustached, poetry-spouting fanatics who roamed the misty mountains stirring up quarrelsome tribesmen in the guise of religion.

His own observation of Britannia now led Ruso to suspect that Valens had deliberately lured him here to relieve the boredom.

The bizarre movements of the British seas had been a novelty, but not one with which he desired a better acquaintance. When his ship had docked in Rutupiae, the captain had offered him the chance to stay on board and sail to Deva. He had declined, taken a lift as far as Londinium with an eye surgeon who was on the way to operate on the governor's wife, then hired a horse and spent several days riding north. He had, he now realized, probably passed Chief Administrative Officer Priscus traveling in the opposite direction on his way to discuss contracts for army medical supplies. Had he but known, he would have seized Priscus and wrested the hospital keys from his grasp. As it was, the trip had been an interesting introduction to his new province.

It had been hard to imagine the lush meadows and busy little towns of Britannia as the setting for the ghastly massacres witnessed by the old and toothless who could remember the rebellion. But by the fifth day of traveling, the hills had become steeper, the military traffic heavier, and the towns less welcoming. Here it was easier to see the problem with keeping order. The road passed through stretches of dark woods where the occasional column of smoke in the distance might have signaled charcoal burning or someone cooking breakfast or an unwary tax collector being ambushed. The farmland was rich still, but the houses were primitive: mud-plastered round huts squatting under mushrooms of thatch and not a window or a water tap in sight. At one point he passed a knot of grim-faced civilians being marched along the road under guard from a squad of auxiliaries, and half a day's ride farther north there was a double crucifixion at the roadside. More civilians huddled weeping underneath the bloodied figures, while a military guard gazed on with studied indifference, and an officer's horse, the only creature at the scene who was definitely innocent, raised its head and whinnied to Ruso's mount in the apparent hope that someone had at last come to take it away.

The only trouble he had encountered on the journey north was a minor brawl in a roadside inn, but the civilians Ruso met on the road looked as sullen as the weather when they stepped aside to let him pass. And these were supposed to be the friendly tribes. Still, many a man had made his reputation at this moist and chilly frontier of empire, and Ruso, who had needed a change for reasons he wasn't intending to confide to anyone here, was happy to let it be thought that he considered Britain a smart career move.

"Fresh fish, sir?" A woman who was out of breath from pushing a cart up the slope lifted a cloth to display glistening silver bodies. She grinned, showing a gap where her front teeth should have been. "Just caught in time for dinner!"

Ruso shook his head.

In the space of a hundred paces he also declined a bucket of mussels, a jar of pepper, a delivery of coal, a set of tableware, an amphora of wine, a bolt of cloth to make the finest bedspread in Deva, some indefinable things in the shape of small sausages, and an introduction to an exotic dancer. Stepping onto the quay, he dodged a trolley being pushed by a small boy who couldn't see over it. Behind him a voice shouted, "Tray of plums, sir?"

It was comforting to know that he still had the appearance of a man with money to spend.

The quay stank of fish with undertones of sandalwood. Somebody must have dropped something expensive. The crews were rushing to load cargoes while the tide was in, shifting crates and sacks and baskets of whatever it took to maintain civilization in this corner of the empire before the tide forced the captains to move their vessels farther out or be stranded in the mud. Ruso wove his way between carts and trolleys, skirting a pile of slate that must have come from the western mountains and would probably be someone's roof by the end of the week. The stack of jars labeled SALINAE would be loaded up and shipped out. He knew that not because he was interested in exports but because one of the legionaries guarding the salt springs had somehow managed to impale himself on a fencing spike, and Ruso had made him talk about his duties in great detail as a distraction from the efforts to remove it.

A wide-eyed brown monkey peered at him from a crate, its childlike fingers wrapped around the bars of its prison. Farther along he passed a pale group of chained slaves. They looked even less thrilled to be here than the monkey was. A couple of them seemed to be gazing at the water heaving against the legs of the jetty and wondering whether to fling themselves into it. He hoped they would have enough sense to realize that since they were chained, they would only be fished out again and revived to have TENDENCY TO SUICIDE written on their sale tags. A warning to buyers that might as well read, PLEASE WORK ME TO DEATH.

None of the ships moored along the quayside was the one he sought. Ruso turned and added his footsteps to the dull thunder of boots making their way along the jetty.

The second ship out bore the name *Sirius* in jaunty blue letters, and beside it Ruso recognized the figure leaning back on a chair with his feet up on a small upturned table.

"Bad news," said Valens, rising to greet him. "Some sort of mixup." He waved one hand toward the carved chair he had been sitting on. It was facing two large trunks, on top of which the table had been up-ended. Ruso saw his name, and the words LEG XX DEVA BRIT chalked on each item. "You'll have to talk to them," said Valens. "I can't make any sense out of them. They keep telling me this is all there is. Jupiter knows where they've sent the rest of it."

Ruso knelt and checked the seals on the trunks. "No, it all seems to be here."

Valens looked blank. "Where's your furniture?"

"Termites," explained Ruso, who had anticipated the question. "Africa's full of them."

"Termites?" Valens scratched his head and stared at the table. "Termites ate the Lucky Earthquake Bed?"

Ruso shrugged. "Turn your back for a moment over there and the damn things eat everything." Of all the items that were gone, he would miss that bed the most. It had been a reminder of a time when he had, briefly, been mistaken for a Divine Being. Now the Divine Being was reduced to telling lies to explain his lack of furniture.

Valens was leaning down and peering at the locked trunks. "You don't think you've brought any with you, do you?"

"They'll have fumigated it," Ruso assured him. "They'd have to. Long voyage, wooden ship . . ."

"I'll go and get a cart," Valens offered, moving hastily away from the articles that looked like trunks but might turn out to be Trojan horses.

Ruso lowered himself into his chair to wait, and wondered who was now sleeping on the Lucky Earthquake Bed. It had been a wedding present from his father and stepmother. In conventional respects it hadn't been a great success. The only time the earth had truly moved in it for him and Claudia, it had also moved for the rest of Antioch. They had clung to each other under the heavy oak frame while roof beams smashed down on top of it and tiles shattered all around them. When the shaking seemed to be over, they crawled out to find that others had not been as lucky. All around was confusion: screams of pain, shouts for help, people scrabbling at piles of rubble, calling the names of their loved ones, and the smell of smoke in the dusty air as fires took hold in the ruins. Had he but known it, the earthquake had signaled the final collapse of his marriage.

He managed to send Claudia to safety with friends who were heading for the countryside. Then he headed back toward the nearest army base: They would surely be organizing rescue parties.

Moments after he set out, the earth shook again. He flung himself to the ground with his hands over his head and hoped Claudia was somewhere out in the open.

The shaking stopped. For a moment all was silence, save the creak and rumble of more buildings collapsing. Ruso lifted his head. A man close by was calling for help.

No one else seemed to have heard the voice, which was coming from an ornate building that was still partially standing. Squinting through the dust and cupping one hand over his nose, Ruso picked his way around the ruins. The only door he could find had most of a wall collapsed against it. Finally he managed to squeeze himself in through a small window.

The room stank of burning oil. Black smoke was seeping through cracks in one elegantly painted wall. A smartly dressed body was sprawled on the floor. Blood was seeping from beneath a heavy cabinet that lay where the head should have been.

"Over here!" called the voice. "Under the table!"

Through the murk, Ruso saw a corner of a table sticking out from under a pile of plaster and brick. Trying to move quickly without pulling more masonry down on top of himself, he managed to clear a way through to the gap beneath. A figure gray with dust crawled out, grabbed his arm, and started to thank him just as the floor gave a sickening heave. "Move!" yelled Ruso, dragging the man across the room and pushing him headfirst out the window before scrambling after him.

Behind them, what was left of the building seemed to groan in despair before finally crashing in on itself. They were still peering at it through the clouded air when a voice cried, "Your majesty! Oh my Lord, you're safe!" and someone fell at the feet of the man Ruso had just rescued. The man reached down and helped the servant up, still staring at the ruins from which he had so narrowly escaped. That was when Ruso realized why he looked vaguely familiar. He wasn't a half-remembered patient after all. Ruso had just rescued the emperor Trajan.

Over the next few days and nights the tremors had continued, claiming more victims from the rescuers trying to reach people trapped under the rubble. Ruso struggled to save the dying and patch up the injured with no equipment, no water, no sleep, and nowhere to turn for advice. Rumors abounded: that the whole country had been devastated, that nowhere outside the city had been hit, that the army was bringing elephants to clear the streets, that plague had broken out, that Antioch was being punished by the gods, that a man crushed to death had come back to life and that a mysterious being, surely a god, had entered the building where the emperor Trajan was trapped and spirited him out through the window. It never occurred to Ruso to try and set the record straight. For the first time in days, he had found something to laugh about.

Claudia, with whom he unwisely tried to share the joke, later cited it as one of her reasons for leaving. Following *you abandoned me in the earthquake!* was *You had a chance to make something of yourself with the emperor and you refused to do anything about it!*

Three weeks after Claudia moved out, Ruso had signed up to a fresh start in Africa with the army. Now he stared at his pathetic collection of furniture and wondered if his wife had been right.

Valens was back, bringing a gnarled creature who had evidently spent all his money on blue tattoos and couldn't afford to bathe.

"I suppose you'll want to carry on using the spare bed, then?" inquired Valens as the tattooed one moved the table aside, lifted both trunks at once, and set off with them down the jetty.

Ruso picked up the chair. "Just until I get sorted out."

Valens reached for the legs of the table and swung it up over his head like a large sunshade. "With what these people charge," he said, "we ought to give up medicine and take up moving furniture."

They reached the end of the jetty. The trunks had been loaded onto a cart that smelled of old fish and appeared to be held together with greasy twine and dirt.

Valens wrinkled his nose and stepped back from the cart. "Were you serious about those termites?"

"The smell from that cart should finish them off."

"You're not in some sort of trouble, are you?"

Ruso watched the man roping down all that remained of his furniture, and said, "No, of course not."

"You won't find much to buy over here, but we've got a few decent carpenters. I'm thinking of having a proper dining room set made."

"For that house?"

"No. I told you, that one's supposed to have been flattened weeks ago. I mean in my new rooms. The ones I'll get when they promote me to CMO."

"So he's definitely not coming back?" Ruso was aware that no one expected the hot springs of Aquae Sulis to rejuvenate the present chief medical officer, but so far there had been no official word of his retirement.

"He's bound to go before long," said Valens. "I'll save him the bother of trailing back up here and have his things sent on."

"And you think they're promoting you to CMO?"

"Why not?"

"Because they might choose me."

"Bollocks."

"I've got combat experience."

"But you don't know anybody yet, Ruso. Anyway, you don't need the money like I do."

"No?"

"I thought you were supposed to inherit from your father. Aren't you the oldest son?"

"There were a lot of expenses," said Ruso. "You know what funerals are like."

"Didn't he have land in Gaul?"

"My brother's looking after it. The farm has a lot of people to support."

"Giddyup!" The driver gave one of the beasts a flick with his stick and the cart lurched forward. They followed its creaking progress up the slope.

"What you need," said Valens suddenly, "is a rich widow."

Ruso noted this suggestion to add to his list of things he didn't need at all. He had no intention of explaining to Valens that what he *did* need was either the CMO's salary or a collection of lucrative private patients and some peace and quiet to get on with his writing. Now that he was living in a backwater with no earthquakes or family members or ex-wife to distract him, he hoped to complete the work he had already started and abandoned several times. G. Petreius Ruso's *Concise Guide to Military First Aid* would be detailed enough to be useful in the field, and short enough to be copied onto very small scrolls that would fit into a soldier's pack. The copying would be expensive, but once those copies had been sold, there would be a double profit—one in cash, and one, he felt sure, in lives and limbs saved. What he didn't need was Valens making helpful suggestions, or worse still, taking up the idea himself.

"Did I tell you," Valens continued, bringing Ruso back to the subject at hand, "I'm thinking of proposing to the second spear's daughter?"

"Is she a rich widow?"

"Gods, no. She's sixteen. Rather attractive, actually, considering what her father looks like."

Whatever the second spear looked like, he must have been on centurion's pay for some years before he had been promoted to a command in the top cohort. He would be a wealthy man.

"Only child, I suppose?" ventured Ruso.

Valens grinned. "Divorce has turned you sadly cynical, my friend."

"Not divorce," said Ruso. "Marriage."

9

RUSO LAY IN the darkness and listened to the scurry of the mice in the dining room, and then to the patter of the dog. There followed some skidding and squeaking and a crash, then a long silence. It was finally broken by the wail of third watch being blown, and the creak of his bed as he rolled over and vowed to move out of this madhouse as soon as he could afford it.

By the time he woke again, Valens had gone on duty. The house was quiet. As soon as he had breakfasted and bathed (there would be no time later), he would be able to make some progress with his writing.

Ruso wandered into the kitchen and picked up half a loaf of bread and a chunk of cheese that had been left out on the kitchen table. There were, he observed with relief, no mouse droppings on the table this morning. Then he glanced across at the little box on the windowsill and saw that the pile Valens was collecting had grown considerably. Abandoning the idea of food, Ruso strode back to his room, pulled on his overtunic, and went across to the hospital to see his private patient.

The girl was still asleep. He did not wake her. Valens would check on her during ward rounds.

The words CLOSED FOR IMPROVEMENTS had now been chalked on the main fort baths for so long that they had grown faint with age. Apparently half the builders had been called away on more pressing peacekeeping duties. The rest were clearly determined not to be accused of rushing their work. The height of the weeds growing around the feet of the scaffolding struts suggested to Ruso that it would be weeks before they got around to fixing the hospital roof. Months until they demolished the old centurion's house in which he now lived, which Valens had somehow persuaded them to leave standing when the adjoining barracks block was flattened for rebuilding. The rebuilding hadn't even been started. The reopening of the main military baths was surely far more urgent, but even that didn't seem likely to happen this month—let alone this morning.

Using the hospital baths was out of the question. The thought of being trapped naked with a roomful of patients comparing their symptoms made him shudder. He would go out to the public baths. This early, there would be no lines. With no mistreated slave girls to distract him, he should soon return clean, invigorated, and ready to make progress with the *Concise Guide to Military First Aid*.

First he needed a decent breakfast. Recent disappointments at other shops had confirmed that it was worth the trouble of walking across to the bakery opposite Merula's, where he savored the smell before handing over his cash for a fresh roll. The crust crackled as he tore it. Steam rose into the cool morning air. He sat on the bench, leaned back with his legs stretched out over the pavement, and took a mouthful.

The streets were as quiet as was usual in the mornings: so quiet that he could catch the occasional bellow of orders from the parade ground, where most of the legion would be sweating their way through daily training. So far his name had not appeared on the training rota: an oversight that would no doubt be rectified when the administrative officer returned.

A couple of women went into the bakery to load their shopping baskets. A small boy passed down the street, bumping along a cartload of apples cushioned in straw. A settled hen squawked in annoyance as a woman emerged from the doorway where it was sitting and batted it out of the way with a broom. Across the street, the shutters were still closed. Ruso gazed idly at the advertisements on Merula's whitewashed walls.

Beneath a picture of a bowl and a jug, BEST FOOD IN DEVA and FINE WINES, LOW PRICES had been daubed in red for long enough to fade and be refurbished—not very accurately, so the faded paint still appeared at the edges of some of the letters. He was surprised to see Saufeia's name still listed under BEAUTIFUL GIRLS!: a bizarre memorial in sharp fresh paint. Asellina and Irene had evidently moved on and been wiped away with a single coat of white, which left them still faintly legible. Chloe was listed, along with someone called Mariamne, but not the nervous and pregnant Daphne. Customers had scrawled comments next to the names. Most were predictable. Something that looked very much like JUICY! was inscribed next to Chloe. Someone had attempted to scrub off Saufeia's only testimonial, but it was still possible to make out the faint scrawl of SNOOTY BITCH.

An elderly man with one leg was lurching toward the bakery on crutches, managing to balance despite a bulging sack tied over one shoulder. Seeing Ruso's interest in the bar he called, "You're too hasty, boss!"

Ruso turned, but his scowl failed to stop the cackle of laughter and the announcement that, "Them girls don't get up till it's time to go to bed!"

The last thing Ruso wanted this morning was a close encounter with them girls, or indeed with anything female. He was about to leave when another handcart came rumbling along the street. It paused outside Merula's. Its owner, a whistling man in a paint-spattered tunic, unloaded a box and put it down in front of the shutters.

"Don't get up till it's time to go to bed, hah!" chortled the one-legged man for the benefit of anyone who had missed it the first time, and lurched off down the street.

Ruso sat down again. For reasons he could not articulate, he wanted to see the dead girl's name removed from that wall.

The painter fetched a cloth out of the box and cleaned the word SAUFEIA and the scrubbed patch next to it. Then he stepped back and surveyed the rest of the wall.

Ruso stepped across to join him. "You need to take that name off, not clean it up."

The painter squinted at the wall. "*Mariamne Bites*. That'd better go too." He stepped forward again and rubbed at the words, which had been scratched on with charcoal. "Keeping me busy, this lot are. Can't keep the staff, see?"

He bent over the box and lifted a brush. He paused to finger a silver charm in the form of a phallus which was slung around his throat, then, with one stroke, he reduced Saufeia's name to a red shadow showing through the white.

"Bad luck, having that up there," he observed. "Might as well finish off the other one too."

"Other one?"

"The one that run off with the sailor." He reached up and obliterated the faint outline of ASELLINA with a fresh brushstroke of white paint. "She won't be back."

"I think I've met somebody who knew her," said Ruso. It had not occurred to him that the porter's missing girlfriend might have worked in a place like this.

The man grinned. " 'Round here, you'll have met quite a few."

Asellina had probably weighed the offers of several admirers, and the luckless porter had not been at the top of the list.

The painter stepped back and squinted at the wall. "Looks a bit patchy, don't it? I told 'em the whole lot wants doing again, but her inside won't part with the money. Knew that Saufeia, then, did you?"

"No."

"Something funny going on there. I reckon she had a premonition."

Ruso, who spent much of his professional life battling against superstition, could not resist asking, "Why?"

"I never took much notice at the time, but she stuck her head 'round the door while I was working, took one look, and said in that posh voice of hers, 'You've spelt me wrong.' I'd gone and put two f's in, see? So I went to put it right and she said, 'You really needn't bother; I shan't be here much longer.' "

The man touched the charm again, then recharged the brush and ran it across the wall again. In its wake, Saufeia's name, correctly spelled with one "f," grew fainter still. "Course, I changed it anyway," he said. "I like to do a proper job." He put the brush back in the pot. "Might as well not have bothered."

He picked up the red brush. "Here's something to cheer the lads up." In the space where MARIAMNE BITES could still faintly be read, he sketched out in large letters the words NEW COOK.

"Merula says I got to put it in big letters," he explained, "So everybody knows. She don't want a bad name after them oysters."

"She's sacked the old cook?" said Ruso.

"Packed her off to the dealer. Lucky that doctor didn't drop dead, or they'd all be facing the inquisitors."

"How many people were ill?"

"Just the one," replied the painter, frowning with concentration as he led the brush down the first stroke of the "N." "That were lucky, weren't it?"

"Not for the doctor."

"That's what they're saying," agreed the painter. "Peculiar, like, just him and no one else. Anyway, won't happen again. New cook, see?"

10

IT HAD BEEN a day where everything was more complicated than it should have been. When he reached the baths Ruso found he was the wrong sex and had to wait outside ("Women only till the sixth hour, sir—it *is* on the door, sir . . .") This afternoon a signaler who had been sent to have a head cut stitched turned out to have tripped on something he hadn't seen. Alerted by the young man's reluctance to meet his gaze, Ruso had insisted on checking his eyesight after the wound was treated. Within seconds he had discovered not only the advancing shadow of cataract in both eyes, but some inkling of the desperate and complex cover-up undertaken by the man and his comrades. Blindness would be the end of any soldier's career, but a signaler with failing eyesight would be invalided out sooner than most.

"I can manage all right, Doc."

"Really?" Ruso gestured toward a notice on the surgery wall. "Read me some of that."

The man turned and stared: not at the notice, but at the blank wall to its left. Then he moved his head and eyed the periphery of the notice from the other side. Finally he said, "The light's not very good in here, is it?"

Ruso said nothing.

The man lowered his bandaged head into his hands. "My girl thinks it's an illness," he said. "She thinks I'll get better."

"Have you spoken to any of the other medics?"

The man shook his head. "I don't need to," he said. "I watched this happen to my father."

It was too early to disclose the idea forming in Ruso's mind. He said merely, "I'll have a word with my colleague."

The man gave a bitter laugh. "Does he work miracles? Because if he does, you tell him I've got a little lad of two and a pregnant girlfriend to support."

Ruso said, "What about other family?"

"None of mine. Her people want me to go for a promotion so we can get properly married." He paused, not needing to explain the irony. He would never be promoted now, and the medical discharge that would free him for marriage would also render him an undesirable son-in-law. He looked up. "We need the money, Doc. Can't you just . . . keep quiet for a bit?"

Ruso frowned. "If you're sent out into the field, you'll be as much danger to us as to the enemy."

"I've managed so far."

"And who's been covering up for you?"

The signaler said nothing.

Finally Ruso said, "You've had a serious bang on the head. I'm recommending you stay here for two days for observation."

Ruso sent the man down to one of the wards. As soon as the rest of his patients were dealt with he went straight to the records room and scrawled an urgent letter to the eye specialist he had met on the ship. He was not optimistic. Even if the specialist agreed to take the case, the delicate surgery required would be terrifying for the patient and difficult for the doctor, and would possibly hasten the blindness it was supposed to cure.

On the way back to his lodgings, Ruso glanced across at the builders working on the roof of the bathhouse. He wished he had chosen a trade where almost anything that went wrong could be fixed with a hammer.

He was about to turn the corner when a voice called after him, "Sir?"

He stopped. One of the hospital orderlies was hurrying after him. "You're wanted, sir!"

"Officer Valens is on duty now," said Ruso, who had been hoping to get on with the *Concise Guide.*

"No, sir, it's you who's wanted."

"Who by?"

"The second spear, sir. You're to report to him straightaway."

11

"STAND EASY, DOCTOR." The second spear settled into his seat, rested muscular arms on a desk that seemed too small for him, and gave Ruso the kind of look that said nonsense would not be tolerated.

Ruso decided he did not envy Valens the challenge of persuading this man to hand over his daughter in marriage.

"We've had a complaint," continued the second spear. "About a body."

"Sir?"

"A girl from a bar."

"Yes, sir. Merula's."

"You took it in?"

"Yes, sir. Nobody knew who she was at the time."

The second spear nodded. "Probably just as well. It might have been somebody's wife. Most of us keep our women well guarded, but you always get the odd one who thinks she knows better. So, then what happened to it?"

Ruso explained. His pauses were punctuated by grunts of assent from across the desk, followed by, "Right. So who cut the hair off?"

"I don't know, sir. It was like that when she was brought in."

"And you didn't think to warn the owner?"

"No, sir."

"Well, they're not happy. They got a bit of a shock when they saw it and they want to know if we did it."

"Absolutely not, sir. You can check with the gate guards. She was found by a couple of fishermen. You could ask them."

The second spear shook his head. "Doesn't matter. As long as we can't be blamed for it. I'll send someone over to calm them down. And tell them to forget any ideas about compensation."

"Thank you, sir. Any luck finding the culprit yet?"

"No. Don't expect we ever will. We'll keep an eye open, but I doubt much will turn up. No witnesses, of course. It's the usual story: These people are quick enough to complain, but blind, deaf, and dumb when you start asking questions. Turns out the girl was offered protection and chose not to take it."

"She might not have understood the dangers, sir. She'd only been here ten days." It was about the same length of time that Ruso had been here himself.

"Hmph. Not what you'd call bright, these locals. Did she think they'd got two of our lads down there on security for fun?"

Ruso said nothing.

"This will knock a bit of sense into the rest of them," the second spear went on. "At least for a month or two. Bloody nuisance, all of them. Haven't been here long, have you?"

"No, sir."

"In a civilized country—even in parts of Britannia—we'd leave the town council or tribal elders or what-have-you to sort this kind of thing out. 'Round here, just because they're living on army land, they expect us to wipe their backsides for them. If it was up to me, I'd have a curfew and flog anything that moves after dark. Still, we should have a bit of peace and quiet for a while. You won't find many women hanging around the streets tonight."

"No, sir," agreed Ruso, who had not planned to look for any.

The second spear leaned back in his chair and folded his arms. "When I was up with the Ninth," he said, "one of the medics took in a body. Thought he was being helpful. The natives got the idea he was cutting it up for anatomy lessons. Caused a riot. Ended up with a whole lot more bodies, three of them ours. My advice, Doctor, is not to get involved with the locals if you can help it."

"Yes sir," said Ruso, glad the second spear did not know who was in Room Twelve.

12

RUSO HAD DISCHARGED his duties for the day. There was nothing further he could do about the signaler's cataracts. His superiors would make any decisions about the dead girl, and he had left orders that he was to be called if there was a crisis with the live one. Alone in his bedroom, he was free to get on with drafting the next section of the *Concise Guide to Military First Aid*. Unfortunately, it was proving more difficult than he had expected.

He had imagined that once his reference books arrived, he would get straight back to work, freshly motivated after so long a break. Instead, he was sitting in his room scowling at a writing tablet on which he had written a title and two lines of notes before delving into the trunk to look up something that turned out to be in a different scroll from the one he expected and to be less relevant than he had remembered it. The bed was now scattered with unraveled scrolls and note tablets and a few scraps of broken pot on which he had scribbled passing thoughts when nothing else had been handy, and he was still stuck on line three. His mind, apparently unwilling to apply itself to ordering his work, seemed to be seizing every chance to wander off. It was futile and unproductive to wonder why a slave with a "posh voice" and the ability to read her own name had been working in a bar in the first place. No wonder Merula had said she was not suited to the job. But then why—

A shout of laughter from beyond his bedroom door brought Ruso back to his task. He reread what he had written, picked up the stylus, then paused to glance over his notes again. It didn't help that Valens was on call this evening, unable to leave the house unless summoned by duty. Across in what passed for a dining room (they had not bothered to shut the door, of course), his colleague was discussing horses with a couple of friends who had loud voices and even louder laughs. Valens had invited him to join them, but as soon as he explained that he had work to do they seemed to have forgotten all about him.

At least they didn't keep popping in to ask how it was going. The *Concise Guide* had been conceived—the only thing that was, thank the gods—during his marriage to Claudia. It had been a welcome retreat. The early work had progressed fluently, but several chapters in, it had occurred to him that he was no longer being "concise." Instantly, the flow of words seemed to dry up. While he waited for inspiration to return, he went back to the beginning and edited the first chapters to half their original length. That was when Claudia asked to see how much he had written.

"Is that all?"

"It's supposed to be concise."

"So is it finished now?"

"No."

"Well, when will it be?"

"Later."

"You ought to talk to Publius Mucius if you're stuck. He writes books."

"I am not stuck!" To prove it, he had begun to devise an Overall Plan. This was what he should have done in the first place. He had entangled himself too early in the detail.

Ruso stared gloomily at the four versions of the Overall Plan, which he had removed from the trunk and stacked on the corner of his writing table. Each version had made good the shortcomings of its predecessor, but some new drawback had soon become apparent. He had kept all the versions in case he wanted to refer to them later—it would be a nuisance to find he'd rubbed something flat only to have to rewrite it—but incredibly, considering the hours he had spent poring over each one, he could not now remember which was which. He did not know whether the tablet claiming to be the LATEST VERSION really was, or whether he should be working from the NEW. And what was AMENDED amending?

Ruso sighed. The truth was, despite all the hours he had spent on it, the Overall Plan had been a waste of time. Maybe the whole project—no, he couldn't abandon the *Concise Guide* after all this work. Any fool with a stylus and a modicum of education—even Publius Mucius—could write a book, and plenty of them seemed to make money at it. Unlike most of them, he actually knew something worth passing on. He must simply get on with it. He picked up the stylus, frowned at the title "Treatments for Eye Injuries," and began to write.

One of the dogs was scratching at his door. Ruso reread what he had just written and realized he had left out a vital word. He upended the stylus and flattened the wax.

There was another shout of laughter from outside. When it died away there was a brief moment of peace, then the scratching started again. Ruso made a conscious decision to ignore the dog, rewrote line three, and mentally arranged the essential points of "Treatments for Eye Injuries" into the right order.

The scratching stopped. A plaintive whine came from under the door. Ruso wrote "Next, check for . . ." With the writing end of the stylus poised above the wax but no patient in front of him as a reminder, he realized he couldn't remember what to check next. He flung the stylus down and made for the door, managing as he went to stub his toe on the corner of a trunk that didn't quite fit under the bed.

When he opened the door the terrier bitch rushed in and then stopped dead, sniffing, while several small shapes bounded past her and disappeared under the bed. Ruso narrowly missed treading on another one in the doorway.

One of Valens's friends, a veterinary surgeon, was waving his arms in the air, demonstrating the height of a jump taken by a filly with the potential to be one of the best horses in the province.

"Ruso!" Valens paused to pick out a date from a bowl propped on the arm of the couch. "Want to buy a horse?"

"Not today."

"How's the work going?"

"Well, the dog was eager to read it."

"Oh, sorry!" Valens gestured toward Ruso's room with the date. "I meant to tell you . . ." Ruso waited while Valens bit one end off the date. "I think you've got a mouse in there. She was at the door this afternoon. If you leave her, she'll flush it out for you."

"Right."

"Something else bothering you?"

Ruso leaned against the doorpost. "Tell me something," he said, "If you were buying a girl to work in a bar, would you choose someone with a respectable accent and some education?"

Valens shrugged. "Why not? She could help with the books."

"Add a bit of class," suggested the owner of the filly.

"Might pull in one or two officers, I suppose," added another voice. Its owner was prone on the floor next to a jug of wine. Ruso recognized the duty civilian liaison officer who had been too busy to break bad news to Merula. "Personally, Ruso, I'd think twice. Invest in a bar by all means, but don't get involved in running it. It won't go down too well higher up."

"I'm not running a bar, I—"

"He's just collecting women," Valens explained. "Which reminds me. We need a girl who can cook. Anybody who finds us one gets an invitation to dinner."

Ruso returned to his room. Hastily whisking a valuable scroll away from the nose of a curious puppy, he tidied up and stored all his work back in the trunks and fastened the lids. He piled everything else that was chewable onto the top of the cupboard. Then, since he had no money and nowhere else to go, he headed for the hospital.

Ruso lit the lamps in the records room, closed the door quietly, and lifted the box labeled CURRENT PATIENTS, ROOMS VI TO X onto the desk. He pulled up a stool, seated himself, leaned on his elbows and stared at CURRENT PATIENTS. A true philosopher would not give way to exasperation at the waste of an evening. A true philosopher, a man determined to apply the power of reason to every circumstance, would welcome this chance to catch up with his records.

There were footsteps outside the window. The low murmur of conversation. As the sounds faded, the smell of fried chicken wafted in through the shutters.

Ruso flipped through the record tablets with his forefinger until he reached Room Nine. He removed and opened the first one. "Crush injury to left foot." After consulting his rough notes, he dipped his pen into the ink and scrawled, "Day 3, still swollen, extensive bruising visible, no mobility in toes, henbane, repeat compress." Putting it aside to dry, he consulted his notes again and wrote "Day 4, breathing improved," on a chest infection.

The smell of chicken was still there. Reminding himself how much money he had saved by dining on hospital stew, Ruso recorded the symptoms of a blacksmith who had been admitted this afternoon with an unfortunately located boil, which he would be lancing in the morning.

Outside, men were strolling about with their comrades, eating fried chicken. Inside, Ruso was spending his free evening writing about other people's boils. A less philosophical man would have been depressed.

The slave girl was sitting up in bed. On the table, the lamplight glinted on the contents of a bowl of broth, which must have sat there untouched for several hours. Ruso's greeting of "Good evening. How are you feeling?" met with the usual serious stare and silence. The lack of response was beginning to irritate him. She was lucky to be alive. Once her arm had healed and she had been properly cleaned up and fed, she could be worth money. But her value would be limited if she remained silent and uncooperative. So, instead of pointing and saying, "How is the arm?" as a prelude to his usual inspection of the hand and check of the bandaging, he sat on the end of the bed.

"So. Tell me why you haven't eaten your dinner."

As he scrutinized her, he had the uncomfortable sensation that she was doing the same to him. He wondered how long she had been a slave. There must have been a time when she—or her owner—had been rich enough to afford jewelry for the pierced ears. Just as someone in Saufeia's past had thought she was worth the trouble of teaching her to read. He supposed the fortunes of slaves rose and fell, just like those of their owners. But unless he could find some way of communicating with this one, he would never find out how she had slid low enough to be dragged about by Claudius Innocens.

"I know you can speak," he insisted, although if he had not heard her shout out in the poppy-induced dreams, he would have begun to wonder.

No response.

"Are you always this quiet?"

No response.

"Well, silent one," he said, "my dining room is full of horsemen and my bedroom is full of dogs. So a little peace is a welcome change."

He took out his own writing tablet and opened it. The space under "Treatments for Eye Injuries" seemed even emptier than before. He sniffed. He glanced across at the girl. "How long is it since you had a trip to the baths? In fact, have you *ever* bathed?"

Moments later Ruso nudged the sign aside with his foot and opened the door of the hospital bathhouse with the hand that wasn't supporting the girl. Inside, he lowered her onto a bench and went back out to find a light. On the way back in he repositioned the sign against the foot of the wall: CLOSED.

The changing room was still warm although the fires would have been banked up for the night some time ago. Ruso began to light the lamps. The girl was watching him, clutching her arm, breathing the air that was thick with damp and sweat and perfumed oil. She was taking in the blue-painted walls, the niches and hooks for clothes, the white piles of discarded towels. He considered collecting the towels himself, then realized how inappropriate that would look. The master tidying for the slave.

"Wait there." His voice echoed around the room as he made the gesture that Valens made when telling the dog to "sit."

He lit only one lamp in the cold room: just enough to see by to walk through it. Ladies did not need a cold plunge. Claudia had always been very firm about that. Presumably slave girls could do without too.

The atmosphere in the warm room made his tunic stick to his skin. He tripped on a discarded wooden shoe and almost turned his ankle. The lamp he was carrying swayed and spat as the oil spilled out onto the floor. He sent the shoe clattering across the tiles toward the hot room door, where the rising light revealed an empty rack looming over a jumble of discarded footwear. Another used towel dangled over the side of the massage couch. A strigil, edge glistening with the last oily scrapings of dirt, skin, and hair, lay on the rim of the tub. Ruso, who never used these baths and had never thought to inspect them, was willing to bet they didn't leave this sort of mess when the chief administrator was around. Evidently they weren't expecting him back before morning.

He wiped the strigil on the towel, then dropped the towel to mop up the spilled lamp oil. The light caught an end-of-the-day rainbow sheen dappling the surface in the tub, but at least the water was still warm. He sniffed the contents of a couple of bottles that had been left on the shelf. Spice. Lavender. The girl could take her pick.

The coals in the brazier of the hot room were almost out. The room smelled of overheated men. He had barely stepped inside when something landed on his head. He flinched and shot up a hand to brush it away, then realized, shook his head, and smiled. This was not Africa. There were so few biting and stinging creatures here that the hospital didn't even have its own poisons expert. What he had felt was only condensation dripping from the ceiling.

Ruso abandoned the hot room, guessing the girl would not linger in there.

When he went back he found she had edged along the bench and was huddled in the corner. She looked bewildered. It struck Ruso that since she had been unconscious when he carried her in, this was the first time she had seen anywhere outside Room Twelve.

He turned to find her a clean towel, only to find himself facing an empty shelf. He did the *sit* gesture again and stepped out into the corridor just as an orderly was passing with a tray of water jugs.

"Where's the clean linen kept?"

"Third door on the left, sir." The orderly disappeared into a side corridor.

Ruso flipped the latch and collided with the door, which had failed to open as expected. He rattled it to no avail, then realized there was a keyhole. When the orderly reappeared with an empty tray he said. "Where's the key?"

"Officer Priscus will have it, sir."

"He took the key to the *linen closet*?"

"Officer Priscus is in charge of all the keys, sir."

"That's ridiculous!"

The orderly was too wise to comment. Ruso was wondering what to do next when he heard a familiar voice.

Evidently Valens's social evening had been interrupted. He found him arguing about racing teams with a grizzled veteran whose leg was swathed in bandages from the hip down. Ruso said, "How do we get hold of clean linen when the administrative officer's not here?"

Valens glanced up. "He usually leaves enough out to last till he gets back. There'll probably be some up from the laundry in the morning."

"Surely he can't just disappear like this?"

"Excuse me a minute," murmured Valens, and left the man's bedside.

As they approached the door, Ruso heard a dog bark somewhere inside the hospital building. "Did you hear that?"

"What?"

Ruso wondered if he was starting to imagine things. "Never mind."

"Priscus has a system," explained Valens. "Jupiter knows what it is, but nobody likes to interfere because as long he's left alone, everything turns up more or less when you need it."

"I need it now. Why the hell isn't he here anyway?"

"Apparently he went to Viroconium to negotiate a contract for delivery of hospital blankets."

"Blankets? Gods above, surely any peasant with a couple of sheep and a wife can knock up a few blankets?"

"Ah," agreed Valens, "you and I might think so. But they have to be the right specification to fit hospital beds."

"Does anyone really believe that?" said Ruso.

Valens shrugged. "You'll have to pinch what you want from someone else."

Back in the corridor, Ruso contemplated the silent door of the linen closet. He had yet to meet Officer Priscus, but already he hated him. The man seemed to have turned hospital administration into an art form—something incomprehensible, overpriced, and useless. In the meantime, a sick girl was huddled in a corner of the changing room, facing a pile of wet towels.

Ruso stood back, contemplated the latch for a moment, and moved. A splintering crash echoed down the deserted corridor. He helped himself before anyone could arrive to see who had just bypassed the hospital administration with a military boot.

"Towels!" he announced, presenting them to her with a flourish.

She seemed less impressed than he had hoped. He took her good arm and helped her up. As he opened the cold room door she tried to pull away. He tightened his grip. "You need to bathe," he insisted, walking her through into the warm room. He thought again how thin she was as he lifted her onto the edge of the massage couch. As he approached with the cleaned strigil and the two bottles of oil, her eyes widened. She raised herself up with her good arm and tried to sidle away down the couch.

Ruso did the "sit" gesture again. "Stay still." He walked around to the other side of the couch, leaned across, and began to untie the sling that was knotted behind her slim neck. He felt her shoulders tighten and remembered how the pregnant Daphne had frozen at the touch of the doorman. "It's all right," he assured her. "You're safe here. Nobody is going to hurt you."

He had carried this girl in through the east gate. He had put her to bed, and dressed her in the washed-out gray tunic she now wore. He had already seen the protruding ribs, the breasts shrunken by hunger, the yellowing bruises that shouldn't be there. He knew the sight of her body would arouse nothing in him but sympathy. Unable to explain that to her, he tapped the splint and said, "Don't get water on the bandages," then put the towels over her good arm and told her he would come back later.

He had finished his records and there was not enough time to settle into "Treatments for Eye Injuries," so Ruso strolled down to the nearest of his wards. He looked at an abscess, got a concussed man to count the number of fingers he held up, ordered another poultice for the crushed foot, listened to a worrying cough, chatted to the signaler, checked up on recent surgical patients, and told the surprised staff not to expect this every night. In a small side room he examined a veteran centurion who had been brought in after collapsing, and decided he had been right this afternoon: It was pneumonia. The man was sixty-six. There was little they could do beyond trying to make him comfortable.

He dared not leave the girl for too long in case she fainted in there. When he had made sure the gasping centurion was propped up on his pillows and had instructed the orderlies to check him every hour, he made his way back down the corridor to the bathhouse.

His announcement of, "It's the doctor!" echoed through the rooms. The only response was the flicker of the lamps in the draft from the door.

He found her perched on the side of the warm bath wrapped in a towel, skinny legs dangling, matted wet hair dripping down her face. "Enjoy that?" he asked, more out of habit than in any hope of an answer. He stood in front of her and frowned at the rough surface of the tangled hair. "Time we sorted this out," he announced. "Can't have you harboring lice." The girl's eyes met his. She showed no sign of understanding.

He reached behind him for the shears he had tucked into his belt. They were usually used for cutting clothes off accident victims, but they were fairly small and sharp and he knew he had a steady hand. He lifted one side of the mat away from her ear. "Keep still."

"No!"

The shriek echoed around the empty blue walls.

Ruso paused with the shears in midair. In his surprise he had let go of the hair. The girl was bent double, her good arm shielding the back of her head.

The sound of the scream died away. The girl began to rock backward and forward, making a soft moaning sound.

"I'm not going to hurt you!" Ruso insisted, hoping no one had heard the scream and wishing he had left this for another day. "I'm cutting the tangles out so you can tidy it up and let it grow back."

The rocking continued. The moaning formed itself into, "No, no, no." The sniff that followed led Ruso to suspect that she was crying.

"Oh, for goodness' sake!" He tucked the shears back into his belt. He was never sure how to deal with crying women, who roused within him an uncomfortable mixture of guilt and exasperation. The "No, no," had finally died into silence by the time it dawned on him that she might have overheard and understood something about the state of the girl dumped in the river.

"Nobody here is going to hurt you," he repeated. "But you can't leave your hair in that mess. What do you want to do about it?"

The girl sat up. She gave another loud sniff and rubbed her eyes with the back of her hand. Then she squared her shoulders and looked him in the face.

In a voice lower and hoarser than he had expected, she said, "I want to die."

13

AN ORDERLY WAS helping the blacksmith down from the treatment table early the next morning when Ruso put his head around the door to investigate the cause of the raised voices and running feet. The corridor was blocked by a crowd of cavalrymen. An unconscious man was being dragged along, his comrades simultaneously yelling for help and shouting at one another to get out of the way. Ruso was grabbed by a wild-eyed rider who insisted, "You'll look after him, right? There wasn't nothing we could do, I'm really sorry, right?"

He learned later that they had been practicing a close-formation gallop when the patient's horse had stumbled. He had fallen under the hooves of the animals behind. There was, as the unfortunate rider had said, nothing the other men could do. There was nothing Ruso could do either. Despite everyone's efforts, the youth was on his way into the shadows even before they pulled the chain mail off to check his injuries.

Ruso had hoped to spend any free moments of his duty with the girl. Instead, the crushed foot was looking worse, the old centurion was putting up a determined fight to die as slowly as possible, and he had to put a frightened patient into an isolation ward until Valens could confirm his diagnosis of leprosy. By the end of the afternoon he had managed only to hand the girl a bowl of porridge and a comb and say, "I'll be down later. I don't want to see that food when I come back," before heading back to the records room to write up his part of the Fatality Report.

He was reaching for a pen when he distinctly heard something that was not human pattering across the tiled entrance hall. He leaped up from the desk and flung open the door. The corridor was empty. He took the few strides to the corner, around which he caught sight of Decimus the porter strolling in through the main doors.

The man paused. "Can I help you, sir?"

"I could have sworn I heard a dog."

"Dog, sir?"

"Running across the entrance hall."

The man looked around as if the dog might leap out from behind Aesculapius. "Across the entrance hall, sir?"

Ruso sighed. "Don't repeat everything I say. You were told to get rid of it."

The man eyed him for a moment, evidently weighing what to say next. Finally he settled on, "I know we should have, sir, but me and some of the lads—"

"We've got enough to cope with here. We don't need a dog running around the hospital."

"Ah, but it's not an ordinary dog, sir. It does tricks. Cheers the patients up. And it's a champion ratter. We don't want rats running around the hospital either, sir, do we?"

"You were told you couldn't keep it here."

"Oh yes, Officer Valens told us what you said, sir."

"What *I* said?"

"Only he doesn't much mind it himself, sir. So we thought if it didn't get in the way—"

"I've seen it. That's enough. And it barks."

"But it never gets in the way, does it, sir? Me and the lads feed it on scraps. It's a grand dog, sir. It'd be a shame to get rid of it."

Ruso closed his eyes. He had had to explain to a bunch of distraught and disbelieving cavalrymen that there was nothing he could do for their comrade. Now he had to go over it all again in writing. He was not in the mood to discuss the comparative desirability of dogs and rodents, and he could hardly point out that Officer Valens was using him as an excuse to wriggle out of giving an unpopular order. It seemed that the porter, having mislaid a woman, had replaced her in his affections with a dog. Perhaps it was a sensible exchange. When he opened his eyes the porter began again.

"Sir—"

"Just keep it out of the treatment rooms and out of sight, you understand? The minute it's a nuisance, it goes."

"Right-oh, sir," agreed the porter. "You won't have no bother with it. It'll be an invisible dog."

"Well, if it becomes visible to Officer Priscus, you're on you own."

Ruso thought he detected a slight hesitation before the porter said, "It's not true, then, sir, that he's got a posting with the governor?"

"Not as far as I know. Now push off. I've got work to do, and I suppose there is a faint chance that you have as well."

"Sir?"

"What now?"

"You don't happen to know when he's coming back?"

"I haven't a clue," said Ruso. "Go and make sure the room lists are up to date in case he turns up this afternoon."

Ruso shut the door of the records room and sat down again. Just as he picked up the pen, the latch clicked and Valens strolled in. He helped himself to the spare chair before enquiring whether Ruso had seen the younger sister of a recently appointed centurion. "She is *stunning*."

"Even more stunning than the second spear's daughter?"

Valens grinned. "That's a long-term project." He settled himself in the chair. "I heard you had a problem?"

Ruso gave him a short run-down of the afternoon's events, leaving out the dog.

"Not good," summarized Valens, putting his feet up on the desk and treating his friend to a display of gleaming hobnails surrounded by dried mud. "By the way, I dropped in on your Tilla just now. Since you were too busy."

Ruso frowned. "My what?"

"Tilla," repeated Valens. When there was no reply he shook his head sadly. "Gods above, Ruso, you are hopeless. What have I told you? First rule with women: Get the name right. Anyway, it looks as though you've got away with that arm. Too early to say whether it'll be of any use, of course."

"Are you sure she's called Tilla?" persisted Ruso. "It doesn't look anything like that on the note of sale."

Valens shrugged. "She said that's what you called her."

"I didn't call her anything. I can't pronounce her name. It's got about fifteen syllables stuffed with g's and h's in odd places."

"She seems to think you told her she'd be Tilla from now on. She seemed quite cheerful about it."

"Did she?" There was no justice in the ways of the world. Ruso, who had saved the girl's life, was rewarded with weeping and "Let me die." Valens, who would have fixed her broken arm with a sharp saw, was granted a pleasant chat.

"Well, she was smiling."

"Good," said Ruso, with as much grace as he could muster.

He should have guessed that Valens's idea of a medical checkup would include an attempt to charm the patient with his boyish good looks and his smooth bedside manner. He would probably smarm his way into the CMO's job in the same fashion. Even without any combat experience. Ruso folded his arms and leaned back against the wall. "I had an interesting conversation myself just now," he said. "Did you tell the staff they could keep that dog?"

Valens scratched his head. "I may have said it didn't bother me. I can't remember."

"Thanks very much. You're not the CMO yet, you know."

"I did tell them what you'd said."

"Only I hadn't, you had. And anyway they completely ignored it. Do we really want animals running around the hospital?"

"Don't be miserable, Ruso. It's only a dog. Which reminds me"—Valens thrust out one foot and kicked the door shut before leaning closer—"speaking of miseries, have you heard this rumor about Priscus getting a posting with the governor?"

"Just now. Is it true?"

"You'd better hope so. Then he might not find out you've demolished his linen closet."

"Gods above, he's only a pen-pusher! Who runs this place?"

Valens pondered that for a moment and then said, "He doesn't interfere with the medical decisions."

Outside, there was a clank of buckets. Someone called out something about stocking up dressings and footsteps trod down the wooden boards of the corridor.

"*Utilis*, said Ruso suddenly. "Useful. Her Latin's a bit shaky. She got into a bit of a state last night. Thought she was never going to get better and wanted to be off with the ancestors, or something. I told her she'd be *utilis* to me."

"Well, that must have been a big comfort. So you aren't going to sell her, then?"

"Of course I am. I don't need her."

"She's cleaned up rather well, don't you think? A bit skinny, but surprisingly good teeth. Why don't we hold on till she's mended and give her a try?"

"No."

"So how is she going to be useful to you?"

"How much would you say an attractive female slave would fetch here?"

Valens's face betrayed his amusement. "Claudia would never have approved of this line of business, you know."

"One of childbearing age?" persisted Ruso.

Valens shrugged. "Two thousand, if you can find the right buyer. Three or four maybe, if she can actually do something."

"Exactly," said Ruso, and dipped the pen in the inkwell.

Finally alone, Ruso started the Fatality Report. The first stroke of the first letter slid down the sheet and ended in a quivering black blob. He rested the pen on the edge of the desk while he blotted the page with a soft rag. A glance at the shelf told him there were no spare sheets. Of course not. The chief administrator had probably taken the key to the stationery cupboard too. Ruso held the sliver of wood over the lamp flame to hurry the drying of the blot and wondered what the girl's smile was like.

The blot was obliterated by a scorch mark. He swore.

This time the stroke started well enough, but the ink began to falter halfway down. He pressed harder. The nib scraped the wood, leaving a blank indentation like a dry riverbed. The dead cavalryman deserved better than this. He dipped the pen in the inkpot and tapped it against the edge.

Gods above, Ruso, you are hopeless.

He wasn't *completely* hopeless. He'd managed three years of marriage. Whereas Valens was still single at thirty-two and any woman willing to marry him would need her sanity examined. So would the second spear, if he gave his permission.

A fine neat stroke this time, cutting across the sepia edge of the scorch mark. That was better. He was making progress now.

The pen jolted between his fingers and stopped working. A second attempt at the stroke made an inkless scratch. Ruso lifted the pen to eye level and squinted at the nib. It was bent at an impossible angle. He flung it into the corner where it made a splash of black as it bounced off the plaster, missed the wastebasket, and rolled across the floor.

Claudia would never have approved of this line of business, you know. He must stop showing an interest in slave girls. He would become a source of amusement.

The next pen had a nib that wobbled about. The third proved to be an inky stick with no nib at all.

Ruso sent the stool crashing back onto the floorboards, wrenched open the door, and roared, "Can't anybody get anything organized in this bloody place?" to an empty corridor.

14

A THRUSH WAS singing its early song in the hospital garden. The girl who had decided they could call her Tilla lay with her eyes closed, letting the music lift her above the dull ache in her arm. The bed was comfortable. She felt clean for the first time in weeks. It occurred to her that she was happy.

The feeling was followed by a flush of shame. She had no right to be happy. This white room with the square window was only a temporary resting place.

The Roman healers had, for reasons that were not clear to her, chosen to delay her arrival in the next world. Three times now she had allowed her thirst to defeat her resolve, reached out her good hand and drunk the barley water they had left in the black jug. When the serious one had sat on the bed and fed her with a spoon like a child, she had accepted a few mouthfuls of salty broth. After he had gone, she had struggled out of the bed, picked up the bowl, and tipped the contents out the window.

She opened her eyes. This morning's bowl of gruel was still untouched on the table. This time there was a plain bone comb beside it. She swung her feet down onto the wooden floor and paused with her head bowed until the giddiness passed. Moments later, the thrush's song died as the latest meal slid out of the bowl to join the others under the lavender bush.

By the time she fell back onto the bed she was sweating and exhausted. She closed her eyes and leaned against the white wall. She must not weaken. In the next world, the others were waiting.

15

RUSO PAUSED IN the doorway of the admissions hall and eyed the three very young soldiers who were standing stiffly against the wall. Over the murmur of conversation that echoed around the hall he inquired, "Are you here for me?"

"Yes, sir," they chorused in badly timed unison.

"Ah." It struck him that this answer was less than helpful since everyone in the hall was there for him in one way or another. "So, you're the new bandagers who are supposed to be following the doctor around this morning?"

"Yes, sir."

"Good. Keep your eyes open and your mouths shut, and you might learn something. I'll try and make time for questions afterward."

There were about twenty patients already lined up on the three benches. Half a dozen still stood in the line at the orderlies' table by the main entrance, waiting to be processed. Each man already seated had been assigned to a bench depending on the apparent urgency of his case. Several of the men on the nearest bench were slumped forward with their heads in their hands. A couple were clutching at injuries with bloodstained rags—one eye, one foot—and one was shivering and coughing.

"Not so busy this morning," observed Ruso, eyeing the empty seats.

"Word gets around, sir," said one of the trainees.

Ruso turned and raised his eyebrows. The other two shrank back as if they were hoping to melt into the wall.

"I mean, sir," the lad stumbled, "only the men who are really ill bother coming."

Ruso was conscious of the patients' eyes on him as he led his little troop across the hall and into his surgery.

Ruso's working space contained three shelves, a collection of unmatched stools and chairs, an examination table by the window, and a desk whose migratory tendencies had been curbed by a previous incumbent with a hammer and several large nails. One wall held a scatter of faded notices and a collection of colored diagrams showing muscles and bones. The students looked uncertain whether to stand to attention or demonstrate their keenness by trying to memorize the diagrams.

"Stand where you can see," he instructed them, laying his case on the desk and unfastening the clasps, "and don't get in my light." As they shuffled awkwardly around the stools, he lifted the lid of the case and repositioned the bronze probe, which always slipped out of its place as soon as the case was vertical. He glanced up at them. "Ready?"

The nods were a little too eager.

The feverish man was summoned, swiftly examined, and sent down to an isolation ward with a prescription. The moment the man had been escorted out of the room, there was another knock on the door. Instead of the next patient, it turned out to be the porter who was part owner of the invisible dog.

"Could I just have a quick word, sir?"

"Can't it wait, Decimus?"

"Very quick, sir."

"Go ahead."

"Sir, I thought you might like to know, Officer Priscus was seen arriving at the street of the Weavers this morning. He's back at his lodgings, sir."

Ruso stared at him. "That's it?"

The man glanced at the students. "We wondered if you wanted anything shifted, sir. Being as he might be here any minute."

Ruso frowned. "Why would I want anything shifted?"

"We're cleaning up a bit, sir. So if you've got anything cluttering up any of the rooms, we could move it for you. Sir. If you tell us where to put it."

Ruso scratched his ear. "If Officer Priscus finds anything cluttering up any of the rooms, you can tell him I put it there."

"Yes, sir." The man hesitated.

"Well?"

"Sir, we think Officer Priscus might ask who helped you put it there in the first place. If there was anything. And then some people who were just trying to be helpful might be in hot water, sir."

Ruso glanced at his students to make sure they were at least pretending not to listen. "I'll deal with it in a moment," he said. "Send in the next man."

Next in was the *optio* with the bloodstained rag clutched to one eye. Ruso looked at his students and grinned. This would take their minds off any speculation about things cluttering rooms. This, he knew, was the patient they had all been dreading.

The *optio* did not disappoint. By the time Ruso had sent him off on a stretcher to be prepared for surgery, one of the students had fainted and the other two were looking as though they wished they could join him on the floor. Ruso supervised the revival of their fallen comrade and gave them all a brief lecture on the importance of not frightening the patient.

Next in was a pale standard-bearer with a recurrence of acute abdominal pain on the right-hand side. He left clutching a prescription for a more powerful medicine. Privately, Ruso hoped that it wasn't gallstones. They were the devil to treat and he dreaded elective surgery almost as much as his patients did. Recovery was at the whim of the gods, but no matter how careful he had been, the blame for failure always lay with the doctor.

The rest of the urgent bench consisted of a man who had stepped on a nail and an unremarkable collection of conditions painful to the owner but mercifully palatable to the medical student.

"Finish your notes," he ordered the observers. "I'll be back in a minute."

The imminent arrival of Officer Priscus seemed to have had the same effect on the staff as a heat wave on a nest of ants. They had all emerged from wherever they hid during the day and were scurrying around clutching blankets and bandages and bedpans and brooms.

The girl's room was quiet. She was sitting on the bed with her knees drawn up under her chin, apparently listening to the sounds of activity around her. Ruso glanced out into the courtyard garden. One man was busy scything the grass and another was on his knees ripping weeds out of the herb bed.

"I need to move you," he said, automatically glancing around the room to see what possessions needed to be gathered up before realizing that she had none. Even the rags she came in with had been burned. He retrieved his comb from beneath the window and wondered if she had been trying to throw it out. Glancing at her hair, he concluded that it had sacrificed several teeth in vain.

He leaned down and placed one arm around her shoulders, the other beneath her knees. He was acutely aware that, underneath the rough wool of the old tunic, she was naked. He was going to have to face the business of finding more clothes for her very soon.

"Up!"

She seemed no heavier than when he had carried her in. The matted hair rested against his cheek. He hoped he had been wrong about the head lice. He hooked one toe around the door and pulled it open, stepping out into the side corridor and pausing to crane around the corner and make sure no one was approaching.

The hospital formed a large square around the courtyard garden, with the long admissions hall and the operating rooms on one side of the square and the wards and other rooms along the remaining three. The quickest way out was to turn right and carry the girl up toward the admissions hall. They could then escape through the side door beside the baths, which would surely be unlocked for the maintenance staff to get in and out during the day.

He had made it about twenty feet along the corridor when an unfamiliar voice sounded in the distance. The tone sounded authoritative and it was growing louder as the owner rounded the corner behind him.

Ruso dodged into another side corridor like the one he had just left. On either side of him were doors to isolation rooms. The voice was growing louder. ". . . and have it all scrubbed through immediately," it was saying.

"Yes, sir!"

"Isolation rooms," announced the voice, almost upon him now. "Your responsibility, Festus Junius."

Moments later Ruso emerged from one of the rooms, alone. At the sight of him, a tall thin officer whose face was ten years older than his hair paused in the doorway of the room opposite.

Pulling the door closed behind him, Ruso said, "*Optio* Priscus, I presume?"

"Indeed," replied the man, inclining the hair slightly toward him. The orderlies with him were stone-faced.

Ruso introduced himself. "New surgeon."

"Ah, good morning, Doctor. Welcome to the hospital. I am your administrator. We conduct a daily ward inspection so if there is anything you require . . ."

Ruso jerked a thumb back toward the door he had just closed. "Leave this one till later, will you? The old boy's only just got off to sleep."

A flicker of something that might have been displeasure moved the muscles of the administrator's face. Then the hair inclined toward Ruso again and the man murmured, "Of course."

Back in the isolation room, Ruso gathered up the girl from where he had dumped her on the end of the bed. The old centurion had woken up. His eyes were wide and his chest was heaving with the effort of drawing breath to speak.

"Wrong room," said Ruso swiftly, "Sorry."

The man's mouth opened.

"Don't try to talk." Ruso gestured toward the bedside. "Do you need me to ring the bell?"

The man shook his head.

"I'll be in later." The old boy had deteriorated since earlier this morning. Ruso left the door ajar so the staff would hear the bell and, as he left, heard a wheezy voice suggest, "You can—leave her behind—if you like."

Priscus had turned right. As soon as the corridor was empty Ruso turned left and hurried back past the girl's former room, narrowly missing a big basket of dirty linen that someone had abandoned just around the corner and promising a voice which called, "Doctor!" that he would be back later.

The girl seemed to have drifted off to sleep as he strode down the corridors. He took a shortcut across the garden. A man who was standing in a lavender bed and scrubbing the wall beneath what had been the girl's window glanced up but said nothing. Finally he reached the hospital kitchens. Ignoring the stares of the staff, he marched through the steamy atmosphere, wrenched open the back door, and stepped out into the street.

Valens had gone out but fortunately forgotten to lock the house door. Welcomed by enthusiastic puppies, Ruso carried the girl over the threshold—a feat that required much less effort than it had with Claudia in his arms—and dumped her on his bed. The house smelled abominably of dogs and mold. He forced open his ill-fitting bedroom shutters and wondered how he could have failed to notice how bad it was before.

In the kitchen he poured a cup of water and hacked a lump of cheese from the end without small teethmarks.

He left the food with the girl and added a scrawled note on the slate which was supposed to be the house message system: SLAVE IN MY ROOM TEMPORARY ARRANGEMENT.

He sprinted most of the way back to the hospital, entered through the front door, nodded to Aesculapius, and made a determined effort to silence his breathing as he strolled across the admissions hall toward his surgery where his students were waiting. Pausing by the door, he turned and saw two benches full of men, all watching him.

"Right!" he said. "Who's next?"

16

THE WOLF WAS very large and very dead. Its skin was splayed against the white wall. Its fangs were bared in a snarl and the lively glint in its glass eyes suggested that it was about to leap up and attack the damp patch on the hospital administrator's ceiling. Priscus, presumably used to the sight, snapped open a folding chair for Ruso. He slid himself into position behind his desk as neatly as if he had been one of his own files on the shelves.

"Ah," he said, smiling in a manner that made Ruso glance back at the wolf for comparison. "I see you've noticed my little trophy, Doctor."

"Is it local?"

"Oh yes. I ran into it a couple of years ago on my way to Eboracum. Quite a fine specimen, don't you think?"

"Very impressive," agreed Ruso, noting that the administrator had a better office than any of the medical staff.

"You'll find there is excellent hunting in Britannia," said Priscus, running a hand lightly over the top of his head, as if to check that the hair was still there. "Although personally I find it rather difficult to set aside the time."

"I imagine you find plenty to do here," suggested Ruso, not adding *especially if you don't give anyone else the keys.*

Priscus smiled again. "Organization," he said, indicating a large board nailed up above the shelves. Each notice on it was spaced an exact inch from its neighbor. "Organization and teamwork," he continued. "The key to a pleasant and successful hospital. Don't you agree, Ruso?"

"I find a steady hand with a scalpel quite useful, myself."

"Precisely!" Priscus spread his fingers to grasp an invisible quantity of precision that he seemed to think was hovering just above his desk. "Efficiency stems from a clear understanding of our various roles and responsibilities. So perhaps you will allow me to give a brief outline of the administrative arrangements."

The administrative arrangements were impressive in their complexity: so impressive that once Ruso had spotted the underlying theme—that every decision was referred back to the hospital administrator—he stopped listening. He was wondering whether Priscus knew who was responsible for breaking into the linen closet when something caught his attention.

"I'm sorry, what did you just say?"

"As I was saying, a scribe could be extraordinarily useful. I think we can find a suitable man."

Ruso frowned. "A scribe?"

"My men aren't used to African writing, I'm afraid."

The man had only been back for a day, and already he had found time to scrutinize the patient records. "It's the same as any other writing," said Ruso. "The dispensary's never complained."

Priscus's head inclined in agreement. "No, they are very professional. But I took the liberty of discussing the matter with them just now and they agree that a scribe would be the best way forward. And of course, so much more convenient for you. Many of the medical staff with whom I have had the honor of serving have found it very useful. No need to keep stopping to take notes. Nothing to carry. Both hands free."

Ruso scratched his ear. "I suppose I could give it a try."

"That's the spirit, Doctor." As Priscus moved to indicate a stack of writing tablets on one side of his desk, a reflection of his hand glided across the polished surface. "I'm sure it won't take long to copy these."

"You're intending to rewrite all my notes?"

"It will give your man a chance to learn what's required. He won't bother you unless there's something he can't make out."

"Is this really necessary?"

"It would be extremely useful for the hospital. There must be a great deal of valuable information in there."

"I suppose so," said Ruso, realizing how neatly he had been outmaneuvered.

"Excellent! Now . . ." Priscus leaned across the desk and lowered his voice. "Let me tell you, in confidence of course, something I heard in Viroconium. I was told on good authority that not only do the procurator's office have orders from Rome to prepare for a major audit, but it is quite possible that our new emperor may inspect the province in person."

Ruso said, "I see," since the man was clearly waiting for him to express amazement before carrying on.

"In the meantime," continued Priscus, "every unit is to be scrutinized. Any waste and inefficiency is to be rooted out."

This was hardly a surprise. Hadrian was reputed to be the sort of officer much approved by poets and taxpayers: a man who marched bareheaded with his troops, wearing the same clothes and eating the same food, perpetually inspecting and commenting and suggesting improvements. The sort of leader who was either an inspiration or a pain in the backside, depending upon your point of view.

"So naturally, Doctor," the administrator concluded, "we will need to reconcile any irregularities in the hospital books before they are opened for scrutiny."

"Naturally," Ruso agreed. As he was wondering if Priscus really expected the emperor to read his medical records, the administrator reached down beside his desk and brought up a file. Ruso recognized the admissions log from the porter's desk.

"On the subject of efficiency, Doctor, perhaps you could help me with this? We seem to have a duplicate entry. Back on . . ."

Ruso gazed at the top of the administrator's head as his finger traced down the columns. As if he could read Ruso's thoughts, Priscus lifted his hand from the records and ran it lightly over his hair again as he said, "Five days before the Ides of September . . ." He glanced up.

Ruso tried to pretend he hadn't been staring. Priscus returned his attention to the admissions log.

"This entry says quite clearly, *Female, 18–25 years*. Then a word that perhaps you could help me with, then farther down the list on the same day, *Female, 18–25 years* again—and this time the entry states, *to set broken arm*."

He's painted his head. That's it. It's not only the hair that's dyed, it's . . .

"Shall I delete the first as a clerical error?"

"No," said Ruso, "there were two of them."

The eyebrows rose toward the hair. "I see."

Ruso reached for the log. "Dead," he read. "The first one was dead when we got her."

"I see." Priscus sat back in his chair. "I shall have a word. Someone should have explained that we never accept civilian patients here unless we have a reasonable prospect of treating them."

"I've been through this with the second spear. We didn't know who it was. By the time we got her she'd obviously been in the river for some time. Plus, she was stark naked and practically bald."

Priscus glanced up sharply. "I beg your pardon?"

"Bald. No hair." Ruso paused to savor his own tactlessness before adding, "She'd had it all cut off."

The administrator's hand stopped halfway to his head and returned to rest on the desk. He stared at it for a moment, then said, "I shall have to look into this. We can't have unidentified—"

"We know who she was. She turned out to be one of the local barmaids. Somebody had murdered her."

Priscus's hand rose to smooth his hair. "I see. How very, uh . . ." He seemed to be searching for a word. Finally he settled on, "Unpleasant."

"Yes."

"I should have been made aware of any inquiry."

Ruso shook his head. "It's over. The second spear dealt with it. Apparently the girl was a runaway and the owner wasn't in the mood to make a fuss, so since they aren't blaming the army, that's probably the end of it."

Priscus's gaze met his own. "You sound a little dissatisfied, Doctor."

"It's none of my business."

"But are you suggesting the officer in charge could have done more?"

Ruso was not going to be led into criticizing the second spear. "He couldn't find any witnesses," he said. "What more could he do?"

"What indeed?" Priscus made a note. "So, the name will appear in the mortuary list instead of the discharge log."

"Exactly," said Ruso, with more confidence than he felt.

"Excellent. So there only remains the female with the broken arm. I am sorry to trouble you with all this, Doctor, but the discharge log has no record of her either, and without the proper records for civilians we are unable to bill the correct fees."

"Are you?" Ruso scratched his ear and wondered whether that should be, *aren't you?*

He looked the man in the eye. "All this will be very much easier when I have a scribe who knows how the system works, Priscus."

The smile reappeared. "I'm sure it will, Doctor. I'm sure it will."

On his way back to the surgery Ruso walked past the entrance to the linen closet. A carpenter was sweeping up wood shavings. The door had been mended.

17

THE LAMPLIGHT PICKED out the white sling resting on top of the gray army blanket. Beneath it, the girl lay asleep on Ruso's borrowed bed. He watched the sling lift softly with each breath. Four days ago, this sight had been cause for celebration. Now it was cause for concern. By now she should either have died or perked up. Instead, apart from the brief revival sparked by his attempt to chop her hair off and the smile wheedled out of her by Valens's bedside charm, the girl had shown little interest in anything. Not even her own recovery.

He had not been entirely sorry to see Valens proved wrong about the comb ("Ruso, *all* women are interested in their hair!"), but his own tactics had been no more successful. His inquiries about native cuisine had reassured him that she would be no stranger to gruel. Yet despite his carefully prescribed convalescent diet—following which his notes recorded disappointingly scant use of the bedside bucket—the girl was recovering neither strength nor spirit. Nor was she putting on weight. Ruso frowned. Tomorrow, he would repeat the worm treatment. Tonight, he had other things to think about.

He leaned back, relishing the familiar creak of his favorite chair as the front two legs lifted off the ground. He banished a fleeting regret. Claudia would never find out that he had now been sitting on this chair exactly how he liked for the past two years, and he still hadn't broken it.

He stared at the box he had just collected from the porter's desk at the hospital, trying to guess what might be inside. Figs? Olives? Not peaches. Peaches would still be in season, but they wouldn't travel. If he'd had any money, he would have paid well for the simple pleasure of a tray of peaches. To feel the flesh pop between his teeth . . . the rich flavor flood onto his tongue . . . the sticky juice run down his chin . . .

He cleared his throat and reminded himself that if he had been born this far north he would never have tasted a peach. A peach was one of those things he didn't need.

What else would he find? A letter. There would definitely be a letter. And some gloves. His sister-in-law had promised gloves for the British winter, and his nieces a picture for him to hang on his wall. Since his nieces were only four and five, that should be interesting.

He expected nothing from his stepmother, a woman whose interests were restricted to personal grooming and home improvements, about which she knew everything except how they were paid for. *Publius dealt with all that, dear.* Nor was he expecting a greeting from either of his half sisters, since he was not in a position to buy them anything they were likely to want.

Ruso had already missed his father's funeral when the news of the death came. The sea passage from Africa was a tricky one and it had taken him almost a month by ship via Athens, Syracuse, Ostia . . . Under different circumstances, it would have been an interesting sight-seeing cruise. As it was, by the time he reached Gaul, Lucius had started to unravel their father's affairs—or, more accurately, their father's affairs had begun to unravel around him.

According to their stepmother, Publius had "investments." The family had always assumed these investments were funding the very grand—and currently half-built—shrine to Diana the Huntress, which Publius had commissioned for the center of the town. "Investments," however, turned out to mean "loans." Examining the documents stored in the trunk to which he had kept the only key, Publius Petreius's sons soon discovered that everything their father did had been done on an elaborate system of credit.

Initially the brothers tried to keep their dreadful discovery secret while they quietly shored up the loans. But they found themselves in the position of the children Ruso had seen playing on a British beach on the day he arrived, building dams against the incoming tide: Every time they secured one area, chaos broke out in another.

Valens's letter telling him about the vacancy with the Twentieth at Deva had come as a gift from the gods. It was all arranged by post with surprising speed. Using the excuse of the move, Ruso sent instructions to have all his surplus belongings sold. A suitable buyer was found for both his housekeeper and his valet. When the deals were complete Ruso withdrew as much money from his account as the army would allow (they insisted on keeping enough to bury him, just in case) and used it to pay off one of the few creditors who genuinely needed the money.

While he was making these arrangements Lucius paid all the small-but-irritating debts. Then the brothers visited each of the large creditors individually, pointing out that slow payment was better than no payment, that the farm would produce a steady income, and that Ruso was earning a good salary. If they wanted their money back they must keep quiet, keep faith and keep funding the building of the shrine to Diana, which the brothers were obliged to finish as it was their father's dying wish.

This last was a lie. The truth was that six different lenders thought they were funding the building of a shrine, when in fact most of them had been funding personal grooming and home improvements. No wonder Publius Petreius's heart had given out under the strain. Within days of his return home, Ruso was glad he had missed the funeral. His grief was frozen beneath a hard layer of anger.

He clunked the chair back onto all four legs, cracked the seal on the box, and prized it open with his knife.

Over on the bed, the girl stirred, sighed, and settled back into sleep.

Ruso groped in the rustling straw. His fingers closed over a jar. He drew it out. OUR OLIVES was chalked on the side in Lucius's hand.

The next find was a rolled piece of white fabric showing a smeared charcoal sketch. It was a wobbly oval topped with a pile of sticks—or perhaps a range of mountains, or a storm at sea. The center of the oval contained an arrangement of blobs and in one corner of the fabric were two outlines of small hands. Ruso turned the picture to several different angles and could make no sense of any of them.

Next out: a pair of thick brown lambskin gloves. He brushed the straw off them and slid his right hand into the soft embrace of the fleece. Cassia had measured well.

Finally, the expected letter. Despite being sealed into the box, the writing tablet had also been closed and sealed individually.

"Greetings, brother," announced black letters so closely crammed onto the thin wood that Ruso had to lean toward the lamp to make them out. "I hope this finds you well. Cassia and the children send their good wishes and our stepmother . . ." Ruso ran his forefinger hastily along the formalities and slowed down for, "On the subject which concerns us all, you will be pleased to hear that there are no further adverse developments." So, no more debts had come crawling out from dark corners. "The girls have drawn a picture of you, which I trust you will enjoy." That was him? Heavens. He must get his hair cut. "The harvest has been as good as we hoped," continued the letter, "and you will be as delighted as I am to know that Cassia is expecting another child in the spring."

As delighted as I am, indeed. A neatly ambiguous statement from the man who had earnestly requested the latest advice on contraception after the birth of the last baby.

"I pray that you remain in good health despite the climate in Britannia," continued Lucius, "and hope you will write soon, brother!" The final sentiments, having reached the bottom right-hand corner too early, performed a sharp turn and twisted up a narrow column of space between the ends of the previous lines and the edge of the letter. "Do not forget our arrangement," Ruso deciphered, turning the page sideways. The way the pen had skidded and fallen off the cut edge of the wood while forming the tails of the longer letters somehow added to the urgency of, "We all depend upon you. Farewell."

Ruso glanced around the shadowy walls of his small but relatively private bedroom, and knew he was lucky. *Do not forget our arrangement.* Lucius was in charge of four children, a wife, a farm, a stepmother, and two goose-brained half sisters, and now there was another baby on the way. All Ruso had to do was carry out his work and send home all the money he could muster every quarter to help keep a roof over his family's head.

Outside, the trumpet sounded the change of watch. It was getting late. Ruso stood to put the box away. Then he lifted the unconscious slave girl and carried her to the kitchen, where he laid her on a rug beside the warm embers in the hearth. She hardly stirred as he slid a cushion under her head and put his own cloak over her for a blanket.

He leaned against the wall with his arms folded and gazed down at her. The surgery had been the easy part. If she perked up, she would have to be fed and sheltered through a long—and possibly unsuccessful—recuperation.

It was not difficult to see why some people threw out useless slaves. He had wondered briefly whether that was what Merula had done with Saufeia—the girl who "wasn't really suitable for this kind of work"—but that would not have made sense. Merula had not suggested that the girl was physically incapable of working, just that her attitude was poor. There were all sorts of jobs that a fit slave could be coerced to do, whatever her attitude. The girl would have been salable to somebody, and her flight and subsequent death must have meant a financial loss to the business. Merula had received the news calmly not because she was indifferent, but because she had expected the worst and prepared herself.

Merula had made one effort to claim compensation—the complaint about the hair—but when that had failed, it seemed she had given up. Since the army provided most of her income, he supposed it was a wise decision. In fact the only person who had shown any interest at all in the question of who had murdered Saufeia was the girl with the ankle chain, the one they called Chloe. He had wished he could promise her that the army would find the culprit and punish him. But if Merula was not going to make a fuss, it was unlikely anyone else would make any effort to narrow down the suspect list from the several thousand men currently in Deva. Besides, now that he thought about it, the murderer might have been a woman.

The girl shifted and murmured something in her sleep.

Ruso's collecting women.

He was glad he didn't have to explain any of it to Lucius.

18

THE GRAY LIGHT of dawn was making its way around the shutters of a house that contained three people. Two were asleep. The third was grappling with the problem of women's underwear. Where could a man get hold of some? Discreetly? As if that were not bad enough, there would be the monthly business to deal with at any moment.

Ruso wished, not for the first time, that he had been blessed with a useful sort of sister. According to Claudia, a man's only role in the mystery of feminine hygiene was to purchase a capable maid and then stay out of the way. So, although his training had covered the theory, in three years of marriage Ruso had evaded the practice so diligently that he had never really been sure what arrangements were necessary. Valens, of course, was bound to know, but he was not going to ask Valens.

Ruso stared at a cobweb that was trembling in the draft from his bedroom window and thought: *landlady*. The girl couldn't stay where she was much longer anyway. The obvious answer was to find a room in a house with a sympathetic landlady. A dispenser of nourishing meals and womanly advice who didn't charge too much. A landlady was the thing. He would go out this morning and find one. In the meantime, he would wander into the kitchen and see if his property had woken up yet.

He had grasped his overtunic between finger and thumb and was about to give it a good shake when he remembered again that this was Britain, where there were no scorpions to creep into dark crevices during the night. Buckling his belt and wondering if he would ever entirely break the wary habits of Africa, he made his way toward the kitchen. The couch, which would have been the obvious place for the girl to sleep, was still being shared by one of Valens's cronies and the dog.

He opened the kitchen door quietly. Something ran across his foot and shot into the corner. He sighed, then started as his eyes adjusted to the shuttered gloom and he realized the hearth was empty. Instead, there was a figure curled up on the table.

"Good morning."

The girl stirred. A tangle of hair slid across her cheek. She blinked sleepily and stretched her good arm above her head. Ruso had a sudden urge to seize her and take her to his own bed, where she would be warm and sleepy and—since he owned her—obedient. He swallowed hard and pushed the thought aside, not wishing to ponder the level of desperation it revealed.

He said, "Why are you on the table?"

She stared at him for a moment, as if trying to remember who he was, and then gave a heavy sigh of recognition. She slid her good hand forward to grasp the edge of the table and leaned forward, surveying the floor.

Ruso followed her gaze. "Are you afraid of the mice?"

He saw her fist tighten. She looked up at him. "Mice do not hurt."

"No," he agreed, "but falling off the table will."

It was a question of simple economics. The longer her recovery took, the longer it would be before he saw his money. "You won't spend the night here again," he promised. "I'll find a proper room."

It was a promise he would regret by the end of the morning.

Several would-be landlords had chalked up advertisements on the amphitheater walls.

The smell of urine and old cabbage stew, which hit Ruso as soon as the first door opened, failed to mask the personal odor of the toothless crone who announced,

"He an't here, I dunno where he is, and he an't done nothing."

"I'll keep looking," said Ruso.

"Did have," said the next one. "We did have a room. Somebody should have rubbed the notice off."

The third room was still having its walls plastered, but the owner's wife promised it would be ready by nightfall.

"How much?"

She told him. Ruso laughed and walked away, and she let him go.

As the morning wore on and his boot studs wore down, it became clear to Ruso that he had a problem. He was here because Rome had decided that Britannia was worth the trouble of holding on to and had stationed just about enough troops here to crack together the skulls of any Britons who refused to cooperate. Side by side with the stick, however, went the carrot. Civilization. Not only the fort, but Deva itself was undergoing a massive modernization project. Every man not currently engaged in keeping an eye on the hill tribes had a trowel in his hand or a hod over his shoulder. It seemed the legion's orders were to hack out all the available stone, saw up all the local trees, and pipe water to every conceivable outlet. Until the last dog kennel had underfloor heating or the new emperor came up with a new plan, the Twentieth Valeria Victrix was to keep on building.

It was not the soldiers themselves who were causing Ruso's difficulties: They were either off skull-cracking or living in the barracks that they were slowly working their way around to modernization. It was the women and children, widowed mothers and spinster aunts the men collected around them. The women and children and mothers and aunts—not to mention the veterans with nowhere else to retire to, who had women and children of their own—all needed beds to sleep in. Then there were all the hangers-on who congregated wherever there were soldiers to be separated from their wages. Hangers-on needed beds too.

The wail of a trumpet from the other side of the fort wall announced that the morning was almost at an end. Ruso was on duty in an hour and he was still no nearer to keeping his promise to the girl. He was going to have to try Valens's suggestion after all.

Earlier that morning, he had pointed out that he had no intention of lodging his slave in a bar that was effectively a brothel.

"Ah, but it isn't," Valens had explained. "Not technically. We had a tax collector in here the other day. Broken wrist: fell off his horse.

Anyway, he said lots of those sort of places don't register their girls so they don't have to pay the tax on their earnings, and when anybody official asks why there's so many bedrooms then, they say that it's because that take in lodgers. It's worth a try. Just don't let her eat the oysters."

"A tax-dodging brothel. Marvelous."

"You could always have a nice chat with Priscus. I hear his new place is rather spacious. Perhaps he'll find you a spare room."

"Maybe I will," agreed Ruso, just to see the expression on Valens's face.

As Merula swayed across the empty barroom in another stylish silky creation, Ruso mused that this was not the sort of landlady he had envisioned.

The elegantly plucked eyebrows rose at his question. Evidently he was not the sort of tenant she was used to either.

"It's not for me," he explained.

"For a friend?"

"Not exactly." He was aware that he was scratching his ear again. He really must try to stop that. Claudia used to say she knew it meant he was lying, which showed how little they understood each other. He lowered his fist onto the barroom table just below the initials of one CLM, who had felt it necessary to carve not only the first letters of his name but a majestic phallus as well, and said, "I have a female slave whom I can't use at home and who is in need of lodgings. One of my colleagues suggested you might be able to find somewhere for her."

"Ah. An officer at the hospital?"

"Yes," said Ruso, suddenly seeing a way forward. "I believe you know him. He was here a short while ago and he had to have some time off work as a result."

Merula managed to look surprised, as if virulent food poisoning were something she could have hoped to keep secret. "So you know about, uh . . . ?"

"I suggest we say no more about it."

Ruso was satisfied to see relief on the woman's face. He was right: She had been afraid Valens would sue. When she said, "I think we can find a place for her," his problem appeared to be solved.

His problem appeared to be solved until Merula asked, "Is the girl experienced in this kind of work?"

Ruso shook his head. "She can't work. She's sick."

"She can't work?" The painted eyes met his. "So why did your friend tell you to send her to me?"

"I can't have her at my place, she needs to recuperate, and I can hardly billet her in a barracks room."

Merula pursed her lips. "This sickness. Is it fever?"

"She's recovering from surgery on an injured arm."

"And before long you expect her to be fit to work."

"I see no reason why not. In the meantime all she needs is a quiet room and regular meals. You do rent out rooms?"

"Oh, yes!" After this confident assertion she paused. "We don't have anything very comfortable just at the moment . . ."

"But you do have a private room?"

"We do, but—"

He followed her up the open staircase and along the creaking wooden landing that looked down over the bar. Several of the upstairs doors were ajar, revealing small cubicles with beds covered in bright blankets and cushions. It all looked reasonably clean. Ruso consoled himself with the thought that at least he was doing business with the best possible class of tax-dodging brothel.

In the gloom at the end of the corridor was a closed door. Merula scraped a key into the lock.

The room was bare except for a bench against one wall and a mattress in the corner. Merula glided forward and unlatched the shutters.

Before he could remark on the bars across an upstairs window, she said, "We sometimes use this room for secure storage." The light revealed the rings of old drinks and drips of candle wax on the surface of the bench. Underneath, one leg had been replaced with a new chunk of yellow wood that was much too heavy and the whole thing had been clumsily nailed to the floorboards. Ruso crouched and turned over the stained mattress. The straw was even lumpier than the one he was borrowing from Valens and it didn't smell good.

Merula started to explain that the room had not been used for a while. He interrupted her.

"Do you have mice?"

She frowned. "The girl is on a special diet?"

"I don't mean on the menu. I mean running around. Wild mice."

As soon as she told him they didn't, he said, "Put in a clean bed and I'll take it."

19

SHE WAS PRETTY. Old women said so to her mother, and her mother always laughed and replied, "And she knows it." Her brothers knew it too, although they would die before they said so. Sometimes her father came into the house smelling of beer, roared, "Where's my beautiful girl?" and lifted her onto his shoulders while her mother shouted at him to *mind that child's head on the door.* And for a few moments she would be a giant, lurching around the houses, reaching for the edges of the thatch, taller than the horses, and seeing right over the tops of people's fences until he put her down and ignored her pleas for "More!" because parents had things to do and because being pretty did not make you important.

When her mother muttered and sighed and tugged at the tangles with the comb, it was because shiny golden curls needed a lot of looking after. She tried not to smile. Her mother would want to know what she was smiling about, and she already knew it wasn't her cousins' faults that they were ordinary little girls whose hair fell down in straight brown lines and she had to remember to be nice to them and . . .

And the smell was wrong.

Somewhere outside, a man's voice was making ugly, solid sounds that fell like rough logs.

Someone was trying not to pull her hair. Someone was—

She remembered the stink of the bathhouse. The glint of metal blades.

"NO!"

Her eyes snapped open as her free hand lashed out and clouted a crouching girl across the face. A jolt of pain shot through her injured arm as the girl squealed and fell backward in a flurry of brown skirt and dirty bare feet.

She had managed to pull herself up and lean against the wall by the time the other girl, who was dark and heavily pregnant, had managed to maneuver herself onto all fours and then haul herself up to sit on the wooden bench.

She remembered the bench. She remembered the room. She remembered what her name was supposed to be. She looked at the girl's hands, which were empty, rough, and red with work. Then she looked around the floor. There was no sign of any shears. She said, "Who are you?"

The girl shook her head and pointed to her mouth.

The question in Latin produced exactly the same gesture.

In Latin again: "Are you dumb?"

The girl nodded, raised her eyebrows in a question and pointed at her, but she did not answer. A name, even one you had only acquired yesterday, should not be so easily given.

"Did they tell you to cut my hair?"

The girl shook her head with a look of alarm. The hand pointed again, this time at a section of hair that had now been untangled. At the far end dangled a comb, trapped in a knot. The girl had been trying to help.

"My name," she said in Latin, "Is Tilla." This produced a welcoming smile, but the traditional request for help in her own language—"I am a stranger here"—was either not understood or ignored.

The girl heaved herself up from the bench, took the one pace necessary to cross the room, and lowered herself to sit next to the mattress. She had begun to attack the tangle again when the door burst open and two men walked into the room.

One had gray eyes and cropped iron-gray hair above a thick neck. The thinner one's hair had once been ginger. The deep brown of his eyes added to the impression that the rest of him was fading into middle age. Tilla had time to observe this while both men stood calmly examining what they could see of her. She also observed that the dumb girl had stopped work and shrunk back to sit beside her with her back to the wall. Instead of staring back at these men who had not had the manners to knock (and whose muscle, Tilla noted, was running to fat around the belly), the girl had her eyes firmly fixed on the gray one's heavy army sandals.

"Stand up," ordered the gray one.

When Tilla failed to move, the girl tapped her arm and translated the order into a hasty scoop of one hand toward the ceiling, at the same time nodding encouragement.

"You want to listen to Daphne," suggested the gray one. "She don't say a lot but she knows what's good for her."

Tilla, noting the girl's anxiety, pulled her knees up and managed to get to her feet on the mattress. Slowly, she forced her trembling legs to push her upward. Her head felt as if it were full of dry sand that was draining away down her body as she stood. Fighting to stay upright, she slumped against the wall. With her eyes closed, she did not see him approach. She was only aware of the sudden cold as the hem of the tunic was lifted, the struggle to keep her balance as the hands groped and probed, and the urge to vomit as the hands withdrew and a voice whispered in her ear, "Show us your smile."

Clenching her teeth, she managed to open her eyes.

"Smile," repeated the gray man, who was not smiling.

The other girl was on her feet now, moving around to where Tilla could see her, nodding eagerly and grinning, making upward gestures at the corners of her mouth.

As Tilla's eyes drifted shut she thought, *Whatever you do to me here will speed me on my way to the next world,* and it was this thought that made her beam with pleasure.

By the time she was alone again, the light through the barred window was fading. Food had been brought, but no one had offered a light. The rattle of the lock had confirmed that she could not leave this darkening room until someone came to let her out.

Tilla fingered the long braids that now held her hair under control and listened to the many voices downstairs. She heard the tramp of feet on stairs. The creak of the floorboards. The false laughter. She understood what sort of place the Roman healer had brought her to. She understood too that none of this mattered, because she had lost all sense of hunger now, surely a sign that she would be in the next world very soon. But she had matters to attend to here first. The gray one had said he would come back.

She reached for the bowl and balanced it against the bandaged arm. Then she picked up the spoon. The lukewarm soup slipped down her throat, sending the strength of the slaughtered ox into her body. She closed her eyes and promised her mother and brothers that she would see them in the next world very soon. In the meantime she would not be shamed in this one. It seemed she was, after all, destined to die in a fight.

20

THE KITCHEN BOY took Ruso's message to Merula, who paused with the kitchen door half-open, reached up to a shelf inside, and handed over a heavy iron key.

Ruso frowned. "My girl is locked in?"

The painted eyes widened. "You don't want her locked in?"

"I appreciate your caution," he said, understanding that a business that had lost two girls in a few months would be nervous, "but she's not in a fit state to run away."

"It's for her own protection," said Merula. "Some of the customers like to go exploring."

Ruso clattered briskly up the wooden stairs with a lamp in one hand and a medical case in the other, trusting it would be apparent to the idlers lolling at the tables beneath that he was not a customer going exploring, but a doctor come to treat a patient. He strode along the landing, passing two cubicles with their doors closed. From behind one came a male voice and a female giggle that sounded like the girl Chloe.

He had to probe with the key before it engaged and he could push the bolt out of place, swing the door open, retrieve his case, and enter the room.

His greeting died as something hard smacked against his head. The case fell from his hand. His foot exploded in pain. He was staggering sideways, trying to keep his grip on the lamp, when something shoved him off balance and he crashed onto the floorboards.

For a moment he lay stunned, blinking at the wavering flame of the lamp, which had somehow remained upright. Cutting through the reverberations inside his skull was a pulsing agony in his foot. He managed to lift his head. The girl was squatting behind the door, wide-eyed, hands to her mouth.

He rolled over. The big toe of his right foot, which should surely have been a bloody pulp, looked pale but otherwise surprisingly intact. He rubbed the back of his head. A lump was developing already, and blood was making a sticky mess of his hair. Ruso brought his hand forward and squinted at the damp fingers. The blood seemed an odd color.

The girl was still in the corner, apparently too frightened to move. Ruso sniffed at the blood, diagnosed soup, rubbed his head again, curled forward, and sat up to clutch his injured foot. His case lay on the floor, undamaged after his toe had broken its fall. Scattered across the floor were the shards of what appeared to be a bowl. It occurred to him that the bowl must have been what she had used to hit him. It also occurred to him to ask himself whether he was seeing double, whether any dancing lights were appearing in front of him, or whether he felt sick. He was disappointed to note that despite deserving all these symptoms, he did not seem to have any of them.

He heaved himself up on one leg and hopped to the doorway. No one seemed to have noticed that he had been attacked. He closed the door and leaned against it, keeping one eye on the girl as he unlaced his sandal and made a closer assessment of the damage. The toe was turning crimson now. When he put the foot back on the floor it felt as though someone was boring into the toe with a hot fire iron.

He sensed a movement and glanced across to see the girl crawling toward him. He made a grab for her wrist just as she pulled the medical case out of his reach. The lid fell back. The pain banged at the back of his skull. He watched the girl's hand hovering above the neat rows of sharpened instruments. It occurred to him that perhaps she was mad. The unlovely Claudius Innocens might, after all, have been sorely provoked.

He was tensed, ready to kick the scalpel out of her hand, when he saw that what she had picked up was a white roll of wadding.

The girl dipped the wadding into a cup beside the bed. Then she reached up and stroked it across the back of his head, exclaiming as she felt the lump.

Ruso snatched the wadding from her. "I'll do that."

The girl retreated to sit on her bed. He pressed the cool damp wadding against the back of his head and rested his head on his knees. There was some water left in the cup. He splashed some of it across his toes. It made cold trails inside his sandal but no difference to the pain.

He could make no sense of it. He had done everything in his power to help this girl.

He sat up straight. The girl shrank farther back into the corner, eyes darting between his face and his hands, evidently waiting for the beating to start. He noted for the first time that her hair now hung in two long braids that left wispy curls around her temples.

"Well?" he demanded.

"Master?" she whispered, twisting the end of one of the braids around her finger.

"Are you insane, or do you have a good reason for wanting to murder me?"

"No, Master." Her Latin, he noted, seemed to have undergone a sudden improvement. He wondered in what other ways she had tried to deceive him.

"Do you know what happens to slaves who attack their masters, Tilla?"

The braid twisted tighter. Her lower lip began to tremble. "No, Master."

He hoped she wasn't about to cry. "Well let me tell you," he growled, his head and his toe throbbing in grim unison. "First every slave in the household is arrested. Then the questioners are sent for. It is the questioners' job to extract the truth, and they will carry on their work for several hours, whether their victim talks or not"—in fact it felt as if they were currently in action in the area of his big toe—"because nobody believes that a slave will tell the truth without torture. And because it is not enough to punish the guilty. A message must be sent to all the other slaves who might be thinking of knocking their masters and mistresses on the head. An example must be set." He glared at her. "Is that what you want? To be an example? Or can you explain yourself?"

He removed the wadding and cooled it again in the cup. The pain was clanging inside his skull like a clapper in a bell.

The girl swallowed. "I am going to the next world."

"If I call the questioners, young woman, you will go very, very slowly. And be hard to recognize by the time you get there."

She seemed to be giving this careful thought. Finally she said, "I do not think it is you who comes."

"You thought I was somebody else? I suppose it didn't occur to you to find out first?"

She lifted her good hand to touch one ear. "Soldier boots," she said, pointing to his feet. "Bad man."

Ruso stared at the pale figure with sudden comprehension. He said, "You were going to fight off one of Merula's customers with a soup bowl?"

She nodded.

He cleared his throat. "You are completely wrong," he informed her, arranging his words carefully because the ringing in his head was growing louder and threatening to jumble them. "You are my patient, under my protection. I apologize if that was not explained to you. Clear up the mess and get back into bed. You will not be punished—this time."

The girl crawled across the floor, gathering the broken shards of the bowl. Then she eased herself onto the mattress and pulled up the covers. Ruso noted that the bright blankets seemed to be reserved for the public rooms: This one was ordinary sheep-brown.

"You are here to rest until you get better," he said. "The door is locked to keep you safe."

The girl glanced at the bars on the window, then closed her eyes, as if she was tired of trying to understand.

"Is your arm painful?"

She nodded.

He crouched beside her and checked the bandages. She was lucky: The splint had held. There was no sign of movement. He placed his fingers and thumb around her upper arm. No swelling or heat. He laid her hand between his.

"Move your fingers." He felt the ends of the fingers twitch between his palms. "Good. Are you eating the food?"

She nodded again.

"Light diet, no flesh, no strong drink, no seafood, and you must drink plenty."

"Beer," she ventured.

"Beer?" He cleared his throat, aware that a professional should not allow wispy curls and a borrowed tunic slipping down over one shoulder to distract him from his work. He recalled his mind to his duty. "Absolutely no beer, nor anything like it." He gestured toward the lidded bucket in the corner, glad that she had not had the strength to use it as a weapon. "Are you passing water?"

She nodded.

"Good."

He reached into the open case. "I'll give you something for the pain, then you can sleep." He measured a few drops into the empty cup and handed it to her.

She took a sip and wrinkled her nose.

"Drink," he ordered, miming the gesture.

She tipped her head back. He retrieved the cup and measured himself a potent dose of the same painkiller, then stood up and closed the shutters. The room was chilly. She had only one blanket.

Downstairs, a lyre player was competing with the din of voices, the to-and-fro slap of the kitchen door, and the clatter and scrape of crockery. From the balcony Ruso could see only two serving girls for all the tables. Both looked harassed. There was a shout of laughter from the far side of the room, where Merula was pouring drinks for a group of officers.

Ruso turned away. The noise was making his head worse. There was still one cubicle with an open door. He limped in and whipped a rich blue blanket off the bed. He picked up a cushion as well. In the doorway he paused and tossed the cushion back onto the bed. There was no point in making her too comfortable.

When he returned the girl was lying flat on the bed with her eyes closed. He laid the blanket over her and tapped her shoulder. "Before you go to sleep," he said, sliding the key into her hand, "make sure you use this."

21

RUSO WAS TRYING to make his way down Merula's stairs without it being obvious that he had acquired a limp during his visit when he recognized Decimus, the hospital porter. The man was slumped over the crowded bar, wiping his eyes with a grimy fist. He also recognized the signals the barmaid was making to the doormen over the man's head. Ruso sighed. His head hurt. His foot hurt. His dignity was injured. He would not normally have interfered with an off-duty soldier's right to make a fool of himself in a public bar. But it was Decimus who had warned him about Priscus's imminent return yesterday morning, and he supposed he owed the man some sort of favor.

Hoping nobody would tread on his toe, he threaded his way between the tables. Finally close enough not to be overheard, he said, "Time to go, soldier."

The man looked at him wetly, sniffed, and informed him that he wouldn't understand.

"You're drunk."

"You don't know what it's like, sir."

"Go now, Decimus, before you get into trouble."

"You never liked him anyway. You always said get rid of him."

"Ah." Ruso rubbed the back of his head where what remained of the soup was setting his hair into stiff clumps. "The invisible dog."

"Bastard." The porter twisted on his stool and spat noisily onto the floor.

"Oy!" A bald man whose toes he had just missed spun around and glared at him.

"Bastard made us knock him on the head. He was a good dog. He was my best friend. He was faithful, that's what he was." The orderly waved an arm in the air. "He was faithful! None of you lot, you don't know what faithful means!"

"Get a grip, man!" urged Ruso, feeling pain dance around his skull as he grabbed the man's arm and hauled him toward the door. Unfortunately for them both, Decimus's feet did not follow. Instead, with another shout of "Bastard!" he toppled sideways onto Daphne, who screamed as her tray of drinks slid into the bald man's lap.

The bald man leaped up and shoved her aside, roaring, "I warned you, sunshine!" at the porter.

"He was the best dog in the legion!" yelled the porter. "He was—ow!"

"Out!" ordered the ginger-headed doorman, ramming the porter's arm up behind his back while his colleague clamped a forearm around the bald man's throat and offered him the chance to be next if he wanted.

The man struggled to turn. "You! Where's Asellina? You let somebody steal my Asellina! You let all the girls run away!"

"Out, pal," repeated Stichus. "You're banned."

"All gone. All run away. He was the best girl in the—ugh!"

The porter, assisted by Stichus, made an impressive exit. As the man floundered and grumbled in the street, Ruso paused in the entrance.

"We've had trouble with him before," said Stichus, settling back onto his stool. "Me, I wouldn't have let him in."

"I need to leave a message for your mistress."

Stichus gave him a look that said he was too busy to run messages. Ruso ignored it. "I've given my patient the key to her room," he said.

"You what?"

"So she can choose who to let in."

Stichus shrugged. "Please yourself. But we can't be watching her day and night. If she's a runner, it's your problem."

"She's not in a fit state to run anywhere," Ruso insisted, although it had crossed his mind that if the girl managed an escape like Asellina's rather than Saufeia's, it might be better for both of them. "And ask your mistress to keep a note of any refusal to eat and drink."

"Starving herself, is she? Don't worry, we've seen it all before. Merula'll soon sort that out."

"Good," said Ruso, trusting the landlady's attempts to stimulate the girl's appetite would not stray too far from the diet.

His business here now at an end, he gathered up his case and limped out into the street. He had barely taken a step when a voice called, "Sir!"

Ruso watched an unsteady salute being performed from a sitting position against the closed shutters of the bakery.

"Man in need of assistance, sir!"

Sir closed his eyes to the sight of the porter. He prayed for patience and for the poppy juice to work quickly.

Despite Ruso's efforts at guidance, the porter's progress was as much sideways as forward. Not five paces down the street he stopped to deposit much of what he had drunk in the gutter. Ruso sighed, leaned back against the bakery wall with the weight on his good foot, and observed that some wit had added the words SAME OLD POISON to the words NEW COOK! beneath the torch illuminating Merula's doorway.

Finally they swayed back up the dark street and in through the south gates of the fort. Ruso gave the password for both of them and they were almost through the passageway when the porter seemed to realize where he was. He hauled himself to attention and shouted, "Request to report a murdering bastard, sir!"

"He's drunk," explained Ruso, as if the grinning guards were not able to see this for themselves.

"I'm drunk!" agreed the man. "I'm drunk, sir, but at least I'm not a murdering bastard with a painted head and a—"

"Shut up!" snarled Ruso. "That's an order."

The man swung around to inspect Ruso's face in the light of the gatehouse torches. After a moment he announced with apparent surprise, "I know who you are! You're the new doctor, Doctor. You bring dogs in, but they aren't as lovely as my Asellina."

Ruso glanced across at the gate guards. "One of you take his other arm, will you?"

Between them they dragged the man into the middle of the perimeter road. To Ruso's relief, the painkiller was beginning to take effect. He dismissed the guard, assuring him that he could cope, although the man plainly seemed to doubt him. "I'm perfectly sober," he explained, steadying himself as he shifted to take the weight off his sore foot. "I've just had a bit of a bang on the head."

"Are you sure you don't need some help, sir?"

"No, I'm fine," Ruso assured him, leaning closer to explain, "I'm the doctor. I've prescribed myself something."

He was starting to feel far more relaxed now. Confident that his command of the situation was secure, he began to half-drag and half-carry the man along the road, taking the shortest route up by the deserted scaffolding of the baths and around the corner past the streaks of light that marked the shutters of the senior officers' houses.

A couple of passersby offered to help, but he dismissed them with a cheery smile and a wave. There was no problem. He was enjoying himself. He really ought to learn to relax more. See the funny side of things.

When he finally let go the orderly slumped against a post at one end of the dark lane between two barracks blocks.

"You're a good man, sir."

"Go and lie down, Decimus," said Ruso.

"You don't know nothing about dogs, but you're a good man."

The man staggered away into the gloom, leaning on the uprights of the portico for support. Finally he paused outside a door and fumbled with the latch. "Drink plenty of water before you go to sleep," called Ruso, feeling a rush of kindness toward the whole of humankind, encapsulated in this one drunken hospital porter, but the man was too busy falling through the doorway to hear him.

Ruso was still smiling when he climbed into his own bed, and so relaxed he decided not to bother taking his boots off.

22

RUSO SHAMBLED ALONG to the kitchen wondering which was more painful: his sore head or his sore foot. Wretched woman. He needed a long cool drink of—

Damn. The jug was empty. Valens had thoughtfully moved it to weigh down the lid of the breadbin against invading mice but hadn't bothered to nip out and fill it first. Inside the bin was a chunk of bread so hard that the mice could have sharpened their teeth on it. There seemed to be nothing else edible in the kitchen. He chose the least dirty of the cups on the shelf and limped to the dining room. Beer would be better than nothing.

A gang of puppies bounced at his feet as he dipped the cup into the barrel. He was replacing the lid when there was a knock at the door. Still clutching the cup and with puppies licking up the drips in his wake, he went to explain to whoever it was that Valens was out.

The moment the door opened, the arm of the young soldier outside shot up in a salute.

Ruso transferred the beer to his other hand, put out his good foot to prevent a puppy escape and lost his balance slightly before returning an untidy salute and asking, "What do you want?"

"Albanus, sir, reporting for duty."

Ruso frowned, trying to imagine what the man's duty might be. "Have you come to help out?"

"Yes sir."

"Oh. Good. Well, you can start by getting some water. I've got a mouth like a sand dune and there's nothing to drink."

The man looked puzzled. "Water, sir?"

Ruso jerked a thumb over his shoulder. "Jug's in the kitchen."

He stepped aside, but the man did not move.

"Come in," ordered Ruso. "Shut the door before the dogs get out."

"Sir?"

"What?"

"I'm your scribe, sir."

Ruso stared at him and noticed the clues for the first time. The ink-stained fingers. The slight bulge to the eyes caused by peering at documents by lamplight. "Oh."

The man held up a satchel. "I've brought my equipment, sir."

"Well, you can take it away again," said Ruso. "I'm not on duty till this afternoon." He paused. "Report to me at the hospital at the seventh hour."

"Yes, sir." There was a pause. "What would you like me to do until then, sir?"

Gods above, Priscus had sent him an enthusiast. "Haven't you got some old records to copy?"

Yes, sir, he had.

"Then you can get on with that. Anything you can't read, ask me this afternoon. Don't make it up."

"Yes, sir."

The wretched man was still standing there.

"Anything else?"

"No, sir."

There was a silence, then Ruso remembered to say, "Dismissed."

After another snappy salute Albanus spun around, sending his satchel swinging outward and crashing back against his side, and marched off in the direction of the hospital. Ruso shut the door, sniffed the beer, and decided it wasn't better than nothing, after all. He limped back into the kitchen to fetch the jug. He had the feeling Albanus would have copied all the records in triplicate by lunchtime and be pestering him for more work. He could have given him the *Concise Guide* to copy. It was a pity that most of it wasn't written yet.

Ruso was carrying the jug out the door when there was a crash and a skitter of paws across floorboards. He turned. Several puppies were running for cover. One was perched on a side table, peering over the edge at fragments of a cup lying in a spreading pool of beer.

Ruso shut the door quietly, limped down the street to the water fountain, and stuck his head under it.

23

TILLA COULD SMELL fresh bread. She pulled the blanket tighter around her shoulders and peered out between the window bars. Across the street, a pigeon was perched on the roof of the bakery. Beneath it, someone swung back the first panel of the door shutters. A plump woman appeared in the gap, bending to apply her bottom to the rest of the shuttering. The panels shifted on their hinges and the pigeon swooped away as the whole apparatus began to screech back along its groove.

Tilla watched the pigeon until the frame of the window blocked her view. Then she returned to her bed, slid her hand underneath, and pulled out the iron key the healer had given her the night before. She had felt sorry for the healer, who had done nothing to deserve being smacked on the head and who should have had her beaten—since it seemed she did, after all, still belong to him. Evidently she was not yet the property of the ill-mannered bullies who had sauntered in yesterday with the clear intention of sizing her up for their own use.

The question was, what should she do now? She had the key. If she could find clothes, if she ate and built up her strength, if she could judge the right moment—she could escape. Or, she could choose not to eat, to cheat the work of the healer, and step forward toward her death. What honor, though, would she have in the next world if she had been offered a chance of freedom in this one and refused to take the risk?

A clunk from the loose board in the corridor warned her that someone was outside. Moments later there was a soft knock at the door. Tilla pressed her face against the door frame and squinted through the crack. She could just about make out a shape that was not tall enough to be either of the men.

"Daphne?"

The form moved and the hand knocked again.

Tilla slid the key into the lock, positioned one foot an inch away to hold the door while she assured herself it was only the girl, and then let her in.

"Daphne," she said, locking the door again. "Thank you."

The girl put the tray down on the bench.

"Did you sleep well?"

Daphne shrugged, and indicated her belly in a way that suggested her expectations of sleep were limited.

"When is your baby due?"

A second shrug indicated that this was not a subject of great interest.

"My master has given me the key," explained Tilla, "so I can decide who comes in. I do not want those men in here. If you come alone, knock like this." She demonstrated three short taps on the windowsill. "Understand?"

Daphne reached out a hand and gave three short taps on the door.

"Only if you are alone, yes?"

Daphne nodded and pointed to herself. For a moment Tilla thought she was about to smile, but a yell of, "Daph*ne*!" from downstairs reminded her of her duties. Tilla let her out, locked the door, and retreated to see what they had given her for breakfast.

24

THE OUTSIDE DOOR to the hospital kitchen was propped open to let out the heat as usual. Ruso nodded a greeting to the cooks as he passed, pausing long enough to light a taper on the grilling coals but not long enough to answer any questions, either about why he was limping horribly or about why he didn't use the front door like everyone else.

He waited until the corridor was empty before making his way down to the courtyard door. Clutching his case in one hand and the taper in the other, he managed to hobble across the courtyard garden and enter by the consulting rooms without being accosted by either patients or staff.

Ruso leaned back on the closed door of the consulting room and contemplated his toe. Such a small part of the body. Such disproportionate agony.

He lit a stub of candle. Then he unlatched his case and retrieved the thinnest of the bronze probes which had, as usual, fallen out of its place. He propped the thicker end of the probe on the top of an inkwell and moved the candle so the tip of the probe was being lapped by the flame.

While he waited for the instrument to heat, he unlaced his sandal, glanced around the room, and then moved a chair away from the wall under the window. This was a quick and straightforward procedure.

There was no need for painkillers or restraints. There was also no need for furniture for him to fall off if things didn't turn out to be quite as straightforward and quick as when he did this to other people.

Shielding his fingers from the heat with a cloth, Ruso picked up the cooler end of the probe. He sat himself on the floor below the window and braced his back against the wall. He took a deep breath. Then he placed the tip of the probe against his toenail.

The door burst open. His hand jolted. The probe slipped out of his grasp and rolled across the floor.

"Ruso!" exclaimed Valens. "They told me you were in here. What are you doing down there?"

He explained.

Valens examined the toe. His face brightened in a manner that Ruso found faintly unsettling. "Shall I do it?"

"No thank you."

"Well, can I bring a couple of chaps in to watch?"

It was an unwelcome, but not an unreasonable, request. "If you must," said Ruso. He got to his feet with some difficulty, and repositioned the probe over the flame.

Moments later Valens returned with the couple of chaps. Either he had lost the ability to count, or each of the chaps had invited a couple more chaps of his own.

"See how the blood's built up under the nail," explained Valens as his audience shuffled about to get a better view of Ruso's blackened toenail. "How does it feel?"

"Painful," grunted Ruso. He could feel himself starting to sweat.

"It's the pressure that's causing the pain," explained Valens. "You, pass that probe over, will you?"

There was movement in the corner. A voice said, "Shall I put the candle out, sir?"

"Not yet," ordered Valens cheerfully. "He might want to have several stabs at it."

Ruso, who hoped fervently that he would not need more than one stab at it, told himself that this was only a very small amount of additional pain. It would, as he assured his patients, bring instant relief. Suddenly, however, this logic did not seem to offer a great deal of comfort. But he could not change his mind now. Nor could he postpone the moment any longer. The probe was being held out for him to take between forefinger and thumb.

He adjusted his grip, positioned the tip of the probe over the dark blister that had formed under his toenail during the night, and pressed.

He gasped as an excruciating wave of pain shot up his foot. Sweating, he forced himself to hold the probe steady and keep pressing as he smelled the nail burning. He closed his eyes, clenched his teeth, and pushed harder.

Suddenly the resistance to the probe gave way. He withdrew it and gave an involuntary sigh of relief as the blood welled out of the burned hole and the pain began to subside.

He looked up, surveyed the silent faces, and grinned. "Thank you, gentlemen. Any questions?"

After the students had been shooed out, Valens said, "Before you distracted me, I came to tell you I've been invited out to dinner tonight."

"Really?" Ruso wiped his toe with a damp cloth and wondered if dinner invitations were so rare in Britannia that guests felt the need to boast about them.

"And," Valens continued, "it's a pity you've already performed your party trick, because so have you."

25

A SMALL INFORMAL dinner, as arranged by the wife of Centurion Rutilius, was one where Ruso was required to make conversation with seven people he didn't know plus one he'd seen too much of, while eating a selection of elaborate dishes that bore little or no resemblance to their stated ingredients.

He had been introduced to his fellow guests and promptly forgotten most of their names. This was a situation he was hoping to salvage by not speaking unless spoken to. He would ask Valens afterward. Valens would know what everyone was called, particularly the two daughters of their host. Obviously they were both Rutilia something, but Ruso was damned if he could remember what. The younger one wasn't supposed to be there anyway: She had been summoned at the last minute when the second spear, who turned out to be her uncle, arrived alone. Apparently his daughter had a bad head cold and wouldn't be coming after all.

Valens, who might conceivably have been disappointed at this news, seemed to accept it stoically enough when etiquette now demanded a rearrangement of the seating plan and he found himself lounging between the plump and giggly wife of another centurion and the elder Rutilia, who must have been of marriageable age.

Ruso took another spoonful of something soft and eggy and wondered how long it would be before Valens offered the second spear's daughter a house call. Around him, his fellow diners were finding ways of informing one another that they thought Hadrian would make a fine emperor, largely because nobody was yet drunk enough to dare say anything else. It was an example of the meaningless conversation that, as Ruso had once tried to explain to Claudia, was one of the reasons he could not see the point of dinner parties.

"What's wrong with people being nice? I suppose you'd rather stay at home and be grumpy?"

"I'm not grumpy. I'm busy."

"Well, just because you're busy, why do I have to stay at home by myself and be miserable?"

Claudia's parents, Ruso felt, had done their daughter a serious disservice. It was clear that they had never introduced her, either by education or example, to the words "obedience" and "duty."

His hosts were going to have similar problems with the other Rutilia, who was not much younger than her sister, if they were not careful. While the plump wife moved on from praising the emperor to admiring the catering and the decor of the dining room, Rutilia the Younger was beckoning the wine jug over for the third time. The slave, who should have had the sense to refuse, didn't.

Ruso licked meat sauce off his fingers and realized his hostess was speaking to him. "I'm sorry, you said . . . ?"

"I said, are you enjoying our venison gravy, Doctor?"

He nodded. "Excellent." (So that was what it was.)

"I'll have the recipe sent over."

He thanked her, wondering what sort of sauce would be produced by two medics who between them could barely boil an egg. Across the table, Valens caught his eye and grinned.

The plump woman, casually propping one hand under her jaw to disguise her chins, leaned forward and peered at Ruso. He was diagnosing short sight as she said, "So, how long have you been in Britannia, doctor?"

"Two weeks," replied Ruso.

The woman appeared to be waiting for more. He felt there was something else he should add to this reply to pad it out a little, but since he had fully answered the question he could not think what the something might be. This was another reason why he disliked dinner parties.

Claudia would insist that attending them was for his own benefit ("You must put yourself forward, Gaius! How will you advance if you never meet the right people?"), but afterward she would complain about his refusal to chatter mindlessly to the right people when he met them. It had just struck him that he could pass the baton by asking this woman the same question back, when she gave up waiting and asked, "And what do you think of it?"

He hesitated. Britannia was dilapidated, primitive, and damp, but some of these men might have chosen to serve here. "It's interesting," he said.

"Our mother doesn't think it's interesting," piped up a young voice from across the table. "Our mother says it's the Back of Beyond."

"Rutilia Paula!" The woman frowned at her daughter across the top of the tureen. Her earrings glittered in the lamplight as she turned to Ruso. "And what do you make of the natives, Doctor?"

"I haven't met many yet," said Ruso, omitting the fact that he owned one of them.

"Are you married?" inquired Rutilia Paula.

"Divorced," replied Ruso as one of Rutilia the Elder's sandals gave her little sister a hefty kick and her mother reinforced the message with, "Paula, dear, really!"

The mother turned back to Ruso. "I'm so sorry, Doctor. You were saying?"

Ruso shook his head. "I'd finished."

Rutilia Paula, evidently encouraged by this response, said, "Is it true you came from Africa and all your things were eaten by ants and now you're very poor?"

Her mother said loudly, "They're not very interesting, I'm afraid."

"Terribly primitive and superstitious," put in the woman with the chins. "They put their enemies inside great big men made of sticks and burn them alive, you know."

"Not now they don't," pointed out her husband. "We've put a stop to all that sort of carrying-on."

"I certainly hope so," replied the wife.

"Now they're just bloody argumentative," put in her husband. "Half the trouble we get is trying to stop them fighting each other."

"They don't want to pay the taxes," put in Rutilius, "but they expect us to turn up when there's trouble."

Ruso deduced that they were talking about the natives. "Is there much trouble?" he asked.

"The lowland tribes don't give us much these days," said the second spear, "but the higher the mountains, they worse they get."

"And they are so terribly *dirty*."

To Ruso's relief the mention of dirt turned the conversation to the vexed question of who was responsible for the slow completion of the work on the fort bathhouse. As the finger of blame moved around the fort and beyond, Valens remarked to their hostess how nice it was to meet someone socially who wasn't in the medical profession. "Most people think we're either going to poison them or slice them up," he explained, "So we end up just socializing with one another." He glanced at Ruso. "Except those of us who don't socialize with anybody, of course."

"You're another of these medical fellers, then?" inquired the second spear, eyeing Valens through the steam rising from a roast bird (duck? large hen? small goose? It had been announced on arrival, but Ruso had been distracted by the sight of Rutilia the Elder clamping her hand across the top of her sister's wineglass until the water jug appeared).

"I am," Valens was saying. "I was wondering—"

"Never believed in doctors, myself," said the second spear. "Bunch of squabbling buffoons."

Valens shook his head sadly as if in total agreement. "It's not a well-regulated profession, I'm afraid."

"Bloody right," agreed the second spear. "Killed my father. Only had a bit of a cough. Could have lived to be eighty. That lot started at him with the blood-cupping and the silly diets and shoving stuff up his backside, and he was dead within the week."

The younger Rutilia started to giggle.

"Very unfortunate," said Valens.

"That's what they said too."

Their hostess stepped in. "Marcus, Doctor Valens was marvelous to Aulus when he was ill. Wasn't he, Aulus?"

Aulus Rutilius grunted assent.

"We were lucky to get him and Doctor Ruso here tonight. They work very hard at that hospital."

"It'll be easier when we get the CMO back," said Ruso.

The plump woman looked puzzled. "The chief medical officer," Valens explained. "He's on long-term sick leave."

There was a "Hmph" from the second spear as Valens added, "Frankly, he's not likely to come back," and Rutilia Paula could be heard whispering to her sister, "Was that the hairy old man with cold hands?"

"Shut up!" hissed the sister.

As Rutilius beckoned a sharp-faced slave and murmured something in her ear, the plump woman said, "I'm sure one of you doctors would make a lovely chief medical officer."

Valens grinned at Ruso. "One of us would," he agreed. He gestured toward the bird. "This duck is excellent," he said. "Which reminds me, does anyone know somebody wanting to hire out a good cook?"

Neither of the ladies could suggest anyone. "It is terribly hard to get good staff here," sympathized the wife with the chins.

"This is the best meal we've had in ages," said Valens. "When we're off duty we tend to eat out, but you never know what you're getting when you eat in public bars. The other day I was nearly killed by a dish of oysters."

Encouraged by the interest this aroused, Valens went on to explain the effect of the oysters in the sort of detail that demonstrated another reason why people didn't socialize with doctors. Ruso took a long drink of well-watered wine. He was praying for a medical emergency that would require his immediate presence when he heard Paula suggest, "Perhaps they used poisoned oysters to murder that girl in the river."

Rutilia shot his wife a look as the sister retorted, "Don't be silly. She was strangled."

Before anyone could reply, the wife said brightly, "Girls! It has been lovely to have you dining with us but unfortunately—"

"Is it true she was bald?"

"—it's time for bed," continued her mother, gesturing toward the slave. "Atia will take you to your room."

The sharp-faced woman stepped forward and Ruso heard the elder girl hiss to her sister, "Now look what you've done!"

"Lovely girls!" enthused the woman with the chins after they had been ushered out of the room.

"Huh," grunted their father. "Need some discipline." He turned to Ruso. "Sorry about Rutilia Paula. I'll be having words with her."

There was a pause and Ruso realized he should say something. "Your daughter is . . ." he began, "she's, ah—very, ah . . ." The woman with the chins emitted a burp. A servant reached forward and removed an empty dish. "She's actually quite funny," he said.

The man scowled. "I'm not raising a comedian: She needs to learn to behave herself." He turned to his wife. "How did she get hold of that business about the murder?"

The earrings swayed and sparkled as she shook her head. "This is a very small place, dear. People talk."

"It's nothing for you ladies to go worrying about," put in the second spear. "Just a runaway barmaid."

"I wouldn't be surprised if it was her own people," said the woman with the chins, "They have some very odd ideas here, you know." She leaned closer to Ruso and her voice dropped to a loud whisper. "I didn't like to mention it with the girls here, but some of them *share their wives.*"

"Really?" said Ruso. "Who with?"

The woman gave an alarming giggle that suggested she thought he was flirting with her. "Each other, of course."

Ruso, sensing that some reaction was needed, said, "Glad I'm not a native."

"Some of them," she continued, "don't like the girls mixing with our men. You see, the truth is, Doctor, our men are a much better prospect than theirs." She turned to her husband. "Aren't they, dear?"

"Much."

"Our men have education and training and discipline, you see. Not that theirs couldn't join the auxiliaries if they wanted to, but most of them are too lazy to work their way up. I suspect she was strangled by a jealous native."

Ruso scratched his ear. The idea that Saufeia had been killed because the locals were jealous of the army's suave sophistication was something he had not considered.

Their hostess leaned forward. "Wasn't there another girl from a bar who went missing?"

"It was the same bar," put in Valens.

"Really?" demanded the woman with the chins. "The same bar? Perhaps there's a madman lurking there, pretending to be a customer!"

"Must be mad if he goes to the bother of getting them out past the doormen," put in her husband.

"Perhaps he *is* one of the doormen. You never can tell with those types."

The man ignored her. "If he wants to murder women why doesn't he just snatch 'em off the street?"

Their hostess looked alarmed. "We make sure our girls never, ever go out without a chaperone."

"We're not talking about daughters of decent families," pointed out the second spear. "And the bar's just having a run of bad luck. The owner reckons the first one eloped with a sailor."

The woman with the chins assured the second spear that he was bound to catch the murderer soon.

He took a sip of wine and said, "We'll see. Trouble is, nobody's got time to turn the place upside down looking for him. It's not as if the girl was anybody important."

"Not to us, perhaps." The words were out before Ruso had thought about them. Suddenly he was aware of a silence and the eyes of everyone around the table were trained on him. "What I mean is," he continued, realizing this apparent questioning of the second spear's judgment was just the sort of thing that would have annoyed Claudia, "she must have been important to somebody, once. She had some education."

Valens grinned. "Ruso's been making inquiries."

"Really?" The eyes above the chins were wide.

"No," he said, glaring at Valens, who had now managed to imply that he didn't trust the second spear to investigate properly. "I just happened to pick it up in conversation."

"Well, you have to expect these things from time to time," observed the husband of the woman with the chins. "We've got three or four thousand men stationed here at the moment. We don't pick them to be country gentlemen."

"What a very sad end," murmured their hostess. "The doctor's right. Somebody must have cared about her."

"Somebody ought to ask the servants what happened to her," ventured the plump woman, dabbling her fingers in the bowl held by a patient slave and drying them on the towel over his arm. "Servants always know everything, you know. It's amazing."

As Ruso dipped his hands into the warm water, he glanced at the face of the slave holding the bowl. The man's expression gave nothing away.

26

RUSO HAD JUST persuaded his stomach to calm down after the unaccustomed riches of a good dinner when the answer to his prayers arrived, much too late. He was woken with the message that he was needed at the hospital. The unlucky patient had been on the way back to barracks from guard duty. In the dark he had tripped, landed badly, and dislocated his shoulder. He was finally drugged into semi-consciousness, then painfully and forcefully reshaped and bandaged. Ruso trod the couple of hundred steps back to his bed with more care than usual, only to be summoned an hour later to prescribe medicine for a man having a seizure. On return he left the message slate propped against his bedroom door with SLEEPING IN, DO NOT DISTURB scrawled across it.

Thus it was with neither joy nor enthusiasm that he opened the front door to urgent knocking shortly after dawn and found his clerk calling to ask whether there was anything he wanted done.

"What I want done," explained Ruso, summoning all the patience he could muster and wondering what sort of a clerk could fail to understand a staff rotation, "is for you to push off and not bother me until I tell you to. Is that clear?"

"Yes, sir."

"Dismissed."

"Yes, sir," replied the man, saluting, but instead of pushing off as ordered he remained on the doorstep.

"I said, *dismissed.*"

"Yes, sir."

"So?"

"Are you ordering me not to come, sir?"

"Of course I'm ordering you not to come! Is there something the matter with your hearing?"

"No, sir."

Ruso leaned against the door frame and yawned. "Albanus," he said, "are you deliberately trying to annoy me?"

The man looked shocked. "Oh no, sir."

"Do you want to be charged with insubordination?"

"Oh no, sir!"

"Then what is the matter with you?"

Albanus's shoulders seemed to shrink as he glanced around to make sure there was no one listening in the street. "Officer Priscus's orders, sir."

"Officer Priscus," explained Ruso, "has seconded you to me. So you do what I tell you."

"Yes, sir."

"So what's the problem?"

"Sir, he's my superior. So when he tells me to report to you in the morning, I have to do it."

Ruso sighed. "He only meant the first morning."

Albanus shook his head. "No, sir. He told me again yesterday."

Ruso ran a hand through his hair. "I'll talk to him. Now get lost."

Albanus nodded eagerly. "Shall I get lost anywhere in particular, sir?"

27

PRISCUS SNAPPED OPEN one of the folding chairs and held it out to Ruso before inserting himself behind the polished desk. As he sat down Ruso noticed two things: that the glass eyes of the wolf pelt were now glaring up at a coat of fresh limewash instead of a damp patch and that the chair he had been given had surprisingly short legs. He was obliged to look up at Priscus in order to speak to him, although since the administrator was busy aligning his bronze inkwell against the edge of the desk, there did not seem to be much point in starting yet.

Priscus lifted his hands and held them just above the inkwell, as if poised to catch it should it try to jump back to its original position. Finally satisfied, he smoothed his hair, which did not seem quite as black today. "Really," he remarked, "one would think that most men were capable of obeying a simple order to leave things where they find them." Finally he looked at Ruso. "Oh dear. I seem to have given you the wrong chair. Would you like to . . . ?"

Ruso lounged in the chair, tipping it onto its back legs. "This is fine," he assured Priscus, enjoying the look of disapproval.

"I'm glad you've come to see me," said Priscus. "I need a word."

"Albanus," suggested Ruso.

Priscus's eyebrows rose in a surprise that might have been genuine. "Are you dissatisfied with his work?"

"His work is fine. He's keen, he knows Latin and Greek, and he's the only clerk I've ever met who could spell *phthisis* right without asking."

"Excellent. I thought you would find him useful."

"He's too useful. He follows me around like a shadow. I can hardly take a pee without him being there to record the event."

"Ah." Priscus inclined his head slowly as if he were afraid any sudden movement might dislodge the hair. "This will be the result of my reassigning his other duties so he can concentrate on helping you settle in."

"Fine. He's assigned to me. Agreed?"

"Indeed."

"So I should be giving him his orders."

Priscus entwined his fingers and leaned forward across the desk. "Is there some difficulty of which I'm not aware?"

"I think we've just sorted it out."

"Excellent. We try and run a tidy administration here, Ruso, but I do appreciate that the complexities are a little hard to grasp. So if there are any difficulties with which Albanus can't help you, I hope you won't hesitate to come straight to me."

Ruso saw the man watch as he lowered the chair back onto all four legs. "There is one thing," he said.

"How can I help?"

"We'd be able to use the supplies much more efficiently if the staff didn't have to keep finding you to ask for keys."

Priscus placed both hands on the edge of the desk. "The men are not permitted to help themselves to supplies," he said. "If I expect to be away for any length of time, I arrange for adequate stocks to be available."

"But . . ."

"Sadly, Ruso, this a policy we have been forced to adopt. There are people in and out of the building at all hours and even the staff are not always above reproach, so I find it wisest not to tempt them. Lock it or lose it, I'm afraid."

"I've never had this problem before."

"No. But there was an unfortunate incident with an inventory check some time ago, and the chief medical officer was . . ." He hesitated, appearing to grope for a word. "Most dissatisfied. My predecessor was given a dishonorable discharge. Not wishing to follow him, I instigated a policy of supervised access to storage areas."

As he spoke there was a knock on the door. Having nothing further to say, Ruso started to get up. Priscus motioned him to sit. "If you wouldn't mind waiting, Ruso? Just a couple more things . . ."

Ruso contemplated the wolf as its killer countersigned dockets for orders to the pharmacy and questioned the need for a new set of scales.

When the pharmacist had gone—leaving behind his request for the scales on a substantial pile labeled FURTHER CONSIDERATION—Priscus turned back to Ruso.

"I do apologize for the interruption," he said. "I'm sure you must be rather busy at the moment."

"I'm told it will improve when we have a CMO."

Priscus raised one eyebrow. "Someone in this room, perhaps?"

"I'm the second medicus," Ruso pointed out.

"But only in terms of date of arrival, surely?" Priscus attempted a smile. "I hear you have combat experience. I would imagine that would stand you in good stead."

Ruso, wishing to discuss neither the ghastly mess of the Jewish rebellions in Cyrenaica nor his own job prospects, said, "What was the other thing you wanted to see me about?"

The administrator turned to one side and pulled a file down from the shelf. "Just a couple more small matters that need to be straightened out in time for the auditors . . ." He flipped open the file and ran his finger down the columns. "Yes, here we are. Charge for private use of isolation room and facilities, five days, immediate payment requested. Perhaps the bill has been mislaid?"

"I don't think I've ever had one."

"Really? I shall have to look into it. This is exactly the sort of slackness the auditors will pick up on."

"Let me have the bill and I'll take care of it."

"Thank you. I am sorry to have to mention it, but we must tighten up on expenses. Otherwise we may be forced to cut back on the services the hospital offers."

"Ah," said Ruso, wondering which service Priscus would be proposing—reluctantly, of course—to cut.

"In fact, I was hoping to have a word with you and Doctor Valens about some suggestions for cutting costs."

"Well, here I am."

"Simple economies, Doctor. Matters which I assure you will add no burden at all to the medical staff." Priscus spoke with an intensity that reminded Ruso of the gleam in the glass eyes of the wolf. "For example, by insisting that most of the hospital business is conducted during the daylight hours, we could save a considerable amount on candles and lamp oil over the course of a year."

"So I imagine," said Ruso, who had often wished he could find a way to stop people from inconveniently falling ill during the night.

"Small savings soon add up, provided one makes a thorough budget first," continued Priscus, moving his hands in a parallel motion as if caressing a small saving in the air above his desk. "Let me give you a simple example. Boiling dressings in larger quantities gives an economy of scale, but we need to invest more in stock in order to keep the supply up. Short-term expense against long-term gain. Which is why . . ."

Ruso braced himself.

"We are instigating a system that will account for the resources each individual uses."

"How many man-hours will it take to add that up?"

"That's the beauty of it, Ruso." Priscus seemed genuinely enthusiastic. "The men are here anyway. It's simply a matter of putting them to the best possible use. A short-term concentrated expenditure analysis will allow us to set consistent spending policies. Which will in turn make it possible to exercise some form of budgetary control."

"Are you telling me the army's running out of money?"

"Oh dear me, no! But we should be making the best use of available resources, don't you agree?"

"I suppose so."

"And these days the idea that everyone has the authority to order whatever strikes his fancy just won't do. If everyone 'just' orders in one thing extra, the budgets are out of control. Let me give you an example. Only yesterday I caught one of the orderlies changing pillows between patients."

"Aren't they supposed to?"

Priscus positively beamed at him. "The stock of pillows and covers," he explained, "is calculated to balance with the timing of the laundry. Unless they are noticeably soiled, pillows are changed on Fridays. Yesterday was Tuesday."

"I ordered the change."

Priscus looked surprised. "Desirable, no doubt, but surely not medically necessary?"

Ruso frowned. It probably hadn't been necessary, but he was not prepared to concede that to Priscus. "Fresh beds cheer people up. People get better quicker when they aren't miserable. It's a medical decision."

"But one that has an effect on the laundry bills." Priscus sighed. "I appreciate your point, but the next time there is a major call on our resources—an epidemic, or a serious accident, or more trouble with the locals—if the budget has been frittered away on inessentials, we'll have no contingency funds to deal with the crisis."

Ruso scratched his ear. "Well, if a plague or a war breaks out, won't someone in Rome notice and send us some more cash?"

Priscus shook his head sadly. "Unfortunately, things are never quite that simple. But of course, nobody takes the trouble to discover the real reasons for difficulties: instead everybody blames the administrators. The fundamental problem we have, you see, is that the people who do the spending are not the ones who have to explain it to the camp prefect. I have to do that. And very shortly the camp prefect will have to explain it to the imperial audit inspectors, and believe me, Ruso, no one wants to fall out of favor with the imperial audit inspectors. They go through the books like terriers hunting a rat."

"Hospital administrators hunting a wolf," suggested Ruso.

"You may have heard that the hospital administrator of the Second Augusta fell on his sword after one of their visits."

"Wasn't he the one who was selling the medicines and keeping the cash?"

Priscus looked offended. "All I ask, Ruso, is that if you make decisions affecting my budgets, you should clear them with me first."

"You want me to prescribe whatever's cheapest?"

"The medical decisions are yours," Priscus assured him. "But I would be grateful if you would keep me informed. Perhaps we could ask Albanus to copy any relevant items from your notes."

Gods above, the man had been planning this ever since his return! Ruso frowned. "I can't have patient records put in the hands of the requisitions clerk."

"Simply the treatments."

"No. You could track them. If you want to know how medicine stocks are going, ask the pharmacy. If you want to know how many pillows are being used, get someone to check your cupboards. That's your job. My job is to get the men here back on their feet as quickly as possible."

Priscus drew a long breath in through his nose and said nothing.

Ruso suppressed a smile. He had never before seen himself as an irresponsible spendthrift. He was quite enjoying the notion.

His enjoyment was short-lived. Priscus reached for another file. Apparently in future the administration would be obliged if he would sign for meals taken when on duty.

"I shouldn't have to pay for them. They deduct enough for food as it is."

"Precisely. Which is why I have seen to it that Albanus has spent the morning going through the rosters to give the pay office separate lists of meals the kitchen has served you when on and off duty. Because payday, as we are all aware, is almost upon us. And otherwise they would have charged you for all of them."

Ruso stared at him for a moment and then said, "Oh," and forced himself to follow it with, "Thank you."

Priscus inclined his head slightly. "A pleasure to be of service," he said.

28

TILLA WAS PONDERING the question of food—how much she could save and hide without arousing anyone's suspicions—when there was a thump low down on the door as if someone had kicked it and a small voice announced in Latin, "It's Lucco, missus. I can't knock, I'll drop your tray."

The ginger-haired kitchen boy had brought a steaming bowl of broth, half a loaf of bread, and a cup of water. He placed the tray on the bench and watched as she tore a chunk of bread away with her teeth. She placed it on the windowsill before breaking it awkwardly into crumbs with one hand and pushing it out between the bars.

Finally he said, "What do you do that for?"

"I have guests."

The boy looked anxious. "Cook didn't say nothing about guests."

"You can wait and see them if you like," she offered, moving the stool to use it as a table and seating herself on the bench. She gestured toward the tray and offered him some bread.

He shook his head. "Mistress says you're too skinny and you got to eat it all."

She tore off another chunk and watched the glistening brown of the broth soak up and darken the bread. By the time she had eaten it, the first sparrow had arrived. Lucco said, "I could get Stichus to find a trap," and at the sound of his voice the sparrow flew away.

Tilla frowned. "I do not trap my guests. Sit still and say nothing."

Moments later several sparrows returned and there was frantic action on the windowsill until a male blackbird brought order by frightening the sparrows away and helping himself to the last remaining crumbs. When he had gone Lucco said, "We could have had sparrow pie."

"Is it good?"

"We'd find out."

Tilla fished out a dripping chunk of bread with her spoon.

"I had dormouse once," Lucco announced. "And swan. Stichus brought me some back from a dinner party."

Romans, Tilla reflected, would eat anything that moved. She could almost believe the rumor that they fattened snails in milk and ate them.

"How long have you worked here, Lucco?"

"I was born here," he told her.

"In this place?"

"In this room."

She glanced around at the bare walls and felt sorry for a child who had been given such a poor welcome into the world. "How old are you?"

"Eight winters."

She dipped the spoon to capture more bread. "You have the same name as one of my uncles, Lucco, you measure your age in winters like me, and yet you speak in the tongue of the army." She switched to her own language. "Who are your people?"

The boy shook his head. "We talk Latin here. We honor the emperor."

"But among ourselves?" she persisted.

Still clinging to the Latin, the boy answered that the mistress did not like them to "talk like natives," adding, "The customers don't like it neither."

Convinced that he understood, she continued, "Where can I find people around here who are not ashamed of their own tongue, Lucco?"

The boy looked at her for a moment, then stepped across to pick up the bucket in the corner. "I forgot," he said, "Mistress says I got to empty you out." Moments later he was gone.

She had not been alone for long when there were three short raps on the door. Instead of Daphne, the ample young woman with the silver ankle chain was lolling against the doorpost. "Tilla," she said. "Is that your real name?"

"Is Chloe yours?"

"Of course not. Let me in."

As soon as she was inside, she closed the door. "I hear you've been asking questions."

"I like to learn." So Lucco had talked. And Daphne had not kept the signal a secret. She would have to be more careful.

Chloe said, "Leave the boy alone. If you must ask questions, ask me. And if you're thinking of running away, my advice is, don't bother."

"I did not say what I was thinking."

"They all think about it. I suppose you've heard the tale about Asellina and her sailor."

"There is a girl who ran away with a sailor?"

Chloe shrugged. "So they say. You did well to get ahold of the key. Nobody's done that before. But if you think it'll be easy . . ." She opened the door a fraction and checked the landing before closing and locking it, "it's time somebody told you what happened to Saufeia."

It seemed that the ill-fated Saufeia had thought she was clever. Clearly she had not realized the dangers that lurked beyond the doors of Merula's.

Tilla said, "Does no one know who killed her?"

Chloe shrugged. "They had an investigation. Lined us all up and asked if anybody saw anything. Of course nobody was stupid enough to say yes. So the soldiers helped themselves to whatever they fancied, pushed off back to the fort, and we've never heard a word."

"Surely it does not end there?"

"Where's it going to go?"

"To find out the truth."

Chloe gave a bitter laugh. "The truth isn't going to bring her back, is it? 'Round here you learn to keep your mouth shut."

Tilla shook her head. "Poor Saufeia, with no one to avenge her."

Chloe looked at her strangely. "They couldn't. They don't know who did it."

"And no family to mourn her passing."

"Look, we did our best. Merula paid for the funeral. Nobody knew what gods she served so we said prayers to all the ones we could think of while Stichus dug the hole, then we threw flowers in and poured a cup of wine over the urn. We even planted violets on top of the grave. Anybody would think we liked her."

29

MOMENTS AFTER RUSO had emerged from Priscus's office, he spotted Albanus at the far end of the corridor. The clerk dodged around the corner as if he was attempting to stay out of sight. Puzzled, Ruso continued down the corridor until he reached the corner, then turned to find the man pressed flat against the wall.

"Albanus, are you avoiding me?"

The clerk swallowed. "You're not supposed to be here yet, sir."

"Perhaps you'd like me to go away again?"

"Oh no, sir! But you told me to stay out of your way."

Ruso sighed. "I didn't mean you have to run off every time you see me."

"No, sir. Sorry, sir. I could fetch my things and start now if you like, sir."

"Please do."

Albanus brightened. "I'll fetch your post as well, sir, shall I?"

"Post?"

Ruso had been known to ignore his pigeonhole for weeks and then find something important and out of date in there. Watching Albanus bustle off in the direction of the records office, it occurred to him that having a personal clerk might even turn out to be useful. Although he hoped he would not have to admit as much to Priscus. In fact, he was intending to keep well clear of Priscus in future. Merely thinking about the administrator gave him an urge to beat the man over the head with his inkwell. Which, for a professional healer attempting to follow the dictates of reason, logic, and philosophy, was more than a little disappointing.

The first letter was from a seller of medical texts advertising his latest stock, none of which Ruso could afford. The second was from one of his former trainees in Antioch, asking for a letter of recommendation. The third was a fresh and unexpected letter from home.

He settled on a stool in the corner of his surgery and read them all. Then, with a calm he did not feel, he dictated a letter of recommendation. He left Albanus to copy it and to tell anyone who asked that he would be back in time for afternoon clinic.

When he reached the cashier's office, the length of the line suggested to Ruso that he would, after all, have to keep his patients waiting. At the counter, the duty clerk and a dim but determined soldier were locked in an argument about receipts. Ruso leaned against the wall and reread the letter which was the cause of his being here.

"Greetings, brother," he deciphered mostly from memory since as usual Lucius had crammed the lines together to fit everything on the page.

I trust you have sent us the package we are expecting. I thank you and eagerly await its arrival. Unfortunately I am now wondering whether our present course of action remains appropriate. Perhaps the full burden of responsibility for the farm is too much for the pair of us to sustain. As you are our father's heir I am writing to ask your permission to seek a buyer. I will endeavor to find someone who requires a sitting tenant and thus save the family any unnecessary upheaval.

You will be interested to hear that the oldest daughter of Germanicus Fuscus is to be married in the spring. Naturally Fuscus will be providing his daughter with a suitable wedding celebration and will wish to make a generous gift to the happy couple, as will we.

We are all in good health, brother, and hope you are the same. Write soon, I beg you.

Fuscus! Ruso certainly was interested to hear about what Fuscus was planning, although not about the marriage. Not two months ago, he and Lucius had shaken Fuscus's hand over an agreement to extend the terms of the loan. Now the man had changed his mind, and clearly Lucius had failed to persuade him to hold off.

"Sir?"

A second clerk had appeared at the counter and was beckoning him forward. Ruso did not look at the faces of the men he bypassed. One day, when they were officers, they would jump the line too.

"I'd like a word with the cashier," he said. "In private."

Afternoon clinic was busy, evening ward round was even busier, and although Lucius's letter was on his mind, Ruso was unable to find the privacy to reply to it. It was several hours after dark when he finally escaped from the hospital—and from Albanus—and made his way back to the house accompanied only by the smell of someone else's fried bacon.

Still pondering his brother's hint about the generous gift, he reflected that he did not have to stay in this inhospitable corner of the empire. As a surgeon, he was not committed to serve out the twenty-five years of a career soldier. He could try to resign and make the crossing to Gaul before the winter storms set in. There, he could exploit the tax-free status of a civilian doctor, take on his full responsibilities as Pater Familias, and support the family on the ailments of neighbors rich enough to pay him.

The trouble was, would it be enough? What if Fuscus's failure to honor his agreement signified a general loss of faith? If all the debts were called in, there would be no farm to go home to. He would have given up a job he enjoyed, with a regular and very reasonable salary, for nothing. Maybe he should tell Lucius to sell and invite them all to join him in Britannia. It was no worse than his stepmother deserved.

What he needed, of course, was the salary of the chief medical officer. Valens was shamelessly jockeying for the job on the flimsy basis of having been here first, but Ruso's experience was far wider and Claudia had always insisted he could do better for himself if he just made more effort to be polite to people. He had taken little notice of her complaints. A man's work should speak louder than his words. The trouble was, hardly anyone here knew much about his work.

He had been wasting too much time messing about with injured and deceased slave girls. For the sake of his family, he was going to have to find ways to impress the right people. He needed to make useful contacts. Get his face known. Gods above, if he was CMO he could even hunt down a rich widow and persuade her to marry him. He could be the sort of man who gave—the words rang through his head like the blast of a warning trumpet—*dinner parties.*

In the meantime, Lucius was waiting for an answer.

Safely shut away in his bedroom, Ruso opened one of the blank writing tablets he had persuaded a dubious Albanus to part with *(I have to sign for them, sir)*, and scrawled,

> *Greetings, brother. Thank you for your suggestion, but I am not prepared to relinquish the burden just yet. Interested to hear about the wedding plans. Are there any more on the horizon? Keep me informed. I am eager to hear all the latest news from home. In the meantime, I am arranging to send three thousand denarii, which I trust will fund a suitably substantial gift.*

30

WHEN SOMEONE THUMPED on the door early the next morning, Ruso rolled over in bed, groaned, and pulled the covers over his head. Surely he had made himself quite clear yesterday? His bed was warm, it was almost comfortable, and he was not going to get out of it. Sooner or later, even Albanus would give up. If he tried opening the door, the dogs would frighten him off.

Instead of being frightened off, the man let himself in past the excited dogs and made his way into the kitchen. Moments later he was crashing about with the fire irons. Worse, he was whistling.

Ruso wrenched open the door of his bedroom and roared, "Albanus!"

The whistling stopped. A rotund stranger appeared in the kitchen doorway. " 'Morning, sir. Beautiful morning!"

"Who the hell are you?"

"Justinus, sir. Officer Valens said would I drop by and lend a hand, sir. Get the fire lit, fetch the water, let the dogs out, that sort of thing, sir."

"Did he tell you to make as much noise as possible?"

"Sorry, sir. Didn't know you were in."

Ruso, who felt he had earned the opportunity to sleep in, went back to bed. He had barely drifted back to sleep when he was woken by a knock on his bedroom door. The rotund man handed him a closed writing tablet. "From one of the centurions, sir. Thought it might be urgent."

Ruso undid the tie and squinted at the letters scraped in the wax. "Marvelous," he said. "Thank you."

"You're welcome, sir. Mind if I ask how you're getting on with the inquiries, sir?"

Ruso frowned. "What inquiries?"

"I heard you were looking into the murder of that girl, sir. Or is it supposed to be a secret?"

"No," growled Ruso, "because I'm not. I'm going back to sleep."

The man failed to secure the door properly. Moments later it swung open and a puppy bounded in. It disappeared under the bed and rushed out again with one of Ruso's sandals in its mouth. Ruso leaned over the side of the bed and flung the writing tablet after it. So he did, after all, have a use for the recipe for venison gravy.

31

THE WOMAN AT the bakery handed Ruso his breakfast roll without being asked and remarked that it was a good day for a celebration.

"Is it?" inquired Ruso, still resentful at being woken to see it..

The woman looked surprised. "It's the birthday of the noble emperor Trajan, sir, may he walk with the gods. We're closing early today."

"So it is," said Ruso, who now vaguely recalled some notice to that effect and, feeling some other comment was needed, added, "Very good."

"And the gods have blessed us with good weather."

It struck Ruso that if the gods kept this up, he might not have to buy Tilla any winter clothes. "When do you think it'll start getting cold?"

The woman assured him there would be no frost for a couple of months. She then contradicted herself by adding that you could never really tell, could you? And if he didn't mind her saying so, it was nice to hear that somebody was still taking an interest in the business of that girl who was murdered, and had he caught anybody yet?

"No," said Ruso, wondering who had started this rumor and how he could stop it before it reached the ears of the second spear.

"We'd help you if we could, but she was hardly here more than a few days and we don't pay much attention to what goes on over there. It's not very nice sometimes, you know. Especially when it gets late."

"I can imagine."

"Shouting and swearing and banging on the shutters."

"Mm," said Ruso, groping in his purse for his money so he could escape.

"Those doormen do their best to keep order but really, it's terribly noisy. We keep ourselves to ourselves. All we knew about that one was that she had a pretty face and a foul mouth."

Ruso looked up. "Really?"

"Oh, yes!" The woman looked pleased at his interest. "She came across the street one day wanting to say something to us. So the doorman, the ginger-haired one—Stichus, is it?—he called her straight back. Which was quite right. We've told that Merula woman we can't have them hanging around here, you see, it puts the customers off, so he was quite within his rights. And when she didn't take any notice he came over and got her, and to be honest, Doctor, she seemed quite a nicely spoken girl up till then—but you should have heard what she said to him! Well, I expect you hear it every day in the barracks, but we don't expect it in the street. And from a young woman. We were quite shocked."

"And then what happened?"

"What happened?" Evidently the woman had already reached the climax of the story and Ruso was supposed to be impressed. "Well, nothing. He took hold of her and got her in and straight up those stairs and we didn't hear any more about it. The Merula woman did have the decency to come over later to apologize. I will say that for them, they do realize what a lot of trouble they cause for the neighbors."

"Tell me about the girl's hair," said Ruso, suddenly curious.

"Her hair?"

"Was it . . ." Ruso tried to think what questions he could ask, and resorted to, "Could you describe it for me?"

"It was red. Very red, not ginger. Natural, I think. But of course you can never tell."

"It was natural," said Ruso, without thinking. Luckily the woman did not pause to wonder how he knew.

"I don't know about the curls," she said. "They could have been done with tongs. And I think it was probably quite long, but it was all pinned up, so I couldn't really see."

"And it was definitely her own hair? Not a wig?"

"Oh yes, I think so. People say you can always tell, don't they, but of course if you couldn't tell you wouldn't know you couldn't, if you see what I mean, would you?"

"Right."

"To tell you the truth, I wasn't surprised when I heard what happened to her."

"No?"

"But I was sorry. Nobody deserves to die like that, do they?"

"No," agreed Ruso, handing over his money, "they don't."

"I wish I could be more help to you."

To his relief another customer arrived at the counter. "You're not alone," Ruso assured the woman. "Nobody else saw anything either."

She pressed the change into his hand and leaned closer to him. "Never mind, Doctor," she said. "I'm sure you'll catch him in the end."

Ruso sat on the sunlit bench outside the bakery to finish his breakfast and wondered what Saufeia had been so eager to say to the bakery staff. Probably nothing of any consequence. He decided he had been wrong about Saufeia. She was not a girl with education who had fallen on hard times, but a creature from the gutter who was sharp enough to pick up a cultivated accent and a few letters. He was aware that this should not have made a difference to his attitude: that the bakery woman was right and nobody deserved to die like that. But there were many worse ways. He had seen several of them. Perhaps everyone else had been right too. Saufeia had been offered protection. She should have had the sense to take it.

In the meantime, he had more pressing things to think about. He needed to decide whether to order some winter clothes now or wait until payday, when the legion would be besieged by traveling merchants eager to relieve it not only of its quarterly wages but also of any advance on Hadrian's promised bonus. When could a buyer secure the best deal? Claudia would have known. His former valet would have known. Until now, Ruso had never needed to know. Now that he had made the grand economy of selling his staff, he was finding day-to-day penny-pinching not only aggravating but quite baffling.

Reminding himself that Lucius had far worse difficulties to contend with, he brushed the crumbs off his tunic and crossed over into the shadow cast by Merula's bar. The shutters were half-open but there seemed to be no one around.

"They're out," called Bassus from somewhere in the gloom at the back of the bar. Everyone seemed to be up early this morning.

"I've come to see my patient." Ruso strode past the tables and started up the stairs.

"You won't find her up there, mate. Try the baths."

Ruso paused. Perhaps he had been too impulsive when he handed over the key. "I didn't say she could go out."

Bassus emerged from the kitchen door, polishing an apple on the front of his tunic. "You didn't say she couldn't."

"Did anybody go with her?"

The doorman took a bite out of the apple and stopped chewing long enough to say, "You don't want to worry about her, mate. We got the best-kept girls in town here." He paused to swallow. "Bathed three times a week, chaperoned everywhere they go . . . Anybody out there messes with our girls, they've got me and Stich to answer to."

"I see," said Ruso, politely refraining from observing that two of the best-kept girls in town had chosen to run away.

Bassus grinned. "If they want to mess with our girls, they got to come over here and show us the money first. Got to build up a retirement fund somehow, haven't I?"

"How's it going?"

The man shook his head. "Born too soon, mate." He slid a heavy knife out of the sheath at his belt and began to dig at a brown patch in the apple. "Born too soon. Me and Stich, we do twenty-five years in the Legion, spend another five years scratching our backsides in the reserves, and all we get is the discharge grant." He flicked the rotten section of the apple out into the street. "Now we got pimply kids been in the army a week, coming in here telling us how they're going to spend the emperor's bonus."

"That's very bad luck," agreed Ruso.

Bassus squinted at the remainder of the apple and, apparently satisfied, wiped the knife on his tunic and slid it back into the sheath. "Tell you what, though. You and me might be able to do a bit of business."

"We might?"

"That girl. You don't want to let her go to Merula. Feed her up a bit, she'd be worth something."

"The thought had crossed my mind."

"Let me know when you're thinking of cashing in." He took another bite out of the apple. "I'll put the word out for you."

"You know a good dealer?"

The man shook his head. "The dealers 'round here, they'll rob you blind. I know some people."

Ruso said, "I'm waiting till she's fit before I make any decisions."

The man shrugged. "Whenever you're ready. Let Merula get her smartened up and see how she turns out."

"Right." Ruso paused. "You're not going to ask me about the investigation?"

"What investigation?"

"There's a rumor going around that I'm investigating the death of your Saufeia."

"And?"

"And it's not true. So if you come across anything, you need to talk to Civilian Liaison. Not me."

"And what are they doing?"

Ruso scratched his ear. "They're uh—as far as I can tell, they've completed the first stage of the investigation and now they're waiting for developments."

"Huh. I won't hold me breath, then."

"So, when will the girls be back?"

"Shouldn't be long."

Ruso nodded. "I'll wait."

The girl's room was much the same as before except that a stool had been brought in and set by the window. On the seat was a faded red cushion with a patched cover. Ruso wondered if Merula had supplied this comfort so his patient could sit and gaze out between the window bars, or whether the girl had slipped out and helped herself.

Ruso glanced out at the street. The only people around were the woman at the bakery counter, a girl carrying a basket of eggs nested in bracken, and a small boy leading a goat. There was no sign of Merula's staff returning from their escorted bathing trip.

Ruso settled himself on the rough bench and took out the *Concise Guide*. He persisted in carrying this one writing tablet, despite having his own clerk following him around like a lost dog.

It had been a pity about that dog at the hospital, he thought. He should have been firmer in the first place. Made them give it away. Instead, it had fallen victim to the tidying urges of a man who seemed to have everything under control except his own bald patch. To be fair, the place was a lot cleaner since Priscus had returned. The hospital baths were neat, tidy, and hot. The wards were swept every morning. Buckets were filled, candles replaced, shelves stocked, and spills instantly swooped on by men clutching mops. In the drive to root out inefficiency, two more clerks had taken up residence in the records room and now the medical staff had to ask to see patients' files and wait to have them fetched. It was all very impressive, and Ruso supposed he ought to be pleased about it.

He opened the tablet, slid the stylus out of its holder, and yawned. Glancing around at the bare walls, he wondered what the girl did in here all day. She did not seem to know anyone who would visit, which was unfortunate but not surprising. The ill-named Innocens must have traveled long distances with his trade. He could have picked her up anywhere in the province. Gazing out the window was all very well, but if she became idle and dispirited, it would slow her recovery. Fresh air and a short stroll to the baths three times a week would do her good, but in between times, he needed to find something useful to occupy her.

What did women do?

Claudia, as far as he knew, spent a few minutes each day giving orders to the servants and then went shopping, or sat exchanging mindless gossip with other wives, or tried a new hairstyle. When this became too tiring she retired to a couch with a selection of honey cakes and a scroll of trashy poetry. Since this girl had no servants, no money, and no friends, Claudia's example was not much help. With only one arm working she would not be able to fiddle with her hair, and the only use she would have for a scroll would be to light the fire with it.

The little he knew about useful but sedentary tasks like spinning and darning suggested that they too needed both hands. After a moment of staring at the cracks in the plaster, Ruso realized that he did not have a clue what a servant would do all day if she were unable to work.

He glanced back down at the blank sheet of wax. It was surprisingly quiet in here. Bassus, while he might have other unappealing habits, was not a whistler, and the crashing din of the construction sites had barely started. Most of the builders would still be at daily training with their units.

Ruso yawned again and tried to remember what should come next in the *Concise Guide*. It was difficult to think concisely when one had not had more than three hours' uninterrupted sleep in the past three days.

He put the stylus and the tablet down on the bench. He would just have a quick doze to refresh his mind before pressing on with his work.

The blankets were folded neatly on the mattress. When he pulled them back, two apples tumbled out and rolled across the floor.

The mattress was no less comfortable than his own, which was scant recommendation. He pulled a blanket up over his shoulders and closed his eyes.

He was just drifting into a blissful sleep when he was pulled back into the room by the sound of something scuffling close by. He resolved to have a good look at the floor later. If he found any mouse droppings, he would demand a discount.

A flurry of wings and frantic cheeping told him the noise was not mice. He opened his eyes. Small birds were squabbling outside the window. When he sat up they flew away. Rising to close the shutters, he noticed a torn scrap of crust and a scatter of breadcrumbs on the wooden sill. He reached through the bars and flicked the crust down into the street, then bent to blow the crumbs away before pulling the shutters across and latching them firmly against the bright morning.

Before long he felt the peaceful floating sensation of a man vaguely and happily aware that he is falling asleep.

He was dreaming in a world suffused with a gentle scent. In the dim light of the dream he could make out a woman sitting in front of him. She was wrapped in a dark blue shawl, and holding a splash of bright yellow flowers against a long blue tunic. She had blond wispy curls pinned back to frame a pretty face, and her eyes were closed. She seemed familiar, as strangers often do in dreams. Then he noticed that under the shawl, the hand holding the flowers was in a white sling.

Ruso flung back the blanket, sprang to his feet, and clapped the shutters apart. The girl's eyes opened.

"I was just waiting for you," he told her. "I need to check your dressings."

In the improved light he observed that her color seemed better than yesterday. When she removed the shawl he also noted with approval that the tunic—which he supposed he would have to pay for—was not new but patched at the elbows.

She reached through the bars to place the flowers on the empty windowsill before seating herself.

The splints seemed to be undisturbed and the sling was providing even support all along the length of the lower arm and not cutting into the wrist. Whoever had retied it for her at the baths had evidently used some common sense. He said, "Where did you get the clothes?"

She pointed at the floorboards.

"Merula?"

The curls bounced as she nodded.

"I expect you to speak when I ask you a question, Tilla."

She cleared her throat. "Yes."

"Yes, sir, or yes, my Lord, or yes, Master."

"Yes."

Ruso sighed. He knew she knew better, but he could not be bothered to argue. Standing beside her, he began the list of daily observations. Hands and feet: cold—and the feet were far from clean. "Did you wear shoes to go to the baths?"

The curls swayed sideways this time. "No."

He would definitely need to explain some rules to Merula. He didn't need her all decorated until she was healthy. The money wasted on perfume and hairpins could have been usefully put toward a pair of winter boots, and the draft from the window suggested that she would need a cloak before long. Would he be expected to pay extra for a brazier in the room? He didn't know. What he did know was that owning a sick slave was just one expense after another.

"Eating well?"

"Yes."

The color of the hand was normal. He took it between his palms. "Move your fingers for me."

He felt them twitch more strongly than before and would have returned her flicker of a smile had it not been inappropriate. Instead, he said, "Very good," made a mental note to point out his patient's progress to Valens, and put her through the usual questions about bowels and urine and sleep and pain. Finally he said, "Right, let's take a look," and reached behind her neck to untie the sling.

She began to roll back the sleeve of the tunic with her good hand.

The woolen sleeve of the tunic was clinging to the surface of the bandaging. He moved closer to help. "If it's all doing well under here," he said, concentrating on unwinding the grubby outer bandage and careful not to be distracted when he accidentally brushed his arm against her breast, "we should be able to take the splints off in about twenty days."

The outer bandage was removed. There was still no sign of infection.

The smell was only of the cerate he had used in the dressing. The alignment of the splints was good. "So," he said, reaching into his case for a fresh bandage, "before your arm was broken, what work could you do?"

Again there was the flicker of a smile. "I grow wheat and beans," she replied with surprising eagerness. "I milk cows and goats. I make butter and cheese. I spin wool. I help when my mother brings out babies."

"Anything else?"

She hesitated. "I make blessings."

He said, "Claudius Innocens . . ." and saw her eyes widen at the mention of her former owner, "said you were an excellent cook."

The eyes met his. "Yes, my Lord."

"Good!" he said, because he did not know anyone who wanted their garden tended or their cows and goats blessed, but an attractive and respectful girl with midwifery skills who was a good cook . . . He was glad, after all, that she had not seized her chance to run away. If he could get that arm fully functional, and if Bassus's judgment was sound, maybe Innocens's claim of four thousand denarii would not sound so ridiculous after all.

32

HE WAS ON the way to frighten Albanus again by arriving earlier than expected at the hospital when a voice called across the street, "Ruso! Just the man!" One of Valens's friends emerged from a side street, hurried up to him, and seized him by the arm. "You've got to help me, Ruso. We've got a bit of a problem."

Ruso, who had already done this officer's job for him once by breaking bad news to Merula, offered only a cautious, "What sort of problem?"

The man moved closer and breathed in his ear, "You know that derelict building over where they're putting the new shops up—the one that had the fire?"

Ruso nodded. He had just left his purchase from that particular row of shops sitting in the drab little room at Merula's.

"Well. A demolition gang went in yesterday and started pulling it down. When they were packing up to go home for the day one of them was looking around what's left of the back room and noticed an odd shape in the corner."

"I see."

"It's not an odd shape when you know what it is. It's a body."

Ruso remained carefully impassive. To his relief, the man let go of his arm.

"I don't know why this sort of thing always happens when it's me on duty," the man grumbled. "Now they want me to find some way to get rid of it."

"Why didn't someone deal with it last night?"

The officer scowled. "Because the idiots wanted to get back for their dinner instead of hanging around answering questions. So they decided not to report it till this morning." He glanced toward the street behind him. "I hope they had nightmares."

"Well, it's a nuisance, but I don't see what it's got to do with me. Or you, in fact."

"Ruso, it's Trajan's birthday. The town council are organizing some sort of do this afternoon. Priests in fancy dress parading about and slicing up animals. The legate's inviting important people to dinner. This isn't the day to announce that there's an unburied body lurking in the back streets, is it?"

Ruso scratched his ear. The man was right. The news that a departed spirit was wandering loose in the town would cause an upset: the fact that its corpse had turned up during the honoring of a recently deceased emperor would be seen as a terrible omen. "Can't they wait a day and find it tomorrow?"

The man shifted uneasily. "How much do you know about ghosts?"

"Nothing."

"But would you want to annoy one?"

"I wouldn't want to annoy whatever's left of Trajan either."

"Exactly. We need to get out of this without upsetting anybody—or the ghost, if there is one—and the only way I can see is to give the body a decent send-off right away."

"Fine."

"Only we can't get anyone to do it because no one's allowed to know it's there."

"What about the builders? They should be good at digging."

"They're refusing to go near the place. They think it's bad luck."

"The mortuary's no use," put in Ruso swiftly before the man could suggest it. "It's not private enough." Besides, admitting another unknown corpse would mean a fresh encounter with Priscus.

"I thought if we could find out who it was," continued the officer, "we could ask a couple of its family or friends to come and shift it quietly, and then get the priests to purify the place first thing tomorrow morning so the builders can go back in. We just need to find out who it is without telling anyone it's there."

"We?"

"I've made a start. The family who used to rent the place are all alive and well and HQ's got nobody reported missing."

"I don't see what else you can do."

"It doesn't narrow it down much, I know. You see my problem."

"Yes, but I don't see how I can help you with it."

The liaison officer cleared his throat. "Neither do I," he admitted, "but you're the one who knows about this sort of thing. Even the builders told me to fetch the doctor from the hospital who investigates suspicious deaths."

"I don't! And I'm supposed to be at the hospital by the seventh hour."

"Oh come on, Ruso—don't be modest!"

"Really. I'm not the least bit interested in investigating suspicious deaths."

"But everyone thinks you are. Come on, man. Don't leave me on my own with this. We've all got to do our best for Trajan's birthday, haven't we?"

Any faint hopes of being able to identify the body were dispelled as soon as Ruso's boots crunched across the debris-strewn site of the burned building. At first glance it was difficult to distinguish the human form, which was the same color as the blackened timbers in which it lay curled. He glanced back through the gap that had once been a doorway to see the liaison officer standing at a safe distance. "You didn't tell me it died in the fire!"

The liaison officer winced. "Keep your voice down!"

"How long ago was that?"

"Sometime in late spring. The building was already boarded up ready for demolition so they didn't bother trying to save it. Just pulled down the one next door to stop the fire spreading and left it to burn. "

Ruso glanced around him. The undemolished remains formed a chaotic jumble that reminded him of the collapsed houses of Antioch. This would have been one of the old single-story buildings: mostly wood with rough plaster, probably straw or dried bracken on the floor, and a thatched roof. It would have gone up like a torch. Anyone caught inside would have had to move fast, and whoever this was hadn't moved fast enough.

He picked his way across the wreckage, testing the charred timbers to ensure they would take his weight, and crouched to take a closer look from a different angle. He was not sure what he was supposed to be looking for. Yes, it was a body. Yes, it was dead. No, there was no way even its own mother would recognize it. Ruso murmured a quiet assurance to its spirit that he came as a friend. Just in case.

The liaison officer had untied his neckerchief to hold over his nose. He was making no effort to approach. Ruso scrutinized him for a moment, thinking. Then he unsheathed his knife and dug away a loose flake of charcoal. The fire had been fiercely destructive of human flesh but surely something must have survived that would give a clue to the identity of the body. A knife, a belt buckle, a cloak pin . . . maybe nails from the boots . . . All of these were things that could have been found by anybody prepared to make the effort. All were things that Ruso should be finding, and wasn't.

"Any ideas?"

Ruso shook his head. "I really haven't got much to go on here." He straightened. "And I haven't the faintest idea whether it's suspicious. You'll have to . . ." His voice trailed into silence. He bent down again and poked at something with the point of his knife, then reached forward and pinched it between his thumb and forefinger. Then he dropped it into his palm, spit on it, and tried to rub away the soot.

"What have you got?"

Ruso sheathed his knife and made his way over to the liaison officer. "I can't tell you who it is," he said, glancing around to make sure no one in the street could hear him, "but I think it's a female."

"Another one? Gods, that's the second one found this month. And you've no idea at all who it is?"

"I'm a doctor, not a fortune-teller," said Ruso, skirting the question rather than admit a tentative thought that he would be investigating tomorrow. "Whatever they tell you, I don't investigate deaths, suspicious or otherwise. You'll have to start asking around in the morning."

"Damn. It's going to have to stay here till then, isn't it?"

"Unless you have a better idea," said Ruso. Unable to resist, he added, "Good luck finding somebody to guard it."

33

RUSO NODDED TO Aesculapius and then to Decimus the porter on his way into the hospital. He was going to have to talk to Decimus, but not now.

Albanus seemed relieved to see him. It was now well past the seventh hour, and the clerk seemed to think the patients lining up along the benches were blaming him for the delay.

Ruso had strapped a broken finger and dismissed its owner with instructions to send in the next patient when an expensive smell wafted into the surgery. He looked up. "Priscus! Are you ill?"

"Fortunately, no," was the reply. "But I do need to see you."

"I'm busy."

"Of course. Perhaps you would be good enough to drop by my office when it's convenient?"

"Later," said Ruso, not specifying a time.

Priscus closed the door. Ruso pictured him gliding away down the corridor, perfuming the rest of the hospital.

He was occupied with patients for most of the afternoon, but a discreet inquiry as he slipped out of the fort—avoiding Priscus—suggested that the public celebration of Trajan's birthday had been a success. No rumors of ill omens seemed to have reached the men on duty at the east gatehouse. If the liaison officer had bothered to mount a guard, it must have been very discreet.

Relieved that he would not have to face questions about a cover-up, he hurried down the street toward Merula's. It occurred to him as he strode through the scatter of bruised petals, fallen leaves, and animal droppings, which marked the course of Trajan's birthday parade, that he would not normally visit a broken arm twice in one day. On the other hand, neither would he normally lodge a female convalescent above a disreputable bar guarded by two ex-legionaries intent on a quick profit.

He was almost there when a female voice shouted, "Doctor!"

He looked up. A pregnant belly, followed by its owner, also clad in vibrant yellow and blue check, was lurching across the street toward him.

"Doctor!"

The woman, who was wearing only one shoe, halted and glanced down at his case again. "Doctor?"

Ruso closed his eyes briefly and dreamed of a world where women stayed quietly at home and sewed things and understood the value of Modesty and Obedience—not to mention Not Turning Up Dead Under Suspicious Circumstances. When he opened them again, he was still in Britannia. He said, "Do you need help?"

"Doctor!"

"Midwife?" he suggested. Perhaps he had an immediate use for Tilla after all.

A vigorous shake of the head suggested exasperation as well as denial. She stabbed a forefinger into his chest, then waved her arm back in the direction he had just come. "Hospital."

"From the hospital, yes."

"Hospital!" She turned her head aside and spat in disgust.

"Ah," said Ruso, feigning understanding and wondering whether her guardians knew she had escaped.

"Soldier!" The arm waved back toward the fort and then indicated her own large form. "Soldier!" she repeated.

Ruso shook his head in a manner which he hoped looked suitably regretful, and lied. "I'm afraid I have no idea what you're talking about."

"Tell her he'll marry her," prompted a voice from across the street. Ruso looked up to see a veteran seated behind a workbench. "She'll only have to wait twenty-five years."

"Eyes!" declared the woman, ignoring him.

It was not the word, but the gesture, that sparked Ruso's sudden attention. "Eyes?" he queried, repeating the gesture so that both hands gradually shaded his vision. He wished he could remember the man's name. "The signaler? You're the signaler's girlfriend?"

She nodded. "Signaler! Hospital! Pah!"

Another blob of saliva spattered onto the stones. He turned to the man, who he now realized was mending the woman's other shoe. "Can you speak British?"

"Not me," replied the man, not looking up from his work. "Time they all learned a civilized language. We've been around here since Nero was in nappies."

Ruso glanced in both directions, but the only people around seemed to be off-duty soldiers and a slave who was discovering that the street was too narrow for the oxcart he was attempting to lead down it.

"How near are you to finishing that shoe?"

The man lifted the shoe to his face, bit through a thread, and held it out. "Done."

Ruso turned to the woman. "Come with me."

He knew where to find a translator.

"Tilla!" Ruso called up to the barred window with the little pot of yellow flowers on the sill.

Stichus, lounging by the entrance with his arms folded, eyed the large form in vivid check before wrinkling his nose and turning to Ruso. "Merula won't want that one, Doc. We got one that shape already."

"I need to see Tilla," said Ruso, just as her face appeared behind the bars. "Tilla? Come down here."

Moments later she threaded her way between the tables, ignoring the attention of several occupants who seemed keen to engage her in conversation and one who offered to kiss her arm to make it better.

Not wishing to entertain Stichus any longer, he led both women away from the bar. By the time they reached the fountain, a rapid and energetic exchange in British had made his first question redundant.

"Stop!" he ordered. "Now that we know you understand each other, I want to know who she is and what she wants."

"She is woman of the Cornovii," replied Tilla, seating herself on a bench without asking his permission. Ruso placed himself at a suitable distance and the woman settled on the other side of Tilla and peered around at him.

"A woman of the who?"

Tilla reached out her good arm and swept it in an arc to indicate their surroundings. "All around here is Cornovii land. Until the army take it away."

"I take it that's not what she's come to complain about?"

"Her man is Catuvellauni. They are a tribe who try to take over—"

"I know who they are," said Ruso, who had ridden through the pleasantly civilized lands of the Catuvellauni tribe on the way north from Londinium, but was no nearer to understanding what this woman wanted.

"Her man is here in the legion," continued Tilla, in a tone that suggested this was nothing to be proud of, and adding, "He is soldier whose eyes are fading. She says, Are you the doctor who say he can go to have his eyes mended?"

"I said we could try. It's a risky procedure. He understood that."

"She wants to know," said Tilla, "why you change your mind."

"I haven't changed my mind."

Tilla conveyed this to the woman, who had plenty to say in response. "She says," was the translation, "that her man tells her the new Doctor sends him to Londinium to mend his eyes and he shows her the letter—"

Ruso had given the signaler a copy of the referral letter, not because he needed one but because it gave Albanus something else to do.

"And she has packed all the bags and taken her son to her sister's house and borrowed money to go with him and more money for lodgings and today he goes to collect his . . ." Tilla frowned. "Something to say he can go on the road?"

"Travel warrant."

"He goes to collect the travel warrant, but the officer will not sign because he is not going. So now he is in trouble with his centurion for not saying his eyes are fading and she has two children and a blind man to care for and everything is worse than—" She broke off, interrupted by the woman. For a moment the two of them were trying to talk over each other. Finally Tilla swiveled around to turn her back on the woman. Her mouth was clamped shut. She folded her good arm over the sling.

"Perhaps," suggested Ruso, "you would be good enough to translate?"

"She is a very rude person."

"That is for me to judge."

"She says things about you. I say you are a good doctor."

The signaler's girlfriend splayed her knees to accommodate her belly and leaned farther out from her seat. Ruso found himself being glared at by two women. He got to his feet. "Tell her," he said, "that I am going back to the fort and I will have her man report to me immediately."

Tilla stood and relayed this message with an impressive air of hauteur, then reported, "She says he did not send her and she wants to know what you will say to him."

"Tell her," replied Ruso, "that what I say to my patients is confidential. And that insulting a Roman officer is a very serious matter. She should learn to curb her tongue."

The signaler looked pale when he showed up at the hospital. His tone veered between respectful and aggrieved as he explained the mysterious reversal of fortune that had fallen upon him. His centurion was now issuing a request for a medical discharge, but not before he and the comrades who had covered up for him had completed a month of ditch digging fueled by nothing but barley bread and water as punishment. Possibly in an attempt to avert further disaster, he apologized on behalf of his girl. She might, he said, have been "a bit overexcited" due to the circumstances and her condition.

It was dusk by the time the signaler had gone. Albanus offered to fetch a light, but Ruso told him not to bother and dismissed him for the day. Gathering up his medical case, he wondered what the signaler's girl had actually said, and whether he should insist on a translation, but then dismissed the thought. He was responsible for a mass of family debt, a sick slave, a list of hopeful patients he often didn't know how to help, and now word had got around that he had insulted the second spear by undermining his investigation into the suspicious death of the barmaid. In a moment he was going to have to sort out this business about the travel warrant, and tomorrow he would have to have a quiet word with Decimus. That was not going to be a pleasure for either of them. He had enough to worry about without wasting time on the opinions of hysterical women.

34

CONTRARY TO PRISCUS'S own policy, there was a yellow glow from beneath his office door. Ruso, hoping the man's expensive smell had faded during the afternoon, took a deep breath of fresh air before knocking and entering. "Priscus," he said, relieved that the smell was not as bad as he had feared, "I don't know what you want, but I want to talk about cataract surgery."

Priscus indicated the folding chairs. "Do please sit down, Doctor. I was wondering at what time I might have the pleasure of your company."

"I recommended a patient for examination by a specialist," said Ruso, snapping open the taller of the two chairs and ignoring the hint that it was his own fault Priscus was being forced to use artificial lighting. "Now I'm told his travel warrant has been refused. Perhaps you could explain."

"Ah."

"That was a medical decision."

"Indeed."

"We've had this discussion before."

"Indeed we have, but—"

"I believe I made my position quite clear."

"Perfectly. And I made clear to you that I would appreciate being consulted before costly decisions are made."

"If you had been here," pointed out Ruso, "I would have mentioned it. As it was, nobody could tell me when you'd be back and the surgeon's heading off to Rome at the end of the month. If the auditors don't like it, you can blame me. Now can we stop playing games and get this travel warrant signed?"

Priscus leaned his elbows on the desk and placed his fingers together at the tips. "I'm afraid this is a rather delicate matter."

"We can sort the delicacies out after he's gone."

Priscus sighed. "I realize that the decision was made in my absence, before we had our little talk. I was only made aware of it yesterday when the man's centurion referred the sick leave request back here to confirm your signature. Evidently he had not realized we had a new doctor. Under the circumstances, I would not normally have intervened. Especially since you are particularly sensitive about this sort of thing. However, as you may be aware, I have the honor of supervising the Aesculapian Thanksgiving Fund."

Ruso grunted. This was no surprise. Priscus seemed to have the honor of supervising everything remotely connected with the hospital.

"The fund," Priscus continued, "is used to pay for items or services of benefit to the patients that it is not possible to cover within the normal hospital budget."

"Of course. Is this relevant?"

"I believe loaning out amounts that are currently surplus to the needs of the fund represents good stewardship."

"So do I. I borrowed some of them."

"I was delighted to note," continued Priscus as if his speech had been prepared in advance, "that in my absence you took advantage of the very favorable terms we can arrange."

"Is that some sort of a problem?"

"No. No, indeed. Although of course we do have to make sure that should the funds be required for an emergency, they can be swiftly replenished."

Ruso leaned back in the chair. "Are you telling me," he said, "that you've managed to lend out so much money we can't pay for one man to visit an eye surgeon?"

"No, no! Of course not. Although, if I had not been away on business, I would have made sure the present level of the fund was checked before the loan was granted."

Ruso shrugged. "If the auditors pick it up, I'll tell them it wasn't you who handed out the cash. And by the time the bill comes in from the surgeon, we'll be past payday and you'll have your money back."

"Thank you." Priscus reached for a writing tablet. "I'm afraid I must ask you to sign another voucher. Just a formality, of course, but we do have to show that we have some sort of guarantee."

"What for? The pay clerks can subtract the money from my bonus."

Priscus's lips twitched. "Of course," he said. His teeth appeared in a smile. "But in view of the second loan you arranged yesterday, based also on the emperor's bonus, I think it would be wise."

Ruso blinked. How in the name of all the gods did Priscus know what he had been doing at headquarters yesterday?

"Rest assured that this is entirely confidential, Ruso."

Was that smile supposed to be reassuring?

"But you understand, with such a substantial loan, certain inquiries have to be made. Normally the inquiries would stay within the cashier's office, but since we have now won our battle to keep the Aesculapian fund largely under hospital control—"

"Priscus, if this is some sort of turf war between the Hospital and HQ—"

"Of course as your colleague on the hospital staff, I said nothing to the cashier's office that might cause you any difficulty. I thought you might prefer to settle this matter between ourselves. But as you see, that then leaves me in an awkward position. If we are to retain control of the Aesculapian fund for the benefit of the patients, the auditors will want to see that correct procedures are followed and some form of security is agreed for the loans."

"I see." He saw only too clearly. He saw that Priscus was wondering why he was borrowing large sums of money. He saw that he did not have his father's cunning and if he was not careful, his attempts to save the family from the legacy of that cunning would quickly prove disastrous.

"Of course if you would prefer," Priscus was saying, "we could ask the camp prefect to authorize a suspension of the normal conditions."

Ruso had to admire the way the threat had been made to sound like an offer of assistance. "As you've no doubt been told," he said, "I'm in the process of replacing my household effects." It struck him that he was starting to talk like Priscus. "But I do have an excellent library of medical texts," he said, "which I think you'll find more than outweigh the value of the loan."

Priscus hesitated. "There would be a slight difficulty there."

"Really?"

"The market for medical texts is a little—restricted. Valuable, of course, but not instantly salable. I'm afraid the auditors would be looking for something that could be turned into ready cash should the need arise."

"It won't."

"Of course not. As I said, this is just a formality." Priscus's lips drew back to show his teeth again. "I'm sure we can think of something suitable."

Ruso could, but he was not going to admit to owning the title to the farm. If he did that, it would only be a matter of time before someone—and Priscus was bright enough, and nosy enough—would put everything together and realize how many layers of loans rested on that one small patch of land in southern Gaul.

Priscus moved a candle closer and made a show of rereading the loan docket. "We really don't want to trouble the camp prefect if we don't have to, do we?" Still reading, he ran one hand lightly over the top of his head, as if to make sure all was firmly in place, and then glanced up. "I believe you do own a girl?"

"She's a liability."

"But rather attractive, I hear."

There seemed to be very little Priscus had not heard.

"She would fetch a good price."

"Not immediately."

"No matter. As you say, the need will not arise." The teeth reappeared. "Shall we say the girl, then, Doctor?"

Ruso gave Aesculapius an especially careful nod on the way out and hoped, as he often did, that the god did not have the power to see into his thoughts. Was using the girl as a loan guarantee any way to repay the divine being who had kept her alive at his request? On the other hand, perhaps Aesculapius was in charge of the whole business. The god of healing was working beyond his usual field: He had looked ahead and saved the girl for the very purpose of helping Ruso solve his family's cash problems.

Ruso made sure he was well clear of the hospital before he allowed himself to admit a suspicion that the figure in the hall did not care one way or the other.

35

RUSO YAWNED AND put the *Concise Guide*—which had advanced precisely three lines this evening—away in the trunk. As he turned he caught sight of his purse on the bedside table. It occurred to him that the blue glass bead he had removed from the body was still inside. He had meant to leave the bead in the mortuary for the night, but this evening's clash with Priscus had driven the plan from his mind. He was too tired to tramp over there now. The thought that it could bring bad luck had been a superstitious whim and one of which he was faintly ashamed. Fear, he mused, was definitely contagious. And sometimes convenient. He had no doubt that the builders were frightened of the corpse, but they had probably enjoyed the day off work.

As he rolled onto his side he felt a series of small movements around him. The puppy that had scrambled onto his bed while he was writing must have sneaked under the covers. He stretched one arm out and felt for the latch on the door. The puppy could make its way out later if it wanted. Finally settled, he yawned again and pulled the blankets up over his shoulders. Valens was on call tonight. What a lot of things a man didn't need when he could feel delight at the simple prospect of an uninterrupted night's sleep.

Ruso had no idea how much time had passed when he found his mind being dragged to a place it didn't want to go by something bouncing around on the bed. He wriggled in annoyance. There was a yelp and a skitter of movement across the floor. Reluctantly his mind registered that whatever it was had gone away. The word *puppy* drifted past him. Wretched dogs. Moments later he thought: *This is one of those dreams where you think you are awake.* He must make some notes on it in the morning. Dreams were interesting. Many people claimed to have been healed during dreams.

This dream was not about healing. It was full of barking dogs. In it he reached up and pulled the pillow around his ears. Dream or no, Valens would deal with it. It was Valens's job to get up, silence the dogs, and put out the—great Jupiter!

Ruso opened his eyes and scrambled out from under the covers. Fire!" he bellowed, grabbing his pillow and beating at the flames that were shooting up from the foot of his straw mattress. "FIRE! VALENS! WAKE UP!"

36

THE TUNIC WAS a pleasing color. Blue suited her. Rianorix from the next valley had told her so. Of course she had ignored him and walked on, because she could do better for herself than an apprentice basket maker and because the last time she had smiled at a compliment, the giver had burst out laughing and demanded payment from his friends. Her response had won him his bet. But Rianorix's words had stayed with her. "Blue is a good color for you, daughter of Lugh."

So when the woman they called Merula had held up three colors against her this morning and chosen the blue one, she was not surprised. The fabric was a coarser weave than anything she would have worn at home, and it had reached the patched stage at which she would normally have handed it on to one of the servants. But it was infinitely better than the scratchy rust red army tunic that was wide in all the wrong places and much too short, and in which she had always felt like a curious exhibit in a cage.

Tilla blew out the candle and lay down on the bed. She closed her eyes. It was the will of the goddess that she should escape: She saw that now. Her prayer was answered. People were being sent to help her. Merula had provided clothes. And now the medicus had told her the splints could come off in twenty days. In her own mind, in the plan he knew nothing about, that gave her eighteen days to find a good pair of shoes and a cloak with a hood to cover her hair. On the nineteenth day she would slip out, release her arm from the bandages, and walk away, just another pedestrian in the street, while the man who thought he owned her would be searching for a woman wearing a sling.

She had wondered where she would go, but today the outraged girl in the awful yellow and blue check had provided her the answer.

Before the medicus had interrupted and insisted on asking his own questions, Tilla had learned with very little prompting that not everyone around here was as progressive as this girl with her soldier boyfriend. Even some of the girl's own family were still trying to pretend the legion would go away if they ignored it. Whereas, although the signaler was a Briton by birth, he had chosen to join up and make something of himself. No man born a Roman citizen could have served the emperor with more dedication—and now the army had betrayed him.

Privately Tilla thought the girl should have known better than to involve herself with anyone from the Catuvellauni, a tribe who would sell their own grandmothers if the price was right. Nor was she interested in the woes of the boyfriend, who had probably done something he should be ashamed of to become a Roman citizen in the first place. What interested her was that the girl's family lived less than half a day's walk from here, and apparently they were not sympathetic to the army. She had her first destination.

She would have to be careful, though. There were few people in these streets who would recognize her, but she must make sure she did not run into the medicus who thought he owned her, or his goodlooking friend who was in love with himself, or, worst of all, the hideous Claudius Innocens. In the meantime, she must use her time here to watch and learn. She must find out how Asellina and Saufeia had managed to elude the men who guarded the doors. After that, she would be on her own. And in order to give herself the best possible chance, she needed to find out whether anyone here really did know what had happened to Saufeia.

37

RUSO'S SOOT-SMIRCHED HAND was shaking only a little as he placed the little ointment pot on the ledge of the mortuary window. "Rest in peace," he murmured, then backed out swiftly and closed the door behind him. As he strode away down the hospital corridor, the blue glass bead remained in the pot, safely inside the mortuary. As—he hoped—did any spirit who might be feeling attached to it.

He took another long drink of water before washing off the worst of the soot in the bathhouse, wondering what Priscus would have to say in the morning around the blackened state of the towels and the feathers floating around in the cold plunge. But minutes later, surveying the little hospital room that was his for the remainder of the night, he felt almost grateful for the administrator's insistence on cleanliness, tidiness, and the readiness of all beds at all times.

Ruso placed the candle on the table next to the cup of water and made sure it was steady. He sniffed at the trunk he had brought across with him from the house and wiped at a couple of feathers stuck to its wet surface. Apart from the odd dark trickle, the water did not seem to have penetrated inside. His books were safe, thank the gods. He left the lid open. He would have to put everything outside to air tomorrow. It would all dry sooner or later, but he would be living with the smell of smoke for weeks.

He delved into the trunk and took out one of his father's old letters. He placed it on the table beside the candle and thought how narrowly he had escaped joining him tonight. Then, finding the scroll he sought, he climbed into bed and pulled up the white hospital blankets. If anything could lull a man back to sleep, Hippocrates' musings *On Airs, Waters, and Places* was it.

The problem with Hippocrates, as Ruso realized some minutes later, was that he was not interesting enough to distract his reader from mulling over an eventful night.

After the scorched pillow had exploded in a snowstorm of feathers, Ruso had abandoned firefighting and dragged his burning mattress into the street. Yelling for help, he then rushed back into the house. Dogs raced around barking and yelping as he stamped out the wisps of burning straw the mattress had scattered in his wake. He wrenched open Valens's door, shouting into the darkness for him to get up and finally thumping him only to find his fist landing on an empty bed. As he ran back into the hall there was a commotion outside. Relieved, he hurried to greet the night watch and was hit in the face by a shock of cold water. Six men clutching buckets then stampeded past him into the house and proceeded to fling water around his bedroom in a manner that suggested they were enjoying themselves while he fought his way through them, desperate to save his books. Despite turning his bedroom into a swamp, the watch captain then insisted the house be abandoned for the night in case the fire should break out again.

"Well," said Valens as he and Ruso made their way to the hospital later, lugging as many of their valuables as they could carry, "it's a shame about the stink, but at least you managed to save most of the stuff. And your very fine self, of course."

"I can't understand it," confessed Ruso. "I went to bed as usual . . ."

"Ah well, it's easily done. And you have been rather busy lately, what with all your women."

"But I didn't leave anything burning!"

They stepped inside the hospital entrance hall, returned the greeting of the surprised night porter, and paused to nod to Aesculapius. Over the sound of their boots in the empty corridor Valens said, "You'll have to take back everything you said about dogs, you know."

"I've got nothing against dogs!" Unlike the captain of the watch, who had found plenty to say after the terrier bitch had bitten him in the excitement.

"Where did they go, by the way?"

Ruso shifted his grip on the trunk. "The watch asked the vets to take them in and check them over. Listen, I'm sure I didn't—"

"Ruso, it doesn't matter. Really. They're sending a gang to help clean up in the morning and I expect the stores will lend you some bedding until you can replace mine. Frankly, for a chap who's just nearly had his house burned down—and I could have been in it, did you think of that?—I'm really extremely calm." He paused in the doorway of an empty room. "I'll take this one. You can have the one around the corner. Don't snore too loud or Priscus will complain."

"Priscus?"

"He's here somewhere. Monitoring levels of after-hours activity."

Ruso checked to make sure Priscus was not lurking in the corridor, and cleared his throat. "Valens?"

Valens flung his armful of possessions onto the floor. "Gods, those feathers are everywhere. What now?"

"What if it wasn't me?"

"Ruso, you're overwrought. What do you mean, what if it wasn't you? Next you'll be blaming the dogs. Just try and be more careful in the future, will you?"

Ruso put down *On Airs, Waters, and Places*, rubbed his eyes, and squinted into the candle flame. Perhaps he really had forgotten to pinch out his light. Perhaps the puppy had grabbed it, carried it down to the end of the bed, and . . . and Valens was right, he was overwrought. He turned back to Hippocrates. Moments later he found himself mulling over the conversation with the civilian liaison officer.

How much do you know about ghosts?

Nothing.

But would you want to annoy one?

He did not believe in ghosts, but neither did he believe in mattresses that set themselves on fire. That was why he had deposited the bead in the mortuary. And why, although he could scarcely believe he was doing it, he now stepped out of bed and gazed around the little room, wondering what he could find that had a connection with the emperor Trajan.

Eventually he delved into his purse and took out a bronze coin. He placed it on the trunk that had been with him in Antioch. Trajan gazed sideways from the surface of the coin while Ruso stood facing him with his arms outstretched.

"Noble Trajan," he said to the trunk, keeping his voice down in case anyone should overhear, "Noble Trajan, this is Gaius Petreius Ruso. We met in Antioch. I was there when you . . ." He paused.

You must put yourself forward, Gaius!

"I saved your life in the earthquake," he said. Just in case there was any doubt, he added, "We got out through the window. Now, my Lord, they tell me you may be with the gods, and I am in need of your help. I pray you will keep me safe through this night from any spirits who wish me harm, and I ask you to grant peace"—How very, very much he hoped Priscus was not lurking outside the door—"I ask you to grant peace to the spirit of the woman who died wearing the blue glass—oh, this is ridiculous!" He flung himself back on the bed. There was no sense in being logical about the gods in daylight only to abandon oneself to superstition and trembling during the hours of the night. A man did not become a god just by dying, no matter what his successor might decree.

Ruso perched himself on the bed with the blanket around his shoulders, splashed cold water on his eyes, and settled down to spend the rest of the night with Hippocrates.

38

THE MAN WHO came to crash open Ruso's shutters and wish him a hearty good morning found him propped against the wall with his head lolled to one side. An abandoned scroll lay beside him on the bed and a solid pool of wax marked the site of a dead candle.

"How are you today, sir?"

Ruso rubbed his neck and tried to maneuver his head back to an upright position. As he did so he suddenly realized why he was here. "I'm still alive!" he announced to the surprised orderly.

The pleasure was short-lived. He had just remembered his first job this morning: to go and retrieve the contents of that pot from the mortuary and find Decimus.

How quickly a man's hopes could crumble. The porter clutched the little bead in his heavy fist as he tried to rub away the tears spilling over into the creases between his fingers.

"I'm sorry," said Ruso.

The porter nodded and managed, "Thank you, sir." He sniffed. "How did you know it was her?"

"I didn't. But I knew your girl had disappeared some time ago and I thought you'd be able to identify her jewelry."

"I wish I hadn't said them things about her."

"You were the only one who kept looking for her."

The porter sniffed again. "Did she suffer, sir?"

"I'm told there were people on the scene very quickly, but nobody heard any cries for help. It's quite possible she lit a fire to keep warm, fell asleep, and knew nothing about it." Had it not been for the dogs, would he have woken last night? Would he have realized what was happening? He didn't know.

The man had opened his fist and was rolling the bead around in his palm with the tip of a finger. "I bought this for her in Viroconium when I was on leave, sir. It was on a necklace. Just a cheap thing."

"She must have valued it to wear it."

"She told me not to waste a lot of money on presents. I was saving up. I was going to get her out of there. She promised me she'd wait."

Ruso said nothing.

"Why didn't she tell me she was going to run away?"

"Perhaps she went on the spur of the moment," suggested Ruso. "She didn't have time to send a message."

The porter sighed. "She was a good girl, my Asellina. I know what people said. But it wasn't her fault she had to work in that place. I was going to buy her out. We had plans." The man looked up suddenly. "All that about the sailor. I knew it wasn't true. First they tried to blame me for stealing her, then they just made up that sailor to shut me up. What do you think made her run away, sir?"

"I don't suppose we'll ever know," said Ruso, not voicing the thought that finding the girl's remains proved nothing: She could have been hiding while waiting for any number of sailors. Or soldiers. Or even a well-heeled local. He put his hand on the man's shoulder. "I'm very sorry, Decimus."

The man picked up the bead between his forefinger and thumb. "Can I keep this, sir?"

"Of course." Ruso coughed, and wondered how much smoke he had inhaled the night before. "Tell me some more about her," he suggested." She sounds . . ." He paused, not sure how to phrase it. "She sounds like a kindhearted sort of girl."

"Wouldn't hurt a fly, sir. She never had no enemies, Asellina. Got on with everybody." The man paused. "Except . . . well, you know. But she never meant no harm."

"There were people she didn't like?"

"Oh, no, sir. She liked everybody. Well, near enough. They have customers down at the bar that nobody likes. But they have to be nice to them, it's their job. The thing was, sir, she used to see the funny side of things. She used to make me laugh. But not everybody knows how to have a good laugh, do they, sir?"

"No," agreed Ruso, relieved. Clearly Asellina had not been vindictive in life: Even if there were such things as ghosts, there was no reason to suppose that in death she would be any different.

Decimus wiped his nose on his fingers and got to his feet. "She deserves a decent funeral, sir."

"Now we know who she is, I'll get the civilian liaison to go and see Merula. Then you'll have to talk to her about funerals."

Decimus nodded and squared his shoulders. "I'll see to it. Are you all right yourself now, sir?"

"Fine, thank you."

"I was sorry to hear about your troubles last night. And now they go and find my Asellina this morning. What do you make of that, sir?"

"Nothing," said Ruso, to whom daylight had brought the conclusion that he must have left the candle burning. "It's just a coincidence." The puppy must have then knocked it over and rolled it across the floor, where the flame had caught a trailing edge of his blanket. "One last thing, Decimus."

"Sir?"

"If you're going to drown your sorrows, don't do it at Merula's. And don't go alone."

The porter managed a weak smile. "Yes, sir. Thank you, sir."

After Decimus had left, Ruso thought about the girl who had always seen the funny side of things, who had lain cold and unburied for all those months while the rest of Deva carried on its business around her. The second girl from Merula's bar whom he had met only in death. Now, surely, there would be a proper investigation. In the meantime, he had to go and see what was being done about making his lodgings fit to live in.

39

IT WAS EARLY evening by the time Ruso found time to check on his slave. He found men crowded around the bar, blocking the entrance. As he approached, he heard the twitter of flutes. Evidently the bad news about Asellina had not been allowed to disrupt business. Finding a place in the crowd, he was in time to see the object of everyone's interest display a length of shapely leg through a slit in a silky outfit that left just enough to be imagined. The dancer arched her back and slid one hand slowly up her thigh. Ruso felt the surge of a desire too long denied.

A voice said, "Good, ain't she, our Chloe?"

He had not noticed Bassus moving over to stand next to him.

"Very," agreed Ruso, hoping he had not been watching with his mouth open.

"I'll get her to give your girl some lessons."

Chloe was swaying across the room toward them. Ruso, making an effort to concentrate, said, "I don't want her working here."

" 'Course not," agreed Bassus as Chloe entwined one braceleted arm around Ruso's neck. "But a bit of private dancing, that's an extra skill, see?"

Ruso felt the flicker of Chloe's tongue against the lobe of his ear.

Bassus was saying something about it all being money in his purse.

"Yes," said Ruso thickly, his mind not on his purse at all.

Suddenly he was deserted: Chloe had moved on to work the tables. A legionary was grinning with embarrassment as she ran her hand down his chest. His companions jeered and whooped as the hand slid lower.

Ruso tightened his grip on his medical case. He was making his way to the stairs—ignoring complaints from customers whose view he was blocking—when Bassus's "Not that way, Doc!" registered. He turned to find the man pointing him to the kitchen door.

Ruso retraced his steps to loud suggestions that he should make up his mind.

"She didn't have nothing to do up there," explained Bassus. "She's helping the cook out instead."

"I said she wasn't to—"

The doorman's hand was heavy on his shoulder. "Don't you worry, Doc, I'm protecting our little investment. She's well out of sight." He winked. "I told Merula we got to keep her as a surprise."

Ruso wondered which was worse: having Bassus as an enemy or having him as a friend. "And untouched," he insisted.

"You leave it to me, Doc." Bassus's words would have been more reassuring if he had not added, "She'll be as untouched as the day she come in here."

As Ruso entered the kitchen a cloud of smoke and steam that reminded him uncomfortably of last night billowed from the griddle. A stocky figure swung away with one arm raised to protect her eyes. Lucco swerved to avoid a collision. The dishes piled against his small chest swayed and rattled, but he managed to keep them balanced. Across the kitchen, Daphne set down her rolling pin beside an expanse of flattened pastry and paused to massage the small of her back with floury hands. Both she and Lucco looked as though they had been crying. The cook, who would not have known Asellina, seemed only to be squinting because of the smoke. When it cleared she turned back toward the spitting griddle with a look of determination and a spatula, while Lucco resumed his journey to the crockery shelves. No one seemed interested in Ruso's arrival, and the figure seated at the table with her fair hair in two long plaits did not look up.

Tilla had steadied the bowl on her lap by trapping it between her knees and the tabletop. In front of her on the scrubbed wooden surface was a heap of untouched bean pods: by her feet a bucket of hollow green halves. Ruso, feeling his tunic beginning to stick to him in the heat, watched unnoticed as she reached for a fresh pod. She pinched one end until it burst open, then widened the gap with her thumb, and finally twisted her wrist so the pod was upside down before maneuvering the thumb back down the inside of the pod to send the beans bouncing into the bowl. A couple shot over the rim. Tilla dropped the empty pod into the bucket and picked up another.

Ruso retrieved a bean that had rolled toward his feet. So, this was what a servant with one hand could do. He hoped the cook was not in a hurry for the vegetables. He stepped forward and dropped the escaped bean into the bowl. Tilla looked up at him in surprise just as the back door opened, sending in a gust of welcome cool air, and with it Merula's voice. "Doctor! Just the man we need!"

"Give me something, Doctor."

The hand that grabbed at Ruso's was cold.

Ruso, who had never expected to see its owner again, disentangled himself from the feeble grasp. The two men stood eyeing each other in the middle of Merula's back yard. The sweaty strands of hair that were usually combed flat across Claudius Innocens's head were dangling around his nose. His skin had a greenish tinge, which Ruso found both professionally interesting and, on a personal level, deeply satisfying. The silence was interrupted by Innocens's need to bend over the bucket again.

Ruso commended Merula for keeping the patient away from anyone else. It could be contagious.

Merula turned. "Phryne!"

A blond girl who was barely more than a child appeared from the open doorway of an outhouse and sidled into the yard. A nervous smile flitted across her face. One hand instinctively rose to cover crooked teeth.

"Get a bed made up in there."

"Yes, Mistress."

"Well, what are you waiting for?"

"Please, Mistress, I don't know where—"

"Then ask someone!"

The girl fled.

Merula turned back to the merchant. "I hope she isn't going to be another disappointment, Innocens."

"She's just a little nervous, madam," he assured her. "She'll settle down—ah!" He bent over, clutching at his stomach.

Merula asked Ruso what he thought the problem was, adding, "He hasn't eaten here," before he could speculate.

Ruso scratched his ear. "It's hard to say," he said. "It could be anything, really." He turned to the patient, who was now slumped against the wall. "It might just pass by itself. You really want me to prescribe you something?"

"Anything, Doctor, sir. I'm in your hands." Innocens's head drooped, swayed toward Merula, and lifted again. "Excellent doctor. Business acquaintance of mine."

"He sold me a half-dead slave," explained Ruso.

Innocens made an attempt to plaster the strands of hair back in place. "And you got a bargain, sir. She's turned into a fine-looking girl."

"No thanks to you." Ruso had a sudden thought. "Innocens, do you come to Deva regularly?"

"I pass through, sir. From time to time."

"Were you here in late spring?"

"Ah—possibly, sir. Possibly."

Ruso wished he had bothered to find out the specific date of the fire. "How long had you been here before you sold me that slave?"

"Oh, dear . . ." The strands of hair fell down again and dangled while their owner struggled to form an answer. Finally he said, "About two or three days, I suppose, sir. I really don't feel very—"

"Did you ever know a girl called Saufeia?"

Merula turned to stare at Ruso.

"Me, sir? Saufeia? I don't think so, sir. But these girls' names change like the wind, sir. If you're after something special I could—"

What Claudius Innocens could do was never made clear: He was too busy lunging for the bucket.

Ruso had to hurry back to his hastily cleaned but still smelly lodgings to fetch one of the ingredients for Innocens's medicine. By the time the ailing man had swallowed it, a bowl of pale damp beans was resting on the table where Tilla had sat. Ruso knocked on her door without success and then, hearing her weeping, hurried downstairs to see if there was a spare key. That was when he learned that Tilla was no longer occupying the shabby little upstairs room. Merula had moved her in to sleep with the other girls.

"That isn't what we agreed."

"I'll give you a discount," conceded Merula, placing a jug of wine and four cups onto a tray. "We needed the room." She glanced around the bar area and shouted, "Daphne? Table four!"

"Whoever's in there now doesn't sound very happy."

Merula handed the tray across the bar to Daphne, who had changed from her kitchen clothes and had tied a green ribbon in her hair. "I don't buy girls to make them happy," said Merula. "I buy them to work. Yours is in with the others. Through the kitchen and turn left."

On a lone chair festooned with discarded clothes sat Chloe, now huddled in a brown blanket, her feet soaking in a bowl of water. Tilla, who had been lying on one of the lower bunks, swung her legs off the bed and stood up. Chloe stayed where she was.

Ruso had never considered where bar staff might live when they were off duty, but if he had, he would have expected something better than this. The room was dingy and cramped. What little floor was visible between the three sets of bunk beds was presumably mud beneath the covering of dried bracken. The walls had once been cream but were badly stained with soot. Limp feminine laundry had been draped over a length of twine tied between the bunks. The girls had made attempts to brighten things up: Two cheerful red bows adorned the latches of the shutters and a familiar-looking cup filled with yellow flowers sat on the one shelf. Around the flowers lay a scattering that reminded him of Claudia: combs, mirrors, hairpins, jars of makeup.

He had the feeling of being too big for the room; as if any misjudged movement would knock over something precious and break it.

The girls, as was proper, were waiting for him to speak first. Trying not to think about Chloe's tongue exploring his ear, he cleared his throat and said, "Good evening."

Tilla bowed her head and murmured with a pleasing—and surprising—display of respect, "My Lord."

Chloe reached for a towel. She looked tired. The black around her eyes was smudged. It was hard to imagine her as the seductress he had seen writhing in the bar.

Ruso coughed again. "I hear there was a funeral today."

Chloe lifted one foot out of the water. "Some of us are starting to wonder who's next."

"I am sorry for the loss of your colleague."

"That's more than the management were. And I wouldn't call it much of a funeral. If it hadn't been for Decimus I bet they'd have dumped her in a ditch."

Not sure how to reply, Ruso turned to his slave. "Show me where you are sleeping now."

Tilla indicated a rolled-up mattress stashed between two bunks. As Ruso checked to make sure it was the clean one, she said, "A new girl is here."

"Asellina's been replaced," put in Chloe. "They were starting to run out of staff."

"The new girl is locked in the room," Tilla continued.

It was not an unreasonable precaution. "You should stay away from her for a day or two," suggested Ruso. "If she came here with Innocens she may have the same illness."

"I hope he is very ill and then he dies," said Tilla.

Ruso, who could not agree with this sentiment aloud even though he might share it, instructed her to sit down. He knelt awkwardly in front of her to check the alignment of the splints. Chloe did not offer him the chair.

As he felt along the length of the lower splint, he said, "I gather Innocens did not eat here?"

"If that's what Merula said," put in Chloe before Tilla could answer, "then he didn't."

Ruso glanced at her. "I'm not trying to accuse anyone. Nothing you say will leave this room, but it will help me do my job."

He saw the two girls look at each other. Chloe shrugged, tossed the towel aside, and reached for her sandals.

"He takes from the kitchen," explained Tilla. "When the mistress is not there."

"What did he take?"

"Wine, apple pie, and Mariamne," said Chloe.

"Mariamne?"

"He might have made *her* feel sick," continued Chloe, winding the thongs of a sandal up her calf, "but not the other way around. There's nothing wrong with the wine, and other people have had the apple pie."

Ruso pondered the possibilities as he checked the limited movement of the bandaged hand. He was paying no attention to Chloe groveling for something under one of the bunks, which was why when he turned to find her hidden behind a golden cavalry mask and brandishing a sword, it was a shock.

Chloe raised the mask. "It's blunt," she assured him, lifting the sword toward the fading light from the window before sliding it back into its scabbard. "You wouldn't believe what rubbish you have to put on here just so the customers can look at you taking it off again. Want to come and see the show?"

"I'm sure it'll be very, uh . . ." Ruso paused, looking for a word. "Artistic."

" 'Course it will," said Chloe. "That's why they come to watch."

When she had gone he turned to his patient. "Tilla, tell me what you know about Claudius Innocens."

"He is a patch of slime."

"Yes, but do you know what he was doing in Deva before I met him?"

Tilla shrugged. "He stays at an inn. He leaves me locked up there when he goes to do business. He tells me he will fetch a healer but I never see one."

"And some of his business was here with Merula?"

"I do not know, my Lord. If you ask him, he will lie to you."

"Did he ever mention any other girls?"

"He says I am the most ungrateful girl he has ever met."

"Hm. So he doesn't lie all the time, then. Tell me one more thing. Do you know why he is ill?"

The eyes that reminded him of the sea were wide with innocence. "Perhaps he is cursed, my Lord."

"What would make you think that?"

"Perhaps your medicine will make him better."

"Perhaps."

There was a pause, then she said, "What medicine do you give?"

Ruso looked at the door to the kitchen, which was closed. He looked at Tilla, and at the complex bandaging that covered the very best work he had been able to do, but which even now would probably not return her the full use of her arm. He said, "I gave him medicines that are recommended by several authorities."

She raised her eyebrows, waiting.

He took a deep breath and said, "Some of my colleagues recommend chewing several cloves of raw garlic." Although not necessarily to cure vomiting. "And then to sweeten the breath, the patient should take honey containing ashes of burned mouse droppings."

Her eyes widened. "And this is what you give for sickness of the stomach?"

"There are men who recommend these things," he responded, wondering what had possessed him to administer this ludicrous and disgusting treatment in which he had no faith at all, and scarcely able to believe that he had just admitted this weak—but oh, so enjoyable!—moment to a slave.

From somewhere in the yard outside the window came the sound of retching. Tilla said, "I think it did not work."

"No," agreed Ruso solemnly. "Perhaps he is cursed."

40

RUSO'S THOUGHTS AS he lined up with the First Century on the damp parade ground were a mixture of apprehension and annoyance. The apprehension was such as any man who has not recently undertaken serious physical training might feel at the prospect of a ten-mile run. The annoyance was partly with Valens, who could surely have found a more sensible way to impress the second spear. It was also with himself for rising to the challenge of Valens's "I would have signed you up too, but after a summer off I don't suppose you'd be up to it."

Pride had prevented him from asking exactly what he would be signed up for. Valens was obviously out to create an impression of being Enthusiastic and Committed, and it would not do to be seen as less enthusiastic or less committed than his rival in the race for promotion. So when Valens had asked him which of them should go first while the other remained on duty, he had volunteered. Now, standing on the parade ground surrounded by the fittest, fastest, fiercest, and best-trained unit in the legion, he knew he should have listened to his common sense rather than his vanity.

A centurion was bawling orders. The second spear was nowhere to be seen. It occurred to Ruso that a more suspicious mind might have described his friend and colleague as a devious bastard. It also occurred to him that there had been no need for him to do this run, but now he was here he had to finish it or risk public humiliation and serious damage to his hopes of promotion.

When the men first set off the shock to his system was as bad as he had feared, but once he had forced his thoughts away from the prospect of the next ten miles, his body settled back surprisingly quickly into the familiar anonymity of the training run. He was no longer an individual. He was part of a many-legged creature moving forward over the relentless crunch of boots on gravel. His lungs shared the heavy breathing of men keeping step. His own sweat mingled with the smell of others wafting through the afternoon drizzle as they passed the competing stinks of laundry and tannery. As they followed the East road out between the green fields that were the territory of the Cornovii, his mind was free to wander.

It wandered back to the cheering sight of the signaler waving at him from the departing wagon to Londinium that morning. Tonight, if his legs were still capable of holding him up, Ruso would stand before the healing God and offer up a prayer for courage for the signaler, steady hands for the surgeon, and the large measure of luck that was needed for successful cataract surgery. And a prayer that for all their sakes, the girlfriend would not deliver while they were on the road.

The thought of the woman led his mind down darker paths: back to the moment when he had realized that Claudius Innocens was supplying slaves to Merula's and might have been around when both of the dead girls disappeared. The thought that his own Tilla had narrowly escaped being offloaded to the highest-bidding bar owner had filled him with fury. That fury had led him over a boundary he had never imagined he would cross. Until yesterday, he had honestly been able to claim that, no matter how unlovely or annoying they were, he had always done his best to help his patients. Now he felt—not shame exactly, but a sense of being stained by the dirt of others.

He had not harmed Innocens. To his relief and Tilla's probable disappointment, the man had recovered overnight and had sent a message of thanks to the hospital this morning. Perhaps the purveyors of mouse droppings had a point after all.

Mouse droppings? There was another boundary he had never imagined he would cross. Not to mention his newfound doubts about ghosts and his sudden rush of faith in Trajan. Ruso wiped a drip of drizzle off the end of his nose. Perhaps the damp climate was making him soft in the head.

He must concentrate on what was important. His duty to his family was no less just because they were far away, but with all the distractions here—slave girls, house fires, arguments with Priscus—he had given them scant thought recently. He must organize himself. He must adopt a logical approach. Observation, diagnosis, treatment.

Observations

No cash
Short-term extra costs of long-term investment (Tilla)
Large debts in Gaul
Small debts in Brittania
Grim (and dangerous?) living quarters
No housekeeper

Increasingly distracted, impulsive, and unprofessional behavior. He was constantly finding his mind wandering away from whatever he was supposed to be doing. As if Tilla were not enough of a diversion, this morning he had found himself wondering if the two girls' deaths were not connected at all, and whether Decimus had lied to him. He only had the man's word for it that there had been no contact from Asellina. What if the porter really had received a message that his girlfriend had run away to join him? Would it have been welcome? His dreams of a future with her would not have included harboring and supporting her as a fugitive slave or having to desert from the legion to flee prosecution from her owners. What if he hadn't been prepared to take the risk? What if he had been afraid of being punished for encouraging her? What if . . .

Gods above, he was doing it again!

Diagnosis

A man burdened with too many responsibilities

Treatment

Long term, concentrate on getting the family out of debt
In the meantime, stay calm

Hold out for eleven days until payday
Use Hadrian's bonus to clear all of the loan from the Aesculapian fund and most of the one from HQ

Find—
private patients
ways to campaign for promotion
somewhere cheap and civilized to live. (The CMO's quarters will do nicely.)

Avoid—
hospital administrators
rogue slave traders
destitute or deceased females, and any temptation to find out what happened to them
civilian liaison officers
any more bright ideas from Valens

Eventually, he would be able to realize his investment in Tilla. He would do it without the help of Bassus, whose bar-trade contacts would probably all be as seedy as Claudius Innocens. He had noticed an advertisement for a traveling slave trader chalked up on a couple of walls on the way out of town, but he did not want to take that route either. Bassus's claim that the local dealers would rob him blind was not the only reason for his reluctance. Having kept her alive, he felt some responsibility toward the girl. He wanted to have some control over where she ended up. If there really were a shortage of good staff in Britannia then some respectable household would have a suitable vacancy. By the time the arm was healing—say, in six to eight weeks—that officer would have turned up.

Ruso, counting three steps to a breath now instead of four, sniffed at the fresh drop of drizzle perching on the end of his nose and glanced at the men slogging forward around him, who had now summoned enough breath to join in the indecent lyrics of marching songs. They would be earning a fraction of his salary, and many of them were supporting families. How did they do it? Were a poor family's needs less than those of the comfortably well off? Were they all closet philosophers, assuring their women that there were lots of things they didn't need? Or was Priscus right, they simply stole whatever they wanted?

Underlying all these was a deeper question: How could one be an educated and intelligent man and not know this sort of thing?

On the first day of Ruso's apprenticeship, his uncle had warned him that a little knowledge would unlock the gates to vast and unsuspected deserts of ignorance. No matter how diligent he was in study, how careful in observation, and how keen to learn from others, the causes of most diseases and the reasons why some patients recovered and some didn't would remain a mystery. The difference between a real doctor and the latest quack who shambled into town offering miracle cures in a bottle was that a real doctor knew his limitations. This speech the fourteen-year-old Ruso had regarded with a level of scorn that he was later glad he had kept to himself.

A true philosopher, he mused now, would be delighted instead of taken aback at every new revelation of his ignorance. A true philosopher would understand that the path to knowledge lay first with the discovery of new questions.

Did continuous rasping of short breaths signify swelling lower down in the throat and was it possible to kill oneself by running until one's airways closed up?

Ridiculous. Of course not. It just felt as though it was.

What caused the head to pound during exercise, and why, despite careful strapping to ward off blisters, did old boots always rub in new places?

You can do this, he told himself. *You have done it many times before. Count.* Each step a bonus. Each step an achievement. Set small targets. One and two and three and four and . . .

"Out of practice, Doc?" Ruso glanced at the fresh-faced young optio who had fallen in step beside him.

"Good to get—" He tried not to sound out of breath, "—out again. Haven't had much—time lately."

"Busy over at the hospital?"

"Short-staffed." He must get the optio to do the talking. "Been with the—legion long?"

"Ten years this winter. My people are from Baetica, but my father was a centurion in the Twentieth."

"Born in Deva?"

"No, no. My father got married after he retired back home."

"Like it here?"

"You get used to it. Hey, are you the doctor that's investigating the murder?"

"No," said Ruso. He had neither the breath nor the desire to elaborate.

They were passing some native houses now. These were set well back from the road, beyond the wide shoulder where brown sheep lifted their heads as the soldiers approached then bounded away to graze at a safer distance. Smoke curled from thick cones of thatch squatting on round stumpy houses. Several small children of indeterminate sex were fighting over a rope swing dangling from the branch of a tree. Chickens wandered in the mud and a boy was leading a reluctant goat past an untidy stack of hay with a pole sticking out of the top. Ruso saw all this but heard none of it. The sounds of these other lives were muffled beneath singing accompanied by the thump of legionary boots and the jingle of buckles.

Aware that his "no" had sounded abrupt, Ruso said, "What are the locals like?"

"We've got both sorts 'round here," explained the optio. "One or two who know what a bathhouse is for."

"And?"

"And a bunch of thieving sheep-shaggers."

"Ah."

"You'll find some of the girls friendly, but you'll need to watch your step."

"Really?"

"Half of them have a string of brothers who want to knife you to restore the family honor. The other half are sent by those honorable families to latch on to an army salary so they can move out of the mud hut. Not much of a choice, is it?"

Ruso smiled. "I hear the second spear has a daughter."

The optio laughed aloud. "You won't get near that one."

"Not me. A friend."

"Not a chance, Doc. Not a chance."

Ruso glanced across at the native huts just as a shapely girl emerged from a gateway carrying two buckets. Moments later he was aware of confusion ahead of him: the sort of confusion caused by someone tripping and the men behind not being able to stop in time. The singing gave way to shouting and swearing. Later runners saw what was happening and parted to flow around the sprawled bodies. Ruso sidestepped to the left, glancing at the playing children who had stopped to stare. The girl had vanished. The optio stayed behind, yelling abuse at the tangle for watching the bloody natives instead of where they were going.

Minutes later a breathless man caught up with Ruso and conveyed the optio's message that one of the fallen men had a suspected broken ankle. Ruso muttered a silent prayer of respect to whichever fate had cursed the unfortunate legionary and hurried back to help. He no longer had to pretend now. He really was both enthusiastic and committed.

41

YOU'RE DOING *WHAT*?"

Valens's hand, clutching his spare underpants, paused above his kit bag. "Seems they're paying a visit to some hairy mountain chieftain whose resolve needs stiffening."

"And they want you to go along?"

Valens resumed his efforts to stuff underwear into the few remaining crevices in his kit bag. "I can do a quick tour of the outpost units while I'm there. It's time somebody checked them over."

"That's going to leave the hospital a bit short, isn't it?"

"I did think about that," said Valens, ramming the last sock down and hauling on the drawstring to close the bag, "But then I thought it would give you a chance to shine, so you probably wouldn't mind."

Ruso's weary mind groped toward a suitable reply, and failed to find it. In the end he said, "Very decent of you."

"You're welcome!" It was not clear whether Valens was ignoring the sarcasm or had simply failed to notice it. "I know you want the CMO post, so it's only fair to let you have a crack at getting yourself noticed."

Ruso yawned. This afternoon, having rendered first aid and organized a party to carry the injured man, he had rejoined the returning runners of the First, and just about kept pace with them for the four miles back to the barracks. His legs were stiff. His feet were blistered. He could not be bothered to point out that his efforts to sustain three men's work single-handed at the hospital would only be noticed if something went wrong.

"Well," continued Valens, "I can't stay up talking, I've got an early start. They're leaving at sunrise, but I want to get down there early and snag a decent horse."

Ruso said, "You'll be missing your turn with the training run, then?"

"But I'll be with them," pointed out Valens, as if he were intending to march with the First instead of ride past them on a borrowed horse. "Now. Do you want me to wake you when I go or will you be enjoying sleeping in in your lovely new redecorated bedroom?"

42

IN THE ABSENCE of Valens, it was Ruso who hurried across to HQ just after dawn for the morning briefing. He was not overjoyed to find Priscus already standing at the back of the hall. Each acknowledged the other with a curt nod.

Ruso frowned. He was unwilling to leave a man who would not know a plague from a pimple as the official representative of the medical service, but it was ridiculous for the hospital to be left to manage itself while both of them stood around listening to notices. He was about to give Priscus a departing wave—that surely would help to mend relations between them, as well as given him a chance to snatch breakfast—when there was an untidy shuffle of men standing to attention, followed by silence. The camp prefect's voice echoed in the rafters, bidding the assembled officers good morning and announcing that he was in charge for four days while the legate was away.

Ruso struggled to concentrate on the notices and ignore the gurgling of his empty stomach and the stifled heavings of a man in front of him who was trying not to cough. Finally the prefect announced his chosen password for the day—*tiger stripes*—and paused to take questions. Only as the briefing was declared closed did it strike Ruso that he should have raised his hand. It was what Valens would have done. It was the sort of thing Claudia would have encouraged. The camp prefect was directly responsible for the hospital and asking questions was a way of getting yourself noticed. The trouble was, there was nothing he actually wanted to know. No, that was not true. There was something he wanted to know, but he couldn't ask it in public.

He asked it later of Albanus, who looked uncomfortable. "I'm not sure I can tell you, sir."

"Why not?"

Albanus coughed and looked to make sure the surgery door was shut. "Well, they gave us a talk about security the other day. All about not telling anyone anything they don't need to know, and how the officers might test us, and . . ."

"Do you actually know the answer?"

Albanus looked even more miserable. "Yes, sir."

"Well, if somebody's already blabbed it to you, it can't be that secure, can it?"

The scribe's face brightened. "Is this a test, sir?"

"Yes. Well done, Albanus. You've passed."

"Thank you, sir."

"Now can you tell me whether the legate has gone off on the same tour as Officer Valens?"

"Yes, sir."

"Yes he has, or yes you can tell me?"

"Both, sir."

"Thank you." Ruso paused. "I suppose you'll be wondering why I wanted to know that."

"Oh no, sir."

"No? Good!" Ruso put his hand on the doorknob. "Ready for ward rounds?"

By the end of the morning Ruso realized he was starting to like Albanus. The man made himself genuinely useful during a full ward rounds and busy clinic, taking a pride in the swift production of whatever information was needed and apparently enjoying his chance to boss the other clerks around.

Ruso made a point of thanking him and was amused to see Albanus blush. "Go and get something to eat," he told him. "We'll start again at the seventh hour."

The scribe hesitated. "Will you be here, sir?"

"At the seventh hour."

"But between now and then, sir . . ."

"I will be somewhere else."

"Yes, sir. Sorry, sir. Only Officer Priscus said I was to know where you were at all times. In case there's an emergency."

"If the bandagers can't deal with it," explained Ruso, "get the watch to sound a call for me. I won't be far away."

Ruso lingered only to leave brief instructions with the guards and then hurried out under the east gatehouse, long strides taking him swiftly down the busy lunchtime street and away from the sound of all but the most energetic of trumpeters.

Moments later he heard a familiar voice calling his name. He kept walking. He had done his very last favor for the civilian liaison people. If they had a problem, he didn't want to know about it. He had enough problems of his own.

"Ruso, wait!"

He turned. "I'm in a hurry."

"Oh, I don't want you to do anything!" said the civilian liaison officer, falling into step with him. "I just want a quick word."

"Very quick, then."

The man broke into a jog to keep up. "I just wanted to say I was sorry to hear about your fire. And to thank you for your help with naming that body the other day."

"Oh," said Ruso, slowing down to negotiate the ladder of an off-duty soldier painting the front of a house. "Right. It was just good luck that I'd spoken to the porter."

"They've finished clearing the site now. There aren't any more bodies."

"Well, I suppose that's good news."

"I went down to the bar to tell them myself," continued the liaison officer, as if this were not his job but someone else's.

"How did they take it?"

"The owner wasn't too happy about paying for another funeral."

"No, so I hear."

"I told her she ought to keep a better eye on her girls."

"Maybe we need to keep a better eye on our men. This is the second runaway who's been found dead."

"We are aware of that, Ruso. We aren't quite asleep over in HQ, you know."

"You might also want to look at a part-time slave trader who supplies girls to bars. He's called Claudius Innocens."

"Really? What do you know about him?"

"Not much," said Ruso. "I just don't like him, that's all."

"I'll mention it," said the officer. "If there's an investigation."

"You mean there isn't?"

"It's not up to me," said the officer. "I just write reports. But thanks for the tip."

As they parted company it struck Ruso that it was no wonder the men of the Twentieth needed to be given talks about security. They had been stationed here far too long. The staff weren't quite asleep in HQ, but there were certainly corners over there where a man with limited ambition could lie down and snooze undisturbed, except when he roused himself to pass on a piece of interesting gossip. He supposed it was the liaison officer who had told Valens that the legate would be leading the First's mission in person. No wonder Valens had wormed his way onto the list. Valens, not Ruso, was seizing the chance to shine. Valens, the army doctor with no combat experience.

Not, by all accounts, that there was much chance of any combat on this trip. If the local chief were to have a change of heart about his loyalty to Rome, he would hardly be likely to have it during a visit from the legate and the First Century. Which, of course, was the point of the trip. Anyone who really wanted to see some action, Ruso had been assured, would seek a posting up north to join in the fun the army were having with the Brigantes.

Ruso had long ago lost any illusions about combat being fun, but it occurred to him that it would do no harm to check out the state of the medical service in the north. If he could cook up some excuse for a few days away, he could return Valens's favor by leaving him to manage all the medical work on his own. In the meantime, Ruso was going to take advantage of his housemate's absence to save himself some cash.

43

TILLA WAS SHREDDING cabbage. She was doing it carefully, slowly, and badly. No matter how hard she tried to hold the knife steady with her left hand, it faltered. Before they toppled onto the scored wood of the kitchen table and broke into untidy shreds, the slices of cabbage were tapered like door-wedges. This mattered to no one else—the cabbage was to be stewed anyway—but Tilla's mind was traveling far ahead of tonight's supper.

She put down the knife, grasped at the air to flex her stiff fingers, and picked it up again. Her work was slow, but it pleased her. She needed to train her left hand into some sort of dexterity if she were to escape and survive. Even if the Roman healer had rebuilt her shattered arm perfectly—which seemed unlikely—her right hand would be feeble after being bandaged for so long. Besides, with every rasp of the knife through the crisp green flesh she could imagine it was not a cabbage she was slicing up, but a man.

To her relief Innocens had gone, leaving the girl Phryne locked in the upstairs room. Phryne, pale but apparently not ill, had been let out to join the other girls on the morning trip to the baths. Tilla had held a brief conversation with her on the way, but Merula had moved close enough to overhear, and they had fallen silent.

Inside the baths, Phryne was the last to take her clothes off. For a moment Tilla wondered if she was going to refuse, but Chloe murmured something in her ear that persuaded her to cooperate. Finally undressed, Phryne sat in the corner of the hot room with her child's body huddled in a towel, watching the other girls as they strolled about in the steam, chatting and laughing, their naked flesh glistening with sweat. Her eyes kept returning to Daphne's blue-veined breasts and enormous rounded belly, taking in the dark line that ran down from the protruding navel and the silver streaks that showed where the skin was stretching and splitting. The girl brought one hand to her mouth as Daphne flopped down splay-legged on the bench, poured oil into one palm, rubbed her hands together, and began to massage the surface of the bulge.

Two girls Tilla did not recognize wandered into the hot room. As soon as they saw who was in there, they retreated. A few moments later some older women wrapped in towels paused in the doorway, looked around, glanced at each other, and then ventured in. They clopped past Merula's girls in wooden bath shoes—they had brought their own, Tilla noticed—and seated themselves in the farthest corner, turning very straight backs toward the rest of the room.

Not long ago, Tilla would have shared these women's contempt for Merula and her girls. Yet now that she lived among them, she had begun to realize things were not as simple as she had supposed. The girls were kept to serve the same army that had built this bathhouse, which the respectable women were now enjoying. This morning, when a man in the street had shouted an insult at them, the same Bassus who had grabbed Tilla as if she were an animal went across to him, said something to him, and then with one swift movement smacked the flat of his hand against the man's ear. Several passersby hurried on while Bassus stood over the fallen man with his arms folded, looking around as if he were daring anyone else to insult his girls. When Merula thanked him he shook his head sadly. "People 'round here," he said. "They don't know nothing about respect."

The hairdressers were plying their trade at the baths as usual. To Tilla's relief nobody showed much interest in her. Her hair was left in anonymous plaits.

Phryne had to sit on the stool while her flat blond locks were sprung into curls with the hot tongs and pinned behind her head in a complicated knot. She managed something like a smile when she was shown the results in the mirror, pursing her lips quickly to hide her teeth. The effect was soon over because Merula told them to take it all down again. "That's not what we want," she said. "You've made her look older."

Merula had gone shopping while Bassus escorted the girls back to the bar and ordered Daphne and Chloe to open up. As he took up a position by the door, Stichus emerged from the kitchen and looked Phryne up and down. He glanced across at Bassus, who shrugged indifference. Stichus seized Phryne by the wrist and dragged her toward the stairs.

Before she could consider the wisdom of it, Tilla had shouted, "Leave her alone!"

The room fell silent. For a moment the only sound was the crackling of the fire under the hot drinks counter. Stichus, still keeping a grip on Phryne's wrist, looked at Bassus as if waiting for guidance. Everyone had stopped what they were doing to watch.

Tilla squared her shoulders. Still addressing Stichus, she said, "She is only a child."

Bassus's stool scraped the tiles. He made his way across the room, a slow smile spreading across his face. Tilla took a deep breath and stood her ground.

Bassus reached out a forefinger and lifted her chin. "And you," he said quietly, "are only a slave. Who won't always have that nice doctor around to look after her." He withdrew the finger. "Remember that."

Stichus jerked Phryne toward the stairs. Tilla felt an arm around her shoulders. "Into the kitchen," urged Chloe. "Cook needs you."

Tilla plunged the knife into another cabbage and tried not to think about Phryne, or how easily the girl's fate might have been her own. She would not wait to find out what might happen when she did not have the doctor to look after her. In fifteen days, she would be gone.

Since the few windows that opened onto the street were barred against burglars, there were only two ways out of Merula's. The main entrance was shuttered and locked at night and guarded by Bassus or Stichus—or both—during the day. The kitchen door led to a gloomy yard from which a door in a high wall opened onto a side street. The door was barred except when kitchen deliveries came in, and the bar secured with a padlock whose key swung from Merula's belt. Even if she managed to steal the key, she would have to fiddle with the padlock in full view of the kitchen window, the upstairs cubicles (not that much window-gazing went on up there), and the row of private rooms occupied by Merula and the doormen, which ran all along the opposite side of the yard to join the building behind. The front entrance was the only realistic way out. She would have to find an excuse to go out into the bar in the evening, wait until the doorman was distracted, and slip away into the night. Most people seemed to think this was the route Asellina and Saufeia had taken, although no one had actually seen them leave.

Strangely enough, it might be easier to escape now that Asellina had been found. The other girls had said little about the circumstances of her death, but they were clearly shocked and frightened by it. And, though only Chloe had dared to say so, upset to realize how little they would be mourned if the same fate befell them. The doormen would not be expecting anyone to venture out alone now.

A door opened behind her. She did not look up.

"Tilla!"

She twisted around, looked up into Merula's painted eyes for a moment, then put down the knife and scrambled to her feet. There was no one else in the kitchen.

"Tilla," said Merula, folding her arms. "I don't suppose for a moment that's your real name, is it?"

"My master says I am Tilla."

"Don't stare at me like that, girl! Haven't you learned anything?"

Tilla lowered her gaze and stared at the rings that looked too heavy for Merula's thin fingers.

"You look well, Tilla."

"I am well, Mistress."

"Many people have helped you to recover. You should be grateful to them."

"Yes, Mistress."

Merula reached forward and raised a tangle of untidily shredded cabbage. "Is that the best you can do?"

"Yes, Mistress."

"If you were one of my girls, you would be better trained."

Tilla resisted the urge to look her in the eye. "I am not one of your girls, Mistress."

The cabbage fell back onto the table. "No," agreed Merula. "None of my girls would dare to question the actions of her superiors, or to speak of what did not concern her."

"No, Mistress."

"Learn this for your own good, Tilla. Slaves who cannot control their tongues may lose them."

"Yes, Mistress."

"Remember my advice. Now go and collect your things. Your master has come to fetch you."

44

RUSO GLANCED BACK to make sure the girl was keeping up. He was glad to get her away from that place. He had explained that he was in a hurry and since they had not yet added up the bill for Tilla's lodgings, Merula had agreed to have it sent over to the hospital. On the way out Bassus had given Tilla a smile that she did not return, said he was sure that they would meet again, and said, "You won't forget us, will you?"

Tilla looked him in the eye and said, "I will not."

Bassus turned his attention to Ruso. "When d'you think she'll be fit?"

"Not for some time."

Bassus's grin reappeared. "You doctors. Never commit yourself, do you?"

"Not if we can help it," said Ruso.

He was swerving out into the street to avoid the painter's ladder when he heard the approaching rhythm of boots on gravel.

He looked up to see a unit of infantry whose front men had now begun to clatter along the flagstoned street behind him. Ruso turned and called, "Step back!" to Tilla. She might not know that a tired column within sniffing distance of its barracks had all the braking ability of a boulder rolling down a mountain. The painter, seeing their approach, wisely scrambled down his ladder and moved its base closer to the house. A wandering hen jerked its head up, glared at the disturbance, and scuttled out of the way.

Tilla stood with her back to the wall as the column began to pass. Judging from the mud, the sweat-streaked hair, and the volume at which the centurion and his optio were berating the stragglers, these men were returning from the regulation twenty-mile full-kit training march.

Several men were looking across at Tilla and grinning. One or two winked at her. Instead of lowering her head like a modest woman, Tilla folded her good arm over her bandaged one and stared back boldly. Ruso moved to stand next to her just as the centurion spotted what was happening and bellowed, "Eyes front!"

"Look away!" Ruso ordered her.

He surveyed the grimy faces of the legionaries trudging past. Any of them could have squeezed the life out of the unlucky Saufeia.

"Tiger stripes," said Ruso to the gate guard without being asked, swiftly followed by, "So, have there been any calls for the doctor?"

"Not a thing, sir."

Ruso handed the man a coin. He beckoned the girl in past the heavy studded gates and led her under the arch. "I'll organize a gate pass for you so you can do the shopping," he said. "Do you understand what your duties are?"

She nodded. "I cook and clean and mind the dogs."

"Good." He unhooked the front door key from his belt and handed it to her. "What can you cook?"

She looked at him. "Soup?"

"Fine," he agreed.

"What in soup?"

Ruso thought about that for a moment. There was unlikely to be much in the kitchen, and if there was, the mice would have found it by now.

"Something tasty," he said, untying his purse. He picked out three coins and put them into her hand. "Buy something for breakfast as well."

Tilla picked up the coins and examined them on both sides as if she wasn't sure they were genuine. "Soup should start in the morning," she remarked.

"Well, do your best," he said. "I won't be back before dark anyway."

They passed into the main street of the fort. "This is the sort of route you are to take back and forth," he instructed her, sweeping one arm in the general direction of the legate's residence. "No exploring, you understand? Deva is not a place for a young woman to wander around on her own."

Tilla's head rose. "If a soldier touch me, my Lord, he will be punished."

"Perhaps," said Ruso, without a great deal of confidence, "but by then it will be too late. Listen to me. Both inside and outside the fort, you are to stick to busy streets where there are plenty of people. If a man pays attention to you, walk away. Don't try to put him in his place. You may get away with boldness wherever you come from, but it won't work around here."

Tilla said, "I pray to the goddess to protect me."

"Well, help her by using a little common sense. Two lone girls have died and I assume you know that at least one of them was murdered?"

"The goddess will punish that man, my Lord. I have put a curse on him."

"I see."

"Also, I will put a blessing on my Master."

"Let's hope your goddess is listening, then."

The girl smiled. "She is listening, my Lord. You see already what she do to Claudius Innocens."

45

THE HEAVY DOOR of the hospital swung shut and the latch dropped with a clank. The skies had cleared into a chilly night. Ruso nodded to the guards as he passed the legate's house. The great man himself was away, but his family would be asleep beyond that grand entrance. In moments of weakness, Ruso envied men who lived in married quarters: men who went home every night to a home-cooked meal and the pleasure of a woman to warm the bed. In such moments he usually took a firm hold of his imagination and brought it to heel by picturing the woman to be Claudia. Tonight, he had no cause for envy. He was going back to warm lodgings and hot food. There would be no one in his bed—he had told the girl to use Valens's room—but there would be no one nagging him in the morning, either.

What a lot of things a man doesn't need.

He shivered, and turned to head toward his supper.

The house was pleasantly cozy, but only the dogs came to greet him. Evidently his servant had gone to bed. He lifted the lamp that had been left burning by the door, and sniffed. Leeks? Onions? It was hard to say. He carried the lamp into the kitchen. Then he cleared a space on the table, laid out the wooden bowl, the spoon, and some bread, which had been placed in the box with the lid weighted down, and settled down to enjoy his first home-cooked meal in Britannia.

The soup was lukewarm.

It was watery.

It was bland.

He took a mouthful of bread and then tried again.

This time the spoon brought out something rounded and hard. Exploring it with his tongue, he found peculiar soft strings attached to it. He returned the object to the spoon and held it up to the lamp to examine it. In the yellow light he saw the top of a carrot with most of the leaves still attached.

Gaius Petreius Ruso sighed deeply and pushed the bowl away. Truly, he was alone in a barbarian land.

46

THE BEDROOM door was wide open but she sidled in, singing softly to keep her courage up. Her eyes scanned the floor as she moved forward with the broom held out in front of her. Satisfied that the floor was clear, she ran clumsily in the medicus's big boots, twisted around, and landed on the bed with her feet in the air, the boots still on. Then she laid the boots and the broom on the bed and crawled around the mattress on her knees, bending to check that none of the covers were hanging down. Finally safe, she turned to the dog standing in the doorway, and said, "Are you ready?"

The medicus had told her to sleep in this room last night. It was the room of the other doctor, the friendly one, who had gone away. She had not slept well. To begin with she had lain rigid in the dark, listening for the sound of the medicus coming home and wondering if he would bed her, because he was a man, or beat her, because she was not a cook, or both.

Instead of the medicus's footsteps she had heard a faint pattering that she tried to tell herself was the sound of her own fear. As soon as she moved, it stopped. As she was drifting off to sleep, it began again. Then it squeaked. Fear might patter, but it did not squeak. So she had to keep listening, moving at short intervals, rolling over, kicking her legs or sighing, hearing the trumpet blowing the watches just as she had on bad nights in the hospital and trying to reason with herself that all houses had mice. No one died because of mice. She had grown up in a house where mice crept through crevices in the walls and nested in the thatch. At night she had heard them rustling the bracken on the floor, and she had gone to sleep with the blanket over her head, knowing that Bran would protect her. But Bran was dead, and the dog in this house was not as fast. Even the Romans, with all their organization, could not control mice.

It was past the middle hour of the night when the medicus came home. She watched a bright line appear and fade around the door as he carried the lamp into the kitchen. He did not spend long there. As soon as she heard his bedroom door scrape across the floor, she counted to ten, flapped the blankets to frighten the mice into their holes, and fled on tiptoe to the dining room, where the dog—after some shoving on both sides—had finally assented to sharing the couch. She had lain beside it, pondering the strangeness of Romans.

When she had first been carried into this house—before he had taken her to Merula's—she had been too weak to observe much beyond that the place smelled bad and looked cluttered. She had assumed that the servant was lazy, or away, or perhaps ill. It had come as a surprise to find that there was no servant except herself. It seemed that despite being surrounded by all this wealth, Roman doctors lived in poverty.

A healer among her own people would be better treated. Her mother was given gifts. Eggs or a hen. A pot of honey. A shawl. A goat. A mirror and comb set. Beer. Once, when she had safely delivered a son to an elder whose wife had been in labor for three days, a pregnant cow. They had lived well. They had a cook and a herdsman. Even when the harvests had failed, she could count on one hand the number of times the family had gone hungry. Whereas this medicus, with all his skill and authority, lived in a vermin-infested ruin and was reduced to bargaining for an injured slave in a back street. Small wonder that Romans had no respect for different tribes. They still had to learn respect for one another.

She must have fallen asleep on the couch, because the next thing she could remember was the sound of someone moving around in the kitchen. She rose to find the medicus helping himself to the bread rolls she had bought for breakfast.

"That soup," he said, without looking up.

She swallowed. "Is—good?"

"Is that the sort of thing you eat over here?"

"Britannia cooking, Master," she ventured.

"Gods above. With that and the weather, I wonder you people have the will to live." He had given her more coins and said, "I haven't got time to go into it now. Get something from a shop for supper. Not a British shop. Understood?" When he left he was clutching his case in one hand and an apple in the other.

Now she was back in the bedroom, determined not to pass another night like the last one. She had already used the broom handle to pull out the clothes that had been thrown under the bed. She had found among them a dish with greasy remains bearing small teethmarks and two cups with fluffy green pillows growing inside them. Now, from the safety of the bed, she bent and jabbed the broom at what looked like an old linen saddlecloth stored underneath the cupboard in the corner. Nothing happened. She pushed the broom farther in and began to slide the saddlecloth sideways, out from between the legs of the cupboard. The dog moved forward to sniff at it. A couple of puppies wandered in to see what was happening. The linen, once red and now faded at the folds to orange, was gathering a rising tide of gray fluff and little black mouse droppings around its leading edge as it moved.

How could anyone live like this? Once she had cleared this last corner, she would give all the floors a good sweep and block all the holes where the boards had warped or knots had fallen out or the mice had gnawed their way in.

She pulled the broom out from under the cupboard, repositioned it on the folded fabric that had emerged, and began to push sideways again. The fabric strained but did not move. It was snagged on the base of the cupboard. She crawled farther up the bed and poked at it from a better angle, putting more of her weight behind the stick. Soon there would be no hiding places left. Tonight, if she brought the dog in and sealed the gap under the door, she might be able to get a better night's—

It was so fast she barely saw it. As the dog shot under the bed in pursuit, the broom jerked in her hand and the fabric pulled clear. Tiny gray shapes leaped out of a tangled nest and scattered in all directions. The broom clattered to the floor. Puppies yelped and skidded. Tilla clapped a hand over her mouth to stifle her scream.

The narrow lane was empty. Tilla twisted the key in the lock and tested the door. Shut. She was safe now. Out of that horrible house. Before long, her heart would stop pounding and her breath would calm down. Out here, the sun was shining and a fresh breeze brought the smell of the tide over the wall of the fort. A gull wheeled overhead, screaming. Somewhere in the distance was the clang of a blacksmith at work. She tied the key on to her belt like a proper housekeeper, picked up the empty shopping basket, and hooked it over her injured arm. Then she slid the loop of the dog lead down from where she had secured it in the crook of her elbow. Grasping the lead firmly in her hand, she drew in a deep breath of the clean air and looked around her.

The house was set on its own at the end of a long open space that separated the hospital and the next barracks block. In the space, nettles had sprouted through what looked like the angular footprints of vanished buildings. The nettles might be useful, although it was late in the season now. Thistles, groundsel, dandelions, and scattered tufts of broad-bladed grass had poked through the black of an old bonfire patch. In the middle of the graveled alley that led past the front door was another scorched area. It seemed an odd place for a bonfire. She supposed it had something to do with the smoke stains and the burned smell in the medicus's house.

The lead pulled against her hand. The dog strained toward the open area and promptly squatted to add its own contribution to the collection of droppings dotting the ground. Tilla wrinkled her nose and decided not to bother gathering the nettles.

To her right, at the end of the alleyway, a wide street paved in stone ran parallel to the high outer wall of the fort. A crow, suddenly alarmed, opened its wings and flapped away from the top of the wall. Two sentries appeared, walking along a high path set behind the top rows of stones. They passed without showing any sign of noticing her.

It struck her that she was the only person in her family who had ever been welcomed behind the walls of a Roman fort. The thought of the gate pass in the leather purse strung on her belt made her feel uneasy. It was not an honorable thing to be trusted by the legions. Throats had been cut for less. And yet, the medicus had made it so easy for her to escape! It must be the work of the goddess, who was more powerful than the gods of the Romans, even though she had hidden her face from her people for such a long time. The goddess was helping her to escape. Chloe had finally told her what little the girls knew about the loss of

Saufeia. Tilla had not made the same mistakes. As for what had happened to Asellina: That was a mystery. But the goddess must know. The goddess would protect her.

Tilla pursed her lips and allowed herself a moment of pity for the medicus, powerless before the will of the one who had chosen to answer her prayers. The medicus had treated her well. She would serve him as best she could in the few days she had left here. She would do what she could to cheer up that dreadful house. In the meantime, she would find out how to cook something.

47

THE THIRD MORNING of Valens's absence dawned to the sound of musical weather. Walking through the fort, a listener could enjoy the sound of water drumming on roofs and splashing from the eaves, streams tinkling down gutters, drains gurgling and backing up. Inside the hospital were the complex rhythms of leaks dripping at different speeds punctuated with the occasional *ping* where the staff had placed metal basins because they had run out of buckets. It had been raining since before dawn, as Ruso well knew since he had been called out while it was still dark. Everywhere with a working brazier now smelled of wet wool hung up to dry. Adding to the cheerless mood of the staff was the knowledge that the planned modernization of the hospital building had receded by another day as the weather held up the work over at the bathhouse. Even Priscus's powers, it seemed, had not extended beyond getting his own office ceiling dried out.

Ruso was dictating notes to Albanus in a mood of grim determination when the morning porter interrupted to announce a visitor. Ruso's temper did not improve when the visitor turned out to be the civilian liaison officer, come to ask if he could borrow Valens's hunting net.

"On a day like this?"

"We're making an early start in the morning. Just me and a few friends. Why don't you join us?"

"I'm busy," said Ruso. "Valens is away."

"Oh, sorry. I suppose you are. We're busy too, you know. Not like you, of course. Our work isn't life or death. Well, not usually."

"No."

"And frankly, if we do anything too fast, it just encourages them. They're supposed to take responsibility for themselves, you know."

"Yes."

"But of course they don't. Sometimes I wonder what they have a town council for. Anything that isn't keeping the drains clean and organizing jolly festivals gets sent to us. Widows who've had their prize goat stolen. Shopkeepers who've been punched on the nose by a soldier they can't quite identify. Natives who—"

His flow was interrupted by a knock on the door. "What do you want?" he demanded of the orderly whose head appeared around the door.

The orderly glanced at Ruso and then back at the liaison officer as if not sure which of them he was supposed to be addressing. "Another visitor for the doctor, sir."

"They all want an immediate investigation, you know," concluded the liaison officer, lifting his wet cloak from his arm and slinging it round his shoulders. "And it's always when I'm on duty. Oh by the way, I put your Claudius Innocens on the second spear's list for a little chat."

"He'll have to move fast. Innocens travels around."

"Really? Well, if we don't catch him this time, we'll nab him when he comes back."

Ruso turned his attention to the orderly. "Who wants me now? I'm trying to get some work done."

"It seems to be a native girl, sir. We would have sent her away, but she's insisting on seeing you."

Ruso sighed. "Send her in."

Tilla appeared, busy rubbing her hair with a towel. Her shawl had done little to prevent the rain soaking into the blue tunic that was now clinging to her with an appealing precision that Ruso did his best to ignore. Her feet were muddy up to the ankles.

The liaison officer looked her up and down as they passed in the doorway, then paused to address Ruso from the corridor. "I meant to say earlier," he said, "glad to hear you found your cook. Very nice. I'll look forward to an invitation."

"Do," said Ruso, calling after him, "wait till you try her soup!" He turned his attention to Tilla. "Who gave you a towel?"

She frowned. "Tall, thin, old. His hair . . ." She paused, then raised her hand in a gesture Ruso recognized.

"Officer Priscus, sir," put in Albanus.

"I see," said Ruso, not altogether pleased at the thought of Priscus sniffing round Tilla. "Is there a problem?"

"I need money, Master."

He saw that she was trying not to shiver. "I gave you money the other day."

"Is spent."

"What—all of it?"

She nodded, slung the towel over her shoulder, and began to count on her fingers. "Bread, apples, onions, carrots, eggs, milk—"

"All right," he interrupted. "I haven't got time for a shopping list." He loosened the strings of his purse and tipped a quantity of pitifully small coins into his hand. "Take this," he said, adding something he remembered Claudia saying, "I shall expect an account at the end of the week." As she bent to pick the coins out of his palm, he realized that the tails of her plaits were dripping. He could not imagine how long it would take to dry that much hair in a climate like this, and so far she had only walked the short distance from the house.

Moments later he watched his own cloak walk out of the surgery with Tilla underneath it. At least part of her would stay dry. He hoped she would not catch a serious chill before he could afford to buy her some footwear.

"Her name is Tilla," he said, turning to his clerk. "If I'm out I may leave the key at the desk for her to collect."

"Yes, sir."

"And wipe that silly grin off your face, Albanus. Anybody'd think you'd never seen a housekeeper before."

48

BY THE FOURTH morning of her stay with the medicus, Tilla had begun to wonder if he lived this way by choice. She had the floors of the usable rooms clear, the mess stacked up in the driest part of the empty room, and the mice in retreat. She had found the best snack shop in Deva, and slipped into Merula's for a quick lesson with the cook while both doormen were out escorting the girls to the baths. Her repertoire was not extensive, but it was edible. Omelette. Poached salmon. Sausages. Boiled cabbage. Porridge. Stewed pears. Baked apples with honey drizzled into the space where the core had been. Yesterday, after the rain had stopped, she had shoved all the dirty clothes in the house into a bag and lugged them out along the Eboracum road to the laundry. Then, feeling she deserved a rest, she and the dog had finished off the beer stored in the dining room. It had been kept too long anyway—but even this the medicus did not appear to notice. He seemed to have no interest in anything beyond eating, working, and sleeping.

Asked what the names of the dogs were, he looked as if he had never thought of that before. They had no names, he said. The bitch belonged to the man who had lived in the house before his colleague. She said, "The pups are old enough to leave," but all he said was, "Good," as if he hoped they would go off and find new homes by themselves.

When he was at home—which was not often—he ate, and then retreated to his room, or sat hunched on the couch scraping rows of figures into a writing tablet, pausing to add the numbers up with a frown that deepened the crease between his eyebrows. Last night he had fallen asleep at the kitchen table. His chin was growing darker each day. It was another thing he did not appear to notice.

As far as Tilla could tell the medicus did not have a woman, but her fears that she would be expected to fill the space had been unfounded. He had made no approach. Maybe he did not like women. Maybe, like many doctors, he was Greek. Everyone knew about the Greeks. But in the past she had caught him looking at her in a way that was not at all Greek. Perhaps he was just too busy. Whatever the reason, she was glad of it. The goddess was watching over her.

She finished laying the kindling in the kitchen hearth. She dampened the grubby bandage around her right hand—she had no wish to set herself aflame—unwrapped the fire steel and prayed for success before settling the dry fragments of scorched lint in the middle of the tinder and bringing the steel down onto the flint. For the first time since she had been forced to do this left-handed, one of the sparks caught straight away. Breathing gently on the glowing edges of the lint, she prayed again for what she was about to do.

She had wondered many times why she had been saved. Visiting Merula's this morning, she had found out. There were now eleven days before her arm would be freed from the splints, so ten days more in the service of the medicus. Ten days in which to perform the new task the goddess had given her.

Tilla fed the tiny fire with dried grass and watched the smoke curl toward the ceiling.

49

JUPITER OPTIMUS MAXIMUS!" muttered Ruso blasphemously, pausing in the doorway of the house and wondering whether to walk away again. It had been one of those days when Aesculapius had not been on his side. A bad day for the doctor and a worse one for his patients, whose sufferings had included emergency abdominal surgery that was unlikely to succeed, the extraction of a glass splinter from an eye, and the amputation of an infected foot. He was supervising the cautery of the stump by a nervous junior medic when an orderly interrupted to tell him there were five stretchers in the hall, bearing the victims of a loading crane that had broken loose down at the docks. In the midst of this no one thought to mention the retired trumpeter who had come in complaining of chest pains and who was only brought to Ruso's attention after he had dropped dead on the floor of the admissions hall. As soon as the man's distraught wife had stopped shrieking at Ruso and been escorted away in tears, someone tapped him on the shoulder and whispered that the surgical patient had died and Officer Priscus was conducting an urgent review of admissions procedures.

Ruso spoke to the comrades of the abdomen patient, saw to it that he was properly laid out, and went home for dinner.

He took a deep breath and entered the house. The sound of a meandering melody came from the kitchen. Exactly what his servant was doing in there—other than singing—was a mystery to Ruso, who flung open the door and demanded, "What on earth is that stink?"

The singing faltered to a halt. Tilla, flushed from leaning over whatever was boiling in the blackened pan above the coals, observed, "My Lord is home early."

He said, "Is that my dinner?"

By way of answer she pointed toward a shelf beyond the reach of the dogs. A coiled string of pink, glistening sausages were an unwelcome reminder of today's abdominal surgery.

"Dinner," she explained. "Soon." There were damp wisps of hair stuck to her forehead.

Ruso returned his gaze to the coals. An unpleasant suspicion began to grow. "Tilla, are you boiling socks in the same pan that you cook in?"

She shook her head vigorously. "I do not boil socks."

"It had better not be another one of your British recipes."

She glanced back at the pan as if she were wondering whether to lie to him, then drew herself up to her full height, looked him in the eye, and said, "Is medicine, Master."

Medicine? Ruso sighed. He was tired of medicine. He was not interested in medicine. He had come here seeking respite from other people's troubles and the last thing he wanted was a sick person in his own house. Mustering his sense of duty, he said, "Do you need something else for your arm?"

"No, Master."

"Is there another problem I should know about?"

"No, Master. I make dinner now."

"Good. Give that pot a thorough scrub before you use it again."

Those eyes were looking straight at him. The expression in them was not one of cooperation.

"Medicine is a tricky business, Tilla," he told her. "It isn't a case of boiling up a few weeds. You could end up poisoning yourself. I work with pharmacists who have trained for years, and even they don't get it right all the time."

She turned away from him, gave the pan a vigorous stir, and banged the spoon on the rim.

Ruso rubbed his hand over his tired eyes. He was being defied. He needed to do something about it. The something was probably not picking his servant up, shaking her, and roaring, "I want my dinner!" So instead he said with all the calm he could muster, "If you are ill, you must tell me about it. I am your doctor."

"Yes, Master."

"Are you ill?" *Please, almighty gods, let it not be something female and complicated . . .*

"No, Master."

"Good." He reached for the cloth that was lying on the table and wound the ends around his hands. "Open the door," he ordered, gripping the hot metal handles through the cloth and lifting the pan carefully off the coals. Beneath the steam was a greenish black goo that heaved and spat as a final bubble came to the surface.

She followed him outside and stood on the gravel of the alley in her bare feet as he tipped the pot over the bonfire patch. The pan clanged as he scraped out the last vestiges of goo with the wooden spoon. Seeing her standing there with her good arm folded over her bad one—he must change that bandage, it was filthy—he wondered if she had been conducting some bizarre magic ritual in his kitchen. Best not to ask. He said, "You have done good work tidying the house, Tilla."

"Yes, Master."

"But I don't want to catch you making medicine again, do you understand?"

"You will not, Master."

It only dawned on him later, as he sat down in front of a dish of sausages shortly to be followed by a bowl of boiled cabbage and an apple (a three-course dinner!) that this was not an entirely satisfactory reply.

50

VALENS RETURNED FULL of tales of wild and wily tribesmen and how he had impressed both the locals and the officers by curing a fever in the hairy chieftain's youngest son. The next morning Ruso gave him a swift summary of the current hospital cases, told him to ask his friend at HQ if he wanted to know anything about the latest body, then escaped to enjoy some time off and catch up on some of the things he had been meaning to do for days. He did not want to waste most of the rare sunny weather standing in the line at the barber's, so while he waited for a shave he strolled down the street and dropped in to a weaver's shop to inquire about the cost of woolen trousers.

He pushed his foot down inside the hole for the second leg, distentangled his boot at the far end, and tugged the rough wool up around his waist. Holding everything in place with the spare fabric bunched in his fist, he tried a few experimental steps across the shop floor.

They seemed ludicrously baggy compared to riding breeches. "Are they supposed to be like this?"

"If you just fasten your belt around the top, sir . . ."

"I look like a bloody native."

"A lot of gentlemen lace their boots up around the legs and pop in a bit of sheepskin, sir. You'll find them very comfortable in the cold weather. Much warmer than leather."

Ruso rubbed his growth of beard and looked down at his toes. His ankles were hidden under the rust-colored wool that was already beginning to irritate his skin in unaccustomed places. He felt ridiculous dressed like this, but Valens had recommended this man and Valens, he had to admit, usually looked surprisingly well turned out for one so disorganized. Presumably when the cold set in, the two of them would look no more outlandish than anyone else.

He glanced out of the doorway in the vague hope of seeing someone dressed like himself. Instead, he saw a young woman walking past, carrying a faded blue military cloak draped over a loaded shopping basket. A young woman with curly fair hair, a bandaged arm, and bare feet. A young woman for whom he had only this morning asked the cobbler to set aside a pair of second-hand boots, and who needed to try them on. She was heading out of town and he guessed she was on the way to the laundry.

"I'll take them," announced Ruso.

"I can show you some other fabrics," offered the weaver, with the sudden anxiety of a man who suspects he could have sold something more expensive.

"They're fine. You can send me the bill care of the hospital." Payday was in less than a week, which was why Ruso now felt it was safe to buy a few small necessities.

"If you'd just like to slip them off—"

"I'll wear them," declared Ruso, pausing only to scribble his signature on the bill before snatching up his belt and hurrying out of the shop.

When he reached the street Tilla was already too far ahead for him to attract her attention without bellowing down the street like a drill sergeant. Acutely aware of the trousers flapping around his ankles with every step, Ruso decided to catch up with her when she stopped at the laundry, which was the only possible place where she could have any business out here. He passed the clanging din of a metalworker's shop where a display of pots and pans swinging in the breeze sounded a chaotic chorus over the steady rhythm of the hammer. Beyond it were a few tumbledown houses, which might have been pleasantly positioned on the edge of town were it not for the stench that was already hinting at the nearness of his destination. He stepped aside for an ancient veteran shuffling along on two sticks, then looked up and realized she must have crossed over to walk in the sunshine. She was hidden by a heavy cart rumbling past in the middle of the street.

The owner of the laundry was taking advantage of the sunshine too. The yard was crisscrossed with loaded washing lines. Navigating by smell, he ducked to avoid being slapped in the face by a sheet and turned left to make the customary contribution in the Vespasianus. Gazing down into the yellow depths, he reflected that the greatest of men could be brought low by one simple act of stupidity. The general who had conquered much of Britannia, stifled a Jewish revolt, and risen to the rank of emperor was chiefly remembered for his attempt to put a tax on public pisspots. His musings were interrupted by a more practical thought: He had not checked for any exit arrangements in the trousers. Perhaps he had better practice in private first. Turning on his heel, he ducked back around the flapping sheets and into the steamy atmosphere of the laundry to meet his slave.

The counter clerk shook his head and managed to look even more vacant than he had before Ruso spoke to him.

"She must be here somewhere," Ruso insisted. "I just saw her. Fair hair. Broken arm."

The youth scratched his head and then examined his fingernails, as if the information were hiding somewhere under his hair and he might have dislodged it.

"She's collecting my laundry," prompted Ruso, glancing around. The only other people he could see were laundry workers: a couple of well-muscled women wringing out towels and child slaves trampling the urine vats.

The clerk had picked up a ledger. "Name?"

Ruso told him. "Or it might be under hers. Tilla. Or Doctor. It's not the laundry I'm after, it's the girl."

The clerk ran a finger down the ledger, paused, squinted, and walked across to check the labels dangling from the necks of linen sacks lined up on the rack behind him. Then he went back along the rack and read them all again. Finally he returned to the ledger and said, "Medicus. Are you the doctor who—"

"No. You're quite sure you haven't seen her?"

"It's still wet. Only came in yesterday. You have to give us—" But Ruso was already out the door.

Back on the street, he spotted her immediately. Although she had been expressly forbidden to wander, Tilla had passed the laundry and kept walking. She was now a distant figure, moving briskly along the side of the road in the manner of a woman who knew exactly where she was going and was anxious to get there.

Ruso was conscious of the fact that there were plenty of things he should be doing this morning, most of which began with a shave and a haircut and none of which included trotting along the Eboracum road in a pair of ridiculous trousers, following a disobedient slave. Common sense dictated that he should shout to call her back now. Curiosity tempted him to continue just a little farther and find out where she was going.

She was approaching the cemetery. He was catching up with her. He wondered whether he had time to duck behind one of the grander gravestones and slip off the trousers. He had settled on a six-foot monument when the sound of wailing alerted him to a group of mourners approaching beyond a clump of trees, close enough to be offended.

Tilla was clearly in a hurry. She hardly bothered to step aside for a couple of cavalrymen trotting past: one of the horses, obedient to instinct rather than its rider, shied to avoid her at the last minute. The rider twisted in the saddle and appeared to shout something at her back. She took no notice. She bustled past a row of carts trundling into town under a weight of timber, and mercifully had the sense to cross to the opposite shoulder while a military road gang downed their picks to watch her pass. A voice bellowed at them to get back to work. Ruso was relieved. It meant they were too busy to gawk at his clothing.

Even if he had managed to put them on properly, it was entirely the wrong weather for trousers. He was beginning to understand why people said the climate here was as unpredictable as the natives. Yesterday the rain had been torrential. Today, sunlight flashed on the metal heads of the picks as the road gang swung back into action. The feathery seed heads of the grasses on the road's shoulder waved gently in a light breeze. His encumbered legs carried him along behind Tilla, feeling hotter with each movement.

He tried to imagine what his servant could be doing out here. Several possibilities came to mind, none of them reassuring. Despite the fate of Saufeia and now apparently Asellina, she could have taken it into her head to run away. But in that case surely she would have spent his grocery money on shoes. Whereas she seemed to be carrying a full shopping basket—which was puzzling in itself. If she was intending to return, why shop first and haul it all the way out of town? Unless, of course, she had used his money to stock up for her journey.

On the other hand, she could be on a repeat expedition to gather whatever she had found yesterday to put in that stinking medicine. In which case he would be faced with the uncomfortable task of punishing her.

He tried to remember what he had seen out here on the training run. Beyond the stubbled fields where a couple of plough teams were now plodding muddily along behind their oxen lay an area where the road and its wide shoulder had been cut through thick woods. Beyond the woods he could remember very little. Pasture? Scrub? He knew there was a native settlement about four miles from the fort, because they had passed the milestone just before the broken ankle incident. Could she be intending to carry the shopping all the way out there?

A worse possibility occurred to him: that she was on the way to some sort of rendezvous. Surely she would have more sense than that? But Tilla seemed to have more faith in her goddess than in any of the practical steps he had suggested to keep herself safe, and any number of unsavory characters could have crawled into her confidence while she was at Merula's. If there really was a madman, he could have come back for a second—or was it a third?—victim, this time choosing an isolated spot away from the danger of witnesses. Well, whoever he was, he would be getting a surprise visit from the medical service.

She was still about fifty paces ahead, showing no sign that she realized she was being followed. This, he told himself, is ridiculous. If he had never downed that cup of fake Falernian, if he had never decided to interfere at the fountain, if he had kept his mouth shut and let events take their course, he would not now be wasting his morning running around after his own slave.

He was glad Valens couldn't see him now. Valens already thought he was crazy. Valens had arrived home last night, tipped the contents of his kit bag onto his bedroom floor, and wanted to know where all his stuff had gone. Ruso had explained about Tilla moving in and he had grinned. "I thought you'd never get 'round to it. So, tell me. What's it like with a one-armed woman?"

Ruso had given him the look he usually gave malingerers. "She's a patient."

Valens crouched down and let the dog lick his face. "I suppose you could give her some interesting hand exercises."

"I told you, she's a—"

"You smell better," Valens informed the dog as he pushed her away so he could stand up. "Has somebody bathed you?"

Ruso shrugged. "I think Tilla took it for walks. Can you bathe a dog when you've only got one arm?"

"She seems to be able to do most things. You're a lucky man. She hasn't got a sister, has she?"

"I wouldn't introduce you if she had."

"Dear me, you are grumpy." Valens lifted the lid of the beer barrel. "I see you've developed a taste for this stuff at last."

Ruso peered into the empty barrel. "Tilla must have thrown it out," he said. "She wasn't too impressed with our housekeeping arrangements."

"I'll ask for wine next time." Valens dropped the lid back down. "Well done, Ruso. I knew I could rely on you to come up with a decent servant in the end."

"I told you, we're not keeping her."

"*We're* not keeping her," Valens had repeated in triumph. "There you are. She's become *our* housekeeper. Excellent! I'll chip in with the costs if you like. I promise not to bed her without asking first."

"Nobody's going to bed her!"

Valens had eyed him curiously before shaking his head. "Ruso, Ruso. You are a good chap and I love you dearly, but you really must learn to relax and enjoy yourself a little."

Ruso scowled at the hems of his trousers. It was all very well for Valens to say he should relax. Valens didn't have the responsibility of shoring up a secretly bankrupt family in Gaul and finding a decent place for a slave over here. A slave who was, he now realized, too attractive for her own good.

Claudia had often complained that her maids were stupid and lazy but never once, as far as he could recall, that they weren't pretty enough. He was beginning to see that Bassus was right. There was a market for beautiful slave girls. It was not in the homes of happy families. He was not proud of it, but the people who depended on him were going to need the kind of price that market would pay.

He glanced up. Apart from a group of cavalry horses approaching in the distance, the road ahead of him was empty. Tilla had turned left, crossed the ditch, and was making her way over the open expanse of the shoulder toward a patch of woodland.

If she had turned to look, she would have seen him step onto the heavy tree trunk that provided a dry foothold across the ditch, then scramble up onto the narrow, muddy path that led through the long grass. Instead she took not the slightest precaution, hurrying into the woods like a woman late for an appointment.

Anxious not to lose her among the trees, he lengthened his stride until there were only twenty or thirty paces between them. The path twisted and turned through the gloom of the woods. The road he had just left was out of sight. Moments later he could barely hear the shuffle of hoofbeats on gravel as the cavalry troop passed. His own boots padded along on mud made slippery by damp leaves. Knotted roots had broken through the surface of the path. Brambles snatched at his trousers. More than once he had to adjust his stride suddenly to avoid snapping a dead branch. Several times he stopped to listen, and was reassured that Tilla was making no effort to be silent. Whoever she had come to meet would know she was approaching. As long as he was careful, Ruso would be able to take him by surprise.

The sunlight filtering through the branches caught the blue of the cloak moving ahead of him. Ruso hurried on, stepping over another dead branch while his right hand moved to unlatch the knife at his belt.

It wasn't there.

In place of the knife was an uncomfortable bundle of trouser fabric. He was cursing himself for leaving the weapon on the counter back at the weaver's shop when he realized the path was leading into an empty clearing. Ahead of him lay open grass dappled with sunlight. The blue cloak was there, dangling from a branch. Tilla was nowhere to be seen.

Ruso stepped off the path and hid behind a broad tree trunk that trembled with ivy. He held his breath, straining unsuccessfully to hear the sound of footsteps. Peering though the ivy, he surveyed the clearing.

Grass. Bushes. Bracken. The folds of the empty cloak shifting slightly in the breeze. There seemed to be at least two paths leading away, but he could not believe she had had time to take either of them unseen and there was no sign of unnatural movement among the leaves. Nor was there any sign of anyone else. He would have heard if she had greeted a friend, and she could hardly have been attacked without him noticing. This was the woman who had planned to knock out a legionary with a soup bowl. She must be hiding somewhere, waiting for whomever she had come to meet. Or perhaps she had seen Ruso after all, and was hoping if she kept out of sight for long enough, he would give up and go away.

Somewhere ahead of him, he could hear the trickle of a stream running though the woods. He hoped Tilla's patience would give out quickly. He was due on duty at the seventh hour and it must be past noon by now.

A black bird with a yellow beak hopped across the clearing. Gently, slowly, Ruso shifted his weight into a more comfortable position. Undisturbed, the bird continued to stab at something in the grass. There was no other sign of movement.

Hiding behind a tree trunk with his back exposed to the rustling undergrowth, it occurred to Ruso that following a native into the woods unarmed had not been a sensible thing to do. He was beyond shouting distance from the road. If there were more than one man to deal with, or if that man were carrying a weapon, he was in trouble.

That was probably why the voice terrified him. Only for a second, though, as he assured himself later. Of course he had not believed for more than a glancing moment that he was hearing the triumphant war cry of a native about to hack him to pieces. Or that a vengeful ghost had come to steal his spirit away in the depths of the woods. He had known, as soon as he had recovered from the surprise, that the sound was nothing to fear. Unfortunately his head did not communicate this knowledge to his heart, which continued to pound against the wall of his chest as if he were being pursued through the forest by a pack of howling wolves, instead of leaning against a tree trunk listening to a woman singing.

Tilla's singing in the kitchen had never been like this. At first shrill and ululating and eerie, then gradually descending, becoming breathy and resonant and peculiarly intimate. Ruso moved slowly forward to peer through the leaves again. He could see her now. She seemed to be alone. He frowned with confusion before guessing she must be standing down in a dip, which was hidden by the undergrowth on the far side of the clearing. Her good arm was raised to the sky. Her face glistened with water. Darkened tendrils of wet hair stuck to her forehead. Her eyes were closed in concentration. The expression on her face was little short of ecstatic. He released a long breath. His servant had not ventured into the woods to meet a lover, but a god.

A thin trail of smoke rose into the air. The question of how Tilla had lit a fire in the middle of the damp woods merged in his mind with the question of what she had been carrying in the basket. He suspected he was now going to have to add "theft of firewood" to her list of misdemeanors.

The song rolled on. It was, in a peculiar barbaric way, beautiful. Sometimes there were strains of a tune Ruso felt he should recognize, then the notes soared away in unexpected directions. Sometimes the same tune seemed to repeat and tangle around itself before giving way to a different one. Another high eerie section gave way to huskiness and a tune that meandered about in a sequence he thought he remembered from the kitchen.

Ruso retreated behind the tree and surveyed the damage to his new trousers. They were now snagged in several places. The bottoms hung limp and muddy around his feet. As he watched, a beetle scurried across the front of his boot. He shifted his foot. The beetle scuttled off and buried itself under a leaf.

The song, or collection of songs, was still going on. Ruso began to experience a familiar sensation. It was the feeling that usually crept over him during the first few verses of after-dinner poetry recitals: the sense that time was slowing down around him and that this damned performance was going to go on all night. Tilla, however, seemed to be enraptured.

Although he could not share it, there were times when Ruso was jealous of the comfort other people seemed to draw from their religion. Patients who retained a calm hope in the face of desperate and painful situations. One man had even offered to pray for Ruso's soul while Ruso amputated two of his toes. So although he had troubling doubts about Aesculapius, very little faith in Jupiter and his ilk, and—usually—silent contempt for the so-called divinity of emperors, Ruso had a solid belief in the value of religion. Leaving aside the water engineer who had to be tied to his bunk until he lost faith in his ability to fly from the top of his aqueduct, even the craziest of beliefs seemed to do less harm than any effort to dislodge them. So he would, if asked, have given Tilla permission for some sort of religious worship. But he had not been asked, and now he was witnessing blatant disobedience of a kind he had never encountered in a servant before. He had excused the attack with the soup bowl as a mistake. The business of cooking up medicines in his kitchen had been more of a misunderstanding. This was nothing short of defiance. He was now obliged, for the first time in his life, to administer a serious beating.

He was not sure what to use. Claudia had usually marked her displeasure by snatching up whatever came to hand—a spoon, a hairbrush, a shoe. He would have to use his belt. To that end, and because he was uncomfortable in them anyway, he would let the singing warble on while he climbed out of the trousers.

He was out of one leg and easing the second boot through the tube of fabric when he felt something drop into his hair. Logic vanished. Both hands shot up to sweep away the scorpion before it stabbed him in the scalp. The movement threw him off-balance. He hopped sideways, grabbing at the tree trunk to stop himself from falling. A bird flew up, squawking in alarm, and as Ruso realized that the thing that had fallen on his head was an autumn leaf, the song stopped.

He flattened himself back against the trunk, scarcely breathing.

In place of the song came a peculiar chanting, as if she were repeating the words of a spell over and over again. The chanting grew nearer. She was walking toward him.

There was no point in trying to hide. He stepped out from behind the tree.

The chanting stopped. Tilla was staring at him. At his face. At his feet. At his trousers. Then at his face again.

"Tilla."

"My Lord."

"You are supposed to be at work."

"Yes, my Lord."

"Instead, you are here."

"Yes, my Lord." She lowered her gaze again. For a moment neither of them spoke. Then she said quietly, "My Lord's trousers are fallen down."

Ruso slowly unrolled the belt from his palm and buckled it around his tunic, trying not to speculate on his servant's perception of what he was up to behind the tree. The punishment would have to wait until he had recovered some dignity.

51

RUSO LOOKED UP from the whetstone and put the scalpel down. "Come in, Albanus."

The door opened. Albanus appeared. "How did you know it was me, sir?"

"Magic," said Ruso, who had recognized the knock. "Any luck?"

Albanus advanced into the surgery. "Sir, the pharmacist says he doesn't know anything that uses all those ingredients."

"Did you ask if you could use them separately?"

"Yes, sir. Or in any combination. And he said yes, it was dog's mercury, and you could use it as a purgative but you'd be safer using hellebore because too much would cause severe gastric problems and coma. The wood sorrel—he said he didn't know any uses for it but if you took lots of it you'd probably be ill, and he said the best thing to do with garlic mustard and nettles is to mix them with scrambled egg and eat it while it's still hot."

"Good. Thank you." Ruso retrieved the scalpel and began work on the other side of the blade.

A wax tablet and a collection of wilted leaves appeared by the whetstone. "I wrote it down, sir."

Ruso glanced across. The notes inscribed in the clerk's neat handwriting really did end with "eat while still hot."

"Very thorough as usual, thank you."

"And there's somebody to see you, sir."

Ruso cleared the greenery to one side of his desk. "Send him in. Have you got his notes?"

"It's a her, sir." Albanus left a slight pause before adding, "I think you've got the notes already."

Albanus had gone, leaving Ruso alone with his slave.

"Close the door, Tilla."

The latch clanked into position.

He carried on stroking the triangular blade across the stone, conscious that she was waiting for him to speak. Her feet were in his line of vision. She was wearing the new boots.

He had asked her to report to him here as soon as she had finished the shopping. By this time, he felt, he would have worked out what disciplinary measures were appropriate. But despite mulling it over throughout their swift and silent walk back to town, and again in the few minutes since he had finished ward rounds, he had failed to make a decision.

He drizzled more oil onto the stone. As it soaked into the worn gray surface in the wake of the blade, he reflected that at least she had turned up as instructed. He had thought she might go gallivanting back to the woods in search of the plants he had confiscated from the basket. Garlic mustard and nettles. Edible and harmless, as the pharmacist had confirmed. Mix with scrambled egg. Eat while still hot. Perhaps he had done her an injustice. But dog's mercury? Severe gastric problems and coma? Surely it was a common enough plant for no one—especially the daughter of a midwife—to mistake it for something else?

He glanced up to find those eyes looking directly into his. Her mouth was set in the sort of line that suggested a direct approach would be a waste of time. Instead he said mildly, "Are the boots a good fit?"

He could see he had taken her by surprise. She lifted her skirt to look at them. "They are, my Lord," she said, and then added, "I thank you."

He nodded. "Good." She had tidied her hair. He noticed for the first time that she had made beads from three acorns: one brown flanked by two green, threaded on a length of thin twine to form a necklace. As her doctor, he should have been pleased to note that she was starting to take an interest in her appearance. As her owner, he had more pressing concerns. He laid the scalpel on the whetstone and pushed it to one side. "Now bring the basket over here and let's see what you've bought me."

She had bought him bread, apples, five eggs, cheese, bacon, and green beans. He glanced into the greased leather pouch that held his own flint and steel, and which she had no business bringing out of the house. He put it back without comment and said, "Tell me, Tilla. What tribe do you come from?"

She laid the folded cloak back across the top of the basket and put them both on a stool. "The Brigantes, my Lord."

The ones who were causing trouble. Somehow this was not a surprise. "They are from the hills north and east of here?"

"Yes, my Lord."

"And are they a very religious people?"

She shook her head. "Not all of them, my Lord."

"But you are faithful to your gods."

"The goddess protects me."

"And when you make medicine, is that something to do with your goddess?"

No reply.

"I'm interested in your medicine. Some of your plants here are new to me. Maybe I have something to learn."

No reply.

He lifted up one of the wilted stalks. "What is the use of wood sorrel?"

No reply. Her good hand was picking at a frayed strand of linen at the end of the bandage.

He put the first plant down and picked up the second. "I'm told this is dog's mercury. What would you use that for?"

No reply.

"You were in the kitchen when Claudius Innocens was taken ill. You put a curse on him."

"Yes, my Lord."

"Had you also made medicine for him?"

"No!"

"So if I ask the other people who were there, they'll confirm that you didn't go near Innocens or his food?"

Tilla pursed her lips as if she were about to spit, then cast a sideways glance at the floorboards and thought better of it. She said, "I do not wish to go near Claudius Innocens."

"No," said Ruso, "that's quite understandable." He ran a forefinger through the stubble he still hadn't found time to have shaved. Perhaps he should give up and hope beards would come into fashion when Hadrian's famously hairy chin began to appear on the coinage. He said, "Who were you making medicine for yesterday?"

No reply. The hand went back to the bandage.

Ruso sighed. "This blessing and cursing business, Tilla. Cooking up potions. Chanting. Wandering off into the woods. It's got to stop. People will think I'm harboring a Druid."

No reply.

"Am I?"

"The Druids are all gone."

"Am I, Tilla?"

"The army kill them all."

Ruso was quite well aware of the official line. The Druids, chased out of Gaul generations ago, had taken refuge in Britannia and made their last stand on a far western island in the territory now covered by the Twentieth. It was rumored that some had escaped, but Rome had taken comfort in the fact that Druid knowledge was not only secret and murderous, but complicated and coupled with a widespread refusal to write anything down. It took, they said, twenty years to train a Druid. So instead of hunting down hidden copies of documents, all the army had to do was keep culling the Druids on a regular basis and they would finish them off, like chopping down weeds before they had a chance to seed.

"Those songs," he said. "What are they about?"

"They tell stories."

"About Druids?"

"About my people. We sing of our ancestors. If we do not sing, our story is lost."

Ruso pondered that for a moment. It was plausible. The locals seemed to have no proper statues or tombstones. A people without that tradition would have to keep the memories alive in another way. "Somebody should write it down," he suggested.

She looked at him as if he had just said something very naïve. "My Lord, the people could not read it."

"They could learn."

"But why would they want to when they can sing?"

"Refusing to learn to read and write," said Ruso, determined to win at least one point, "is a very shortsighted view."

"Saufeia could read and write."

"Indeed," said Ruso. "Even women can learn."

"Saufeia is dead."

He scratched his ear. This was the sort of illogical leap that made women so difficult to deal with. "Saufeia wasn't murdered because she could read and write."

"If you say, my Lord."

"She was murdered because she met a bad man."

"She was stupid. I am not stupid like Saufeia."

"Wandering off into the woods by yourself is hardly clever, Tilla. Especially at the moment. Did anyone suggest you go there?"

"No, my Lord."

"You found the place by yourself? Nobody helpfully told you where to find a nice stream?"

"No, my Lord."

"Even so. If I could follow you, so could someone else. Now explain to me about the medicine."

No reply.

"I have to know. I can't leave a servant I can't trust in charge of my house."

The loose thread on the bandage began to unravel. She wound it around her forefinger.

"The medicine, Tilla."

Finally she said, "Is for someone else."

"Who?"

The end of her forefinger was turning pink.

Ruso sighed. "I don't want to have to punish you, Tilla," he said, wondering what sort of doctor contemplated beating his patients. Besides, he was not sure where to hit her. On the back? On the legs? Across her one usable hand? "I also assume," he said, buying time, "that you stole my firewood."

"No, my Lord. I took from a pile by the hospital."

"Oh, marvelous. You stole the hospital's firewood." Priscus had probably counted the logs and was in the process of billing him for them. "Now. Tell me about the medicine."

The finger tugged more thread loose and then jerked to a stop as the unraveling reached the knot where the bandage was tied. "Is the goddess!" she said suddenly. "The goddess tell me to do it!"

"Who did the goddess tell you to give it to?"

"I cannot say."

Slowly, Ruso pushed back his chair and stood up. He put both hands on the buckle of his belt. "I don't want to do this, Tilla," he said. "Tell me."

She shook her head. "I cannot."

He sighed again and unfastened the belt. He had spoken the truth: He did not want to do this. Discipline was like surgery: unpleasant but necessary. He wrapped the heavy buckle end around his right hand, making sure the studded straps were safely clutched in his palm and would not flail about. He did not want to injure her. But neither could he allow any suspicion that his servant might be poisoning people at the whim of some mad native god.

He grasped the loose end of the belt in his left hand and stretched it out so she could see it. The belt was supple with age. He knew, from years of polishing, every scar in the deep brown of the leather; every scratch on the silver of the trim. He had never before considered using it to inflict pain. Now he snapped it taut and stepped out from behind the desk. "Tell me," he said, seeing the color fade from her cheeks. "Now."

She bowed her head.

Someone was knocking at the door.

Ruso felt his voice rise to a shout. "Not now, Albanus!"

"Sir, a message from Officer Priscus!"

"In a minute!"

"Right-oh, sir! Sorry, sir!"

Ruso closed his eyes for a moment and attempted to compose himself. He heard the whisper of fabric. When he opened his eyes she was kneeling at his feet with her head still bowed, as if pleading for mercy.

He was beginning to feel exasperated. He had put up with far more than most owners would tolerate. Now, because he had tried to treat her fairly, this wretched girl had assumed she could get away with whatever she liked and he found himself having to fill a role he found deeply distasteful.

He took a long breath. "You have been collecting poisonous plants," he said. "If there is an innocent explanation, you must give it to me. Otherwise, I will have to report you. I have already told you about the questioners. You will beg for mercy, and they will not listen."

In the silence that followed, he prayed she was not going to tell him something he would have to report anyway. The cursing would not go down well if it were made public. If the questioners got hold of her, the best she could hope for was a swift end.

A dark tear splash appeared on the floorboards in front of her. A second fell beside it. Ruso clenched his fists. This was not fair. She was doing it on purpose to avoid answering questions. Sooner or later, this was the trick they all resorted to. Gods, how he hated having to deal with women! It was as if they sensed that he wouldn't know what to do.

Tilla sniffed and lifted both fists, still held together by the thread of bandage, to wipe her eyes.

"Oh, for pity's sake!" He turned and flung the belt at the desk. It skidded across the top and sent the whetstone and the scalpel clattering onto the floor. "Get up!" he snapped. "Sit on a chair and stop fiddling with that bandage."

Tilla sniffed again and scrambled up onto the nearest stool.

Ruso retrieved the scalpel from under a chair, lifted her hands, and stroked apart the thread that held them together. The limp forefinger lifted as he unraveled the binding, then fell back into her lap. The white indentation that ran around it gradually turned pink.

Tilla said flatly, "I have failed."

This so accurately mirrored his own feeling that he paused before asking, "At what?"

"If I speak," she said, not looking up, "I will be punished. If I do not speak I will be punished."

Ruso sat on his desk and folded his arms. He was almost sure she was telling the truth about Innocens. She could not have picked anything more dangerous than a dandelion around Merula's and anyway the girls never went out without the protective supervision of one of the doormen. So what on earth could she have to confess? As gently as he could he said, "Then you may as well tell me now."

"If I tell," she said, "my tongue will be cut out."

Ruso frowned. "Is this some Druid nonsense? The Druids are finished, Tilla. We're in charge here now."

"Is not Druids!" she blurted in exasperation. "Is Merula!"

Ruso felt his shoulders drop. "Merula?"

"You have seen Daphne!"

He stared at her. "The pregnant one?" He tried to grasp the connection. "Are you telling me Merula cut out her tongue?"

"Daphne asks a customer to help her run away. He says he will help, then he tells Merula. You see what happens to slaves who talk!"

He slid off the desk, crouched in front of her and gripped her by the shoulders. "Tell me," he insisted. "Tell me exactly what's going on. I'm going to put a stop to this nonsense right—" There was another knock at the door. "I said, not now, Albanus! Is this life or death?"

"Yes, sir! No, sir!"

"Which?"

"Yes, not now, sir, no it's not life or death, sir." There was a pause, then the clerk's voice said uncertainly, "Shall I come back in a minute, sir?"

"Don't bother," said Ruso. "I'll come and find you."

He returned his attention to his servant. "Quickly," he urged.

52

"SO," SAID RUSO, scratching one ear and trying to make sense of what his servant had just told him. "This new girl at Merula's, Phryne—"

"Is not her real name."

"Well, just pretend it is for the moment. This is a girl from your own tribe who accepted a lift from Innocens and then found herself kidnapped and sold to Merula."

"She is not a slave. She is freeborn. Her father is carpenter."

"These are serious allegations, Tilla."

"Yes, my Lord."

"And are you saying that Merula knows her history?"

"She tell her."

"These are *very* serious allegations."

"Yes, my Lord. Merula—"

"Threatened to have your tongue cut out if you talked. I know. How was she going to explain that to me?"

She shrugged.

"Clearly she didn't expect to have to do it. So you're convinced that your goddess has given you the job of saving this girl, but rather than have your tongue cut out, you were encouraging her to run away and making magic potions and prayers to protect her from the same fate as the other girls."

"And I put—"

"Don't say it!" he interrupted. "If you've been putting curses on Merula or anyone else, I want you to keep quiet about it. I happen to think it's nonsense but there are people who won't. You could get yourself into a lot of trouble."

Suddenly she looked up as if a bright idea had occurred to her. "My Lord could buy Phryne!"

He frowned. "Buy Phryne? What would I want to buy her for?"

"Or my Lord's friend, the good-looking one, he could buy her!"

"Even if we wanted to," Ruso pointed out, unable to imagine the good-looking one exerting himself for a slave he didn't want, "neither of us can buy her if she's stolen, can we?"

"Then you send her home, and Merula does not know that I tell you!"

"And the lightness in my purse is counterbalanced by the weight of moral righteousness."

She looked at him blankly. "Is what?"

"Never mind."

"You get your money back," she said. "I tell her family, they pay you."

"Marvelous. I'll go into business with Claudius Innocens. He can be the muscle man, and I'll send you to do the extortion."

She said, "Oh."

He was conscious of time moving on. He really should go and deal with whatever Priscus wanted. "There's no need for all these complicated schemes, Tilla," he told her. "I know your people have trouble believing it, but this part of Britannia is under Roman protection. A man can't steal a freeman's daughter and sell her into slavery, and an owner certainly can't buy a slave and put her to work knowing her to be stolen. You've acted correctly in reporting a crime. I'll pass on the report and it will be dealt with in the proper way."

"But my Lord, Merula—"

"Don't worry about Merula. The law says that slaves are the property of their owners. Merula might get away with bullying her own girls but nobody's going to cut out the tongue of my property. I'll make it clear to the bar staff that they're to leave you alone in future. Understood?"

She nodded. "Yes, my Lord."

"Now go over to the house and get started on dinner. And don't steal anybody else's firewood."

"Yes, my Lord." She stood and gathered up the cloak and the basket. Her hand was on the door latch when one last question occurred to him.

"Tilla?"

She turned. "My Lord?"

"You are legally a slave yourself, aren't you?"

She raised her hand to the place on her upper arm where the tunic hid the copper slave band. "I am, my Lord."

"And Innocens didn't steal you?"

"He paid money, my Lord."

"Hm. Not as much as he told me he did, I'll bet."

She smiled. "No, my Lord. I think not."

53

To Ruso's surprise and mild embarrassment, the urgent message from Priscus had been a referral to a private patient with a toothache. By the time he arrived at the office the administrator had gone out, but Albanus introduced him to a small boy who had been waiting to take the first available doctor to his grandmother.

He followed the boy out through the fort gates and down a street behind the amphitheater to a barber's shop. A veteran with a spectacular scar running down into a patch over one eye was perched on a stool by the entrance, steadily stropping a wicked-looking razor and ignoring the sound of raised female voices from somewhere in the depths of the building. He stood up as Ruso entered the shop.

"I was told you needed a doctor."

The veteran's one good eye glanced down from Ruso's growing beard to his medical case, then across at the boy who had brought him. He said something to the boy in British. The boy's reply seemed to satisfy him.

"It's the mother-in-law." The man jerked his head toward the back of the shop. "Needs a tooth pulled. Good luck."

The boy picked up a broom and began to sweep clumps of hair off the floor. Ruso made his own way past shelves stacked with towels and basins and stoppered jars. He rapped on the door.

The younger of the two voices in the back room launched into a fierce tirade of British that seemed to be aimed at someone else. The only word he understood was *medicus*.

"I'm the doctor," he announced, and pushed open the door in search of his patient.

The room smelled of smoke and boiled cabbage. It contained a table, two stools, an unmade bed, and an exasperated woman. The woman was standing by another door that led to the back of the house. This door was closed. From behind it came a speech in which he could again make out the word *medicus*. This time it sounded like an accusation.

The woman pushed a strand of hair out of her eyes. "Well, Doctor, you've worked a miracle already. My mother is out of bed."

"I understand she wants a tooth pulled."

"She doesn't. We do."

Ruso said, "Ah."

"All week," announced the woman, still in Latin but slowly, and loud enough to be understood from the other side of the closed door, "All week she has been tormented with worms in her tooth. We have tried everything we can think of. We have bought medicines to drive the worms out. My husband offered to pull it. We have taken her to the healer. She is still in pain. Now my husband has called for a medicus . . ."

The stream of British from the other side of the door contained the words *Roman* and *medicus* in a tone that suggested they were interchangeable with *bloodthirsty* and *maniac*.

"My husband," continued the woman, "whose life was saved by a Roman medicus, has hired a surgeon for my mother at his own expense, and my mother shames us all by refusing to see him."

"Sit down, Doctor," offered the veteran's voice from behind him. "The wife will pour you a beer."

"I've told her he's here," explained the woman, unnecessarily. "She still won't open the door."

"This often happens with toothache," observed Ruso, suspecting he was only a transient player in a long-running dispute. He offered to leave some paste to pack around the tooth. For answer, the woman placed one of the stools in front of him. Then she took down a cup from the shelf and poured beer from the jug on the table.

"How do you usually get them out?" inquired the veteran.

"The worms?"

"The patients."

Ruso took a sip of the beer and decided it would have been better used on the tooth worms, which, if they existed, must be devious little beasts because neither he nor anyone he knew had ever seen one. "I don't," he said.

The woman banged a cup down in front of her husband and poured more beer. The husband peered at it with his one eye. "Steady on, woman. You could drown a fly in that."

The woman shrugged and returned to her station by the door. She seemed to be listening for movement. The veteran helped himself to more drink, evidently not troubled by the mysterious objects floating in it. "Women, eh?"

Ruso braved another mouthful of the beer. "Tell me something," he said, "you do women's hair as well as men's?"

The barber shook his head. "Never had much chance to practice in the army. I'll do a quick trim on the locals, but we don't go in for all that fussing with pins and curling tongs."

"I just wondered if you'd had anyone in asking about selling hair."

The barber hooked something out of the beer with his little finger and wiped it off on the edge of the table. "I might look at something valuable. Blond, or red. Mouse brown you might as well use for stuffing cushions."

"Have you had anyone in asking about red?"

The one eye met his. "Is this about that tart in the river? I heard some doctor was poking around."

"This isn't official. I was the one who took the body in. I just wondered how far the inquiry had got."

"Well, nobody's come bothering me."

"Right." Ruso was beginning to wonder if the second spear was doing anything at all about the dead girls. At this rate Innocens would die of old age before anyone found the time to question him. "Well, if you should happen to hear anything—"

"If we get anyone around here, I'll tell them what I'm telling you. I don't want nothing to do with it."

The woman began to pound the door with the heel of her hand.

The man leaned forward to be heard over the din and said, "From what I heard, those girls were well looked after at Merula's. Compared to some of the places down the Dock road, Merula's bar is a palace. They took it into their heads to run off—" He broke off. "Will you stop that, woman? The old bat might be daft but she's not deaf!" He turned back to Ruso. leaving the wife to deliver another tirade in British. "Don't take a genius to work out what happened to them, does it?"

"I know what happened to them, and at least one of them didn't die by accident. What nobody seems to be able to find out is who did it."

"If I was you, Doctor, I'd stay out of it. You start asking too many questions, you upset people. I know who I buy from. I don't buy from murderers."

"I wasn't suggesting—"

"'Course you weren't. But you should be careful who you ask. People who go around poking into other people's business can end up in a whole lot of trouble."

"Why would anybody shelter a murderer?"

"I'm not saying they would. I'm just saying, watch out. Me, I mind my own affairs and I don't let my woman wander around this place after dark." The man rocked his stool back to lean against the wall and turned to the aforementioned woman. "Did I just hear you tell her I'd take the door down?"

The woman stabbed a finger toward Ruso. "Our money is sitting there, doing nothing!"

"Do you *know* how much it costs to fix a door, woman?"

Ruso rubbed his chin and decided to ask now before he or the barber drank any more of the beer. He gestured toward the shop, which since it opened westward onto the street would still catch the best of the daylight. "Any chance of a shave while I'm waiting?"

An hour or so later the patient lay on her bed in a drugged stupor, minus two disgusting black molars that had now vanished into the dusk along with her grandson. Ruso had a smooth chin, short hair, and he hadn't been bitten once.

As he closed his case he was still weighing whether to knock the cost of the haircut off the fee. Charges tended to fluctuate depending upon the means of the patient, but asking too little was as bad as asking too much. Word got around. Precedents were hard to break.

"About the fee . . ."

The barber frowned. "I know you had a bit of a wait, Doc. But you did have professional services during the waiting time."

"Exactly."

"The other officer told the lad it was a flat rate."

Ruso's face must have betrayed his confusion. "The other officer?"

"Old whatshisname—Priscus. Up at the hospital. Recommended you very highly."

"I see."

"He said you'd got an arrangement. We pay him and he passes it on to you."

"Ah," said Ruso, "*that* arrangement."

Ruso strode across the paved area toward the fountain, the fall of each boot on the flagstones coinciding with the rhythm of the speech he was rehearsing for Priscus. "And ex*act*ly what *right* have *you* . . . ?" He was distracted by a gaggle of children gathered by the steps that ran up the outside of the amphitheater. On the wall behind them he could just make out the white of a chalk scrawl announcing the forthcoming visit of L. CURTIUS SILVANUS, DEALER IN SLAVES: RELIABLE STAFF FOR THE DISCERNING EMPLOYER. Below, half a dozen children were scrabbling to peer into the hand of a boy whom he recognized as the barber's son.

"Ugh, look, there's roots!"

"Look at the blood on them!"

"Did you see the worms wriggling?"

He was passing the entrance to the oil merchant's when one of them shouted, "Hey, mister! Got a penny, mister?"

Ruso ignored him. Others joined in the chorus. He could hear their footsteps running up behind him. "Mister! Mister!"

Ruso spun on his heel and the gang stopped dead, a small and ragged bunch gathered just out of arm's reach. He pointed to the barber's son. "Does your father know you beg in the street?"

The boy hesitated, then grinned. "I know something you don't," he said.

"No doubt."

"I'll tell you, but you got to pay me first."

"Why would I do that?"

The boy glanced at his comrades, then sidled closer to Ruso. "I know something about red hair."

Ruso stared at him.

"I heard you ask. You want to know about somebody selling red hair."

"Somebody sold red hair to your father?"

The boy held out one hand, and made a show of clamping the other over his mouth.

Ruso sighed, and filched out the one meager coin inside his purse.

The boy took it and removed his hand from his mouth to let out the words, "It was a man."

"Do you know his name?"

"No."

"What sort of a man? What did he look like?"

The boy looked at his friends for support. "I don't know. He was just a man."

"Old, young, fat, thin? It's no good holding out, I haven't got any more money."

The boy frowned. "He was old."

"Was he a soldier?"

"I don't know," said the boy, backing away.

"When was this?"

The boy's friends closed around him. "He was just a man!" he called as they turned and fled.

A man. Ruso frowned at the backs of the retreating children. With a little effort civilian liaison could have found that out—and probably more—days ago. In the morning HQ would be receiving another report, and might even have to interrupt their hunting trips to go and question the barber. In the meantime, Ruso had told the boy the truth. Despite treating his second private patient in Deva, he had no cash in his purse.

Another thought struck him. Priscus's lodgings were somewhere on the east side of the town. He might be at home. According to Decimus, who was not as discreet as Albanus, the miserable old weasel had gone home to keep an appointment with his decorator.

Ruso tightened his grip on the handle of his case. Why wait for morning? He spun around. He was going to straighten out this business of the fees right now.

"Ow!"

The girl he collided with stumbled back against the wall. He made a grab to steady her and knocked something from her hand. It clanged as it hit the pavement. "Sorry," he said as the noise reverberated down the narrow street. "I didn't see you."

The girl shook off his hand and bent to retrieve the item she had dropped. "If this bloody thing's broken again, you'll pay for it. It's only just been—"

"Chloe?"

"Oh! Hullo, Doctor." Chloe held a large saucepan up for inspection. She wiggled the handle experimentally. "Still attached. No harm done."

Ruso frowned. "Should you be wandering alone out here? It's getting dark."

He was conscious of an arm snaking around the back of his neck. "Mm," Chloe murmured, "you never know who you might run into." Cheap perfume wafted over him as a husky voice whispered in his ear, "Fancy a little stroll?"

"No," said Ruso's mouth before the rest of him had a chance to argue.

Chloe detached herself and shrugged. "Oh well, it was worth a try. Sweet dreams, Doctor." Swinging the pan by her side, she set off in the direction of Merula's.

She had not gone ten paces when Ruso caught up with her.

"Change your mind?"

"I need to know where the street of the Weavers is."

"Ask me nicely."

"Tell me and I'll walk you back. Why didn't they send someone with you?"

"What for? I'm not going to run away, am I?"

"That wasn't what I meant," he said, falling into step with her.

"I'm going straight back." Chloe lifted the saucepan. "And I'm armed."

"I'm serious."

"Asellina was unlucky," she said. "Saufeia was clueless."

"I heard she was quite bright."

"Not in any ways that were of any use to her."

"No, I gather she wasn't brought up for, uh . . . for your kind of life."

"Not many people are, are they? Some of us just find we have a natural talent."

Ruso smiled. "Tilla seems to have convinced herself that Saufeia was doomed by the curse of being able to read and write."

For a moment Chloe did not answer, then she said quietly, "No offense, Doctor, but if you want to do Tilla any favors, you tell her to keep out of what doesn't concern her."

It was his second warning in one evening. "Chloe," he said, "do you know something about what happened to Saufeia?"

"Me? I don't know a thing. And if anybody asks, you can tell them I said so."

They walked on in silence. When they reached the bakery, Chloe paused and turned. The light from the torch outside Merula's was making a halo in her hair. "Thanks for walking me back, Doc. I appreciate it."

"Be careful," he urged her.

"Do me one more favor, eh? Don't mention my little offer to the management."

"I wouldn't dream of it," said Ruso, who had already guessed that Chloe's efforts at private enterprise would be frowned upon by her owners.

Chloe laughed. "Tilla said you were all right, and you are."

"So, where do I find the street of the Weavers?"

She took his arm and pointed down the alleyway that ran alongside the bar. "Just down there."

"You don't happen to know which house the hospital administrator lives in?"

"You ask a lot of questions, don't you?"

"Tall, thin, interesting hair," prompted Ruso. "I won't be mentioning anything to your management, remember?"

"Bad smell under his nose?"

"That's the one."

"Sounds like our new neighbor," said Chloe. "Try the first house you come to on the right."

54

SOMEONE WAS IN: There was a yellow streak of light where the door didn't fit the top of the frame. While he was waiting for Priscus to open up Ruso observed that the man had made a smart choice of neighbors. His house backed onto Merula's bar, but the noise which the woman at the bakery found so disturbing would all be out at the front, where the shutters opened onto the road. Priscus's house would back onto the kitchen yard and the private apartments occupied by Merula and her "boys." Beside Priscus's front door were shutters covering the storefront of a basket maker and on the opposite corner a weaver had gone home for the night. Even when the shops were busy, the hospital administrator's peace would hardly be disturbed by the sounds of weaving or fiddling about with willow wands. Ruso pondered, not happily, the irony of Priscus enjoying peaceful and private lodgings while the men who actually dealt with the sick shared a vermin-infested dump awaiting demolition.

The administrator not only had peaceful and private lodgings, but a slave whose limbs were all in working order. Admittedly, a dumb slave. The man stood silhouetted in the doorway, communicating by the shaking of his head and the raising of one palm that his master was not at home to visitors.

"I'll wait," said Ruso, putting one boot inside the door and indicating his medical case.

The slave made an effort to shut the door.

"It's business," said Ruso, pushing in the opposite direction.

The slave looked thin and tired, as if the effort of communication was wearing him down. He glanced around, perhaps hoping someone was coming to back him up. Seeing the whitewashed corridor behind him empty, he stood back to let Ruso enter.

Ruso followed the slave into a spacious reception room that smelled of lavender and lamp oil. To one side a chest of drawers held a lamp burning in front of the household gods. In the center, two wicker chairs sat at a spindly-legged table bearing a fruit bowl, a jug, and a cup. They were arranged as if someone was about to paint them. Priscus was nowhere to be seen.

The man motioned Ruso to a chair and indicated the cup. Ruso shook his head. The wicker chair creaked as the weave adjusted to his weight. He looked around him. This was one of the new houses, and far more spacious than the place where the barber's family lived. One door led to the back of the building, another to the side. From behind one of them there was a faint cry: too indistinct to tell whether it was male or female, pleasure, pain, or surprise. The slave glanced at the doorway leading deeper into the house, then at Ruso. He stepped forward and offered the fruit bowl.

Ruso helped himself to a couple of grapes and wondered how far they had traveled. "Will he be long?"

The man gave an expansive shrug and retreated to the side room, which Ruso guessed was a kitchen. Ruso had the feeling he had gone to hide from Priscus rather than fetch him.

Ruso put a grape into his mouth and burst it with his tongue. The juice flooded his mouth with memories. The grapes would be in at home now. Lucius, who wouldn't have received his letter yet, must be wondering whether this was the last batch of their own wine they would ever make.

He was just enjoying the second grape when there was a shrill and terrible scream from the rear door. A howl of rage cut across it, followed by Priscus yelling, "You filthy little bedbug!"

Ruso had leaped out of his chair when the door burst open and Priscus emerged.

The administrator did not look happy. His hair was awry. His face, and most of the rest of him, seemed to have been splattered with something that might once have been edible, and which he was attempting to wipe off with a hospital blanket. He staggered as he trod on the untied thong of one of his own sandals and roared, "Tadius!" at the closed door before turning and clutching the blanket to his chest at the sight of Ruso.

"What are you doing here?"

The slave emerged from the other room.

"Get a cloth and a bucket of water!" ordered Priscus, "and find me a clean tunic."

The slave hurried away. Priscus bent over, trying to wipe his face on a corner of blanket and adjust his hair at the same time. The smell of fish sauce was almost, but not quite, overpowering his bath oil.

"I seem to have called at a bad time," remarked Ruso, noting that Priscus's attempts to rearrange his hair had succeeded in leaving it resting in a clump above one ear. "Have you had an accident?"

"It's nothing," snapped Priscus, following Ruso's eyes to where a shadow was moving in the doorway behind him. He turned and slammed the door shut. The slave, who had been hurrying toward it clutching a bucket and cloth, retreated in confusion.

"Seems we've both had a busy evening," said Ruso. "You've been seeing your decorator and I've been pulling teeth."

Priscus scowled. "This is really not a convenient time—"

"I can see that. I just dropped by to collect my fee."

"Your—?"

"Professional fee. Apparently we have an arrangement."

The slave reappeared holding a folded tunic. Priscus turned to Ruso. "We'll discuss this in the morning."

"We'll discuss it when you've got clean clothes on."

Priscus glanced at the slave as if he was wondering whether to ask him to throw his unwanted visitor out, then thought better of it and shuffled across to the kitchen in his unfastened sandals, beckoning the man to follow him.

Ruso helped himself to a couple more grapes and seated himself in the creaky chair. From behind the kitchen door came the sound of Priscus complaining and the sharp crack of a slap as Tadius evidently failed to please. From behind the other door, Ruso thought he could make out the sound of someone moving about. Whoever it was did not emerge.

"Disgraceful," Priscus was saying as he emerged clean from the kitchen wearing a neatly pressed tunic and a realigned hairstyle. "Utterly disgraceful. If the owner doesn't come up with some very acceptable compensation I shall cancel my order and have my meals delivered from somewhere else. Tadius? Make sure you give the floor a good scrub, put on a clean bolster cover and have the other one laundered first thing in the morning." He closed the kitchen door and turned back to Ruso. "Now, what was it you wanted?"

"My fee," said Ruso. getting to his feet. For the tooth extraction."

"Ah. The tooth extraction. Yes." Visibly making an effort to take control of himself once more, Priscus indicated the table. "Would you like a drink?"

"No, I would like my fee."

Priscus sighed. "We seem to have got off on the wrong foot, Ruso. Do sit down."

Reluctantly, Ruso resumed his seat.

Priscus, who seemed to have made an impressively swift recovery of his composure, adjusted the position of the other chair and lowered himself into it. "You are obviously most unhappy."

"I was told by my patient that you and I have an arrangement. Apparently I go out on house calls and you pocket the fee."

"Oh, dear, no. I can see we've had a little misunderstanding." Priscus smoothed the top of his hair with his hand and explained that it was hospital practice to make deductions at source for loan repayments. "I would have spoken to you about it, but the boy said it was an emergency. I don't have the documents at hand, of course, but I can show you the account in the morning."

"This was a private patient!"

"Ah, but the boy came to the hospital to ask for a doctor."

"A couple of denarii is hardly going to make much of a dent in the loan, is it? Or are you expecting me to work it off?"

"No, no, of course not. But when it was sanctioned I was not aware that the camp prefect would be ordering an inspection of the hospital accounts prior to the arrival of the auditors."

"We've been through this. I've already signed over a guarantee."

"The loan is perfectly in order. But I do need to be able to show some repayments on the account and this seemed the simplest way. Of course I would have asked for your approval, but the boy said it was an emergency and you were not available for discussion."

Ruso sighed. He couldn't imagine the camp prefect having the slightest interest in a reduction of two denarii from the loan account of the Aesculapian Thanksgiving Fund, especially since he had already signed over his slave in the event of default. He could well believe, however, that Priscus was taking revenge for Ruso's persistent attempts to avoid him.

"All right," Ruso conceded. "We'll leave things as they are. But in future I'll negotiate and collect my own fees."

"Of course." Priscus paused. "And perhaps we could agree to conduct hospital business within the confines of the hospital? This really was a most unfortunate time to call."

55

RUSO HAD INTENDED to dictate a note about the Brigantian girl, but the business of the red hair complicated matters. In the end he decided to request an appointment with the second spear to explain things in person. Granted a brief audience, he passed on his information about the barber—although not its source—and was acknowledged with a grunt that might have been encouragement but did not sound like it. He then went on to explain that a stolen girl, knowingly supplied by one Claudius Innocens, was in imminent danger. To his relief, this aroused a better response. The second spear could not be expected to have much interest in the welfare of Brigantian carpenters' daughters, but he was shrewd enough to agree that action needed to be taken before some scruffy native with a grudge spotted the girl and used her as an excuse to stir up trouble. "We've had enough problems with that bar," he growled. "We'd shut it down, but the others are worse. Just do me a favor and don't find any more bodies."

The sun came out as Ruso strode back to the hospital. He found himself feeling surprisingly cheerful, and murmured a prayer of thanks for all that had happened to him in Britannia. There were only four more days until payday, and despite some worrying moments, he was going to reach it with his credit intact. He had been given the chance to run the hospital single-handed on two occasions, he was more or less in favor with civilian liaison, and if there were any justice in the army (which was doubtful), he would be well in line for the CMO post. He had rescued one girl and saved her arm, and now he had taken steps to retrieve another and put a stop to a filthy trade in stolen human flesh. This evening he would have the satisfaction of pointing out to Tilla that there was no need for all that cursing and howling and mumbo-jumbo over the cooking pot. He would not go into the details of why the army was going to investigate Phryne's case even though they had not received an official complaint. He would simply explain that . . . In fact, he wouldn't have to wait until this evening, because she was walking toward him.

"Tilla!" He was glad to see she had chosen this route. It was wide, it was busy, and the progress of any passing female would be closely supervised by numerous builders clambering about on the scaffolding of the bathhouse.

"Tilla, good news!" He waited until she joined him before beginning his explanation of how, in a civilized society, criminals were dealt with by the law.

He was halfway through his first sentence when she flung herself at him. Off balance and bewildered, he staggered backward and was thrust flat against the wall as something spattered the gravel just inches from his feet.

"Sorry!" shouted a voice from the scaffolding.

Ruso found himself gazing at a shuddering trowel, its point embedded deep in the road where he had just been walking. Moments later he realized that he was still clutching Tilla against his chest, almost as if he had saved her instead of the other way around. In fact, anyone walking around the corner now would get quite the wrong impression of what was going on. Unable to back away, he placed his hands on her shoulders and moved her to a more acceptable distance. "Are you—" He glanced across at the trowel, paused to clear his throat, and began again. "Are you all right?"

"I am, my Lord."

He let go. "Thank you."

They stepped away from each other, both turning aside to brush down the creases in their clothing as footsteps clattered on the planking above them. Tilla glared at the builder who was making his way down the ladder. "You are very careless!"

The builder glanced from one to the other of them, said, "Sorry, sir," then added, "Miss."

"You could kill my Master!" continued Tilla. "Why do you throw this—this *thing*?" She flapped a hand at the trowel, evidently frustrated at not knowing enough Latin to give him a fluent scolding.

"I didn't throw it," said the man, stepping across to retrieve it. "It was an accident." He wiped the gravel-spattered remnants of mortar off the trowel onto a leg of the scaffold, and turned to Ruso. "Sorry about that, sir. Slipped out of my hand. Lucky you got her out of the way."

"I didn't," said Ruso, squinting up at the high walls of the refurbished bathhouse. "What's your name, soldier?"

"Secundus, sir. From the century of Gallus."

"Well, Secundus. You need to be more careful."

"Yes, sir."

"When's this work going to be finished?"

Ignoring Tilla's scowl, the man pointed out that it was only a month over schedule, as if this were something to be proud of. This week they had been held up because a batch of tiles had arrived in the wrong size. Once the roof was done, the plumbers and plasterers and painters would be finished in about ten days. They were working right up to dark to get finished.

"Good. Then perhaps somebody will fix our hospital roof."

"You're next on the list, sir," promised Secundus with an ease that suggested he had said it many times to many people.

After he had gone Tilla said, "That man is a liar."

"I know," agreed Ruso. "But there's no point in arguing with them or they'll take even longer."

Tilla frowned. "I am not talking about the roof," she said.

56

As Tilla left the room carrying the cleared dishes, Valens pushed the nearest light away with his toe, put his feet up on the table, and went back to his favorite topic of the evening. "Are you sure there was somebody there?"

"Positive," said Ruso. "He was shouting at them."

Valens chuckled. "I don't know which is more amazing. Priscus and a secret assignation, or Priscus stealing the hospital bedclothes. Dear me. What a shame you couldn't see who it was. Male or female, do you think?"

"I couldn't tell. All I had was a glimpse of a shadow in the doorway."

There was a crash from the kitchen. Ruso winced. Valens said, "Don't be too hard on her, old man. It must be tricky washing up with one hand."

"She's got some use in the right hand now," pointed out Ruso.

"Which you *very* kindly saved for her," acknowledged Valens. "And I suppose she *has* got all evening to do the pots." He leaned back on the couch, yawned, and stretched his arms above his head as the dog scrambled out from behind him. "Do you realize," he observed to the ceiling, "this is the first time we've both had dinner at home? You are a remarkable chap under that dour exterior, Gaius Petreius."

Ruso poured himself more wine and maintained the silence of his dour exterior.

"First you wander down a back alley and find us a housekeeper, then you pay a visit to the hospital administrator and—gods, I wish I'd seen the expression on his face. Silly old fart!" Valens, who was on call this evening, bent forward and poured a generous amount of water into his own wine before raising it to his lips. "So, he tried to pretend he was just having his dinner delivered?"

"Well, there was certainly food involved."

"Dear me. He can't have imagined you'd believe him."

Ruso swilled the wine around in his cup. "I don't want to guess what might be in Priscus's imagination," he said. "He's probably crouched in a corner of his web right now, plotting revenge."

"Well. Old Priscus, eh?"

"I'd be grateful if you'd keep your mouth shut for a while. He's got it in for me already."

"Me? Soul of discretion. But I must say, it's all quite wonderful. Priscus! The last man I would suspect of having a wild private life."

"He does have that wolf on his wall."

"I'd always assumed he bought that from a hunter. Well. Perhaps I'm wrong about that too. Maybe there's more to our diligent pen-pusher than we all thought." Valens took a long drink from his cup.

Ruso said, "Do you know a roofer named Secundus? His centurion's called Gallus."

Valens frowned. "I can't recall him. Why?"

"He dropped a trowel on my head this afternoon. From the top of the scaffolding."

"Why didn't you say so? Want me to take a look?"

"He missed," explained Ruso. "He said it was an accident. But I'm starting to wonder."

"Really? You're usually such a sensible sort of chap."

"After that business with the fire . . ."

"You've just had a run of bad luck, that's all. Go and offer a pigeon to Fortuna if you're that worried."

"Do you really think that would help?"

Valens grinned. "Of course not. But it might make you feel better. You're probably a bit out of balance. Have you tried a purge?"

"No."

"Are you watching your diet?"

"No."

"Getting enough sleep?"

"Not really."

"There you are, then. I don't go around thinking somebody was trying to poison me with those oysters. It was just an accident. It doesn't do to brood on things, you know."

There was another crash from the kitchen. This time it sounded as though something had broken.

Ruso shouted, "Be careful in there, Tilla!"

The only reply was the swish and tinkle of a broom chasing broken crockery across the floor.

"Never mind," said Valens, indicating the wine jug. "We've got the important stuff in here. Drink up, you're not on duty."

Ruso rocked the front legs of his favorite chair off the ground—he had moved it in here for dinner—and put his feet up opposite Valens's.

"I must say," observed Valens, "your Tilla may be a bit ham-handed but she's not doing a bad job with the cooking. For someone who hasn't done it before."

"She has done it before," Ruso corrected him. "Just not our sort of food."

"Really?" Valens's brows lowered in puzzlement. "That's funny, because she told me—"

He was interrupted by the sound of someone banging on the front door. "Damn," he muttered, swinging his feet down from the table.

There was a brief and largely inaudible conversation at the door, then it closed and Valens reappeared clutching his cloak. "Got to go," he said, "Tribune with a tummy ache. Tell the lovely Tilla she can warm up my bed if she wants."

"What was it she told you?"

"What? Oh." Valens flung his cloak over his shoulders. "Before her home was raided by some rival tribe or other, her family owned a cook." His voice distorted as he squinted to see where he was pushing the fastening pin. "So, she never bothered to learn. I thought you knew."

After Valens had clattered the door shut, Ruso remained in his chair, gazing at the lamp. "I thought I knew too," he informed it. Well. He hoped the army would investigate Claudius Innocens very thoroughly.

Preferably with a sharp implement. Innocens had promised him that Tilla could cook.

Which reminded him. He needed to talk to her.

He paused in the doorway. Tilla carried on drying a spoon with a cloth and then flung it down with such force that it bounced.

"The chicken stew was very good, Tilla."

"Thank you, my Lord." She snatched up another spoon and gave it a swift wipe.

"I have some news for you."

The second spoon clattered down beside its mate.

Ruso cleared his throat. "Is something the matter?"

She glanced at him. "No, my Lord. I am very lucky."

"Indeed you are."

She tossed the cloth over the hook by the hearth. "I am very lucky not to be Phryne."

"That's what I came to tell you about," he said. "When I saw you this afternoon I was on the way back from reporting the problem. I've been assured there will be some action very soon."

She turned. "Tonight?"

"Not that soon." It was hardly the sort of emergency that would persuade the second spear to miss his dinner.

"So Phryne is still at Merula's tonight."

Ruso had not expected thanks, but he had expected that his slave would be pleased. "She will be a lot safer there than she would be out on the streets," he said.

"With the men."

"Yes," said Ruso, exasperated. "With the men. Who are unlikely to do her serious harm, because if she's laid up she can't earn any money for Merula. Now stop throwing our things about." As Tilla opened her mouth to speak he said, "And don't start wailing and cursing either, because I have work to do."

He snatched up his wine in one hand and his chair in the other. He was heading toward his room when he heard her say, "I will be silent. I will control my tongue."

"Good!" A leg of the chair banged into the wall and the wine lurched toward the side of the cup. "Get on with your work, and don't break anything else."

"I know what happens to slaves who talk too much!"

"Yes!" he shouted back. "And I'm beginning to understand why!"

Ruso placed a lamp on his desk, kicked the bedroom door shut, and blew the dust off the pile of writing tablets. He flipped open the first one and sat down. "Treatment of Eye Injuries." Gods above, he had been on this section for months. Tonight he was going to finish it.

He moved the lamp to a better angle and began to read through what he had written so far. Halfway down the page he paused to note with satisfaction that Tilla had stopped crashing around in the kitchen. No doubt she was regretting her display of temper. He thought he had handled it rather well. Now he had the rest of the evening for "Treatment of Eye Injuries."

His finger had reached the bottom of the first page before it struck him that he could not remember what he had just read. This was not encouraging. If he found it boring, what about his readers? He picked up his stylus, tweaked the wick of the lamp with the sharp end, and reassured himself that the author of a book whose content was worthwhile need not concern himself with elegant style. People who wanted to know something useful would not want to hunt through pages of authorial showing off to find it. The task of a medical writer—particularly a concise one—was to offer immediate and practical help, not tell jokes. He took another gulp of wine and started to read again in the brighter light.

Perhaps he should leave the bedroom door open, just in case there was some very quiet wailing and cursing going on.

Perhaps not.

He had more important things to do than waste his evening wondering what his servant was up to.

The trouble with women was that no matter what you did, they were never satisfied. Instead of being grateful for the efforts made on their behalf—sometimes quite considerable, and at no small inconvenience—they chose to pick on one small matter that had not been attended to, and complain about it.

What else was he supposed to have done about that girl? Stride into the bar and demand that Merula hand her over? What Tilla did not seem to understand was that in the absence of an official complaint by someone willing to take up her case—which Ruso certainly wasn't, since the girl was none of his business—no one was obliged to do anything at all about Phryne. Not tonight, not next week, not ever.

In the meantime, while the medicus to the Twentieth sat in the wavering light, pondering the welfare of local barmaids over a cup of wine and a bellyful of chicken stew, there could be a frightened legionary lying injured out in some dark and distant outpost, unable to summon even a bandager, wishing to the gods that either he or his companions knew something about first aid.

Ruso straightened his chair, cleared his throat, and began to fill the central leaf with writing.

He wrote steadily to the foot of the wax, read it through, and was correcting it when he heard the front door open. He and Valens grunted a mutual good night and moments later he heard the other bedroom door shut. There was no sound from the kitchen.

Ruso flipped the wooden leaf over and began to fill the other side.

He was surprised when a distant trumpet sounded for the next watch, which told him he had been writing for a couple of hours now.

The lamp was starting to sputter as he finished the last sentence. He pushed the wick down to conserve the oil, propped the tablet beside the lamp, and reread his work. It was good. He slapped the tablet shut and put it back on the top of the pile. He would get Albanus to make a clean copy in the morning.

His thoughts returned to Tilla's concern for Phryne. She had a point. The girl's situation was not a happy one, and it would doubtless be getting worse with every hour she spent in that place. At least, though, she had the protection of being the daughter of a freeman. The law would—eventually—help her in a way that it would never have helped Saufeia, or Asellina, or the unfortunate Daphne. Neither the law nor the army offered any hope to slaves whose owners expected them to work as prostitutes. Their only choices were to cooperate, kill themselves, or run away. And if the escape went disastrously wrong, there seemed to be few who would care. He hoped the business about the hair had whetted the second spear's appetite for investigation. And that Phryne would not take it into her head to run away tonight.

Ruso picked up his cup of wine. He blew out the struggling lamp before the flame scorched the dry wick and headed for the door.

He stood for a moment, breathing in the warm air of the dining room. As his eyes adjusted to the dark he could make out a bundle huddled on the couch, faintly outlined by the dull glow of the dying embers in the fire. He held his breath, but he already knew how quietly she slept. He could hear only a faint crackle of burning and the thud of his own heart. He took a step forward.

There was the rustle of fabric and the bundle moved. "My Lord?"

He groped for a taper and knelt to push the end into the embers. "That business this afternoon, Tilla. The near miss."

"Is not an accident, my Lord."

"Whatever it was, you did well. That's all. Go back to sleep now."

"Good night, my Lord."

The end of the taper caught into a yellow flame. He lifted it out and set it to the candle on the table.

"My Lord?"

"Yes?"

"I know you try to help Phryne."

He paused, candle in hand, by the kitchen door. "I am sorry if you were hoping for more."

"I am not hoping for anything, my Lord."

Ruso poured himself a cup of water in the kitchen. *I am not hoping for anything, my Lord.* Considering the fortunes of the slaves he had come to know since moving to Deva, that was hardly surprising.

He paused by the couch on his way back to the bedroom, setting the candle and the water on the table. "Before you sleep, Tilla," he said, "I have something to ask you. No—" he held out a hand, "don't stand up."

She pulled the blankets around her shoulders, curled her feet in beneath her, and stifled a yawn. The dog must be sleeping on Valens's bed: There was room beside her on the couch. Ruso chose the edge of the table instead. One of his feet brushed against something. He glanced down to see two small boots set in a neat pair. "I have been told more than once," he said, "that Saufeia could read and write."

"Yes, my Lord."

"There is something people are not telling me."

She frowned. "I am telling my Lord everything he asks."

"I want to know why it matters. Does it have something to do with what happened to her?"

From outside the house the sound of boots on gravel rose and rapidly faded as the guard relieved from the last watch took a shortcut on their way back to bed.

"What about the other girl? Do you know anything about that?"

"Asellina. She ran away."

"Was she meeting someone?"

"Her man says it is not him. Nobody knows another man."

"What do the girls think happened to her?"

"Nobody knows anything, my Lord."

"And what about Saufeia? Does anybody know anything about her?"

She did not answer.

"Merula isn't going to hurt you, Tilla. She's no fool. She wouldn't dare touch someone else's slave."

Her hair was loose over her shoulders. She began to twirl a strand around her forefinger.

"You told me about Phryne, and something will be done about it. If someone would tell the truth about Saufeia, perhaps something could be done about that too."

"The truth will not bring her back."

"The truth may save some other girl from the same fate."

There was a crackle from the grate as the embers shifted and sent up an orange fountain of sparks. The finger stopped twirling. "The truth I know, my Lord," she said, "is not enough. You will ask more questions, and people will hear the questions and know I tell you, and the person who tell me will be very sorry."

"The person who tell—who *told* you is Chloe, isn't it?"

"Whatever you say, my Lord."

"You are a very stubborn woman."

"Yes, my Lord. Whatever you say."

He shrugged. "I'm not staying up to argue. In the morning, I want you to tell me."

He was almost at the door when he heard her voice, low and urgent. "Nobody knows who Saufeia's letter is to, my Lord. Nobody knows what it says. To ask questions is to dig in a wasps' nest where there is much danger and nothing to eat at the end of it. Saufeia is gone to the other world. Leave her in peace."

As Ruso pulled up his blankets and pinched out the lamp it occurred to him that he was lucky to be blessed with a sensible friend like Valens. And a strong sense of logic. Otherwise, he might be thinking that the fire had not been an accident or a haunting but the work of someone who did not like him asking questions. Someone who had forced open his ill-fitting shutters and tossed something burning onto his bed.

57

NO FILE COPY, sir?" Albanus looked surprised.

"Just one for me. I'll have the notes back with it when you've finished."

Albanus turned over the top leaf of the *Concise Guide.* "There's quite a lot of work here, sir."

"I'll see you're rewarded," promised Ruso, reminding himself that it was only three days until payday.

"Oh, I didn't mean that, sir!" Albanus seemed genuinely shocked. "Three pages is nothing. What I mean is, I wouldn't recommend keeping the only fair copy and the notes together in one place. If there's a fire, or the roof leaks over them, you could end up having to start all over again."

"Are you telling me," said Ruso, incredulous, "that you keep file copies of everything?"

Albanus shook his head sadly. "No, sir. There isn't room. We have a list of priority items to keep, which end up in HQ—men's records, that sort of thing—and the rest is stored for a time depending on what it is, and then burned."

Something stirred at the back of Ruso's mind. "And is that just the hospital, or the whole fort?"

Albanus blinked. "I think that's what everyone does, sir. You simply can't keep everything, there wouldn't be space."

"So a letter that came in would be kept for—how long?"

"I don't know, sir. I could find out. I suppose it depends on what it is. And obviously there's no control over personal letters to the men."

"Ah." Of course. Even if Saufeia had addressed her mysterious letter to a legionary boyfriend, she was hardly likely to have been corresponding via the official post. He was not thinking clearly.

"They just go on the daily lists," added Albanus.

Ruso stared at him. "Daily lists?" he repeated. "Are you telling me someone sits down with the post sacks and makes a list of every letter received in the fort?"

Albanus nodded. "Ever since a letter got lost that told the camp prefect his mother had died, sir. There was a bit of a fuss. So now if it comes through the gate, it gets noted down—recipient and sender—and signed for."

"And who has access to these lists?"

"The HQ clerks, I suppose, sir. To be honest I don't think anybody looks at them much. It's one of those things you don't need because you've got it."

Ruso scratched his ear. "And how easy would it be," he asked, "for someone to make a discreet inquiry?"

"For someone like you, sir? I think the clerks would want to know why you were looking. In case you were going to put in a complaint about them."

"I see."

"But you wouldn't need to do it, would you, sir?" Albanus's face brightened. "You've got me."

58

TILLA HAD DELIBERATELY left the baker's for last and now, as she rounded the corner, there was Lucco sweeping the opposite pavement in front of the drawn shutters and the red writing on the wall. The boy sloshed a bucket of gray water across the stones, picked up the broom, and chased trickles of bobbing dirt down crevices toward the street drain.

Tilla glanced up and down the street and checked that the upstairs window of Merula's was shuttered. "Lucco!"

The boy gave the broom a final swish and looked up. "You've missed them," he said. "They've gone to the baths."

The goddess had granted her prayer: Bassus was safely out of the way. She moved closer to Lucco so she would not be overheard, "Do you know if Phryne was with them?"

The boy shrugged. "Dunno."

"No," said a voice. Strong fingers clamped around her bandaged arm and Bassus slid out from behind the shutters. He told Lucco to get lost. The boy scuttled into the bar. "Phryne's feeling a bit under the weather this morning," said Bassus.

Tilla felt a stab of pain as he squeezed her arm.

"Nice of you to ask, though."

She dared not move. She had thought the goddess would keep her safe. Now it seemed she was expected to manage on her own.

"Surprised to see me, are you?" he asked. "Stich took the girls out this morning."

Two women with baskets were standing chatting at the bakery counter across the street. Tilla announced loudly, "You are hurting my arm!"

One of them turned.

"I am not afraid of you!" she added, ashamed that the words were not true.

Bassus followed her gaze to where everyone had now stopped talking to watch what he was doing.

"If you hurt me," added Tilla, struggling to keep her voice level, "my master will have you punish with the law!"

There was a sharper stab as he pulled her against his chest. " 'Round here, girl," he hissed, "I *am* the law."

Before she could decide whether to scream, Bassus burst into laughter and released her. "It's all right, ladies," he called to the audience across the street, holding up both hands in mock surrender. "Just a lovers' tiff."

He turned back to Tilla. "Cheer up, gorgeous. You're worth too much to damage. Me and your doctor friend done a deal, did you know that?"

"You are lying."

"Am I? I'm going to introduce him to some people I know. We should get a good price for you."

She stared at the man's heavy, seamed face. She took a deep breath. "My master will never deal with a man like you!"

Bassus shrugged. "Ask him yourself." He cocked his head to one side and examined her face. "What's the matter?" He smiled and shook his head. "Oh dear, oh dear. Gone soft on him, eh? You thought he was going to *keep* you, didn't you?"

59

HERE YOU ARE!" declared Valens, settling himself on the wooden lid of the row opposite Ruso in the hospital latrine. "I'll tell them I haven't seen you."

"Who?"

"Apparently the second spear wants your balls roasted on a spit."

Ruso washed the sponge out in the water-channel, shook it, and tossed it back into the bowl. "Any particular reason?"

"Seems he spent a whole afternoon looking for a kidnapped girl."

Ruso pulled his tunic straight and adjusted his belt. "Good. So what's the problem?"

"The problem, Ruso, is that when they found her she insisted she wasn't kidnapped at all."

Before he could reply, an orderly appeared in the doorway and exclaimed, "There you are, sir!" as if he too thought Ruso had reason to hide.

Ruso sighed and waited for what he knew must be coming. But instead of an urgent summons to report to the second spear, he was told there was a veteran waiting to see him at the east gate.

"Tell them to take a message," said Ruso.

"They said he wants to see you personally, sir."

"I'm busy. If he wants to see me he'll have to come back after the tenth hour."

The orderly disappeared. Ruso dipped his hands in the basin, shook off the water, and headed for the surgery.

Albanus handed him the record for the first patient and returned to perch on his stool by the door. Ruso surveyed the notes from the recruiting panel. Under "Lucius Eprius Saenus, age twenty, height five feet eight inches, medium build, distinguishing features, scar on left temple," the scribe of the recruiting panel had written: "general physique satisfactory, eyesight good, hearing good, teeth—three missing in upper jaw, two in lower, genitals normal, no sign of disease, feet not flat." The examining doctors at the recruitment panel had already done most of the work. Ruso's job was merely to prod Lucius Eprius Saenus in places he didn't wish to be prodded again, look at places he still wouldn't want looked at, and generally confirm that his health had not deteriorated since he had been confirmed fit to join the army. This performance would have to be repeated for the other twenty-two stubble-headed recruits lined up on the benches in the hall, all of whom would resent him by the end of the afternoon, but not as much as they would loathe and dread their centurions by the end of the week. Almost as much, in fact, as Ruso was dreading his next encounter with the second spear.

"Right," said Ruso, opening his case and extracting a tongue depressor. "Let's get started."

Albanus leaned out the door and said something to someone. An orderly who was evidently afraid the recruits had gone deaf bellowed, "FIRST MAN TO SEE THE DOCTOR!"

A pale and skinny youth in a loincloth appeared in the doorway and stood to attention.

"Come in," suggested Ruso. "I can't see much of you from out there."

The youth entered and stood to attention before the desk. His flesh was goosepimpled. His eyes roved over the array of instruments in Ruso's case.

"Lucius Eprius Saenus," said Ruso, closing the case. "Strip."

The youth looked at him as if he didn't understand the instruction.

Ruso gestured toward the loincloth. "The army needs to see all of you, Saenus."

"Yes, sir," agreed the youth, not moving.

"That's an order."

"Yes, sir."

"Well, what are you waiting for?"

The youth swallowed. "I'm not Lucius Eprius Saenus, sir."

Ruso glanced at Albanus. "You're not?"

"No, sir."

"Well why didn't you say that in the first place?"

"You didn't ask."

Ruso got to his feet and walked in a slow circle around the youth, who was clearly a couple of inches short of five feet eight. There was no sign of a scar on the temple. "Who are you, then?"

"Quintus Antonius Vindex, sir."

Albanus bent down and began to scrabble through the records box.

"Quintus Antonius Vindex," continued Ruso, "have you ever heard the expression, *rhetorical question*?"

"No, sir."

"No. Well, the correct answer to *Why didn't you say so in the first place?* was, *Sorry, sir.*"

"Yes, sir. Sorry, sir."

Albanus had given up scrabbling and was now kneeling in front of the box, pulling the records out and heaping them onto the floor.

"Go and find Saenus," Ruso suggested to the youth. "I'll call you in when I'm ready."

They must have realized the mistake outside, because Ruso was still returning to his seat when the next man entered.

"Lucius Eprius Saenus?" inquired Ruso, rereading the description carefully and taking no chances this time.

"Do I look like it?" demanded a familiar voice.

Albanus leaped to his feet with the eagerness of a man seeing a chance to redeem himself. "You can't come in here!" he cried. "The doctor's busy!"

"I can go where I like 'round here, mate," retorted Bassus. "Know a lot of people, don't I?"

"It's all right," Ruso reassured Albanus, who had sized up Bassus and was moving toward the door to call for reinforcements. "Go and find Saenus, will you? I'll be back in a minute."

Safely beyond the front door of the hospital and overhearing ears, he turned to Bassus. "So you're the veteran who wants to see me. What's going on?"

Bassus frowned. "I come here to ask you that. We've had investigators crawling all over the bar like cockroaches and now I'm having to trail over to HQ with a bunch of slave documents. And what I'm wondering is, who was it told them they might find something?"

Ruso took a careful breath. He could feel his heart pounding. "Are you telling me," he said, "that you have the official ownership documents for that new girl?"

"I was right, then. I thought it was you. 'Course we have. Merula just couldn't find them this morning, what with the girls screaming and lads crashing around all over the place."

Ruso got to his feet and said quietly, "I owe Merula an apology."

"I wouldn't go near her right now, mate. Keep your mouth shut and stay out of the way. That's what I come to tell you."

"Thank you," said Ruso, not entirely sure why Bassus seemed to be defending him. "I will."

"Next time you got any problems, Doc, you talk to me first. We're business partners. Right?"

Ruso scratched his ear. "I seem to have been misinformed."

"That's what I thought," said Bassus.

"I'll see to it that my informant is dealt with."

"Bloody women," sympathized Bassus. "Always stirring things up. You can't believe a word they say. People think I'm hard on 'em, but they don't have to put up with it like I do."

Ruso nodded. There seemed to be nothing he could add.

60

BY THE TIME Ruso had formed the opinion that all twenty-three recruits were fit enough to be driven to exhaustion, despair, and finally to usefulness, the message he had been expecting had arrived. He was to report to the second spear.

One of the qualities needed for promotion through the centurionate was the ability to single-handedly compel eighty trained killers to do things they didn't much want to do, and to do them instantly. In this respect, as in many others, the second spear was generally reputed to be heading for the very top. As Ruso entered the man's office, he was conscious of adopting the stance of legionaries he had seen being humiliated on the parade ground: shoulders square, head high, eyes straight ahead, focused on nothing.

"Doctor Gaius Petreius Ruso, sir," announced the orderly.

The second spear ordered his man to wait outside. When the door was closed, he got to his feet. "Well, Doctor? What have you got to say for yourself?"

"I'm sorry about what happened, sir. I was misinformed."

"I'm not talking about that farce in the whorehouse, Ruso. All you did there was upset a local trader, waste my time, and make the army look ridiculous. The camp prefect will deal with all that. And if you're expecting me to go running around hunting down slave traders and hair dealers on your say-so, you're a bigger fool than you look."

"Yes, sir," said Ruso, wondering what else the second spear could want to talk about. He was staring at a point just to the right of the man's shoulder and silently bidding farewell to any hopes of the chief medical officer post when he was conscious of a sudden movement. A hand grabbed his throat. He was knocked backward. His head crashed against the wall. The second spear's face filled his vision. The mouth opened. "Give me one reason," it growled, "why you aren't about to have a very nasty accident."

Shocked, winded, struggling for air, Ruso attempted to wheeze, "Don't know what you mean, sir."

"Don't treat me like an idiot, son. You might be able to fool them down at that hospital but you're not fooling me." Each sentence that followed was punctuated by a tightening of the grip around his throat. "Thought you could get away with it, did you? Thought you'd try your luck? Thought she might talk me 'round?"

Realizing too late what this was about and that his rank was not going to protect him, Ruso mouthed, "No."

The second spear relaxed his grasp for a second and Ruso was gulping in air when the grip clamped back around his throat and his bruised skull was slammed back against the wall. Over the ringing in his ears, a voice roared, "Don't lie to me! You were seen!"

61

RUSO STUMBLED THROUGH the front door and across the room. He dragged a blanket off the couch and stretched out, laying his throbbing head on a cushion that smelled of dog and stale beer.

"Tilla!" he croaked. "Get me some water."

The sound of his head bouncing off the wall was still echoing in his skull. His throat felt as though the slightest twist would split his windpipe and crack his neck bones apart.

He had almost begged Tilla's goddess for help as the strength drained out of him like desert sand sifting through his fingers. A distant voice was shouting, "Sir! Sir, you'll kill him!" and finally the vice around his throat had loosened and he'd collapsed to the floor.

She had not heard his request for water. He couldn't call any louder. He rolled onto his side and tried again, the word rasping in his throat and ringing through his aching skull.

"Tilla!"

Still no reply. Too tired to lift himself off the couch, he closed his eyes and waited for her to find him.

Something was jumping on his stomach. An African drummer was practicing on the inside of his skull. Something was bouncing on his chest. A chisel was being scraped up the inside of his throat. A rough tongue was licking his face. He lifted an arm and batted away a small warm body. The licking stopped. The body yelped as it landed.

A voice called, "Off, boys and girls! He doesn't want to play!" The bouncing ceased. The drumming and scraping didn't.

Ruso opened one eye to see Valens scoop up a whining puppy. "You're not hurt," Valens assured the puppy after a perfunctory check. He turned to the couch. "Are you all right there, Ruso?"

The water helped. He was less sure about the liniment. "I got it from one of the vets," explained Valens. "He says it's marvelous stuff. I've been waiting for a chance to try it out."

Ruso grimaced.

"Don't worry about the smell; you won't notice it after a minute or two. So, what happened?"

Ruso pointed to his throat and moved his head carefully from side to side.

"Write it down," suggested Valens. "Hold on, I'll find something . . . if the lovely Tilla hasn't chucked it all . . . Where is she, by the way?"

Ruso lifted both palms in an exaggerated shrug. Valens disappeared into his room and began throwing things about in his hunt for writing materials. Ruso hauled himself to his feet and shuffled across the floor.

The kitchen fire was dead. There was no sign of any attempt to prepare supper. The water jug was almost empty and there was no bread in the bin. The wretched girl must be up to her old tricks with the goddess. She could not possibly have the meal ready on time if the fire wasn't lit by now. He wondered if she knew what had happened at Merula's and was hiding from him.

Ruso wandered into his bedroom. Rubbing the lump on the back of his head, he stood in the doorway and tried to remember whether he had put his best cloak away or whether it was missing from the hook on the wall.

Valens appeared, clutching a slate. "So. Talk to me."

There were many things he wished to say to Valens, but the slate was not big enough. Instead he scrawled, "My throat hurts, my head hurts, I have no money, my servant has disappeared, and I am about to do ward rounds smelling like a sick horse."

"Ah." Valens reached for the slate. He licked his forefinger, rubbed out the word *horse*, and wrote, *donkey*.

Carefully, Ruso tipped his head back toward the pharmacy ceiling, gargled the last of the foul mixture, and spat. Watching it slide down the side of the waste bucket, he pondered the efficiency of military communications. It was a mystery why the army bothered with a signal system when its men were so good at gossip. He had left the second spear's house barely an hour ago, and just now the pharmacist, after expressing sympathy for his sudden cold, waited until the last patient had left to murmur between gargles, "Sorry to hear about the second spear's daughter, sir. That was bad luck."

Ruso turned to him and rasped, "What about the second spear's daughter?"

"If it's any consolation, most of us think she wouldn't be your type, sir."

"I'm not bloody interested in the . . ." Ruso paused and lowered his voice. "Any rumors about myself and the second spear's daughter are groundless. I'm sure she's a lovely young lady but I've never actually set eyes on her. So go back to whomever told you this nonsense, and tell them if they spread any more lies I'll deal with them myself."

Halfway through late-ward rounds, he met Valens in a corridor. "How's it going?" demanded Valens.

Ruso paused to insert another throat lozenge before strong-arming him into an empty isolation room and latching the door.

"Jupiter!" Valens wrinkled his nose. "You'd think that salve would have worn off by now, wouldn't you?"

"I've been thinking," said Ruso. "Have you been smarming around the offspring of the second spear?"

"I did have a pleasant chat with her the other day. Nice girl."

"Well, don't. Her father thinks you're me, and he doesn't like it."

"No? Well, I wouldn't either. Look at the state of you. Your eyes are bloodshot, your hair's sticking up, and you smell like something they clean the drains with."

"I know. And it's your fault!"

"She hasn't complained to him, has she?"

"*She* hasn't. You were seen."

Valens smiled. "I didn't think she would. I knew she'd be a sensible sort of girl. She's got a sensible sort of nose."

Ruso opened his mouth to argue, then decided it would only make his throat worse.

"I'll tell you all about it later," suggested Valens. "Over tonight's supper served by the lovely Tilla."

"I can't find Tilla."

"Dear me. You are having a bad day."

"I am," growled Ruso. "But it'll improve when I kill you."

62

THE HOUSE FELT chilly as he entered. The dog offered him the briefest of greetings and then dodged past his legs and out the door. Ruso sniffed and glanced around at the floor. The puppies must have been locked in for hours.

The kitchen hearth was a blackened void where the fire should have been. Ruso sniffed again and crouched to inspect the floor. Beneath the table was a small brown turd.

Outside, he heard Valens whistle for the dog. Moments later there were footsteps on the gravel. The main door slammed and Valens appeared in the kitchen, surveying the empty shelves and the dead fire. "Where is she?"

"I don't know. The dogs haven't been let out."

"So where's our dinner?"

Something in Ruso's expression must have told Valens that this was the wrong question.

"She's probably gone shopping," suggested Valens. "Met up with a friend or something. You know how women talk. Perhaps she's dropped around to Merula's."

"I'd be amazed if she'd gone there. Anyway, she'd know to come back by now."

"Well, I can't wait till she turns up. If you get the fire going, I'll go and talk nicely to the kitchen staff. See if they can sneak something past Priscus." Valens paused. "I wouldn't worry, old man. She's bound to show up before long."

"It's getting dark. Something's wrong."

"Then she'll be back any minute, won't she?" Valens grinned. "Cheer up. You'll be able to give her a good spanking."

"Thanks."

"I'll do it if you like."

Ruso scowled. "Just disappear, will you?"

By the time men, dog, and puppies had eaten Valens's gleanings from the hospital kitchen ("This is just like old times, isn't it?"), it was time to light the lamps. Leaving Valens to cover his on-call duties, Ruso put a lead on the dog and went out to look for his servant.

It was not as dark outside as it had seemed in the house. As he waited for the dog to finish sniffing around the shadowy nettle patch, Ruso's eyes adjusted to the gloom. He could pick out the rectangular shape of the next barracks block, the roof of the hospital, and, turning, the outline of the main wall at the end of the street across the perimeter road. As he watched, he heard the tramp of guards. Two shapes moved steadily toward each other along the top of the wall, crossed, and continued in opposite directions.

A breeze plucked at the fabric of his spare cloak and suggested there was rain on the way. "That's enough, dog," urged Ruso, eager to move but not sure of his direction. He did not want to imagine what might have happened to Tilla, but imagination was his only tool in deciding a sensible pattern for the search. If she had run into the wrong man—and the gods knew, he had tried many times to warn her—she could be anywhere. Alive or dead. Inside the fort or out. Inside, he felt, was less likely. The men's lack of privacy and propensity to gossip would serve as some protection.

He stopped at the hospital in case there was a message, but there were no notes at the desk. Decimus's assurance of "I'm sure she'll turn up soon, sir!" was bright rather than confident, and Ruso wondered how many people had said the same thing to him about Asellina.

"Decimus, what do you know about a builder called Secundus—century of Gallus?"

Decimus frowned. "Nothing, sir. Gallus's men haven't been back long."

"Where from?"

"I don't know exactly, sir. Somewhere in the north."

"When did they get back here?"

"Last week sometime, sir. They brought a couple of wounded in for treatment."

"Oh."

"I could find out which day if you like, sir."

"No," said Ruso, "last week is good enough."

In the end he headed toward the east gate. A couple of times along the way he called her name experimentally into the night air, as if he were calling a lost pet. There was no reply.

There was a brief flash of hope at the gate when one of the guards said, "Ah, you mean Tilla, sir!" He and his comrade had seen her leave clutching a shopping basket at her usual time in the morning. He sounded as though they looked forward to these morning sightings. Disappointingly, they had been elsewhere since then and had only just come back on duty.

"Have you lost her, sir?"

"No," said Ruso. "She's just very late. If you see her, tell her to report directly to my house."

He passed through the gates and made his way across the open area that separated the fort from the civilian buildings. At this time of night the town was little more than a huddle of angular shapes illuminated by the occasional glimmer of a torch. Somewhere among the buildings, a dog barked. There was the faint sound of a baby crying. He heard the approach of voices and stepped sideways onto the road's shoulder. Three men ambled past, too deep in a disagreement about horse racing to notice him. When they had gone, the street was empty. Ruso stepped back onto the paved surface and tried not to imagine what might be happening to a girl who was wandering the streets at this time of night.

The entrance to Merula's was lit by the usual pair of torches. Someone was playing twittering flute music inside but a quick glance from the safety of the shadows across the street confirmed what Ruso suspected: There were few customers tonight. He wondered whether the security raid had frightened them off, and whether Merula had guessed as much as Bassus had.

Stichus was leaning back against the bar with his arms folded, looking bored. Behind him, Daphne paused from pouring drinks to press her hands into the small of her back and stretch her expansive belly. A girl whom Ruso vaguely knew as Mariamne emerged from the kitchen with a loaded tray. She carried it across to the table in the corner where Merula was mercifully busy with a couple of customers whom Ruso recognized from the early-morning officers' briefing. There was no sign of Tilla.

A pair of heavy boots appeared on the stairs. Bassus made his way down to the bar, ordered a drink from Daphne, and emerged to drink it outside under the torch. Ruso crossed the street and stood beside him, out of sight of the bar.

Bassus frowned. "I thought you weren't going to show your face 'round here?"

"I came to ask if you'd seen Tilla."

Bassus slapped at something on his neck. "Bloody gnats. You'd think they'd be gone by September. She's not run out on you, has she?"

"Is she here?"

Bassus took a long pull on his drink. "She *was* here," he said. "Dropped by this morning. Just before our visit from the lads. We had a nice little chat. You know what? I think she fancies me."

"Did she say where she was going?"

"You haven't gone and lost her, have you? What about our agreement?"

"Not lost," promised Ruso. "Just—temporarily mislaid. Did she meet anyone here that she would have gone off with?"

"You told us to keep her away from the customers, remember?"

"Do you have men from the century of Gallus in here?"

"Not at the moment."

"Recently?"

"Had a bunch of them in a few days ago. Just got back from the north. Celebrating."

Ruso scratched his ear. Bassus had confirmed what he already suspected: Secundus could not have been involved with the death of Saufeia. Valens was right: He had been off-balance. The accident with the trowel had been a simple coincidence. As for the fire—he did not have time to worry about the fire now. He said, "Would any of the girls know where she was going?"

"The girls didn't see her. I did. And then she left. And if you don't want to get me into trouble, you'll do the same."

Tilla had still not returned when Valens and he went to bed. Ruso heard the third and fourth watch sounded. Once he got up to investigate a noise that might have been someone knocking, but when he opened the door there was nobody there. He called her name into the darkness. The only reply was a blustery spatter of rain.

He woke with an uneasy feeling that there was something he should remember. When he remembered it, the unease blossomed into an anxiety that lifted him out of bed before dawn to pace about in a house where her absence was almost tangible. He tried to silence his imagination by telling himself she had chosen to leave. Her arm was recovering: She didn't need him anymore.

Instead of being worried, he should be pleased. He owed it to his family to sell her, but he had not been looking forward to it. Now she had solved his dilemma by running away. The tale about Phryne had been a cover for some sort of primitive good-luck potion she was cooking up for herself. Tilla had fled from Deva and was safely on her way to the hilly lands of the Brigantes.

Valens came wandering into the kitchen, rubbing his eyes. "No breakfast, then?"

Ruso shook his head. "Can you manage without me this morning?"

Valens's eyes squeezed shut and his mouth widened in a lopsided and unstifled yawn that displayed a couple of missing teeth and distorted his agreement into something like, "Yuhhhh."

Ruso wished the girls who called him "the good-looking doctor" could see him now.

"Wretched girl might have bothered to send a message," remarked Valens.

"I think she might have run off," confessed Ruso.

"Even so."

Ruso nodded. His relationship with the girl had been awkward, hesitant, and frequently bad tempered, but he thought they had developed some level of mutual respect.

"You did fix her arm for her," Valens continued, voicing Ruso's own thoughts.

"And paid money for the privilege," he grumbled. Damn it, if he hadn't rescued her from Innocens there might well have been a third dead girl found in Deva.

Immediately he wished he had not brought to mind the image of those bodies: the one strangled and bloated and the other barely recognizable as human. Why would Tilla have chosen to leave before her arm was healed? He had no evidence that she was on her way back to the Brigantes. Her soul could already have begun the journey to a darker place. If that was true, then he wanted to know. He wanted to bury her himself. And then he would not only hunt down whoever had killed her: He would seek out the people who should have investigated the previous deaths, and hadn't. The trouble was, he was one of them.

He turned abruptly. "I'm going out," he announced.

In the gloom of his bedroom, he pulled on his overtunic without thinking once about scorpions. He flung his old cloak around his shoulders and paused to run a finger over the smooth, cold hilt of his knife.

63

ONCE HE HAD passed the cemetery, Ruso urged the borrowed horse into a canter. It was a broad-backed beast, recently retired as the mount of a tribune, who, according to the groom, was not the steadiest of horsemen. It was mild-tempered, comfortable, and too staid to be in great demand. It was the ideal horse for a man who needed an animal that could carry an extra rider.

He slowed it to a trot to pass a string of heavy carts, then wove around a road gang and a couple of mounted men leading a string of shaggy ponies. A local family was heading into town carrying baskets of vegetables. Half a dozen legionaries were heaving against the tilted side of a vehicle that had one wheel in the ditch, evidently determined to right it without unloading it first. A couple of them glanced hopefully up at him, realized he was an officer, and bent back to their task.

Farther out, the traffic grew lighter. Sheep were grazing beside the road, watched over by a small boy with a large stick. Ruso concentrated on the opposite shoulder, looking out for the path that led across to the woods.

The horse seemed surprised at being asked to jump the ditch—evidently the tribune had demanded very little of it—but it landed on the other side in a reasonably tidy fashion. A couple of birds flew up from the trees in alarm as it approached. Apart from birds, the woods appeared to be deserted. The horse slowly picked its way forward along the narrow path, apparently unperturbed by its rider's occasional lurch forward to lie along its neck as they passed under overhanging branches.

There was no smell of smoke among the trees: only that of damp earth and rotting leaves. A better tracker than Ruso would have known whether anyone had passed this way recently. Unable to read the signs, he concentrated on making his way safely through the undergrowth and strained to catch any sounds beyond the brush of leaves, the creak of the saddle, and the warble of distant birdsong.

He emerged from the woods picking twigs out of his hair and circled the horse around the clearing, trying to look into the trees and over the bracken to the muddy patch where the spring originated. There was no sign of her.

"Tilla!"

His shout died away into silence. The birdsong had stopped.

"*Tilla!* Can you hear me?"

He tried several times, twisting in the saddle to call in different directions, waiting each time for a response that did not come.

He swung down off the horse and left it to graze while he pushed his way through the bracken to the spring. The remains of a small fire lay in the grass, sodden and cold. The fire could have been lit on her last visit or last night: He had no way of knowing. What was certain was that it had not been active this morning.

Ruso got to his feet, took a deep breath, and shouted, "Tilla! Where are you?" one last time.

He turned to face the spring. He raised one hand in the air as he had seen his servant do. Glad that no one but the horse could hear him, he offered a prayer to the goddess of the spring, asking her to keep safe her faithful servant whose name was . . . he pulled the document from his tunic and read out, "Dar . . . lugh . . . dach . . . a," and then added, "but who is known to me as Tilla."

His approach to the native houses was announced by several excited dogs. As he drew closer, chickens scuttled to safety under a gate on which a small boy sat staring with his mouth open. A couple of squawking geese made experimental runs at the horse. It flattened its ears but plodded forward.

Ruso dismounted and led the horse toward the gate. The boy scrambled down the other side of the gate and fled into the houses. Women appeared in the doorways. An old man emerged from behind a haystack and shouted an order. The dogs, which to Ruso's relief were tethered, fell silent.

When he turned after fastening the gate, the occupants of the houses had all gathered in a silent line. Several women had their arms folded. One, white up to the elbows with flour, rested a reassuring hand on the head of the small boy, who was now hiding behind her skirts. To the right of the people, swinging gently in the morning breeze, Ruso saw the reason why the dogs were tied up. The carcass of a freshly slaughtered sheep dangled, still dripping, over a tub of thick blood. As the natives stared at him in silence it struck him that the outer skin of civilization was very thin here. He had no doubt that not so very long ago, these people would have slaughtered him with as little compunction as they had killed the sheep, and cheerfully nailed his severed head to the gatepost.

Surveying the eight pairs of eyes watching his every move, he wondered where the men and the rest of the children were. The girl whose appearance had distracted the First Century on its training run was nowhere to be seen. There must be people still hiding in the houses. He wondered if he should have unlatched the safety strap on his knife. He wondered if he could vault onto the horse before they reached him. He wondered whether the horse could clear the gate. Then he began.

"My name," he announced, "is Gaius Petreius Ruso, Medicus with the Twentieth Legion. I have come here to look for a woman." He stopped. It was, he realized, an unfortunate start. Worse, his audience showed no sign of understanding it. Faced with impassive stares, he asked, "Does anyone here speak Latin?"

The small boy blinked. There was no other response.

"I am looking for the woman who is my servant," he said, pulling out the sale document. "Her name is . . ." He read out the complicated name again, suspecting that he was pronouncing it all wrong. "She is missing. She has curly fair hair"—with a twirling motion he indicated his own, which was indeed hair, but entirely the wrong color—"and her arm is—" He made a chopping motion with his left hand on his lower right arm, and then mimed winding a bandage around it. "Her arm is broken." Although by now they probably thought he was threatening to chop it off. "I want her to know that if she comes home she will not be punished." *Even though,* he wanted to add, *she very much deserves it.*

He cleared his throat. "I am anxious to know that she is safe," he said.

A cockerel strutted across the mud that separated him from his audience. The small boy tried to stuff a fistful of his mother's skirt into his mouth. Without taking her eyes off Ruso, the woman crouched and gathered the child into her floury arms.

"I want to know that she is safe," Ruso repeated. He surveyed the blank faces. "If I had any money," he continued, "I would be offering a reward. But I don't, so I can't. And if I thought any of you understood a word I was saying, I would tell you that even if I can't find Tilla, I'd like to find out what the condition is underneath that splint. I'd like to find out because I want to know whether there's anything I've done since I came to your miserable country that has made it worth the bother of coming here. So. There you are. Well, thank you all for being so tremendously helpful."

As he tramped out through the mud in the gateway—he was not going to pick his way around the edge as if a Roman officer were afraid of getting dirty—the dogs began to bark again. This time no one tried to stop them. A few yards beyond the gate he looked over his shoulder.

They were still watching.

64

THERE WAS NO sign of her at the house, where he only stopped long enough to clean off the mud before going to the hospital. There he found two messages: Albanus was trying to track him down, and Priscus wanted an urgent meeting. Ruso managed to find Albanus first. As they entered the surgery the clerk asked,

"Any word on your housekeeper, sir?"

"Nothing. What did you want me for?"

"Officer Priscus says—"

"Yes, I know. Urgently. Was that it?"

"No, sir, not entirely." Albanus checked to make sure the surgery door was closed. "It's about that delicate matter, sir," he began. "I told them at HQ that I'd lost a document and it was all rather embarrassing, and they let me have a private hunt through the post records. You'd be amazed at the volume of correspondence, sir."

"And?"

"I've been through every list for the last two months, but I can't find a letter from a Saufeia anywhere."

"Damn," muttered Ruso.

"Would you like me to go back any farther, sir?"

Ruso shook his head. "There's no point."

"If there's anything I can do to help you find your housekeeper, sir . . ."

Ruso settled himself on the corner of his desk and folded his arms. There were things he needed to know, but he was more likely to acquire a broken jaw from the second spear than any information. Valens had offered to sound out his friend in civilian liaison, but the only sounds forthcoming were negative ones. Ruso was going to have to consult a source he despised: army gossip.

"Albanus," he said, "who or what do the men think was responsible for the deaths of those two girls?"

Albanus's eyes widened. "Do you think the same person might have taken your housekeeper, sir?"

"I hope not. But I'm running out of other ideas."

Albanus thought for a moment. "To be honest, sir, nobody seems to know. Most people just think there's a madman around who likes killing women."

"I've been through that. Why two from one bar?"

"It could be a very important customer. Somebody the management is scared of."

"How important?"

Albanus scratched his head. "I can't see the legate or any of the tribunes frequenting there, to be honest, sir, can you? It's more likely somebody with a grudge against the management."

"Right. How many people would that include?"

"If you count all the men who've ever been thrown out of Merula's? Quite a lot, sir. That's before you consider the staff there."

Ruso decided not to mention doctors who had been poisoned by the food. Even if both the girls had been victims of one man with a grudge, that grievance must have been incurred long before his own arrival in Deva. His chances of discovering the right complainant—and quickly—were slim.

"Of course, there might be no connection at all, sir."

"Do you think Asellina really did try to run off with a sailor?"

"To tell you the truth, sir, most people think she led poor old Decimus on a bit of a dance. It would have taken him years to save up enough to buy her. And he's still got fifteen years to serve, so he couldn't run away with her instead—not unless he deserted, and then what would they have had to live on? So, she decided to go with the sailor instead."

"Does anyone know anything about this sailor? Nobody seems to have seen him."

Albanus frowned. "I don't know, sir. It was all looked into at the time. Then it all blew over and everybody forgot about it. Except Decimus, of course. And I suppose the people at the bar." He glanced up. "Perhaps that was why Saufeia thought she'd give it a try, sir. Because she thought Asellina had gotten away with it."

It suddenly occurred to Ruso that he might have been looking in the wrong place for a letter. What if Saufeia had been trying to contact the last successful runaway? "Do you happen to know," he said, "whether Asellina could read and write?"

Albanus shook his head. "I shouldn't think so, sir. From what I hear, Saufeia was a bit unusual."

"She certainly doesn't seem to have been as popular as Asellina."

"No, sir. Of course there are the other theories about Saufeia."

Ruso was beginning to suspect that the hospital staff had spent more time considering this case than the official investigators. "Tell me."

"Well, one is that her own people killed her because of the shame she'd brought on the family by working at Merula's, sir. Which does sort of make sense, because what was a girl who could read and write doing in a place like that?"

"I don't know. From what I hear, she'd probably been hanging around with soldiers for years. Anything else?"

"I did hear a rumor that it was one of the married officers who'd had a fling with her and didn't want his wife to find out what he was up to."

"No name, I suppose?"

"No, sir. But most people seem to think she wandered off, then had an argument with a client who didn't want to pay and he turned nasty."

"Hm," said Ruso. "Well, that seems to cover every possibility."

"Cheer up, sir. If it was any of those, then your housekeeper's disappearance has nothing to do with the others, does it?"

"No," agreed Ruso, scratching his ear. "It doesn't." The thought should have been reassuring, but it wasn't, because it left him with nowhere to look.

"Unless there really is a madman, of course."

"Yes. Thank you, Albanus."

"Sorry, sir. I didn't mean to—"

There was a rap on the door. Albanus opened it and a familiar voice said, "Didn't you get my message, Ruso?"

"Ah," said Ruso. "Priscus. There you are."

Glaring at Albanus, Priscus added, "I specifically stressed that this was *most urgent.*"

"I was just sending him to find you," said Ruso, noting inwardly that his ability—and readiness—to tell lies had improved dramatically since he had come to Britannia. He dismissed Albanus, then motioned the administrator to a stool, while he himself remained seated on the corner of his desk, reversing their usual positions. "How can I help?"

"I haven't come here to ask for help, Ruso. I have come here to tell you how I am going to help you out of a very awkward situation."

Ruso, wondering which of his many awkward situations Priscus had found out about, raised his eyebrows and waited.

"Your missing servant," Priscus continued, unaware of the relief these words offered to his listener. "I take it she hasn't been found?"

"Not yet."

"Very well. I have had notices drawn up. They are being distributed as we speak."

Ruso found himself scratching his ear again. "Notices?"

"Missing slave notices. The usual sort of thing. I'm surprised you haven't done it yourself."

"I was hoping she would turn up," said Ruso, feeling he probably should have.

"Frankly, Ruso, I was also surprised not to be notified of her loss. As custodian of the Aesculapian fund."

Ruso looked him in the eye. "The loan will be paid in full," he insisted. "On the due date."

Priscus inclined his hair in his usual careful manner, and said, "Of course."

Ruso remembered that hair sticking out in a wild clump during his visit to Priscus's house, which it seemed the administrator was going to pretend had never happened. "So, from your point of view," he continued, forcing himself to concentrate, "the girl is irrelevant."

"Nevertheless, as a responsible custodian—"

"Priscus, the auditors can't hold you responsible for my slave running off."

The hand that smoothed the hair trembled slightly, and for the first time Ruso wondered if the man was genuinely frightened of the imperial auditors. "Nevertheless," Priscus was repeating, "as a responsible custodian I should be seen to be taking precautionary measures."

"Very thorough of you," said Ruso, wondering if the administrator stuck his nose this far into everyone's affairs, or whether he was particularly unlucky. Surely this couldn't still be revenge for the linen closet? Standing up to terminate the interview, he said, "I seem to be in your debt, Priscus. Let's hope your notices will do the trick, eh?"

65

ANOTHER NIGHT PASSED, and still there was no sign of Tilla's return. During a brief lull in morning surgery Albanus ventured to ask whether his officer was feeling all right.

"Perfectly well, thank you," replied Ruso crisply. "Is there a problem?"

"No, sir," said his clerk, too tactful to point out what Ruso already knew: that several times he had asked patients the same question twice. Sometimes it was because he had forgotten the answer. At other times it was because he had not only failed to register the answer, but had forgotten that he had already asked the question.

By the end of surgery and ward rounds he had seen forty-two patients and had made at least three final and utterly contradictory decisions about where Tilla had gone and what he should do about it.

Midday saw him leave the fort by the west gate, for no other reason than that he had not been that way recently. He had no real hope of catching sight of Tilla. She was either long gone or hiding or . . . he recalled this morning's vow not to speculate about worse fates. Whatever had happened to her, he was going to find her. He strode down to the docks.

The elegant houses stared out through a thin drizzle at a view that held none of the charm it had offered on the morning that the *Sirius* had brought his belongings. The tide had sunk away to reveal a weed-strewn and smelly expanse of mud flats. The farthest legs of the jetty reached out into the river channel, where a couple of bulbous merchant ships were moored. The sound of hammering came from one of them, and a figure jolting one arm a heartbeat before each of the blows was dangling on a rope slung from the bows. A couple of figures sat on the jetty, swinging their feet in the air and their fishing lines into the water. Closer to shore, a man and a group of barefoot boys were plodding slowly across the mud, heads down, searching for whatever they were collecting in their buckets. A sail mender was plying his trade, sheltered from the drizzle by one of his own creations stretched over a wooden frame. Ruso felt bizarrely disappointed, as if he had expected Tilla to be sitting down at the dockside like a parcel, waiting to be collected.

As he turned to make his way back up the hill, he scanned the many offerings scrawled on the wall of the warehouse on the corner. Amongst the advertisements for lodgings, hot food, the visiting slave trader, and BEAUTIFUL GIRLS AND BOYS! DANCING FOR YOU! he read in the much clearer script of a clerk who was used to posting official notices,

RUNAWAY SLAVE
ATTRACTIVE FEMALE, AGE ABOUT 20. FAIR CURLY HAIR.
SLIM. 5 FEET 4 INCHES TALL. RIGHT ARM INJURED, MAY BE BANDAGED.
MISSING SINCE 3RD BEFORE KALENDS OF OCT.
REWARD FOR RETURN OR INFORMATION LEADING TO CAPTURE:
CONTACT G. POMPEIUS PRISCUS, ADMINISTRATOR, AESC. THANKSGIVING FUND, LEG XX HOSPITAL.

He scowled. The notice read as if Priscus owned her himself. Not even a mention of his own name. The man's presumption passed all bounds of decency. The notice was skillfully worded, though. The words *attractive female* would blind the eyes of many a potential searcher to the fact that the amount of the reward was not specified—which was just as well. He supposed he, as the owner, would end up having to pay it. He wouldn't put it past Priscus to send him a bill for the signage as well.

He paused on the way up the hill to ask a fearsomely painted female lolling on a bench outside a whorehouse whether she had seen a woman answering Tilla's description. He had barely got half a sentence out when her owner appeared in the doorway behind her and assured him that yes, they had a girl just like that. If the gentleman would just step inside she would be very pleased to meet him.

"I don't want a girl like her," explained Ruso, "I want the girl herself."

"She'll be whoever you want her to be," promised the owner, leaning closer and leering, "new to the business but keen as mustard—and fresh as a daisy."

A hideous thought crossed Ruso's mind in the wake of this unlikely description. "Let me have a look at her."

The man's smile widened as he beckoned him forward. "Right this way, sir. Satisfaction guaranteed."

"I'm not coming *in,*" explained Ruso. "You've just told me you've got a new girl who answers the description of my missing slave." The man's smile dropped away. "I want you to send her out here."

The man frowned. Ruso heard a creak and a sigh as the painted female got up from the bench. A heavy hand landed on his shoulder and a husky voice said, "Want me to get rid of him, boss?"

The man nodded in her direction and introduced her. "Elegantina," he said. "Champion lady wrestler in three provinces. Recently retired."

Ruso twisted around and nodded a greeting to a face held uncomfortably close to his own. "Ruso," he said. The woman was as tall as he was, and probably heavier. He turned back to her owner. "I heard Merula's got raided the other day," he said.

"They didn't find nothing," pointed out the owner.

"No, but they're obviously in the mood to look."

"All my staff are registered."

"I don't doubt your honesty, but you could have been deceived. Let me put your mind at rest."

The man glared at him for a moment, then said, "All right, Ellie." The weight lifted off Ruso's shoulder as the owner turned into the doorway and yelled, "Camilla! Here! Now!"

Moments later a small creature with badly bleached hair was blinking pink-rimmed eyes into the daylight.

Ruso shook his head. "It isn't her." He leaned forward and put a coin in the hand of the wretched girl, who promptly and automatically handed it to her owner. "If you see or hear anything," he added, wondering how many more miserable creatures were caged like animals in places like this, "the details are posted on the wall down there. There's a reward."

Four days' growth of stubble on his chin gave him a good excuse to visit the barber. Conversation during the shave was limited to the weather and inquiries after the mother-in-law, who was apparently still a mad old bitch but no longer a mad old bitch with a toothache. Once the blade was put away Ruso ran a thumb along the newly-smooth line of his jaw and said, "Have you seen the notices about the missing slave girl?"

The barber untied the towel and shook it. "I heard another one ran off," he said. "Expect she'll bob up before long. If she hasn't cremated herself."

Ruso rose from the stool. "This one is my housekeeper."

The man paused. "Sorry, Doc. No offense meant."

"I know what you think of people who ask questions, but this is important. If anyone knows anything at all about what happened to the other girls, it's his duty to say something. In confidence, of course."

The man shrugged and looked away. "Sorry, Doc. Wish I could help."

Ruso fixed his gaze on the one eye. "Try harder. I heard you bought some red hair not long ago."

"Who told you that?"

"Never mind."

"I buy and sell all the time. It's my business."

"It was brought in by a man. I need to know who he was. My girl could be in danger."

The man folded his arms. "Like I said before. I don't buy from murderers. And like I told you, you're going to get yourself into trouble, going around accusing people."

"I'm not saying he did it. I'm saying he could have information."

"If you know so much, why isn't this an official investigation?"

This was getting nowhere. "She's a Briton," said Ruso, pulling open his purse to pay for the shave. "She comes from somewhere up in the hills. I'm hoping she just decided to head for home."

"More than likely," agreed the barber.

Ruso handed over the last of his cash and thanked the gods that tomorrow was payday. "If your wife hears anything . . ." He hesitated, not wanting to say, *If anyone offers you any blond curls that aren't their own . . .* "Just ignore the official name on the notices," he concluded. "Send a message directly to me. There's a reward."

She'll bob up before long. It was not a cheering thought with which to lean on the damp rail of the bridge and stare downstream at the water swirling along the channels in the mud flats. Ruso had not been gazing for long when he was aware of movement and saw a pair of long brown plaits dangling down over the rail to his left.

"My husband," announced the stranger, "is a good man."

Not sure where this was leading, Ruso decided not to encourage the woman by replying. This was a ploy he regretted as soon as he risked a glance and recognized the barber's wife.

"He looks after his family," she continued, evidently not put off by the silence. "He keeps us all. Even my mother, who treats him like a bad smell. He has done nothing wrong."

Ruso said carefully, "I haven't accused him of anything."

"It was nothing to do with him, you understand? He was not involved. People sell hair all the time. It is business."

"I'm just trying to find my housekeeper," said Ruso. "I'm not interested in anything else."

"They are very loyal to one another," said the woman. "You know what the men are like. Stupid, sometimes, but loyal."

"I understand."

"Would you betray a comrade?"

Ruso watched a dead branch drifting down one of the channels. "If I thought it would save a life, I might."

The branch caught on a mud bank and swung around in the current. A spur caught in the opposite bank and the branch was stuck, straddling the flow.

He said, "So, it was a soldier."

"A veteran."

"And this was shortly after the last girl disappeared?"

The woman nodded. "My husband didn't know the girl was dead, you understand? It was just business."

Water was pouring over the branch in a long shimmering curl that crashed down into a line of foam.

Ruso said, "I have no money with me, but I will see to it that you are—"

The bar of the bridge gave a sudden shudder as the woman's fist landed on it. "I am not doing this for money! You Romans, you think everything is for money!"

"I need more help," he explained. "I need a description. A name, if you have one."

"I came to speak with you," said the woman, ignoring his words with a haughtiness that reminded him painfully of Tilla, "because I think you are a good man."

"I'll be grateful for anything you can tell me that might help my servant."

"I do not know," she said, "how the man got the red hair. For all I know, the girl may have cut if off by herself and given it to him to sell. He is the only one who can tell you that; you must ask him."

"How do I find this man?"

"I do not know his name," she said, "but he works at Merula's bar."

66

AT MERULA'S MOST of the lunchtime customers had gone, leaving only a few hangers-on who had nowhere better to go, or else no inclination to go there. Tomorrow would be different, insisted Stichus as he palmed the coins Ruso had just borrowed from Valens. Tomorrow was payday. Stichus indicated the girls seated around the bar. Today, a customer could take his pick.

Ruso was glad there were few witnesses to see Chloe rise from the table with a smile, slide her hand into his, and lead him up the stairs.

The cubicle was, he knew, the best the place had to offer. The wide bed was strewn with plump blue cushions. Chloe pulled the door shut behind them and the yellow glow of a lamp rose to help the light that struggled in through a small pane of bubbly glass. Ruso found himself trying to work out a tangle of naked bodies painted on the walls in various uncomfortable-looking combinations as Chloe's arms slid around his waist. He felt her breath against his ear. "I knew you'd change your mind," she murmured.

Ruso grasped both her hands and held them still. He opened his mouth to speak and found himself suddenly hoarse, but managed, "I just want to talk."

"You can talk to me," whispered Chloe, nuzzling the back of his neck. "I'm a good listener. It's nice and private here. You can tell me anything you want." He felt a gentle push toward the bed. "Let's get comfortable, shall we?"

As he felt himself sink into the cushions, he reasoned that it would do no harm. Chloe was very attractive. She was warm. She was willing. She was a professional, and he had paid. He could always talk to her afterward.

She was curled around him on the bed, pressing herself against him. He glanced down to watch her foot sliding up his thigh. The charms on her ankle bracelet trembled with each movement. Her skin was smooth. Her toes were perfect. She was nibbling his ear.

Ruso closed his eyes. At last: a woman who understood what he needed. What he deserved. And the beauty of it was, there was no commitment. He could have this whenever he wanted. Because this was a professional service. A business transaction. Like the buying of someone's hair . . .

Restraining Chloe's exploring hand, he pulled himself up to sit with his back against the wall. "When I said I wanted to talk," he growled, hoping there was no one listening behind the door, "that's what I meant."

Chloe arched her back and stretched, draping herself across his lap and looking up at him. "But you're so *nice,*" she said, pursing her lips and miming a kiss.

"No," he said, heaving at her shoulders to lift her away from him. "I'm not nice. And I'm tired of being lied to."

She swung her legs off the bed and sat up. "Suit yourself."

"Do you know where Tilla is?"

"No." She bent to fiddle with one of the pins that held her curls in place. "Is that it? Can I go now?"

"No. Is she here?"

Chloe pushed the pin back into place and sighed. "You don't learn, do you?" She turned to face him. "It was you who told them about Phryne, wasn't it?"

When Ruso said nothing, she continued, "Well, you were a big help to her. She'd tell you how much herself if she was well enough to receive visitors."

"Is she all right?"

"Of course she's not all right."

"I could—"

"You've caused enough trouble already. Lucky for her, it's payday coming up. They aren't stupid here. She'll be fit to work by tomorrow."

Ruso found himself staring at the tangle of bodies painted on the walls. For a girl in a place like this, being fit to work was a dubious blessing. Perhaps the child had indeed pretended to be stolen in the vain hope of escape. Or perhaps he had been right the first time: The whole thing had been a story concocted by Tilla to cover her own escape. He no longer knew whom to believe. "Chloe," he said, "do you think Tilla's run away?"

"I don't know."

"The last person to see her was Bassus. He said she came here while you were out at the baths."

"Well, she's not here now. Ask him where she went."

"Are you not telling me because you don't know, or because you're afraid?"

She gave a snort of derision. "You know the first thing you learn in this place? Never show fear. Something Phryne needs to learn. And you know the second thing? Mind your own business."

"If one of your management's done something to Tilla . . ."

Chloe shook her head. "I can tell you one thing about Bassus, Doctor. He won't damage anything that might turn him a profit."

"I heard that somebody here hurt Daphne."

"So? You don't have to be much of a talker to do this job. They'll have her back to work after they've sold the baby."

Ruso took a deep breath. "And what about Asellina? Or Saufeia? Did they really run away, or were they allowed out like you are?" He paused. "Do the girls do home visits? Private parties, that sort of thing?"

"What's that got to do with Tilla? It's you she's run away from, not us."

"Because she's missing like the other two. And the only thing that links them all is this place. What's going on here, Chloe?"

Chloe stared at him for a moment, then got to her feet. "I don't know what you think you're stirring up," she said, "but I don't want anything to do with it." She stepped forward and lifted the latch on the door. "Time's up." She walked out onto the landing. "Get out now, or I'll call the boys. And don't come here again."

Chloe's sandals clattered away down the stairs. Ruso sighed, gave a parting glance at the tangled bodies—the participants looked depressingly bored—and followed her down to the bar.

"Bassus!"

The man turned. "Back again, eh? Come to pay your bill?"

"Come for a chat," said Ruso. "Can we go somewhere private?"

"No thanks. You're not my type."

Ruso shrugged. "I can say it in front of everyone, if you like."

Bassus glanced around. The bar held four members of the staff, three customers, and, in a cage beside one of them, a jackdaw. Bassus jerked a thumb toward the door. "Outside."

On the way out they passed Stichus. "You're getting soft," Bassus told him. "Letting bloody caged birds in."

"It talks," retorted Stichus.

"Show me something round here that don't."

"Daphne," suggested Stichus, with what he clearly thought was wit.

"Take a walk a minute, Stich? Me and the doc have got business."

Stichus retreated into the bar. Bassus leaned against the painted wall, folded his arms, and glowered at the woman behind the bakery counter as if he were daring her to eavesdrop. "Make it quick," he said. "I'm a busy man."

"So am I," said Ruso. "But you said next time I had a problem to come to you. So here I am."

Bassus sighed. "What is it now?"

"I still haven't found Tilla."

"How many times have I got to say it? I don't know where she is! If I knew, I'd tell you. I got a couple of nice buyers lined up. If she don't turn up soon I'm going to have to let them down."

"But in the course of looking for her, I've run across some troubling information."

There was barely a hesitation before he said, "And this information would be?"

"I'll get to that in a minute. I'm trying to stop Tilla from meeting the same fate as the other two runaways. Tell me, is it true that Saufeia wasn't much good at her job?"

"What's that got to do with it? She was useless. Even when she was trying, which weren't often."

"And what do you do with girls who don't please the customers?"

"Sell them, of course."

Ruso nodded. "That's what I thought."

"Sounds to me like you thought we take them out back and strangle them."

"What I can't understand," said Ruso, "is why her hair was all shorn off. She wouldn't do it herself if she was planning to work the streets or run away with a lover, and Merula certainly wouldn't do it if she was planning to sell her."

Bassus shrugged. "Sorry. Can't help you there."

"What I'm thinking," explained Ruso, watching him carefully, "and correct me if I'm wrong, is that it must have been done after she was dead. Perhaps not by the murderer, but by someone else who knew him. Who might be able to point me in his direction." He paused. "Someone who then went and sold the hair."

Bassus was staring at the pavement opposite, scratching his neck with one finger.

"If something's happened to Tilla," said Ruso, "I want to know about it."

Bassus continued to ponder for a moment. Finally he gave a sigh. "All right. This is it. I don't know nothing about Tilla but I know a bit about the other thing. You keep your mouth shut, agreed?"

"Agreed."

"When Merula noticed Saufeia weren't around, me and Stich took a couple of torches and went to look. We found her in a back alley."

"Which back alley?"

"Over by the amphitheater. Propped sitting up in a corner like she was waiting for somebody. The bastard had only just got away. I reckon he heard us coming. She was still warm."

"You didn't call for help?"

Bassus looked him in the eye. "I know dead when I see it, Doc. Besides . . . I'm not known for being a patient man. Twenty-five years in the legion, I believe in discipline, see? People don't know what we have to put up with, with these girls. Strangled runaway, dark night, back alley—who'd have believed us?"

"But she was your own slave." Executing one's own slaves was officially frowned upon, but fellow slaves were not in a position to complain and it was hard to see who else would bother.

"She weren't ours," explained Bassus. "She belonged to the business. And if Merula thought we'd done it she'd have gone mad." He paused. "I know what you're thinking. We should've just walked away. I wish I had. Only Stich, he decides to be clever."

This seemed an unlikely proposition, but Ruso let it pass.

"He says, if we just leave her here, then some greedy bastard's going to find her and nick all her fancy clothes and everything. What all belong to the bar. That hair was worth something too. So we took what was ours and we give her a decent send-off."

"In the river?"

"We weren't to know she'd come back, were we? But we didn't kill her. I swear. And I don't know who did."

Ruso nodded. "And would you know anything about an accident happening to someone who asked too many questions?"

Bassus folded his arms. "Could be arranged. Who you thinking of?"

"Never mind." If the man had known anything about the fire or the incident with the trowel, he was a good actor. "One last question. Do you know anything about a letter?"

There was a slight pause before he said, "What letter?"

"There's a rumor that Saufeia wrote to somebody. I know she was telling everyone she wouldn't be here much longer. I assume she was arranging to meet someone."

Bassus shook his head. "I don't know nothing about no letter," he said. "And she wouldn't have been here much longer 'cause we'd have traded her on. But your Tilla couldn't be writing to nobody, that I do know. Look. Asellina was unlucky. Saufeia run into a customer what didn't want to pay, and whoever he was he didn't bother taking her far to finish her. If he'd got your Tilla you'd have found her by now. I reckon she's run off, like it says in the notices. You ask me, you want to stop wasting time poking around with dead tarts and hire yourself a slave hunter."

67

PAYDAY DAWNED AT last. There was still no sign of Tilla. Ruso spent the morning trying to do justice to the needs of his patients, which were as pressing as ever. Outside, however, it was apparent that the Twentieth was working itself up to a level of excitement that heralded a busy night for the medical service. The enthusiasm raised by the quarterly arrival of cash had been swelled by the anticipation of at least the first installment of Hadrian's bonus to his loyal troops. The bathhouse scaffolding was abandoned, its occupants presumably waiting in other jostling lines like the one he was now passing outside a centurion's quarters. A neglected noticeboard at the head of a barracks block announced an interunit sports event this afternoon in the amphitheater—a gallant but probably doomed attempt to direct the Twentieth's payday energy into useful channels. If this unit was anything like any of the others Ruso had known, by evening the real entertainment would be in full swing. The bars would be overflowing with off-duty soldiers, and men who ought to know better would be doing things they would very much regret in the morning. If Tilla was still somewhere in the town, he hoped she would have the sense to stay behind closed doors.

Minutes later, he walked away from the camp prefect's office still staring at the bottom figure on the copy of his account. *Perhaps you'd like to take some time to check the figures, sir.* This couldn't be right. There must be some mistake.

She had not miraculously returned to the house while he was out. He sat on his one chair and ignored the puppy that scrambled up his leg and danced around before settling on his lap. Outside, a shout of laughter echoed along the street from one of the barracks blocks. Ruso dipped his hand into the jar Valens had been given by a grateful patient and groped around for the last of the olives.

The figure at the top of the sheet was fine. The "Brought forward" figure was correct. Miraculously, the army had managed to send his records across two seas and two continents in time for the clerks to do the arithmetic. The down payment on the gift to celebrate the accession of the noble emperor Hadrianus was most welcome, except that a large chunk of it had been compulsorily diverted into his savings account. "Deductions," read the line underneath. That was where the trouble started.

Following all the usual deductions for his keep and the legionary celebration at Saturnalia was a figure for "Loan repayment"—they'd taken the whole advance back at once, of course—and an item called "Expenditure." The amount defied all his attempts to live frugally. The details were listed on a separate sheet and included "Meals taken at the hospital" and "Private use of hospital facilities."

Perhaps you'd like to take some time to check the figures, sir. Ruso licked the olive brine off his fingers and began to count. Three attempts brought three confirmations of the impossible figure against "Makes a total of." Next he deducted the amount he owed the Aesculapian Thanksgiving Fund. Then he took off the sum he had arranged to be sent to Lucius. Finally he subtracted enough to cover his bill at Merula's.

Ruso leaned back in his chair and stared gloomily at the empty olive jar. What would remain in his purse was barely enough to see a civilized man through the next three weeks, let alone three months. No wonder men on basic pay resorted to stealing from Priscus's linen closets. He could not live for three months on this. He must take the time to find more private patients. He must get on with his writing. He must get promoted. He must find Tilla alive—and when he had, he must sell her.

As he framed this thought in his mind, two things occurred to him simultaneously. One was that he didn't want to sell her and he never had. The other was that today he had somewhere new to look.

Ruso had never bought a slave at a market. There had always been someone else—father, uncle, wife, other slaves—to deal with that sort of thing. The only time he had needed to buy his own staff was after his divorce, when he had taken the post in Africa. That had been a simple matter of moving into the house occupied by his predecessor and handing over a sum of cash to retain the slave couple who already worked there. He had, of course, bought Tilla, but that had not been a planned purchase. He had never been called upon to assess the suitability of strangers to join his household, and he had never paid any attention to how it was done. Which was why, he supposed, he was surprised to see that the notice announcing the arrival of the slave trader had now been amended to read, VIEWING FROM 6TH HR TODAY, AUCTION AT 9TH HR.

Deva, being less a town than a collection of houses outside a fort, did not have a forum. Instead, the action had been crammed into the space between the amphitheater and the fountain. Peering above the heads of the shoppers, Ruso could make out stalls offering jewelry, EFFICIENT SCRIBE SERVICES, hot pies, FORTUNE-TELLING, and PORTRAITS PAINTED WHILE YOU WAIT. A succession of bright balls rising and falling in the air marked the passage of a juggler, and the area by the oil shop had been cordoned off to make a performance space for a dancing bear, currently sitting in its cage with its back to the crowds.

Ruso pushed his way toward the huge open-sided marquee that filled one side of the open space. From its roof swung a sign announcing L. CURTIUS SILVANUS, DEALER IN SLAVES: RELIABLE STAFF FOR THE DISCERNING EMPLOYER. The people crowded into it fell into four categories. The merchandise were the cheerless ones with chains around their ankles and labels around their necks. The customers were the ones peering and poking at the merchandise and asking them to open their mouths, flex their arm muscles, or prove they could speak Latin. The security staff appeared to be doing nothing at all, while a couple of clerks fluttered around a makeshift office formed by a row of folding desks.

Ruso shoved his way to the desks and arrived just as an African with a lined face and a thick gold rope around his neck pushed his way in through a flap at the back of the marquee.

"Are you the owner?"

The man bowed. "Lucius Curtius Silvanus, at your service."

Ruso explained about Tilla.

"I assure you, sir, my staff take great care. We very rarely buy in the street and only then with full documentation and references." He indicated the stock with a sweep of his arm. "All purchases come with a money-back guarantee for a full six months. We certainly wouldn't take on anything with an obvious injury."

Ruso nodded. "And is this everyone? Or do you have a special collection?"

The man smiled, revealing a wide gap between his two front teeth. "Ah, sir, I'm afraid they are for inspection by appointment only. But all our present collection have been with us for at least ten days."

"Nevertheless—"

The man's expression hardened. He summoned a clerk and ordered him to show Ruso the list of the private collection. There were a couple of Greek tutors, a geometry teacher, a painter, a family physician (Ruso would have liked to meet that one), three "beautiful young boys" whose talents were not listed, and a set of fourteen-year-old twin girls, described as "very beautiful, black hair, green eyes, good figures, soft-spoken, and eager to please."

"How much are the girls?" he inquired, wondering what prices were like here.

"More than you can afford," said the clerk—evidently a sharp judge of character.

Nothing here seemed likely to lead to Tilla. He was about to leave when a woman's voice said, "Good afternoon, Doctor!" and he turned to find Rutilius's wife smiling at him.

"We heard about your housekeeper," put in Rutilia the Younger. "Have you come to buy another one?"

"Such a shame," sympathized her mother. "It's so difficult to find good staff."

The daughter said, "I hope the madman hasn't got her. Have you looked in the river?"

"Really, dear!" chided the mother. She was apologizing for her daughter's tactlessness when Ruso heard a distinct cry of "Doctor!" from somewhere across the marquee. "I'm sorry," he interrupted, relieved. "I have to go. Someone's calling me."

"Doctor!"

The boy was perhaps eight or nine years old. He had ginger-colored hair and his face was blotched with pink, as if he had been crying. He was dressed in a plain brown tunic. Like all the other slaves, he was barefoot. The iron cuff looked as though it could snap his thin white ankle. He was chained to a massive bearded native on one side and an elderly man with a bent back on the other. Ruso stared at him, trying to remember where he had seen him before.

The boy sniffed, wiped his nose on the back of his hand, and said, "It's me, Doctor. Lucco."

Ruso frowned. "Lucco? From Merula's?"

The boy nodded. "Yes, sir."

"What are you doing here?"

The boy's eyes glistened with tears. "I'm being sold, sir." He swallowed hard and squared his shoulders. "I'm a good worker, sir. And I'm quick to learn. Really I am."

Ruso gazed at the skinny form with a mounting sense of dismay, knowing he could not say what the boy was hoping to hear. What could a man with no money possibly say or do to reassure a child who was chained like an animal, waiting to be auctioned to the highest bidder? He closed his eyes and fought the urge to utter a curse on the spirit of his weak-willed father, on his spendthrift stepmother, on his half sisters, who combined the worst qualities of both. He wanted to lay a hand on Lucco's shoulder and assure him that all would be well. Only it probably wouldn't.

At least he could save the boy from being poked and peered at for a few minutes. He said, "Why are you being sold, Lucco?"

The boy eyed him for a minute, as if he was wondering what to answer. Ruso groaned inwardly as he realized his mistake. The child thought he was being interviewed for a job. "Lucco," he explained gently, crouching down to speak to him face-to-face, "I can't buy you. I'm sorry. I may look rich to you, but the truth is, I'm not."

The boy sniffed again. "Yes, sir."

The old man burst into a fit of coughing. In his efforts to stifle the cough he staggered backward, dragging the chain and jerking Lucco's ankle sideways. The boy winced and bent to rub his leg. The big native turned and growled something at the old man, who ignored him.

"Lucco," said Ruso, wishing he did not have to ask this, "you remember my slave, Tilla?"

"She used to feed her dinner to the birds."

"Well, now she's missing. I'm afraid that whoever hurt Saufeia might hurt her. If you know anything at all about what happened to Saufeia, or to Asellina, you must tell me. Nobody's going to punish you for talking now."

The boy shook his head. "I don't know nothing about Saufeia, sir. Everybody thought Asellina had gone to live somewhere nicer. All the girls cried when they found her."

"I see."

"I like it at Merula's," said the boy. "I don't want to go nowhere else."

"You're a bright boy, Lucco," said Ruso. "You'll do well wherever you go."

The boy replied politely, "Yes, sir."

Ruso stood up straight, glancing around him and wondering if it would be kinder to get out of the way and let potential buyers assess the boy's worth. The more the better. A slave for whom there were several bidders would fetch a higher price and logic dictated that a valuable asset would be well treated. The trouble was, logic rarely dictated what people did in the privacy of their own homes.

"Sir?"

He turned.

"Sir, please could you give my mother a message?"

"Your mother?"

"Please could you tell her Bassus told Merula about the oysters?"

Ruso frowned. "Bassus told Merula about the . . . ?"

"The oysters, sir. So Merula told him to take me to the trader." An energetic sniff was followed by, "Bassus said he was going to find a nice family for me, but now he's gone and told Merula about the oysters. My mother doesn't know."

Ruso was now thoroughly confused. "You mother doesn't know about the oysters?"

"She doesn't know I'm here." The boy glanced over at the clerks behind the desks. "Do you think they'll let me go and say good-bye?"

Ruso doubted it very much. "You are being sold because of oysters?"

The boy nodded. "I didn't mean to do it, sir. I mean, I didn't mean . . ." His voice tailed into silence.

Ruso scratched his ear. This story was beginning to sound familiar. He lowered his voice so they could not be overheard. "Wasn't Merula's last cook sold because of serving bad oysters?"

Lucco nodded, dumb.

"And now Merula's found out you were involved?"

Something approaching panic entered the boy's eyes. "Please, sir!" he muttered, barely audible above the hum of conversation in the marquee. "I won't ever do it again!"

"I'm not going to tell anyone, Lucco." If no one had seen to it that the damnation of "attempted poisoner" was written on the child's label, he was certainly not going to do it himself.

"I didn't mean it, sir," whispered Lucco. "Somebody said the officer from the hospital was there. I thought they meant the nasty one."

Ruso was having difficulty following him again. "Tell me about these oysters," he suggested.

"Cook had them on the side to throw away."

"And you sent them out to a customer?"

He nodded. "It was just a bit of a joke, sir."

A bit of a joke that could have ended in a charge of attempted murder and a gruesome execution for its perpetrator. As it was, Valens had suffered acute food poisoning and Ruso had been obliged to do the work of three men and had ended up so far out of his senses that he had bought a girl on a building site.

He put his hand back on the boy's shoulder. "I'll go and see your mother right away. Where do I find her?"

"She'll be working, sir."

"Yes, but where?"

The boy stared at him. "Where she always works, sir. At Merula's."

It was Ruso's turn to stare.

"You know her, sir," said the boy. "They call her Chloe."

68

EARLIER THAT SAME morning, two young women in local dress were walking away from the huddle of native houses that Ruso had visited two days before. They were making their way down the track that led to the main Eboracum road. The taller of them was carrying a small sack over her shoulder.

Her companion turned to glance at her. "It's not too late. You could stay."

"And repay kindness with trouble?"

"No one knows you're here."

"Sabrann, sooner or later someone will talk. Now the worst they can say is that I came, and I went."

They walked on in silence for a few steps, then the smaller girl frowned. "Stop a moment." She reached up and tugged at her companion's hood. There had not been enough plant dye—or time—to disguise the whole of the hair. Brown wisps curled around the temples, but beneath the hood was a long blond plait. "You must remember to keep this forward," she warned. "I can't pin it any tighter. I don't know how you're going to manage tomorrow"

The taller girl shrugged. "Someone will be sent to help."

"You'll have to keep moving. It's a good fifteen miles and the state of the tracks will slow you down."

They reached the edge of the road. The only traveler they could see was leading an oxcart back in the direction of the fort.

"Do you have all you need?"

The hooded girl lowered the sack to the ground. "Bread, a comb, a blanket. Everything I asked for, and your mother gave me cheese and bacon."

Sabrann put a hand on her shoulder. "May the goddess walk beside you."

"And keep you ever in her gaze."

Their embrace was awkward, the hooded girl careful to keep her right arm concealed beneath her inconspicuous gray cloak. "I must go," she said, fingering her acorn necklace before raising the sack to her shoulder. "While the road is empty."

"Don't forget!" Sabrann waved an arm in an easterly direction, raising it to indicate distance. "Beyond the bridge, after the oak tree, take the track to the left. You must be careful not to stay on the road any longer than you have to."

The hooded girl stepped onto the gravel surface. When she turned, Sabrann was already on her way back to the houses. She was alone on the road once more.

Three days earlier, the walk to this place from Deva had tired her more than she had expected. She had been relieved to be offered water and, after the briefest of introductions, summoned to the big house to be inspected by the grandmother, who was head of the family.

Led over to face a chair near the fire, she had knelt in the bracken that covered the floor. As her eyes adjusted to the familiar gloom of a house with no windows, she found herself being peered at by a wizened old woman with sparse white hair pulled back behind large ears.

"Darlughdacha," said the old woman, repeating the name that had been shouted into one of her ears by her interpreter, the girl Sabrann. The grandmother shared the girl's strangled accent and her speech was distorted by the absence of teeth to trim the ends of the syllables, but the name was clear enough. "Daughter of Lugh," continued the grandmother. "Why have you come to us? Do we know you?"

"I spoke with a woman who was born near here, grandmother!" shouted the young woman who had been Tilla for a few weeks, and before that had been nobody for so long that being addressed by her own name now made her feel that someone else must be kneeling beside her. "Her name is Brica! She told me I could find people of honor here!" It was difficult to shout without sounding angry.

"It's no good," said Sabrann. "I have to shout everything right into her ear."

The old woman, realizing that she was missing something, turned to Sabrann, then squinted at her and frowned. "Where is your hair, girl?"

Sabrann grinned. "I pinned it up!" she shouted, twisting to show the back of her head and miming a stabbing action with her fingers, then turning back to shout, "Hairpins!"

The grandmother shook her head in disbelief. "This will all come to an end when you have a husband and some proper work to do!" She aimed a forefinger at Tilla. "What did she say?"

Sabrann leaned close to the old woman again and shouted, "She has heard that we are people of honor!"

"Yes," snapped the old woman, "but who says so?"

Sabrann hesitated before shouting, "Brica, grandmother!"

"Aha!" The woman smacked one blue-veined hand onto the blanket that was tucked around her knees. "So, my brother's family remember what honor is!" The chin rose and the creased lips clamped together. After a pause they opened again. "I hear Brica's man is losing his sight," she declared. "The gods are just."

Behind her back, Sabrann gave Tilla a look that was somewhere between weariness and apology. Tilla prayed silently to the goddess that she would not be turned away because of someone else's quarrel. She had nowhere else to go.

Sabrann bent down again. "She asks hospitality for nine nights!" she shouted. "Until her arm is healed! Then she will leave!"

"Why does she not go to my brother's family?"

"Because she seeks people of honor!" yelled Sabrann, clearly embarrassed at her grandmother's rudeness. "She does not want to stay with friends of the Romans!"

The grandmother plucked at the edge of the blanket, tugging it higher up on her lap, then returned her attention to the figure kneeling in front of her. "Tell me, daughter of Lugh," she said, "who are your family?"

Relieved, Tilla who was now Darlughdacha again had begun the business of naming her tribe, then her parents and her grandparents and her great-grandparents while the old woman frowned and put in occasional questions about brothers and cousins and who was married to whom and who had fought beside which warriors and eventually they found the connection they were both seeking: an obscure second cousin who had once sold cows to the old woman's late husband's brother. "Now we know who you are," declared the woman, nodding with satisfaction. "You are welcome to stay with us while your arm heals, Daughter of Lugh, child of the Brigantes. You may sleep with this one who stabs herself with hairpins."

Tilla inclined her head. "It is an honor, grandmother."

"She says it's an honor!" yelled Sabrann.

Extra bracken had been hauled from the drying racks and thrown down to make a bed on the floor of the small house where the unmarried girls slept. On that first night, comfortably fed, stretched out on a borrowed blanket, covered by the medicus's cloak—she would have to get rid of that, a problem she would think about later—Tilla had lain listening to strangers chattering in her own tongue. She rolled over to watch the glow of the firelight. A hound had wandered in earlier and settled close to the warmth. One of its ears twitched and it gave a sudden shudder as it dreamed. It occurred to her that there must be mice, and to her surprise it also occurred to her that she did not care. She took a deep breath, savoring the familiar smells of wool and wood smoke and muddy dog. As she thought, "I am happy," she was aware of a voice nearby in the darkness suggesting, "Perhaps she is sleeping."

"Are you sleeping, daughter of Lugh?" demanded a second voice.

"Shh, Sabrann!" urged a third girl. "Don't wake her!"

She closed her eyes and said nothing. She did not want to answer questions about where she had come from. She did not want to think about where she was going, or what she might find when she finally reached home. She wanted to lie here, in this bed, and remind herself over and over again: *I am free.*

The questions had followed soon enough, though, as had the expressions of sympathy when they found out her family was dead and her arm had been broken when she tried to defend herself against a Roman merchant who had brought her down from the north to sell her.

It was as much of the truth as it was safe for them to know, and it would have satisfied them, if only a Roman officer had not arrived that afternoon on an elderly horse and announced that he had come to look for a woman.

The blank expressions with which he was faced were a defense the family had used many times. In truth several of them understood what he was saying and all grasped what he wanted, but none chose to reveal that the woman he sought was inside a house not ten steps from where he stood.

The Roman had finally given up and tramped back through the gateway. It was not until he was out of sight that the arguments started.

By this time the men had arrived, summoned from the fields by those nearest to home who had heard the dogs.

Their guest, it seemed, had lied to them. (Her objection of "I told no lies!" was ignored.) She was a runaway. It was against the law to harbor runaways. She must go.

No, insisted other voices, she must stay. She was a Brigante, true, but not a complete foreigner. She was nearly one of their own people. It was a matter of honor not to betray her.

Tilla, realizing she was not expected to be a part of this argument, slipped back inside the house and sat by the door, listening as indignation rose on both sides of the debate. A couple of the women tried to intervene. Nobody took any notice.

Someone cried that it was a disgrace to deny hospitality to an injured woman.

"Her master is a healer. Let him deal with it."

"Her master is a Roman!"

"She has brought the army to our doors!"

"One man on an old horse?"

"Romans are like rats. Where there is one there are more."

"What if they decide to search the houses?"

"What, for one slave?"

"Enough!" It was the voice of the old woman, quavering but loud enough to silence the debate. "Enough," she repeated. Tilla wondered who had gone to fetch her and how much they had managed to explain. "The girl will stay here tonight. We will discuss this matter after dark. You all have work to do. Go."

The arguers did not bother to mute their grumbling as they dispersed, and Tilla overheard someone say, "She's not his slave, you fool."

"He said *ancilla*. *Ancilla* means slave."

"Never mind what *ancilla* means. She's not his slave. She's his woman."

The evening meal was finished. The other girls had gone to mind younger brothers and sisters. The adults had carried rush lights across to the big house and closed the door behind them. Tilla was squatting by the fire in the girls' house, busying herself grinding corn while she waited to be told her fate. It was a job that could be done, albeit slowly, with one hand.

As the stone scraped and rumbled round on its base she thought about the people she had left behind. She thought about the girls at Merula's, and the boy Lucco, who did not know that it was forbidden to eat swan, and Bassus, and Stichus with the ginger-colored hair, and the woman she had got to know at the bakery. She thought about the pregnant Brica whose man might lose his sight, and the handsome doctor who always smiled at her, but mostly she thought about the medicus, who hardly smiled at all. She supposed he was smiling even less now. It served him right. Behind her back he had made arrangements to have her sold. At first she had not believed Bassus, but later she had arrived back inside the fort with the shopping and there he was, standing in the street outside the hospital, chatting to the medicus as if they were old friends. That was when she finally understood what the medicus had meant when he had told her she would be useful to him. He had mended her arm not out of kindness, but out of greed. Instead of going to his house to prepare supper, she had turned around, made her way back out through the east gate, and kept walking.

The dog lying beside her suddenly lifted his head and turned toward the door. Moments later, a hinge creaked and a figure slipped in.

"My cousins are seeing to the little ones," announced Sabrann. "And my aunt is shouting for the grandmother." She dropped the sack on the ground. "I brought you some more corn, daughter of Lugh."

"Thank you."

It was the first time they had been able to speak privately since the argument erupted. Sabrann said, "They are talking about you."

"I know."

"I would have you stay."

"Others would have me leave."

Sabrann reached a hand inside the sack and trickled a fistful of corn into the hole in the center of the stone. "He was quite good-looking," she observed.

Tilla tightened her grip on the handle and carried on swiveling the top stone back and forth in a half circle over the lower one. "Who?"

"Your Roman. And not as short as most of them."

"No," Tilla agreed, stilling her arm as the girl reached a hand forward to scoop up the speckled flour that was trickling out from between the stones to form little mounds on the cloth.

Sabrann dropped the handful of flour into the bowl. "*Are* you his slave?"

The stone began to move again. "He thinks so."

"Did you go inside the fort?"

"Yes."

"Is it true what they say about the granary?"

Tilla frowned. "The granary?"

Sabrann nodded. "Everyone says they have a great big building filled with enough corn to stuff themselves for a year."

"It's possible. They like making great big buildings."

"Can you imagine how many families that would feed? And still they take the taxes."

"Is this why your grandmother is angry with Brica?"

"It was bad enough my great-uncle's family chose to trade with the army. Now one of them allows a soldier to father her children." Sabrann paused to watch the stone's movement around and back. "They say," she said, "that most of them have to pay women to lie with them."

"They speak the truth."

"Why would any woman do that? I would never do it."

"If you thought they would kill you," said Tilla slowly, "you might consider it."

The stone ground away and back, away and back before the girl murmured, "Forgive me. Everyone says I speak before I think."

Tilla shook her head. "No need. The goddess was protecting me. The medicus is not like that."

"People are saying you are his woman."

There was a grating sound from the millstones. Tilla let go of the handle and flexed her stiff fingers. "People are wrong."

Sabrann reached into the sack and gave a sudden giggle. "Can you keep a secret?"

"Always."

"Before we sent the corn tax in, we all took turns spitting in it."

Tilla smiled. "This was to wish them luck?"

"Of course." Sabrann cupped her hands to trickle more corn into the opening. "The boys wanted to piss in it, but Da said they would notice the smell. And they'd see it was damp. Spit, you can stir in."

Their eyes met, and both girls grinned.

"Your medicus might be eating spit," observed Sabrann.

"Good luck to him," said Tilla, seizing the handle and scraping the millstone faster back and forth on its half circle.

"My cousin could put a curse on him for you if you ask," Sabrann offered.

"Your cousin has the power of words?" Tilla had no intention of enlisting the cousin's help. If there were any cursing to be done, she would do it herself. Fortunately Sabrann, who was nodding eagerly, did not seem to have noticed that she had dodged the question.

"Not ten days ago," announced Sabrann, "my own cousin made a whole squad of soldiers fall over."

Tilla's hand paused. "How did she do that?"

"She was carrying water up to the house when about a hundred and fifty of them came running past, all squashed up together like they do, and you know how they stare at you?"

Tilla nodded.

"My cousin was tired of being stared at so she spoke a curse. And the moment the words were ended one of the soldiers tripped and all the ones behind him landed on top of him in a big heap. And when they got up one of them couldn't walk and had to be carried away with his leg strapped up. We were all laughing so hard we had to run and hide behind the fence."

"Daughter of Lugh!" It was a man's voice.

Enjoying the tale, they had noticed neither the dog nor the door announce his arrival.

Tilla got to her feet. "I am here."

"I am to take you to the grandmother."

There must have been twenty people gathered around the fire in the big house. The grandmother sat straight-backed in her chair and motioned for Tilla to kneel in front of her.

"Daughter of Lugh," she said, "everyone here has spoken about you. Now I wish to hear you speak for yourself."

Tilla got to her feet, brushing the bracken off her knees. She looked around at all the faces turned toward her, silent in the flickering firelight. She took a deep breath, raised her hands, and began a song.

"She is singing!" shouted a woman in the grandmother's ear.

"I know!" snapped the grandmother. "I can hear it!"

She sang some of the story of her ancestors. She sang a blessing on the grandmother and her family. And she sang a farewell.

69

EVEN AT THIS distance, Ruso could hear the roar from the amphitheater. The sports must be well under way; some of the Twentieth burning off energy and the others merely reaching a height of excitement that would wash over the town like a wave when the exit gates opened.

At Merula's, they were getting ready for a busy night. Bassus and Stichus were outside nailing the torches into their brackets ("Bastards pinch 'em else"). A few early customers were in, being served by Mariamne. Daphne was lumbering up the stairs with a pile of fresh sheets.

Behind the bar, Merula was tasting the offering from the hot drinks cauldron. She winced. "Not enough cinnamon," she snapped to a girl who was lining up jugs behind the bar.

Ruso reached for his purse as he approached. Merula saw the gesture, and her scowl gave way to a professional smile.

When he had settled his bill he said, "I need a word with Chloe."

The frown returned. "She's not working at the moment."

"I just need to give her a message."

"She's ill."

"I'm a doctor," Ruso pointed out.

The lines around Merula's mouth deepened, but she waved a hand in the direction of the kitchen. "If you can get her back to work," she said, "I'll be the one paying you."

Unusually, both doors of the kitchen were propped open, but despite the passage of air, the smoke and steam still made Ruso cough. One end of the table was covered in dirty bowls and discarded onion skins, and at the other a pale squad of uncooked pies was lined up ready to march into the oven. None of the staff who were attempting to work and argue at the same time took any notice of him. Ruso suspected that the decision to sell the kitchen slave on the eve of one of the busiest nights of the year had not been a popular one.

He rapped on the side door that led to the room where the girls slept, paused briefly, and then strode into the room.

A figure in one of the lower bunks rolled over to face him. The face was red and wet. The eyes were swollen with weeping.

"Chloe?"

"Don't come near me!"

"Chloe, about Lucco—"

"He's gone! They took him away!"

"I know."

"They promised I could keep him! They promised!" She sniffed violently. "He's all I've got!"

"I've seen him."

Chloe did not appear to have heard. With a sudden movement she swung her feet to the floor and leaped at him. "You did this!" she shrieked, pounding him with her fists. "You did this!"

Ruso made a grab for both arms and held them still. Instead of pulling away, Chloe thrust her distorted face into his. "You couldn't keep your nose out!" she wailed. "You had to show off what you'd found out, didn't you?"

Ruso held her at arm's length and looked her in the eye. "Sit down, Chloe," he ordered, "and listen to me."

"I won't sit down! Lucco is my life! It's your fault he's gone!"

"My fault?"

"Why did you have to interfere?" she shrieked. "Look what happened to Phryne! Everything you do causes trouble!"

"SIT DOWN!" roared Ruso, pushing her roughly onto the bed and narrowly missing banging her head on the top bunk.

She was silent now. Her hands were shaking as she lifted them to cover her face.

"He's gone," she moaned, "my little boy, my little boy, my baby . . ."

Ruso shifted a pile of clothes and a hairbrush and seated himself on the only chair. "I've seen him," he said. "He's with a visiting trader."

Chloe shuddered, then managed to say, "Is he all right? He'll be frightened."

"He wanted me to—"

He was about to explain about the message when the door burst open and Stichus announced, "I know where he is!"

"With the trader," groaned Chloe.

"I'm going down there to get him."

"I haven't got any money," said Chloe, reaching down to unfasten her ankle chain. "I've got this, and a bit saved up, but it's nothing."

"Don't matter," announced Stichus, "me and Merula have had words. I'm leaving. I get my share after closing time tonight. I'll go down there, put a bid on the boy, and pay up in the morning."

Chloe reached for his hand. "You'd do that? Really?"

Stichus grinned. It was not a pretty sight, but Ruso guessed it was kindly meant. The man, whom he had always thought of as Bassus's shadow, was showing commendable initiative. There was only one problem.

"They may not give you credit," he said. "There's a sign saying 'cash only.'"

Stichus stared at him as if only now noticing he was there. Finally he said, "Fine," and turned on his heel. "It's my money; I'll have it now."

When he had gone Ruso said, "Your son says to tell you that Bassus told Merula about the bad oysters."

"I know that already, bless him," said Chloe. She sniffed and groped for something to wipe her nose on, finally settling on a soggy ball of rag that she shook open and applied to her blotchy face. "It's all my fault."

Ruso, relieved that he was no longer being blamed, said nothing.

"I should never have said anything about Saufeia's stupid letter," said Chloe, unexpectedly. "Then you wouldn't be poking your nose in and asking questions . . ." She paused to sniff. "And Bassus wouldn't know I'd talked. He told Merula about Lucco's silly trick with the oysters so she'd sell him. And he did it to get back at me."

Ruso let out a long sigh. It was his turn to lower his head into his hands. He should have had more sense than to question Bassus about the letter. "I'm sorry," he said. "I'm just trying to find out what's happened to Tilla."

Chloe stretched herself out on the bunk and lay with her eyes open, gazing at the slats holding the mattress above. "I knew it would all go wrong in the end," she said.

From beyond the kitchen door there was a crash and a shout of exasperation. Ruso took a deep breath. He stared at his toes. He wished he were somewhere else. Another country. Another lifetime. Anywhere he might never have met the girl he called Tilla. If he had ignored the fuss around the fountain, none of this would have happened. But Chloe was right: He *had* to interfere. And from that moment everything had gone wrong. It was as if he was cursed from the moment those beautiful eyes had . . . gods above! Now he was starting to believe all that rubbish himself.

Stichus reappeared, looking angry. "I can't get the cash," he said. "Miserable cow says it's locked in a strongroom and she hasn't got the key. I'm going down there anyway."

"Stop!" Ruso was reaching for his purse. "How much are you expecting from your wages?"

Stichus waved a hand to indicate that anything Ruso could offer was nothing compared to his need. "A bloody sight more than you've got."

For answer, Ruso knelt on the floor and upended his purse. Chloe gasped.

Ruso glanced at Stichus. The man opened his mouth and closed it again as if he had lost the power of words.

"I'm about to repay a loan," explained Ruso. "But that can wait a day." Since Tilla had vanished, Priscus could hardly seize her if the Aesculapian loan was not paid on time.

When Stichus had hurried out with the money, Chloe said, "I'm sorry for the things I said. I think you do try to do the right thing."

"I'm beginning to wonder why I bother."

He glanced at her. Chloe had managed a weak smile.

"I examined Saufeia's body after they pulled her out of the river," he told her. "Someone said to me that no one should die like that. And it's true."

Chloe sat up and put her bare feet on the floor. "If I knew where Tilla was," she said, "I would tell you. I don't. But I can tell you some of what you want to know. If you promise, really really promise, to keep quiet about it now? You won't tell anyone or ask any more questions?"

"If it will help someone, I can't stay silent."

"How can it? It's about Saufeia, and she's dead."

"Very well."

"I don't know who killed her in the end. But I do know the thing they're so frightened of everyone finding out. Saufeia was a Roman citizen."

Ruso felt himself blink. "A citizen?" he repeated. A citizen could not be a slave, let alone a slave forced to work as a prostitute. "How could she be . . . ?"

"What she told us—what she started to tell everybody before Bassus gave her one of his little private coaching sessions—was, she was a centurion's daughter who'd run away with her boyfriend after a fight with her stepfather."

A centurion's daughter. So that explained the smattering of education. And the knowledge of army expletives.

"Then she fell out with the boyfriend—that was the one thing she was good at, falling out with people—and he dumped her on the road. She had no money, of course. So she went to an inn to ask for help and got picked up by some lowlife who said he'd take her home. Well, of course he didn't. So she ended up here.

"As soon as she got here she started whining about who she was, but Merula was short-staffed so she told her to shut up and they put her to work. They must have known they'd done a stupid thing, but by then they were in serious trouble anyway, so they just kept on serving her to the customers and everybody was too scared to talk because Merula said we'd all be arrested and whipped. Of course they couldn't ever let her out. She must have realized they were just going to work her to death. Or sell her on to someplace worse." Chloe gave a bitter laugh. "Don't believe any of those stories about girls from places like this being rescued by men who fall in love with them. I've been here longer than all of them, and I can tell you, it doesn't happen."

"Tilla told me about Daphne's punishment."

"Daphne should have had more sense. Most of the men we meet aren't as soft as poor old Decimus."

"She was trying to copy Asellina?"

"I always thought it was odd that Asellina didn't get in touch," said Chloe. "The truth is, the only way you can go from here is down."

Ruso wondered if the men who came to relax with these girls realized the true ghastliness they were paying to support. "You've been fortunate."

"I've been determined," she said. "I have a child to think of." She dropped her head into her hands. "What if someone outbids him?"

"He has plenty of money," said Ruso, whose own unspoken question was, *What if he runs off with it?* "Tell me some more about Saufeia."

Chloe nodded. "The cook took pity on her and got her some writing things. She wrote a letter to the legate at the fort asking to be sent home. The cook was supposed to deliver it, but Bassus saw it and said he'd take it instead. We all thought she'd get a beating when he read it, but it looked as though he'd just gone and delivered it, 'cause a couple of days later some official lackey arrived here with a letter for her. Said he wouldn't hand it over to anybody else. She burned it as soon as she'd read it and she wouldn't tell anybody what was in it, but I got the idea she thought somebody was coming to save her."

Ruso scratched his head. "But if someone was coming to get her, why did she run away? Surely if she'd waited they'd have sent an officer down with a whole squad, made arrests . . ."

"Like they tried with Phryne."

Ruso scratched his ear. "I truly meant well, Chloe. I was told the child was kidnapped."

"You were told that by Tilla?"

He nodded.

"She should have known better."

Ruso shrugged. "She was convinced it was true. She was cooking up potions to help."

"I meant, she should have known better than to tell you. Of course Phryne was kidnapped."

"What?"

"I tell you, if they ever get their hands on that Claudius Innocens, he's a dead man. After Saufeia you'd think they'd learn, but he offered them Phryne cheap and they didn't ask too many questions. And nobody 'round here was going to say anything, not after everything that had happened."

"But I was told the second spear questioned Phryne in private!"

Chloe pursed her lips. "Your second spear's men aren't very bright. One of them told our lovely management why he was here before he sent them to fetch her. So they had time to have a word with her before they brought her downstairs. They told her a string of lies about how much trouble she'd be in if she didn't say what they wanted. She was too scared to know who to trust."

"So where did Bassus get her documents?"

"Bassus and Innocens between them," said Chloe, "must know every forger in the province."

Ruso shook his head slowly from side to side, as if trying to settle all this jumbled information in his brain. "Tilla told me I was poking about in a wasps' nest," he observed.

"We did try to warn you."

Ruso frowned. "Let me get this straight. You're telling me Saufeia knew help was coming but she still ran away?"

"No," said Chloe, "that's not what I'm saying."

"It was staged!" said Ruso suddenly. "They couldn't get rid of her here without everyone knowing so they forged an official letter telling her someone would meet her outside."

Chloe gave a weak smile. "Does it take you this long to diagnose all your patients?"

"Without the letter or any witnesses to the murder, nobody can prove anything."

"Of course," Chloe agreed. "Saufeia was stupid, but they aren't. The letter probably held instructions for her to burn it."

"Which she did because she thought she was keeping it secret." Ruso paused. "This is only a theory. It could be wrong."

"It isn't," said Chloe. "Listen. They've always let me out because they knew I'd come back for Lucco. But after Asellina went one or two girls started to get ideas, so they tightened up. I'm the only one who gets past them now. All that stuff about escorting girls for their own safety? It's rubbish. It's so nobody makes a run for it. Every slave here is in chains, Doctor. They just aren't the sort you can see. Saufeia wouldn't have got out of here unless they wanted her to."

"The doormen let her out, followed her, and then killed her."

Chloe shrugged. "I don't know. If they didn't, they know who did. It doesn't much matter, does it? Nobody knows who her family was or what her real name was, and it won't bring her—" She broke off to look up as the door opened. "Lucco!" she shrieked, leaping to her feet and pulling the boy into her arms. "Oh, Lucco, my baby!"

Stichus, standing in the doorway, caught Ruso's eye and grinned. "Bet you thought I'd run off with the cash," he said.

"It never crossed my—" Ruso's lie was stifled by an enthusiastic kiss from Chloe, who then flung herself at Stichus in a similar fashion before seizing her son again and ordering him to say thank you.

"It was nothing," said Ruso, finding his mouth stuck in a foolish grin and relieved that at last he seemed to have gotten something right. He was heading for the door when Stichus said, "Stay a minute, Doc, all right? I got something to say and I want a proper witness." He stepped in and closed the door.

Chloe glanced at him, puzzled.

"I should have said this a long time ago," announced Stichus. He placed a hand on Lucco's head. "I don't know what your mother's told you but I know she knows. And she's never said nothing to me but I know she knows I know too."

Lucco, Ruso felt, was making a good job of trying to look impressed without having the faintest idea what his rescuer was talking about.

Stichus cleared his throat. "This here young man," he said, addressing Chloe and Ruso, "is my legal property as of today. But I don't think of him that way. You and I both know" (here he glanced at Chloe, who was looking apprehensive) "that this here young man is my own flesh and blood."

Lucco's eyes widened. He turned to his mother. "Am I?"

Chloe reached up and tweaked Stichus's fading red hair, then grinned at Lucco. "You never guessed?"

Lucco scratched his head, giving his father—who now seemed not to know what to do—a hint to remove the hand.

"That all right with you, then?" Stichus asked him.

"I *knew* there was something," said Lucco. "You were always nicer to me than the others were."

Ruso, not needed here and due at the hospital, tried to slip around Stichus toward the door. Stichus's hand landed on the latch before he got there. "Right," he announced, "busy night ahead, got to get back to work. You coming, son?"

After they were gone Chloe took Ruso's hand. "I'm grateful, Doctor. I know you won't let me show you how much, but I'll see he pays you back in the morning."

"It was nothing," Ruso repeated. "I have to go now, there are patients . . ."

"If Tilla was here I'd ask her to put a blessing on you."

"If Tilla were here I wouldn't have had the money," he observed. "The gods move in strange ways."

"They do," agreed Chloe. "Who would have guessed that for all these years old Stichus has been thinking my boy was his son?"

Ruso paused with his hand on the door latch. "Isn't he?"

Chloe grinned. "He is now," she said.

70

TILLA WAS SINGING quietly to herself. The sack of provisions swung and bumped against the small of her back with each step. Its weight was a pleasure. It meant independence. There was no one out here to give her orders or ask where she was going.

She was not entirely sure where she was going herself. After two years she had little idea whether anything was left of her home. Whatever she found, though, would be better than the place she had left: a place built by foreign warriors who fought not for honor but for money and hid their shame by bullying everyone else. In the end even the medicus had turned out to be little better than his companions. She had begun to think he could be trusted. She had even begun to grow fond of him. Now she realized what a fool she had been. The time she had spent with Sabrann had opened her eyes anew to the twisted thinking of the emperor's men and all those who served them. She was lucky to have escaped before she had been hopelessly corrupted like Merula, a woman who survived by trampling on others. Or Chloe, who had no vision of anything beyond the walls of the bar.

She wished she had been able to bring the child with her: the one they had called Phryne. When she reached home she would spread the word of what had happened to her. Perhaps the child's people would send warriors. Perhaps not. There were cowards among the Brigantes too. Elders who acted out of fear and called it being sensible, or abandoned their own ways and called it progress. The taint of Rome was like rot spreading through a crate of apples.

There was a dip in the road ahead. She could see the tops of wooden rails that must be the sides of a bridge. Beyond them, set well back—the Romans were afraid of ambushes, and always chopped down everything close to the road—stood a massive tree that was the right shape for an oak. That must be the marker for the track Sabrann had told her to follow.

As she looked, two cavalry horses appeared over the brow of the next rise. Tilla tugged the sack into a new position on her shoulder and kept an eye on the riders, who were progressing toward her at a leisurely trot. She slowed, not wanting to meet them on the narrow bridge.

It occurred to her that if she had a horse, she could make the journey far more easily. The weak arm would make it hard to mount, but once she was up, she would manage one-handed. She was a good rider. She had been allowed to ride her father's horses as a child. Perhaps someone would lend her a pony. Perhaps, if they wouldn't, she would wait until no one was looking and help herself.

She heard the clump of hoofbeats on the wooden bridge. She kept walking, head down, close to the shoulder so the horses would have plenty of room to pass.

Something inside the sack was poking into her back. As she shifted the weight the sack pulled at the fabric on her shoulder. She felt the gray hood slip backward. Quickly, she lifted her right hand to pull it forward again, but the cloth was caught under the weight of the sack and her weak arm did not have the strength to tug it free.

The horses were only about thirty paces away now. She turned to one side, swung the sack to the ground, and bent over, busying herself with adjusting the hood and pinning it back into place. She could hear the approaching crunch of hooves on the gravel. The men were talking to each other.

The hood was back in place. The horses were almost level with her now. She slid her right arm in under the cloak, realizing as she did so that two or three inches of grimy bandage had been poking out of the end of her sleeve.

The horses were next to her. The riders were still chatting as if they had noticed nothing. The bandage had probably looked like a glimpse of undertunic.

They had passed. She grabbed the neck of the sack and swung it back over her shoulder.

Behind her, the hoofbeats faltered and began to grow louder. The riders were coming back.

"Halt!"

Tilla froze.

"What's your name, girl?"

She turned, keeping her head bowed in a pretense of respect. "Brica, sir."

"Brica, eh? What are you doing all the way out here, Brica?"

Tilla stared at the polished hooves of the front horse. "I go to visit my aunt, sir. She is sick."

The second rider moved around to take up a position beside her.

"What do you think?" said the first rider to him. "She look like a Brica to you?"

"Hm." There was a creak of leather as the second rider bent down from his saddle to examine her. "Chin up, girl."

Tilla lifted her head a fraction.

"You know what she looks like to me?" offered the first rider, circling his horse behind her and nudging her forward into the middle of the road. "She looks like 'Attractive female, age about 20.' "

"Slim, about five feet four inches," continued his companion as if they were quoting from something. "Hold out your arm, gorgeous."

Tilla slid the sack off her shoulder and held out her left arm.

"The other one."

Her left hand darted inside the cloak and tugged down the offending sleeve before she reached out her right arm. "If you touch me," she said, "my master will have you punish."

A sword swished out of its scabbard. A blade glinted in front of her. Its tip plucked back the fabric of her sleeve, revealing the dirty linen bandage.

"I think you're the one who gets to be 'punish,' gorgeous." Both horses were circling her now. "We're the ones who get the reward."

Tilla let the sack fall, grabbed her skirts, and dodged through the gap between the two horses. Leaping across the ditch, she scrambled up onto the rough grass and raced toward the woods. If she could just get between the trees, she stood a chance . . .

Over the rasp of her own breath she heard cheering. Then the approach of hoofbeats. There was a horse cantering on either side of her now. She slowed: They slowed. She speeded up: They increased their pace. The men were laughing. Playing with her. She stopped dead, spun around, and ran back the other way, but it was hopeless. There was no cover ahead of her now: only the open road. The thud of hooves on turf surrounded her once more. The horses were crowding her. Hands reached down and flung her cloak back over her shoulders. "Now!" shouted one of the men. She ducked. Too late. They grabbed her under both arms and scooped her up with a swift, practiced movement. Legs flailing helplessly, boots brushing the tips of the grasses, she dangled between the two horsemen as their mounts cantered back to the road.

71

RUSO SHOULD HAVE gone straight to the hospital, but instead he hurried to the house and spent several minutes scratching notes onto a tablet, which he then thrust into the trunk with all the versions of the *Concise Guide*.

Albanus was waiting for him with the look of anxiety that seemed to be his permanent expression lately. "Lots of people have been asking for you, sir. There's a line waiting in the hall."

"Where's Valens?" Ruso was still breathless after sprinting from the house.

"Officer Valens has been taking the urgent cases and telling the rest you'll be back any minute, sir. And Officer Priscus said you had an appointment with him—about the Aesculapian Thanksgiving Fund?"

"Yes, I know about that one. Anything else?"

"I need a word with you too, sir."

"Is it urgent?"

"Not really, sir."

"Good. Let's get working on this line."

He had almost emptied the bench in the hall when there was a commotion in the corridor and the door shuddered as someone fell against it. Ruso glanced up. "Put the bar across, Albanus, will you?"

The clerk leaped to secure the door and Ruso carried on cleaning up a nastily torn ear as the shouting faded away down the corridor. "How did you get this?" he asked.

"Over at the wrestling," explained its owner. "We're cheering our lad on and there was a bit of an exchange with some lads sitting behind, and next thing I know I'm upside down with somebody's boot kicking the side of my head."

"Ah," said Ruso. "Sport. Always brings out the best in a man. Albanus, just poke your head into the corridor and make sure there's nobody lying dead out there, will you?"

Moments later Albanus returned to report that some plasterers from the Twentieth had got into a dispute with a visiting crew of sailors. Knives were out before the centurial staff had been able to wade in and restore order. Now the wounded of both groups had been brought in for treatment and, having tried to carry on the fight in the corridor, had been sent to wait under guard in separate rooms.

"Idiots," observed the man with the torn ear.

"What a joy payday is," remarked Ruso. "I'll just pop a few stitches in this ear, then you can go and have a nice nap while I have the pleasure of meeting the navy."

In fact it was Valens who dealt with the sailors while the plasterers were assigned to Ruso. Only one was seriously injured: a stab wound that had probably penetrated a lung. The man required some immediate and careful patching before he was admitted for observation, nursing care, and an outcome whose uncertainty would have frightened him if he had been sober. The others he released into the care of their centurion, who looked willing to inflict a few injuries himself if anyone showed any more signs of misbehaving.

"We'll be seeing that group lined up outside HQ tomorrow," observed Ruso as they left. "What's next?"

" 'Evening, Ruso." Valens appeared around the door in a gruesomely bloodstained tunic. "Good of you to turn up."

"Nice outfit," Ruso observed.

"Don't insult me; I've taken time off from my onerous duties to bring you some news. They've found Tilla."

"Where? Is she all right? Where is she?"

Valens shrugged. "According to my sources, a road patrol found her taking a stroll eight or nine miles out of town."

"Where is she? Is she all right?"

"I imagine they've taken her to Priscus in the hope of a reward. As advertised."

A dreadful thought crossed Ruso's mind. "To Priscus?"

"That is what it said on the advertisements, isn't it?"

Ruso turned to Albanus. "What time is it?"

"I think I heard the eleventh hour just now, sir."

"Is the cashier's office still open?"

Albanus frowned. "I doubt it, sir. They'll have locked up some time ago and gone to the sports."

"Tell the next patient to wait a minute. I need to go and see Priscus."

Ruso sprinted along the corridor, narrowly missing a collision with a couple of orderlies carrying a man on a stretcher. When he reached the office, it was locked. One of the records room clerks informed him that Officer Priscus had been called away. The clerk's tone suggested that it was very convenient for Officer Priscus to be called away early on pay-day while everyone else had to stay behind and work.

"Where are the records for the Aesculapian fund?"

The clerk looked surprised. "In Officer Priscus's room, sir."

"And if someone wanted to make a payment while he was out?"

"We'd tell him to come back tomorrow, sir. We aren't allowed to handle cash. We don't have the facilities."

Valens had gone by the time Ruso got back to his surgery. "Albanus," he said, "I need to get at the records of the Aesculapian fund. I need to, uh—find out how much I owe. I was supposed to pay it back today and I haven't had time."

Albanus frowned. "They'll be in the administrator's office, sir. Nobody can get in there."

Ruso looked him in the eye. "Is that definitely true, Albanus? Surely a man as thorough as Priscus would arrange for a spare key somewhere in case one got lost?"

Albanus was chewing the end of his stylus. "I really couldn't say, sir. Officer Priscus wouldn't tell the clerks anything like that."

"No, because he's a secretive bastard. But you know where it is, don't you?"

"Sir, I really can't—"

"Albanus, I am your superior officer and this is an order. Find a way to get me into that room."

Albanus stood at attention. "Yes, sir!"

"I'm sorry, sir. I don't think it's here."

They had been through the whole of the Aesculapian Thanksgiving Fund file twice, the second time struggling to read by lamplight. Ruso sighed. "It's no use. He's taken it with him."

"Is there anything I can do, sir? Shall I keep looking?"

Ruso shook his head. "Put all this stuff away and lock up. I've got to go out for a while. I'll go and warn Valens he's on his own."

Valens was predictably annoyed but unable to prevent his colleague from leaving.

Making his way down to the south gate Ruso heard footsteps running along behind him in the darkness. "Doctor, sir!" gasped a breathless Albanus.

"I'm in a hurry, Albanus. Can't it wait?"

"No, sir, I don't think it can."

"Walk with me."

The clerk fell into step with him. "Sir, you remember I said there was that one thing I needed to say to you?"

"What was it?"

"Well, sir, you know I went through all the incoming post logs looking for a letter from Saufeia and I didn't find one?"

"You've found one?"

"Not exactly, sir. But I thought, maybe it came in some other way and somebody replied to it. So I went back and looked through the outgoing logs instead."

"And?"

"And I found it. A letter to Saufeia. Dated two days before she died."

"Is there a file copy?"

"No, sir, just a listing in the log. Date, who to, who from."

"And are you going to tell me who it was from, or do I have to guess?"

"Yes, sir! No, sir! I'd be glad to tell you, sir. To tell you the truth I was a bit concerned."

"Albanus, *who is it*?"

Albanus told him. Ruso turned to look at the shadowy figure of his clerk. "Are you absolutely sure?"

"Yes, sir."

"Who else knows about this?"

"I haven't said anything to anybody else, sir."

"Don't. Don't say anything to anyone unless . . ." Ruso hesitated. They were approaching the torches of the main gate now. A couple of men passed them in the dark. "Don't say anything unless I, uh—unless I appear to have got into difficulties tonight. If that happens, go to my house tomorrow morning and go through my documents very thoroughly. Then I want you to tell the whole damn province."

72

LET THE DOCTOR through!" roared a guard as the gates swung open and an untidy jumble of men surged in under the torchlit archway, eager to be out of the rain that was now cooling the payday fervor of the Twentieth. Ruso shouldered his way against the flow.

"Let the doctor through!" echoed a second guard, helpfully shoving the nearest man aside and dragging Ruso forward.

Once outside, he sprinted along the street, weaving in and out of groups of off-duty legionaries. Several were under escort and attempting to step smartly. A couple had abandoned their legs altogether and were being carried home by their comrades. The bars must be closing. So, this was civilized Britannia. A place where the army felt it could trust the locals enough to relax in their presence. Ruso was willing to bet that these sort of antics were not going on in the hill country.

There was a rectangle of light around Priscus's front door but no one answered his knocking. He slammed the flat of his hand three times against the wooden paneling so the whole door shook. "Priscus! It's Ruso!"

"Oy! You!" bellowed a voice from down the street. "Get away from that door!"

Ruso slammed his hand against the door again. "Priscus! Open up!" He spun around to explain, "Doctor. Medical emergency," just as the pair of junior officers moved apart in the darkness to each grab an arm.

"Name?" demanded one of them.

He told them.

"Where's your bag of tricks?"

"I came straight here," said Ruso, truthfully enough.

"Why aren't they letting you in, then?"

"I don't know. This is definitely the house." He turned and hammered on the door again. "Priscus!"

"There's someone in," observed one of the men, bending to try and peer through the gap at the side of the door. "There's a light. Perhaps he's too ill to get to the door."

Ruso lifted one boot to crash it against the lock, but Priscus's house was made of stronger stuff than the linen closet. The door shuddered and held firm.

"Don't you worry, Doc," one of the men assured him. "We'll get you in. Ready?"

Moments later the three of them were picking themselves up from Priscus's door, which was now detached from its splintered frame and lying flat on the hall tiles.

Insisting that he didn't need a stretcher team, he dismissed his helpers and strode down the hallway to where a figure—not the one he had expected—was standing with folded arms in the doorway of Priscus's living room.

"Bassus! Where is she? What's he done with her?"

"He can't see you," said Bassus, showing no sign of surprise at the unusual form of entry. "He's talking to me. Put the door back on your way out."

The veteran's silhouette filled the narrow corridor. He was a fraction shorter than Ruso but a lot heavier, and he was a professional doorman. Ruso wished he had not dismissed his eager comrades in arms. If it came to a struggle, he was not going to get in.

"The army won't let you sell her," he said. "He's trying to take her for the hospital fund."

"Who?"

"Tilla. He's found Tilla. Didn't he tell you?"

From somewhere behind Bassus came a cry of "Doctor!" Surprisingly, Priscus sounded relieved that he had arrived.

"Miserable bastard's not telling me anything," observed Bassus. "Yet."

"She was picked up earlier today," said Ruso. "He's got her somewhere. Let me talk to him."

Bassus appeared to think about it for a moment, then said, "Be my guest," and stepped aside to allow Ruso past.

Priscus, hair awry, was huddled in one of the wicker chairs. He half rose to exclaim, "Doctor!" then shrank back into the chair as Bassus approached.

"Pull up a seat," suggested Bassus, gesturing to a stool in the corner.

"I haven't come here for a rest," retorted Ruso. "I've come to find my servant."

"Suit yourself." Bassus flung himself into the second wicker chair. Priscus closed his eyes to shut out the sight of the doorman's large boots being planted on the delicate table.

Underneath the table, the fruit bowl lay in pieces. Its contents rested where they had rolled across the floor. The servant was nowhere to be seen. Ruso, who had no idea what was going on and no time to find out, said, "Priscus, where's Tilla?"

The administrator cleared his throat. "As steward of the Aesculapian fund—"

"Where is she?"

"As steward of the Aesculapian fund, I have a duty to . . ."

Ruso's steps made a sharp sound on the tiled floor. Standing over Priscus, he emphasized each word. "Where is Tilla?"

Priscus sat up in the chair and made an attempt to push his hair back into place. "As I have just been telling this . . . man," he said, glancing at Bassus, "I will not be bullied. The girl is in a safe place and I must remind you that following default of a loan repayment, I have a perfect right as steward of—"

"I want to see her. Now."

The wicker creaked as Priscus squirmed in the chair and glanced at Bassus. "Under the circumstances," he said, "I could perhaps arrange release of the girl on receipt of immediate cash payment. With an additional sum as penalty for a missed deadline plus the cost of recovery."

It was Bassus who demanded, "How much?" as Ruso said, "The girl. Now. You'll get the money first thing in the morning."

"Oh dear, no, I'm afraid not. It has to be a simultaneous—"

"Don't be ridiculous," snapped Ruso, wishing he had not lent all of his spare money to Stichus. "Nobody's going to walk around at night carrying that much cash. You've got my signature on the agreement. Just hand her over and you'll get your money in the morning."

Bassus was shaking his head sadly. "He needs the money tonight, Doc. He's got a few debts to pay himself." He reached down into the chair and waved a writing tablet at Priscus. "Haven't you, sunshine?"

Priscus sighed and looked up at Ruso as if hoping for support. "I have already explained," he said, "that the money is in long-term investments. I am not in a position to withdraw such investments without warning, and certainly not at this hour of the night."

"Long-term investments? Hah! You've been feathering your nest!"

"Bassus," said Ruso, feeling he should show more loyalty than he felt, "you're talking to an officer. Watch what you're saying."

"I know what I'm saying." Bassus lifted his legs and gave the table a swift kick. It toppled over. The crash as it landed on the tiles echoed around the room. "Oops," he said, "there goes another long-term investment."

Priscus sprang to his feet. "Really! I must protest!"

Bassus moved surprisingly fast for such a heavy man. The chair skidded backward on the tiles as Priscus landed in it, gasping for breath.

"Now listen to me, you scraggy-faced runt," growled Bassus, "me and Stich, we work our balls off out there, and we don't get nothing from you except trouble and promises."

Ruso looked from one to the other of them, baffled. He had assumed Bassus was collecting a debt. Why would Merula's doormen be expecting anything from Priscus?

Bassus was thrusting the writing tablet forward so that it was almost touching Priscus's nose. "There it is, see? All written down. All agreed. My retirement fund. You told us it was there."

"It is there."

"Good. Because I want it now. And if you don't hand it over, I'll have the girl instead."

"The girl is the property of the Aesculapian Thanksgiving Fund!" insisted Priscus. "She's legionary business."

"Legionary business, huh? I'll bet the legion don't know how much it's chipped in to the cost of *this* place. Where is she?"

"She's not here."

Bassus leaned forward and hauled Priscus out of the chair. He was saying, "Well, tell me where she is and we'll go and get her, shall we?" but

Ruso was not listening. He was moving toward the sound that had just turned his stomach. It was the muffled sound of a woman screaming.

It was the shrill, tormented shriek of a woman in terrible pain. By the time he burst into Priscus's bedroom it had stopped. There was nobody in the room. Just the empty bed, a few cupboards too small to hide a prisoner, and . . .

He stepped forward and tugged aside the curtain covering part of the back wall. This should surely have been the rear boundary of the property, but instead of blank plaster there was a door. It had already been forced: The lock was hanging loose. As he dragged it open, another scream filled his ears.

The dark space in front of him seemed to be a corridor. "Tilla!" he yelled, heading toward faint streaks of light that marked a doorway. "Tilla!" He collided with something that fell over with a crash of broken crockery. It barely masked the screaming. Holy gods, what were they doing to her?

"Leave her alone!" he roared.

All three occupants of the room looked up as he burst in: the naked, sweating, and breathless woman squatting on the floor and the people either side of her, holding her by the arms.

"You'll be all right," one of them assured her. "The doctor's here."

In reply the naked woman grimaced, flung her head back, and gave a terrible groan of pain. It was the pain of a woman in labor. Instead of Tilla, Ruso had found Daphne. He glanced around the room, mystified.

"What are you doing here?"

"She can't give birth in the bar, can she?" retorted one of the girls supporting Daphne. "So they've dumped us back here, out of the way. We don't know what to do."

"It's stuck," added Phryne, who was holding Daphne's other arm.

Ruso stared at Daphne. He was an army surgeon. He was a medic. He was a man. A man who knew the limits of his knowledge, and a difficult delivery might well be beyond them, even if he had his case with him. "Where's the midwife?"

"On another call," explained the girl grimly.

Ruso lifted a candle from its stand and squatted in front of Daphne. "I'm just going to take a quick look and see what's going on," he explained.

It was worse than he had feared. It was not even a breech. What he could see of the child was not a head nor a pair of buttocks, but a tiny hand. The baby was wedged sideways. There was no way to bring it out at this angle. If it would not turn, he would have to improvise a scalpel with the knife slung at his belt. And someone would have to decide which should be allowed to live: the mother or the child.

Before he could say anything, the cords in Daphne's neck tightened, her mouth opened, and she let out another long and piercing shriek, as if all the pain and horror of her mutilation were finally being released to reverberate around the room.

There was a brief silence as Daphne paused for breath. He put his hand on her arm. "Try not to push," he urged. "I'm going to get help." He had no idea how much Tilla knew about delivering babies. He prayed that it was more than he did.

He realized where he was on the way back to find Priscus. They had put Daphne in one of the rooms that looked out onto Merula's narrow back yard: the private living quarters that joined onto the building behind. The bedrooms used by Merula and the doormen.

It was becoming clear to Ruso that he had underestimated Priscus. The man's tentacles stretched far beyond the hospital. It seemed that the administrator employed the doormen at Merula's. Quite possibly he controlled Merula herself. What had the civilian liaison officer said? *Invest in a bar by all means, but don't get involved in running it. It won't go down too well higher up.* With the help of his builder, Priscus had contrived a private entrance through which his every appetite could be indulged while his respectable front door remained unsullied by the taint of the bar trade.

Ruso heard the administrator before he saw him. The man was still protesting, the pitch of his voice rising with fear. Bassus, not distracted by Daphne's screams, had him pinned against the wall of the living room. Priscus peered around as Ruso approached. "Ruso! Help me! He's gone mad! He'll kill me!"

Ruso addressed himself to Bassus. "If we don't get Tilla in there in the next few minutes," he said, "Daphne will be dead and so will the baby. That's not going to help your retirement fund."

"See?" grunted Bassus, making a sudden movement that resulted in a howl of pain from the administrator. "He's not going to help you. He's on my side. Where is she?"

With something like a sob, Priscus said, "She's quite safe. I promise. Let me go."

Bassus tightened his grip. Priscus gasped.

"Where?" demanded Bassus.

Priscus seemed to be having trouble getting the words out. "In the—in the storeroom. Behind the shop—" The sentence ended with a shriek.

"Which shop?"

"Next door!" screamed Priscus. "The basket maker's!" He twisted awkwardly to look across the room. "That key on the hook."

73

TILLA HAD SAT exhausted on the floor of the little storeroom for some time, wondering what to do next. She did not understand why the officer with the many long words and the odd hair had ignored her requests to send a message to the medicus. Nor did she understand why he had brought her to this place outside the fort. She knew where she was. Even if she had not recognized the route from the glimpses afforded by a badly tied blindfold, she would have guessed from the rattle of the brittle willow wands that rolled away beneath her as she sat down.

It must be dark outside now. The shop had fallen silent. She had heard the shutters being dragged across and the clank of the lock. It seemed no one would come for her until morning.

Then, not long ago, there had been shouting and banging nearby. She thought she recognized the voice of the medicus. She had leaped up and begun hammering on the door. "My Lord! It is Tilla! I am here, my Lord! Help me!"

From somewhere outside there was a loud crash, and then the voices faded. No one came. Perhaps it was not him. Perhaps he would not have helped her anyway.

Not long after that came the sound of voices raised in anger. The words were muffled by the stone of the wall. She could not make out what was happening.

Her captors had left her necklace in place. She ran a forefinger along the smooth curve of one of the acorns. She would not taste the poison yet. But if she could escape no other way, it was ready.

The willow wands rattled as she stood up. The officer had ordered the man in the shop to help him drag something heavy across the door after she was shut in. Tilla felt around for the latch, running her fingers around the cold metal shapes and trying to understand how the mechanism worked. The latch was the kind that could be opened from both sides. It seemed the officer had not bothered to wedge it shut, relying on the weight of whatever they had put against the door to hold it closed. She bent down and snapped the end off a willow wand, then poked it under the latch to hold it up. She cleared the rest of the wands back to make a space for her feet. Then she braced herself with her back against the door and the boots the medicus had bought her planted firmly on the floor, and pushed.

Nothing happened.

Tilla relaxed, took a deep breath, and heaved again. Something behind her moved a fraction, then fell back into place as her strength gave out. She stood up, shrugged her bruised shoulders to loosen them, shook each leg in turn, then braced herself a third time, took a deep breath, pursed her lips, and heaved. The door moved farther, but not far enough. The fourth attempt was worse than the first. She was sliding down in despair when she heard someone jangling the lock on the shutters. A man was shouting her name. A man she had once hoped she could trust. She held her breath.

"Are you in there? Tilla, it's me! Ruso! Can you hear me?" And then, to someone else, "Can you see how this damned thing works?"

The medicus had planned to sell her. But he was a better prospect than the one with the odd hair, who reminded her of a dead spider. "I am here, my Lord!" she cried, banging on the door again. "Help me!"

Moments later she was almost knocked backward by the enthusiasm of his embrace. "Tilla! Thank the gods! Where have you been? Are you all right?" He drew back. "What's the matter?"

She shook her head. She must remember why he was pleased to see her. It would be so easy to be deceived again. "It is nothing, my Lord." If she explained how the cavalrymen had left her bruised and stiff, he would pretend to care.

"I was afraid you were dead." The dark eyes were searching hers. "Where have you been?"

She swallowed. "You would sell me."

"What? No, you don't understand—I never wanted to—"

From somewhere back in the shop, Bassus's voice cut him short. "You never wanted to? Are you joking? We had a deal!"

"Nobody will be selling her," put in another voice. "That slave is the legal property of the Aesculapian Thanksgiving Fund."

The medicus turned and demanded to know how long she had been locked up here. "Until the deadline ran out, I suppose?"

They both ignored the torrent of words that followed.

"So," she said to him, "it is true. You would sell me."

She tried not to flinch as the medicus took her by the shoulders. He looked as he must look when he was trying not to tell a patient bad news. "No," he said. "I mean, I didn't . . ."

She raised one hand to her throat.

"Well, yes . . ." Ruso stumbled on, correcting himself. "But I didn't—what are you doing?"

She put the acorn up to her mouth. "Why should I live as a slave in this world when I can be free in the next?"

His grip on her shoulders tightened. "What are you talking about?"

Her lips brushed against the curve of the acorn as she made the words. "Let me go, or I will take the poison."

"Tilla, for pity's sake!" He was looking at the acorn, trying to decide whether he could grab it before she put it between her teeth. He would not be fast enough. They both knew it.

"You are as bad as the others," she told him. "You are worse. You pretend to have honor."

For a moment he said nothing. Then he raised his head. "Daphne needs you, Tilla. The baby is coming and she's in trouble. I think she's going to die."

"Go and help her yourself," she told him. "You are the medicus."

"That's how I know," he said.

"You lie to me. You are lying now about Daphne."

"Daphne will die," he urged. "I'm begging you, Tilla. If you know how to help her, come now."

She knew what he was thinking. He was wondering if she had lied about bringing out babies just as she had lied about being able to cook.

"Why do you care for Daphne? She is a slave. You are a medicus to the soldiers."

"If you can't help," he said, "say so now and I'll go and do my best."

He was afraid, but not for himself. He was afraid for Daphne.

"You will make it worse," she told him. "Let go of me and show me where she is." She raised her voice so the other men could hear. "If anyone comes near, I will go to the next world."

The medicus turned to the men. "Stand back," he ordered. "Let her pass."

74

BY THE TIME they reached Daphne, she seemed barely conscious of what was going on. Her head was hung down, her hair plastered flat with sweat. The girls holding her looked weary and frightened. Merula was standing over them, hands on hips. She looked relieved to see Ruso. "Doctor! Do something, will you? The customers can hear her in the bar!"

Ruso knelt beside the pale form and put one hand over hers. "Daphne, it's the medicus. Can you hear me?"

The girl's eyelids flickered and fell still again. "Daphne, Tilla's here. We're going to help you. Just hold on."

Daphne's head lifted for a second. Her lips parted but instead of a cry of pain a misshapen vowel sound emerged.

"That's the spirit!" urged the older girl.

Ruso glanced up. "What did she say?"

The girl grinned. "She said piss off."

"Take no notice!" ordered Merula, turning to glare at Tilla. "What's she doing here?"

Tilla stepped forward and knelt by Daphne, talking in her own tongue as she examined her. Without looking up, Daphne stretched out a trembling hand and Tilla grasped it.

"You need to wait outside," Ruso said to Merula.

Beyond folding her arms, Merula failed to move. "Of all the nights," she remarked, eyeing the unfortunate Daphne. "Three girls out of action back here while we're rushed off our feet in the bar. And now the door staff are playing up. We've even had to borrow a servant from one of the neighbors. Not that he's much help."

This, Ruso supposed, explained why Priscus's man had not been at home. It was hard to imagine the timid house slave being much use as a security guard. "Go back to work," he urged. "We'll manage here."

"It's too late now. Madam here's made so much fuss she's frightened all the customers away."

Tilla turned. "You must all get out."

Ruso said, "I'll stay in case you need any—"

"Out!"

"Who do you think you are?" demanded Merula. "He is a doctor, and this is my room!"

Tilla put her hand to her throat. "There is poison inside," she explained, fingering the acorns as she glanced between Ruso and Merula. "If anyone comes near, I will eat it. I will die. And her," she pointed at Daphne, "and the child. Understand?"

Ruso grasped Merula's arm and forced her out into the corridor. "We understand," he said, and closed the door behind them.

"She's bluffing," said Merula.

"No, she isn't," said Ruso. "She knows about poisons."

They heard the thud of the bar dropping on the other side of the door. "Bitch!" muttered Bassus, who had apparently been lurking outside with Priscus. "We'll sort her out later." He glanced at Merula. "Busy night, was it?"

"Yes. No thanks to you, or to madam back there. Stichus is closing up. You might think of helping him."

"He can work for free if he wants," retorted Bassus, heading off down the corridor. "I'm going to pick up a bit of what's owed to me."

"Don't you dare touch that money!" shouted Merula, running after him. "It isn't yours. I have to take out costs, pay the bills . . . !"

Priscus turned to Ruso. "I don't think we need you now."

Ruso hesitated just long enough to bid his promotion a silent and sad good-bye, and to wonder how many night duties he would owe Valens because of this. Then he said, "I'm not leaving here without Tilla."

"The girl belongs to a legionary welfare fund. If you attempt to remove her, you will be put on a charge and she will be taken from you."

Ruso was about to argue when there was a roar of, "Bastard!" from somewhere at the far end of the corridor.

He asked, "What time did they find her?" but Priscus was already hurrying toward the sound, calling over his shoulder, "I have the documents, Ruso!"

Ruso followed him along the corridor, through the empty kitchen, and into the brighter light of the bar.

Bassus was still shouting. "Bastard! Thieving sniveling ginger bastard!" The top of his head was visible as he rummaged behind the counter. Everyone except he and Merula seemed to have gone.

Merula flung herself across the counter, elegant bottom in the air, arms flailing, reaching for something. As Ruso watched she slid back to the floor. In her hand was the box in which the earnings were kept secure behind the bar. She upended it above her head. A sprinkle of dust and a small brown feather drifted to the floor. She gave a howl of despair. "The entire payday money!"

Priscus was saying, "But who—?" when Bassus rose from behind the bar and hurled a jug across the room. "Him and that cheap tart!" The jug hit the wall opposite with a dull crack and shattered on the floor.

A couple of late-night customers who had crept in around the unlocked shutters made a hasty retreat.

"But who—?"

"Stichus and Chloe, of course!" exclaimed Merula. "I should never have trusted him once that little vixen got ahold of him."

Ruso closed his eyes and let out a long, slow breath. He had been relying on Stichus to give him back the money to pay the Aesculapian fund. Instead, it was clear the man had stolen the bar takings and fled. Without the money to cover the loan, even if Tilla were released tonight, Ruso would have to hand her back to Priscus tomorrow.

There was a scrape of wood on tile and a clatter of tumbling cups as Priscus shoved a table aside. "They won't get away with this!" he announced, peering around the shutters into the dark street. "We'll have them followed."

"In the middle of the night?" snapped Merula.

"This is your fault!" said Bassus to Priscus. "If it weren't for you and your tight-fisted money-saving schemes, none of this would have happened."

Priscus glared at him. "You were supposed to be at the door!"

"And you're supposed to be the one with the brains!"

Priscus sighed and lowered himself onto a bench. "Merula. Find me something to drink."

"The good wine's in the kitchen," said Merula, heading toward it.

"And two cups!" shouted Bassus after her. He seated himself beside Priscus. "I've had enough of this. I want my money." He slid along the bench until he was pressed against the administrator, who visibly braced himself to avoid being pushed off the end and onto the floor. "So until you come up with it . . ." Bassus gave a smile that was truly frightening, "you got the pleasure of my company. Give me the girl and we'll call it even."

"The girl isn't his to give," put in Ruso, stepping forward.

The two men looked up at him. "As I have explained, Ruso," said Priscus, "she is not yours either."

Ruso, hoping neither of them knew that he had lent his money to the vanished Stichus, said, "Give her back to me, Priscus. Women aren't safe with you. You don't want someone tracking down Saufeia's family and telling them how she died, do you?"

"Saufeia?"

"You know what I'm talking about."

"Nobody knows how that girl died!" snapped Priscus. "She was just a slave who ran away. Tilla is a slave who is signed over as guarantee for a loan. The two are not connected."

"Both were bought on the cheap without asking too many questions."

Priscus shrugged. "I have no idea what you mean, Ruso. Nor do I know how you can justify wasting time here when you should be on duty at the hospital."

Ruso did not know the answer to that one himself. Instead he said, "How much did you know about Saufeia when you bought her?"

Priscus frowned. "Don't be ridiculous. I am not responsible for buying bar staff."

"Of course you are. It's your bar."

"Merely a business investment. I arrange the finances. I employ a manager to do everything else."

"Including the deals with cockroaches like Claudius Innocens? Or do you do those yourself?"

"I have quite enough responsibilities at the hospital without taking on any more."

"Where do you think those girls come from, Priscus? Don't you stop to wonder why the prices are so low?"

Bassus rammed an elbow into Priscus's ribs. "See? What did I tell you?"

"Hold your tongue!" ordered Priscus, moving to another seat and bending to rub the bruised side of his chest. "You should never listen to malicious gossip, Ruso. Merula's bar is a respectable business."

"It's easy enough to buy a cheap girl, isn't it?" Ruso continued. "I've done it myself. But I didn't force mine to work in a place like this. Whereas your people were stupid enough to do that even after Saufeia had told them she was a citizen and asked for help."

There was only a slight pause before Priscus clasped his hands in apparent dismay. "Are you telling me," he said, "that that poor Saufeia girl was a Roman citizen?"

Bassus snorted. "Don't pretend you didn't know." He turned to Ruso. "He knew all right."

"Don't be ridiculous!"

"I was there when Merula told him," Bassus continued, ignoring the interruption. "He said we'd got to shut the girl up."

"What did he mean by that?"

"How should I know? I did what I always do when they act up. I explained a few things to her for her own good. In a way that would help her remember. Only instead of being sensible she went and wrote a letter asking for help and tried to send it to the legate. What was I supposed to do then?"

"I don't know," said Ruso. "What did you do?"

"I went to the management," said Bassus. "I told them we ought to be careful. With her being a citizen."

Unlike the unfortunate Daphne, thought Ruso, whose talkativeness had been cured with a sharp knife.

"I'm only the head doorman," continued Bassus, nodding toward his employer. "I gave the letter to him. Then it all happened like I told you."

"He's lying," insisted Priscus. "I never saw any letter. I had nothing to do with what happened to that girl. I told you, I leave all that to the manager."

"But Merula couldn't deal with this, could she?" said Ruso. "The girl wanted protection from a legionary officer."

"I don't know what she wanted!" snapped Priscus.

"And when an officer wrote back to her, offering to help, she didn't have the sense to realize it was a trap." Ruso turned to Bassus. "Did she really give you the slip, or were you told to let her out?"

"What do you think?" growled Bassus. "You think I can't do my job? 'Course we were told."

"Not by me!" insisted Priscus.

"No," agreed Bassus. "But I don't reckon Merula dreamed it up by herself. I reckon she thought you were letting the girl go."

"Letting her go?" demanded Priscus. "Merula would know better than that! The girl would have gone back to her family, raised a complaint, created a scandal—you would all have been in serious trouble!"

"So would you," pointed out Bassus. "You bought her."

"Nonsense!" retorted Priscus. He turned to Ruso. "You see the difficulty I'm in, Ruso? My staff made a terrible mistake and tried to cover it up. I only found out when it was over. It was too late to save that poor girl, and now they're trying to save themselves by blaming it on me."

"It weren't me what killed her," insisted Bassus. "And it weren't Stich either." He glowered at Priscus. "We just got orders to go and clean up your mess. Again."

The hand that rose to smooth Priscus's hair was shaking. "I am not responsible for any of this," he insisted. He turned to Bassus. "If you try to claim I was involved, I will tell the whole story and you will be tried and executed. And as for you, Ruso—you've been trying to undermine me ever since you came here. If you attempt to pass this slander on to anyone else, I will sue."

"Fine," said Ruso. "And I'll produce the evidence of the letter, and we'll let the governor decide."

"There was no letter!"

Ruso shook his head. "The trouble with terrorizing your staff, Priscus, is that they're too scared to bend the rules. I don't know what you said to the clerks, but one of them was so thorough he made sure your reply to Saufeia was entered in the official record."

"You're joking!" exclaimed Bassus. "He used the official post?"

"Shut up!" Priscus scowled at Ruso. "You're lying."

"You said she wasn't going to bother us again!" shouted Bassus. "You said you'd dealt with her and nobody would know!"

Priscus leaped to his feet. "Keep your mouth shut, you fool! He's lying!"

They were both looking at Ruso now. He paused, savoring his sudden feeling of power and wishing he had the money to back it up. "You know what I'm like with administration, Priscus," he said. "Not my strong point, is it? Do you really think I would have dreamed up a tale about post logs? And before you start to think about strangling me in a back alley . . ." he glanced at Bassus, "or performing tongue surgery, or arranging any accidents, you should know that I've followed your example and made a file copy of all this." He made his way toward the kitchen door. "It's to be opened later this evening if I don't return. So," he added, "I'll be leaving with Tilla as soon as she's finished."

He left them to argue. The last words he heard as the kitchen door swung shut were from Bassus. "The official post? Are you really that stupid?"

The kitchen was still empty. The staff seemed to have abandoned the mess and retreated to bed. There was no sign of Merula either, nor the wine she had gone to fetch. Beyond it, the corridor that led to the back of the building was in darkness. Ruso paused, waiting for his eyes to adjust, listening for any sound from Daphne or the child. There was none. Suddenly he had the odd conviction that there was someone else there with him.

He held his breath. His right hand moved slowly and silently toward his knife. From behind him came the faintest rustle of fabric. He spun around, knife pointed at where someone's throat might be. "Don't move!"

"Don't hurt me!" It was Merula's voice.

He said, "Why are you hiding?"

"I thought you might be one of the others."

Ruso lowered the knife. "How's Daphne?"

"I don't know," she said, "and I don't care." She bent down and heaved up some sort of bag. "This place is finished. I'm not staying around to take the blame for what they did to that girl."

Ruso said, "Did they kill Asellina as well?"

"That was Priscus. The gods alone know why. That's what started all this. We had to find a replacement."

"So you did a deal with Innocens?"

"It wasn't me. I'd have had more sense. I worked my way up here, Ruso. Seventeen years in the trade: I know what I'm doing. Then Priscus went and bought the place and started interfering. Never paying full price for anything. I told him, if you're going to run a business like this, you have to invest. But he wouldn't listen."

Ruso slid the knife back into the sheath. "Was it you who put Saufeia to work?"

"We all make mistakes, Doctor."

"True."

"I should have left when Priscus took over."

"Yes," agreed Ruso, "I know exactly what you mean."

He was on his way to the end room when he heard the squeal of a hinge out in the yard and then the gate slam shut. Ahead of him was the angry, scratchy cry of a newborn child.

75

TILLA SAT BACK against the wall, clutching her arm to try and ease the ache. Beside her, Daphne lay exhausted but alive on the bed that was soaked with blood and the water of the birth. Phryne was kneeling by the bed, holding a blanket around the squalling and slimy child they had laid on its mother's belly. Now that the thick cord joining mother and baby was no longer blue, the other girl tied it as Tilla instructed. They had not been able to find anything suitable in the room, so the cord was strangled with the leather thongs removed from her boots.

Tilla leaned forward and wiped her hands on the filthy bedspread. Her work was almost done. Soon the men would come back for her, and she would have to decide what to do.

So many days had passed since she had met the medicus, and yet her choice was the same as before. She was not afraid of death. The poison had failed her today on the road. Startled by her capture, she had not thought to reach for it before they tied her arms. Now, at last, she understood. The goddess had kept her in this world not to save Phryne but to welcome Daphne's child. Praying now for Daphne who had been kind to her, she closed her eyes.

She was wakened by the medicus's voice outside the door. Startled, she rubbed her eyes. She must not sleep. They knew now about the poison that was her freedom. As soon as she dropped her guard, they would take it away from her. She had to leave for the next world tonight, or find a reason to linger in this one.

He was banging on the door now. Calling her. The girls were looking at her, and at the bar across the door, not sure what to do.

She straightened her back. "Are you alone?"

"Yes."

She nodded to the girls. "Let him in."

Once inside he stood awkwardly, eyeing the figure on the bed. "Is she—"

"She is alive."

He said, "You did well."

"I need your knife," she said.

Without question, he crouched down and slid it along the floorboards. After she had severed the cord, Phryne swaddled the child in the shawl they had found in the trunk under the window and she settled it on its mother's breast, where it finally fell silent. "Be proud of yourself," she told Daphne in their own tongue. "Be proud of your son."

When she turned back she saw the medicus was resheathing his knife. "There's blood on that bandage," he said, frowning at her arm.

As she said, "Not mine," Daphne gave a soft moan. Tilla slid her hand under the blanket and felt the belly harden.

"Soon you can rest," Tilla told her, lifting the blanket up to see if the afterbirth was coming yet. "You are a strong girl. You have done well."

They were waiting in silence when they heard footsteps outside. The one with the odd hair appeared in the doorway, trembling and asking the medicus to look at a wound on his head. As usual, he was full of words. This time he was talking about working out a plan.

"We can extend the terms of the loan," he was saying as the medicus lifted one of the lamps to get a better view of the back of the head, from which a trickle of blood glittered black in the light. The wound had not stopped his talking. "You can keep the girl," he continued, "she's too much trouble." Tilla turned her head to listen. "Too much trouble" surely meant they were talking about her.

He was sounding excited now. "We can say Stichus killed Bassus in a fight over the takings—"

The medicus interrupted to say the wound needed cleaning before he could examine it, and he would have no part of killing anyone.

"No, Ruso, no. You don't understand. It was self-defense. You saw him attack me earlier."

The afterbirth was coming now. "Good girl," she urged, crouching to watch. It was important that it should be whole. Daphne should not be allowed to slip into the next world now. Not after such a struggle.

Daphne groaned.

"Good girl," Tilla repeated, wishing the men would have the sense to leave them in peace. "It is nearly done."

"It was terrible," the one with many words was insisting, as if anything could be terrible compared to what the girl on the bed had just been through. "I was frightened for my life. He grabbed me by the throat and banged my head against the counter. A stone counter, Ruso. I could have died! I still feel dizzy."

She glanced around. The medicus was scratching his ear in the way he did when he was uncertain. He said, "Are you telling me—?"

"I was all on my own with him! You deserted me, you abandoned a fellow officer . . . I had to wait till he went to find a drink and get a knife from the kitchen. It was terrible!"

"You stabbed Bassus with a kitchen knife? Gods in heaven, Priscus! Let me past, I'll have to—"

But the talkative one was clutching his arm, still complaining.

It was whole. She tied the towels in place, tucked Daphne into the blanket, and murmured a prayer of thanks to the goddess, with a final plea that the bleeding would stop soon. Behind her, the men were arguing in the doorway. The one called Priscus was promising the medicus that the man was quite dead and would not be telling any more tales.

An evening of blood.

She stroked Daphne's forehead and tidied a strand of hair that had fallen over her eyes. "The goddess has favored you with courage, sister. You did well. He is a fine healthy baby." It was not the time to be asking if there was a father to be told the news. Instead, she turned to the men in the doorway. "We need help."

The medicus glanced at them. "We need help," she repeated, raising her voice over that of the one with many words. "She needs to be carried to a clean bed."

She stepped aside. The medicus eyed her for a moment as if he were not used to taking orders, then told Phryne to bring the child and said stiffly, "Congratulations, Daphne," before stooping to gather her up in his arms. Tilla let the girls guide the medicus to a clean bed. The one called Priscus scurried after them, talking faster and faster.

Alone, she took a long cool drink of water from the jug. She had not eaten since breakfast. The soldiers had taken her food and eaten it while she walked behind them, tethered like a donkey, all the way back to Deva. She leaned back against the wall and slid down it until she was sitting on the floorboards with her legs stretched out in front of her. The boots were flapped open, thongless, useless for running even if she had the strength. She fingered the filthy bandage the medicus had put on her arm—how many days ago now? So much trouble, and for what? To bring her here to save one unborn child?

She felt her eyes flutter shut, and rubbed them hard. She must not sleep. Her hand moved to the twine fastened around her throat. She must decide tonight. She must ask for a sign from the goddess. She must get up and bar the door. In a moment, she would do all these things. She would just sit here for a while first, surrounded by the mess that comes with the welcoming of a new life, and recover her strength.

76

BASSUS WAS SLUMPED over the counter, his head in a dark pool of red wine mingled with the blood that had welled through the fabric of his tunic. No breath stirred the surface of the pool. Ruso's fingers moved slowly around the warm flesh of the neck, pressing for the throb of a pulse. He shook his head. The doorman was, as Priscus had claimed, quite dead. He lifted the man's shoulders, then lowered him onto the counter again and stepped away. There appeared to be more than one wound, and all were in the back. It did not look like self-defense.

"It could have been Stichus," Priscus was saying. "It all fits, do you see? Stichus wanted to steal the earnings and—"

Ruso turned on his heel and strode out of the bar.

Tilla was asleep. Priscus, who had followed him, was now talking about having the connecting door blocked up and selling the business. "Frankly, it was always something of a disappointment. Terribly difficult to find the right staff. As you know yourself, of course . . ."

Ruso knelt beside Tilla and ran a finger through the brown curls that she must have hoped would disguise her. Her eyelids flickered, then she settled back into sleep. Priscus was saying something about learning from one's mistakes and putting this unfortunate affair behind them.

Ruso stood up and stepped away. He would let her sleep a little longer. He was now so late that a few more minutes would make no difference. "Accessory to kidnap and rape of a native girl, accessory to repeated rape of a citizen of Rome, strangling that citizen, and now stabbing a veteran in the back," he said. "Plus I gather the other mess Bassus had to clear up for you was Asellina."

Priscus scowled. "I really can't be held responsible for having to put an end to that girl. I warned her more than once to pull herself together. She was quite insane."

"Really? I heard she was a cheerful and popular member of the staff."

Priscus tightened his lips. "She was warned! She was ordered to show appropriate respect!"

Ruso glanced at Priscus's hair and tried to imagine the effect it would have on a girl who was prone to giggling. "You mean she wouldn't stop laughing?"

"I told you. She was insane."

Not everyone likes a good laugh, do they, sir? Poor Decimus had been wiser than he realized. "Did you invent the story about her running off with the boyfriend?" Ruso asked. "Or was that someone else?"

"How was I supposed to know the wretched girl had an admirer? When Merula made a fuss I told her to make up some sort of reason why the girl had gone, and I gave her an example. A better manager would have used some initiative. Instead she just repeated what I'd said."

"So when her boyfriend turned up and demanded to know where she was, Merula told him she'd run off with the mysterious sailor."

"That girl was the property of the business. My property."

"And you didn't like your property laughing at you."

Priscus glared at him for a moment, clenching and unclenching his fists as if he was making a conscious effort to rein in his temper. Finally he said, "What does it matter? What happened was a little unfortunate, but as her owner, the only loss was mine."

"This whole business has been more than a little unfortunate, Priscus."

Priscus took a deep breath and appeared to recover his composure. "It has been an extremely difficult episode," he agreed. "But I think we can both feel relieved now." The hand that smoothed his hair was hardly shaking at all now. "We just need to tidy up a little. Then we can put everything behind us and make a fresh start. I'll confirm that you were called to an emergency here so your absence won't damage your promotion prospects."

Tilla stirred and murmured something in her sleep. Ruso stared at Priscus, wondering if the man's calm attempt to reason his way out of terrible crimes was a sign of insanity. Wondering too if he had collected any more weapons on his way back through the kitchen. "You expect me to keep quiet about this?"

"Of course." Priscus's mouth twisted into his wolf smile, and for the first time Ruso felt afraid of him. "What a terrible waste it would be," continued Priscus, "to ruin both of our careers over something like this. Because no matter what price you get for the girl—and, be honest, Ruso, even if you redeem her now, you will have to sell her—it will not make up the deficit in your personal finances, will it?"

"You know nothing about my personal finances."

"Really? Were you hoping no one would find out? Of course you were. Each of your creditors finding out about the others would cause a total collapse. If my informants are correct, you might be forced to sell that rather lovely farm in Gaul, leaving your brother and his expanding family homeless and penniless."

"You wouldn't!"

"Only with the deepest reluctance, I assure you."

One of the candles dimmed and drowned in a pool of wax. Ruso wondered if Valens had gone to bed yet. He took a deep breath. "If I keep quiet now," he said, "I'll be in your hands. I'll never know when you might decide to talk."

"Nor I you," Priscus pointed out.

"Is that any way to live?"

"On the other hand," said Priscus, "as I suggested, we could extend the terms of the loan. I can arrange to mislay the guarantee document. So you can sell your slave whenever you like."

There was a movement. Before Ruso realized what was happening, Tilla had put one hand to her throat and snapped the twine that held the poison around her neck.

"Stop!" he urged, lunging toward her and freezing a step away as she put the package to her lips once more. "Tilla. Please."

"Daphne is safe," said Tilla, looking first at Ruso and then at Priscus. "Now one of you will sell me. For greed, or for debt."

He did not dare to move. She could slip the acorn into her mouth and crush it in an instant if he tried to snatch it from her. "Please, Tilla, don't take whatever it is you've got there."

Those eyes were looking into his. The eyes that had first looked at him, unseeing, as she was being dragged down a back street by the greasy Claudius Innocens. "Daphne does not need me," she said. "Why should I not take it?"

And suddenly, clear and so obvious he could not understand how he had overlooked it, he knew why. "Tilla, listen. Do you trust me?"

The poison was held steady. "You take me in. You mend my arm," she said.

"Yes. You see?"

"So you can sell me for money."

"No! I had no idea . . ." He was about to say, "I had no idea you would turn out to be so valuable," but that was more truthful than helpful. He closed his eyes and prayed for the sort of persuasive powers the gods gave to other men. Men like Valens. When he opened them, no inspiration came. In desperation he whispered, "You must trust me." Then he turned back to Priscus. "I won't keep silent," he said. "This has got to stop."

Priscus frowned. "I'm offering you your precious slave back, Ruso. Surely you can't be thinking of sacrificing your family to prove a point about a couple of dead whores? There are hundreds of them! You said it yourself: Anyone can buy a girl in a back street."

"Anyone can," said Ruso, "but once you have, you're responsible for her." Without looking, he stretched one hand back toward Tilla, palm open. "Give me the poison, Tilla."

The hand remained empty in the air.

A muscle began to twitch in Priscus's cheek. "You're not seeing things clearly, Ruso," he said. "Think about it overnight. We'll discuss it in the morning."

"There's nothing to discuss."

"Ruso, I am the hospital administrator. I have served with the legion for fifteen years. You are a visiting medic with a record of damaging hospital property, a reputation for lateness, and a known penchant for hanging around bars with loose women. Which of us will be believed?"

"I don't know," said Ruso. "We'll have to see. Give me the poison, Tilla." A long streak of muscle in his arm was beginning to ache, and still his hand remained empty.

Priscus was watching Tilla. The wolfish smile began to spread across his face again. "Have you ever seen a slave market, Tilla? Rows of bodies chained up to be inspected and auctioned to the highest bidder. Of course he wants you to live. I imagine you will fetch quite a price."

"Don't listen to him, Tilla. Give it to me." Ruso, not daring to turn, tried not to think about what would happen to her, and to Lucius and the rest of the family, if she did not do as she was told. But then, when had Tilla ever done as she was told?

"She's grown fond of you, Ruso," said Priscus. "She doesn't want you to sell her to a stranger. She would rather die. You need to realize that the locals have no fear of death. That's why we have so much trouble with them. They would rather go to the next world than live dishonored in this one."

"I think they may have a point."

"You see, Tilla? Even your medicus thinks it is shameful to live without honor. Just one little bite, and you can be free."

"Tilla, please! Trust me."

"The two of us can come to an understanding, Ruso." The twitch in Priscus's cheek had begun again. "For the sake of the medical service."

Ruso felt something touch the palm of his hand. His fingers closed over three smooth warm shapes.

"It's your duty to support me, Ruso!" cried Priscus. "They were just slaves! They were of no importance!"

Ruso took Tilla by the arm and helped her to her feet. When he turned back, Priscus was clutching a kitchen knife. Ruso backed away, cursing his carelessness and snatching at the empty space where his own weapon should have been. "Stay back, Tilla!"

Instead, Tilla pushed him out of the way and stepped forward, her good arm pointed toward Priscus. In her hand was Ruso's knife, still stained with the blood of the birth.

"Careful, Priscus," Ruso warned, suddenly inspired. "Her tribe train all their left-handed people to be warriors."

"I'll have you arrested and sold!" Priscus shouted at Tilla. He waved the kitchen knife at Ruso. "He signed the documents!"

"You could do that," agreed Ruso, moving toward the foot of the bloodstained bed, "but it wouldn't keep me quiet, would it?"

He opened his hand and placed the poison on the bedcovers. Still defended by Tilla, he made for the door. "Perhaps you're the one who needs to think about it overnight, Priscus," he said. "Shut the door behind us, will you, Tilla?"

77

RUSO, HUNCHED IN his room with his spare cloak around his shoulders and his feet warmed by a sleeping dog, reached for another tablet of the *Concise Guide*. He flipped it open and squinted at the lettering in the lamplight. Then he breathed on the wax to warm it and ran the flattened end of the stylus across the sheet to wipe away the writing he had spent so many hopeful hours composing.

Stacked at a safe distance from the lamp were the final plans of the *Concise Guide* and a couple of tablets full of notes. These were the only parts he intended to keep. The rest was being finally and irrevocably scrapped. He was never going to finish it: he realized that now. Even if he had not been as tired as he was—and it had taken a lot of night duty to pacify Valens for being left alone on payday—he knew he was not blessed with the powers of concentration that a real author needed. A real author would not have sat for hours in front of an uncompleted work, pondering the answers to irrelevant questions like what had happened to his former servant and whether she was safe. Wondering if she might think of him occasionally. Wondering whether he would ever find out where she was. Wondering whether, if he had been more insistent, she would have stayed. And if she had stayed, what might have happened.

Ruso picked at the twine tying the two leaves of the next tablet, tugged at the end, and scowled as it tightened into a knot. He had managed without Tilla before she came. He would manage without her now that she was gone. In time—and it was obviously going to take longer than the thirty days he had so far been without her—she would become no more than an interesting memory. In time he would stop feeling a fool for having offered her a choice in the hope that she might want to stay. Perhaps in time he would forget the whole business. Perhaps in time he would even be able to walk the streets of Deva without feeling tainted by the human misery that he now knew lay behind the entertainment of the legion he served.

He glanced across at the damp stain that had blossomed beneath his bedroom window. Of course she wouldn't have wanted to stay. Even Valens would have had trouble enticing a woman to stay in this moldering excuse for a home. Ruso, the man who had considered selling Tilla for a profit, had not stood a chance. No wonder the last he had heard of her was a message saying she had gone north and taken Phryne with her.

He sliced the tip of his knife through the knot and breathed warmth onto the next sheet. The stylus scraped across the surface, filling the scratches and catching up the misted droplets where his breath had condensed on the cold wax. His careful thoughts on "where a broken bone is suspected" sank into the past.

He had signed the death warrant of the *Concise Guide* three weeks ago, when the camp prefect had called him and Valens in separately for "a chat." The chat had not been a cozy experience. Evidently the camp prefect knew more than Ruso would have wished about his performance since joining the Twentieth. There was nothing to be gained by explaining that he was normally very reliable and that the downhill slide was the result of his colleague eating a dish of bad oysters. When the prefect had said, "And if you were in charge of the medical service, what would you change?" he had come up with the brightest idea he could think of at the time, which was that practical first-aid training for every man in the unit would mean faster treatment of injuries, less time off sick, and less pressure on the hospital.

The chief medical officer had been appointed the following day. He was a Greek medic from the Second Augusta, based farther south. He was generally agreed to possess connections, competence, and no charm whatsoever. Unfortunately, though, Ruso's bright idea had not died with his ambitions. The prefect passed it on to the new CMO, who congratulated Ruso on his initiative and gave him the job of organizing the training. Since no legionary would pay for something the army would give him for free, Ruso found himself organizing the destruction of the market for his own work.

Valens's response to being overlooked was to announce that he was glad to be able to carry on practicing real medicine, instead of being mired in administration like the CMO. Apparently the second spear's daughter was very impressed with his devotion to his calling. Ruso was impressed too: not with Valens's devotion but with his ability to weave a useful lie in with the truth. The new man had indeed taken over the reins at a difficult time, following the suicide of the hospital administrator.

It was a month since Priscus's manservant had gone to wake him and found him dead in his bed. A doctor was called. According to Valens, the sight of the administrator's ghastly grimace of pain beneath his beautifully combed hair was the stuff of nightmares. The note on the bedside table had given typically detailed instructions for his funeral—Priscus was an administrator to the last—but no reason for the taking of his own life. The second spear, charged with investigating both this death and a murder on the same night in the adjoining bar, dismissed Ruso's suggestion that the two were connected with, "You again! I suppose you're going to tell me you saw him do it?"

"No, sir."

"Then don't come bothering me with any more of this rubbish. The pen-pusher from the hospital killed himself for reasons I know but you needn't, and from what I hear, the doorman was a nasty piece of work who could cheerfully have been knifed by a couple dozen suspects. And since the woman who owns the place has run off, it's pretty bloody obvious which one of them did it."

"Sir, with respect—"

But the look on the face of the second spear told Ruso that respect was not required. What was required was to shut up, go away, and stop being a nuisance.

It occurred to Ruso that only he, Tilla, and possibly Merula would ever know the real story behind Priscus's suicide. Ruso had been ignored, Tilla had gone away, and Merula, wherever she was, was certainly not going to say anything that would reveal her own failure to protect the

Roman citizen whom they had all known as Saufeia. As for Asellina, the slave put to death by her owner for having a fit of the giggles—Ruso tried to find something comforting to say to Decimus, and failed.

In the absence of fact, speculation was both rife and confident. Even Albanus could not resist hinting to Ruso that irregularities had been found in the hospital accounts and in the Aesculapian Thanksgiving Fund. "And when you hear what's in his will, sir, you'll see what I mean."

At Priscus's request the funeral had been attended by all the hospital staff. As instructed, a clerk read the will to the assembled company. The wish that his manservant be granted his freedom was of scant interest to the mourners. The desire that all his property be sold for the benefit of the Aesculapian fund, however, caused raised eyebrows and the exchange of more than one knowing glance. Ruso caught Albanus looking at him before both resumed a dutifully funereal expression. The camp prefect, who was turning out to be a more perceptive man than Ruso had imagined, described Priscus in his funeral oration as "an outstanding administrator and a man of many contradictions."

To Ruso's intense relief, the money loaned to Stichus had been repaid shortly after Stichus and Chloe reappeared from wherever they had been hiding. He had waited in vain, though, for a demand to pay it back to the Aesculapian fund. Finally his conscience sent him to see the unfortunate clerk who had been given the task of wrestling Priscus's outstanding administration into a shape presentable to the imperial auditors.

The man hunched over onto one elbow while he ran a chewed fingertip down the accounts. Finally the finger paused.

"You did have a loan," he agreed. "It was paid back on the twelfth before the Kalends of October."

"No, that's not right."

"Well, that's what it says."

"There must be some sort of mix-up."

The man sighed, swiveled the record around, and slid it across the desk, the finger pointing to an entry in Priscus's precisely-spaced hand. "Look."

Ruso read it twice. The meaning was unmistakable. About the same time as the administrator had persuaded him to sign over Tilla as guarantee, Ruso's loan had been repaid in full. There was no mention of a slave in the fund records. The only explanation Ruso could think of was that Priscus had chosen to take over the debt himself. If Ruso failed to pay up, Priscus would take Tilla for his own purposes—and as he must have guessed, when he tired of her she would still be worth far more than the loan had cost. But if the loan had been paid, Priscus would merely have broken even . . . Ruso paused. He had never been able to settle the business of the fire in his own mind, nor that accident under the bathhouse scaffolding. But now that he thought about it, the fire had happened just after he had signed the loan guarantee. Priscus had been in the hospital that night and could have slipped out to push something burning through the shutters of the bedroom window. He had not been on the building site, but he had been a man of wide influence. Perhaps Ruso would go and have a chat about him with Secundus from the century of Gallus. Because, of course, if Ruso had burned to death or had his skull split by the trowel, he would never have paid and Priscus would have had his signature on the document handing over Tilla . . . A document that he had not bothered to read before signing it. Had he signed Tilla over to the fund itself, or to its administrator?

"Satisfied?"

"Mm." Ruso scratched his ear. "I suppose," he said, "as all Priscus's money was bequeathed to the fund, I'm morally obliged to consider paying it myself anyway."

The man looked horrified. "You can't do that! I've only just got it to balance. You'll mess up the whole system."

So instead, he had sent the money to another good cause: a family in southern Gaul.

Ruso wiped out the final line of "in cases of fever" and reflected that truth might be an honorable concept, but very few men actually wanted to hear it. And of those who did, some would regret having asked. He leaned back in his chair and eyed the pile of tablets waiting to be erased. Months of work. Ahead of him, several tedious and penny-pinching hours saving the cost of tablets he would never need again because he was not going to write a book. Ever. He reached forward, scooped them up, pulled his feet from under the dog, and strode into the kitchen.

The embers in the kitchen hearth were still glowing. The first tablets were beginning to smoke as he threw the last one on. A yellow flame popped up through a gap, wavered, and grew tall.

The *Concise Guide* was illuminating the kitchen with a merry blaze when the main door scraped open and Valens called, "Darling! I'm home!" before appearing in the kitchen doorway and giving an exaggerated sniff. "What's that you're burning?"

"Just some rubbish I didn't need."

"Well, burn some more and perhaps we'll be rehoused sooner than we thought." Valens, his ambition for the CMO's house thwarted, was now eagerly trying to engage better lodgings. He bent to peer at the contents of the fire. "That reminds me. I was supposed to bring you a letter."

Ruso reached out his hands to warm them over his disappearing masterpiece. "From?"

"Londinium. That chap you sent to get his cataracts looked at. Albanus gave it to me and I left it in the surgery. Big handwriting. Did it himself, apparently. They're naming their son after you. The worst eye's been done and it seems to have worked."

"Good."

"They'll discharge him anyway, you know. The sight will never be up to much."

"I know," said Ruso, recalling the battle with Priscus about the cost of the operation. The administrator had been right, but for all the wrong reasons.

Valens lifted the lid of the bread bin.

"It's empty," said Ruso, reaching for the poker to prod at the settling flames.

Valens lowered the lid with a disappointed sigh. "I can't eat out, I'm on call. I'll have to wander back to the kitchen and see what I can scrounge up. We're going to have to do something about another slave, Ruso."

"Yes," agreed Ruso, not adding that they had agreed this more than once, but neither of them had done anything about it. They needed a slave to go and find them a slave.

"Oh, and there was another message. Apparently Albanus thinks I've become his assistant. He said to tell you something about a girl being home safe."

Ruso stopped. "Tilla?"

Valens looked pained. "I would have remembered if it was the lovely Tilla, Ruso, whom you so rashly allowed to abandon us with an empty bread bin. No. This is another of your many women. Let me think . . . something Greek."

"Phryne?"

"That's it. Phryne."

"Who brought the message?"

Valens shrugged. "Some urchin brought it to the gate, apparently."

The poker clattered back on the hearth. Ruso snatched up his cloak from the chair where he had thrown it. "I've got to go out."

"Do I know this Phryne? Can she cook?"

Ruso squeezed the shaft of his cloak pin into the catch. "No," he said, answering both questions with one word on his way out of the house.

78

STICHUS NODDED A greeting from his old place on the door. From his shadow, a small figure in an identical tunic grinned at Ruso. A quick inquiry confirmed that Lucco had not been the urchin. He had, as he announced with pride, been at work all day. "I've been helping the painter." He pointed at the outside of the wall beside him. "Look." The torch lit up freshly painted lettering. "I can read all the letters," added the boy. "It says: 'Chloe's.' "

"Very good," observed Ruso, stepping inside. The bar was doing a brisk trade. Ruso nodded to Mariamne, who was serving at the tables. He reached for his purse and waited while a youth tried unsuccessfully to haggle over the price of a beer. After the youth had lost—but still bought the beer—Ruso asked a girl he did not recognize to pour him a large cup of the best wine Chloe's had to offer.

It was the first drink he had ordered here since the day he bought Tilla, and the first time he had been back to the bar since the dreadful events of payday. He had just enough money for the wine. On the way over he had promised himself he was not going to buy anything or anybody else, and if there was the least hint of trouble anywhere near him, he was going to walk away without a second glance.

He was handing over the cash when Chloe's voice cut across the hubbub. "Don't let him pay for that!" Moments later she was kissing him on the cheek like a long-lost friend. "Come and see the baby!" she urged. "Where have you been?"

Steadying his wine as she dragged him by the arm, he followed her toward the kitchen and a fine smell of stewed lamb. "I got your package," he said. "Thank you."

Chloe laughed. "I bet you were worried when you found out we'd gone."

"Just a little."

"I told you he'd pay you back."

Ruso nodded, wondering who really did own the money he had finally sent to Lucius.

Daphne was standing at the kitchen table, cracking brown eggs into a bowl two at a time with a swift and economical technique that made him suddenly nostalgic for Tilla's frustrated struggles to manage his kitchen left-handed. Daphne looked up at his approach, smiled, and pointed toward the other end of the table where a drawer rested on the tabletop. Inside, a small fuzz of dark hair was visible under one end of a blanket.

Ruso said the things people were supposed to say about babies. Indeed, this one was a particular miracle, even though it looked just like all the others and its cloths smelled as though they needed changing.

He glanced from Chloe to Daphne. "I came to see if you'd heard the news. Phryne is safely home."

Daphne's thumbs-up sign trailed a long string of egg white.

"Do you know who brought the message?"

Chloe shook her head. "Nobody's been here." She took his arm again. "Come and eat," she urged, pausing to exchange a word with the cook and inspect the contents of a couple of steaming pans before leading him back into the bar and beckoning Mariamne over. "Whatever the doctor wants," she said as the girl gathered empty cups onto a tray. "And the Falernian. He's our guest of honor. And tell Flora to smile, will you? People come here to enjoy themselves."

Ruso glanced at the customers and the girls clustered around the lamplit tables and reflected that a couple of months ago, he would have been embarrassed to be made welcome in a place like this. Now he was happy about it. He had nowhere to go this evening and all he had eaten was two sausages scrounged from a patient who wasn't eating his food. He placed his cup on the table and settled into an empty seat as

Mariamne placed another cup and a brimming wine jug beside him and went to fetch him a bowl of lamb stew.

Chloe sat down beside him, helped herself to his wine, and was pouring him a fresh cup from the jug when a large hand landed on the table and a swaying legionary leaned over her. "That bitch over there," he announced, waving at a table across by the bar, "won't go upstairs with me."

Chloe put the jug down and placed a hand over his. "Marcus, I hope you were a gentleman and offered her something nice in exchange?"

"You're in charge. Tell her to do her job."

Chloe shook her head. "All our girls work for themselves, Marcus." She leaned closer to him. "And they're specially selected and trained by me. You might find she's asking a little bit more than you'd pay somewhere else, but I promise, you won't be disappointed."

The legionary stared at her for a moment. "She's asking a bloody fortune! Forget her. What else have you got?" He looked her up and down. "You working tonight?

Chloe smiled and pointed toward the door, where Stichus was glaring across at them. "I'm a one-man woman these days, my love. Isidora!" She beckoned over the girl who had turned at the mention of the name. "Isidora, this is my very good friend Marcus. Marcus, this is the girl for you." She reached for their hands and joined them.

When they had gone Chloe sank back in her chair with a sigh of exasperation. "Silly bitch, I'll have to talk to her. If it's not one thing here, it's another." She leaned her elbows on the scarred wood and opened her hands to indicate the sweep of the bar. "Well? What do you think?"

"I take it you're the new Merula?"

"A girl can't keep working for ever, you know. I always wanted to get out before everything started to sag."

Ruso, not sure if a compliment was expected at this point, mumbled something, took a long drink of the wine she had poured him, then drew back and asked, "What's this?"

"Weren't expecting that, were you?" asked Chloe, clearly proud of it. "It's Falernian. A present from a client. Don't ask, because I won't tell you. We're very discreet here."

It wasn't, but he didn't have the heart to tell her. At least it was a better imitation than Merula had sold him. He said, "You seem to be doing well."

She nodded. "We lost a few girls to start with, people who went back home, but most of us either haven't got homes or wouldn't be welcome if we went there. And there's been no trouble recruiting. Not now that word's got around I'm not running things the way that old cow did. The girls work here for their keep. If they take a customer upstairs, they pay me to use the room and they hold on to the rest themselves."

"I see."

"It should all work very nicely, if the girls just use a bit of common sense. They provide a good service, they get the cash. Before, everything got handed over to the management."

"That's very enterprising."

Chloe grinned. "And I can tell the tax man we're letting out rooms. So it's all nice and legal."

Ruso looked at her over the rim of the wine cup. " Really?"

She leaned across him and adjusted the fold of his cloak over his shoulder. "It is unless somebody tells, Doctor."

"It's none of my business. But someone's going to figure it out before long."

"From what I heard," said Chloe, "the bar wasn't mentioned in Priscus's will."

Ruso nodded. "I imagine he didn't trust his witnesses to keep it quiet. Being involved in running a, um—"

"Whorehouse," put in Chloe.

"It wouldn't have done much for his reputation."

"Exactly," said Chloe. "That's why he always let everybody think the business belonged to Merula. Even a lot of the staff didn't realize. So as far as anybody knows—anybody except you me and Stich, that is—the name's only been changed because murder's bad for trade, and she's left me in charge till she gets back."

"Is she coming back?"

"I wouldn't hold your breath. She took all her jewelry with her and she won't want to be tried for what she did to Saufeia."

Chloe reached out a manicured fingernail, lifted his chin, and pouted a kiss. "Cheer up, Doctor. Lucco's safe, Daphne's got her baby, and everyone's glad those bastards aren't in charge here anymore."

Ruso took another long drink and swilled the not-quite-precious wine dangerously close to the rim of the cup. "Asellina is dead and her boyfriend doesn't know why. Saufeia's family will never know where she's buried. And I don't know what's happened to Tilla."

"Asellina died in an accident, Doctor, still wearing the necklace poor old Decimus gave her as part of their tragic love affair. She loved him to the end. That's what I told him, and if you tell him anything else, we'll have him down here every night getting drunk and picking fights."

"True."

"Tilla and Phryne were from the same people, weren't they?"

"The Brigantes."

"So if one's home safely, then the other must be as well. Look, here comes your supper. Now have a taste of that and tell me if it isn't the best lamb stew in town. And don't think about Saufeia. You can't tell her family anything that'll be of any comfort to them."

Mariamne placed a steaming bowl on the table. "Compliments of the house, sir."

"When you've finished," added Chloe, getting to her feet and leaning forward to stroke one fingertip along his cheek, "choose yourself a girl and tell her Chloe sent you for the special."

79

RUSO TROD HEAVILY down the moonlit street, his stomach full of stew and his mind full of dark thoughts. He had lingered as long as he could over the meal and consumed the entire jug of Chloe's fake Falernian, but he had not taken up the offer of a girl. Even a desperate man had to have standards.

A family emerged from a side street and turned on to the road ahead of him. A child who should have been in bed at this hour was perched on its father's shoulders. The mother had a baby cradled against her hip. They seemed to be hurrying somewhere. Moments later they turned off to the right and disappeared.

Ruso walked on, in no particular direction. A rat scurried across the street in front of him and vanished into an alley that smelled of sewage. Even the rats had somewhere to go and something to do. Whereas he was facing another evening sitting in a cold house with only the dogs and the ashes of his failed work for company.

A man needed a family, Ruso decided. Or a religion. Something to cling to. His own family were far away and as for religion—he was not sure that he and Aesculapius were on good terms at the moment. Especially if the god had found out that his fund had been short-changed to help a small farm in Gaul out of debt.

A man needed a family or a religion. He felt a long way from both.

He was thinking about her again. He was thinking that he should have given her instructions about keeping in touch. She was still, technically, his property. But it was obvious that after all that had happened to her in Deva she would not choose to stay here. He had only himself to blame.

He heard voices behind him and turned to see a group of five or six youths striding purposefully down the street. Their conversation was in British. He stepped aside. They passed him without seeming to notice he was there.

He supposed he could go to the hospital and do late ward rounds, but he was more than a little drunk and besides, it would only bring out more "Haven't you got a home to go to?" comments. He had discharged the last patient who had asked that, on the premise that anyone able to sit up in bed and make sarcastic remarks was well enough to be sent back to barracks in the morning.

Glancing up to see where he was—it would not be a good idea to wander down the Dock road at this hour—he was surprised to see the building ahead silhouetted against an orange sky. He drew in a sharp breath and paused to stare. Somewhere toward the distant cemetery, sparks were flying upward, fading to black specks, and floating down through the disturbed air. It was too big for a funeral pyre, and much too late at night. He was too far away to hear the shouting but he could see well enough. Somebody's house was on fire.

He had promised himself he would walk away from trouble, but this was different. Hurrying through the shadowed streets he overtook another family and was surprised to hear, " 'Evening, Doctor! Are you going where we're going?"

It was a moment before he recognized the barber, who seemed to be out for a stroll with his family.

"There's a fire," explained Ruso, wondering how they could have failed to notice.

"Looks good, don't it?" observed the barber. He fell in step with Ruso. "I wouldn't bother meself, but we'll never hear the last of it if we don't take the ma-in-law."

Ruso winced. For all they knew, people could be injured or dead. Clearly the barber had been right to assess his mother-in-law as a mad old bitch. "We'd better hurry," he said.

"Oh, it'll go on for a bit yet," observed the barber. "Mind your step!"

He pushed Ruso to one side just in time to stop him from stepping in a pile of animal droppings. "Once that lot get going with the dancing and the stories you can be up till daylight." The man lifted his left hand to reveal the dark shape of a tankard, "Still, there's usually a good drop of beer to be had."

Ruso's legs carried on in the same direction while his head rearranged his assessment of where he was going. His suspicions were confirmed when the barber said,

"One thing you can say for the locals, they know how to do a good bonfire."

Ruso said, "What are they celebrating?"

"The new year."

"But it's only the end of October!"

"Ah, to you and me and the rest of the empire, Doc, but the wife's family's new year is tomorrow. And tonight for one night only—this is according to the old bag, mind—the doors are open between the living and the dead."

"I see," said Ruso. They were closer to the fire now. He could hear faint strains of chanting and the wail of pipes, hopefully from the living. He wondered whether, miles away across the damp green hills of Britannia, Tilla was singing one of her interminable ancestor songs beside a bonfire of her own.

The crowd had gathered on a patch of empty land between the last houses and the cemetery. The size of the crowd surprised him, but the Twentieth had been here for many years now and he supposed most of their women would be local. People had gathered well back from the leaping flames of a colossal bonfire. Those closest to him were silhouettes and around the fire he could make out the pale shapes of faces. The flames lit up the movements of the musicians, who were standing on some sort of platform.

Around him, knots of people were wandering across the grass to where a couple of lamplit carts were serving food and—judging by the numbers of men and women clutching cups—beer. He glanced back at the entrance to the lot and saw, as he had expected, a glint of moonlight on polished armor. The legionaries standing guard on each side of the gate would be the visible ones. He supposed others would be stationed farther back, discreetly positioned so as not to provoke trouble but ready to rush forward and quell it if it seemed to be starting without them. The chances of any trouble here, though, were minimal. Most of these people would have connections with the army. This, he thought, surveying the crowds, was just the sort of event Rome would approve. Happy natives enjoying a night out under the watchful eye of their benevolent imperial guardians. He wondered what the imperial guardians would do if the old woman was right, and the dead decided to walk back through the open door and join in.

The thought reminded him of something. He felt for his purse and fingered the coin inside. Then he strode across to join the line at the drinks stall.

Ruso disliked talking to people about death. They usually asked questions he didn't know the answers to. Wherever possible, he left that sort of thing to the priests. The priests didn't know the answers either, but they thought they did, which usually seemed to please grieving relatives. When there was no priest available, he would pull out some sort of platitude about the deceased having gone to a better place and being out of pain now. But had they? Were they? How could anyone know?

He had seen many people die, and he could still make no sense of it. One moment the body was a person with a will and a future and a sense of humor and a liking for honeyed dates or goat cheese or other men's wives. Then—and the change could take a second, or hours, or days, but the end was always the same—the body was just a mass of flesh which had to be disposed of before it stank. And whatever anyone said about ghosts or open doors or crucified Judean carpenters, nobody had ever come back, so how could anyone say with any confidence that there was a better place—or any place at all?

He knelt, stretched out his hands, and let the cold dry earth run through his fingers. Plants had begun to grow on the grave. He assumed they were weeds, although in the moonlight it was impossible to tell. It had been difficult enough to make out the name burned along the wooden post that was hammered into the top of the grave as a marker, but finally he had picked out all the letters: SAUFEIA. Spelled correctly. One "f."

He had never met this young woman in life. He had only seen the battered and decaying husk of a body from which the soul was long gone. He owed her no duty beyond that of a doctor to a patient. He had more than fulfilled that duty. Yet still he felt guilty.

The people who buried Saufeia's ashes had not left a spout to connect the dead to the living, so he lifted the cup of wine he had bought from the stall—how Roman these people had become!—and held it at arm's length above the grave. He listened for a moment to the sounds of celebration drifting over from the bonfire. Then he began to tilt the cup until a thin stream of wine ran from it to soak into the soft earth. As it trickled into the ground he said quietly, "May you rest in peace, sister. May you enjoy a better life in the next world than you suffered in this one. May you forgive us all for not avenging you sooner, and . . ." He paused to clear his throat, "and may the dead be kind enough to forgive me for not telling the whole truth, because I have a duty to the living."

"Sometimes," murmured a girl's voice, "is good not to tell too much truth."

Ruso felt his whole body begin to shake. The night when the doors are open between the living and the dead . . . And yet it was the wrong voice. He knew that voice. He knew it very well indeed. Slowly, he lowered the cup onto the grave and was relieved to press his hands onto the solid earth. He told himself he was not losing his mind. He was simply confusing his memories: an understandable mistake brought on by the strange surroundings of the moonlit cemetery and too much free wine at the bar.

"Hail and farewell, Saufeia," he whispered, then scrambled hastily to his feet.

"Are you finish?" The words were spoken by a woman in native dress with a shawl pulled over her head.

He stared at her, squinting in the moonlight. "You aren't really here," he informed her. "I've had too much to drink. I am going to walk to the real world now, past next year and back into this one, and then I am going to bed, and when I wake up tomorrow morning you won't be there."

The girl eyed him solemnly and then said, "My Lord is afraid he is losing his mind."

"I'm not losing my mind," he insisted, "I'm drunk."

"My Lord is drunk," she agreed, "but I am here. She pushed back the shawl and held out one bare arm. "See?"

He rubbed his eyes and looked at the pale arm. Then he took it and turned it over, marveling at its straightness.

"I have seen you go to the bar," explained Tilla. "I wait outside for a very long time while you drink, and I follow you."

He had thought many times about what he would say to Tilla if he ever saw her again. He could not remember what he had decided. Instead, he found himself slipping back into the role of doctor. "The muscles in the arm will be weak," he heard himself telling her. "You must do exercises every day to build them up again. Clench your fist for me. Good. Do you have full movement in the hand?"

She gave a deep, throaty chuckle. "Now will you will ask me if my bowels are open today?"

He let go of the arm. "No. I'm sorry, Tilla, I—" He glanced around them at the deserted cemetery. "I can't believe you're here. I thought you were never coming back."

"The first time I meet you," she said, "I am thinking I wish to die. I want to go to the next world. You, with your bandages and your exercises and eat your dinner and have you use the pot yet, you keep me here."

Ruso scratched his ear. "I'm not sure about the next world," he said. "That's why I prefer to keep people in this one, just in case."

"Then I find out that you want to sell me."

"That was a mistake," said Ruso. "I wasn't thinking straight."

"A mistake, yes."

"Did you bring the message about Phryne?"

"I send a boy to the gate. I have to find out what has happened to that Priscus man. To know if it is safe to come."

"I thought you would stay at home with your people."

She paused. "I think about you and the other good-looking doctor," she said. "In that terrible house."

"Valens is trying to engage a better one," said Ruso.

"My arm is mended," she said. "I am still in this world, and I have to thank you. If you sell me, you can get a better house. Then I will find a way to the next world and you will have money."

He stared at her. "You mean I sell you, I get lots of money, and if you don't like the new owner you kill yourself? What sort of an arrangement is that?"

"Is honorable."

"Is ridiculous. I told you, I don't believe in the next world. And I wouldn't dream of sending anyone to it so I can have a better house. That was never what I needed the money for." He hesitated. "If you really want to do something for me, come home."

She looked him up and down. "You have not shave. There are dark rings under your eyes." She placed a finger close to the pin on his chest. "There is a hole in your cloak."

"I've been doing a lot of night duty."

The sound of cheering and laughter drifted over from the bonfire. She said, "Will your better house have mice?"

He took a deep breath. "If you come back," he said, "you will not be sleeping with the mice. You will be sleeping with me."

Another burst of distant laughter broke the silence. He was beginning to think he had made a serious mistake when she reached forward, took his hand, and turned to address the grave.

"We must leave now, sister," she said. "We will pray for you. Watch over us in the new year from the next world."

They were almost back at the fort gates when Tilla said, "I must tell you some truth, my Lord. You could not sell me anyway."

"Why not?" said Ruso, happy to launch into an argument now that he was assured of her company. "I have the documents. You told me yourself that Innocens bought you in a legitimate sale."

There was a slight pause before she replied, "I told you he pay money for me."

"Exactly."

"The woman he pay is not the one who—"

"Stop!" ordered Ruso. "Whatever it is, I don't want to hear it. I'm tired of the truth. Just carry on the way you are, Tilla. That's an order."

Author's Note

Ancient accounts of Roman Britain are tantalizingly patchy, and everything we have—even passages purporting to tell us what the Britons were thinking and saying—comes from the conqueror's pen. The earliest British stories were not recorded until an era as far removed from Hadrian as we are from Shakespeare. However, many of the gaps are still being filled by archaeology, and anyone in search of reliable information about our ancestors should most definitely look there rather than within the pages of an entertainment such as this.

The layout and remains of Deva can be seen in the streets of modern day Chester, although the port silted up many years ago. The Twentieth Legion really did carry out major rebuilding there during Trajan's reign, but the schedule, the delays, and the bad behavior were imposed upon their innocent ghosts by me. I should also confess that while the administration portrayed here was inspired by the Roman army's meticulous record keeping, some of the arrangements might come as a surprise to scholars. They might be less surprising to anyone who has attempted to plait the fog of public finance for a living.

The word *medicus* was used to describe men of various ranks, and the hierarchy Ruso is attempting to climb is pure conjecture. What is not in doubt is that the doctors of antiquity were remarkably skilled.

Cataract surgery might have been terrifying, but it was possible. However, there were no modern antibiotics or anesthetics, and accurate knowledge sat alongside such beliefs as Pliny's suggestion that snakebites could be cured with human earwax. Small wonder, then, that the sick turned to Aesculapius, the god of healing, who may or may not have had a Thanksgiving fund, but who certainly deserved one.

As for the rescue of Trajan, Cassius Dio records that he was saved from the Antioch earthquake by a mysterious stranger. Whether this stranger was Ruso or the god Jupiter, I leave to the reader to decide.

The goings-on at Merula's bar were partly inspired by Pompeii, where the names of long-dead girls remain on the walls of their workplaces. Two thousand years later, of course, we have moved on. Slavery is illegal. Yet I fear that is scant comfort to any young woman a long way from home who is forced to provide "personal services" while the trafficker who holds her passport pockets her earnings. This appalling trade is going on right now, in our own cities, and it survives because it finds customers. I didn't need to make it up. Unfortunately.

Acknowledgments

People whose names are not on the cover helped with this book, and I am indebted to the friends and family who offered encouragement in the face of my frequent assertions that it was going Very Badly.

A few people deserve a special mention. Richard Lee and the Historical Novel Society helped to conjure the early chapters out of a very different story. Peta Nightingale and Araminta Whitley encouraged me to finish it—something I failed to do until the good folk at BBC Scotland threatened to come and inquire about its progress. Mari Evans at Michael Joseph and Gillian Blake at Bloomsbury USA provided much-needed guidance—and, thank goodness, a title.

Bill Hancock supplied the quotation from Horace. Nina Palmer, Guy Russell, Kate Weaver, and Dr. Martin Weaver were all kind enough to read through the text, and saved me from much of my own ignorance.

Three books provided particularly fascinating background: David J. P. Mason's *Roman Chester: City of the Eagles*, Ralph Jackson's *Doctors and Diseases in the Roman Empire*, and Alan K. Bowman's *Life and Letters on the Roman Frontier.*

Needless to say, none of the above is responsible for any factual errors, misinterpretations, deliberate tweakings, or wild flights of fantasy that readers may encounter in the preceding pages.

KEEP READING!

More intrigue and bad luck lie ahead for Gaius Petreius Ruso. Turn the page for a sneak preview of the next installment in the *Medicus* series,

TERRA INCOGNITA

It is spring in the year 118, and Gaius Petreius Ruso has been stationed in the Roman-occupied province of Britannia for nearly a year. After his long and reluctant investigation of the murders of a handful of local prostitutes, Ruso needs to get away. With that in mind, he has volunteered for a posting with the army in Britannia's deepest recesses—a calmer place for a tired man.

But the edge of the Roman Empire is a volatile place; the independent tribes of the north dwell near its borders. These hunterlands are the homoland of Ruso's slave. Tilla, who has scores of her own to settle there: Her tribespeople are fomenting a rebellion against Roman control, and her former lover is implicated in the grisly murder of a soldier. Ruso, filling in for the domented local doctor, is appalled to find that Tilla is still spending time with the prime suspect Worse, he is honor-bound to try to prove the man innocent—and the army wrong—by finding another culprit. Soon both Ruso's and Tilla's lives are in jeopardy, as is the future of their burgeoning romance.

The new novel by Ruth Downie

TERRA INCOGNITA

Hardcover $23.95
Bloomsbury USA
Available wherever books are sold

HE HAD NOT expected to be afraid. He had been fasting for three days, and still the gods had not answered. The certainty had not come. But he had made a vow and he must keep it. Now, while he still had the strength.

He glanced around the empty house. He was sorry about that barrel of beer only half drunk. About the stock of baskets that were several weeks' work, and that he might never now sell at market.

He had nothing else to regret. Perhaps, if the gods were kind, he would be drinking that beer at breakfast tomorrow with his honor restored. Or perhaps he would have joined his friends in the next world.

He would give the soldier a chance, of course. Make one final request for him to do as the law demanded. After that, both their fates would lie in the hands of the gods.

He closed the door of his house and tied it shut, perhaps for the last time. He walked across and checked that the water trough was full. The pony would be all right for three, perhaps four days. Somebody would probably steal her before then anyway.

He pulled the gate shut out of habit, although there was nothing to escape and little for any wandering animals to eat in there. Then he set off to walk to Coria, find that foreign bastard, and teach him the meaning of respect.

1

MANY MILES SOUTH of Coria, Ruso gathered both reins in his left hand, reached down into the saddlebag, and took out the pie he had saved from last night. The secret of happiness, he reflected as he munched on the pie, was to enjoy simple pleasures. A good meal. A warm, dry goatskin tent shared with men who neither snored, passed excessive amounts of wind, nor imagined that he might want to stay awake listening to jokes. Or symptoms. Last night he had slept the sleep of a happy man.

Ruso had now been in Britannia for eight months, most of them winter. He had learned why the province's only contribution to fashion was a thick cloak designed to keep out the rain. Rain was not a bad thing, of course, as his brother had reminded him on more than one occasion. But his brother was a farmer, and he was talking about proper rain: the sort that cascaded from the heavens to water the earth and fill the aqueducts and wash the drains. British rain was rarely that simple. For days on end, instead of falling, it simply hung around in the air like a wife waiting for you to notice she was sulking.

Still, with commendable optimism, the locals were planning to celebrate the arrival of summer in a few days' time. And as if the gods had finally relented, the polished armor plates of the column stretching along the road before him glittered beneath a cheering spring sun.

Ruso wondered how the soldiers stationed up on the border would greet the arrival of men from the Twentieth Legion: men who were better trained, better equipped, and better paid. No doubt the officers would make fine speeches about their united mission to keep the Britons in order, leaving the quarrels to the lower ranks, and Ruso to patch up the losers.

In the meantime, though, he was not busy. Any man incapable of several days' march had been left behind in Deva. The shining armor in front of him was protecting 170 healthy men at the peak of their physical prowess. Even the most resentful of local taxpayers would keep their weapons and their opinions hidden at the sight of a force this size, and it was hard to see how a soldier could acquire any injury worse than blisters by observing a steady pace along a straight road. Ruso suppressed a smile. For a few precious days of holiday, he was enjoying the anonymity of being a traveler instead of a military—

"Doctor!"

His first instinct was to snatch a last mouthful of pie.

"Doctor Gaius Petreius Ruso, sir?"

Since his other hand was holding the reins, Ruso raised the crumbling pastry in acknowledgment before nudging the horse to the edge of the road where there was room to halt without obstructing the rest of the column. Moments later he found himself looking down at three people.

Between two legionaries stood a figure that gave the unusual and interesting impression of being two halves of different people stuck together along an unsteady vertical line. Most of the left half, apart from the hand and forearm, was clean. The right half, to the obvious distaste of the soldier restraining that side, was coated with thick mud. There was a bloodied scrape across the clean cheek and a loop of hair stuck out above the one braid that remained blond, making the owner's head appear lopsided. Despite these indignities, the young woman had drawn herself up to her full height and stood with head erect. The glint in the eyes whose color Ruso had never found a satisfactory word to describe—but when he did, it would be something to do with the sea—suggested someone would soon be sorry for this.

All three watched as Ruso finished his mouthful and reluctantly rewrapped and consigned the rest of his snack to the saddlebag. Finally he said, "Tilla."

"It is me, my lord," the young woman agreed.

Ruso glanced from one soldier to the other, noting that the junior of the two had been given the muddy side. "Explain."

"She says she's with you, sir," said the clean man.

"Why is she like this?"

As the man said, "Fighting, sir," she twisted to one side and spat on the ground. The soldier jerked her by the arm. "Behave!"

"You can let go of her," said Ruso, bending to unstrap his waterskin. "Rinse the mud out of your mouth, Tilla. And watch where you spit. I have told you about this before."

As Tilla wiped her face and took a long swig from the waterskin, a second and considerably cleaner female appeared, breathless from running up the hill.

"There she is!" shrieked the woman. "Thief! Where's our money?" Her attempt to grab the blond braid was foiled by the legionaries.

Ruso looked at his slave. "Are you a thief, Tilla?"

"She is the thief, my lord," his housekeeper replied. "Ask her what she charges for bread."

"Nobody else is complaining!" cried the other woman. "Look! Can you see anybody complaining?" She turned back to wave an arm toward the motley trail of mule handlers and bag carriers, merchants' carts and civilians shuffling up the hill in the wake of the soldiers. "I'm an honest trader, sir!" continued the woman, now addressing Ruso. "My man stays up half the night baking, we take the trouble to come out here to offer a service to travelers, and then *she* comes along and decides to help herself. And when we ask for our money all we get is these two ugly great bruisers telling us to clear off!"

If the ugly great bruisers were insulted, they managed not to show it.

"You seem to have thrown her in the ditch," pointed out Ruso, faintly recalling a fat man behind a food stall—the first for miles—at the junction they had just passed. "I think that's enough punishment, don't you?"

The woman hesitated, as if she were pondering further and more imaginative suggestions. Finally she said, "We want our money, sir. It's only fair."

Ruso turned to Tilla. "Where's the bread now?"

Tilla shrugged. "I think, in the ditch."

"That's not our fault, is it, sir?" put in the woman.

Ruso was not going to enter into a debate about whose fault it was. "How much was it worth?"

There was a pause while the woman appeared to be assessing his outfit and his horse. Finally she said, "Half a denarius will cover it, sir."

"She is a liar!" put in Tilla, as if this were not obvious even to Ruso.

He reached for his purse. "Let me tell you what is going to happen here," he said to the woman. "I will give you one sesterce, which is—"

"Is too much!" said Tilla.

"Which is more than the bread was worth," continued Ruso, ignoring her. "My housekeeper will apologize to you—"

"I am not sorry!"

"She will apologize to you," he repeated, "and you will go back to your stall and continue charging exorbitant sums of money to travelers who were foolish enough not to buy before they set out."

Ruso dismissed the grinning soldiers with a tip that was not enough to buy their silence but might limit the scurrilous nature of their exaggerations when they told the story around tonight's campfires. The women seemed less satisfied, but that was hardly surprising. Ruso had long ago learned that the pleasing of women was a tricky business.

By now the bulk of the legionaries had gone on far ahead, followed by a plodding train of army pack ponies laden with tents and millstones and all the other equipment too heavy to be carried on poles on the soldiers' backs. Behind them was the unofficial straggle of camp followers.

Ruso turned to Tilla. "Walk alongside me," he ordered, adding quickly, "Clean side in." She sidestepped around the tail of the horse and came forward to walk at its shoulder. Ruso leaned down and said in a voice which would not be overheard, "None of the other civilians is causing trouble, Tilla. What is the matter with you?"

"I am hungry, my lord."

"I gave you money for food."

"Yes, my lord."

"Was it not enough?"

"It was enough, yes."

She ventured no further information. Ruso straightened up. He was not in the mood for the I-will-only-answer-the-question-you-ask-me game. He was in the mood for a peaceful morning and some more of last night's chicken in pastry, which he now retrieved and began to eat. He glanced sideways. Tilla was watching. He did not offer her any.

They continued in silence along the straight road up and down yet another wooded hill. British hills, it seemed, were as melancholic as British rain. Instead of poking bold fingers of rock up into the clouds, they lay lumpy and morose under damp green blankets, occasionally stirring themselves to roll vaguely skyward and then giving up and sliding into the next valley.

Somewhere among those hills lay the northern edge of the empire, and even further north, beyond the supposedly friendly tribes living along the border, rose wild cold mountains full of barbarians who had never been conquered and now never would be. Unless, of course, the new emperor had a sudden fit of ambition and gave the order to march north and have another crack at them. But so far Hadrian had shown no signs of spoiling for a fight. In fact he had already withdrawn his forces from several provinces he considered untenable. Britannia remained unfinished business: an island only half-conquered, and Ruso had not found it easy to explain to his puzzled housemate back in Deva why he had volunteered to go and peer over the edge into the other half.

"The North? Holy Jupiter, man, you don't want to go up there!" Valens's handsome face had appeared to register genuine concern at his colleague's plans. "It's at—it's *beyond* the edge of the civilized world. Why d'you think we send foreigners up there to run it?"

Ruso had poured himself more wine and observed, "When you think about it, we're all foreigners here. Except the Britons, of course."

"You know what I mean. Troops who are used to those sorts of conditions. The sort of chap who tramps bare chested through bogs and picks his teeth with a knife. They bring them in from Germania, or Gaul, or somewhere."

"I'm from Gaul," Ruso reminded him.

"Yes, but you're from the warm end. You're practically one of us." This was evidently intended as a compliment. "I know you haven't exactly shone here in Deva, after all that business with the barmaids—"

"This has got nothing to do with barmaids," Ruso assured him. "You know I spent half of yesterday afternoon waiting for a bunch of men who didn't turn up?"

"I believe you did mention it once or twice."

"And it's not the first time, either. So I tracked down their centurion today. Apparently he and his cronies have been telling the men they can go for first aid training if they want to."

"If they *want to*?"

"Of course they don't want to. They want to spend their spare time sleeping and fishing and visiting their girlfriends."

"I hope he apologized."

"No. He said he couldn't see the point of teaching ordinary soldiers first aid. He said it's like teaching sailors to swim—just prolongs the agony."

Valens shook his head sadly. "You really shouldn't let a few ignorant centurions banish you to the—" He was interrupted by a crash from the kitchen and a stream of British that had the unmistakeable intonation of a curse. He glanced at the door. "I suppose you're intending to take the lovely Tilla as well?"

"Of course."

"That *is* bad news. I shall miss her unique style of household management." Valens peered down at his dinner bowl and prodded at something with the end of his spoon. "I wonder what this was when it was alive?" He held it up toward the window to examine it, then flicked it off the spoon and onto the floor. One of the dogs trotted forward to examine it. "So," continued Valens. "Where exactly is this unholy outer region?"

"It's a fort called Ulucium. Apparently you go up to Coria and turn left at the border."

"You're going to some flea-bitten outpost beyond the last supply depot?"

"I'm told the area's very beautiful."

"Really? By whom?"

Ruso shrugged. "Just generally . . . by people who've been there." He took refuge in another sip of wine.

Valens shook his head. "Oh, Ruso. When I told you women like to be listened to, I didn't mean you should take any notice of what they say. Of course Tilla says it's very beautiful. She probably wants to go home to visit all her little girlfriends so they can paint their faces blue and dance around the cooking pot, singing ancestor songs. You didn't promise you'd take her home?"

"It's only for a few months. There's a couple of centuries going up to help revamp the fort, fix their plumbing, and encourage the taxpayers."

"You did! You promised her, didn't you?"

Ruso scratched the back of his ear. "I think I may have," he confessed. "It seemed like a good idea at the time."

Ruso took another mouthful of cold pie and wondered whether he should have listened to Valens rather than Tilla. From what he could gather, the principal activities of Tilla's tribe were farming and fighting, fueled by rambling tales about glorious ancestors and a belief that things you couldn't see were just as real as things you could. None of this had mattered much down in the relatively civilized confines of Deva, but as they traveled farther north, Tilla's behavior had definitely begun to deteriorate.

Ruso glanced downward. Tilla's muddy tunic was flapping heavily around her ankles. Thick brown liquid squelched out of her boots with every step.

He sighed, and balanced the remains of the pie on the front of the saddle. He reached out and touched her cheek just above the scrape. "I'll clean that up when we stop. Are you hurt anywhere else?"

"It was a soft landing, my lord. I do not see him coming, or I would fight back."

Ruso was not as sorry about this as his housekeeper seemed to be. "Why didn't you buy food before we set out this morning?"

"There was a woman in labor in the night. I forgot."

"One of the soldiers' women?"

"Yes."

"What on earth was she doing traveling in that condition?"

Tilla shrugged. "When a man marches away, who knows if he will come back? He might find a new woman. The army might send him across the sea. Then what will she do?"

Ruso, who had no idea what she might do, said, "So what happened to her?"

His slave jerked a thumb backward over her shoulder. "She is giving her daughter a bumpy welcome on a cart."

"She's a very lucky woman," observed Ruso.

"The goddess has been kind to her."

Ruso retrieved the crumbling remains of the snack and passed them across. "It's a bit dry. Sorry."

She wiped her mouth and hands on a clean patch of tunic before accepting it. "Thank you, my lord."

"There's to be no more stealing from now on, Tilla. Is that quite clear?" He gestured toward the mud. "You see where it leads."

A smile revealed white teeth in the unusually brown face. "I know where it leads." She patted the outside of her thigh. From beneath her clothing he heard the chink of money. Ruso was not impressed. "I had to pay that woman more than you saved to get you out of trouble," he said.

Tilla eyed him for a moment as if she were considering a reply, then crammed the remains of the food into her mouth, dropped into a crouch at the roadside, and began to scrabble about under her clothing. Ruso glanced around to see one or two people watching, and decided the most dignified reaction was to ride on and pretend he had not noticed.

Moments later he heard her running up behind him. He turned. "Was that really necessary?"

She nodded, and drew breath before announcing, "I have been waiting a long time to tell you something, my lord."

A sudden and deeply worrying thought crossed Ruso's mind. A thought he had been trying to ignore for some months.

He had been careful. Extremely careful. Far more careful than his slave, who on first being introduced to modern methods of contraception had fallen into a fit of disrespectful and uncontrollable laughter. He had insisted, of course, citing three years of successfully child-free marriage—something Tilla evidently thought was nothing to boast about. He had finally persuaded her to complete her part by squatting on the floor, taking a cold drink, and sneezing, but over the months Tilla had proved just as reluctant as Claudia to face the chill of a winter bedroom. Her sneezing too had shown a disappointing lack of commitment. He had given up trying to argue with her. Now he supposed he was going to have to face the consequences.

The horse, sensing his tension through the reins, tossed its head.

"Do you really think," Ruso said, "that this is the best time to tell me?"

"No, but you must know one day, and you will be happy."

"I see."

"Close your eyes, my lord."

"What for?"

"It is nothing bad."

"But why—"

"Is nobody looking."

Ruso glanced around to verify this before obeying. As the view faded away he was conscious of his body shifting with the pace of the horse. Something touched his thigh with a chink, and rested there.

"Is for you, my lord."

He opened his eyes. Hooked over one of the front saddle horns was the leather purse he had given her for the housekeeping money. He felt the muscles in his shoulders relax. Whatever this was, it was not what he had feared.

As he lifted the purse he glanced at his slave. Tilla was watching him, and looked very pleased with herself.

He loosened the drawstring, slid two fingers into the pouch, and pulled out a large warm coin. "What's this?"

"A sesterce."

"I can see that." He really must have a word with Tilla about this literal interpretation of questions. It was bordering on insolence, but so far he had failed to find a way to phrase the reprimand that did not suggest he could have worded his questions better. "Why," he tried again, framing the sentence with care, "are you stealing when you have this much cash?"

Her smile broadened. "I know my lord has no money."

"That's my business, not yours. You aren't going to help by pinching bread and getting into fights."

She pointed at the purse. "All for you."

Ruso tugged at the drawstring and peered inside.

'Gods above!' he exclaimed, weighing the purse in his hand again. He lowered it quickly as an army slave leading a string of pack ponies looked across to see what was happening. When the man had lost interest he investigated the contents of the purse again and leaned down to murmur, "This is a lot of money. Where did you get it?"

Tilla's shrug turned into an expansive gesture that suggested the coins had mysteriously fallen upon her in a rain shower.

"This can't possibly belong to you!"

"I save up."

Ruso sat up and frowned. He had little spare cash. He had certainly not offered any of it to his slave. He assumed she was sometimes paid for helping to deliver babies, and it was quite normal for slaves to try and build up enough funds to buy their freedom. But why would she hand him her personal savings? Besides, this was too much for a handful of babies, no matter how grateful their parents. He glanced at her. "Tilla, how have you . . ." The answer crept up on him as he spoke, stifling the final words of the question.

Tilla had become his housekeeper not long after his arrival in Britannia. Since she knew more about shopping than he did—in fact, almost everyone knew more about shopping than he did—he had never bothered to inquire too deeply into the relationship between cash and catering. He had begun by insisting that she render a weekly account. But after the first week she seemed to have forgotten about it and he had been too busy to insist. In any case, what was the point of having a slave to look after the house if he still had to do all the thinking himself?

A voice rose unbidden from the depths of his memory. *For goodness' sake, Gaius,* it said. *If it weren't for me the staff would walk all over us!*

He was glad Claudia was not here to see him now.

"Tilla," he murmured, "Tell me you don't make a habit of stealing."

She looked surprised. "Oh no, my lord."

"Good. So what is this?"

"I am your servant," she continued. "I will not let you be cheated."

"What?"

"I make things fair."

"Are you telling me," said Ruso, glancing around again to make sure he could not be overheard, "that if you don't approve of the price you help yourself?"

"Is not right that people grow fat on cheating when my lord is a good man and has no—"

"That's hardly the point, Tilla!" Ruso sat back in the saddle, frowned at the whiskery ears of his horse, and wondered how to explain something so fundamental it had never occurred to him to question it. "Ever since I began my work as a doctor," he observed, "I have done my best to build up a good reputation."

"Yes, my lord."

"I want men to say, 'There is Gaius Petreius Ruso, the medicus who can be trusted.' "

"Yes, my lord."

" 'He doesn't pretend to know everything, but he does his best for his patients.' "

"Yes, my lord."

"This has been my ambition."

"Yes, my lord."

"If it ever becomes my ambition to have them say, 'There is Gaius Petreius Ruso, the man who sends his servant out to steal for him,' I will let you know."

"I understand this," came the reply. "I am doing it before you tell me."

A NOTE ON THE AUTHOR

In 2004 Ruth Downie won the Fay Weldon section of BBC3's End of Story competition. *Medicus* is her first novel. She is married with two sons and lives in Milton Keynes, England.

P9-DFA-784

Praise for Donald Ray Pollock's

The Devil All the Time

"Disarmingly smooth prose startled by knife-twists of black humor. . . . Expertly employs the conventions of Southern Gothic horror." —*The Wall Street Journal*

"Reads as if the love child of O'Connor and Faulkner was captured by Cormac McCarthy, kept in a cage out back and forced to consume nothing but onion rings, Oxycontin and Terrence Malick's *Badlands*."
—*The Oregonian*

"[Pollock] doesn't get a word wrong in this super-edgy American Gothic stunner." —*Elle*

"A systematic cataloguing of the horror and hypocrisy that festers in the dark shadow of the American dream." —*The Portland Mercury*

"Features a bleak and often nightmarish vision of the decades following World War II, a world where redemption, on the rare occasions when it does come to town, rides shotgun with soul-scarring consequences."
—*The Onion*, A.V. Club

"Mr. Pollock's new novel is, if anything, even darker than *Knockemstiff*, and its violence and religious preoccupations venture into Flannery O'Connor territory."
—*The New York Times*

"Donald Ray Pollock's engaging and proudly violent first novel . . . suggests a new category of fiction—grindhouse literary. Subtle characterization: check. Well-crafted sentences: check. Enthusiastic amounts of murder and mayhem: check, check."

—*The Daily Beast*

"Beneath the gothic horror is an Old Testament sense of a moral order in the universe, even if the restoration of that order itself requires violence."

—*The Columbus Dispatch*

"For a first novel so soaked in stale sweat and bright fresh blood, Pollock's sweat is well-earned, and his blood is wise." —*Philadelphia Citypaper*

"A gallery of reprobates and religious fanatics . . . are multidimensional, flawed human beings."

—*Dayton Daily News*

"[*The Devil All the Time* is] a world unto its own, a world vividly and powerfully brought to life by a literary stylist who packs a punch as deadly as pulp-fiction master Jim Thompson and as evocative and morally rigorous as Russell Banks." —*Philadelphia Inquirer*

"Stunning . . . . One wild story . . . gives us sex, murder, mayhem and some of the most bizarre characters in fiction today." —*Richmond Times-Dispatch*

DONALD RAY POLLOCK

The Devil All the Time

Donald Ray Pollock, recipient of the 2009 PEN/Robert Bingham Fellowship, made his literary debut in 2008 with the critically acclaimed short story collection *Knockemstiff*. He worked as a laborer at the Mead Paper Mill in Chillicothe, Ohio, from 1973 to 2005.

www.donaldraypollock.com

ALSO BY DONALD RAY POLLOCK

Knockemstiff

The Devil All the Time

A NOVEL

DONALD RAY POLLOCK

ANCHOR BOOKS
A DIVISION OF RANDOM HOUSE, INC.
NEW YORK

FIRST ANCHOR BOOKS EDITION, JULY 2012

Copyright © 2011 by Donald Ray Pollock

All rights reserved. Published in the United States by Anchor Books, a division of Random House, Inc., New York, and in Canada by Random House of Canada Limited, Toronto. Originally published in hardcover in the United States by Doubleday, a division of Random House, Inc., New York, in 2011.

Anchor Books and colophon are registered trademarks of Random House, Inc.

This is a work of fiction. Names, characters, businesses, organizations, places, events, and incidents either are the product of the author's imagination or are used fictitiously. Any resemblance to actual persons, living or dead, events, or locales is entirely coincidental.

The Library of Congress has cataloged the Doubleday edition as follows:
Pollock, Donald Ray
The devil all the time / Donald Ray Pollock.—1st ed.
p. cm.
I. Ohio—Rural conditions—Fiction. I. Title.
PS3616.O5694D48 2011
813'.6—dc22
2010053322

Anchor ISBN: 978-0-307-74486-9

Book design by Pei Koay

www.anchorbooks.com

Printed in the United States of America
10 9 8 7

ONCE AGAIN
FOR
PATSY

The Devil All the Time

PROLOGUE

ON A DISMAL MORNING near the end of a wet October, Arvin Eugene Russell hurried behind his father, Willard, along the edge of a pasture that overlooked a long and rocky holler in southern Ohio called Knockemstiff. Willard was tall and raw-boned, and Arvin had a hard time keeping up with him. The field was overgrown with brier patches and fading clumps of chickweed and thistle, and ground fog, thick as the gray clouds above, reached to the nine-year-old boy's knees. After a few minutes, they veered off into the woods and followed a narrow deer path down the hill until they came to a log lying in a small clearing, the remains of a big red oak that had fallen many years ago. A weathered cross, fitted together out of boards pried from the back of the ramshackle barn behind their farmhouse, leaned slightly eastward in the soft ground a few yards below them.

Willard eased himself down on the high side of the log and motioned for his son to kneel beside him in the dead, soggy leaves. Unless he had whiskey running through his veins, Willard came to the clearing every morning and evening to talk to God. Arvin didn't know which was worse, the drinking or the praying. As far back as he could remember, it seemed that his father had fought the Devil all the time. Arvin shivered with the damp, pulled his coat a little tighter. He wished he were still in bed. Even school, with all its miseries, was better than this, but it was a Saturday and there was no way to get around it.

Through the mostly bare trees beyond the cross, Arvin could see wisps of smoke rising from a few chimneys half a mile away. Four hundred or so people lived in Knockemstiff in 1957, nearly all of them connected by blood through one godforsaken calamity or another, be it lust or necessity or just plain ignorance. Along with the tar-papered shacks and cinder-block houses, the holler included two general stores and a Church of Christ in Christian Union and a joint known throughout the township as the Bull Pen. Though the Russells had rented the house on top of the Mitchell Flats for five years now, most of the neighbors down below still considered them outsiders. Arvin was the only kid on the school bus who wasn't somebody's relation. Three days before, he'd come home with another black eye. "I don't condone no fighting just for the hell of it, but sometimes you're just too easygoing," Willard had told him that evening. "Them boys might be bigger than you, but the next time one of 'em starts his shit, I want you to finish it." Willard was standing on the porch changing out of his work clothes. He handed Arvin the brown pants, stiff with dried blood and grease. He worked in a slaughterhouse in Greenfield, and that day sixteen hundred hogs had been butchered, a new record for R. J. Carroll Meatpacking. Though the boy didn't know yet what he wanted to do when he grew up, he was pretty sure he didn't want to kill pigs for a living.

They had just begun their prayers when the sharp crack of a branch breaking sounded behind them. As Arvin started to turn around, Willard reached over and stopped him, but not before the boy caught a glimpse of two hunters in the pale light, dirty and ragged men whom he'd seen a few times slouching in the front seat of an old sedan scabbed with rust in the parking lot of Maude Speakman's store. One carried a brown burlap sack, the bottom stained a bright red. "Don't pay them no mind," Willard said quietly. "This here is the Lord's time, not nobody else's."

Knowing that the men were close by made him nervous, but Arvin settled back down and closed his eyes. Willard considered the log as holy as any church built by man, and the last person in the world the boy wanted to offend was his father, even though that seemed like a losing battle at times. Except for the dampness dripping from the leaves and a squirrel cutting in a tree nearby, the woods were still again. Arvin was just beginning to think the men had moved on when one of them said in a raspy voice, "Hell, they havin' them a little revival meeting."

"Keep it down," Arvin heard the other man say.

"Shit. I'm thinking now would be a good time to pay his old lady a visit. She probably laying over there in bed right now keeping it warm for me."

"Shut the fuck up, Lucas," the other said.

"What? Don't tell me you wouldn't take a piece of that. She's a looker, damned if she ain't."

Arvin glanced over uneasily at his father. Willard's eyes remained shut, his big hands woven together on top of the log. His lips moved rapidly, but the words he said were too faint for anyone but the Master to hear. The boy thought about what Willard had told him the other day, about standing up for yourself when someone gave you some shit. Evidently, those were just words, too. He had a sinking feeling that the long ride on the school bus was not going to get any better.

"Come on, you dumb sonofabitch," the other man said, "this thing's getting heavy." Arvin listened as they turned and made their way back across the hill in the direction from which they'd come. Long after their footsteps faded away, he could still hear the mouthy one laughing.

A few minutes later, Willard stood up and waited for his

son to say his amens. Then they walked back to the house in silence, scraped the mud off their shoes on the porch steps, and entered the warm kitchen. Arvin's mother, Charlotte, was frying slices of bacon in an iron skillet, beating eggs with a fork in a blue bowl. She poured Willard a cup of coffee, set a glass of milk down in front of Arvin. Her black, shiny hair was pulled back in a ponytail, secured with a rubber band, and she wore a faded pink robe and a pair of fuzzy socks, one with a hole in the heel. As Arvin watched her move about the room, he tried to imagine what might have happened if the two hunters had come on to the house instead of turning around. His mother was the prettiest woman he'd ever seen. He wondered if she would have invited them in.

As soon as Willard finished eating, he pushed back his chair and went outside with a dark look on his face. He hadn't said a word since he'd finished his prayers. Charlotte got up from the table with her coffee and stepped over to the window. She watched him stomp across the yard and go into the barn. She considered the possibility that he had an extra bottle hid out there. The one he kept under the sink hadn't been touched in several weeks. She turned and looked at Arvin. "Your daddy mad at you for something?"

Arvin shook his head. "I didn't do nothing."

"That ain't what I asked you," Charlotte said, leaning against the counter. "We both know how he can get."

For a moment, Arvin considered telling his mother what had happened at the prayer log, but the shame was too great. It made him sick to think that his father would listen to a man talk about her that way and just ignore it. "Had a little revival meeting, that's all," he said.

"Revival meeting?" Charlotte said. "Where did you get that from?"

"I don't know, just heard it somewhere." Then he got up

and walked down the hallway to his bedroom. He closed the door and lay down on the bed, pulling the top blanket over him. Turning on his side, he stared at the framed picture of the crucified Jesus that Willard had hung above the scratched and battered chest of drawers. Similar pictures of the Savior's execution could be found in every room of the house except the kitchen. Charlotte had drawn the line there, the same as she'd done when he started taking Arvin over to the woods to pray. "Only on the weekends, Willard, that's it," she'd said. The way she saw it, too much religion could be as bad as too little, maybe even worse; but moderation was just not in her husband's nature.

An hour or so later, Arvin was awakened by his father's voice in the kitchen. He jumped off the bed and smoothed the wrinkles out of the wool blanket, then went to the door and pressed his ear against it. He heard Willard ask Charlotte if she needed anything from the store. "I got to gas up the truck for work," he told her. When he heard his father's footsteps in the hall, Arvin moved quickly away from the door and across the room. He was standing by the window pretending to study an arrowhead he'd picked up from the small collection of treasures he had lying on the sill. The door opened. "Let's take a ride," Willard said. "No sense you sitting in here like a house cat all day."

As they walked out the front door, Charlotte yelled from the kitchen, "Don't forget the sugar." They got in the pickup and drove out to the end of their rutted lane and then turned down Baum Hill Road. At the stop sign, Willard made a left onto the stretch of paved road that cut through the middle of Knockemstiff. Though the trip to Maude's store never took more than five minutes, it always seemed to Arvin as if he had entered another country when they came off the Flats. At the Patterson place, a group of boys, some younger than himself, stood in the open doorway of a dilapidated garage passing cigarettes back and forth and taking turns punching a gutted deer carcass that hung from a joist. One of the boys whooped and took several swings at the chilly air as they drove past, and Arvin scooted down in his seat. In front of Janey Wagner's house, a pink baby crawled around in the yard under a maple tree. Janey was standing on the sagging porch pointing at the baby and yelling through a broken window patched with cardboard at someone inside. She was wearing the same outfit she wore to school every day, a red plaid skirt and a frayed white blouse. Though she was only a grade ahead of Arvin in school, Janey always sat in the rear of the bus with the older boys on the way home. He'd heard some of the other girls say that they allowed her back there because she'd spread her legs and let them play stink finger with her snatch. He hoped that maybe someday, when he was a little older, he would find out exactly what that meant.

Instead of stopping at the store, Willard made a sharp right up the gravel road called Shady Glen. He gave the truck some gas and whirled into the bald, muddy yard that surrounded the Bull Pen. It was littered with bottle caps and cigarette butts and beer cartons. An ex-railroader spotted with warty skin cancers named Snooks Snyder lived there with his sister, Agnes, an old maid who sat in an upstairs window all day dressed in black and pretending to be a grieving widow. Snooks sold beer and wine out of the front of the house, and, if your face was even vaguely familiar, something with a lot more kick out the back. For his customers' convenience, several picnic tables were set up under some tall sycamores off to the side of the house, along with a horseshoe pit and an outhouse that always appeared on the verge of collapse. The two men that Arvin had seen in the woods that morning were sitting on top of one of the tables drinking beer, their shotguns leaning against a tree behind them.

With the truck still rolling to a stop, Willard pushed the door open and leaped out. One of the hunters stood up and threw a bottle that glanced off the truck's windshield and landed with a clatter in the road. Then the man turned and started running, his filthy coat flapping behind him and his bloodshot eyes looking around wildly at the big man chasing him. Willard caught up and shoved him down into the greasy slop pooled in front of the outhouse door. Rolling him over, he pinned the man's skinny shoulders with his knees and began pounding the bearded face with his fists. The other hunter grabbed one of the guns and hurried to a green Plymouth, a brown paper sack under his arm. He sped away, bald tires slinging gravel all the way past the church.

After a couple of minutes, Willard stopped beating the man. He shook the sting out of his hands and took a deep breath, then walked over to the table where the men had been sitting. He picked up the shotgun propped against the tree, unloaded two red shells, then swung it like a ball bat against the sycamore until it shattered into several pieces. As he turned and started for the truck, he glanced over and saw Snooks Snyder standing in the doorway with a stubby pistol pointed at him. He took a few steps toward the porch. "Old man, you want some of what he got," Willard said in a loud voice, "you just step on out here. I'll stick that gun clear up your ass." He stood waiting until Snooks closed the door.

When he got back inside the pickup, Willard reached under the seat for a rag and wiped the traces of blood off his hands. "You remember what I told you the other day?" he asked Arvin.

"About them boys on the bus?"

"Well, that's what I meant," Willard said, nodding over at the hunter. He tossed the rag out the window. "You just got to pick the right time."

"Yes, sir," Arvin said.

"They's a lot of no-good sonofabitches out there."

"More than a hundred?"

Willard laughed a little and put the truck in gear. "Yeah, at least that many." He started to ease the clutch out. "I'm thinking it best if we keep this between us, okay? No sense gettin' your mom all upset."

"No, she don't need that."

"Good," Willard said. "Now how about I buy you a candy bar?"

For a long time, Arvin would often think of that as the best day he ever spent with his father. After supper that evening, he followed Willard back over to the prayer log. The moon was rising by the time they got there, a sliver of ancient and pitted bone accompanied by a single, shimmering star. They knelt down and Arvin glanced over at his father's skinned knuckles. When she'd asked, Willard had told Charlotte that he'd hurt his hand changing a flat tire. Arvin had never heard his father lie before, but he felt certain that God would forgive him. In the still, darkening woods, the sounds traveling up the hill from the holler were especially clear that night. Down at the Bull Pen, the clanging of the horseshoes against the metal pegs sounded almost like church bells ringing, and the wild hoots and jeers of the drunks reminded the boy of the hunter lying bloody in the mud. His father had taught that man a lesson he'd never forget; and the next time somebody messed with him, Arvin was going to do the same. He closed his eyes and began to pray.

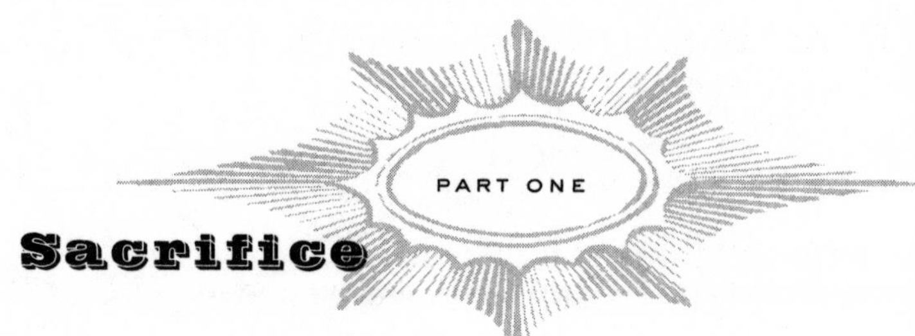

PART ONE

Sacrifice

I

IT WAS A WEDNESDAY AFTERNOON in the fall of 1945, not long after the war had ended. The Greyhound made its regular stop in Meade, Ohio, a piddling paper-mill town an hour south of Columbus that smelled like rotten eggs. Strangers complained about the stench, but the locals liked to brag that it was the sweet smell of money. The bus driver, a soft, sawed-off man who wore elevated shoes and a limp bow tie, pulled in the alley beside the depot and announced a forty-minute break. He wished he could have a cup of coffee, but his ulcer was acting up again. He yawned and took a swig from a bottle of pink medicine he kept on the dashboard. The smokestack across town, by far the tallest structure in this part of the state, belched forth another dirty brown cloud. You could see it for miles, puffing like a volcano about to blow its skinny top.

Leaning back in his seat, the bus driver pulled his leather cap down over his eyes. He lived right outside of Philadelphia, and he thought that if he ever had to live in a place like Meade, Ohio, he'd go ahead and shoot himself. You couldn't even find a bowl of lettuce in this town. All that people seemed to eat here was grease and more grease. He'd be dead in two months eating the slop they did. His wife told her friends that he was delicate, but there was something about the tone of her voice that sometimes made him wonder if she was really being sympathetic. If it hadn't been for the ulcer, he would have gone off to fight with the rest of the men. He'd have slaughtered a whole platoon of Germans and shown her just how goddamn delicate he was. The biggest regret was all the medals he'd missed out on. His father once got a certificate from the railroad for not missing a single day of work in twenty years, and had pointed it out to his sickly son every time he'd seen him for the next twenty. When the old man finally croaked, the bus driver tried to talk his mother into sticking the certificate in the casket with the body so he wouldn't have to look at it anymore. But she insisted on leaving it displayed in the living room as an example of what a person could attain in this life if he didn't let a little indigestion get in his way. The funeral, an event the bus driver had looked forward to for a long time, had nearly been ruined by all the arguing over that crummy scrap of paper. He would be glad when all the discharged soldiers finally reached their destinations so he wouldn't have to look at the dumb bastards anymore. It wore on you after a while, other people's accomplishments.

Private Willard Russell had been drinking in the back of the bus with two sailors from Georgia, but one had passed out and the other had puked in their last jug. He kept thinking that if he ever got home, he'd never leave Coal Creek, West Virginia, again. He'd seen some hard things growing up in the hills, but they didn't hold a candle to what he'd witnessed in the South Pacific. On one of the Solomons, he and a couple of other men from his outfit had run across a marine skinned alive by the Japanese and nailed to a cross made out of two palm trees. The raw, bloody body was covered with black flies. They could still see the man's heart beating in his chest. His dog tags were hanging from what remained of one of his big toes: Gunnery Sergeant Miller Jones. Unable to offer anything but a little mercy, Willard shot the marine behind the ear, and they took him down and covered him with rocks at the foot of the cross. The inside of Willard's head hadn't been the same since.

When he heard the tubby bus driver yell something about a break, Willard stood up and started toward the door, disgusted with the two sailors. In his opinion, the navy was one branch of the military that should never be allowed to drink. In the three years he'd served in the army, he hadn't met a single swabby who could hold his liquor. Someone had told him that it was because of the saltpeter they were fed to keep them from going crazy and fucking each other when they were out to sea. He wandered outside the bus depot and saw a little restaurant across the street called the Wooden Spoon. There was a piece of white cardboard stuck in the window advertising a meat loaf special for thirty-five cents. His mother had fixed him a meat loaf the day before he left for the army, and he considered that a good sign. In a booth by the window, he sat down and lit a cigarette. A shelf made of poplar ran around the room, lined with cloudy antique bottles and tarnished kitchenware and cracked black-and-white photographs of bygone people for the dust to settle on. Tacked to the wall by the booth was a faded newspaper account of a Meade police officer who'd been gunned down by a bank robber in front of the bus depot. Willard looked closer, saw that it was dated February 11, 1936. That would have been four days before his twelfth birthday, he calculated. An elderly man, the only other customer in the diner, was bent over at a table in the middle of the room slurping a bowl of green soup. His false teeth rested on top of a stick of butter in front of him.

Willard finished the cigarette and was just getting ready to leave when a dark-haired waitress finally stepped out of the kitchen. She grabbed a menu from a stack by the cash register and handed it to him. "I'm sorry," she said, "I didn't hear you come in." Looking at her high cheekbones and full lips and long, slender legs, Willard discovered, when she asked him what he wanted to eat, that the spit had dried in his mouth. He could barely speak. That had never happened to him before, not even in the middle of the worst fighting on Bougainville. While she went to put the order in and get him a cup of coffee, the thought went through his head that just a couple of months ago he was certain that his life was going to end on some steamy, worthless rock in the middle of the Pacific Ocean; and now here he was, still sucking air and just a few hours from home, being waited on by a woman who looked like a live version of one of those pinup movie angels. As best as Willard could ever tell, that was when he fell in love. It didn't matter that the meat loaf was dry and the green beans were mushy and the roll as hard as a lump of #5 coal. As far as he was concerned, she served him the best meal he ever had in his life. And after he finished it, he got back on the bus without even knowing Charlotte Willoughby's name.

Across the river in Huntington, he found a liquor store when the bus made another stop, and bought five pints of bonded whiskey that he stuck away in his pack. He sat in the front now, right behind the driver, thinking about the girl in the diner and looking for some indication that he was getting close to home. He was still a little drunk. Out of the blue, the bus driver said, "Bringing any medals back?" He glanced at Willard in the rearview mirror.

Willard shook his head. "Just this skinny old carcass I'm walking around in."

"I wanted to go, but they wouldn't take me."

"You're lucky," Willard said. The day they'd come across the marine, the fighting on the island was nearly over, and the sergeant had sent them out looking for some water fit to drink. A couple of hours after they buried Miller Jones's flayed body, four starving Japanese soldiers with fresh bloodstains on their machetes came out of the rocks with their hands up in the air and surrendered. When Willard and his two buddies started to lead them back to the location of the cross, the soldiers dropped to their knees and started begging or apologizing, he didn't know which. "They tried to escape," Willard lied to the sergeant later in the camp. "We didn't have no choice." After they had executed the Japs, one of the men with him, a Louisiana boy who wore a swamp rat's foot around his neck to ward off slant-eyed bullets, cut their ears off with a straight razor. He had a cigar box full of ones he'd already dried. His plan was to sell the trophies for five bucks apiece once they got back to civilization.

"I got an ulcer," the bus driver said.

"You didn't miss nothing."

"I don't know," the bus driver said. "I sure would have liked to got me some medals. I figure I could have killed enough of those Kraut bastards for two anyway. I'm pretty quick with my hands."

Looking at the back of the bus driver's head, Willard thought about the conversation he'd had with the gloomy young priest on board the ship after he confessed that he'd shot the marine to put him out of his misery. The priest was sick of all the death he'd seen, all the prayers he'd said over rows of dead soldiers and piles of body parts. He told Willard that if even half of history was true, then the only thing this depraved and corrupt world was good for was preparing you for the next. "Did you know," Willard said to the driver, "that the Romans used to gut donkeys and sew Christians up alive inside the carcasses and leave them out in the sun to rot?" The priest had been full of such stories.

"What the hell's that got to do with a medal?"

"Just think about it. You're trussed up like a turkey in a pan with just your head sticking out a dead donkey's ass; and then the maggots eating away at you until you see the glory."

The bus driver frowned, gripped the steering wheel a little tighter. "Friend, I don't see what you're getting at. I was talking about coming home with a big medal pinned to your chest. Did these Roman fellers give out medals to them people before they stuck 'em in the donkeys? Is that what you mean?"

Willard didn't know what he meant. According to the priest, only God could figure out the ways of men. He licked his dry lips, thought about the whiskey in his pack. "What I'm saying is that when it comes right down to it, everybody suffers in the end," Willard said.

"Well," the bus driver said, "I'd liked to have my medal before then. Heck, I got a wife at home who goes nuts every time she sees one. Talk about suffering. I worry myself sick anytime I'm out on the road she's gonna take off with a purple heart."

Willard leaned forward and the driver felt the soldier's hot breath on the back of his fat neck, smelled the whiskey fumes and the stale traces of a cheap lunch. "You think Miller Jones would give a shit if his old lady was out fucking around on him?" Willard said. "Buddy, he'd trade places with you any goddamn day."

"Who the hell is Miller Jones?"

Willard looked out the window as the hazy top of Greenbrier Mountain started to appear in the distance. His hands were trembling, his brow shiny with sweat. "Just some poor bastard who went and fought in that war they cheated you out of, that's all."

WILLARD WAS JUST GETTING READY to break down and crack open one of the pints when his uncle Earskell pulled up in his rattly Ford in front of the Greyhound station in Lewisburg at the corner of Washington and Court. He had been sitting on a bench outside for almost three hours, nursing a cold coffee in a paper cup and watching people walk by the Pioneer Drugstore. He was ashamed of the way he'd talked to the bus driver, sorry that he'd brought up the marine's name like he did; and he vowed that, though he would never forget him, he'd never mention Gunnery Sergeant Miller Jones to anyone again. Once they were on the road, he reached into his duffel and handed Earskell one of the pints along with a German Luger. He'd traded a Japanese ceremonial sword for the pistol at the base in Maryland right before he got discharged. "That's supposed to be the gun Hitler used to blow his brains out," Willard said, trying to hold back a grin.

"Bullshit," Earskell said.

Willard laughed. "What? You think the guy lied to me?"

"Ha!" the old man said. He twisted the cap off the bottle, took a long pull, then shuddered. "Lord, this is good stuff."

"Drink up. I got three more in my kit." Willard opened another pint and lit a cigarette. He stuck his arm out the window. "How's my mother doing?"

"Well, I gotta say, when they sent Junior Carver's body back, she went a little off in the head there for a while. But she seems pretty good now." Earskell took another hit off the pint and set it between his legs. "She just been worried about you, that's all."

They climbed slowly into the hills toward Coal Creek. Earskell wanted to hear some war stories, but the only thing his nephew talked about for the next hour was some woman he'd met in Ohio. It was the most he'd ever heard Willard talk in his life. He wanted to ask if it was true that the Japs ate their own dead, like the newspaper said, but he figured that could wait. Besides, he needed to pay attention to his driving. The whiskey was going down awful smooth, and his eyes weren't as good as they used to be. Emma had been waiting on her son to return home for a long time, and it would be a shame if he wrecked and killed them both before she got to see him. Earskell chuckled a little to himself at the thought of that. His sister was one of the most God-fearing people he'd ever met, but she'd follow him straight into hell to make him pay for that one.

"WELL, WHAT IS IT EXACTLY you like about this girl?" Emma Russell asked Willard. It had been near midnight when he and Earskell parked the Ford at the bottom of the hill and climbed the path to the small log house. When he came through the door, she carried on for quite a while, grabbing onto him and soaking the front of his uniform with her tears. He watched over her shoulder as his uncle slipped into the kitchen. Her hair had turned gray since Willard had seen her last. "I'd ask you to get down with me and thank Jesus," she said, wiping the tears from her face with the hem of her apron, "but I can smell liquor on your breath."

Willard nodded. He'd been brought up to believe that you never talked to God when you were under the influence. A man needed to be sincere with the Master at all times in case he was ever really in need. Even Willard's father, Tom Russell, a moonshiner who'd been hounded by bad luck and trouble right up to the day he died of a diseased liver in a Parkersburg jail, ascribed to that belief. No matter how desperate the situation—and his old man had been caught in plenty of those—he wouldn't ask for help from on High if he had even a spoonful in him.

"Well, come on back to the kitchen," Emma said. "You can eat and I'll put on some coffee. I made you a meat loaf."

By three in the morning, he and Earskell had killed four pints along with a cupful of shine and were working on the last bottle of store-bought. Willard's head was fuzzy, and he was having a hard time putting his words together, though evidently he'd mentioned to his mother the waitress he'd seen in the diner. "What was that you asked me?" he said to her.

"That girl you was talkin' about," she said. "What is it you like about her?" She was pouring him another cup of boiling coffee from a pan. Though his tongue was numb, he was sure he'd already burned it more than once. A kerosene lamp hanging from a beam in the ceiling lit the room. His mother's wide shadow wavered on the wall. He spilled some coffee on the oilcloth that covered the table. Emma shook her head and reached behind her for a dishrag.

"Everything," he said. "You should see her."

Emma figured it was just the whiskey talking, but her son's announcement that he'd met a woman still made her uneasy. Mildred Carver, as good a Christian woman as ever there was in Coal Creek, had prayed for her Junior every day, but they'd still sent him home in a box. Right after she heard that the pallbearers doubted that there was even anything in the casket, as light as it was, Emma started looking for a sign that would tell her what to do to guarantee Willard's safety. She was still searching when Helen Hatton's family burned up in a house fire, leaving the poor girl all alone. Two days later, after much deliberation, Emma got down on her knees and promised God that if He would bring her son home alive, she'd make sure that he married Helen and took care of her. But now, standing in the kitchen looking at his dark, wavy hair and chiseled features, she realized she'd been crazy to ever pledge such a thing. Helen wore a dirty bonnet tied under her square chin, and her long, horsey face was the spitting image of her grandmother Rachel's, considered by many the homeliest woman who ever walked the ridges of Greenbrier County. At the time, Emma hadn't considered what might happen if she couldn't keep her promise. If only she had been blessed with an ugly son, she thought. God had some funny ideas when it came to letting people know He was displeased.

"Looks ain't everything," Emma said.

"Who says?"

"Shut up, Earskell," Emma said. "What's that girl's name again?"

Willard shrugged. He squinted at the picture of Jesus carrying the cross that hung above the door. Ever since entering the kitchen, he had avoided looking at it, for fear of ruining his homecoming with more thoughts of Miller Jones. But now, just for a moment, he gave himself over to the image. The picture had been there as long as he could remember, spotty with age in a cheap wooden frame. It seemed almost alive in the flickering light from the lantern. He could almost hear the cracks of the whips, the cruel taunts of Pilate's soldiers. He glanced down at the German Luger lying on the table by Earskell's plate.

"What? You don't even know her name?"

"Didn't ask," Willard said. "I left her a dollar tip, though."

"She won't forget that," Earskell said.

"Well, maybe you ought to pray about it before you go traipsing back up to Ohio," Emma said. "That's a long ways off." All her life, she had believed that people should follow the Lord's will and not their own. A person had to trust that everything turns out just as it's supposed to in this world. But then Emma had lost that faith, ended up trying to barter with God like He was nothing more than a horse trader with a plug of chew in his jaw or a ragged tinker out peddling dented wares along the road. Now, no matter how it turned out, she had to at least make an effort to uphold her part of the bargain. After that, she would leave it up to Him. "I don't think that would hurt none, do you? If you prayed on it?" She turned and started covering what was left of the meat loaf with a clean towel.

Willard blew on his coffee, then took a sip and grimaced. He thought about the waitress, the tiny, barely visible scar above her left eyebrow. Two weeks, he figured, and then he'd drive up and talk to her. He glanced over at his uncle trying to roll a cigarette. Earskell's hands were gnarled and twisted with arthritis, the knuckles big around as quarters. "No," Willard said, pouring the last of the whiskey into his cup, "that never hurt none at all."

2

WILLARD WAS HUNGOVER and shaky and sitting by himself on one of the back benches in the Coal Creek Church of the Holy Ghost Sanctified. It was nearly seven thirty on a Thursday evening, but the service hadn't started yet. It was the fourth night of the church's annual weeklong revival, aimed mostly at backsliders and those who hadn't been saved yet. Willard had been home over a week, and this was the first day he'd drawn a sober breath. Last night he and Earskell had gone to the Lewis Theater to see John Wayne in *Back to Bataan*. He walked out halfway through the movie, disgusted with the phoniness of it all, ended up in a fight at the pool hall down the street. He roused himself and looked around, flexed his sore hand. Emma was still up front visiting. Smoky lanterns hung along the walls; a dented wood stove sat halfway down the aisle off to the right. The pine benches were worn smooth by over twenty years of worship. Though the church was the same humble place it had always been, Willard was afraid that he had changed quite a bit since he had been overseas.

Reverend Albert Sykes had started the church in 1924, shortly after a coal mine collapsed and trapped him in the dark with two other men who'd been killed instantly. Both of his legs had been broken in several places. He managed to reach a pack of Five Brothers chewing tobacco in Phil Drury's pocket, but he couldn't stretch far enough to grab hold of the butter and jam sandwich he knew Burl Meadows was carrying in his coat. He said he was touched by the Spirit on the third night.

He realized he was going to soon join the men beside him, already putrid with the smell of death, but it didn't matter anymore. A few hours later, the rescuers broke through the rubble while he was asleep. For a moment, he was convinced that the light they shined in his eyes was the face of the Lord. It was a good story to tell in church, and there were always a lot of Hallelujahs when he came to that part. Willard figured he'd heard the old preacher tell it a hundred times over the years, limping back and forth in front of the varnished pulpit. At the end of the story, he always pulled the empty Five Brothers pack out of his threadbare suit coat, held it up toward the ceiling cradled in the palms of his hands. He carried it with him everywhere. Many of the women around Coal Creek, especially those who still had husbands and sons in the mines, treated it like a religious relic, kissing it whenever they got a chance. It was a fact that Mary Ellen Thompson, on her deathbed, had asked for it to be brought to her instead of the doctor.

Willard watched his mother talking to a thin woman wearing wire-rim glasses set crooked on her long, slender face, a faded blue bonnet tied under her pointy chin. After a couple of minutes, Emma grabbed the woman's hand and led her back to where he was sitting. "I asked Helen to sit with us," Emma told her son. He stood up and let them in, and as the girl passed by him, the odor of sour sweat made his eyes water. She carried a worn leather Bible, kept her head down when Emma introduced her. Now he understood why his mother had been going on for the last few days about why good looks were not all that important. He would agree that was true in most cases, that the spirit was more important than the flesh, but hell, even his uncle Earskell washed his armpits once in a while.

Because the church had no bell, Reverend Sykes went to the open door when it was time for the service to start and shouted to those still loitering outside with their cigarettes and gossip and doubts. A small choir, two men and three women, stood up and sang "Sinner, You'd Better Get Ready." Then Sykes went to the pulpit. He looked out over the crowd, wiped the sweat off his brow with a white handkerchief. There were fifty-eight people sitting on the benches. He'd counted twice. The reverend wasn't a greedy man, but he was hoping on the basket bringing in maybe three or four dollars tonight. He and his wife had been eating nothing but hardtack and warbled squirrel meat for the past week. "Whew, it's hot," he said with a grin. "But it's bound to get hotter, ain't that right? Especially for them that ain't right with the Lord."

"Amen," someone said.

"Surely is," said another.

"Well," Sykes went on, "we gonna take care of that shortly. They's two boys from over around Topperville gonna lead the service tonight, and from what everyone tells me, they got a good message." He glanced at the two strangers sitting in the shadows off to the side of the altar, hidden from the congregation by a frayed black curtain. "Brother Roy and Brother Theodore, get on over here and help us save some lost souls," he said, motioning them forward with his hand.

A tall, skinny man stood up and pushed the other, a fat boy in a squeaky wheelchair, out from behind the curtain and near the center of the altar. The one with the good legs wore a baggy black suit and a pair of heavy, broken-down brogans. His brown hair was slicked back with oil, his sunken cheeks pitted and scarred purple from acne. "My name is Roy Laferty," he said in a quiet voice, "and this here is my cousin, Theodore Daniels." The cripple nodded and smiled at the crowd. He held a banged-up guitar in his lap and sported a soup-bowl haircut. His overalls were mended with patches cut from a feed sack, and his thin legs were twisted up under him at sharp angles. He had on a dirty white shirt and a brightly flowered tie. Later, Willard said that one looked like the Prince of Darkness and the other like a clown down on his luck.

In silence Brother Theodore finished tuning a string on his flattop. A few people yawned, and others began whispering among themselves, already fidgety with what seemed to be the beginning of a boring service by a motley pair of shy newcomers. Willard wished he'd slipped out to the parking lot and found someone with a jug before things got started. He had never felt comfortable worshipping God around strangers packed together inside a building. "We ain't passing no basket tonight, folks," Brother Roy finally said after the cripple nodded that he was ready. "Don't want no money for doing the Lord's work. Me and Theodore can get by on the sweetness of the air if we have to, and, believe me, we've done it a many a time. Savin' souls ain't about the filthy dollar." Roy looked to the old preacher, who managed a sick smile and nodded in reluctant agreement. "Now we gonna summon the Holy Ghost to this little church tonight, or, I swear to you all, we gonna die trying." And with that, the fat boy hit a lick on the guitar and Brother Roy leaned back and let out a high, awful wail that sounded as if he was trying to shake the very gates of heaven loose. Half the congregation nearly jumped out of their seats. Willard chuckled when he felt his mother jerk against him.

The young preacher started pacing up and down the center of the aisle asking people in a loud voice, "Now what is it you most afraid of?" He waved his arms and described the loathsomeness of hell—the filth, horror, and despair—and the eternity that stretches out in front of everyone forever and ever without end. "If your worst fear is rats, then Satan will make sure you get your fill of 'em. Brothers and sisters, they'll chew your face off while you lay there unable to lift a single finger against them, and it won't ever cease. A million years in eternity ain't even an afternoon here in Coal Creek. Don't even try and figure that up. Ain't no human head big enough to calculate misery like that. Remember that family over in Millersburg got murdered in their beds last year? The ones had their eyes cut out by that lunatic? Imagine that for a trillion years—that's a million million, people, I looked it up—being tortured like that, but never dying. Having your peepers plucked out of your head with a bloody ol' knife over and over again, forever. I hope them poor people was right with the Lord when that maniac slipped in their window, I surely do. And really, brothers and sisters, we can't even picture the ways the Devil's got to torment us, ain't no man ever been evil enough, not even that Hitler feller, to come up with the ways Satan is gonna make the sinners pay come the Judgment Day."

While Brother Roy preached, Theodore kept up a rhythm on the guitar that matched the flow of the words, his eyes following the other's every movement. Roy was his cousin on his mother's side, but sometimes the fat boy wished they weren't so closely related. Though he was satisfied with just being able to spread the Gospel with him, he'd had feelings for a long time that he couldn't pray away. He knew what the Bible said, but he couldn't accept that the Lord thought such a thing a sin. Love was love, the way Theodore saw it. Heck, hadn't he proved that, showed God that he loved him more than anyone? Taking that poison until he wound up a cripple, showing the Lord that he had the faith, even though sometimes now he couldn't help thinking that maybe he'd been a little too enthusiastic. But for now, he had God and he had Roy and he had his guitar, and that was all he needed to get by in this world, even if he never did get to stand up straight again. And if Theodore had to prove to Roy how much he loved him, he'd gladly do that, too, anything he asked. God was Love; and He was everywhere, in everything.

Then Roy hopped back up on the altar, reached under

Brother Theodore's wheelchair, and brought out a gallon jar. Everyone leaned forward a bit on the benches. A dark mass seemed to be boiling inside it. Someone called out, "Praise God," and Brother Roy said, "That's right, my friend, that's right." He held up the jar and gave it a violent shake. "People, let me tell you something," he went on. "Before I found the Holy Ghost, I was scared plumb to death of spiders. Ain't that right, Theodore? Ever since I was a little runt hiding under my mother's long skirts. Spiders crawled through my dreams and laid eggs in my nightmares, and I couldn't even go to the outhouse without someone holding my hand. They was hanging in their webs everywhere waiting on me. It was an awful way to live, in fear all the time, awake or asleep, it didn't matter. And that's what hell is like, brothers and sisters. I never got no rest from them eight-legged devils. Not until I found the Lord."

Then Roy dropped to his knees and gave the jar another jiggle before he twisted the lid off. Theodore slowed the music down until all that was left was a sad, ominous dirge that chilled the room, raised the short hairs on the backs of necks. Holding the jar above him, Roy looked out over the crowd and took a deep breath and turned it over. A variegated mass of spiders, brown ones and black ones and orange- and-yellow-striped ones, fell on top of his head and shoulders. Then a shiver ran through his body like an electric current, and he stood up and slammed the jar to the floor, sending shards of glass flying everywhere. He let out that awful screech again, and began shaking his arms and legs, the spiders falling off onto the floor and scurrying away in all directions. Some lady wrapped in a knitted shawl jumped up and hurried toward the door and several more screamed, and in the midst of the commotion, Roy stepped forward, a few spiders still clinging to his sweaty face, and yelled, "Mark my word, people, the Lord, He'll take away all your fears if you let Him. Look what He's done for me." Then he cleared his throat and spit something black out of his mouth.

Another woman started beating at her dress, crying out that she'd been bit, and a couple of children started blubbering. Reverend Sykes ran back and forth attempting to restore some order, but by then people were scrambling toward the narrow door in a panic. Emma took Helen by the arm, trying to lead her out of the church. But the girl shook her off and turned and walked into the aisle. She held her Bible against her flat chest as she stared at Brother Roy. Still strumming his guitar, Theodore watched his cousin nonchalantly brush a spider off his ear, then smile at the frail, plain-looking girl. He didn't stop playing until he saw Roy beckon the bitch forward with his hands.

ON THE DRIVE HOME, WILLARD SAID, "Boy, them spiders was a nice touch." He slipped his right hand over and began moving his fingers lightly up his mother's fat, jiggly arm.

She squealed and swatted at him. "Quit that. I won't be able to sleep tonight as it is."

"You ever heard that boy preach before?"

"No, but they do some crazy stuff at that church over in Topperville. I'll bet Reverend Sykes is regrettin' he ever invited them. That one in the wheelchair drank too much strychnine or antifreeze or something is why he can't walk. It's just pitiful. Testing their faith, they call it. But that's taking things a bit too far, the way I see it." She sighed and leaned her head back against the seat. "I wish Helen had come with us."

"Well, wasn't nobody slept through that sermon, I'll give him that."

"You know," Emma said, "she might have if you'd paid a little more attention to her."

"Oh, the way it looked to me, Brother Roy's gonna give her about as much of that as she can handle."

"That's what I'm afraid of," Emma said.

"Mother, I'm going back up to Ohio in a day or two. You know that."

Emma ignored him. "She'd make someone a good wife, Helen would."

SEVERAL WEEKS AFTER WILLARD LEFT for Ohio to find out about the waitress, Helen knocked on Emma's door. It was early in the afternoon on a warm November day. The old woman was sitting in her parlor listening to the radio and reading again the letter she'd received that morning. Willard and the waitress had gotten married a week ago. They were going to stay in Ohio, at least for now. He'd gotten a job at a meatpacking plant, said he had never seen so many hogs in his life. The man on the radio was blaming the unseasonable weather on the fallout from the atomic bombs unleashed to win the war.

"I wanted to tell you first because I know you been worried about me," Helen said. It was the first time Emma had ever seen her without a bonnet on her head.

"Tell me what, Helen?"

"Roy asked me to marry him," she said. "He said God give him a sign we was meant for each other."

Standing in the doorway with Willard's letter in her hand, Emma thought about the promise she'd been unable to keep. She'd been dreading a violent accident, or some horrible disease, but this was good news. Maybe things were going to turn out all right after all. She felt her eyes start to blur with tears. "Where you all going to live?" she asked, unable to think of anything else to say.

"Oh, Roy's got a place behind the gas station in Topperville," Helen said. "Theodore, he'll be staying with us. At least for a little while."

"That's the one in the wheelchair?"

"Yes'm," Helen said. "They been together a long time."

Emma stepped out onto the porch and hugged the girl. She smelled faintly of Ivory soap, as if she'd had a bath recently. "You want to come in and sit for a while?"

"No, I got to go," Helen said. "Roy's waiting on me." Emma looked past her down over the hill. A dung-colored car shaped like a turtle was sitting in the pull-off behind Earskell's old Ford. "He's preaching over in Millersburg tonight, where them people got their eyes carved out. We been out gathering spiders all morning. Thank God, with the way this weather's been, they're still pretty easy to find."

"You be careful, Helen," Emma said.

"Oh, don't worry," the girl said, as she started down off the porch, "they ain't too bad once you get used to them."

3

OVER THE NEXT COUPLE OF YEARS, the only news Emma had from Willard were the few cursory words he scribbled on cards at Christmas time, but in the spring of 1948, she recieved a telegram saying that she was finally a grandmother; Willard's wife had given birth to a healthy baby boy named Arvin Eugene. By then, the old woman was satisfied that God had forgiven her for her brief loss of trust. It had been nearly three years, and nothing bad had happened. A month later, she was still thanking the Lord that her grandson hadn't been born blind and pinheaded like Edith Maxwell's three children over on Spud Run when Helen showed up at her door with an announcement of her own. It was one of the few times Emma had seen her since the girl married Roy and switched to the church over in Topperville. "I wanted to stop by and let you know," Helen said. Her arms and legs were as pale and thin as ever, but her belly stuck out like a pillow, big with child.

"My goodness gracious," Emma said, opening the screen door. "Come on in, honey, and rest awhile." It was late in the day, and gray-blue shadows covered the weedy yard. A chicken clucked quietly under the porch.

"I can't right now."

"Oh, don't be in such a hurry. Let me fix you something to eat," the old woman said. "We haven't talked in ages."

"Thank you, Mrs. Russell, but maybe some other time. I got to get back."

"Is Roy preaching tonight?"

"No," Helen said. "He ain't preached in a couple of months now. Didn't you hear? One of them spiders bit him real bad. His head puffed up big as a pumpkin. It was awful. He couldn't open his eyes for a week or better."

"Well," the old woman said, "maybe he can get on with the power company. Someone said they was hiring. They supposed to be running the electric through here before long."

"Oh, I don't think so," Helen said. "Roy ain't give up preaching, he's just waiting for a message."

"A message?"

"He ain't sent one in a while, and it's got Roy worried."

"Who ain't sent one?"

"Why, the Lord, Mrs. Russell," Helen said. "He's the only one Roy listens to." She started to step down off the porch.

"Helen?"

The girl stopped and turned around. "Yes'm?"

Emma hesitated, not quite knowing what to say. She looked past the girl, down the hill at the dung-colored car. A dark figure sat stiffly erect behind the steering wheel. Have faith, she reminded herself. Everything will turn out all right. "You'll make a good mother," she said.

AFTER THE SPIDER BITE, Roy stayed shut up in the bedroom closet most of the time waiting on a sign. He was convinced that the Lord had slowed him down in order to prepare him for something bigger. As far as Theodore was concerned, Roy knocking the bitch up was the last straw. He began drinking and staying out all night, playing in private clubs and illegal joints hid back in the sticks. He learned dozens of sinful songs about cheating spouses and cold-blooded murders and lives wasted behind prison bars. Whoever he ended up with usually just dumped him drunk and piss-stained in front of the house; and Helen would have to go out at dawn and help him inside while he cursed her and his ruined legs and that pretend preacher she was fucking. She soon grew afraid of them both, and she traded Theodore rooms, let him sleep in the big bed beside Roy's closet.

One afternoon a few months after the baby was born, a squirmy grub of a girl they named Lenora, Roy walked out of the bedroom convinced that he could raise the dead. "Shit, you're just a loony," Theodore said. He was drinking a can of warm beer to settle his stomach. A small metal file and a Craftsman screwdriver lay in his lap. The night before, he'd played for eight hours straight at a birthday party over on Hungry Holler for ten dollars and a fifth of Russian vodka. Some bastard had made fun of his affliction, tried to pull him up out of his wheelchair and make him dance. Theodore set the beer down and started working on the head of the screwdriver again. He hated the whole goddamn world. The next time someone fucked with him like that, the sonofabitch was going to end up with a hole in his guts. "You ain't got it no more, Roy. The Lord done left you, just like He left me."

"No, Theodore, no," Roy said. "That ain't true. I just talked to Him. He was sitting right in there with me a minute ago. And He don't look like the pictures say, either. Ain't got no beard for one thing."

"Loony as hell," Theodore said.

"I can prove it!"

"How you gonna do that?"

Roy paced back and forth across the floor, moving his hands around like he was trying to stir inspiration up out of the air. "We'll go kill us a cat," he said, "and I'll show you I can bring it back." Next to spiders, cats were Roy's biggest fear. His mother had always claimed that she caught one trying to suck his breath away when he was a baby. He and Theodore had slaughtered dozens of them over the years.

"You're kidding me, right?" Theodore said. "A fuckin' cat?" He laughed. "No, you gonna have to get more serious than that before I'll believe you now." He pressed his thumb against the end of the screwdriver. It was sharp.

Roy wiped the sweat from his face with one of the baby's dirty diapers. "What then?"

Theodore glanced out the window. Helen was standing in the yard with the pink-faced brat in her arms. She'd gotten huffy with him again this morning, said she was getting tired of him waking the baby up. She had been bitching a lot lately, too damn much in his opinion. Hell, if it wasn't for the money he brought home, they'd all starve to death. He gave Roy a sly look. "How about you bring Helen back to life? Then we'll know for sure you ain't just talkin' crazy."

Roy shook his head violently. "No, no, I can't do that."

Theodore smirked, picked up the can of beer. "See? I knew you was full of shit. You always have been. You ain't no more a preacher than them drunks I play for every night."

"Don't say that, Theodore," Roy said. "Why you want to say things like that?"

"Because we had it good, goddamn it, and then you had to go and get married. It's drained the light right out of you, and you too dumb to see it. Show me you got it back, and we'll start spreading the Gospel again."

Roy recalled the conversation he'd had in the closet, God's voice clear as a bell in his head. He looked out the window at his wife standing by the mailbox singing softly to the baby. Maybe Theodore was onto something. After all, he told himself, Helen was right with the Lord, and always had been as far as he knew. That could only help matters when it came to a resurrection. Still, he'd like to try it out on a cat first. "I'll have to think on it."

"Can't be no tricks," Theodore said.

"Only the Devil needs them." Roy took a sip of water from the kitchen sink, just enough to wet his lips. Refreshed, he decided to pray some more, and started toward the bedroom.

"If you can pull this off, Roy," Theodore said, "there won't be a church in West Virginia big enough to hold all the people that will want to hear you preach. Shit, you'll be more famous than Billy Sunday."

A few days later, Roy asked Helen to leave the baby with her friend, the Russell woman, while they took a drive. "Just to get out of the stinking house for a while," he explained. "I promise you, I'm done with that closet." Helen was relieved; Roy had suddenly started acting like his old self again, was talking about getting back into preaching. Not only that, Theodore had quit going out at night, was practicing some new religious songs and sticking to coffee. He even held the baby for a few minutes, something he had never done before.

After they dropped off Lenora at Emma's house, they drove thirty minutes to a woods a few miles east of Coal Creek. Roy parked the car and asked Helen to go for a walk with him. Theodore was in the backseat pretending to be asleep. After going just a few yards, he said, "Maybe we ought to pray first." He and Theodore had argued about this, Roy saying he wanted it to be a private moment between just him and his wife while the cripple insisted that he needed to see the Spirit leave her firsthand to make sure they weren't faking it. When they knelt down under a beech tree, Roy pulled Theodore's screwdriver from beneath his baggy shirt. He put his arm around Helen's shoulder and gripped her close. Thinking he was being affectionate, she turned to kiss him just as he plunged the sharp point deep into the side of her neck. He let go of her and she fell sideways, then rose up, grabbing frantically for the screwdriver. When she jerked it out of her neck, blood sprayed from the hole and covered the front of Roy's shirt. Theodore watched out the window as she tried to crawl away. She went only a few feet before falling forward into the leaves and flopping about for a minute or two. He heard her call out Lenora's name several times. He lit a cigarette and waited a few minutes before he hauled himself out of the car.

Three hours later, Theodore said, "It ain't gonna happen, Roy." He sat in his wheelchair a few feet from Helen's body holding the screwdriver. Roy was down on his knees beside his wife, holding her hand, still trying to coax her back to life. At first his supplications had rung through the woods with faith and fervor, but the longer he went without even a twitch from her cold body, the more garbled and deranged they had become. Theodore could feel the onslaught of a headache. He wished he had brought something to drink.

Roy looked up at his crippled cousin with tears running down his face. "Jesus, I think I killed her."

Theodore pushed himself closer and pressed the back of his dirty hand against her face. "She's dead, all right."

"Don't you touch her," Roy yelled.

"I'm just trying to help."

Roy struck the ground with his fist. "It wasn't supposed to be this way."

"I hate to say it, but if they catch you for this, them ol' boys in Moundsville will fry you like bacon."

Roy shook his head, wiped the snot from his face with his shirtsleeve. "I don't know what went wrong. I thought for sure . . ." His voice dwindled away, and he let go of her hand.

"Shit, you just miscalculated, that's all," Theodore said. "Anybody could have done that."

"What the hell am I gonna do now?" Roy said.

"You could always run," Theodore said. "That's the only smart thing to do in a situation like this. I mean, fuck, what you got to lose?"

"Run where?"

"I been sitting here thinking on it, and I figure that old car would probably make it to Florida if you babied it."

"I don't know," Roy said.

"Sure you do," Theodore said. "Look, once we get there, we sell the car and start preaching again. That's what we should have been doing all along." He looked down at pale, bloody Helen. Her whining days were over with. He almost wished he had killed her himself. She had ruined everything. By now, they might have had their own church, maybe even been on the radio.

"We?"

"Well, yeah," Theodore said, "you gonna need a guitar player, ain't you?" For a long time he had dreamed of going to Florida, living by the ocean. It was hard to live the crippled life surrounded by all these lousy hills and trees.

"But what about her?" Roy said, pointing at Helen's body.

"You gonna have to bury her deep, brother," Theodore said. "I put a shovel in the boot just in case things didn't turn out like you expected."

"And Lenora?"

"Believe me, that kid will be better off with the Russell lady," Theodore said. "You don't want your kid growing up running from the law, do you?" He looked up through the trees. The sun had disappeared behind a wall of dark clouds, and the sky had turned the color of ash. The damp smell of rain was in the air. From over around Rocky Gap came a slow, faint rumble of thunder. "Now you better start digging before we get soaked."

WHEN EARSKELL CAME IN THAT NIGHT, Emma was sitting in a chair by the window rocking Lenora. It was nearly eleven o'clock, and the storm was just starting to ease off. "Helen told me they wouldn't be gone more than an hour or two," the old woman said. "She only left one bottle of milk."

"Aw, you know them preachers," Earskell said. "They probably went out and got on a good one. Hell, from what I hear, that crippled boy could drink me under the table."

Emma ran her hand over the baby's thin hair. "I wish we had a phone. There's something about this just don't feel right to me."

Earskell peered down at the sleeping infant. "Poor little thing," he said. "She looks just like her mother, don't she?"

4

WHEN ARVIN WAS FOUR YEARS OLD, Willard decided that he didn't want his son growing up in Meade around all the degenerates. They had been living in Charlotte's old apartment above the dry cleaners ever since they had gotten married. It seemed to him as if every pervert in southern Ohio was located in Meade. Lately, the newspaper was filled with their sick shenanigans. Just two days ago a man named Calvin Claytor had been arrested in the Sears and Roebuck with a foot of Polish sausage tied to his thigh. According to the *Meade Gazette*, the suspect, dressed only in ripped coveralls, was caught brushing up against elderly women in what the reporter described as a "lewd and aggressive manner." As far as Willard was concerned, that Claytor sonofabitch was even worse than the retired state representative the sheriff caught parked along the highway on the outskirts of town with a chicken stuck to his privates, a Rhode Island Red that he'd purchased for fifty cents from a nearby farm. They'd had to take him to the hospital to cut it off. People said that the deputy, out of respect for the other patients or maybe the victim, had covered the hen with his uniform jacket when they marched the man into the ER. "That's somebody's mother the bastard was doing that to," Willard told Charlotte.

"Which one?" she asked. She was standing at the stove stirring a pot of spaghetti.

"Jesus, Charlotte, the sausage man," he said. "They oughta cram that thing down his throat."

"I don't know," his wife said. "I don't see that being as bad as someone messing with animals."

He looked over at Arvin, sitting on the floor rolling a toy truck back and forth. From all indications, the country was going to hell in a hurry. Two months ago, his mother had written him that they had finally found Helen Laferty's body, what little was left of it anyway, buried in the woods a few miles from Coal Creek. He had read the letter every night for a week. Charlotte had noticed that Willard started becoming increasingly upset about the news in the paper right after that. Though Roy and Theodore were the prime suspects, there hadn't been a sign of them anywhere for almost three years, so the sheriff still couldn't rule out that they might have also been murdered and dumped elsewhere. "We don't know, could have been the same one butchered them people in Millersburg that time," the sheriff told Emma when he came with the news that Helen's grave had been found by a couple of ginseng hunters. "He might have killed the girl, then cut them boys up and scattered them. The one in the wheelchair would have been easy pickings, and everybody knows that other one didn't have sense enough to pour piss out of a boot."

Regardless of what the law said, Emma was convinced that the two were alive and guilty, and she wouldn't rest easy until they were locked up or dead. She told Willard she was raising the little girl as best she could. He had sent her a hundred dollars to help pay for a proper burial. Sitting there watching his son, Willard suddenly had an intense desire to pray. Though he hadn't talked to God in years, not a single petition or word of praise since he'd come across the crucified marine during the war, he could feel it welling up inside him now, the urge to get right with his Maker before something bad happened to his family. But looking around the cramped apartment, he knew he couldn't get in touch with God here, no more than he'd ever been able to in a church. He was going to need some woods to worship his way. "We got to get out of this place," he told Charlotte, laying the newspaper down on the coffee table.

THEY RENTED THE FARMHOUSE on top of the Mitchell Flats for thirty dollars a month from Henry Delano Dunlap, a plump, girlish lawyer with shiny, immaculate fingernails who lived over by the Meade Country Club and dabbled in real estate as a hobby. Though at first Charlotte had been against it, she soon fell in love with the leaky, run-down house. She didn't even mind pumping her water from the well. Within a few weeks after they moved in, she was talking about someday buying it. Her father had died of tuberculosis when she was just five years old, and her mother had succumbed to a blood infection just after Charlotte entered the ninth grade. All her life, she'd lived in gloomy, roach-infested apartments rented by the week or month. The only family member she still had living was her sister, Phyllis, but Charlotte didn't even know where she was anymore. One day six years ago, Phyllis had walked into the Wooden Spoon wearing a new hat and handed Charlotte her key to the three rooms they shared above the dry cleaners on Walnut Street. "Well, Sis," she said, "I got you raised and now it's my turn," and out the door she went. Owning the farmhouse would finally mean some stability in her life, something she craved more than anything, especially now that she was a mother. "Arvin needs to have somewhere he can always call home," she told Willard. "I never did have that." Every month they struggled to put another thirty dollars away for a down payment. "You just wait and see," she said. "This place will be ours someday."

They discovered, however, that dealing with their landlord about anything was no easy matter. Willard had always heard that most lawyers were crooked, conniving pricks, but Henry Dunlap proved to be first-class in that regard. As soon as he found out that the Russells were interested in buying the house, he started playing games, raising the price one month, reducing it the next, then turning around and hinting that he wasn't sure he wanted to sell at all. Too, whenever Willard turned in the rent money at the office, money he'd worked his ass off for at the slaughterhouse, the lawyer liked to tell him exactly what he was going to spend it on. For whatever reason, the rich man felt the need to make the poor man understand that those few wadded-up dollars didn't mean a thing to him. He'd grin at Willard with his liver-colored lips and blow off about how it barely covered the cost of some nice cuts of meat for Sunday dinner, or ice cream for his son's pals at the tennis club. The years passed by, but Henry never tired of taunting his renter; every month there was a new insult, another reason for Willard to kick the fat man's ass. The only thing that held him back was thinking about Charlotte, sitting at the kitchen table with a cup of coffee, waiting nervously for him to return home without getting them evicted. As she reminded him time and time again, it didn't really matter what the windbag said. Rich people always thought you wanted what they had, though that wasn't true, at least not in Willard's case. As he sat across from the lawyer at the big oak desk and listened to him prattle on, Willard thought about the prayer log he'd fixed up in the woods, about the peace and calm it would bring him once he got home and ate supper and made his way over there. Sometimes he even rehearsed in his head a prayer he always said at the log after his monthly visit to the office: "Thank you, God, for giving me the strength to keep my hands off Henry Dunlap's fat fucking neck. And let the sonofabitch have everything he wants in this life, though I got to confess, Lord, I sure wouldn't mind seeing him choke on it someday."

WHAT WILLARD DIDN'T KNOW was that Henry Dunlap used his big talk to hide the fact that his life was a shameful, cowardly mess. In 1943, right out of law school, he'd married a woman who, he discovered not too long after their wedding night, couldn't get enough of strange men. Edith had fucked around on him for years—paper boys, auto mechanics, salesmen, milkmen, friends, clients, his former partner—the list went on and on. He'd put up with it, had even grown to accept it; but not too long ago, he'd hired a colored man to take care of the lawn, a replacement for the white teenager whom she'd been screwing, believing that even she wouldn't stoop that low. But within a week, he'd come home in the middle of the day without warning and saw her bent over the couch in the family room with her ass up in the air and the tall, skinny gardener pounding it for all it was worth. She was making sounds that he'd never heard before. After watching for a couple of minutes, he slipped quietly away and returned to his office, where he finished off a bottle of scotch and ran the scene over and over in his head. He pulled a silver-plated derringer out of his desk and contemplated it for a long time, then put it back in the drawer. He thought it best first to consider other ways to solve his problem. No sense in blowing his brains out if he didn't have to. After practicing law in Meade for nearly fifteen years, he'd made the acquaintance of several men in southern Ohio who probably knew people who would get rid of Edith for as little as a few hundred dollars, but there wasn't one of them he felt could be trusted. "Don't get in a hurry now, Henry," he told himself. "That's when people fuck up."

A couple of days later, he hired the black man full-time,

even gave him a quarter raise on the hour. He was assigning him a list of jobs to do when Edith pulled in the driveway in her new Cadillac. They both stood in the yard and watched her get out of the car with some shopping bags and walk into the house. She was wearing a tight pair of black slacks and a pink sweater that showed off her big, floppy tits. The gardener looked over at the lawyer with a sly smile on his flat, pocked face. After a moment, Henry smiled back.

"DUMB AS GOATS," Henry told his golfing buddies. Dick Taylor had asked him about his renters out in Knockemstiff again. Other than listening to Henry brag and make a fool of himself, the other rich men around Meade didn't have much use for him. He was the biggest joke in the country club. Every single one of them had fucked his wife at one time or another. Edith couldn't even swim in the pool anymore without some woman trying to scratch her eyes out. Rumor had it she was after the black meat now. Before long, they joked, she and Dunlap would probably move up to White Heaven, the colored section on the west side of town. "I swear," Henry went on, "I think that ol' boy married his own goddamn sister, the way they favor each other. By God, you should see her, though. She wouldn't be half bad if you cleaned her up some. They ever get behind in the rent, maybe I'll take it out in trade."

"What would you do to her?" Elliot Smitt asked, winking at Dick Taylor.

"Shit, I'd bend that sweet thing over, and I'd . . ."

"Ha!" Bernie Hill said. "You ol' dog, I bet you've already busted it open."

Henry picked a club from his bag. He sighed and looked dreamily down the fairway, placing one hand over his heart. "Boys, I promised her I wouldn't tell."

Later, after they'd returned to the clubhouse, a man named Carter Oxley walked up to the fat, sweating lawyer in the bar and said, "You might want to watch what you say about that woman."

Henry turned and frowned. Oxley was a new man at the Meade Country Club, an engineer who had worked himself up to the #2 position at the paper mill. Bernie Hill had brought him along to be part of their foursome. He hadn't said two words the entire game. "What woman?" Henry said.

"You were talking about a man named Willard Russell out there, right?"

"Yeah, Russell's his name. So?"

"Buddy, it's no skin off my back, but he damn near killed a man with his fists last fall for talking trash about his wife. The one he beat up still ain't right, sits around with a coffee can hanging from his neck to catch his slobbers. You might want to think about that."

"You sure we're talking about the same guy? The one I know wouldn't say shit if he had a mouthful."

Oxley shrugged. "Maybe he's just the quiet type. Those are the ones you got to watch."

"How do you know all this?"

"You're not the only one who owns land out in Knockemstiff."

Henry pulled a gold cigarette case from his pocket and offered the new man a smoke. "What else do you know about him?" he asked. That morning Edith had told him that she thought they should buy the gardener a pickup truck. She was standing at the kitchen window eating a fluffy pastry. Henry couldn't help noticing that the top of it was covered with chocolate icing. How appropriate, he thought, the fucking whore. He was glad, though, to see that she was putting on weight. Before long, her ass would be as wide as an ax handle. Let the grass-cutting bastard pound it then. “It doesn’t have to be a new one,” she told him. “Just something he can get around in. Willie’s feet are too big for him to be walking to work all the time.” She reached in the bag for another pastry. “My God, Henry, they’re twice as long as yours.”

5

EVER SINCE THE FIRST OF THE YEAR, Charlotte's insides had been giving her fits. She kept telling herself it was just the flux, maybe indigestion. Her mother had suffered greatly from ulcers, and Charlotte remembered the woman eating nothing but plain toast and rice pudding the last few years of her life. She cut back on the grease and pepper, but it didn't seem to help. Then in April, she began bleeding on and off. She spent hours lying on top of the bed when Arvin and Willard were gone, and the cramps eased considerably if she curled up on her side and stayed still. Worried about hospital bills and spending all the money they had saved for the house, she kept her pain a secret, foolishly hoping that whatever ailed her would go away, heal itself. After all, she was only thirty years old, too young for it to be anything serious. But by the middle of May, the spotty bleeding had become a steady trickle, and to dull the pain she'd taken to sneaking drinks from the gallon of Old Crow that Willard kept under the kitchen sink. Near the end of that month, right before school let out for the summer, Arvin found her passed out on the kitchen floor in a puddle of watery blood. A pan of biscuits was burning in the oven. They didn't have a phone, so he propped her head up with a pillow and cleaned up the mess as best he could. Sitting down on the floor beside her, he listened to her shallow breathing and prayed it wouldn't stop. She was still unconscious when his father came home from work that evening. As the doctor told Willard after the test results came back, it was too late by that time. Someone was always dying somewhere, and in the summer of 1958, the year that Arvin Eugene Russell counted himself ten years old, it was his mother's turn.

AFTER TWO WEEKS IN THE HOSPITAL, Charlotte raised up in her bed and said to Willard, "I think I had a dream."

"A good one?"

"Yeah," she said. She reached out and squeezed his hand a little. She glanced over at the white cloth partition that separated her from the woman in the next bed, then lowered her voice. "I know it sounds crazy, but I want to go home and pretend we own the house for a while."

"How you gonna do that?"

"With this stuff they got me on," she said, "they could tell me I was the Queen of Sheba and I wouldn't know any different. Besides, you heard what the doctor said. I sure as hell don't want to spend what's left of my time in this place."

"Is that what the dream was about?"

She gave him a puzzled look. "What dream?" she said.

Two hours later, they were pulling out of the hospital parking lot. As they headed out Route 50 toward home, Willard stopped and bought her a milk shake, but she couldn't keep it down. He carried her into the back bedroom and made her comfortable, then gave her some morphine. Her eyes glazed over and she went to sleep within a minute or so. "You stay here with your mother," he told Arvin. "I'll be back in a bit." He walked across the field, a cool breeze against his face. He knelt down at the prayer log and listened to the small, peaceful sounds of the evening woods. Several hours passed while he stared at the cross. He viewed their misfortune from every conceivable angle, searching for a solution, but always ended up with the same answer. As far as the doctors were concerned,

Charlotte's case was hopeless. They had given her five, maybe six weeks at the most. There were no other options left. It was up to him and God now.

By the time he returned to the house, it was turning dark. Charlotte was still sleeping and Arvin was sitting beside her bed in a straight-backed chair. He could tell the boy had been crying. "Did she ever wake up?" Willard asked, in a low voice.

"Yeah," Arvin said, "but, Dad, why don't she know who I am?"

"It's just the medicine they got her on. She's gonna be fine in a few days."

The boy looked over at Charlotte. Just a couple of months ago, she was the prettiest woman he had ever seen, but most of the pretty was gone now. He wondered what she would look like by the time she got well.

"Maybe we better eat something," Willard said.

He fixed egg sandwiches for him and Arvin, then heated up a can of broth for Charlotte. She threw it up, and Willard cleaned up the mess and held her in his arms, feeling her heart beat rapidly against him. He turned out the light and moved to the chair beside her bed. Sometime during the night he dozed off, but woke up in a sweat dreaming of Miller Jones, the way the man's heart had kept on throbbing as he hung on those palm trees skinned alive. Willard held the alarm clock close to his face, saw that it was nearly four in the morning. He didn't go back to sleep.

A few hours later, he poured all his whiskey out on the ground and went to the barn and got some tools: an ax, a rake, a scythe. He spent the rest of the day expanding the clearing around the prayer log, hacking away at the briers and smaller trees, raking the ground smooth. He began tearing boards off the barn the next day, had Arvin help him carry them to the prayer log. Working into the night, they erected eight more crosses around the clearing, all the same height as the original. "Them doctors can't do your mom any good," he told Arvin, as they made their way back to the house in the dark. "But I got hopes we can save her if we try hard enough."

"Is she gonna die?" Arvin said.

Willard thought a second before he answered. "The Lord can do anything if you ask Him right."

"How we do that?"

"I'll start showing you first thing in the morning. It won't be easy, but there ain't no other choice."

Willard took a leave of absence from work, told the foreman that his wife was sick, but that she'd soon be better. He and Arvin spent hours praying at the log every day. Every time they started across the field toward the woods, Willard explained again that their voices had to reach heaven, and that the only way that would happen was if they were absolutely sincere with their pleas. As Charlotte grew weaker, the prayers grew louder and began to carry down the hill and across the holler. The people of Knockemstiff woke up to the sound of their entreaties every morning and went to bed with them every night. Sometimes, when Charlotte was having a particularly bad spell, Willard accused his son of not wanting her to get better. He'd strike and kick the boy, and then later sink into remorse. Sometimes it seemed to Arvin as if his father apologized to him every day. After a while, he stopped paying attention and accepted the blows and harsh words and subsequent regrets as just part of the life they were living now. At night, they would go on praying until their voices gave out, then stumble back to the house and drink warm water from the well bucket on the kitchen counter and fall into bed exhausted. In the morning, they'd start all over again. Still, Charlotte grew thinner, closer to death. Whenever she came out of the morphine slumber, she begged Willard to stop this nonsense, just let her go in peace. But he wasn't about to give up. If it required everything that was in him, then so be it. Any moment, he expected the spirit of God to come down and heal her; and as the second week of July came to an end, he could take a little comfort in the fact that she'd already lasted longer than the doctors had predicted.

It was the first week of August and Charlotte was out of her head most of the time now. While he was trying to cool her off with wet cloths one sweltering evening, it occurred to Willard that maybe something more was expected of him than just prayers and sincerity. The next afternoon he came back from the stockyards in town with a lamb in the bed of the pickup. It had a bad leg and cost only five dollars. Arvin jumped off the porch and ran out into the yard. "Can I give it a name?" he asked as his father brought the truck to a stop in front of the barn.

"Jesus Christ, this ain't no goddamn pet," Willard yelled. "Get in the house with your mother." He backed the truck into the barn and got out and hurriedly tied the animal's hind legs with a rope, then hoisted the lamb in the air upside down with a pulley attached to one of the wooden beams that supported the hayloft. He moved the truck a few feet forward. Then he lowered the terrified animal until its nose was a couple of feet from the ground. With a butcher knife, he slit its throat and caught the blood in a five-gallon feed bucket. He sat on a bale of straw and waited until the wound stopped dripping. Then he carried the bucket to the prayer log and carefully poured the sacrifice over it. That night, after Arvin went to bed, he hauled the furry carcass to the edge of the field and shoved it off into a ravine.

Soon after that, Willard began picking up animals killed along the road: dogs, cats, raccoons, possums, groundhogs, deer. The corpses that were too stiff and too far gone to bleed out, he hung from the crosses and the tree limbs around the prayer log. The heat and humidity rotted them quickly. The stench made Arvin and him choke back vomit as they knelt and called out for the Savior's mercy. Maggots dripped from the trees and crosses like squirming drops of white fat. The ground around the log stayed muddy with blood. The number of insects swarming around them multiplied every day. Both were covered with bites from the flies and mosquitoes and fleas. Despite it being August, Arvin took to wearing a long-sleeved flannel shirt and a pair of work gloves and a handkerchief over his face. Neither of them bathed anymore. They lived on lunch meat and crackers bought at Maude's store. Willard's eyes grew hard and wild, and it seemed to his son that his matted beard turned gray almost overnight.

"This is what death is like," Willard said somberly one evening as he and Arvin knelt at the putrid, blood-soaked log. "You want such as this for your mother?"

"No, sir," the boy said.

Willard struck the top of the log with his fist. "Then pray, goddamn it!"

Arvin pulled the filthy handkerchief from his face and breathed deeply of the rot. From then on, he quit trying to avoid the mess, the endless prayers, the spoiled blood, the rotten carcasses. But still, his mother kept fading. Everything smelled of death now, even the hallway leading back to her sickroom. Willard started locking her door, told Arvin not to disturb her. "She needs her rest," he said.

6

AS HENRY DUNLAP WAS GETTING READY to leave the office one afternoon, Willard showed up, over a week late on the rent. For the last few weeks, the lawyer had been slipping home in the middle of the day for a few minutes and watching his wife and her black lover go at it. He had a feeling that it was an indication of some kind of sickness on his part, but he couldn't help himself. His hope, though, was that he could somehow pin Edith's murder on the man. God knows the bastard deserved it, fucking his white employer's wife. By then, sled-footed Willie was getting cocky, reporting for work in the mornings smelling of Henry's private stock of imported cognac and his French aftershave. The lawn looked like hell. He was going to have to hire a eunuch just to get the grass cut. Edith was still pestering him about buying the sonofabitch a vehicle.

"Jesus Christ, man, you don't look so good," Henry said to Willard when the secretary let him in.

Willard pulled out his wallet and laid thirty dollars on the desk. "Neither do you, for that matter," he said.

"Well, I've had a lot of things on my mind lately," the lawyer said. "Grab a chair, sit down a minute."

"I don't need none of your shit today," Willard said. "Just a receipt."

"Oh, come on," Henry said, "let's have a drink. You look like you could use one."

Willard stood staring at Henry for a moment, not sure he

had heard him right. It was the first time Dunlap had ever offered him a drink, or acted the least bit civil since right after he'd signed the lease six years ago. He had come in ready for the lawyer to give him hell about being late with the rent money, had already made up his mind to knock the fuck out of him today if he got too mouthy. He glanced at the clock on the wall. Charlotte needed another prescription filled, but the drugstore was open until six. "Yeah, I reckon I could," Willard said. He sat down in the wooden chair across from the lawyer's soft leather one while Henry got two glasses and a bottle of scotch from a cabinet. He poured the drinks, handed the renter one.

Taking a sip from his drink, the lawyer leaned back in his chair and gazed at the money lying on top of the desk in front of Willard. Henry's stomach was sour from worrying about his wife. He'd been thinking for several weeks about what the golfer had told him about his renter beating the fuck out of that man. "You still interested in buying the house?" Henry asked.

"Ain't no way I can come up with that kind of money now," Willard said. "My wife's sick."

"I hate to hear that," the lawyer said. "About your wife, I mean. How bad is it?" He pushed the bottle toward Willard. "Go ahead, help yourself."

Willard poured two fingers from the bottle. "Cancer," he said.

"My mother died from it in her lungs," Henry said, "but that was a long time ago. They've come a long way with treating it since then."

"About that receipt," Willard said.

"There's damn near forty acres goes with that place," Henry said.

"Like I said, I can't get the money right now."

The lawyer turned in his chair and looked at the wall away from Willard. The only sound was a fan swiveling back and forth in the corner, blowing hot air around the room. He took another drink. "A while back I caught my wife cheating on me," he said. "I ain't been worth a shit since." Admitting to this hillbilly that he was a cuckold was harder than he thought.

Willard studied the fat man's profile, watched a trickle of sweat run down his forehead and drip off the end of his lumpy nose onto his white shirt. It didn't surprise him, what the lawyer said. After all, what sort of woman would marry a man like that? A car went by in the alley. Willard picked up the bottle and poured his glass full. He reached in his shirt pocket for a cigarette. "Yeah, that would be hard to take," he said. He didn't give a damn about Dunlap's marital problems, but he hadn't had a good drink since he'd brought Charlotte home, and the lawyer's whiskey was top shelf.

The lawyer looked down into his glass. "I'd just go ahead and divorce her, but, goddamn it, the man she's fucking is black as the ace of spades," he said. He looked over at Willard then. "For my boy's sake, I'd rather the town didn't know about that."

"Hell, man, what about kicking his ass?" Willard suggested. "Take a shovel to the bastard's head, he'll get the message." Jesus, Willard thought, rich people did fine and dandy as long as things were going their way, but the minute the shit hit the fan, they fell apart like paper dolls left out in the rain.

Dunlap shook his head. "That won't do any good. She'd just get her another one," he said. "My wife's a whore, been one all her life." The lawyer pulled a cigarette from the case lying on the desk and lit it. "Oh, well, that's enough of that shit." He blew a cloud of smoke toward the ceiling. "Now about that house again. I've been thinking. What if I told you there was a way you could own that place free and clear?"

"Ain't nothing free," Willard said.

The lawyer smiled slightly. "There's some truth to that, I guess. But still, would you be interested?" He set his glass on the desk.

"I'm not sure what you're getting at."

"Well, neither am I," Dunlap said, "but how about you call me next week here at the office and maybe we can talk about it. I should have things worked out by then."

Willard stood up and drained his glass. "That depends," he said. "I'll have to see how my wife's doing."

Dunlap pointed at the money Willard had laid on the desk. "Go ahead and take that with you," he said. "Sounds like you might need it."

"No," Willard said, "that's yours. I still want that receipt, though."

THEY KEPT PRAYING AND SPILLING BLOOD on the log and hanging up twisted, mashed roadkill. All the while, Willard was considering the conversation he'd had with the fat-ass landlord. He'd run it through his head a hundred times, figured Dunlap probably wanted him to kill the black man or the wife or maybe both of them. There wasn't anything else in the world he could think of that would be worth signing over the land and the house. But he also couldn't help but wonder why Dunlap would think that he would do something like that; and the only thing Willard could come up with was that the lawyer considered him stupid, was playing him for a fool. He'd make sure his renter's ass was sitting in jail before the bodies cooled off. For a brief spell, he had thought after talking to Dunlap that maybe there was a chance he could fulfill Charlotte's dream. But there wasn't any way they were ever going to own the house. He could see that now.

One day in the middle of August, Charlotte seemed to

rally, even ate a bowl of Campbell's tomato soup and held it down. She wanted to sit on the porch that evening, the first time she'd been out in the fresh air for weeks. Willard took a bath and trimmed his beard and combed his hair, while Arvin heated some popcorn on the stove. A breeze blew in from the west and cooled things off a bit. They drank cold 7-Up and watched the stars slowly cross the sky. Arvin sat on the floor next to her rocking chair. "It's been a rough summer, hasn't it, Arvin?" Charlotte said, running her bony hand through his dark hair. He was such a sweet, gentle boy. She hoped Willard would realize that when she was gone. That was something they needed to talk about, she reminded herself again. The medicine made her so forgetful.

"But now you're getting better," he said. He stuck another handful of popcorn in his mouth. He hadn't had a hot meal in weeks.

"Yeah, I feel pretty good for a change," she said, smiling at him.

She finally went to sleep in the rocker around midnight and Willard carried her to bed. In the middle of the night, she woke up thrashing around with the cancer eating another hole through her. He sat beside her until morning, her long fingernails digging deeper and deeper into the meat of his hand with each new wave of the pain. It was her worst episode yet. "Don't worry," he kept telling her. "Everything's going to get better soon."

He spent several hours the next morning driving along the back roads searching in the ditches for new sacrifices, but came up empty. That afternoon, he went to the stockyards, reluctantly bought another lamb. But even he had to admit, they didn't seem to be working. On his way out of town, already in a foul mood, he passed by Dunlap's office. He was still thinking about that sonofabitch when he suddenly jerked the truck over and stopped along the berm of Western Avenue. Cars drove by honking their horns, but he didn't hear them. There was one thing that he hadn't tried yet. He couldn't believe that he hadn't thought of it earlier.

"I'D ALMOST GIVEN UP ON YOU," Dunlap said.

"I been busy," Willard said. "Look, if you still want to talk, how about you meet me at your office at ten o'clock tonight?" He was standing in a phone booth in Dusty's Bar on Water Street, just a couple of blocks north of the lawyer's office. According to the clock on the wall, it was almost five. He'd told Arvin to stay in the sickroom with Charlotte, said he might be getting in late. He'd made the boy a pallet on the floor at the foot of her bed.

"Ten o'clock?" the lawyer said.

"That's as early as I can get there," Willard said. "It's up to you."

"Okay," the lawyer said. "I'll see you then."

Willard bought a pint of whiskey from the bartender and drove around listening to the radio. He passed by the Wooden Spoon as it was closing, saw some skinny teenage girl walking out the door with the bowlegged old cook, the same one who had been working the grill there when Charlotte was waiting tables. He probably still couldn't fix a meat loaf worth a shit, Willard thought. He stopped and filled the truck with gas, then went to the Tecumseh Lounge on the other side of town. Sitting at the bar, he drank a couple of beers, watched a guy wearing thick glasses and a dirty yellow hard hat run the pool table four times in a row. When he walked back out into the gravel lot, the sun was starting to go down behind the paper mill smokestack.

At nine thirty, he was sitting in his truck on Second Street, a block east of the lawyer's office. A few minutes later, he watched Dunlap park in front of the old brick building and go inside. Willard drove around to the alley, backed up against the building. He took a few deep breaths to steady himself before getting out of the truck. Reaching behind the seat, he got a hammer and stuffed the handle down his pants, pulled his shirt over it. He looked up and down the alley, then went to the rear door and knocked. After a minute or so, the lawyer opened the door. He was wearing a wrinkled blue shirt and a pair of baggy gray slacks held up by red suspenders. "That's smart, coming in the back like that," Dunlap said. He had a glass of whiskey in his hand and his bloodshot eyes indicated that he'd already had a few. As he turned toward his desk, he staggered a bit and farted. "Sorry about that," he said, just before Willard struck him in the temple with the hammer, a sickening crack filling the room. Dunlap fell forward without a sound, knocking over a bookcase. The glass he'd been holding shattered on the floor. Willard bent over the body and hit him again. When he was sure the man was dead, he leaned against the wall and listened carefully for a while. A car went by on the street out front and then nothing.

Willard put on a pair of work gloves he had in his back pocket and dragged the lawyer's heavy body to the door. He straightened up the bookcase and picked up the broken glass and wiped up the spilled whiskey with the sport coat that was slung over the back of the lawyer's chair. He checked the lawyer's pants pockets, found a set of keys and over two hundred dollars in his wallet. He put the money in a desk drawer, stuck the keys in his overalls.

Opening the office door, he stepped into the small reception room and checked the front door to make sure it was locked. He went into the lavatory and ran some water on Dunlap's jacket and went back to wipe the blood off the floor. Surprisingly, there wasn't that much. After tossing the sport coat on top of the body, he sat down at the desk. He looked around for something that might have his name on it, but found nothing. He took a pull from the bottle of scotch on the desk, then capped it and stuck it in another drawer. On the desk was a photo in a gold frame of a chubby teenage boy, the spitting image of Dunlap, holding a tennis racket. The one of the wife was gone.

Turning out the lights in the office, Willard stepped into the alley and laid the jacket and the hammer in the front seat of the truck. Then he let the tailgate down and started the truck and backed it up to the open doorway. It took only a minute to drag the lawyer into the bed of the truck and cover him with a tarp, weigh the corners down with cement blocks. He shoved the clutch in on the truck and coasted a couple of feet, then got out and shut the office door. As he drove out Route 50, he passed by a sheriff's cruiser parked in the empty store lot at Slate Mills. He watched in the rearview and held his breath until the illuminated Texaco sign faded from view. At Schott's Bridge, he stopped and tossed the hammer into Paint Creek. By three AM, he was finishing up.

The next morning when Willard and Arvin got to the prayer log, fresh blood was still dripping off the sides into the rancid dirt. "This wasn't here yesterday," Arvin said.

"I run over a groundhog last night," Willard said. "Went ahead and bled him out when I got home."

"A groundhog? Boy, he must have been a big one."

Willard grinned as he dropped to his knees. "Yeah, he was. He was a big fat bastard."

7

EVEN WITH THE SACRIFICE OF THE LAWYER, Charlotte's bones began breaking a couple of weeks later, little sickening pops that made her scream and claw gashes in her arms. She passed out from the pain whenever Willard tried to move her. A festering bedsore on her backside spread until it was the size of a plate. Her room smelled as rank and fetid as the prayer log. It hadn't rained in a month, and there was no letup from the heat. Willard purchased more lambs at the stockyard, poured buckets of blood around the log until their shoes sank over the tops in the muddy slop. One morning while he was out, a lame and starving mutt with soft white fur ventured up to the porch timidly with its tail between its legs. Arvin fed it some scraps from the refrigerator, had already named it Jack and taught it to sit by the time his father got home. Without a word, Willard walked into the house and came back out with his rifle. He shoved Arvin away from the dog, then shot it between the eyes while the boy begged him not to do it. He dragged it into the woods and nailed it to one of the crosses. Arvin stopped speaking to him after that. He listened to the moans of his mother while Willard drove around looking for more sacrifices. School was getting ready to start again, and he hadn't been off the hill a single time all summer. He found himself wishing that his mother would die.

A few nights later, Willard rushed into Arvin's bedroom and jerked him awake. "Get over to the log now," he said. The boy sat up, looked around with a confused look. The hall light was on. He could hear his mother gasping and wheezing for breath in the room across the hall. Willard shook him again. "Don't you quit praying until I come and get you. Make Him hear you, you understand?" Arvin threw on his clothes and started jogging across the field. He thought about wishing her dead, his own mother. He ran faster.

By three in the morning, his throat was raw and blistered. His father came once and dumped a bucket of water on his head, implored him to keep praying. But though Arvin kept screaming for the Lord's mercy, he didn't feel anything and none came. Some of the people down in Knockemstiff closed their windows, even with the heat. Others kept a light on the rest of the night, offered prayers of their own. Snook Haskins's sister, Agnes, sat in her chair listening to that pitiful voice and thinking of the ghost husbands that she had buried in her head. Arvin looked up at the dead hound, its vacant eyes staring across the dark woods, its belly bloated and near bursting. "Can you hear me, Jack?" he said.

Right before dawn, Willard covered his dead wife with a clean white sheet and walked across the field, numb with loss and despair. He slipped up behind Arvin silently, listened to the boy's prayers for a minute or two, barely a choked whisper now. He looked down, realized with disgust that he was gripping his open penknife in his hand. He shook his head and put it away. "Come on, Arvin," he said, his voice gentle with his son for the first time in weeks. "It's over. Your mom's gone."

Charlotte was buried two days later in the flat, sun-beaten cemetery outside of Bourneville. On the way home from the funeral, Willard said, "I'm thinking we might take us a trip. Go down and visit your grandma in Coal Creek. Maybe stay for a while. You can meet Uncle Earskell, and that girl they got living with them would be just a little younger than you. You'll like it there." Arvin didn't say anything. He still hadn't gotten over the dog, and he was certain there was no way to get over his mother. All along, Willard had promised that if they prayed hard enough, she would be all right. When they arrived home, they found a blueberry pie wrapped in newspaper on the porch by the door. Willard wandered off into the field behind the house. Arvin went inside and took off his good clothes and lay down on the bed.

When he woke several hours later, Willard was still gone, which suited the boy fine. Arvin ate half the pie and put the rest in the icebox. He went out on the porch and sat in his mother's rocking chair and watched the evening sun sink behind the row of evergreens west of the house. He thought about her first night under the ground. How dark it must be there. He'd overheard an old man standing off under a tree leaning on a shovel telling Willard that death was either a long journey or a long sleep, and though his father had scowled and turned away, Arvin thought that sounded all right. He hoped for his mother's sake that it was a little of both. There had been only a handful of people at the funeral: a woman his mother used to work with at the Wooden Spoon, and a couple of old ladies from the church in Knockemstiff. There was supposed to be a sister somewhere out west, but Willard didn't know how to get in touch with her. Arvin had never been to a funeral before, but he had a feeling that it hadn't been much of one.

As the darkness spread across the overgrown yard, Arvin got up and walked around the side of the house and called out for his father several times. He waited a few minutes, thought about just going back to bed. But then he went inside and got the flashlight from the kitchen drawer. After looking in the barn, he started toward the prayer log. Neither of them had been there in the three days since his mother had passed. The night was coming on quick now. Bats swooped after insects in the field, a nightingale watched him from its nest beneath a bower of honeysuckle. He hesitated, then entered the woods and followed the path. Stopping at the edge of the clearing, he shined the light around. He could see Willard kneeling at the log. The rotten stench hit him, and he thought he might get sick. He could taste the pie starting to come up in his throat. “I’m not doing that no more,” he told his father in a loud voice. He knew it was bound to cause trouble, but he didn’t care. “I ain’t praying.”

He waited a minute or so for a reply, and then said, “You hear me?” He stepped closer to the log, kept the light shining on Willard’s kneeling form. Then he touched his father’s shoulder and the penknife dropped to the ground. Willard’s head lolled to one side and exposed the bloody gash he’d cut from ear to ear across his throat. Blood ran down the side of the log and dripped onto his suit pants. A slight breeze blew down over the hill and cooled the sweat on the back of Arvin’s neck. Branches creaked overhead. A tuft of white fur floated through the air. Some of the bones hanging from the wires and nails gently tapped against one another, sounding like some sad, hollow music.

Through the trees, Arvin could see a few lights glimmering in Knockemstiff. He heard a car door slam somewhere down there, then a single horseshoe clang against a metal peg. He stood waiting for the next pitch, but none came. It seemed like a thousand years had passed since the morning the two hunters had come up behind Willard and him here. He felt guilty and ashamed that he wasn’t crying, but there were no tears left. His mother’s long dying had left him dry. Not knowing what else to do, he stepped around Willard’s body and pointed the flashlight ahead of him. He began making his way down through the woods.

8

AT EXACTLY NINE O'CLOCK THAT EVENING, Hank Bell stuck the CLOSED sign in the front window of Maude's store and turned off the lights. He went behind the counter and got a six-pack of beer from the bottom of the meat case, then stepped out the back door. In his front shirt pocket was a little transistor radio. He sat down in a lawn chair and opened a beer and lit a cigarette. He had lived in a camper behind the concrete-block building for four years now. Reaching into his pocket, he turned the radio on just as the announcer reported that the Reds were down by three runs in the sixth inning. They were playing out on the West Coast. Hank estimated it was just after six o'clock there. The way time worked, that was a funny thing, he thought.

He looked over at the cigar tree he'd planted the first year he worked at the store. It had grown nearly five feet since then. It was a start he'd gotten from the tree that stood in the front yard of the house he and his mother had lived in before she passed, and he lost the place to the bank. He wasn't sure why he'd planted it. A couple more years at the most, and he was planning on leaving Knockemstiff. He talked about it to any customer who would listen. Every week, he saved back a few dollars from the thirty Maude paid him on Fridays. Some days he thought he'd move up north, and other times he decided the South might be best. But there was plenty of time to decide where to go. He was still a young man.

He watched a silvery-gray mist a foot or so high move

slowly up from Black Run Creek and cover the flat, rocky field behind the store, part of Clarence Myers's cow pasture. It was his favorite part of the day, right after the sun went down and right before the long shadows disappeared. He could hear some boys whooping and yelling on the concrete bridge out in front of the store whenever a car drove by. A few of them hung there almost every night, regardless of the weather. Poor as snakes, every one of them. All they desired out of life was a car that would run and a hot piece of ass. He thought that sounded nice in a way, just going through your entire life with no more expectations than that. Sometimes he wished he weren't so ambitious.

The praying on top of the hill had finally stopped three nights ago. Hank tried not to think about the poor woman dying up there, closed up in that room, like people were saying, while the Russell man and his boy went half insane. Hell, they'd damn near driven the entire holler crazy at times, the way they went on every morning and every evening for hours. From what he'd heard, it sounded more like they were practicing some sort of voodoo instead of anything Christian. Two of the Lynch boys had come across some dead animals hanging in the trees up there a couple of weeks ago; and then one of their hounds turned up missing. Lord, the world was getting to be an awful place. Just yesterday, he'd read in the newspaper that Henry Dunlap's wife and her black lover had been arrested on suspicion of killing him. The law had yet to find the body, but Hank thought her lying with a Negro was damn near proof that they'd done it. Everybody knew the lawyer; he owned land all over Ross County, used to stop in the store once in a while sniffing around for moonshine to impress some of his big-shot friends. From what Hank had seen of the man, he probably deserved killing, but why didn't the woman just get a divorce and move up to White Heaven with the coloreds?

People didn't use their brains anymore. It's a wonder the lawyer didn't have her killed first, that is, if he knew about the boyfriend. Nobody would have blamed him for that, but now he was dead and probably better off. It would have been a hell of a thing to have to live with, everyone knowing your wife ran around with a black man.

The Reds came up to bat, and Hank began thinking about Cincinnati. Sometime soon, he was going to drive down to the River City and see a doubleheader. His plan was to buy a good seat, drink beer, stuff himself with their hot dogs. He'd heard wieners tasted better in a ballpark, and he wanted to find out for himself. Cincinnati was just ninety miles or so on the other side of the Mitchell Flats, a straight shot down Route 50, but he'd never been there, hadn't been any farther west than Hillsboro his entire twenty-two years. Hank had the feeling that his life would really begin once he made that trip. He didn't have the details all figured out yet, but he also wanted to buy a whore after the games were over, some pretty girl who would treat him nice. He'd pay her extra to undress him, pull off his pants and shoes. He was going to buy a new shirt for the occasion, stop in at Bainbridge on his way down and get a decent haircut. He'd remove her clothes slowly, take his time with each little button or whatever it was that whores fastened their clothes with. He'd spill some whiskey on her titties and lick it off, like he heard some of the men talk about when they came in the store after having a few up at the Bull Pen. When he finally got inside her, she'd tell him to take it easy, that she wasn't used to being with a man his size. She wouldn't be anything like that loudmouth Mildred McDonald, the only woman he'd ever been with so far.

"One little pop," Mildred had told everyone at the Bull Pen, "and then nothing but smoke." That had been over three years ago, and people still razzed him about it. The whore in Cincinnati would insist that he keep his money after he finished with her, ask him for his phone number, maybe even beg him to take her away. He figured he'd probably come back home a different person, just like Slim Gleason had when he returned from the Korean War. Before he left Knockemstiff for good, Hank thought he might even stop in at the Bull Pen and buy some of the boys a farewell beer, just to show there weren't any hard feelings about all the jokes. In a way, he supposed, Mildred had done him a favor; he'd put away a lot of money since he'd quit going up there.

He was half listening to the game and thinking about the dirty way Mildred had done him when he noticed someone with a flashlight walking up through Clarence's pasture. He saw the small figure bend down and slip through the barbwire fence and head toward him. It was nearly dark now, but as the person got closer, Hank realized it was the Russell boy. He'd never seen the boy off the hill by himself before, heard his father wouldn't allow it. But they'd buried his mother just this afternoon, and maybe that had changed things, softened the Russell man's heart a little. The boy was wearing a white shirt and a pair of new overalls. "Hey there," Hank said as Arvin got closer. The boy's face was gaunt and sweaty and pale. He didn't look good, not good at all. It looked like he had blood or something smeared on his face and clothes.

Arvin stopped a few feet from the storekeeper and turned off the flashlight. "The store's closed," Hank said, "but if you need something, I can open back up."

"How would a person go about getting hold of the law?"

"Well, either cause some trouble or call them on the telephone, I reckon," Hank said.

"Could you call 'em for me? I ain't never used a telephone before."

Hank reached in his pocket and turned the radio off. The

Reds were getting clobbered anyway. "What do you want with the sheriff, son?"

"He's dead," the boy said.

"Who is?"

"My dad," Arvin said.

"You mean your mom, don't you?"

A confused look came over the boy's face for a moment, then he shook his head. "No, my mom's been dead three days. I'm talking about my dad."

Hank stood up and reached in his pants for the keys to the back door of the store. He wondered if maybe the boy had gone simple with grief. Hank remembered the rough time he'd gone through when his own mother passed. It was something a person never really got over, he knew that. He still thought about her every day. "Come on inside. You look thirsty."

"I ain't got no money," Arvin said.

"That's all right," Hank said. "You can owe me."

They went inside and the storekeeper slid the top of the metal pop cooler open. "What kind you like?"

The boy shrugged.

"Here's a root beer," Hank said. "That's the kind I used to drink." He handed the boy the bottle of pop and scratched at his day-old beard. "Now your name's Arvin, ain't it?"

"Yes, sir," the boy said. He set his flashlight down on the counter and took a long drink and then another.

"Okay, so what makes you think there's something wrong with your daddy?"

"His neck," Arvin said. "He cut himself."

"That ain't blood you got on you, is it?"

Arvin looked down at his shirt and his hands. "No," he said. "It's pie."

"Where is your dad?"

"A little ways from the house," the boy said. "In the woods."

Hank reached under the counter for the phone book. "Now look," he said, "I don't mind calling the law for you, but don't be fooling with me, okay? They don't take kindly to wild-goose chases." Just a couple of days ago, Marlene Williams had him call and report another window peeper. It was the fifth time in just two months. The dispatcher had hung up on him.

"Why would I do that?"

"No," Hank said. "I guess you wouldn't."

After he made the call, he and Arvin went out the back door and Hank picked up his beers. They walked around and sat down on the bench in front of the store. A cloud of moths fluttered around the security light that stood over the gas pumps. Hank thought about the beating the boy's daddy had given Lucas Hayburn last year. Not that he probably didn't deserve it, but Lucas hadn't been right since. Just yesterday, he had sat on this bench all morning bent over with a gob of spit hanging from his mouth. Hank opened another beer and lit a smoke. He hesitated a second, then offered the boy one from his pack.

Arvin shook his head and took another drink of the pop. "They ain't pitching horseshoes tonight," he said after a couple of minutes.

Hank looked up the holler, saw the lights on at the Bull Pen. Four or five cars were parked in the yard. "Must be taking a break," the storekeeper said, leaning back against the wall of the store and stretching his legs out. He and Mildred had gone to the hog barn over at Platter's Pasture. She said she liked the rich smell of the pig manure, liked to imagine things a little different than most girls.

"What is it you like to imagine?" Hank had asked her, a hint of worry in his voice. For years, he had listened to boys and men talk about getting laid, but not once had any of them said anything about hog shit.

"That ain't none of your business what's in my head," she told him. Her chin was sharp as a hatchet, her eyes like lusterless gray marbles. Her only redeeming feature was the thing between her legs, which some had said reminded them of a snapping turtle.

"Okay," Hank said.

"Let's see what you got," Mildred said, tugging at his zipper and pulling him down in the dirty straw.

After his miserable performance, she shoved him off and said, "Jesus Christ, I should have just played with myself."

"I'm sorry," he said. "You just had me worked up. It'll be better next time."

"Ha! I doubt very much they'll be a next time, Bub," she said.

"Well, don't you at least want a ride home?" he'd asked as he was leaving. It was nearly midnight. The two-room shack she lived in with her parents over in Nipgen was several hours away if she walked it.

"No, I'm gonna hang around here awhile," she said. "Maybe someone worth a shit will show up."

Hank flipped his cigarette into the gravel lot and took another drink of beer. He liked to tell himself that things had turned out for the best in the end. Although he wasn't a spiteful person, not at all, he had to admit that he got some satisfaction out of knowing that Mildred was now hooked up with a big-bellied boy named Jimmy Jack who rode an old Harley and kept her penned up on his back porch in a plywood doghouse when he wasn't selling her ass out behind one of the bars in town. People said she'd do anything you could think of for fifty cents. Hank had seen her in Meade this past Fourth of July, standing by the door outside Dusty's Bar with a black eye, holding the biker's leather helmet. The best years of Mildred's life were behind her now, and his own were just getting ready to begin. The woman he was going to pick up in Cincinnati would be a hundred times finer than any old Mildred McDonald. A year or two after he moved away from here, he probably wouldn't even be able to recall her name. He rubbed a hand over his face and looked over, saw the Russell boy watching him. "Damn, was I talking to myself?" he asked the boy.

"Not really," Arvin said.

"Hard to tell when that deputy will show up," Hank said. "They don't much like to come out here."

"Who's Mildred?" Arvin asked.

9

LEE BODECKER'S SHIFT WAS NEARLY OVER when the call came through on the radio. Another twenty minutes and he would have been picking up his girlfriend and heading out Bridge Street to Johnny's Drive-in. He was starving. Every night, after he got off, he and Florence drove to either Johnny's or the White Cow or the Sugar Shack. He liked to go all day without eating, then wolf down cheeseburgers and fries and milk shakes; and finish things off with a couple of ice-cold beers down along the River Road, leaned back in his seat while Florence jacked him off into her empty Pepsi cup. She had a grip like an Amish milk maiden. The entire summer had been a succession of almost perfect nights. She was saving the good stuff for the honeymoon, which suited Bodecker just fine. At twenty-one years old, he was just six months out of the peacetime army, and in no hurry to be tied down with a family. Although he had been a deputy only four months, he could already see a lot of advantages to being the law in a place as backward as Ross County, Ohio. There was money to be made if a man was careful and didn't get the big head, like his boss had done. Nowadays, Sheriff Hen Matthews had a picture of his round, stupid puss on the front page of the *Meade Gazette* three or four times a week, often for no conceivable reason. Citizens were starting to joke about it. Bodecker was already planning his campaign strategy. All he had to do was get some dirt on Matthews before the next election, and he could move Florence into one of the new houses they were building on

Brewer Heights when they finally tied the knot. He had heard that every single one of them had two bathrooms.

He turned the cruiser around on Paint Street near the paper mill and headed out Huntington Pike toward Knockemstiff. Three miles out of town, he passed by the house in Brownsville where he lived with his sister and mother. A light was on in the living room. He shook his head and reached in his shirt pocket for a cigarette. He was paying most of the bills right now, but he had made it clear to them when he came back from the service that they couldn't depend on him much longer. His father had left them years ago, just went off to the shoe factory one morning and never returned. Recently, they had heard a rumor that he was living in Kansas City, working in a pool room, which made sense if you had ever known Johnny Bodecker. The only time the man ever smiled was when he was busting a rack of balls or running a table. The news had been a big disappointment to his son; nothing would have made Bodecker happier than discovering that the fucker was still earning his keep somewhere stitching soles onto loafers in a dingy red-brick building lined with high, dirty windows. Occasionally, when he was driving around on patrol and things were quiet, Bodecker imagined his father returning to Meade for a visit. In his fantasy, he followed the old man out into the country away from any witnesses and arrested him on a phony charge. Then he beat the shit out of him with a nightstick or the butt of his revolver before taking him to Schott's Bridge and pushing him over the rail. It was always a day or so after a heavy rain and Paint Creek would be up, the water swift and deep on its way east to the Scioto River. Sometimes he let him drown; other times he allowed him to swim to the muddy bank. It was a good way to pass the time.

He took a drag off the cigarette as his thoughts drifted from his father to his sister, Sandy. Though she had just turned sixteen, Bodecker had already found her a job waiting tables in the evening at the Wooden Spoon. He had pulled over the owner of the diner a few weeks ago for driving drunk, the man's third time in a year, and one thing had led to another. Before he knew it, he was a hundred dollars richer and Sandy had work. She was as bashful and anxious around people as a possum caught out in daylight, always had been, and Bodecker didn't doubt that learning to deal with customers those first couple of weeks had been torture for her, but the owner had told him yesterday morning that she seemed to be getting the hang of it now. On nights when he couldn't pick her up after work, the cook, a thickset man with sleepy blue eyes who liked to draw risqué pictures of cartoon characters on his white paper chef's hat, had been giving her a ride home, and that worried him a little, mostly because Sandy was inclined to go along with whatever anyone asked her to do. Not once had Bodecker ever heard her speak up for herself, and like a lot of things, he blamed their father for that. But still, he told himself, it was time she began learning how to make her own way in the world. She couldn't hide in her room and daydream the rest of her life; and the sooner she started bringing in some money, the sooner he could get out. A few days ago, he had gone so far as to suggest to his mother that she let Sandy quit school and work full-time, but the old lady wouldn't hear of it. "Why not?" he asked. "Once someone finds out how easy she is, she's bound to get knocked up anyway, so what does it matter if she knows algebra or not?" She didn't offer a reason, but now that he had planted the seed, he knew he just had to wait a day or two before bringing it up again. It might take a while, but Lee Bodecker always got what he wanted.

Lee made a right onto Black Run Road and drove to Maude's grocery. The storekeeper was sitting on the bench out front drinking a beer and talking to some young boy. Bodecker got out of the cruiser with his flashlight. The storekeeper was a sad, worn-out-looking fucker, even though the deputy figured they were roughly the same age. Some people were born just so they could be buried; his mother was like that, and he'd always figured that's why the old man had left, though he hadn't been any great prize himself. "Well, what we got this time?" Bodecker asked. "I hope it ain't another one of those goddamn window peepers you keep calling about."

Hank leaned over and spit on the ground. "I wish it was," he said, "but no, it's about this boy's daddy."

Bodecker trained the flashlight on the skinny, dark-haired boy. "Well, what is it, son?" he said.

"He's dead," Arvin said, putting a hand up to block the light shining in his face.

"And they just buried his poor mother today," Hank said. "It's a damn shame, it is."

"So your daddy's dead, is he?"

"Yes, sir."

"Is that blood you got on your face?"

"No," Arvin said. "Somebody gave us a pie."

"This ain't some joke, is it? You know I'll take you to jail if it is."

"Why you all think I'm lying?" Arvin said.

Bodecker looked at the storekeeper. Hank shrugged and turned his beer up and drained it. "They live at the top of Baum Hill," he said. "Arvin here, he can show you." Then he stood up and belched and headed around the side of the store.

"I might have some questions for you later on," Bodecker called out.

"It's a goddamn shame, that's all I can tell you," he heard Hank say.

Bodecker put Arvin in the front seat of the cruiser and drove up Baum Hill. At the top, he turned down a narrow dirt lane lined with trees that the boy pointed out. He slowed the car down to a crawl. "I never been back this way before," the deputy said. He reached down and quietly unsnapped his holster.

"Ain't nobody new been back here in a long time," Arvin said. Looking out the side window into the dark woods, he realized that he'd left his light in the store. He hoped the storekeeper didn't sell it before he got back down there. He glanced over at the brightly lit instrument panel. "You gonna turn the siren on?"

"No sense in scaring someone."

"There's nobody left to scare," Arvin said.

"So this where you live?" Bodecker asked as they pulled up to the small, square house. There were no lights on, no sign that anyone lived here at all except for a rocking chair on the porch. The grass was at least a foot high in the yard. To the left was an old barn with most of its siding stripped off. Bodecker parked behind a rusted-out pickup. Just your typical hillbilly trash, he thought. Hard to tell what kind of mess he was getting into. His empty stomach gurgled like a broken commode.

Arvin got out without answering and stood in front of the cruiser waiting for the deputy. "This way," he said. He turned and started around the corner of the house.

"How far is it?" Bodecker asked.

"Not too far. Maybe ten minutes."

Bodecker flipped on his flashlight and followed behind the boy along the edge of an overgrown field. They entered the woods and went several hundred feet down a well-worn path. The boy suddenly stopped and pointed ahead into the darkness. "He's right there," Arvin said.

The deputy trained his light on a man, dressed in a white shirt and dress pants, crumpled loosely over a log. He took a few steps closer, could make out a gash in the man's neck. The front of his shirt was soaked in blood. He sniffed the air and gagged. "My God, how long he been laying here like this?"

Arvin shrugged. "Not long. I fell asleep after the funeral and then there he was."

Bodecker pinched his nostrils together, tried to breathe through his mouth. "What the hell is that smell then?"

"That's them up there," Arvin said, pointing into the trees.

Bodecker lifted his flashlight. Animals in various states of decay hung all around them, some in the branches and others from tall wooden crosses. A dead dog with a leather collar around its neck was nailed up high to one of the crosses like some kind of hideous Christ-like figure. The head of a deer lay at the foot of another. Bodecker fumbled with his gun. "Goddamn it, boy, what the hell is this?" he said, turning the light back on Arvin just as a white, squirming maggot dropped onto the boy's shoulder. He brushed it off as casually as someone would a leaf or a seed. Bodecker waved his revolver around as he started to back away.

"It's a prayer log," Arvin said, his voice barely a whisper now.

"What? A prayer log?"

Arvin nodded, staring at his father's body. "But it don't work," he said.

PART TWO

On the Hunt

10

THE COUPLE HAD BEEN ROAMING the Midwest for several weeks during the summer of 1965, always on the hunt, two nobodies in a black Ford station wagon purchased for one hundred dollars at a used-car lot in Meade, Ohio, called Brother Whitey's. It was the third vehicle they had gotten off the minister in as many years. The man on the passenger's side was turning to fat and believed in signs and had a habit of picking his decayed teeth with a Buck pocketknife. The woman always drove and wore tight shorts and flimsy blouses that showed off her pale, bony body in a way they both thought enticing. She chain-smoked any kind of menthol cigarettes she could get her hands on while he chewed on cheap black cigars that he called dog dicks. The Ford burned oil and leaked brake fluid and threatened to spill its metal guts all over the highway anytime they pushed it past fifty miles an hour. The man liked to think that it looked like a hearse, but the woman preferred limousine. Their names were Carl and Sandy Henderson, but sometimes they had other names, too.

Over the past four years, Carl had come to believe that hitchhikers were the best, and there were plenty of them on the road in those days. He called Sandy the *bait*, and she called him the *shooter*, and they both called the hitchhikers the *models*. That very evening, just north of Hannibal, Missouri, they had tricked and tortured and killed a young enlisted man in a wooded area thick with humidity and mosquitoes. As soon as they picked him up, the boy had kindly offered them sticks of Juicy Fruit, said he'd drive for a while if the lady needed a break. "That'll be the goddamn day," Carl said; and Sandy rolled her eyes at the snide tone her husband sometimes used, as if he thought he was a better class of trash than the stuff they found along the roads. Whenever he got like that, she just wanted to stop the car and tell the poor fool in the backseat to get out while he still had a chance. One of these days, she promised herself, that was exactly what she was going to do, hit the brakes and knock Mister Big Shot down a notch or two.

But not tonight. The boy in the backseat was blessed with a face smooth as butter and tiny brown freckles and strawberry-colored hair, and Sandy could never resist the ones who looked like angels. "What's your name, honey?" she asked him, after they'd gone a mile or two down the highway. She made her voice nice and easy; and when the boy looked up and their eyes met in the rearview mirror, she winked and gave him the smile that Carl had taught her, the one he'd made her practice night after night at the kitchen table until her face was ready to fall off and stick to the floor like a pie crust, a smile that hinted at every dirty possibility a young man could ever imagine.

"Private Gary Matthew Bryson," the boy said. It sounded odd to her, him saying his full name like that, like he was up for inspection or some such shit, but she ignored it and went right on talking. She hoped he wasn't going to be the serious type. Those kinds always made her part of the job that much harder.

"Now that's a nice name," Sandy said. In the mirror, she watched as a shy grin spread over his face, saw him stick a fresh piece of gum in his mouth. "Which of them you go by?" she asked.

"Gary," he said, flipping the silver gum wrapper out the window. "That was my daddy's name."

"That other one, Matthew, that one's from the Bible, ain't it, Carl?" Sandy said.

"Hell, everything's from the Bible," her husband said, staring out the windshield. "Ol' Matt, he was one of the apostles."

"Carl used to teach Sunday school, didn't you, baby?"

With a sigh, Carl twisted his big body around in the seat, more to take another look at the boy than anything else. "That's right," he said with a tight-lipped smile. "I used to teach Sunday school." Sandy patted his knee, and he turned back around without another word and pulled a road map from the glove box.

"You probably already knew that, though, didn't you, Gary?" Sandy said. "That your middle name is right out of the Good Book?"

The boy quit chomping his gum for a moment. "We never went to church much when I was a kid," he said.

A worried look swept across Sandy's face, and she reached for her cigarettes on the dash. "But you been baptized, right?" she asked.

"Well, sure, we ain't complete heathens," the boy said. "I just don't know any of that Bible stuff."

"That's good," Sandy said, a hint of relief in her voice. "No sense takin' chances, not with something like that. Lord, who knows where a person might end up if he wasn't saved?"

The soldier was going home to see his mother before the army shipped him off to Germany or that new place called Vietnam, Carl couldn't recall which now. He didn't give a damn if he was named after some crazy sonofabitch in the New Testament, or that his girlfriend had made him promise to wear her class ring around his neck until he returned from overseas. Knowing stuff like that only complicated things later on; and so Carl found it easier to ignore the small talk, let Sandy handle all the dumb questions, the pitter-patter bullshit. She was good at it, flirting and flapping her jaws, putting them at ease. They had both come a long way since they'd first met, her, a lonely, scrawny stick of a girl waiting tables at the Wooden Spoon in Meade, eighteen years old and taking shit off customers in hopes of a quarter tip. And him? Not much better, a flabby-faced mama's boy who had just lost his mother, with no future or friends except for what a camera might bring. He'd had no idea, as he walked into the Wooden Spoon that first night away from home, of what that meant or what to do next. The only thing he had known for sure, as he sat in the booth watching the skinny waitress finish wiping the tables off before turning out the lights, was that he needed, more than anything else in the world, to take her picture. They had been together ever since.

Of course, there were also things that Carl needed to say to the hitchhikers, but that could usually wait until after they parked the car. "Take a look at this," he'd begin, when he pulled the camera out of the glove box, a Leica M3 35mm, and held it up for the man to see. "Cost four hundred new, but I got it for damn near nothing." And though the sexy smile never left Sandy's lips, she couldn't help but feel a little bitter every time he bragged about it. She didn't know why she had followed Carl into this life, wouldn't even try to put such a thing into mere words, but she did know that that damn camera had never been a bargain, that it was going to cost them plenty in the end. Then she'd hear him ask the next model, in a voice that sounded almost like he was joking, "So, how would you like to have your picture took with a good-looking woman?" Even after all this time, it still amazed her that grown-up men could be so easy.

After they carried and dragged the army boy's naked body a few yards into the woods and rolled it under some bushes heavy with purple berries, they went through his clothes and duffel bag and found nearly three hundred dollars tucked away in a pair of clean white socks. That was more money than Sandy made in a month. "The lying little weasel," Carl said. "Remember me asking him for some gas money?" He swiped at a cloud of insects gathered around his sweaty, red face, stuck the wad of bills in his pants pocket. A pistol with a long pitted barrel lay beside him on the ground next to the camera. "Like my old mother used to say," he went on, "you can't trust any of them."

"Who?" Sandy said.

"Them goddamn redheads," he said. "Hell, they'll spit out a lie even when the truth fits better. They just can't help it. It's something got fucked up in their evolution."

Up on the main road a car with a burned-out muffler went by slowly, and Carl cocked his head and listened to the *pop-pop* sound until it faded away. Then he looked over at Sandy kneeling beside him, studied her face for a moment in the gray dusk. "Here, clean yourself off," he said, handing her the boy's T-shirt, still damp with his sweat. He pointed at her chin. "You got some splatter right there. That skinny bastard was full as a tick."

After wiping the shirt over her face, Sandy tossed it on top of the green duffel and stood up. She buttoned her blouse with shaky hands, brushed the dirt and bits of dead leaf off her legs. Walking to the car, she bent down and examined herself in the side mirror, then reached through the window and grabbed her cigarettes off the dash. She leaned against the front bumper and lit a smoke, dug a tiny piece of gravel out of one skinned knee with a pink fingernail. "Jesus, I hate it when they cry like that," she said. "That's the worst."

Carl shook his head as he flipped through the boy's wallet one more time. "Girl, you got to get over that shit," he said. "Them tears he shed is the kind of thing makes for a good picture. Those last few minutes was the only time in his whole miserable life when he wasn't faking it."

As Sandy watched him stuff everything that belonged to the boy back into the duffel, she was tempted to ask if she could keep the girlfriend's class ring, but decided it wasn't worth the hassle. Carl had everything figured out, and he could turn into a raging maniac if she tried to flaunt even one little rule. Personal items had to be disposed of properly. That was Rule #4. Or maybe it was #5. Sandy could never keep the order of the rules straight, no matter how many times he tried to drill them into her head, but she would always remember that Gary Matthew Bryson loved Hank Williams and hated the army's powdered eggs. Then her stomach growled and she wondered, just for a second, if those berries hanging over his head back there in the woods were fit to eat or not.

AN HOUR LATER, they pulled into a deserted gravel pit they had passed by earlier when Sandy and Private Bryson were still cracking jokes and making fuck-eyes at each other. She parked behind a small utility shed cobbled together out of scrap lumber and rusty sheets of tin and shut off the engine. Carl climbed out of the car with the duffel bag and a can of gasoline they always carried. A few yards past the shed, he set the bag down and sprinkled some gas on it. After he had it burning good, he went back to the car and searched the backseat with a flashlight, found a wad of gum stuck under one of the armrests. "Worse than some kid," he said. "You'd think the military would teach them better than that. With soldiers like that one, we'll be fucked if those Russians ever decide to invade." He peeled the gum off carefully with his thumbnail and then returned to the fire.

Sandy sat in the car and watched him poke the flames with a stick. Orange and blue sparks hopped and fluttered and disappeared into the darkness. She scratched at some jigger bites around her ankles and worried about the burning sensation between her legs. Though she hadn't mentioned it to Carl yet, she was pretty sure that another boy, one they had picked up in Iowa a couple of days ago, had given her some kind of infection. The doctor had already warned her that another dose or two would ruin her chances of ever having a baby, but Carl didn't like the look of rubbers in his pictures.

When the fire died out, Carl kicked the ashes around in the gravel, then took a dirty bandanna from his back pocket and picked up the hot belt buckle and the smoking remains of the army boots. He flung them out into the middle of the gravel pit and heard a faint splash. As he stood at the edge of the deep hole, Carl thought about the way that Sandy had wrapped her arms around the army boy when she saw him set the camera down and pull the pistol out, like that was going to save him. She always tried that shit with the pretty ones, and though he couldn't really blame her for wanting it to last a while longer, this wasn't just some damn fuck party. To his way of thinking, it was the one true religion, the thing he'd been searching for all his life. Only in the presence of death could he feel the presence of something like God. He looked up, saw dark clouds beginning to gather in the sky. He wiped some sweat out of his eyes and started back to the car. If they were lucky, maybe it would rain tonight and wash some of the scum out of the air, cool things off a bit.

"What the hell were you doing over there?" Sandy asked.

Carl pulled a new cigar from his shirt pocket and started peeling off the wrapper. "You get in a hurry, that's when you make a mistake."

She held her hand out. "Just give me the fucking flashlight."

"What you doing?"

"I got to pee, Carl," she said. "Jesus, I'm about ready to bust, and you're over there daydreaming."

Carl chewed on the cigar and watched her make her way around the back of the shed. A couple of weeks on the road and she was down to nothing again, her legs like goddamn toothpicks, her ass flat as a washboard. It would take three or four months to put some meat back on those bones. Slipping the roll of film he'd shot of her and the army boy into a small metal canister, he stuck it in the glove box with the others. By the time Sandy returned, he had loaded a new roll into the camera. She handed him the light and he stuck it under the seat. "Can we get a motel tonight?" she asked in a tired voice as she started the car.

Carl pulled the cigar out of his mouth and picked at a shred of tobacco caught between his teeth. "We need to do some driving first," he said.

Heading south on 79, they crossed the Mississippi into Illinois on Route 50, a road they'd become mighty familiar with over the last several years. Sandy kept trying to hurry things, and he had to remind her several times to slow down. Wrecking the car and being pinned inside or knocked out was one of his biggest fears. Sometimes he had nightmares about it, saw himself lying handcuffed to a hospital bed trying to explain those rolls of film to the law. Just thinking about it started to fuck with the high he'd gotten off the army boy, and he reached over and twisted the knob on the radio until he found a country music station coming out of Covington. Neither of them spoke, but every once in a while, Sandy hummed along to one of the slower songs. Then she'd yawn and light another cigarette. Carl counted the bugs that splattered against the windshield, stayed ready to grab the wheel in case she nodded off.

After driving through a hundred miles of small, hushed towns and vast, dark cornfields, they came upon a run-down motel built out of pink cement blocks called the Sundowner. It was nearly one o'clock in the morning. Three cars sat in the potholed parking lot. Carl rang the buzzer several times before a light finally popped on inside the office and an elderly lady with metal curlers in her hair opened the door a crack and peered out. "That your wife in the car?" she asked, squinting past Carl at the station wagon. He looked around, could just barely make out the glow of Sandy's cigarette in the shadows.

"You got good eyes," he said, managing a brief smile. "Yeah, that's her."

"Where you all from?" the woman asked.

Carl started to say Maryland, one of the few states he hadn't been to yet, but then remembered the tag on the front of the car. He figured the nosy old bag had already checked it out. "Up around Cleveland," he told her.

The woman shook her head, pulled her housecoat tighter around her. "You couldn't pay me to live in a place like that, all that robbing and killing going on."

"You got that right," Carl said. "I worry all the time. Too many spooks for one thing. Heck, my wife won't hardly leave the house anymore." Then he pulled the army boy's money out of his pocket. "So how much for a room?" he asked.

"Six dollars," the woman said. He wet his thumb and counted off some singles and handed them to her. She left for a moment and came back with a key on a worn and wrinkled cardboard tag. "Number seven," she said. "Down on the end."

The room was hot and stuffy and smelled like Black Flag. Sandy headed straight for the bathroom and Carl flipped the portable TV set on, though there wasn't anything on the air but snow and static that time of night, not out here in the sticks anyway. Kicking off his shoes, he started to pull down the thin plaid bedspread. Six dead flies lay scattered on top of the flat pillows. He stared at them for a minute, then sat down on the edge of the bed and reached inside Sandy's purse for one of her cigarettes. He counted the flies again, but the number didn't change.

Looking across the room, he rested his eyes on a cheap framed picture hanging on the wall, a flowers-and-fruit piece of shit that nobody would ever remember, not one person who ever slept in this stinking room. It served no purpose that he could think of, other than to remind a person that the world was a sorry-ass place to be stuck living in. He leaned forward and set his elbows on his knees, tried to imagine one of his pictures in its place. Maybe the beatnik from Wisconsin with the little cellophane of reefer, or that big blond bastard from last year, the one who put up such a fight. Of course, some were better than others, even Carl would admit that; but one thing that he knew for certain: whoever looked at one of his photos, even one of the lousy ones from three or four years ago, they would never forget it. He'd bet the army boy's wad of greenbacks on that.

He mashed the cigarette out in the ashtray and looked back down at the pillow. Six was the number of models they had worked with this trip; and six was what the old bitch had charged him for the room; and now here were six poisoned flies lying in his bed. The lingering stench of the bug spray began to burn his eyes and he dabbed at them with the end of the bedspread. "And what do these three sixes mean, Carl?" he asked himself out loud. Pulling out his knife, he fiddled with a hole in one of his molars while searching his mind for a suitable answer, one that avoided the most obvious implication of those three numbers, the biblical sign that his crazy old mother would have gleefully pointed out to him if she were still alive. "It means, Carl," he finally said, snapping his penknife shut, "that it's time to head home." And with a sweep of his hand, he brushed the tiny winged corpses off onto the dirty carpet and flipped the pillows over.

II

EARLIER THAT SAME DAY, BACK IN MEADE, OHIO, Sheriff Lee Bodecker sat at his desk in an oak swivel chair eating a chocolate bar and looking through some paperwork. He hadn't had a drink of alcohol, not even a lousy beer, in two months, and his wife's doctor had told her that sweets would take the edge off. Florence had spread candy all over the house, even stuck hardtack under his pillow. Sometimes he woke himself up at night crunching on it, his throat sticky as flypaper. If it weren't for the red sleeping capsules, he never would get any rest. The worry in her voice, the way she babied him now, it made him sick to think of how he'd let himself go. Although county elections were still over a year away, Hen Matthews was proving himself to be a sore loser. His former boss was already playing dirty, spreading shit about lawmen who can't catch crooks any better than they can hold their liquor. But every candy bar Bodecker ate made him want ten more, and his belly was starting to hang over his belt like a peck sack of dead bullfrogs. If he kept it up, by the time he had to start campaigning again he'd be as sloppy fat as his pig-faced brother-in-law, Carl.

The telephone rang, and before he had a chance to say hello, an older woman's reedy voice on the other end asked, "You the sheriff?"

"That's me," Bodecker said.

"You got a sister works at the Tecumseh?"

"Maybe," Bodecker said. "I ain't talked to her lately." From the tone of the woman's voice, he could tell that this wasn't a friendly call. He set the rest of the candy bar down on top of the paperwork. These days, talk of his sister made Lee nervous. Back in 1958, when he had come home from the army, he would have busted a gut laughing if someone had suggested that shy, skinny Sandy was going to turn out wild, but that was before she met up with Carl. Now he hardly recognized her. Several years back, Carl had talked her into quitting her job at the Wooden Spoon and moving to California. Though they were gone less than a month, when she returned something about her was different. She took a job tending bar at the Tecumseh, the roughest joint in town. Now she walked around in short skirts that barely covered her ass, her face painted up like one of the whores he had run off Water Street when he first got elected. "Been too busy chasing bad guys," he joked, trying to lighten the caller's mood. He glanced down and noticed a scuff mark on the toe of one of his new brown boots. He spit on his thumb and leaned over and tried to wipe it out.

"Oh, I bet you have," the woman said.

"You got some kind of problem?" Bodecker said.

"I sure do," the woman said viciously. "That sister of yours, she's been peddling her ass right out the back door of that filthy place for over a year now, but as far as I can see, Sheriff, you ain't never lifted a hand to stop it. Hard to tell how many good marriages she's broke up. Like I told Mr. Matthews just this morning, it makes a person wonder how you ever got elected, you havin' family like that."

"Who the hell is this?" Bodecker said, leaning forward in his chair.

"Ha!" the woman said. "I ain't falling for that. I know how the law operates in Ross County."

"We operate just fine," Bodecker said.

"That ain't what Mr. Matthews says." And with that, she hung up.

Slamming the receiver down, Bodecker pushed back his chair and stood up. He glanced at his watch and grabbed his keys off the top of the file cabinet. Just as he got to the door, he stopped and turned back to the desk. He rummaged around in the top drawer, found an open bag of butterscotch balls. He stuck a handful of them in his pocket.

As Bodecker passed by the front desk on his way out, the dispatcher, a young man with bulging green eyes and a flat-top haircut, looked up from a dirty magazine he was reading. "Everything all right, Lee?" he asked.

His big face red with aggravation, the sheriff continued on without a word, then paused at the door and looked back. The dispatcher was holding the magazine up to the overhead light now, studying some naked female form tightly bound in leather straps and nylon rope, a balled-up pair of panties stuck in her mouth. "Willis," Bodecker said, "don't you let somebody walk in here and catch you looking at that damn cock book, you hear? I got enough people on my ass as it is."

"Sure, Lee," the dispatcher said. "I'll be careful." He started to turn another page.

"Jesus Christ, man, can't you take a hint?" Bodecker yelled. "Put that goddamn thing away."

As he drove over to the Tecumseh, he sucked on one of the butterscotch balls and thought about what the woman on the phone had said about Sandy whoring. Though he suspected that Matthews had put her up to the call just to fuck with him, he had to admit that he wouldn't be that surprised to find out it was true. A couple of banged-up beaters sat in the parking lot, along with an Indian motorcycle crusted over with dried mud. He took off his hat and badge and locked them in the trunk. The last time he'd been here, at the beginning of the summer, he had puked Jack Daniel's all over the pool table. Sandy had run everyone out early and closed the place up. He had lain on the sticky floor among the cigarette butts and hockers and spilled beer while she soaked up his mess off the green felt with towels. She then set a small fan down on the dry end of the table and turned it on. "Leroy's gonna shit when he sees this," she said, her hands on her skinny hips.

"Fuck that sumbitch," Bodecker mumbled.

"Yeah, that's easy for you to say," Sandy said, as she helped him get up off the floor and into a chair. "You don't have to work for the prick."

"I'll shut the goddamn place down," Bodecker said, flailing his arms wildly at the air. "I swear I will."

"Just settle down, big brother," she said. She wiped his face off with a soft, wet rag and fixed him a cup of instant coffee. Just as Bodecker started to take a sip, he dropped the cup. It shattered on the floor. "Jesus, I should have known better," Sandy said. "Come on, I better get you home."

"What kind of goddamn junker you drivin' now?" he slurred as she helped him into the front seat of her car.

"Honey, this ain't no junker," she said.

He looked around inside the station wagon, tried to focus his eyes. "What the fuck is it then?" he said.

"It's a limousine," Sandy said.

12

IN THE MOTEL BATHROOM, Sandy ran the tub full of water and peeled the wrapper off one of the candy bars she kept in her makeup bag for those days when Carl refused to stop and eat. He could go days without food when they were traveling, never thinking about anything but finding the next model. He could suck on those damn cigars and run that dirty knife through his fangs all he wanted, but she wasn't about to go to bed hungry.

The hot water relieved the itching between her legs, and she leaned back and closed her eyes as she nibbled on the Milky Way. The day they came across the Iowa boy, she had gotten off the main highway looking for a place to pull over and take a nap when he jumped up out of a soybean field looking like a scarecrow. As soon as the boy stuck his thumb out, Carl slapped his hands together and said, "Here we go." The hitchhiker was covered with mud and shit and bits of straw like he'd slept in a barnyard. Even with all the windows down, the rotten smell of him filled the car. Sandy knew it was hard to stay clean out on the road, but the scarecrow was the worst they'd ever picked up. Setting the candy bar on the edge of the tub, she took a deep breath and dunked her head under the water, listened to the faraway sound of her heart beating, tried to imagine it stopping forever.

They hadn't driven very far when the boy started chanting in a high-pitched voice, "California, here I come, California, here I come"; and she knew that Carl was going to be extra mean to this one because they just wanted to forget all about that goddamn place. At a gas station outside of Ames, she'd filled the car with gas and bought two bottles of orange screwdriver, thinking that might quiet the boy down some; but once he got a couple of sips in him, he started singing along to the radio, and that made things even worse. After the scarecrow squawked his sorry way through five or six songs, Carl leaned over to her and said, "By God, this bastard's gonna pay."

"I think he might be retarded or something," she said in a low voice, hoping Carl might let him go because he was superstitious that way.

Carl glanced back at the boy, then turned around and shook his head. "He's just stupid is all. Or a goddamn nutcase. There's a difference, you know."

"Well, at least turn the radio off," she suggested. "No sense egging him on."

"Fuck it, let him have his fun," Carl said. "I'll take the songbird out of him directly."

She dropped the candy wrapper on the floor and ran some more hot water. She hadn't argued at the time, but she wished to God now she hadn't touched the boy. She lathered up the washcloth and pushed the end of it inside her, squeezed her legs together. Out in the other room, Carl was talking to himself, but that usually didn't mean anything, especially right after they had finished with another model. Then he got a little louder, and she reached up and made sure the door was locked, just in case.

With the Iowa boy, they had parked at the edge of a garbage dump, and Carl had taken the camera out and started his spiel while he and the boy finished off the second bottle of screwdriver. "My wife loves to play around, but I'm just too damn old to get it up anymore," he told the boy that afternoon. "You know what I mean?"

Sandy had puffed on her cigarette, watched the scarecrow in the rearview mirror. He rocked back and forth, grinning wildly and nodding his head to everything that Carl said, his eyes blank as pebbles. For a moment, she thought she was going to vomit. It was more nerves than anything else, and the sick feeling passed quickly, like it always did. Then Carl suggested that they get out of the car, and while he spread a blanket on the ground, she reluctantly began taking off her clothes. The boy started up his damn singing again, but she put her finger to her lips and told him to be quiet for a while. "Let's have some fun now," she said, forcing a smile and patting a spot next to her on the blanket.

It took the Iowa boy longer than most to realize what was happening, but even then he didn't struggle too much. Carl took his time and managed at least twenty photos of junk sticking out of various places: lightbulbs and clothes hangers and soup cans. The light was starting to fade by the time he set the camera down and finished things off. He wiped his hands and knife on the boy's shirt, then walked around until he found a discarded Westinghouse refrigerator half buried in the trash. With the shovel from the car, he cleared the top off and pried the door open while Sandy went through the boy's pants. "That's it?" Carl said when she handed him a plastic whistle and an Indian head penny.

"What did you expect?" she said. "He don't even have a billfold." She glanced inside the icebox. The walls were covered with a thin coat of green mold, and a mason jar of gooey, gray jam lay smashed in one corner. "Jesus, you going to put him in there?"

"I'd say he's slept in worse places," Carl said.

They folded the boy double and crammed him inside the refrigerator, then Carl insisted on one last photo, one of Sandy in her red panties and bra getting ready to close the door. He squatted down and aimed the camera. "That's a good one," he said, after he clicked the shutter. "Real sweet." Then he stood up and stuck the boy's whistle in his mouth. "Go ahead and shut the goddamn thing. He can dream about California all he wants now." With the shovel, he began spreading trash over the top of the metal tomb.

The water grew cold, and she stepped out of the tub. She brushed her teeth and smeared some cold cream on her face and ran a comb through her wet hair. The army boy had been the best she'd had in a long time, and she planned to go to sleep tonight thinking about him. Anything to chase that damn scarecrow out of her head. When she came out of the bathroom in her yellow nightgown, Carl was lying on the bed, staring at the ceiling. It had been a week, she figured, since he'd bathed. She lit a cigarette and told him that he wasn't sleeping with her unless he washed the smell of those boys off.

"They're called models, not boys," he said. He rose up and swung his heavy legs off the bed. "How many times I got to tell you that?"

"I don't care what they're called," Sandy said. "That's a clean bed."

Carl glanced down at the flies on the rug. "Yeah, that's what you think," he said, heading for the bathroom. He peeled off his grimy clothes and sniffed himself. He happened to like the way he smelled, but maybe he should be more careful. Lately, he was beginning to worry that he was turning into some kind of fairy, and he suspected that Sandy thought the same thing. He tested the shower water with his hand, then stepped into the tub. He rubbed the bar of soap over his hairy, bloated body. Beating off to the photos wasn't a good sign, he knew that, but sometimes he couldn't help it. It was hard for him when they were back home, sitting alone in that crummy apartment night after night while Sandy was pouring drinks in the bar.

As he dried himself off, he tried to recall the last time they had made love. Last spring maybe, though he couldn't be sure. He tried to imagine Sandy young and fresh again, before all their shit started. Of course, he had soon found out about the cook who had taken her cherry and the one-nighters with the pimple-faced punks, but still, there was an air of innocence about her back then. Perhaps, he sometimes thought, that was because he didn't have that much experience himself when he first met her. Sure, he'd slept with a few whores—the neighborhood had been full of them—but he'd only been in his mid-twenties when his mother had the stroke that left her paralyzed and practically speechless. By then, there hadn't been any boyfriends banging on her door for several years, and so Carl was stuck with looking after her. For the first several months, he considered pressing a pillow over her twisted face and freeing them both, but she was his mother after all. Instead, he began applying himself to recording her long downward slide on film, a new photo of her shriveled-up body twice a week for the next thirteen years. Eventually, she got used to it. Then one morning he found her dead. He sat on the edge of the bed and tried to eat the egg he'd mashed up for her breakfast, but he couldn't get it down. Three days later, he tossed the first shovelful of dirt on her coffin.

Besides his camera, he had $217 left after paying for her funeral and a rickety Ford that would run only in dry weather. The odds of the car ever making it across the United States were slim to none, but he had dreamed of a new life almost as long as he had been alive, and now his best and last excuse was finally at peace in St. Margaret's Cemetery. And so, on the day before the rent ran out, he boxed up the curling stacks of sickbed photos and set them by the curb for the garbage truck. Then he drove west from Parson's Avenue to High Street and headed out of Columbus. His destination was Hollywood, but he had no sense of direction in those days, and somehow that evening he ended up in Meade, Ohio, and the Wooden Spoon. Looking back on it, Carl was convinced that fate had steered him there, but sometimes, when he remembered the soft, sweet Sandy of five years ago, he almost wished he had never stopped.

Shaking himself from his reverie, he squeezed some toothpaste into his mouth with one hand while fondling himself with the other. It took a few minutes, but finally he was ready. He walked out of the bathroom naked and a bit apprehensive, the purple tip of his hard-on pressing against his sagging, stretch-marked belly.

But Sandy was already asleep; and when he reached out and touched her shoulder, she opened her eyes and groaned. "I don't feel good," she said, turning over and curling up on the other side of the bed. Carl stood over her for a couple of minutes, breathing through his mouth, feeling the blood leave him. Then he turned the light off and went back into the bathroom. Fuck it, she didn't give a damn that he was asking for something important tonight. He sat down on the commode, and his hand fell between his legs. He saw the army boy's smooth, white body, and he picked up the wet washcloth off the floor and bit down on it. The sharp end of the leafy branch had initially been too big to fit in the bullet hole, but Carl had worked it back and forth until it stayed erect, looking like a young tree sprouting from Private Bryson's muscled chest. After he finished, he stood up and spit the washcloth into the sink. As he stared at his panting reflection in the mirror, Carl realized that there was a good chance he and Sandy would never make love again, that they were worse off than he had ever imagined.

Later that night, he awoke in a panic, his fat heart quivering in its ribbed cage like a trapped and frightened animal.

According to the clock on the nightstand, he had been asleep less than an hour. He started to roll over, but then lurched out of bed and stumbled to the window, jerked the curtain open. Thank God, the station wagon was still sitting in the parking lot. "You dumb bastard," he said to himself. Pulling on his pants, he walked across the gravel to the car in his bare feet and unlocked the door. A mass of thick clouds hovered over him. He took the six rolls of film from the dash and carried them back to the room, stuffed them inside his shoes. He'd completely forgotten about them, a clear violation of his Rule #7. Sandy muttered something in her sleep about scarecrows or some such shit. Going back to the open doorway, Carl lit another of her cigarettes and stood looking out into the night. As he cursed himself for being so careless, the clouds shifted, revealing a small patch of stars off to the east. He squinted through the cigarette smoke and started to count them, but then he stopped and closed the door. One more number, one more sign, that wouldn't change a goddamn thing tonight.

13

THREE MEN WERE SITTING AT A TABLE drinking beer when Bodecker entered the Tecumseh Lounge. The dark room lit up with sunlight for a brief moment, casting the sheriff's long shadow across the floor. Then the door swung shut behind him and everything settled into gloom again. A Patsy Cline song came to a sad, quavering end on the jukebox. None of the men said a word as the sheriff walked past them toward the bar. One was a car thief and another a wife beater. They'd both spent time in his jail, waxed his cruiser on several occasions. Though he didn't know the third man, he figured it was just a matter of time.

Bodecker sat down on a stool and waited for Juanita to finish frying a hamburger on the greasy grill. He recalled that she had served him his first whiskey in this bar not so many years ago. He'd chased after the feeling he'd gotten that night for the next seven years, but never found it again. He reached in his pocket for one of the candies, then decided to hold off. She laid the sandwich on a paper plate along with a few potato chips she scooped out of a metal lard bucket and a long pale pickle she forked from a dirty glass jar. Carrying the plate to the table, she set it down in front of the car thief. Bodecker heard one of the men say something about covering up the pool table before somebody got sick. Another one laughed and he felt his face begin to burn. "You quit that," Juanita said in a low voice.

She went to the register and made the car thief's change and took it back to him. "These tater chips are stale," he told her.

"Then don't eat 'em," she said.

"Now, darling," the wife beater said, "that ain't no way to be."

Ignoring him, Juanita lit a cigarette and walked down to the end of the bar where Bodecker sat. "Hey, stranger," she said, "what can I get—"

"—and by God if her ass didn't drop open like a lunch bucket," one of the men said loudly just then, and the table erupted into laughter.

Juanita shook her head. "Can I borrow your gun?" she said to Bodecker. "Those bastards been in here since I opened up this morning."

He watched them in the long mirror that ran behind the bar. The car thief was giggling like a schoolgirl while the wife beater mashed the potato chips on the table with his fist. The third man was leaned back in his chair with a bored expression on his face, cleaning his fingernails with a matchstick. "I could run 'em out if you want," Bodecker said.

"Nah, that's okay," she said. "They'd just come back later wanting to give me some more grief." She blew smoke out of the side of her mouth and half smiled. She hoped her boy wasn't in trouble again. The last time, she'd had to borrow two weeks' pay to get him out of jail, all over five record albums he'd stuck down his pants at the Woolworth's. Merle Haggard or Porter Wagoner, that would have been bad enough, but Gerry and the Pacemakers? Herman's Hermits? The Zombies? Thank God his father was dead, that's all she could say. "So what can I do you for?"

Bodecker gazed for a moment at the two rows of bottles lined up under the mirror. "You got any coffee?"

"Just instant," she said. "Don't get many coffee drinkers in here."

He made a face. "That stuff hurts my stomach," he said. "How about a Seven-Up?"

After Juanita set the bottle of pop down in front of him, Bodecker lit a cigarette and said, "So Sandy ain't come in yet, huh?"

"I wish. She's been gone over two weeks now."

"What? She quit?"

"No, nothing like that," the barmaid said. "She's on vacation."

"Again?"

"I don't know how they do it," Juanita said, lightening up, relieved that his visit didn't seem to have anything to do with her son. "I don't reckon they stay any place fancy, but I barely make enough here to pay the rent on that ol' trailer I live in. And you know damn well Carl ain't paying for none of it."

Bodecker took a sip of the pop and thought again about the phone call. So it probably was true, but if Sandy's been tricking for over a year, like the bitch said, why in the hell hadn't he heard about it before now? Maybe it was a good thing he had taken the pledge. The whiskey had evidently started turning his brain to mush. Then he glanced over at the pool table and considered other things he might have been careless about the past few months. A sudden cold chill swept over him. He had to swallow several times to keep the 7-Up from coming back up. "Did she mention how long they'd be gone?" he asked.

"She told Leroy she'd be home by the end of this week. I sure hope so. The tight ass won't hire no extra help."

"You got any idea where they were going?"

"It's hard to tell about that girl," Juanita said with a shrug. "She was talking about Virginia Beach, but I just can't picture Carl sunning himself by some ocean for two weeks, can you?"

Bodecker shook his head. "To tell you the truth, I can't picture that sonofabitch doing anything." Then he stood up and laid a dollar on the bar. "Look," he said, "when she gets back, tell her I need to talk to her, okay?"

"Sure, Lee, I'll do that," the barmaid said.

After he walked out the door, one of the men yelled, "Hey, Juanita, have you heard what Hen Matthews been saying about that big-headed bastard?"

14

A CAR DOOR SLAMMED in the parking lot. Carl opened his eyes, looked across the room at the flowers and fruit on the wall. The clock said it was still early morning, but he was already covered in sweat. He got out of bed and went to the bathroom, emptied his bladder. He didn't comb his hair or brush his teeth or wash his face. He dressed in the same clothes he'd worn for the past week, his purple shirt, a baggy pair of shiny, gray suit pants. Sticking the film canisters in his pockets, he sat on the edge of a chair and put his shoes on. He thought about waking Sandy up so they could get a move on, but then decided to let her rest. They'd slept in the car the past three nights. He figured he owed her that, and besides, they were going home anyway. No reason to hurry now.

While he waited for her to wake up, Carl chewed on a cigar and took the army boy's wad of money out of his pocket. As he counted it again, he remembered a time the year before when they were cutting across the lower end of Minnesota. They were clinging to their last three dollars when the radiator on this '49 Chevy coupe they were traveling in that summer blew a hole. He managed to temporarily seal the leak with a can of black pepper he carried for just such an emergency, a trick he'd heard about at a truck stop one time. They found a hick gas station a mile or so off the highway before it busted open again, ended up spending the bigger part of a day waiting around while some grease monkey with a pack of Red Man hanging out of his back pocket kept promising to fix it as soon as he finished a tune-up his boss wanted done yesterday. "Won't be long now, mister," he told Carl every fifteen fucking minutes. Sandy didn't help matters any. She parked her ass on a bench right outside the garage door and filed her nails and teased the poor bastard with glimpses of her pink underwear until he didn't know whether to shit or go blind, she had him so tore up.

Carl finally threw up his hands in disgust and got the rolls of film out of the glove box and locked himself in the restroom behind the station. He sat for several hours in that stinking sweatbox thumbing through a pile of ragged detective magazines stacked on the damp floor next to the filthy, crusted commode. Every once in a while, he heard the bell ring around front, announcing another gas customer. A brown cockroach crawled sluggishly up the wall. He lit one of his dog dicks, thinking that might help move his bowels, but his insides were like cement. The best he could do was dribble a little blood now and then. His fat thighs grew numb. At one point, someone pounded on the door, but he wasn't about to give up his seat just so some no-good sonofabitch could wash his dainty hands.

He was about to wipe his bloody ass when he came across the article in a soggy copy of *True Crime*. He settled back down on the commode, flicked the ash off his cigar. The detective being interviewed in the story said that two male bodies had been found, one stuffed in a culvert near Red Cloud, Nebraska, and the other nailed to the floor of a shed on an abandoned farm outside Seneca, Kansas. "We're talking within a hundred miles of each other," the detective pointed out. Carl looked at the date on the cover of the magazine: November 1964. Hell, the story was already nine months old. He read the three pages over carefully five times. Though he refused to offer any specifics, the detective suggested there was a good chance the two murders were connected because of the *nature* of the crimes. So, judging from the condition of the remains, we're looking at the summer of 1963, thereabouts anyway, he said. "Well, at least you got the year right," Carl muttered to himself. That was their third time out, when they got those two. One was a runaway husband hoping to find a new beginning in Alaska and the other a tramp they'd seen scrounging for something to eat in a trash can behind a veterinarian's office. Those spikes had made for a damn good picture. There'd been a coffee can full of them right inside the door of the shed, like the Devil had set them there knowing that Carl was going to show up some day.

He cleaned himself off and wiped his sweaty hands on his pants. He tore the story out of the magazine and folded it, stuck the pages in his wallet. Whistling a little tune, he wet his comb in the sink and slicked back his thin, graying hair, squeezed a patch of whore bumps on his face. He found the grease monkey talking to Sandy in a low voice inside the garage. He had one skinny leg pressed up against hers. "Jesus Christ, it's about time," she said, when she looked up and saw him.

Ignoring her, Carl asked the mechanic, "Did you get it fixed?"

The man stepped away from Sandy, nervously stuck his greasy hands in the pockets of his coveralls. "I think so," he said. "I filled her up with water, and she's holdin' so far."

"What else did you fill up?" Carl said, eyeing him suspiciously.

"Nothing, not a thing, mister."

"Did you let it run awhile?"

"We ran it for ten minutes," Sandy said. "While you was back there in the can doing whatever you was doing."

"All right," Carl said. "What we owe you?"

The mechanic scratched his head, pulled out his pack of chew. "Oh, I don't know. Does five bucks sound all right?"

"Five bucks?" Carl said. "Hell, man, the way you been playing around with my ol' lady? She's gonna be sore for a week. I'll be damn lucky if you didn't knock her up."

"Four?" the mechanic said.

"Listen to this shit," Carl said. "You like to take advantage, don't you?" He glanced over at Sandy and she winked. "Okay, you throw in a couple cold pops, I'll give you three dollars, but that's my final offer. My wife ain't just some cheap whore."

It was late in the evening by the time they drove out of there, and they slept in the car that night along a quiet country road. They shared a can of potted meat, using Carl's penknife for a spoon; and then Sandy climbed over the backseat and said good night. A short while later, just as he was starting to nod off in the front, a sharp spasm shot through Carl's guts and he fumbled for the door handle. Bolting from the car, he climbed over a drainage ditch that ran alongside the road. He jerked his pants down just in time, emptied a week's worth of nerves and junk into the weeds while holding on to the trunk of a pawpaw tree. After he cleaned himself off with some dead leaves, he stood outside the car in the moonlight and read the magazine story one more time. Then he took his lighter out and set it aflame. He decided not to mention it to Sandy. Sometimes she had a big mouth, and he didn't like to worry about what he might have to do to it on down the road.

15

THE DAY AFTER TALKING TO THE BARMAID at the Tecumseh, Bodecker drove over to the apartment where his sister and her husband lived on the east side of town. For the most part, he didn't give a damn how Sandy carried on her sorry life, but she wasn't going to peddle her snatch in Ross County, not as long as he was sheriff. Fucking around on Carl was one thing—hell, he couldn't blame her for that—but working it for money was something else entirely. Although Hen Matthews would try to shame him with dirt like that come election time, Bodecker was worried about it for other reasons. People are like dogs: once they start digging, they don't want to stop. First, it would just be that the sheriff had a whore for a sister, but eventually someone would find out about his dealings with Tater Brown; and after that, all the bribes and other shit that had piled up since he had first pinned on a badge. Looking back on it, he should have busted that thieving, pimp sonofabitch when he had a chance. A big arrest like that might have nearly wiped his slate clean. But he'd let his greed get the best of him, and now he was stuck in it for the long haul.

Parked in front of the shabby duplex, he watched a flatbed truck bulging with cattle turn into the stockyards across the street. The tangy smell of manure hung heavy in the hot August air. The old beater Sandy had hauled him home in that last night before he took the pledge was nowhere to be seen, but he got out of the cruiser anyway. He was pretty certain it had been a station wagon. He walked around the side of the house and climbed the rickety stairs that led to their door on the second floor. At the top was a little landing that Sandy called the patio. A sack of garbage lay overturned in one corner, green flies crawling over egg shells and coffee grounds and wadded-up hamburger wrappers. Next to the wooden railing sat a padded kitchen chair and underneath it a coffee can half full of cigar butts. Carl and Sandy were worse than the coloreds up on White Heaven and the holler trash out in Knockemstiff, he thought, the way the two of them lived. God, how he hated slobs. The prisoners in the county jail took turns washing his cruiser every morning; the creases in his khaki pants were as sharp as knives. He kicked an empty Dinty Moore can out of the way and knocked on the door, but nobody answered.

As he started to leave, he heard a sliver of music coming from somewhere close by. Looking over the railing, he saw a chubby woman in a flowered swimsuit lying on a yellow blanket in the yard next door. The rusted frames and parts of old motorcycles were scattered around her in the tall grass. Her brown hair was pinned on top of her head, and she held a tiny transistor radio in her hand. She was slathered with baby oil, shiny as a new penny in the bright sun. He watched as she twisted the dial around searching for another station, heard the faint twang of some hillbilly song about heartbreak. Then she set the radio on the edge of the blanket and closed her eyes. Her slick belly rose and fell. She turned over, then raised her head and glanced around. Satisfied that no one was watching, she undid the top of the bathing suit. After a moment's hesitation, she reached down and tugged the lower half up to reveal three or four inches of the white cheeks of her ass.

Bodecker lit a cigarette and started back down the stairs. He imagined his brother-in-law sitting out here in the sun sweating buckets and trying to get his eyes full. It was easy enough to do, the way the woman lay spread out there for anybody to see. Taking pictures seemed to be the only thing that Carl thought about, and Bodecker wondered if he ever took any of the neighbor without her knowing it. Though he wasn't sure, he figured there was a law against shit like that. And if there wasn't, there sure as hell ought to be.

16

BY THE TIME THEY LEFT THE SUNDOWNER, it was noon. Sandy had woken up at eleven, then spent an hour in the bathroom getting ready. She was only twenty-five, but her brown hair was already beginning to show traces of gray. Carl worried about her teeth, which had always been her best feature. They were stained an ugly yellow from all the cigarettes. He'd noticed, too, that her breath was bad all the time now, regardless of how many mints she consumed. Something was starting to rot inside her mouth, he was sure of it. Once they got back home, he needed to get her to a dentist. He hated to think of the expense, but a nice smile was an important part of his photographs, providing a needed contrast to all the pain and suffering. Though he'd tried time and time again, Carl had yet to get one of the models to fake even a little smirk once he took the gun out and started on them. "Girl, I know sometimes it's hard, but I need you to look happy if these are gonna turn out good," he told Sandy, whenever he'd done something to one of the men that upset her. "Just think of that Mona Lisa picture. Pretend you're her hanging up on the wall in that museum."

They hadn't driven but a few miles when Sandy braked suddenly and pulled into a little diner called the Tiptop. It was shaped somewhat like a wigwam and painted different shades of red and green. The parking lot was nearly full. "What the hell are you doing?" Carl said.

Sandy shut off the engine, stepped out of the car, went around to the passenger's side. "I ain't drivin' another mile until I get some real food," she said. "I been eating nothing but candy for three days. Shit, my teeth are getting loose."

"Jesus Christ, we just got on the road," Carl said, as she turned and started walking toward the diner door. "Hold up," he yelled. "I'm coming."

After locking the car, he followed her inside and they found a booth near a window. The waitress brought two cups of coffee and a ragged menu spattered with ketchup. Sandy ordered French toast and Carl asked for a side of crisp bacon. She put her sunglasses on, watched a man in a stained apron try to install a new roll of paper in the cash register. The place reminded her of the Wooden Spoon. Carl looked around the crowded room, farmers and old people mostly, a couple of haggard salesmen studying a list of prospects. Then he noticed a young man, early twenties maybe, sitting at the counter eating a piece of lemon meringue pie. Sturdy build, thick, wavy hair. A backpack with a small American flag sewn on it leaned against the stool beside him.

"So?" Carl said, after the waitress brought the food. "You feeling any better today?" As he talked, he kept one bloodshot eye on the man at the counter, the other on their car.

Sandy swallowed and shook her head. She poured some more syrup on the French toast. "That's something we need to talk about," she said.

"What is it?" he asked, pulling the burnt rind off a slice of the bacon and sticking it in his mouth. Then he took a cigarette from her pack and rolled it between his fingers. He shoved what remained on his plate over to her.

She took a sip of her coffee, glanced at the table of people next to them. "It can wait," she said.

The man at the counter stood up and handed the waitress some money. Then he slung the backpack over his shoulder with a weary groan and went out the door with a toothpick stuck in his mouth. Carl watched him go to the edge of the road and try to thumb a passing car. The car went on without stopping, and the man started walking west at a lazy pace. Carl turned to Sandy, nodded toward the window. "Yeah, I seen him," she said. "Big deal. They're all over the place. They're like cockroaches."

Carl watched the road for traffic while Sandy finished eating. He thought about his decision to head home today. The signs were so clear to him last night, but now he wasn't so sure. One more model would jinx the three sixes, but they could drive for a week and not find another who looked like that boy. He knew better than to fuck with the signs, but then he recalled that *seven* was the number of their room last night. And not a single car had passed by since the boy left. He was out there right now, looking for a ride in the hot sun.

"Okay," Sandy said, wiping her mouth with a paper napkin, "I can drive now." She got up and reached for her purse. "Better not keep the fucker waiting."

PART THREE

Orphans and Ghosts

17

ARVIN WAS SENT TO LIVE WITH HIS GRANDMOTHER right after his father's suicide, and though Emma made sure that he went to church with Lenora and her every Sunday, she never asked him to pray or sing or kneel at the altar. The welfare people from Ohio had told the old woman about the terrible summer the boy had endured while his mother was dying, and she decided not to push anything other than regular attendance on him. Knowing that Reverend Sykes was prone to be overly zealous at times in his attempts at bringing hesitant newcomers into the fold, Emma had gone to him soon after Arvin's arrival and explained that her grandson would come into the faith his own way when he was ready. Hanging roadkill from crosses and pouring blood on logs had secretly impressed the old preacher—after all, weren't all the famous Christians fanatical in their beliefs?—but he went ahead and agreed with Emma that maybe that wasn't the best way to introduce a young person to the Lord. "I see what you're getting at," Sykes said. "No sense turning him into one of them Topperville nut jobs." He was sitting on the church steps peeling a bruised yellow apple with a pocketknife. It was a sunny September morning. He wore his good suit coat over a pair of faded bib overalls and a white shirt starting to unravel around the collar. Lately, his chest had been hurting him, and Clifford Odell was supposed to give him a ride to a new doctor over in Lewisburg, but he hadn't shown up yet. Sykes had overheard someone at Banner's store say that the sawbones had gone to college for six years, and he was looking forward to meeting him. He figured a man with that much education could cure anything.

"What's that supposed to mean, Albert?" Emma asked.

Sykes glanced up from the apple and saw the hard look the woman was giving him. It took him a moment to realize what he had said, and his wrinkled face flushed red with embarrassment. "I'm sorry, Emma," he sputtered. "I wasn't talking about Willard, no way. He was a good man. One of the best. Shoot, I still remember the day he got saved."

"That's all right," she said. "No sense buttering up the dead, Albert. I know what my son was like. Just don't go pestering his boy, that's all I ask."

LENORA, ON THE OTHER HAND, couldn't seem to get enough of her religion. She carried a Bible with her everywhere she went, even to the outhouse, just like Helen had; and each morning, she got up before everyone else and prayed for an hour on her knees on the splintered wooden floor beside her and Emma's bed. Although she had no memory of either of her parents, the girl directed most of the prayers that she let Emma hear on her murdered mother's soul and most of her silent ones on some news of her missing father. The old woman had told her time and time again that it would be best to forget about Roy Laferty, but Lenora couldn't help wondering about him. Nearly every night, she fell asleep with an image of him stepping up on the porch in a new black suit and making everything all right. It gave her a small comfort, and she allowed herself to hope that, with the Lord's help, her father really would return someday if he was still alive. Several times a week, no matter what the weather, she visited the cemetery and read the Bible out loud, especially the Psalms, while seated on the ground next to her mother's grave. Emma had once told her that the book of Songs was Helen's favorite part of the Scriptures, and by the time she finished the sixth grade, Lenora knew them all by heart.

THE SHERIFF HAD LONG SINCE GIVEN UP on finding Roy and Theodore. It was as if they had turned into ghosts. Nobody was able to find a photograph or record of any kind on either of them. "Hell, even the retards up in Hungry Holler got birth certificates," he offered as an excuse, whenever one of his constituents brought up the two's disappearance. He didn't mention to Emma the rumor that he'd heard right after they disappeared, that the cripple was in love with Roy, that there might have been some queer homo thing going on between them before the preacher married Helen. During the initial investigation, several people testified that Theodore had complained bitterly that the woman had taken the edge off Roy's spiritual message. "It's ruined many a good man, that ol' nasty hair pie," the cripple was heard to say after he'd had a few drinks. "Preacher, shit," he'd go on, "all he thinks about now is getting his dick wet." It irked the sheriff to no end that those two sodomite fools might have committed murder in his county and gotten away with it; and so he kept repeating the same old story, that in all likelihood the same maniac that butchered the Millersburg family had also killed Helen and hacked Roy and Theodore to pieces or dumped their bodies in the Greenbrier River. He told it so much that he half believed it himself at times.

THOUGH ARVIN NEVER CAUSED HER any serious trouble, Emma could easily see Willard in him, especially when it came to the fighting. By the time he was fourteen, he had been kicked out of school several times for using his fists. Pick your own time, he remembered his father telling him, and Arvin learned that lesson well, catching whoever his enemy happened to be at the moment alone and unaware in the restroom or stairwell or under the bleachers in the gymnasium. For the most part, however, he was known throughout Coal Creek for his easygoing ways, and to his credit, most of the scraps he got caught up in were because of Lenora, defending her from bullies who made fun of her pious manner and pinched face and that damn bonnet she insisted on wearing. Though just a few months younger than Arvin, she already seemed dried up, a pale winter spud left too long in the furrow. He loved her like his own sister, but it could be embarrassing, walking into the schoolhouse in the morning with her following meekly on his heels. "She ain't never gonna make cheerleader, that's for sure," he told Uncle Earskell. He wished to hell his grandmother had never given her the black-and-white photograph of Helen standing under the apple tree behind the church in a long, shapeless dress with a ruffled hat covering her head. As far as he was concerned, Lenora certainly didn't need any new ideas on how to make herself look more like the shade of her pitiful mother.

WHENEVER EMMA ASKED HIM about the fighting, Arvin always thought of his father and that damp fall day long ago when he had defended Charlotte's honor in the Bull Pen parking lot. Though it was the best day he ever remembered spending with Willard, he never told anybody about it, or, for that matter, mentioned any of the bad days that soon followed. Instead, he would simply say to her, his father's voice echoing faintly in his head, "Grandma, there's a lot of no-good sonsofbitches out there."

"My Lord, Arvin, why do you keep saying that?"

"Because it's true."

"Well, maybe you should try praying for them then," she'd suggest. "That wouldn't hurt none, would it?" It was times like this when she regretted ever telling Reverend Sykes to leave the boy to find the path to God on his own terms. As far as she could tell, Arvin was always on the verge of heading the other direction.

He rolled his eyes; that was her advice for everything. "Maybe not," he said, "but Lenora already does enough of that for the both of us, and I don't see where it's doing her much good."

18

THEY SHARED A TENT DOWN AT THE END of the midway with the Flamingo Lady, a rail-thin woman with the longest nose Roy had ever seen on a human being. "She ain't really a bird, is she?" Theodore asked him after the first time they met her, his usual brash voice turned timid and shaky. Her strange appearance had frightened him. They had worked with freaks before, but nothing that looked quite like this one.

"No," Roy assured him. "She's just putting on a show."

"I didn't think so," the cripple said, relieved to find out that she wasn't real. He looked over and noticed Roy checking out her ass as she walked toward her trailer. "Hard to tell what kind of diseases something like that's got," he added, his cockiness quickly returning once he was satisfied she was out of hearing range. "Women like that, they'll fuck a dog or a donkey or anything else for a buck or two."

The Flamingo Lady's wild, bushy hair was dyed pink, and she wore a bikini that had ragged pigeon feathers glued to the flesh-colored material. Her act consisted mostly of standing on one leg in a little rubber swimming pool filled with dirty water while preening herself with her pointy beak. A record player sat on a table behind her playing slow, sad violin music that sometimes made her cry if she had accidentally taken too many of her nerve pills that day. Just as he had feared, Theodore figured out after a month or so that Roy was tapping it, though try as he might, he could never actually catch them in the filthy act. "That ugly bitch is gonna hatch an egg one of these days," he railed at Roy, "and I'd bet a dollar to a doughnut the goddamn chick will look just like you." Sometimes he cared; sometimes he didn't. It depended on how he and Flapjack the Clown were getting along at the moment. Flapjack had come to Theodore wanting to learn a few chords on the guitar, but then he'd showed the cripple how to play the skin flute instead. Roy once made the mistake of pointing out to his cousin that what he and the clown were doing was an abomination in the eyes of God. Theodore had set his guitar down on the sawdust floor and spit some brown juice in a paper cup. He'd recently taken to chewing tobacco. It made him a little sick to his stomach, but Flapjack liked the way it made his breath smell. "Damn, Roy, if you ain't a good one to talk, you crazy bastard," he said.

"What the hell does that mean? I ain't no peter puffer."

"Maybe not, but you sure as hell murdered your old lady with that screwdriver, didn't you? You ain't forgot about that, have you?"

"I ain't forgot," Roy said.

"Well then, you figure the Lord thinks any worse of me than He does of you?"

Roy hesitated for a minute before answering. According to what he had read in a pamphlet that he had found under a pillow in a Salvation Army shelter one time, a man laying with another man was probably equal to killing your wife, but Roy wasn't sure if it was any worse or not. The manner in which the weight of certain sins was calculated sometimes confused him. "No, I don't reckon," he finally said.

"Then I suggest you stick to your pink-haired crow or pelican or whatever the hell she is and leave me and Flapjack the fuck alone," Theodore said, digging the wet wad of chew out of his mouth and slinging it toward the Flamingo Lady's wading pool. They both heard a tiny splash. "We ain't hurting nobody."

The banner outside the tent read THE PROPHET AND THE PICKER. Roy delivered his grisly version of the End Times while Theodore provided the background music. It cost a quarter to get inside the tent, and convincing people that religion could be entertaining was tough when just a few yards away were a number of other more exciting and less serious distractions, so Roy came up with the idea of eating insects during his sermon, a slightly different take on his old spider act. Every couple of minutes, he'd stop preaching and pull a squirming worm or crunchy roach or slimy slug out of an old bait bucket and chew on it like a piece of candy. Business picked up after that. Depending on the crowd, they did four, sometimes five shows every evening, alternating with the Flamingo Lady every forty-five minutes. At the end of each show, Roy would quickly step out behind the tent to regurgitate the bugs and Theodore would follow in his wheelchair. While waiting to go on again, they smoked and sipped from a bottle, half listened to the drunks inside whoop and holler and try to coax the fake bird into stripping off her plumes.

By 1963, they had been with this particular carnival, Billy Bradford Family Amusements, for almost four years, traveling from one end of the hot, humid South to the other from early spring until late fall in a retired school bus packed with moldering canvas and folding chairs and metal poles, always setting up in dusty, pig-shit towns where the locals thought a couple of creaky whirly rides and some toothless, flea-bitten jungle cats along with a tattered freak show was high-class entertainment. On a good night, Roy and Theodore could make twenty or thirty bucks. The Flamingo Lady and Flapjack the Clown got most of what they didn't spend on booze or bugs or at the hot dog stand. West Virginia seemed like a million miles away, and the two fugitives couldn't imagine the arm of the law in Coal Creek ever stretching that far. It had been nearly fourteen years since they had buried Helen and fled south. They didn't even bother to change their names anymore.

19

ON ARVIN'S FIFTEENTH BIRTHDAY, Uncle Earskell handed him a pistol wrapped in a soft cloth along with a dusty box of shells. "This was your daddy's," the old man said. "It's a German Luger. Brought it back from the war. I figure he'd want you to have it." Earskell had never had any use for handguns, and so he'd hid it away under a floorboard in the smokehouse right after Willard left for Ohio. The only time he'd touched it since was to clean it occasionally. Seeing the elated look on the boy's face, he was glad now he'd never broken down and sold it. They had just finished supper, and there was one piece of fried rabbit left on the platter in the middle of the table. Earskell debated whether or not to save the haunch for his breakfast, then picked it up and started gnawing on it.

Arvin unwrapped the cloth carefully. The only gun his father had kept at home was a .22 rifle, and Willard never allowed him to touch it, let alone shoot it. Earskell, on the other hand, had handed the boy a 16-gauge Remington and took him to the woods just three or four weeks after he came to live with them. "In this house, you better know how to handle a gun unless you want to starve to death," he told Arvin.

"But I don't want to shoot anything," Arvin said that day, when Earskell stopped and pointed out two gray squirrels jumping back and forth on some branches high in a hickory tree.

"Didn't I see you eatin' a pork chop this morning?"

"Yeah."

"Somebody had to kill that hog and butcher it, didn't they?"

"I guess so."

Earskell lifted his own shotgun then and fired. One of the squirrels fell to the ground, and the old man started toward it. "Just try not to tear 'em up too bad," he said. "You want to have something left to put in the pan."

The coat of oil made the Luger shine like new in the wavering light cast from the kerosene lamps hanging at both ends of the room. "I never did hear him talk about it," Arvin said, lifting the gun up by the grip and pointing it toward the window. "About being in the service, I mean." There had been quite a few things his mother had warned him about when it came to his father, and asking questions about what he had seen in the war was high on the list.

"Yeah, I know," Earskell said. "I remember when he got back, I wanted him to tell me about the Japs, but anytime I brought it up, he'd start in about your mother again." He finished the rabbit and laid the bone on his plate. "Hell, I don't think he even knew her name at the time. Just saw her waiting tables in some eatin' place when he was coming home."

"The Wooden Spoon," Arvin said. "He took me there once after she got sick."

"I think he saw some rough things over on them islands," the old man said. He looked around for a rag, then wiped his hands on the front of his overalls. "I never did find out if they ate their dead or not."

Arvin bit his lip and swallowed hard. "This is the best present I ever got."

Just then, Emma entered the kitchen carrying a plain yellow cake in a small pan. A single candle was planted in the middle of it. Lenora followed behind dressed in the long blue dress and bonnet that she usually wore only to church. She held a box of matches in one hand and her cracked leather

Bible in the other. "What's that?" Emma said when she saw Arvin holding the Luger.

"That's Willard's gun he give me," Earskell said. "I figured it was time to pass it on to the boy."

"Oh, my," Emma said. She set the cake down on the table and grabbed up the hem of her checkered apron to wipe back a tear. Seeing the gun reminded her once again of her son and the promise she'd failed to keep all those years ago. Sometimes she couldn't help but wonder if they would all still be alive today if she had only convinced Willard to stay here and marry Helen.

Everyone was silent for a moment, almost as if they knew what the old woman was thinking. Then Lenora struck a match and said in a singsong voice, "Happy birthday, Arvin." She lit the candle, the same one they had used to celebrate her fourteenth birthday a few months ago.

"It ain't much use for anything," Earskell went on, ignoring the cake and nodding at the gun. "You got to be right up on something to hit it."

"Go ahead, Arvin," Lenora said.

"Might as well throw a rock," the old man joked.

"Arvin?"

"The shotgun will do you more good."

"Make your wish before the candle burns out," Emma said.

"Them's nine-millimeter shells," Earskell pointed out. "Banner don't carry them at the store, but he can order them special."

"Better hurry!" Lenora yelled.

"Okay, okay," the boy said, setting the gun down on the cloth. He bent down and blew out the tiny flame.

"So what did you wish for?" Lenora asked. She hoped it had something to do with the Lord, but the way Arvin was, she wasn't going to hold her breath. Every night, she prayed that he would wake up with a love for Jesus Christ glowing in his heart. She hated to think that he was going to end up in hell like that Elvis Presley and all those other sinners he listened to on the radio.

"Now you know better than to ask that," Emma said.

"That's all right, Grandma," Arvin said. "I wished that I could take you all back to Ohio and show you where we lived. It was nice, up there on the hill. At least it was before Mom took sick."

"Did I ever tell you about the time I lived in Cincinnati?" Earskell said.

Arvin looked at the two women and winked. "No," he said, "I don't recall it."

"Lord, not again," Emma muttered, while Lenora, smiling to herself, lifted the stub of the candle off the cake and put it in the matchbox.

"Yep, followed me a girl up there," the old man said. "She was from over on Fox Knob, was raised right next to the Riley place. Her house ain't there no more. Wanted to go to secretary school. I wasn't much older than you are now."

"Who wanted to go to secretary school," Arvin asked, "you or the girl?"

"Ha! Her did," Earskell said. He took a long breath, then slowly let it out. "Her name was Alice Louise Berry. You remember her, don't you, Emma?"

"Yes, I do, Earskell."

"So why didn't you stay?" Arvin said, without thinking. Though he had heard parts of the story a hundred times, he'd never before asked the old man why he had ended up back in Coal Creek. From living with his father, Arvin had learned that you didn't pry too much into other people's affairs. Everyone had things they didn't want to talk about, including himself. In the five years since his parents had passed, he had never once mentioned the hard feelings he held against Willard for leaving him. Now he felt like an ass for opening his mouth and putting the old man on the spot. He began wrapping the pistol back up in the cloth.

Earskell peered across the room with dim, cloudy eyes as if he was searching for the answer in the flowered wallpaper, though he knew the reason well enough. Alice Louise Berry had died in the influenza epidemic of 1918, along with 3 million or so other poor souls, just a few weeks after starting her classes at the Gilmore Sanderson Secretarial School. If only they had stayed in the hills, Earskell often thought, she might still be alive. But Alice always had big dreams, which was one of the things he had loved about her, and he was glad that he hadn't tried to talk her out of it. He was certain those days they spent in Cincinnati among the tall buildings and crowded streets before she took the fever were the happiest ones of her life. His, too, for that matter. After a minute or so, he blinked away the memories and said, "That sure looks like a dandy cake."

Emma took up her knife and cut it into four pieces, one for each of them.

20

ONE DAY ARVIN WENT LOOKING FOR LENORA after school let out and found her backed up against the trash incinerator next to the bus garage, surrounded by three boys. As he walked up behind them, he heard Gene Dinwoodie tell her, "Hell, you're so damn ugly I'd have to put a sack over your head before I could get a hard-on." The other two, Orville Buckman and Tommy Matson, laughed and squeezed in closer to her. They were seniors who had been held back a year or two, and all of them were bigger than Arvin. They spent most of their time at school sitting in the shop building trading dirty jokes with the worthless industrial arts teacher and smoking Bugler. Lenora had shut her eyes tight and begun praying. Tears were running down her pink face. Arvin got only a couple of licks in on Dinwoodie before the others tackled him to the ground and took turns punching him. While he was lying in the gravel, he thought, as he often did when in the middle of a fight, of the hunter that his father had beaten so badly that day in the outhouse mud. But unlike that man, Arvin never gave up. They might have killed him if the janitor hadn't come along with a cart of cardboard boxes to burn. His head ached for a week, and he had trouble reading the blackboard for several more.

Though it took him almost two months, Arvin managed to catch each of them alone. One evening right before dark, he followed Orville Buckman to Banner's store. He stood behind a tree a hundred yards down the road and watched the boy come back out swigging a pop and eating the last of a Little

Debbie. Just as Orville started past him with the bottle tipped up to take another drink, Arvin stepped out into the road. He smacked the bottom of the Pepsi bottle with the palm of his hand and sent the glass neck halfway down the big boy's throat, breaking two of his rotten front teeth off. By the time Orville realized what had hit him, the fight was pretty much finished except for the blow that put his lights out. An hour later, he woke up lying in the ditch along the road choking on blood and a paper sack over his head.

A couple of weeks later, Arvin drove Earskell's old Ford over to the Coal Creek High School basketball game. They were playing the team from Millersburg, which always brought a big turnout. He sat in the car smoking Camel cigarettes and watching the front door for Tommy Matson to show his face. It was drizzling rain, a chilly, dark Friday night in early November. Matson liked to think of himself as the school cock-hound, was always bragging about the pussy he picked up at the games while their stupid boyfriends scrambled up and down the gym floor chasing a rubber ball. Right before halftime, just as Arvin flipped another butt out the window, he saw his next target walk outside with his arm around a freshman girl named Susie Cox and head to the row of school buses parked in the back of the lot. Arvin got out of the Ford carrying a tire iron and followed them. He watched Matson open the rear door of one of the yellow buses and help Susie up inside. After waiting a few minutes, Arvin twisted the handle on the door and let it swing open with a raspy squeak. "What was that?" he heard the girl say.

"Nothing," Matson told her. "I must not got it shut all the way. Now come on, girl, let's get them bloomers off."

"Not until you close that door," she said.

"Goddamn it," Matson grumbled, raising up off her. "You

better be worth it." He walked down the narrow aisle holding his pants up with one hand.

When he leaned out to grab the latch and pull the door back, Arvin swung the tire iron and hit Matson across the kneecaps, toppling him out of the bus. "Jesus!" he yelled when he hit the gravel, landing hard on his right shoulder. Swinging the tire iron again, Arvin cracked two of his ribs, then kicked him until he stopped trying to get up. He took a paper bag out of his jacket and knelt down beside the moaning boy. Grabbing hold of Matson's curly hair, he pulled his head up. The girl inside the bus didn't make a peep.

The next Monday at school, Gene Dinwoodie walked up to Arvin in the cafeteria and said, "I'd like to see you try and put a sack over my head, you sonofabitch."

Arvin was sitting at a table with Mary Jane Turner, a new girl at the school. Her father had grown up in Coal Creek, then spent fifteen years in the merchant marine before returning home to claim his inheritance, a run-down farm on the side of a hill that his grandfather had left him. The redheaded girl could curse like a sailor when the opportunity presented itself, and though Arvin wasn't sure why, he liked that a lot, especially when they were making out. "Leave us alone, you dumb prick," she said, glaring scornfully at the tall boy standing over them. Arvin smiled.

Ignoring her, Gene said, "Russell, after I get done with you, I might just take your girlfriend out for a nice long ride. She ain't no beauty queen, but I gotta say, she's not nearly as bad as that rat-faced sister of yours." He stood over the table with his fists clenched, waiting for Arvin to leap up and start swinging, then watched dumbfounded as the boy closed his eyes and put his hands together. "You got to be shittin' me." Gene looked around the crowded lunchroom. The gym teacher, a burly man with a red beard who wrestled for extra money in Huntington and Charleston on the weekends, was scowling at him. The rumor around the school was that he'd never been pinned, and that he won all his matches because he hated everybody and everything in West Virginia. Even Gene was afraid of him. Leaning over, he said to Arvin in a low voice, "Don't think praying's gonna get you out of this, motherfucker."

After Gene walked away, Arvin opened his eyes and took a drink from a carton of chocolate milk. "Are you all right?" Mary said.

"Sure," he said. "Why you ask that?"

"Were you really praying?"

"I was," he said, nodding his head. "Praying for the right time."

He finally caught Dinwoodie a week later in his daddy's garage changing a spark plug in his '56 Chevy. By then, Arvin had collected a dozen paper bags. Gene's head was tightly encased in them when his younger brother found him several hours later. The doctor said he was lucky that he hadn't suffocated. "Arvin Russell," Gene told the sheriff after he came to his senses. He'd spent the last twelve hours in the hospital believing that he was running dead last in a race at the Indy 500. It had been the longest night of his life; every time he stomped the accelerator, the car slowed down to a crawl. The roar of the engines passing him by was still ringing in his ears.

"Arvin Russell?" the sheriff, a hint of doubt in his voice. "I know that boy likes to scrap, but hell, son, you twice as big as he is."

"He caught me off guard."

"So you seen him before he put that knot on your head?" the sheriff asked.

"No," Gene said, "but he's the one."

"And how exactly do you know this?"

Gene's father was leaning against the wall watching his son with sullen, bloodshot eyes. The boy could smell the Wild Irish Rose wafting off his old man clear across the room. Carl Dinwoodie wasn't too bad if he stuck to beer, but when he got on the wine, he could be downright dangerous. This might come back to bite me in the ass if I'm not careful, Gene thought. His mother went to the same church as the Russell bunch. His father would kick the shit out of him all over again if he heard he'd been harassing that little Lenora bitch. "I could be wrong," Gene said.

"Why did you say the Russell boy did it then?" the sheriff said.

"I don't know. Maybe I dreamed it."

Over in the corner, Gene's father made a sound like a dog retching, then said, "Nineteen years old and still in school. What you think about that, Sheriff? Worthless as tits on a boar hog, ain't he?"

"Who we talking about?" the sheriff said, a puzzled look on his face.

"That no-account thing laying right there in that bed, that's who," Carl said, then turned and staggered out the door.

The sheriff looked back to the boy. "Well, any idea why whoever did do it put them sacks over your head like that?"

"No," Gene said. "Not a clue."

21

"WHAT YOU GOT THERE?" Earskell said, as Arvin stepped up onto the porch. "I heard you over in there shooting that pop gun." His cataracts were getting worse every week, like dirty curtains being slowly pulled shut in an already dim room. A couple more months and he was afraid he wouldn't be able to drive anymore. Getting old was next to the worst goddamn thing that had ever happened to him. Lately, he'd been thinking about Alice Louise Berry more and more. They had both missed out on a lot, her dying so young.

Arvin held up three red squirrels. He had his father's pistol stuck in the waistband of his pants. "We'll eat good tonight," he said. Emma had served nothing but beans and fried potatoes for four days now. Things always got lean toward the end of the month, before her pension check came. Both he and the old man were starving for some meat.

Earskell leaned forward in his chair. "You surely didn't get those with that German piece of shit, did you?" Secretly, he was proud of the way the boy could handle the Luger, but he still didn't think much of handguns. He'd rather have a pepper gun or a rifle any day.

"It ain't a bad gun," Arvin said. "You just got to know how to shoot it." It was the first time the old man had ridiculed the pistol in quite a while.

Earskell laid down the implement catalog he'd been peering through all morning and pulled his penknife out of his pocket. "Well, go fetch us something to put 'em in, and I'll help you clean 'em."

Arvin pulled the skins off the squirrels while the old man held them by their front legs. They gutted the carcasses on a sheet of newspaper and cut the heads and feet off and laid the bloody meat in a pan of salted water. After they finished, Arvin folded up the mess in the paper and carried it out to the edge of the yard. Earskell waited until he came back up on the porch, then pulled a pint out of his pocket and took a drink. Emma had asked him to talk to the boy. She was at her wit's end after hearing about the latest incident. He wiped his mouth and said, "Played cards over at Elder Stubb's garage last night."

"So did you win?"

"No, not really," Earskell said. He stretched his legs out, looked down at his battered shoes. He was going to have to try mending them again. "Saw Carl Dinwoodie there."

"Yeah?"

"He wasn't none too happy."

Arvin sat down on the other side of his great-uncle in a creaky cast-off kitchen chair held together with baling wire. He studied the gray woods across the road and chewed at the inside of his mouth for a minute. "He pissed off about Gene?" he asked. It had been over a week since he'd bagged the son-ofabitch.

"A little maybe, but I think he's more ticked off about the hospital bill he's gonna have to pay." Earskell looked down at the squirrels floating in the pan. "So what happened?"

Though Arvin didn't ever see the point of offering up any details to his grandmother for beating the shit out of someone, mostly because he didn't want to upset her, he knew Earskell wouldn't be satisfied with anything other than the facts. "He's been teasing Lenora, him and his candy-ass buddies," he said. "Calling her names, shit like that. So I fixed his wagon for him."

"What about the others?"

"Them, too."

Earskell heaved a long sigh, scratched at the whiskers on his neck. "You think maybe you should have held back just a little bit? Boy, I understand what you're saying, but still, you can't go sending people to the hospital over some name-calling. Puttin' some knots on his head is one thing, but from what I hear, you hurt him pretty bad."

"I don't like bullies."

"Jesus Christ, Arvin, you going to meet lots of people you might not take a liking to."

"Maybe so, but I bet he won't pick on Lenora anymore."

"Look, I want you to do me a favor."

"What's that?"

"Stick that Luger away in a drawer and forget about it for now."

"Why?"

"Handguns ain't made for hunting. They're for killin' people."

"But I didn't shoot the bastard," Arvin said. "I beat him up."

"Yeah, I know. This time anyway."

"What about them squirrels? I hit every one of them in the head. You can't do that with no shotgun."

"Just put it up for a while, okay? Use the rifle if you want to go after some game."

The boy studied the floor of the porch for a moment, then looked up at the old man with narrowed, suspicious eyes. "He get mouthy with you?"

"You mean Carl?" Earskell asked. "No, he knows better than that." He didn't see any sense in telling Arvin that he had drawn a royal flush on the last and biggest pot of the night, or that he had folded so that Carl could take the money home with two pissy pair. Though he knew it had been the right thing to do, it still made him half sick thinking about it. There must have been two hundred dollars in that kitty. He just hoped the boy's doctor got a chunk of it.

22

ARVIN WAS LEANING AGAINST THE ROUGH RAIL of the porch late on a clear Saturday night in March looking at the stars hanging over the hills in all their distant mystery and solemn brilliance. He and Hobart Finley and Daryl Kuhn, his two closest friends, had bought a jug earlier that evening from Slot Machine, a one-armed bootlegger who operated over on Hungry Holler, and he was still sipping on it. The wind had a bite to it, but the whiskey kept him warm enough. He heard Earskell inside the house moan and mutter something in his sleep. In the good weather, the old man slept in a drafty lean-to he had nailed on the back of his sister's house when he moved in a few years ago, but once it turned cold out, he lay on the floor next to the wood stove on a pallet made up of scratchy, homespun blankets that smelled like kerosene and mothballs. Down the hill, parked in the pull-off behind Earskell's Ford was Arvin's prized possession, a blue 1954 Chevy Bel Air with a loose transmission. It had taken him four years doing whatever kind of work he could get—chopping firewood, building fence, picking apples, slopping hogs—to save enough money to buy it.

Earlier that day, Arvin had driven Lenora to the cemetery to visit her mother's grave. Though he would never admit it, the only reason he went to the graveyard with her now was because he hoped she might recall some buried memory about her daddy or the cripple he ran with. He had become fascinated with the riddle of their disappearance. Although Emma and many others in Greenbrier County seemed convinced that the two were alive and well, Arvin found it hard to believe that two bastards as nutty as Roy and Theodore were purported to be could have vanished into thin air and never be heard from again. If it was that easy, he figured a lot more people would do it. He'd wished many times that his father had taken that route.

"Don't you think it's funny how we both ended up orphans and living in the same house like we do?" Lenora had said after they entered the cemetery. She set her Bible down on a nearby tombstone and loosened her bonnet a bit and pulled it back. "It's almost like everything happened so we'd meet each other." She was standing next to her mother's place looking down at the square marker lying flat to the ground: HELEN HATTON LAFERTY 1926–1948. A small winged but faceless angel was carved into each top corner. Arvin had pushed spit between his teeth and glanced around at the dead remains of last year's flowers on the other graves, the clumps of grass and rusty wire fence that surrounded the cemetery. It made him uneasy when Lenora talked like that, and she had been doing it a lot more since she'd turned sixteen. They might not have been blood relation, but it made him squeamish to think of her any other way than as his sister. Though he realized the odds weren't good, he kept hoping she might find a boyfriend before she said something really stupid.

He weaved a little as he moved from the edge of the porch over to Earskell's rocking chair and sat down. He started thinking about his parents, and his throat got tight and dry all of the sudden. He loved whiskey, but sometimes it brought on a deep sadness that only sleep would erase. He felt like crying, but lifted the bottle and took another drink instead. A dog barked somewhere over the next knob, and his thoughts wandered to Jack, the poor harmless mutt that his father had killed just for some more lousy blood. That had been one of the worst days of that summer, the way he remembered it, almost as bad as the night his mother died. Soon, Arvin promised himself, he was going to go back to the prayer log and see if the dog's bones were still there. He wanted to bury them proper, do what he could to make up for some of what his crazy father had done. If he lived to be a hundred, he vowed, he would never forget Jack.

Sometimes he wondered if perhaps he was just envious that Lenora's father might still be alive while his was dead. He had read all the faded newspaper accounts, had even gone out combing the woods where Helen's corpse had been found, hoping to discover some piece of evidence that would prove everybody wrong: a shallow pit with two skeletons slowly rising side by side up through the earth, or a rusty wheelchair pocked with bullet holes hidden deep in an overlooked gully. But the only things he'd ever come across were two spent shotgun shells and a Spearmint gum wrapper. As Lenora ignored his questions that morning about her father and kept on blabbing about fate and star-crossed lovers and all that other romance shit she read about in books checked out from the school library, he'd realized that he should have stayed home and worked on the Bel Air. It hadn't run right since the day he bought it.

"Damn it, Lenora, stop talking that nonsense," Arvin had told her. "Besides, you might not even be an orphan. As far as everyone around here's concerned, you daddy's still alive and kicking. Hell, he might pop over the hill any day now dancing a jig."

"I hope so," she'd said. "I pray every day that he will."

"Even if it meant he killed your mother?"

"I don't care," she said. "I've already forgiven him. We could start all over."

"That's crazy."

"No, it's not. What about your father?"

"What about him?"

"Well, if he could come back—"

"Girl, just shut up about it." Arvin started toward the cemetery gate. "We both know that ain't gonna happen."

"I'm sorry," she said, her voice breaking into a sob.

Taking a deep breath, Arvin stopped and turned around. Sometimes it seemed as if she spent half of her life crying. He held his car keys in his hand. "Look, if you want a ride, come on."

When he got home, he cleaned the Bel Air's carburetor with a wire brush dipped in gasoline, then left again right after supper to pick up Hobart and Daryl. He had been down all week, thinking about Mary Jane Turner, and he felt the need to get good and sloshed. Her father hadn't taken long to decide that life in the merchant marine was a hell of a lot easier than plowing rocks and worrying about whether it rained enough or not, and so he had packed his family up and headed for Baltimore and a new ship the previous Sunday morning. Though Arvin had kept after her from their first date, he was glad now that Mary hadn't let him in her pants. Saying goodbye had been hard enough as it was. "Please," he'd asked as they stood at her front door the night before she left; and she had smiled and stood on her tiptoes and one last time whispered dirty words in his ear. He and Hobart and Daryl had pooled their money together for the bottle and a twelve-pack of Blue Ribbon and three packs of Pall Malls and a tank of gas. Then they drove up and down the dull streets of Lewisburg until midnight listening to the radio fade in and out and blowing off about what they were going to do after high school, until their voices turned as rough as gravel from all the smoke and whiskey and grandiose plans for the future.

Leaning back in the rocker, Arvin wondered who was living in his old house now, wondered if the storekeeper still stayed by himself in that little camper and if Janey Wagner was knocked up by now. "Stink finger," he muttered to himself. He thought again about the way the deputy named Bodecker had locked him in the back of the patrol car after he had led him to the prayer log, like the lawman was afraid of him, a ten-year-old kid with blueberry pie on his face. They had put him in an empty cell that night, not knowing what else to do with him, and the welfare lady had showed up the next afternoon with some of his clothes and his grandmother's address. Holding the bottle up, he saw that there was maybe two inches left in the bottom. He stuck it under the chair for Earskell in the morning.

23

REVEREND SYKES COUGHED, and the congregation of the Coal Creek Church of the Holy Ghost Sanctified watched a trickle of bright blood run down his chin and drip onto his shirt. He kept preaching, though, gave the people a decent sermon about helping your neighbor; but then at the end he announced that he was stepping down. "Temporary," he said. "Just till I get to feeling better." He said that his wife had a nephew down in Tennessee who had just graduated from one of those Bible colleges. "He claims he wants to work with poor people," Sykes went on. "I figure he must be a Democrat." He grinned, hoping for a laugh to brighten things up a little, but the only sound he heard came from the small clutch of women in the back near the door crying with his wife. He realized now that he should have made her stay home today.

Taking a careful breath, he cleared his throat. "I ain't seen him since he was a boy, but his mother says he's all right. Him and his wife should be here in two weeks, and like I said, he's just gonna help out for a while. I know he ain't from around here, but try to make him feel welcome anyway." Sykes started to weave a bit and grabbed hold of the pulpit to steady himself. He pulled the empty Five Brothers pack from his pocket and held it up. "Just in case any of you need it, I'm gonna hand this over to him." A hacking fit came over him then, bent him double, but this time he managed to cover his mouth with his handkerchief and hide the blood. When he got his breath back, he rose up and looked around, his face red and sweaty with the strain of it all. He was too embarrassed to tell them that he was dying. The black lung that he'd been fighting for years had finally gotten the better of him. Within the next few weeks or months, according to the doctor, he'd be meeting his Maker. Sykes couldn't honestly say that he was actually looking forward to it, but he knew that he'd had a better life than most men. After all, hadn't he lived forty-two years longer than those poor wretches who had died in the mine cave-in that had pointed him toward his calling? Yes, he'd been a lucky man. He wiped a tear from his eye and shoved the bloody rag in his pants pocket. "Well," he said, "no sense keeping you folks any longer. That's all I got for now."

24

ROY LIFTED THEODORE OUT OF THE WHEELCHAIR and carried him across the dirty sand. They were at the north end of a public beach in St. Petersburg, a few miles south of Tampa. The cripple's useless legs swung back and forth like a rag doll's. He was rank with the smell of piss, and Roy had noticed that he wasn't using his milk bottle anymore, just soaking his rotten dungarees whenever he needed to go. He had to set Theodore down several times and rest, but he finally got him to the edge of the water. Two stout women wearing wide-brimmed hats rose up and looked over at them, then hurriedly gathered up their towels and lotions and headed for the parking lot. Roy went back to the chair and got their supper, two fifths of White Port and a package of boiled ham. They had swiped it from a Winn-Dixie a couple of blocks away right after a truck driver hauling oranges let them out. "Didn't we spend some time locked up here once?" Theodore asked.

Roy swallowed the last slice of meat and nodded. "Three days, I think." The cops had picked them up for vagrancy just before dark. They had been preaching on a street corner. America was getting as bad as Russia, a thin, balding man yelled at them as they were escorted past his cell to their own that night. Why could the police throw a man in jail just because he didn't have any money or an address? What if the man didn't want any goddamn money or a fuckin' address? Where was all this freedom they bragged about? The cops took the protestor out of the block every morning and made him carry a stack of telephone books up and down the stairs all day. According to some of the other prisoners, the man had been arrested for vagrancy twenty-two times just in the past year, and they were sick of feeding the Communist bastard. If nothing else, they were going to make him sweat for his bologna and grits.

"I can't remember," Theodore said. "What was the jail like?"

"Not bad," Roy said. "I believe they gave out coffee for dessert." The second night they were there, the cops brought in a big, hulking brute with a carved-up face called the Zit-Eater. Right before bedtime, they stuck him in the cell down at the end of the hall with the Communist. Everyone in the jail had heard about the Zit-Eater except for Roy and Theodore. He was famous up and down the Gulf Coast. "Why do they call him that?" Roy had asked the paper hanger with the handlebar mustache in the cell next to theirs.

"Because the fucker gets you down and pops your pimples if you got any," the man said. He twisted the waxed ends of his black mustache. "Lucky for me I've always had a nice complexion."

"What the hell does he do that for?"

"He likes to eat 'em," another man said, from a cell across the way. "Some claim he's a cannibal, got leftovers buried all over Florida, but I don't buy it. He just likes to get attention, that's what I think."

"Jesus, someone oughta kill a sonofabitch like that," Theodore said. He glanced at the acne scars on Roy's face.

The mustache shook his head. "He'd be a hard one to kill," he said. "You ever see one of them retards that can carry a car on his back? They had one of 'em at this alligator farm where I worked one summer down by Naples. You couldn't have stopped that bastard with a machine gun once he got started. The Zit-Eater, he's like that." Then they heard some commotion down at the end of the hall. Evidently, the Communist wasn't going to give up easy, and that cheered Roy and Theodore a little, but after a couple of minutes all they could hear was his crying.

The next morning, three broad-chested men in white coats came in with billy clubs and hauled the Zit-Eater away in a straitjacket to a nuthouse on the other side of town. The Communist quit bitching about the law after that, didn't complain once about the fresh squeeze marks on his face or the blisters on his feet, just carried his phone books up and down the stairs like he was thankful they'd given him some meaningful work to do.

Theodore sighed, looked out over the blue gulf, the water smooth as a pane of glass that day. "That sounds nice, coffee for dessert. Maybe we could let them take us in, get a little break."

"Shit, Theodore, I don't want to spend the night in jail." Roy kept one eye on the new wheelchair. He'd slipped into an old folks' home a couple of days ago and borrowed it after the wheels on the last one gave out. He wondered how many miles he had pushed Theodore since they had left West Virginia. Though he wasn't good with numbers, he estimated it had to be up around a million by now.

"I'm tired, Roy."

Theodore hadn't been acting right since he cost them the job with the carnival the summer before. A young boy, maybe five or six years old, eating a cardboard scoop of cotton candy, had wandered into the back of the tent while Roy was out front trying to drum up some customers. Theodore swore that the boy asked for help in zipping his pants up, but not even Roy could buy that one. Within minutes, Billy Bradford had loaded them up in his Cadillac and dumped them a few miles out in the country. They didn't even get a chance to say their goodbyes to Flapjack or the Flamingo Lady; and though they had tried to get on with several other outfits since then, word of the crippled pedophile and his bug-eating buddy had spread fast among the carny owners. "Want me to go get your guitar?" Roy asked.

"Nah," Theodore said. "I ain't got no music in me today."

"You sick?"

"I don't know," the crippled boy said. "It's like there's never no letup."

"Want one of them oranges the trucker gave us?"

"Hell no. I've et enough of them damn things to last me till the Judgment Day. They still give me the shits."

"I could drop you off at the hospital," Roy said. "Come back for you in a day or two."

"Hospitals, they worse than jails."

"Want me to pray over you?"

Theodore laughed. "Ha. That's a good one, Roy."

"Maybe that's what's wrong with you. You don't believe no more."

"Don't start in on that shit again," Theodore said. "I've served the Lord in various capacities. And I got the legs to prove it."

"You just need some rest," Roy said. "We'll find us a good tree to sleep under before dark."

"It still sounds mighty nice. Them passing out coffee for dessert."

"Jesus, you want a cup of coffee, I'll go get you one. We still got some change left."

"I wish we was still with the carnival," Theodore sighed. "That was the best we ever had it."

"Yeah, well, you should have kept your hands off that kid if that's the way you feel."

Theodore picked up a pebble and threw it in the water. "It makes you wonder, don't it?"

"What's that?" Roy asked.

"I don't know," the cripple said with a shrug. "Just makes you wonder, that's all."

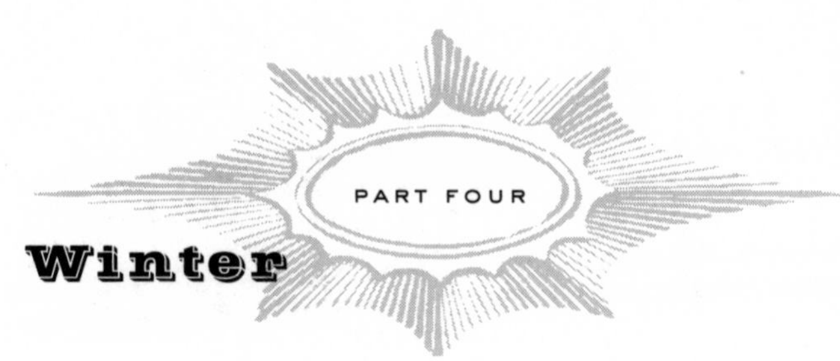

PART FOUR

Winter

25

IT WAS A COLD FEBRUARY MORNING in the early part of 1966, Carl and Sandy's fifth year together. The apartment was like an icebox, but Carl was afraid if he kept knocking on the landlady's door downstairs about turning up the thermostat, he might snap and strangle her with her own filthy hairnet. He had never killed anyone in Ohio, didn't believe in shitting in his own nest. That was Rule #2. So Mrs. Burchwell, although she deserved it more than anything, was off-limits. Sandy woke up a little before noon and headed for the living room with a blanket draped over her narrow shoulders, dragging the ends of it through the dust and dirt on the floor. She curled up on the couch in a shivering ball and waited for Carl to bring her a cup of coffee and turn the TV on. For the next several hours she smoked cigarettes and watched her soap operas and coughed. At three o'clock, Carl yelled from the kitchen that it was time to get ready for work. Sandy tended bar six nights a week, and though she was supposed to let Juanita off at four, she was always running late.

With a groan, she sat up and stabbed out her cigarette in the ashtray and flung the blanket off her shoulders. She turned off the TV, then shivered her way to the bathroom. Bending over the sink, she splashed some water around in the bowl. She dried off her face, studied herself in the mirror, tried vainly to brush the yellow stains off her teeth. With a tube of red lipstick, she made up her mouth, fixed her eyes, pulled her brown hair back in a limp ponytail. She was sore and bruised. Last night, after she closed up the bar, she let a paper mill worker who had recently lost a hand in a rewinder bend her over the pool table for twenty bucks. Her brother was watching her closely these days, ever since that goddamn phone call, but twenty bucks was twenty bucks, no matter how you looked at it. She and Carl could drive halfway across a state on that much money, or pay the electric bill for the month. It still irked her, all the crooked shit that Lee was into, and then him worried about her costing him votes. The man told her he would fork over another ten if she'd let him stick the metal hook up inside her, but Sandy told him that sounded like something he should save for his wife.

"My wife ain't no whore," the man said.

"Yeah, right," Sandy shot back as she pulled down her panties. "She married you, didn't she?" She'd held on to the twenty the whole time he pounded her. It was the hardest she'd been fucked in a long time; the bastard was definitely going for his money's worth. He sounded like he was going to have a heart attack, the way he was grunting and gasping for air, the cold metal hook pressed against her right hip. By the time he finished, the money was wadded up into a little ball in her hand, soaked with sweat. After he backed away, she smoothed it out on the green felt and stuck it inside her sweater. "Besides," she said, as she walked over to unlock the door and let him out, "that thing ain't got no more feeling than a beer can." Sometimes, after a night like that, she wished she was back working the morning shift at the Wooden Spoon. At least Henry, the old grill cook, had been gentle. He'd been her first, right after she turned sixteen. They had lain together on the floor of the stockroom a long time that night, covered with flour from a fifty-pound bag they had knocked over. He still stopped by the bar once in a while to shoot the shit and tease her about rolling out some more pie dough.

When she came into the kitchen, Carl was sitting in front of the stove reading the newspaper for the second time that day. His fingers were gray with ink. All the burners on the stove were lit and the oven door was open. Blue flames danced behind him like miniature campfires. His pistol lay on the kitchen table, the barrel pointed toward the door. The whites of his eyes were laced with red veins, and his fat, pale, unshaven face looked like some cold and distant star in the reflection from the bare lightbulb hanging over the table. He'd spent most of the night bent over in the tiny closet in the hallway that he used as a darkroom, coaxing life into the last of the film he had saved back from the previous summer. He hated to see it end. He'd nearly cried when he developed that last photo. Next August was a long ways off.

"Those people are so screwed up," Sandy said as she searched inside her purse for the keys to the car.

"Which people?" Carl asked, turning another page of the paper.

"Them ones on TV. They don't know what they want."

"Damn it, Sandy, you pay too much attention to those fuckers," he said, glancing at the clock impatiently. "Hell, you think they give a shit about you?" She should have been at work five minutes ago. He had been waiting all day for her to leave.

"Well, if it wasn't for the doctor, I wouldn't watch it anymore," she said. She was always going on about the M.D. on one of the shows, a tall, handsome man whom Carl was convinced must be the luckiest bastard on the planet. The man could fall down a rat hole and climb out with a suitcase stuffed with money and the keys to a new El Dorado. Over the years that Sandy had been watching him, he'd probably performed more miracles than Jesus. Carl couldn't stand him, that fake movie star nose, those sixty-dollar suits.

"So whose dick did he suck today?" Carl said.

"Ha! You're one to talk," Sandy said, as she pulled on her coat. She was sick of always having to defend her soaps.

"What the hell does that mean?"

"It means whatever you think it means," Sandy said. "You were in that closet all night again."

"I'll tell you what, I'd like to meet up with that sonofabitch."

"I bet you would," Sandy said.

"I'd make him squeal like a goddamn pig, I swear to God!" Carl yelled as she slammed the door behind her.

A few minutes after she left, Carl quit cursing the actor and turned the stove off. He laid his head in his arms at the table and dozed off for a while. The room was dark when he woke up. He was hungry, but all he could find in the refrigerator were two moldy heels of bread and a dab of crusty pimento cheese in a plastic container. Opening the kitchen window, he tossed the bread into the front yard. A few flakes of snow drifted through the ray of light coming from the landlady's porch. From over in the stockyards across the street, he heard somebody laugh, the metal clang of a gate being slammed shut. He realized that he hadn't been outside in over a week.

He closed the window and walked into the living room and paced back and forth singing old-time religious songs and waving his arms in the air like he was leading a choir. "Bringing in the Sheaves" was one of his favorites, and he sang it several times in a row. When he was a boy, his mother used to sing it while doing the wash. She had a certain song for every chore, every heartache, every goddamn thing that happened to them after his father died. She did laundry for rich people, got cheated half the time by the no-good bastards. Sometimes he would skip school and hide under the rotting porch with the slugs and spiders and the shreds that remained of the neighbor's cat, and listen to her all day. Her voice never seemed to tire. He would ration the butter sandwich she'd packed for his lunch, sip dirty water from a rusty soup can he kept stored in the cat's rib cage. He'd pretend it was vegetable beef or chicken noodle, but no matter how hard he tried, it always tasted like mud. He wished to hell he had bought some soup the last time he went to the store. The memory of that old can made him hungry again.

He sang for several hours, his loud voice booming through the rooms, his face red and sweaty with the effort. Then, just before nine o'clock, the landlady began pounding furiously with the end of a broom handle on her ceiling below. He was in the middle of a rousing version of "Onward Christian Soldiers." Any other time he would have ignored her, but tonight he sputtered to a stop; he was in the mood to move on to other things. But if she didn't turn the fucking heat up soon, he'd start keeping her up until midnight. He could stand the cold easy enough, but Sandy's constant shivering and complaining were getting on his nerves.

Going back to the kitchen, he got a flashlight from the spoon drawer and made sure the door was locked. Then he went around closing all the curtains, ended up in the bedroom. He got down on his knees and reached under the bed for a shoe box. He carried the box into the living room and turned off all the lights and settled down on the couch in the darkness. Cold air blew in around the loose windows, and he drew Sandy's blanket over his shoulders.

With the box on his lap, he closed his eyes and reached a hand under the cardboard lid. There were over two hundred photos inside, but he pulled just one out. He rubbed his thumb slowly over the slick paper, tried to divine which image it might be, a little thing he did to make it all last longer. After making his guess, he opened his eyes and flipped the flashlight on just for a second. *Click, click.* A tiny taste and he set that photo to the side, closed his eyes again, and took out another. *Click, click.* Bare backs and bloody holes and Sandy with her legs spread. Sometimes he went through the entire box without guessing a single one of them correctly.

Once he thought he heard a noise, a car door slam, footsteps on the back stairs. He got up and tiptoed from room to room with the pistol, peeking out the windows. Then he checked the door and returned to the couch. Time seemed to shift, speed up, slow down, move back and forth like a crazy dream he kept having over and over. One second he was standing in a muddy soybean field outside of Jasper, Indiana; and the next click of the flashlight took him to the bottom of a rocky ravine north of Sugar City, Colorado. Old voices crawled through his head like worms, some bitter with curses, others still pleading for mercy. By midnight, he'd traveled through a large portion of the Midwest, relived the last moments of twenty-four strange men. He remembered everything. It was as if he resurrected them every time he brought out the box, stirred them awake and allowed them to do their own kind of singing. One last click and he decided to call it a night.

After he returned the box to its hiding place under the bed, he switched the lights back on and wiped off the blanket as best he could with her washcloth. For the next couple of hours, he sat at the kitchen table cleaning the pistol and studying his road maps and waiting on Sandy to get off work. He always felt the need for her company after a bout with the box. She had told him about the paper mill man, and he thought about that for a while, what he'd do with the hook if they ever picked up a hitchhiker like that.

He'd forgotten how hungry he was until she walked in with two cold hamburgers slathered with mustard, three bottles of beer, and the evening newspaper. While he ate, she sat opposite him and carefully added up her tips, stacking the nickels, dimes, and quarters into small, neat piles, and he recalled the way he'd acted earlier about her stupid TV show. "You did pretty good tonight," he said, when she finally finished counting.

"Not bad for a Wednesday, I guess," she said with a tired smile. "So what did you do today?"

He shrugged. "Oh, cleaned out the fridge, sang a few songs."

"You didn't piss the landlady off again, did you?"

"Just kidding," he said. "I got some new pictures to show you."

"Which one is it?" she asked.

"The one had that bandanna tied around his head. They turned out pretty good."

"Not tonight," she said. "I'd never get to sleep." Then she pushed half the change over to him. He scooped it up and dumped it in a coffee can he kept under the sink. They were always saving for the next junker, the next roll of film, the next trip. Opening the last beer, he poured her a glass. Then he got down on his knees in front of her and pulled her shoes off, began rubbing the work out of her feet. "I shouldn't have said anything about your damn doctor today," he said. "You watch whatever you want."

"It's just something to do, baby," Sandy said. "Takes my mind off things, you know?" He nodded, gently worked his fingers into the soft soles of her feet. "That's the spot," she said, stretching out her legs. Then, after she finished the beer and a last cigarette, he scooped her skinny body up and carried her giggling down the hallway and into the bedroom. He hadn't heard her laugh in weeks. He would keep her warm tonight, that was the least he could do. It was nearly four in the morning, and somehow, with lots of luck and little regret, they had made it through another long winter day.

26

A FEW DAYS LATER, CARL DROVE SANDY TO WORK, told her he needed to get out of the apartment for a while. It had snowed several inches the night before, and that morning the sun finally managed to break through the thick, gray bank of clouds that had hovered over Ohio like some dismal, unrelenting curse for the past several weeks. Everything in Meade, even the paper mill smokestack, was sparkling and white. "Want to come in for a minute?" she asked when he pulled up in front of the Tecumseh. "I'll buy you a beer."

Carl looked around at the cars in the slushy parking lot. He was surprised it was so crowded in the middle of the day. He'd kept himself shut up in the apartment for so long that he didn't think he could tolerate that many people his first time back out in the real world since before Christmas. "Ah, I think I'll pass," he said. "I figured I'd just ride around for a while, try to get home before dark."

"Suit yourself," she said, opening her car door. "Just don't forget to pick me up tonight."

As soon as she went inside, Carl headed straight back to the apartment on Watt Street. He sat staring out the kitchen window until the sun went down, then walked out to the car. He stuck his camera in the dash and the pistol under the seat. There was half a tank of gas in the station wagon and five dollars in his wallet that he'd taken from their travel money jar. He promised himself he wasn't going to do anything, just drive around town a little and pretend. Sometimes, though, he wished he hadn't ever made up those goddamn rules. Hell, around here, he could probably kill a hick every night if he wanted to. "But that's why you got the rules in the first goddamn place, Carl," he told himself as he started down the street. "So you don't fuck everything up."

As he passed by the White Cow Diner on High Street, he saw his brother-in-law standing beside his cruiser at the edge of the parking lot talking to someone sitting behind the wheel of a shiny black Lincoln. They appeared to be arguing, the way Bodecker was slinging his arms around. Carl slowed down and watched them in his rearview as long as he could. He thought about something that Sandy had said one night a couple of weeks ago, that her brother was going to end up in prison if he didn't stop hanging around guys like Tater Brown and Bobo McDaniels. "Who the hell are they?" he had asked. He was sitting at the kitchen table unwrapping one of the cheeseburgers she had brought him from work. Someone had taken a bite out of one corner of it. He scraped the diced onion off with his penknife.

"They run everything from Circleville clear down to Portsmouth," she told him. "Everything that's illegal anyway."

"Right," Carl said. "And how do you happen to know this?" She was always coming home with another bullshit story some drunk had fed her. Last week she had talked to someone who was in on the Kennedy assassination. Sometimes it irritated the shit out of Carl that she could be so gullible, but then again, he knew that was probably one of the main reasons she had stuck with him all this time.

"Well, because this guy stopped in the bar today right after Juanita left and handed me an envelope to give to Lee." She lit a cigarette and blew some smoke toward the stained ceiling.

"It was plumb full of money, and it wasn't all singles, either. There must have been four or five hundred dollars in there, maybe more."

"Jesus Christ, did you take any of it?"

"You gotta be kidding me, right? These ain't the kind of people you steal from." She picked up one of the french fries from the greasy cardboard container sitting in front of Carl, dabbed it into a glob of ketchup. All evening, she had thought about hopping in the car and taking off with the envelope.

"But he's your brother, goddamn it. He ain't gonna do nothing to you."

"Shit, Carl, the way Lee is now, I doubt if he would think twice about getting rid of us. At least not you anyway."

"Well, what did you do with it then? You still got it on you?"

"Hell no. When he came in I just gave it to him and played dumb." She looked at the french fry in her hand, dropped it in the ashtray. "He still didn't seem none too happy, though," she said.

Still thinking about his brother-in-law, Carl turned onto Vine Street. Every time he ran into Lee, which, thank God, wasn't that often, the sonofabitch asked him, "So where you working, Carl?" He'd give anything to see his ass caught in a jam he couldn't get out of by flashing that big fucking badge around. Up ahead, he saw two boys, maybe fifteen or sixteen years old, moving slowly along the sidewalk. He pulled over and shut off the engine, rolled down the window and took several gulps of the cold air. He watched them split up at the end of the block, one going east, the other west. He rolled down the passenger's-side window and started the car, drove to the stop sign and made a right.

"Hey," Carl said, when he pulled up beside the skinny boy

wearing a dark blue jacket with Meade High School stitched on the back of it in white. "You need a ride?"

The boy stopped and looked at the driver behind the wheel of the dumpy station wagon. The man's sweaty face was shiny in the glare from the streetlight. A brown stubble covered his fat jowls and neck. His eyes were beady and cruel, like a rodent's. "What'd you say?" the boy asked.

"I'm just riding around," Carl said. "Maybe we could go get some beer." He swallowed and caught himself before he started begging.

The boy smirked. "You got the wrong guy, mister," he said. "I ain't built that way." Then he started walking again, faster this time.

"Fuck you then," Carl said under his breath. He sat in the car and watched the boy disappear into a house a few doors down. Though a tad disappointed, he was mostly relieved. He knew he wouldn't have been able to stop himself if he got the punk in the car. He could almost picture it, the little bastard lying in the snow turned inside out. Someday, he thought, he was going to have to do a winter scene.

He drove back to the White Cow Diner, saw that Bodecker was gone now. He parked the car and went inside, sat at the counter and ordered a cup of coffee. His hands were still shaking. "Damn, it's cold out," he said to the waitress, a tall, skinny girl with a red nose.

"That's Ohio for you," she said.

"I'm not used to it," Carl said.

"Oh, so you ain't from around here?"

"No," Carl said, taking a sip of the coffee and pulling out one of his dog dicks. "I'm passing through from California." Then he frowned and looked down at the cigar. He wasn't sure why he said that, unless maybe he wanted to impress the girl. The mere mention of the state usually made him sick. He and Sandy had moved out there just a few weeks after they got married. Carl had thought he would find success there, taking photographs of movie stars and beautiful people, getting Sandy some work as a model, but instead they ended up broke and hungry, and he finally sold her to two men he met outside a fly-by-night talent agency who wanted to make a dirty movie. She had refused at first, but that night, after he plied her with vodka and promises, they drove their old beater up into the foggy Hollywood Hills, came to a small, dark cottage with newspapers taped over the windows. "This might be our big break," Carl said as he led her to the door. "Make some connections."

Besides the two men he'd made the deal with, there were seven or eight others standing along the lemon yellow walls of the living room, bare except for a movie camera on a tripod and a double bed covered with wrinkled sheets. A man handed Carl a drink and another asked Sandy to take her clothes off in a gentle voice. A couple of them took photographs as she stripped. Nobody said a word. Then somebody clapped his hands and the bathroom door swung open. A midget with a shaved head that was way too big for his body led a tall, dazed-looking man out into the room. The midget wore nice slacks rolled up several inches above his pointy Italian shoes and a Hawaiian shirt, but the big man was buck naked, a long, blue-veined penis as big around as a coffee cup dangling between his tanned, muscular legs. When she saw the grinning midget unhook the leash from the dog collar around the man's neck, Sandy rolled off the bed and started grabbing frantically for her clothes. Carl stood up and said, "Sorry, boys, the lady's changed her mind."

"Get that cocksucker out of here," the one behind the movie camera growled. Before Carl knew what was happening, three men had dragged him out the door and put him in his car. "Now you wait here or she's going to get hurt real bad," one of them told him. He chewed on his cigar and watched shadows move back and forth behind the covered windows, tried to convince himself that everything was going to be all right. After all, it was the movie business, couldn't be anything too serious go wrong. Two hours later, the front door opened and the same three men carried Sandy out to the car, tossed her in the backseat. One of them came around to the driver's side and handed Carl twenty dollars. "This ain't right," Carl said. "The agreement was for two hundred."

"Two hundred? Shit, she wasn't worth ten. Once that big sonofabitch got it in her ass, she passed out and laid there like a dead fish."

Carl turned and looked at Sandy lying on the seat. She was starting to come around a little. They had put her blouse on backward. "Bullshit," he said. "I want to talk to them guys I made the deal with."

"You mean Jerry and Ted? Hell, they left an hour ago," the man said.

"I'll call the law, that's what I'll do," Carl said.

"No, you won't," the man said, shaking his head. Then he reached through the window and grabbed Carl by the throat and squeezed. "In fact, if you don't quit your bitching and get the hell out of here, I'm going to take you back inside and turn ol' Frankie loose on your chubby ass. Let him and Tojo make another hundred." As the man walked back toward the house, Carl heard him say over his shoulder, "And don't try bringing her back. She ain't got what it takes for this business."

The next morning, Carl went out and bought an ancient-looking Smith & Wesson .38 at a pawnshop with the twenty dollars the porno man had given him. "How do I know this thing even works?" he asked the pawnbroker.

"Follow me," the man said. He took Carl into a back room and fired two bullets into a barrel filled with sawdust and old magazines. "They quit making this model in 1940 or thereabouts, but it's still a damn good gun."

He went back to the Blue Star Motel, where Sandy was soaking in a tub of hot water and Epsom salts. Showing her the gun, he swore that he was going to plug the two bastards who had set them up; but then he went down the street and sat on a bench in a park the rest of the day thinking about killing himself instead. Something broke in him that day. For the first time, he could see that his whole life added up to absolutely nothing. The only thing he knew how to do was work a camera, but who needed another fat guy with thin hair taking boring pictures of whiny, red-faced babies and sluts in their prom dresses and grim-faced married couples celebrating twenty-five years of misery? When he returned to their room that night, she was already asleep.

They headed back to Ohio the next afternoon. He drove and she sat on the pillows they had stolen from the motel room. He found that he had a hard time looking her in the eye, and they barely said two words to each other all the way across the desert and into Colorado. As they started up into the Rockies, the bleeding finally stopped and she told him that she would rather drive than sit there thinking about being raped by that midget's doped-up slave while all those men cracked jokes about her. When she got behind the wheel, she lit a cigarette and turned the radio on. They were down to their last four dollars. A couple of hours later, they picked up a man smelling of gin thumbing his way back to his mother's house in Omaha. He told them that he had lost everything, including his car, in a whorehouse—just a house trailer, really, with three broads working shifts, an aunt and her two nieces—out in the sand north of Reno. "Pussy," the man said. "It's always been a problem for me."

"So it's like some kind of sickness gets hold of you?" Carl said.

"Buddy, you sound like that head doctor I had to talk to one time." They rode along in silence for a few minutes, then the man leaned forward and laid his arms casually on the top of the front seat. He offered them a drink from a flask, but neither of them were in the mood for a party. Carl opened up the dash to take the camera out. He was thinking that he might as well take some nature shots. Good chance he would never see these mountains again. "This your wife?" the man asked, after he scooted back again in his seat.

"Yeah," Carl said.

"I'll tell you what, friend. I don't know what your situation is, but I'll give you twenty bucks for a quickie with her. To tell you the truth, I don't think I can last to Omaha."

"That's it," Sandy said. She hit the brakes and flipped the turn signal on. "I've had my fill of motherfuckers like you."

Carl glanced down at the pistol in the glove box half hid under a map. "Wait a minute," he said to Sandy in a low voice. He turned and looked at the man, nice clothes, black hair, olive complexion, high cheekbones. A hint of cologne mixed with the smell of the gin. "I thought you lost all your money."

"Well, I did, all I had anyway, but I called Mom when I got to Vegas. She wouldn't buy me another set of wheels this time, but she did send me a few dollars to get home on. She's good about stuff like that."

"How about fifty?" Carl said. "You got that much?"

"Carl!" Sandy screeched. She was on the verge of telling him that he could get his fucking ass out, too, when she saw him slip the gun out of the dash. She turned her eyes back to the road and brought the car back up to cruising speed.

"Boy, I don't know," the man said, scratching his chin.

"Sure, I got it, but fifty bucks oughta buy some fireworks, you know what I mean? You care to throw in some extras?"

"Sure, anything you want," Carl said, his mouth turning dry as his heart started beating faster. "We'll just have to find somewhere private to pull over." He sucked in his gut and slid the gun down in his pants.

A week later, when he finally got up the nerve to develop the photographs he'd taken that day, Carl knew with the first glimpse, with a certainty that he had never felt before, that the beginning of his life's work was staring back at him in that shallow pan of fixer. Though it hurt him to see Sandy once again with her arms wrapped around the whore hound's neck in the throes of her first real orgasm, he knew he would never be able to stop. And the humiliation he had felt in California? He vowed that would never happen again. The next summer they went out on their first hunt.

The waitress waited until Carl lit the cigar, then asked, "So what do you do out there?"

"I'm a photographer. Movie stars mostly."

"Really? You ever took any pictures of Tab Hunter?"

"No, can't say that I have," Carl said, "but I bet he'd be a nice one to work with."

27

WITHIN A FEW DAYS, Carl was a regular at the White Cow. It felt good to be out among people again after spending so much of the winter holed up in the apartment. When the waitress asked him when he was heading back to California, he told her that he had decided to stay put for a while, take a break from all the Hollywood crap. One evening he was sitting at the counter when a couple of men who looked to be in their sixties pulled up in a long black El Dorado. They parked just a few feet from the front door and strutted inside. One was dressed in a Western outfit trimmed in sparkling sequins. His potbelly pushed against a belt buckle designed to look like a Winchester rifle, and he walked bowlegged, as if, Carl thought, he had either just gotten off a mighty wide horse or was hiding a cucumber up his ass. The other wore a dark blue suit, decorated across the front with various badges and patriotic ribbons, and a square VFW cap at a jaunty angle. Both of their faces were flushed red with strong drink and arrogance. Carl recognized the cowboy from the newspaper, a Republican loudmouth on the city council, always complaining at the monthly meetings about the degenerate, wide-open sex scene in the Meade city park. Though Carl had driven through there a hundred times at night, the hottest thing he'd ever encountered was a pair of gawky teenagers attempting a kiss in front of the World War II memorial.

The two men sat down in a booth and ordered coffee. After the waitress served them, they began talking about a man with long hair they had seen walking down the sidewalk on their way over from the American Legion. "Never thought I'd see anything like that around here," the suit said.

"You just wait," the cowboy said. "If something ain't done, they'll be thick as fleas on a monkey's ass within a year or two." He took a sip of his coffee. "I got a niece lives in New York City, and that boy of hers looks just like a girl, hair clear down over his ears. I keep telling her, you send him to me, I'll straighten his ass out, but she won't do it. Says I'd be too rough on him."

They lowered their voices a bit, but Carl could still hear them talking about the way they used to hang niggers, how someone needed to start lynching again, even if it was goddamn hard work, but with the longhairs this time. "Stretch a few of their dirty necks," the cowboy said. "That will wake 'em up, by God. At least keep 'em out of these parts."

Carl could smell their aftershave clear across the diner. He stared at the sugar bowl in front of him on the counter and tried to imagine their lives, the irrevocable steps they had taken to get to where they were on this cold, dark night in Meade, Ohio. It was electric, the sensation that went through him just then, the awareness he had of his own short time on this earth and what he had done with it, and these two old fucks and their connection to it all. It was the same sort of feeling he got with the models. They had chosen one ride or one direction over another, and they had ended up in his and Sandy's car. Could he explain it? No, he couldn't explain it, but he sure as hell could feel it. *The mystery*, that's all Carl could ever say. Tomorrow, he knew, it wouldn't mean anything. The feeling would be gone until the next time. Then he heard water running in the sink back in the kitchen, and the clear image of a soggy grave he'd once dug on a starry night rose to the surface of his memory—he'd dug in a wet spot, and a half-moon, high in the sky and as white as new snow, had bobbed and settled on top of the water seeping into the bottom of the hole and he had never seen anything so beautiful—and he tried to hold on to the image because he hadn't thought about it for a while, but the old men's voices broke in again and disturbed his peace.

His head began to ache a little and he asked the young waitress for some of the aspirins he knew she kept in her purse. She liked to smoke them, she had confessed to him one night, crush them and put the powder in a cigarette. Small-town dope, Carl had thought, and he had to restrain himself from laughing at her, this poor stupid girl. She handed him two tablets with a wink, Jesus, like she was passing him a shot of morphine or something. He smiled at her and thought again about taking her out for a trial run, watch a hitcher get his jollies with her while he took some pictures and assured her that this was the way all models got their start. No doubt she'd believe him. He'd told her some pretty wild stories, and she didn't act embarrassed anymore. Then he swallowed the aspirins and turned a bit on his stool so he could hear the two men better.

"The Democrats gonna be the ruination of this country," the cowboy said. "What we need to do, Bus, is start our own private army. Kill a few of them and the rest will get the idea."

"You mean the Democrats or the longhairs, J.R.?"

"Well, we'd start with the sissies first," the cowboy said. "Remember that crazy sonofabitch had that chicken stuck to him out on the highway that time? Bus, I guarantee you these longhairs is going to be ten times worse than that."

Carl took a sip of his coffee and listened while the two men fantasized about a private militia. It would be their final contribution to the country before they died. They would gladly sacrifice themselves if need be. It was their duty as citizens. Then Carl heard one of them say loudly, "What the hell you looking at?"

They were both staring at him. "Nothing," Carl said. "Just drinking my coffee."

The cowboy winked at the suit and asked, "What you think, boy? You like them longhairs?"

"I don't know," Carl said.

"Shit, J.R., he's probably got one at home waiting on him," the suit joked.

"Yeah, he don't have the grit for what we need," the cowboy said, turning back to his coffee. "Shit, probably never even served in the military. Soft as a doughnut, that boy." He shook his head. "Whole damn country's gettin' like that."

Carl didn't say anything, but he wondered what it would be like to kill a couple of dried-up fuckers like them. For a moment, he thought about following them when they left, have them screw each other just for starters. He bet he could have that cowboy shitting in the suit's little hat by the time he got serious. Those two pricks could look at Carl Henderson and regard him as a nothing all they wanted, he didn't care. They could blow off from now until doomsday about the killing they would like to do, but neither of them had the guts for it. In fifteen minutes he could have them both begging for a seat in hell. There were things he could do that would make them eat each other's fingers for just two minutes of relief. All he had to do was make the decision. He took another sip of his coffee, looked out the window at the Cadillac, the foggy street. Sure, just an old fat boy, boss. Soft as a fucking doughnut.

The cowboy lit another cigarette and coughed up some brown gunk that he spit in the ashtray. "Turn one of them goddamn things into a pet, that's what I'd like to do," he said, wiping his mouth on a paper napkin the other handed him.

"Would you want it to be a man or a woman, J.R.?"

"Hell, they look the same, don't they?"

The suit grinned. "What would you feed it?"

"You know damn well what I'd feed it, Bus," the cowboy said, and they both laughed.

Carl turned back around. He had never thought of that before. A pet. Keeping such a thing wasn't possible right now, but maybe someday. See, he thought to himself, there was always something new and exciting to look forward to, even in this life. Except for the weeks they were out on the hunt, he always had a hard time staying upbeat, but then something would happen that would remind him that it wasn't all shit. Of course, to even consider turning a model into some sort of pet, they would have to move out of town, get a place out in the sticks. You'd need a basement or, at the very least, some sort of outbuilding close to the house, a toolshed or a barn. Maybe he could eventually train it to do his bidding, though he doubted, even at the same time he was considering it, that he'd have the patience. Just trying to keep Sandy in line was hard enough.

28

BODECKER WALKED INTO THE TECUMSEH one afternoon near the end of February, right after Sandy started her shift, and ordered a Coke. Nobody else was in the bar. She poured it for him without saying a word, then turned back to the sink behind the bar where she was cleaning dirty beer mugs and shot glasses left over from last night. He noticed the dark circles around her eyes and the gray streaks in her hair. She didn't look like she weighed ninety pounds, the loose way her jeans hung on her. He blamed Carl for the way she'd gone downhill. Bodecker hated the thought of that fat sonofabitch living off her like he did. Though he and Sandy hadn't been what you'd call close in years, she was still his sister. She had just turned twenty-four her last birthday, five years younger than himself. The way she looked today she'd have a hard time passing for forty.

Lee moved to a stool down at the end of the bar so he could watch the door. Ever since that night he'd had to come in the bar and pick up that bag of money—the dumbest fucking thing that Tater Brown had pulled on him so far, and the bastard had heard about it, too—Sandy had hardly spoken to him. It bothered him, at least a little when he took the time to consider it, that she would think badly of him. He figured she was still pissed off because of all the hell he'd raised about her selling her ass out of the back of this dump. He turned to look at her. The place was dead, the only sound that of glasses clinking together in the water as she picked one up to wash it.

Fuck it, he thought. He began talking, mentioned that Carl sure was spending a lot of time talking to a young waitress at the White Cow while she was stuck here serving drinks to pay the bills.

Sandy set the glass in the plastic drainer and dried off her hands while she thought of something to say. Carl had been driving her to work an awful lot lately, but that was none of Lee's business. What would he do with some girl anyway? The only time Carl got hard anymore was when he looked at his photographs. "So what?" she finally said. "He gets lonely."

"Yeah, he lies a lot, too," Bodecker said. Just the other evening, he had seen Sandy's black station wagon sitting at the White Cow. He parked across the street and watched his brother-in-law flap his jaws with the skinny waitress. They looked like they were having a good time together, and he'd gotten curious. After Carl left, he went in and sat down at the counter, asked for a cup of coffee. "That guy that just left," he said. "You happen to know his name?"

"You mean Bill?"

"Bill, huh?" Bodecker said, trying not to smile. "He a friend of yours?"

"I don't know," she said. "We get along all right."

Bodecker pulled a notebook and a pencil out of his shirt pocket, pretended to write something down. "Quit the horse shit and tell me what you know about him."

"Am I in some kind of trouble?" she asked. She stuck a strand of hair in her mouth, started shuffling nervously back and forth.

"Not if you talk, you ain't."

After listening to the girl repeat a few of Carl's stories, Bodecker glanced at his watch and stood up. "That's enough for now," he said, putting the notebook back in his pocket. "It don't sound like he's the one we're looking for." He thought for a moment, looked at the girl. She was still nibbling on her hair. "How old are you?" he said.

"Sixteen."

"This Bill ever ask you to pose for any pictures?"

The girl's face turned red. "No," she said.

"The first time he starts talkin' that kind of stuff, you call me, okay?" If Carl hadn't been the one trying to fuck the girl, he wouldn't have even bothered. But the sonofabitch had ruined his sister, and Bodecker couldn't forget about it, no matter how often he told himself it wasn't any of his business. It just kept eating at him, like a cancer. The best he could do right now was let Sandy know about this little waitress. But someday he still wanted to make Carl pay big-time. It wouldn't be that hard, he thought, not much different from castrating a hog.

He had left the diner after questioning the girl and drove out to the state park by the prison and waited for Tater Brown to bring him some money. The dispatcher squawked something on the radio about a hit-and-run on the Huntington Pike, and Bodecker reached over and turned the volume down. A few days ago, he had done another job for Tater, used his badge to flush a man named Coonrod from a fish camp where he was hiding out along the Paint Creek bottoms. Handcuffed in the backseat, he thought the sheriff was taking him to town for questioning until the cruiser stopped along the gravel road at the top of Reub Hill. Bodecker didn't say a word, just yanked him out of the car by the metal bracelets and half dragged him into the woods a hundred yards or so. Just as Coonrod switched from yelling about his rights to pleading for mercy, Bodecker stepped behind him and shot him in the back of the head. Now Tater owed him five thousand dollars, a thousand more than the sheriff had charged him the first time. The sadist had beat up one of the better whores who worked upstairs in Tater's strip club, tried to extract her womb with a toilet plunger. It had cost the gangster another three hundred at the hospital to have everything pushed back inside her. The only one who ended up making out on the deal was Bodecker.

Sandy sighed and said, "Okay, Lee, what the fuck are you talking about?"

Bodecker tipped his glass up, started chewing on some ice. "Well, according to this girl, your hubby's name is Bill and he's a big-shot photographer from California. Told her he's good buddies with a bunch of movie stars."

Sandy turned back to the sink, dipped some more dirty glassware in the soapy water. "He was probably just messing with her. Sometimes Carl likes to bullshit people for fun, just to see how they'll react."

"Well, from what I've seen, he's getting a pretty good reaction. I gotta say, I never thought the fat bastard had it in him."

Sandy threw down her drying rag and turned around. "What the hell you doing? Spying on him?"

"Hey, I wasn't trying to tick you off," Bodecker said. "I figured you'd want to know."

"You never did like Carl," she said.

"Jesus Christ, Sandy, he had you whorin' for him."

She rolled her eyes. "Like you don't do nothing wrong."

Bodecker put his sunglasses on and forced a smile, showed Sandy his big white teeth. "But I'm the law around here, girl. You gonna find out that makes all the difference." He threw a five-dollar bill on the bar and walked out the door and got into his cruiser. He sat there for a few minutes, staring through the windshield at the run-down trailers in Paradise Acres, the mobile-home court that sat next to the bar. Then he laid his head back against the seat. It had been a week and so far nobody had reported the plunger bastard missing. He thought maybe he'd buy Florence a new car with part of the money. He wanted so much to close his eyes for a few minutes, but falling asleep out in the open wasn't a good idea these days. The shit was starting to get deep. He wondered how long it would be before he had to kill Tater or, for that matter, before some sonofabitch decided to kill him.

29

ON A SUNDAY MORNING, Carl fixed some pancakes for Sandy, her favorite food. She'd come home drunk the night before in one of her sad-ass moods. Whenever she got tangled up in all those worthless feelings again, there was nothing he could say or do to make things better. She just had to work it out herself. A couple of nights of drinking and whining about it and she'd come back around. Carl knew Sandy better than she knew herself. Tomorrow night, or maybe the next, she would fuck one of her patrons after the bar closed, some crew-cut country boy with a wife and three or four snot-nosed kids at home. He'd tell Sandy that he wished he had met her before he ever married the old sow, that she was the sweetest piece he'd ever had, and then everything would be fine and dandy until the next time she got the blues.

Beside her plate he had laid a .22 pistol. He had bought it a few days ago for ten dollars from an elderly man he'd met at the White Cow. The poor sonofabitch was afraid that he would shoot himself if he kept the gun around. His wife had passed away last fall. He had treated her badly, he admitted, even when she was lying on her deathbed; but now he was so lonely, he couldn't stand it. He told all this to Carl and the teenage waitress while icy snow pinged against the plate-glass windows of the diner and the wind shook the metal sign out by the street. The old man wore a long overcoat that smelled of wood smoke and Vicks VapoRub and a blue watch cap speckled with lint pulled down tight on his head. While he was confessing, it occurred to Carl that it might be good for Sandy to have her own weapon when they went out hunting, just as a backup in case something ever went haywire. He wondered why he hadn't thought of it before. Though he was always careful, even the best fucked up sometimes. He had felt good about buying the gun, thought maybe it meant that he was getting wiser.

You'd have to shoot someone in the eye or stick it directly in their ear to ever kill anyone with a .22, but it would still be better than nothing. He'd done that once with a college boy, stuck a gun in his ear, some curly-haired Purdue prick who had snickered when Sandy told him that she'd once dreamed of going to beauty college, but then she ended up tending bar and everything had turned out just the way it was supposed to. Carl had found a book in the boy's coat pocket after he tied him up, *The Poems of John Keats*. He tried asking the fucker nice what his favorite rhyme was, but by then the smart-aleck bastard had shit his pants and had a hard time concentrating. He opened the book to a poem and started reading it while the boy cried for his life, Carl's voice getting louder and louder to drown out the other's pleading until he came to the last line, which he has forgotten now, some bullshit about love and fame that he had to admit made the hair stand up on his arms at the time. Then he pulled the trigger and a wad of wet, gray brains shot out the other side of the college boy's head. After he fell over, blood pooled in the sockets of his eyeballs like tiny lakes of fire, which made a hell of a picture, but that was with the .38, not some goddamn peashooter .22. Carl was sure that if he could show the smelly geezer the picture of the boy, the sad sack would think twice about ever doing himself in, at least not with a gun. The waitress had thought Carl was pretty slick the way he got the pistol away from the old man before he hurt himself. He could have fucked her that night in the backseat of the station wagon if he'd wanted to, the way she kept going on about how wonderful he was. There was a time a few years ago when he would have been all over that little bitch, but something like that just didn't hold much appeal these days.

"What's this?" Sandy said when she saw the pistol beside her plate.

"It's just in case something ever goes wrong."

She shook her head, pushed the gun across to his side of the table. "That's your job, making sure that never happens."

"I'm just saying—"

"Look, if you ain't got the balls for it anymore, just say so. Jesus Christ, at least let me know before you get us both killed," Sandy said.

"I told you before, I don't like that kind of mouth," he said. He looked at the stack of pancakes getting cold. She hadn't touched them. "And you're going to eat those goddamn griddle cakes, too, you hear me?"

"Fuck you," she said. "I'll eat what I want." She stood up and he watched her take her coffee into the living room, heard the TV come on. He picked up the .22 and aimed it at the wall that divided the kitchen from the couch that she had no doubt plopped her skinny ass down on. He stood there for a couple of minutes, wondering if he could make the shot, then put the gun in a drawer. They spent the rest of the cold morning silently watching a Tarzan movie marathon on Channel 10, and then Carl went to the Big Bear and bought a gallon of vanilla ice cream and an apple pie. She'd always liked the sweets. If he had to, he'd force it down her, he thought as he paid the clerk.

Many years ago, he'd heard one of his mother's boyfriends say that, back in the good old days, a man could sell his wife if he got hard up or sick of her, drag her ass to the town market with a horse collar clamped tight around her lousy neck.

Making Sandy choke on some ice cream wouldn't be that big a deal. Sometimes they didn't know what was best for them. His mother sure didn't. A man named Lyndon Langford, the smartest of the long line of bastards she had gotten messed up with during her time on earth, a factory worker in the GM plant in Columbus who sometimes read real books when he was trying to stay off the sauce, had given young Carl his first lessons in photography. Just remember, Lyndon had once told him, most people love to have their picture taken. They'll do damn near anything you want if you point a camera at them. He would never forget the first time he saw his mother's naked body, in one of Lyndon's pictures, tied to her bed with extension cords, a cardboard box over her head with two holes cut in it for her eyes. Still, he was a halfway decent man when he wasn't drinking. Then Carl fucked everything up by eating a slice of the deli ham that Lyndon kept in their icebox for the nights when he stayed over. His mother never forgave him for it, either.

30

WHEN OHIO STARTED TO TURN WARM and green again, Carl began seriously planning the next trip. He was considering the South this time, give the Midwest a break. He spent evenings studying his road atlas: Georgia, Tennessee, Virginia, the Carolinas. Fifteen hundred miles a week, that's what he always planned for. Though they usually traded cars around the time the peonies bloomed, he had decided that the station wagon was in good enough shape for one more outing. And Sandy wasn't bringing home the money she used to when she was whoring regular. Lee had taken care of that.

Lying in bed late one Thursday night, Sandy said, "I been thinking about that gun, Carl. Maybe you're right." Though she hadn't mentioned it, she'd also been doing a lot of thinking about the waitress at the White Cow. She'd even stopped in there once, ordered a milk shake, checked the girl out. She wished Lee had never told her. What bothered her most was the way the girl reminded Sandy of herself right before Carl walked into her life: nervous and shy and eager to please. Then, a few nights ago, pouring a drink for a man she had recently fucked for free, she couldn't help but notice that he wouldn't even give her a second glance now. As she watched the man leave a few minutes later with some toothy bimbo in a fake fur jacket, it occurred to her that maybe Carl was looking for her replacement. It hurt to think he'd turn on her like that, but then why should he be any different from any of the other bastards she had known? She hoped she was wrong, but having her own gun might not be such a bad idea.

Carl didn't say anything. He had been staring miserably at the ceiling, wishing the landlady was dead. It surprised him, Sandy mentioning the gun after all this time, but maybe she had just come to her senses. Who in the hell wouldn't want to carry a gun doing the shit they did? He rolled over, tossed his share of the bedsheet off his fat legs. It was sixty fucking degrees outside at three in the morning, and the old bitch still had the thermostat cranked up. He was certain that she did it on purpose. They'd had words again the other day about his singing at night. He got up and opened the window, stood there letting the slight breeze cool him off. "What made you change your mind?" he finally asked.

"Oh, I don't know," she said. "Like you said, you never know what might happen, right?"

He stared out into the darkness, rubbed the stubble on his face. He dreaded getting back in the bed. His side was soaked with sweat. Maybe he'd sleep on the floor tonight by the window, he thought. He leaned down near the ripped screen and took several deep breaths. Damn, he felt like he was suffocating. "She's just doing it for spite, goddamn it."

"What?"

"Leaving the fuckin' heat on," he said.

Sandy rose up on her elbows and looked at his dark form crouched by the window, like some brooding, mythical beast about to spread its wings and take off in flight. "But you'll show me how to shoot it, won't you?"

"Sure," Carl said. "That's no big deal." He heard her strike a match behind him, take a drag off a cigarette. He turned back toward the bed. "We'll take it out somewhere on your day off, let you fire a few rounds."

On Sunday they left the apartment around noon and drove

to the top of Reub Hill and down the other side. He made a left into a muddy lane and stopped when they got to the trash dump at the end. "How do you know about this place?" Sandy asked. Before Carl came along, she had spent more than a few nights getting screwed back here by boys she didn't care to remember now. Always, she had hoped that if she put out for this next one, he'd treat her like his girlfriend, maybe take her to one of the dances at the Winter Garden or the Armory, but that had never happened. As soon as they got a nut, they were done with her. Some of them even took her tip money and made her walk home. She looked out her window and saw, lying in the ditch, a used rubber stretched down over the top of a Boone's Farm bottle. Boys used to call the place Train Lane; from the looks of things, she figured they still did. Now that she thought about it, she had never been to a dance in her life.

"Just saw it when I was out driving around one day," he said. "Reminded me of that place in Iowa."

"You mean with the Scarecrow?"

"Yeah," Carl said. "Ol' California, here I come, that cocksucker." He reached across her and opened the glove compartment, grabbed the .22 and a box of shells. "Come on, let's see what you got."

He loaded the gun and set up a few rusty tin cans on top of a soggy, stained mattress. Then he walked back to the front of the car and fired off six shots at thirty feet or so. He knocked four cans over. After he showed her again how to load it, he handed the gun to her. "The fucker goes a cunt hair to the left," he said, "but that's okay. Don't try to aim so much as point, like you'd do with your finger. And just take a breath and squeeze the trigger as you let it out."

Sandy held the pistol in both hands and sighted down the barrel. She closed her eyes and pulled the trigger. "Don't shut your eyes," Carl said. She fired off the next five rounds as fast as she could. She put several holes in the mattress. "Well, you're gettin' closer," he said. He handed her the box of shells. "You load this time." He pulled out a cigar and lit it. When she hit the first can, she squealed like a little girl who'd found the prize Easter egg. She missed the next one, then plugged another. "Not bad," he said. "Here, let me see it."

He had just finished loading the gun again when they heard a pickup coming fast down the lane toward them. The truck stopped with a lurch a few yards away, and a middle-aged, gaunt-faced man got out. He wore a pair of blue dress pants and a white shirt, polished black shoes. Probably been stuck in church all morning, sitting in a pew with his fat-ass wife, Carl thought. Getting ready to eat some fried chicken now, take a nap if the old bag would shut her mouth for a few minutes. Then back to work in the morning, hard at it. You had to almost admire someone who had the wherewithal to stick with something like that. "Who gave you permission to shoot out here?" the man said. The rough tone of his voice indicated he was none too happy.

"Nobody." Carl looked around and then shrugged. "Shit, buddy, it's just a dump."

"It's my land is what it is," the man said.

"We're just getting in some target practice, that's all," Carl said. "Trying to teach my wife how to defend herself."

The man shook his head. "I don't allow no shooting on my land. Hell, boy, I got cattle over in there. Besides that, don't you know it's the Lord's Day?"

Carl heaved a sigh and cast a look at the brown fields that surrounded the dump. There wasn't a cow in sight anywhere. The sky was a low canopy of endless, immovable gray. Even this far out of town, he could detect the acrid smell of the paper mill in the air. "Okay, I get the hint." He watched as the farmer headed back to his truck, shaking his gray head. "Hey, mister," Carl suddenly called out.

The farmer stopped and spun around. "What now?"

"I was wondering," Carl said, taking a few steps toward him. "Would you mind if I took your picture?"

"Carl," Sandy said, but he waved his hand for her to keep quiet.

"What the hell you want to do that for?" the man said.

"Well, I'm a photographer," Carl said. "I just think you'd make a good picture. Heck, maybe I could sell it to a magazine or something. I always keep my eyes peeled for fine subjects like yourself."

The man looked past Carl at Sandy standing beside the station wagon. She was lighting a cigarette. He didn't approve of women who smoked. Most of them he'd known were trash, but he figured a man who took pictures for a living probably couldn't get anything decent. Hard to tell where he had picked her up. A few years ago, he'd found a woman named Mildred McDonald in his hog barn, half naked and sucking on a cancer stick. She had told him she was waiting on a man, just as casual as anything, then tried to get him to lie with her in the filth. He glanced at the gun Carl was holding in his hand, noticed that his finger was still on the trigger. "You better go ahead and get out of here," the man said, then started walking fast toward his truck.

"What you gonna do?" Carl said. "Call the law?" He glanced back at Sandy and winked.

The man opened the door and reached inside the cab. "Hell, boy, I don't need a crooked sheriff to take care of you."

Hearing that, Carl began to laugh, but then he looked around and saw the farmer standing behind the door of the truck with a rifle pointed at him through the open window.

He had a wide grin on his weathered face. "That's my brother-in-law you're talking about," Carl told him, his voice turning serious.

"Who? Lee Bodecker?" The man turned his head and spit. "I wouldn't go around braggin' about that if I was you."

Carl stood there in the middle of the lane staring at the farmer. He heard the squeak of a door behind him as Sandy got in the car and slammed it shut. For a second, he imagined just raising the pistol up and having it out with the bastard, a regular shootout. His hand began shaking a little, and he took a deep breath to try to calm himself. Then he thought about the future. There was always the next hunt. Just a few more weeks and he and Sandy would be on the road again. Ever since he'd heard the Republicans talking in the White Cow, he'd been thinking about killing one of those longhairs. According to the news he'd seen on the TV lately, the country was heading for turmoil; and he wanted to be around to see it. Nothing would please him more than to watch the whole shithouse go up in flames someday. And Sandy had been eating better lately, was starting to fill out again. She was losing her looks fast—they never had gotten her teeth fixed—but they still had a couple of good years left. No sense throwing that away just because some stupid-ass farmer had a hard-on. As soon as he made his decision, his hand stopped twitching. He turned and started toward the station wagon.

"And don't ever let me catch you back here again, understand?" Carl heard the man yell as he got in the front seat and handed Sandy her pistol. He looked around one more time as he cranked the engine, but he still didn't see any fucking cows.

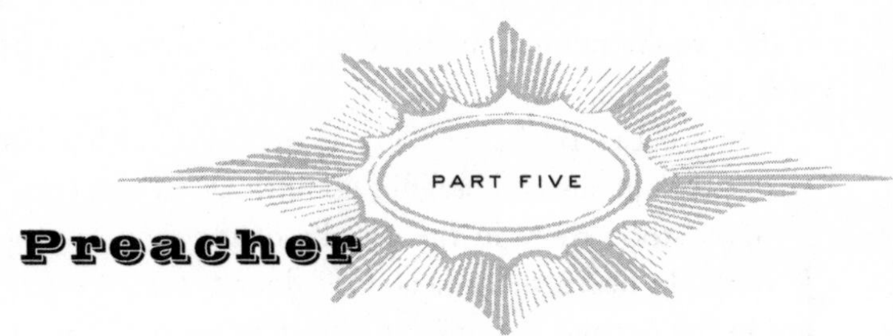

PART FIVE

Preacher

31

OCCASIONALLY, IF THE LAW GOT TOO ROUGH or the hunger bad enough, they would head inland, away from the big water that Theodore loved, so that Roy could find some work. While Roy picked fruit for a few days or weeks, Theodore sat in a lonely grove of trees or under some shady bushes waiting for his return every evening. His body was nothing but a shell now. His skin was gray as slate and his eyes weak. He passed out for no reason, complained about sharp pains that numbed his arms, and a heaviness on his chest that sometimes made him puke up his lunch meat breakfast and the half fifth of warm wine that Roy left him every morning to keep him company. Still, every night, he'd try to come alive for a spell, attempt to play some music, even though his fingers didn't work too well anymore. Roy would walk around their campfire with a jug trying to get some words started, something from the heart, while Theodore listened and picked at the guitar. They'd practice their big comeback for a while, and then Roy would collapse on top of his blanket, worn out from the day's work in the orchard. He'd be snoring within a minute or two. If he was lucky, he'd dream about Lenora. His little girl. His angel. He'd been thinking about her more and more lately, but sleeping was as close as he could get to her.

As soon as the fire died down, the mosquitoes would dive in again, drive Theodore crazy. They didn't bother Roy at all, and the cripple wished he had blood like that. He woke one night with them buzzing in his ears, still sitting in his wheelchair, the guitar lying on the ground in front of him. Roy was curled up like a dog on the other side of the ashes. They had been camping in the same spot for two weeks. Little piles of Theodore's stool and vomit were scattered over the dead grass. "Lord, we may have to think about moving," Roy had said that evening when he got back from the store down the road. He fanned his hand in front of his face. "Gettin' mighty ripe around here." That had been a few hours ago, in the heat of the day. But now a cool breeze, smelling faintly of the salt water forty miles away, brushed against the leaves of the trees above Theodore's head. He leaned over and picked up the wine jug at his feet. He took a drink and capped the bottle and looked at the stars set against the black sky like the tiny chips of a shattered mirror. They reminded him of the glitter that Flapjack used to brush on his eyelids. Up around Chattahoochee one evening, he and Roy had sneaked back into the carnival just for a few minutes, a year or so after the incident with the little boy. No, the hot dog vendor told them, Flapjack wasn't with them anymore. We were set up right outside this redneck town in Arkansas, and one night he just disappeared. Hell, we were halfway across the state the next day before anyone noticed him missing. The boss said he'd show up eventually, but he never did. You boys know how ol' Bradford is, all business. He said Flapjack was starting to lose his funny anyway.

Theodore was so tired, so sick of it all. "We had some good times though, didn't we, Roy?" he said out loud, but the man on the ground didn't move. He took another drink and set the bottle on his lap. "Good times," he repeated in a low voice. The stars blurred and faded from his sight. He dreamed of Flapjack in his clown suit and bare churches lit with smoky lanterns and loud honky-tonks with sawdust floors, and then a gentle ocean was lapping at his feet. He could feel it, the cool water. He smiled and pushed himself forward and began floating out to sea, farther than he had ever been before. He wasn't afraid; God was calling him home, and soon his legs would work again. But in the morning, he awoke on the hard ground, disappointed that he was still alive. He reached down and felt his pants. He'd pissed himself again. Roy had already taken off for the orchard. He lay with the side of his face pressed against the dirt. He stared at a mound of his fly-covered shit a few feet away and tried to slip back into sleep, back to the water.

32

EMMA AND ARVIN WERE STANDING in front of the meat case in the grocery store in Lewisburg. It was the end of the month, and the old woman didn't have much money, but the new preacher was arriving on Saturday. The congregation was having a potluck supper for him and his wife at the church. "You think chicken livers would be all right?" she asked after some more calculations in her head. The organs were cheapest.

"Why wouldn't they be?" Arvin said. He would have agreed with anything by then; even pig snouts would have been fine with him. Emma had been staring at the trays of bloody meat for twenty minutes.

"I don't know," she said. "Everyone says they like the way I do 'em, but—"

"All right," Arvin said, "get them all a big steak then."

"Pshaw," she said. "You know I can't afford nothing like that."

"Then chicken livers it is," he said, motioning for the butcher in the white apron. "Grandma, quit worrying about it. He's just a preacher. I'd say he's et a lot worse than that."

That Saturday evening, Emma covered her pan of chicken livers with a clean cloth and Arvin set them carefully on the back floorboard of his car. His grandmother and Lenora were more than a little nervous; they'd been practicing their introductions all day. "Pleased to meet you," they had repeated anytime they passed each other in the small house. He and Earskell had sat on the front porch and chuckled, but after a while, it started getting tiresome. "Jesus Christ, boy, I can't stand it no more," the old man finally said. He got up from his rocker and went around the back of the house and into the woods. It took Arvin several days to get those four words out of his head, that "pleased to meet you" shit.

When they arrived at six o'clock, the gravel lot around the church was already full of cars. Arvin carried in the pan of livers and placed them on the table near the rest of the meats. The new preacher, tall and portly, was standing in the middle of the room shaking hands and saying, "Pleased to meet you," over and over. His name was Preston Teagardin. His longish blond hair was slicked back over his head with perfumed oil, and a big oval stone glittered on one hairy hand and a thin gold wedding band on the other. He wore shiny powder-blue pants that were too tight and ankle-high boots and a ruffled white shirt that, though it was only the first of April and still cool out, was already soaked through with sweat. Arvin figured him for thirty or so, but his wife appeared to be quite a bit younger, still in her teens perhaps. She was a slim reed of a girl with long auburn hair parted in the middle and a pale, freckled complexion. She stood next to her husband, chomping gum and pulling at the lavender and white polka-dot skirt that kept riding up her trim, round ass. The preacher kept introducing her as "my sweet, righteous bride from Hohenwald, Tennessee."

Preacher Teagardin wiped the sweat off his smooth, broad forehead with an embroidered handkerchief and mentioned a church he had worshipped at for a while down in Nashville that had real air-conditioning. It was clearly evident that he was disappointed with his uncle's setup. Lord, there wasn't even a single fan. By the middle of summer, this old shack would be a torture chamber. His spirits started to flag, and he was beginning to look as sleepy and bored as his wife, but then Arvin noticed him perk up considerably when Mrs. Alma Reaster came through the door with her teenage daughters, Beth Ann and Pamela Sue, ages fourteen and sixteen. It was as if a pair of angels had fluttered into the room and alighted on the preacher's shoulders. Try as he might, he couldn't keep his eyes off their tanned, tight bodies in matching cream-colored dresses. Suddenly inspired, Teagardin began talking to all those around him about forming a youth group, something he'd seen used to great effect at several churches in Memphis. He was going to do his best, he vowed, to get the young people involved. "They are the lifeblood of any church," he said. Then his wife stepped up and whispered something in his ear while staring at the Reaster girls that must have agitated him greatly, some of the congregation thought, with the way he puckered his red lips and pinched the inside of her arm. It was hard for Arvin to believe that this pussy-sniffing fat boy was any relation to Albert Sykes.

Arvin slipped outside to smoke just before Emma and Lenora ventured forward to introduce themselves to the new man. He wondered how they would react when the preacher greeted them with "Pleased to meet you." He stood under a pear tree with a couple of farmers dressed in dungarees and shirts buttoned tight around their necks, watching a few more people hurry inside while listening to them talk about the going price of veal calves. Finally, someone came to the door and yelled, "The preacher's ready to eat."

The people insisted that Teagardin and his wife go first, so the chubby boy grabbed two plates and proceeded around the tables, sniffing at the food delicately and uncovering dishes and sticking his finger into this and that for just a taste, putting on a show for the two Reaster girls, who giggled and whispered to each other. Then all of the sudden, he stopped and passed his still-empty plates to his wife. The pinched mark on her arm was already beginning to turn blue. He looked toward the ceiling with his hand held up high, then pointed at Emma's pan of chicken livers. "Friends," he began in a loud voice, "there's no doubt we're all humble people here in this church this evening and you all have been awful nice to me and my sweet, young bride, and I thank ye from the bottom of my heart for the warm welcome. Now, they ain't a one of us got all the money and fine cars and trinkets and pretty clothes that we would like to have, but friends, the poor old soul that brung in them chicken livers in that beat-up pan, well, let's just say I'm inspired to preach on it for a minute before we set down to eat. Recall, if you can, what Jesus said to the poor in Nazareth those many centuries ago. Sure, some of us are better off than others, and I see plenty of white meat and red meat laid out on this table, and I suspect that the people who carried them platters in eat mighty good most times. But poor people got to bring what they can afford, and sometimes they can't afford much at all; and so them organs is a sign to me, telling me that I should, as the new preacher of this church, sacrifice myself so that you all can have a share of the good meat tonight. And that's what I'm going to do, my friends, I'm going to eat those organs, so you all can have a share of the best. Don't worry, it's just the way I am. I model myself on the good Lord Jesus whenever he gives me the chance, and tonight he has blessed me with another opportunity to follow in his footsteps. Amen." Then Preacher Teagardin said something to his red-haired wife in a low voice, and she headed straight for the desserts, wobbling a little in her cardboard high heels, and filled the plates with custard pie and carrot cake and Mrs. Thompson's sugar cookies, while he carried the pan of livers to his place at the head of one of the long plywood tables set up in the front for eating.

"Amen," the congregation repeated. Some looked confused,

while others, those who had brought some of the good meat, grinned happily. A few glanced at Emma, who stood near the back of the line with Lenora. When she felt their eyes on her, she started to swoon and the girl grabbed her by the elbow. Arvin rushed forward from where he was standing in the open doorway and helped her outside. He sat her down in a grassy spot under a tree, and Lenora brought her a glass of water. The old woman took a sip and started to cry. Arvin patted her on the shoulder. "Now, now," he said, "don't you worry about that pus-gutted blowhard. He probably don't have two nickels to rub together. You want me to talk to him?"

She dabbed at her eyes with the hem of her good dress. "I never been so embarrassed in my whole life," she said. "I could have crawled under the table."

"You want me to take you home?"

She sniffled some more, then sighed. "I don't know what to do." She looked toward the door of the church. "He sure ain't the preacher I was hoping for."

"Hell, Grandma, that fool ain't no preacher," Arvin said. "He's bad as them they got on the radio begging for money."

"Arvin, you shouldn't talk like that," Lenora said. "Preacher Teagardin wouldn't be here if the Lord hadn't sent him."

"Yeah, right." He started to help his grandmother up. "You see the way he was gobbling them livers down," he joked, trying to get her to smile. "Heck, that boy probably ain't had nothing that good to eat in a coon's age. That's why he wanted them all for his own self."

33

PRESTON TEAGARDIN WAS LYING ON THE COUCH reading his old college psychology book in the house the congregation had rented for his wife and him. It was a little square box with four dirty windows and an outhouse surrounded by weeping willows at the end of a dirt path. The leaky gas stove was full of mummified mice, and the cast-off furniture they had provided smelled like dog or cat or some other dirty creature. My God, with the way the people around here lived he wouldn't have been surprised if it wasn't hog. Though he'd been in Coal Creek only two weeks, he already despised the place. He kept trying to look upon his assignment in this outpost in the sticks as some sort of spiritual test coming directly from the Lord, but it was more his mother's doing than anything else. Oh, yes, she had fucked him royally, shoved it right up his ass, the old shrew. Not a penny more allowance until he showed his mettle, she had said after finally finding out—the same week she was getting ready to attend the graduation ceremony—that he had dropped out of Heavenly Reach Bible College at the end of his first semester. And then, just a day or so later, her sister had called and told her that Albert was sick. What perfect timing. She'd volunteered her son without even asking him.

The psychology course he'd taken with Dr. Phillips was the only good thing that came out of his college experience. What the hell did a degree from a place like Heavenly Reach mean in a world of Ohio Universities and Harvard Colleges anyway? Might as well have purchased a diploma through one of those mail-order places advertised in the backs of comic books. He'd wanted to go to a regular university and study law, but no, not with her money. She wanted him to be a humble preacher, like her brother-in-law, Albert. She was afraid she'd spoiled him, she said. She said all kinds of shit, insane shit, but what she really wanted, Preston understood, was to keep him dependent on her, tied to her apron strings, so he'd always have to kiss her ass. He had always been good at figuring people out, their petty wants and desires, especially teenage girls.

Cynthia was one of his first major successes. She was only fifteen years old when he helped one of his teachers at Heavenly Reach dunk her in Flat Fish Creek during a baptism service. That same evening, he fucked her dainty, born-again ass under some rosebushes on the college grounds, and within a year he had married her so that he could work on her without her parents sticking their noses in. In the last three years, he'd taught her all the things he imagined a man might be able to do with a woman. He couldn't begin to add up the hours it had taken him, but she was trained as well as any dog now. All he had to do was snap his fingers and her mouth would start watering for what he liked to refer to as his "staff."

He looked over at her in her underwear, curled up in the greasy easy chair that had come with the dump, her silky-haired gash pressed tight against the thin yellow material. She was squinting at an article about the Dave Clark Five in a *Hit Parader* magazine, trying to sound out the words. Someday, he thought, if he kept her, he would have to teach her how to read. He had discovered lately that he could last twice as long if one of his young conquests read from the Good Book while he nailed her from behind. Preston loved the way they panted holy passages, the way they began to stutter and arch their backs and struggle not to lose their place—for he could become very upset when they got the words wrong—right before his staff exploded. But Cynthia? Shit, a brain-damaged second-grader from the darkest holler in Appalachia could read better. Whenever his mother mentioned that her son, Preston Teagardin, with four years of high school Latin under his belt, had ended up married to an illiterate from Hohenwald, she nearly had another breakdown.

So it was debatable, keeping Cynthia. Sometimes he would glance over at her and, for a second or two, not even be able to recall her name. Gaped open and numb from his many experiments, what had once been fresh and tight was a faded memory now, and so, too, was the excitement she used to arouse in him. His biggest problem with Cynthia, though, was that she no longer believed in Jesus. Preston could abide just about anything but not that. He needed for a woman to believe that she was doing wrong when she lay with him, that she was in imminent danger of going to hell. How could he get turned on by someone who didn't understand the desperate battle raging between good and evil, purity and lust? Every time he fucked some young girl, Preston felt guilty, felt as if he was drowning in it, at least for a long minute or two. To him, such emotion proved that he still had a chance of going to heaven, regardless of how corrupt and cruel he might be, that is, if he repented his wretched, whoring ways before he took his last breath. It all came down to a matter of timing, which, of course, made things all that much more exciting. Cynthia, though, didn't seem to care one way or another. Nowadays, fucking her was like sticking his staff in a greasy, soulless doughnut.

But you take that Laferty girl, Preston thought, turning another page in the psychology book and rubbing his half-hard cock through his pajamas, Lord, that girl was a believer. He'd been watching her closely in church the past two Sundays. True, she wasn't much to look at, but he'd had worse down in Nashville when he volunteered that month at the poor house. He reached over and took a saltine from a pack on the coffee table, crammed it in his mouth. He let it lie on his tongue like a host and melt, turn into a soggy, tasteless glob. Yes, Miss Lenora Laferty would do for now, at least until he could get his hands on one of the Reaster girls. He'd put a smile on that sad, crimped face of hers once he got that faded dress off. According to the church gossips, at one time her father had been a preacher around this county, but then—at least the way they told it—he'd murdered the girl's mother and disappeared. Left poor Lenora just a babe with the old lady who'd gotten so tore up about those chicken livers. This girl, he predicted, was going to be so easy.

He swallowed the cracker, and a little spark of happiness suddenly swept through his body, ran from the top of his blond head down his legs and into his toes. Thank God, thank God, his mother had decided all those years ago that he was going to be a preacher. All the fresh young meat a man could stand if he played his cards right. The old bag had curled his hair every morning and taught him good hygiene and made him practice his facial expressions in the mirror. She'd studied the Bible with him every night and drove him around to different churches and kept him in nice clothes. Preston had never played baseball, but he could cry on cue; he'd never been in a fistfight, but he could recite the book of Revelation in his sleep. So, yes, goddamn it, he'd do what she had asked, help out her sick, sad-sack brother-in-law for a while, live in this shit hole of a house, and even pretend to like it. He'd show her his "mettle," by God. And then, when Albert got back on his feet, he'd ask her for the money. He'd probably have to deceive her, feed her some bullshit story, but he'd feel at least a pang of guilt, so that was all right. Anything to get to the West Coast. It was his new obsession. He'd been hearing stuff on the news lately. There was something going on out there that he needed to witness. Free love and runaway girls living in the streets with flowers stuck in their matted hair. Easy pickings for a man blessed with his abilities.

Preston marked his place with his uncle's prized tobacco sack and closed the book. Five Brothers? Jesus, what sort of person would put their faith in something like that? He'd nearly laughed in Albert's face when the old man told him it had the power to heal. He looked over at Cynthia, half asleep now, a string of drool hanging from her chin. He snapped his fingers and her eyes popped open. She frowned and tried to shut her eyes again, but it was impossible. She did her best to resist, but then got up from her chair and knelt at the side of the couch. Preston pulled down his pajama bottoms, spread his fat, hairy legs a bit. As she began to swallow him, he said a little prayer to himself: Lord, just give me six months in California, then I'll come home and fly right, settle down with a flock of good people, I swear on my mother's grave. He pushed Cynthia's head down farther, heard her begin to gag and choke. Then her throat muscles relaxed and she quit fighting it. He held her there until her face turned scarlet and then purple from lack of air. He liked it that way, he surely did. Look at her go.

34

ONE DAY ON HER WAY HOME FROM SCHOOL, Lenora stopped at the Coal Creek Church of the Holy Ghost Sanctified. The front door was opened wide and Preacher Teagardin's ratty English sports car—a gift from his mother when he'd first gone off to Heavenly Reach—was sitting in the shade, same as yesterday and the day before. It was a warm afternoon in the middle of May. She had ducked Arvin, watched from inside the schoolhouse until he gave up waiting and left without her. She stepped inside the church and let her eyes adjust to the gloom. The new preacher was sitting on one of the benches halfway down the aisle. It looked as if he was praying. She waited until she heard him say, "Amen," and then she began moving slowly forward.

Teagardin felt her presence behind him. He had been waiting patiently on Lenora for three weeks now. He'd come to the church nearly every day and opened the door around the time the school let out. Most days he saw her ride past in that piece-of-shit Bel Air with that half brother or whatever he was, but once or twice he'd seen her walking home by herself. He heard her soft steps on the rough wood floor. He could smell her Juicy Fruit breath as she got closer; he had the nose of a bloodhound when it came to young women and their different odors. "Who is it?" he said, raising his head.

"It's Lenora Laferty, Preacher Teagardin."

He crossed himself and turned to her with a smile. "Well,

what a surprise," he said. Then he peered at her more closely. "Girl, you look like you been crying."

"It's nothing," she said, shaking her head. "Just some kids at school. They like to tease."

He looked past her for a moment, searching for a suitable response. "I suspect they just jealous," he said. "Envy tends to bring out the worst in people, especially the young ones."

"I doubt if that's it," she said.

"How old are you, Lenora?"

"Almost seventeen."

"I remember when I was that age," he said. "There I was, full of the Lord, and the other kids making fun of me day and night. It was awful, the horrible notions that ran through my head."

She nodded and sat down on the bench across from him. "What did you do about it?" she asked.

He ignored her question, appeared to be deep in thought. "Yes, that was a rough time," he finally said with a long sigh. "Thank God it's over." Then he smiled again. "You got anywhere you have to be for the next couple hours?"

"No, not really," she said.

Teagardin stood up, took hold of her hand. "Well, then, I think it's about time you and me take a ride."

TWENTY MINUTES LATER, they were parked on a secluded dirt lane that he'd been checking out ever since his arrival in Coal Creek. It had once led to some hay fields a mile or so off the main road, but the land was now overgrown with Johnson grass and thick brush. His tire tracks were the only ones he'd seen on it for the past two weeks. He judged it to be a safe spot to bring someone. When he shut the car off, he mouthed a short, empty prayer, then laid his warm, meaty hand on Lenora's knee and told her just what she wanted to hear. Hell, every one of them wanted to hear pretty much the same thing anyway, even the ones full of Jesus. He wished that she had resisted a little bit more, but she was easy, just like he had predicted. Even so, as many times as he'd done this, all the time he was peeling her clothes off, he could hear every bird, every insect, every animal that moved in the woods for what seemed like miles. It was always like that the first time with a new one.

When he finished, Preston reached down and grabbed her gray, dingy panties lying on the floorboard. He wiped the blood off himself and handed them to her. He swatted at a fly buzzing around his crotch, then tugged up his brown slacks and buttoned his white shirt as he watched her struggle back into her long dress. "You ain't gonna tell no one, are you?" he said. Already, he wished he'd stayed home and read his psychology book, maybe even attempted cutting the grass with the push mower Albert had sent over after Cynthia stepped on a black snake curled up in front of the outhouse. Unfortunately, he had never been one of those men adept at physical labor. Just thinking about shoving that mower around and around that rocky yard made him feel a little sickish.

"No," she said. "I'd never do that. I promise."

"That's good. Some people might not understand. And I sincerely believe that a person's relationship with their preacher should be a private thing."

"Did you mean what you said?" she asked him bashfully.

He struggled to recall which bullshit line he had used on her. "Well, sure I did." His throat was parched. Maybe he'd drive over to Lewisburg and have a cold beer to celebrate busting open another virgin. "By the time we get done," he said, "them boys at your school won't be able to take their eyes off you. It just takes some breaking in for some girls, that's all. But I can tell you one of them that just gets prettier as they get older. You should thank the Lord for that. Yep, you got some sweet years ahead of you, Miss Lenora Laferty."

35

AT THE END OF MAY, ARVIN GRADUATED from Coal Creek High School, along with nine other seniors. The following Monday, he went to work for a construction crew that was putting a new coat of blacktop on the Greenbrier County stretch of Route 60. A neighbor across the knob named Clifford Baker had gotten him on. He and Arvin's father used to raise hell together before the war, and Baker figured the boy deserved a break as much as anyone. It was a good-paying job, nearly union wages, and though he was designated a laborer, supposedly the worst job on the crew, Earskell had worked Arvin harder in the garden patch behind the house. The day he got his first check, he picked up two fifths of good whiskey from Slot Machine for Earskell, ordered Emma a wringer washer from the Sears catalog, and bought Lenora a new dress for church at Mayfair's, the priciest store in three counties.

While the girl was trying to find something that fit, Emma said, "My Lord, I hadn't noticed before, but you sure are starting to fill out." Lenora turned back to the mirror and smiled. She had always been straight up and down, no hips, no chest. Last winter, someone had taped a picture from *Life* magazine of a heap of concentration camp victims to her locker, wrote in ink, "Lenora Laferty," with an arrow pointing to the third corpse from the left. If it hadn't been for Arvin, she wouldn't have even bothered to take the picture down. But she was finally starting to look like a woman, just like Preacher Teagardin had promised. She was meeting him three, four, sometimes five afternoons a week now. She felt bad every time they did it, but she couldn't tell him no. It was the first time she had ever realized just how powerful sin could be. No wonder it was so hard for people to get into heaven. Each time they met, Preston had something new he wanted to try. Yesterday, he'd brought a tube of his wife's lipstick. "I know it sounds silly, with what we been doing," she said timidly, "but I don't think a woman should paint her face. You ain't mad, are you?"

"Well, heck no, darling, that's all right," he told her. "Shoot, I admire your beliefs. I wish that wife of mine loved Jesus like you do." Then he grinned and pushed her dress up, hooked his thumb over the top of her panties and pulled them down. "Besides, I was thinking about painting something else anyway."

ONE EVENING, AS SHE WASHED THE SUPPER DISHES, Emma looked out the window and saw Lenora coming out of the woods across the road from the house. They had waited on her a few minutes, then went ahead and ate. "That girl sure is spending a lot of time in them woods lately," the old woman said. Arvin was leaned back in his chair drinking the last of the coffee and watching Earskell try to roll a smoke. He was bent over the table, a look of intense concentration on his lined face. Arvin watched his fingers tremble, wondered if his great-uncle was beginning to slip a little.

"Knowing her," Arvin said, "she's probably out talkin' to butterflies."

Emma watched the girl scramble up the bank toward the porch. She looked like she had been running, the way her face was flushed. The old woman had noticed a big change in the girl the last few weeks. One day she was happy, the next day filled with despair. A lot of girls went a mite crazy for a while when the blood started flowing, Emma reasoned, but Lenora had gone through all that two years ago. She still saw her studying her Bible, though; and she seemed to love going to church more than she ever did, even though Preacher Teagardin couldn't hold a candle to Albert Sykes when it came to giving a good sermon. At times, Emma wondered if the man really cared at all about preaching the Gospel, the way he kept losing his train of thought, like he had other things on his mind. There she was, she realized, getting all stirred up about those chicken livers again. She would have to pray on it again tonight when she went to bed. She turned and looked at Arvin. "You don't figure she might have her a beau, do you?"

"Who? Lenora?" he said, and then rolled his eyes as if it was one of the most ridiculous things he'd ever heard. "I don't think you need to worry about that, Grandma." He glanced over and saw that Earskell had made a mess of his cigarette, was just sitting there with his mouth open, staring at the makings on the table. Reaching over for the sack of tobacco and the papers, the boy began rolling a new one.

"Looks ain't everything," Emma said harshly.

"That's not what I'm saying," he sputtered, ashamed that he had joked about the girl. There were already too many people doing that. It suddenly dawned on him that he wouldn't be at school anymore to keep them off her back. She was going to have a rough row to hoe next fall. "I just don't think there's any boys around here she'd be interested in, that's all."

The front screen door opened and closed with a squeak, and then they heard Lenora humming a song. Emma listened closely, recognized it as "Poor Pilgrim of Sorrow." Satisfied for now, she dipped her hands in the lukewarm water, began scrubbing on a skillet. Arvin turned his attention back to the cigarette. He licked the paper and gave it another twist, then handed it to Earskell. The old man smiled and fumbled in his shirt pocket for a match. He searched a long time before he found one.

36

BY THE MIDDLE OF AUGUST, Lenora knew she was in trouble. She had missed her period twice and the dress that Arvin had bought her would hardly fit anymore. Teagardin had broken it off a couple of weeks before. He told her that he was afraid if he kept meeting her, his wife was going to find out, perhaps even the congregation. "Ain't neither one of us wants that to happen, right?" he said. She walked by the church several days before she found him there, the door propped open and his little car sitting under the shade tree. He was sitting in the shadows near the front, his head bowed when she stepped inside, just like that day when she first came to him, three months ago, only this time he didn't smile when he turned around and saw who it was. "You ain't supposed to be here," Teagardin said, though he wasn't totally surprised. Some of them just can't quit it all at once.

He couldn't help but notice the way the girl's tits pressed against the top of her dress now. He had seen it time after time, the way their young bodies filled out once they started getting it regular. Glancing at his watch, he saw that he had a few extra minutes. Maybe he should give her one last good fuck, he was thinking, when Lenora blurted out, her voice cracking and hysterical, that she was carrying his baby. He jumped up with a start, then hurried to the front door and closed it. He looked down at his hands, thick but soft as a woman's. He wondered, in the time it took him to draw a deep breath, if he could strangle her with them, but he knew damn well he didn't have the guts for that sort of business. Besides, if he were to accidentally get caught, prison, especially some loathsome dungeon in West Virginia, would be much too harsh for a delicate person such as himself. There had to be another way. He had to think fast, though. He considered her situation, a poor orphan girl knocked up and half out of her mind with worry. All these thoughts ran through his head while he took his time locking the door. Then he walked to the front of the church where she sat on one of the benches, tears running down her quivering face. He decided to begin talking, which was what he did best. He told her that he had heard of cases like hers, where the person was so deluded and sick over something they had done, some sin they had committed that was so terrible, that they started imagining things. Why, he'd read about people, just common folks, some of them barely able to write their own name, who became convinced that they were the president or the pope or even some famous movie star. Those kinds, Teagardin warned in a sad voice, usually ended up in a nuthouse, getting raped by the orderlies and forced to eat their own waste.

Lenora had quit sobbing by then. She wiped her eyes with the sleeve of her dress. "I don't understand what you're talking about," she said. "I'm pregnant with your baby."

He held out his hands, heaved a sigh. "That's part of it, the book says, not understanding. But you think about it. How could I be the daddy? I've never touched you, not once. Look at you. I've got a wife sitting at home that's a hundred times as pretty and she'll do anything I ask, and I do mean anything."

She looked up with a dumbfounded expression on her face. "You're saying you don't remember all the things we did in your car?"

"I'm saying that you must be crazy to come into the Lord's house and talk such trash. You think anyone's gonna believe you over me? I'm a preacher." Jesus, he thought, standing there looking down at this red-nosed, sniveling hag, why hadn't he just held out and waited until the Reaster girl came around. Pamela had proved to be the finest piece he'd had since the early days with Cynthia.

"But you're the father," Lenora said in a soft, numb voice. "Hasn't been nobody else."

Teagardin looked at his watch again. He had to get rid of this wench fast, or his whole afternoon was going to be ruined. "My advice to you, girl," he said, his voice turning low and hateful, "is you figure some way to get rid of it, that is, if you even are knocked up like you say. It would just be some little bastard with a whore for a mother if you keep it. If nothing else, think of that poor old woman who's raised you, brings you to church here every Sunday. She'll die from the shame of it all. Now you get on out before you cause any more trouble."

Lenora didn't say another word. She looked at the wooden cross hanging on the wall behind the altar, then stood up. Teagardin unlocked the door and held it open, a scowl etched on his face, and she walked past him with her head down. She heard the door quickly close behind her. Though she felt faint, she managed to walk a hundred yards or so before she collapsed under a tree a few feet from the edge of the gravel road. She could still see the church, the one she had gone to all her life. She had felt the presence of God there many times, but not once, it occurred to her now, since the new preacher had arrived. A few minutes later, she watched Pamela Reaster come up the other end of the road and go inside, a look of happiness spread across her pretty face.

That evening, after supper, Arvin drove Emma to the church

for the Thursday night service. Lenora had pleaded sick, said her head felt like it was splitting open. She hadn't touched her food. "Well, you don't look good, that's for sure," Emma said, feeling the girl's cheek for fever. "You go ahead and stay home tonight. I'll have 'em say a prayer for you." Lenora waited in her bedroom until she heard Arvin's car start up, then made sure Earskell was still asleep in his rocker on the porch. She went out to the smokehouse and opened the door. She stood and waited until her eyes adjusted to the gloom. She found a length of rope coiled in a corner behind some minnow traps and tied a crude noose on one end. Then she moved an empty lard bucket over to the center of the small shed. She stepped up on it and wrapped the other end of the rope seven or eight times around one of the support beams. Then she hopped off the bucket and closed the door. It was dark in the shed now.

Stepping back up on the metal bucket, she put the noose around her neck and tightened it. A trickle of sweat ran down her face, and she caught herself thinking that she should do this out in the sunlight, in the warm summer air, maybe even wait another day or two. Perhaps Preston would change his mind. That's what she would do, she thought. He couldn't have meant what he said. He was upset, that's all. She started to loosen the noose and the lard bucket began to wobble. Then her foot slipped and the bucket rolled away and left her dangling in the air. She had dropped only a few inches, not nearly enough to break her neck clean. She could almost touch her toes to the floor, just another inch or so. Kicking her legs, she grabbed hold of the rope, tried her best to raise herself up to the beam, but she didn't have enough strength. She tried to yell out, but the choking sounds wouldn't carry beyond the shed door. As the rope slowly squeezed her windpipe shut, she became more frantic, clawing at her neck with her fingernails.

Her face turned purple. She was vaguely aware of urine running down her legs. The blood vessels in her eyes began to burst, and everything got darker and darker. No, she thought, no. I can have this baby, God. I can just leave this place, go away like my daddy did. I can just disappear.

37

A WEEK OR SO AFTER THE FUNERAL, Tick Thompson, the new sheriff of Greenbrier County, was waiting at Arvin's car when the boy got off work. "I need to talk to you, Arvin," the lawman said. "It's about Lenora." He had been one of the men who helped carry her body out of the smokehouse after Earskell saw the door unlatched and found her. He'd been called to a few suicides over the years, mostly men, though, blowing their brains out over some woman or a bad business deal, never a young girl hanging herself. When he'd asked, right after the ambulance pulled away that evening, Emma and the boy both said she had actually seemed happier lately. There was something about it that didn't add up. He hadn't had a decent night's sleep all week.

Arvin tossed his lunch bucket in the front seat of the Bel Air. "What about her?"

"I figured it might be best to tell you instead of your grandmother. From what I hear, she's not taking things too good."

"Tell me what?"

The sheriff took his hat off, held it in his hands. He waited until the rest of the road crew walked by and got in their vehicles, then cleared his throat. "Well, hell, I don't know how to say it, Arvin, other than just say it. Did you know Lenora was carrying a baby?"

Arvin stared at him for a long minute, a puzzled look on his face. "That's bullshit," he finally said. "Some sonofabitch is lying."

"I know how you must feel, I really do, but I just came from the coroner's office. Though ol' Dudley might be a drunk, he ain't no liar. Near as he can figure it, she was about three months along."

The boy turned away from the sheriff and reached in his back pocket for a dirty rag, wiped his eyes. "Jesus," he said, struggling to keep his upper lip from quivering.

"Do you think your grandmother knew?"

Shaking his head, Arvin took a deep breath and exhaled it slowly, then said, "Sheriff, my grandma would die if she heard that."

"Well, did Lenora have a boyfriend, someone she was seeing?" the sheriff asked.

Arvin thought about the night, just a few weeks ago, when Emma had asked that same question. "None that I know of. Hell, she was the most religious person I ever seen."

Tick put his hat back on. "Look, here's the way I see it," he said. "Ain't nobody has to know about this but you, me, and Dudley, and he won't say nothing, I guarantee it. So we'll just keep it quiet for now. How does that sound?"

Swiping at his eyes again, Arvin nodded. "I'd appreciate that," he said. "It's been bad enough everyone knowing what she did to herself. Hell, we couldn't even get that new preacher to—" His face suddenly grew dark, and he looked away toward Muddy Creek Mountain in the distance.

"What is it, son?"

"Ah, nothing," Arvin said, looking back at the sheriff. "We couldn't get him to say no words at the funeral, that's all."

"Well, some people have strong views on things like that."

"Yeah, I guess so."

"So you got no idea who she might have been messing with?"

"Lenora stayed to herself mostly," the boy said. "Besides, what could you do about it anyway?"

Tick shrugged. "Not much, I expect. Maybe I shouldn't have said nothing."

"I'm sorry, I didn't mean no disrespect," Arvin said. "And I'm glad you told me. At least now I know why she did it." He stuck the rag back in his pocket and shook Tick's hand. "And thanks for thinking about my grandma, too."

He watched the sheriff pull away, then got in his car and drove the fifteen miles back to Coal Creek. He played the radio as loud as it would go and stopped at the bootlegger's shack in Hungry Holler and bought two pints of whiskey. When he got home, he went in and checked on Emma. She hadn't been out of bed all week as far as he knew. She was starting to smell bad. He dipped a glass of water from the bucket on the kitchen counter and made her sip some. "Look, Grandma," he said to her, "I expect you to get out of bed in the morning and fix me and Earskell breakfast, okay?"

"Just let me lay here," she said. She rolled over on her side, closed her eyes.

"One more day, that's it," he told her. "I'm not kidding around." He went in the kitchen and fried some potatoes, fixed bologna sandwiches for him and Earskell. After they ate, Arvin washed up the skillet and plates and looked in on Emma again. Then he took the two pints out on the porch and handed one to the old man. He sat down in a chair and finally allowed himself to consider what the sheriff had told him. Three months along. For sure, it hadn't been some boy from around here got Lenora pregnant. Arvin knew everybody, and he knew what they thought about her. The only place she liked to go was church. He thought back to when the new preacher first arrived. That would have been April, just over four months ago. He recalled the way Teagardin got all excited when the two Reaster girls walked in the night of the potluck. Other than himself, nobody had seemed to notice except the young wife. Lenora had even put her bonnets away not long after Teagardin showed up. He had thought she was finally sick of being made fun of at school, but maybe she had another reason.

He shook two cigarettes out of his pack and lit them, handed one to Earskell. The day before the funeral, Teagardin told some of the church members that he didn't feel comfortable preaching over a suicide. Instead, he asked his poor sick uncle to say a few words in his place. Two men had carried Albert in on a wooden kitchen chair. It was the hottest day of the year, and the church was like a furnace, but the reverend had risen to the occasion. After the service, Arvin went out driving around on the back roads, which was what he always did now when things didn't make any sense. He passed by Teagardin's house, saw the preacher walking to the outhouse in a pair of bedroom slippers and a floppy, pink hat like a woman might wear. His wife was sunbathing in a bikini, stretched out on a blanket in the weedy, overgrown yard.

"Damn, it's hot," Earskell said.

"Yeah," Arvin said after a minute or two. "Maybe we ought to sleep out here tonight."

"I don't see how Emma stands it in that bedroom. It's like an oven back there."

"She's gonna get up in the morning, fix us breakfast."

"Really?"

"Yeah," Arvin said, "really."

And she did, biscuits and eggs and sawmill gravy, was up an hour before they stirred from their blankets on the porch. Arvin noticed that she had washed her face and changed her dress, tied a clean rag around her thin, gray hair. She didn't say much, but when she sat down and began to fix herself a plate, he knew that he could stop worrying about her now. The next day, when the foreman got out of his pickup and pointed at his watch that it was quitting time, Arvin hurried to his car and drove by Teagardin's again. He parked a quarter of a mile down the road and walked back, cutting through the woods. Sitting in the fork of a locust tree, he watched the preacher's house until the sun went down. He didn't know what he was looking for yet, but he had an idea of where to find it.

38

THREE DAYS LATER AT QUITTING TIME, Arvin told the boss he wouldn't be back. "Aw, come on, boy," the foreman said. "Shit, you 'bout the best worker I got." He spit a thick string of tobacco juice against the front tire of his pickup. "Stay two more weeks? We be finishing up by then."

"It ain't the job, Tom," Arvin said. "I just got something else needs taking care of right now."

He drove to Lewisburg and bought two boxes of 9mm bullets and stopped at the house and checked on Emma. She was in the kitchen scrubbing the linoleum floor on her hands and knees. He went to his bedroom and got the German Luger from the bottom drawer of his dresser. It was the first time he'd touched it since Earskell had asked him to put it away over a year ago. After telling his grandmother he'd be back soon, he went over to Stony Creek. He took his time cleaning the gun, then loaded eight shells into the magazine and lined up some cans and bottles. He reloaded four more times over the next hour. By the time he put it back in the glove box, the pistol felt like a part of his hand again. He had missed only three times.

On his way back home, he stopped at the cemetery. They had buried Lenora beside her mother. The monument man hadn't put the stone up yet. He stood looking down at the dry, brown dirt that marked her place, remembering the last time he'd come here with her to see Helen's grave. He could vaguely recall how she had tried, in her own awkward way, to flirt with him that afternoon, talking about orphans and star-crossed lovers, and he had gotten aggravated with her. If only he had paid a little more attention, he thought, if only people hadn't made fun of her so much, maybe things wouldn't have turned out like they did.

The next morning, he left the house at the usual time, acting as if he was going to work. Though he was certain in his gut that Teagardin was the one, he had to be sure. He began keeping track of the preacher's every movement. Within a week, he had watched the bastard fuck Pamela Reaster three times in an old farm lane just off Ragged Ridge Road. She walked through the fields from her parents' house to meet him there, every other day at exactly noon. Teagardin sat in his sports car and studied himself in the mirror until she arrived. After the third time he saw them meet there, Arvin spent an afternoon piling up deadwood and horseweeds to make a blind just a few yards from where the preacher parked under the shade of a tall oak tree. It was Teagardin's custom to hustle the girl away as soon as he was finished with her. He liked to dawdle a bit alone under the tree, relieving his bladder and listening to bubble gum music on the car radio. Occasionally, Arvin heard him talking to himself, but he could never make out the words. After twenty or thirty minutes, the car would start up, and Teagardin would turn around at the end of the lane and go home.

The next week, the preacher added Pamela's younger sister to his roster, but the meetings with Beth Ann took place inside the church. By then, Arvin had no doubts, and when he woke up Sunday morning to the sound of the church bells tolling across the holler, he decided the time had come. If he waited any longer, he was afraid he would lose his nerve. He knew Teagardin always met the older girl on Mondays. At least the horny sonofabitch was regular in his habits.

Arvin counted the money he had managed to put back

from the paving job. He had $315 in the coffee can under his bed. He drove over to Slot Machine's after Sunday dinner and bought a fifth of whiskey, spent the evening drinking with Earskell on the porch. "You sure are good to me, boy," the old man said. Arvin had to swallow several times to keep from crying. He thought about tomorrow. This was the last time they would ever share a bottle.

It was a beautiful evening, cooler than it had been for several months. He went inside and got Emma, and she sat with them for a while with her Bible and a glass of ice tea. She hadn't been back to the Coal Creek Church of the Holy Ghost Sanctified since the night that Lenora died. "I think fall's going to come early this year," she said, marking her place in the book with a bony finger and gazing out across the road at the leaves already beginning to turn rust-colored. "We're going to have to start thinking about getting some wood in before long, ain't we, Arvin?"

He looked over at her. She was still staring at the trees on the hillside. "Yeah," he said. "Be cold before you know it." He hated himself for deceiving her, pretending everything was going to be all right. He wanted so much to be able to tell them goodbye, but they would be better off not knowing anything if the law came hunting for him. That night, after they went to bed, he packed some clothes in the gym bag he used to take to school and put it in the trunk of his car. He leaned on the porch railing and listened to the faint rumble of a coal train over the next swath of hills heading north. Going back inside, he stuck a hundred dollars in the tin box that Emma kept her needles and thread in. He didn't sleep any that night, and in the morning he just drank some coffee for breakfast.

He had been sitting in the blind for two hours when the Reaster girl came hurrying across the field, maybe fifteen minutes early. She appeared worried, kept looking at her wristwatch. When Teagardin showed up, easing his car down the rutted road slowly, she didn't jump in like she had always done in the past. Instead, she stood a few feet away and waited for him to shut the engine off. "Well, get in, honey," Arvin heard the preacher say. "I got a full sack for you."

"I ain't staying," she said. "We got problems."

"What do you mean?"

"You were supposed to keep your hands off my sister," the girl said.

"Oh, shit, Pamela, that didn't mean anything."

"No, you don't understand," she said. "She told Mother about it."

"When?"

"About an hour ago. I didn't think I was going to be able to get away."

"That little bitch," Teagardin cursed. "I hardly touched her."

"That ain't the way she tells it," Pamela said. She looked toward the road nervously.

"What did she say exactly?"

"Believe me, Preston, she told everything. She got scared because the bleeding won't stop." The girl pointed her finger at him. "You better hope you didn't do something so she can't have kids."

"Shit," Teagardin said. He got out of the car and paced back and forth for several minutes, his hands clasped behind his back like a general in his tent planning a counterattack. He took a silk handkerchief out of his pants pocket and patted his mouth. "What do you think your old lady will do?" he finally said.

"Well, knowing her, after she takes Beth Ann to the hospital, the first thing she'll do is call the fucking sheriff. And just so you know, he's my mom's cousin."

Teagardin placed his hands on the girl's shoulders and looked into her eyes. "But you haven't said anything about us, right?"

"You think I'm crazy? I'd rather die first."

Teagardin let go of her and leaned against the car. He looked out over the field before them. He wondered why nobody was farming it anymore. He imagined an old two-story house in ruins, some rusted pieces of antique machinery sitting in the weeds, maybe a hand-dug well of cool, clean water, covered over with rotten boards. Just for a moment, he pictured himself fixing the place back up, settling down to a simple life, preaching on Sundays and working the farm with callused hands through the week, reading good books out on the porch in the evenings after a nice supper, some tender babes playing in the shaded yard. He heard the girl say she was leaving, and when he finally turned to look, she was gone. Then he considered the possibility that perhaps Pamela was lying to him, trying to scare him into laying off her sister. He wouldn't put anything past her, but if what she said was true, he had only an hour or two at best to pack and get out of Greenbrier County. He was just getting ready to start the car when he heard a voice say, "You ain't much of a preacher, are you?"

Teagardin looked up and saw the Russell boy standing right outside the door of the car pointing a pistol of some kind at him. He'd never owned a gun, and the only thing he knew about them was that they usually caused trouble. The boy looked bigger up close. Not an ounce of fat on him, he noticed, dark hair, green eyes. He wondered what Cynthia would think of him. Though he knew it was ridiculous, with all the young pussy he was getting, he felt a pang of jealousy just then. It was sad to realize that he'd never look anything like this boy. "What the hell are you doing?" the preacher said.

"Been watching you screw that Reaster girl that just left.

And if you try to start that car, I'm gonna blow your fucking hand off."

Teagardin let go of the ignition key. "You don't know what you're talking about, boy. I didn't touch her. All we did was talk."

"Maybe not today, but you been plowing her pretty steady."

"What? You been spying on me?" Maybe the boy was one of those voyeurs, he thought, recalling the term from his collection of nudist magazines.

"I know every fuckin' move you've made for the last two weeks."

Teagardin looked out the windshield toward the big oak at the end of the lane. He wondered if it could be true. In his head, he counted the number of times he'd been here with Pamela over the last couple of weeks. At least six. That was bad enough, but at the same time he felt somewhat relieved. At least the boy hadn't seen him banging his sister. Hard to tell what the crazy hillbilly might have done. "It ain't what it looks like," he said.

"What is it then?" Arvin asked. He flipped the safety off the gun.

Teagardin started to explain that the little slut wouldn't leave him alone, but then he reminded himself to be careful with his words. He considered the possibility that maybe this hoodlum had a crush on Pamela. Perhaps that's what this was all about. Jealousy. He tried to recall what Shakespeare had written about it, but the words wouldn't come to him. "Say, ain't you Mrs. Russell's grandson?" the preacher asked. He looked down at the clock on the dash. He could have been halfway home by now. Rivulets of greasy sweat began to run down his pink, clean-shaven face.

"That's right," Arvin said. "And Lenora Laferty was my sister."

Teagardin turned his head slowly, his eyes focused on the boy's belt buckle. Arvin could almost see the wheels spinning inside his head, watched him swallow several times. "That was a shame, what that poor girl did," the preacher said. "I pray for her soul every night."

"You pray for the baby's, too?"

"Now you got it all wrong there, my friend. I didn't have nothing to do with that."

"Do with what?"

The man squirmed around in the car's tight seat, glanced at the German Luger. "She came to me, said she wanted to make a confession, told me she was with child. I promised her I wouldn't tell anybody."

Arvin took a step back and said, "I'll bet you did, you fat sonofabitch." Then he fired three shots, blew out the tires on the driver's side and put the last one through the back door.

"Stop!" Teagardin yelled. "Stop, goddamn it!" He threw his hands up.

"No more lies," Arvin said, moving forward and jamming the pistol against the preacher's temple. "I know you was the one got her that way."

Teagardin jerked his head away from the gun. "Okay," he said. He took a deep breath. "I swear, I was going to take care of everything, I really was, and then . . . and then the next thing I know she'd done herself in. She was crazy."

"No," Arvin said, "she was just lonely." He pressed the barrel against the back of Teagardin's head. "But don't worry, I ain't gonna make you suffer like she did."

"Now hold on here, goddamn it. Jesus Christ, man, you wouldn't kill a preacher, would you?"

"You ain't no preacher, you worthless piece of shit," Arvin said.

Teagardin began crying, true tears running down his face

for the first time since he was a little boy in short pants. "Let me pray first," he sobbed. He started to put his hands together.

"I already did it for you," Arvin said. "Put in one of them special requests you fuckers are always talking about, asked Him to send you straight to hell."

"No," Teagardin said, right before the gun went off. A fragment of the bullet came out right above his nose and landed with a ping on the dashboard. His big body pitched forward, and his face banged against the steering wheel. His left foot kicked the brake pedal a couple of times. Arvin waited until he stopped moving, then reached inside and picked the sticky shell fragment up off the dash and threw it into the weeds. He regretted shooting those other rounds off now, but there wasn't time to dig around for them. He hurriedly scattered the blind that he'd built and picked up the can he'd used for his cigarette butts. In five minutes, he was back at his car. He tossed the butt can in the ditch. As he stuck the German Luger up under the dash, he suddenly thought of Teagardin's young wife. She was probably sitting over in their little house right now, waiting for him to get home, the same as Emma would be doing for him tonight. He leaned back in the seat and shut his eyes for a moment, tried to think of other things. He started the engine and drove out to the end of Ragged Ridge, made a left toward Route 60. The way he had it figured, he could be in Meade, Ohio, sometime tonight if he didn't stop. He hadn't planned any further ahead than that.

Four hours later, about fifty miles outside of Charleston, West Virginia, the Bel Air began making a thumping noise underneath. He managed to get off the highway and into a filling station lot before the transmission went out completely. He got down on his hands and knees and watched the last of the fluid drip from the casing. "Motherfucker," he said. Just as he started to get up, a thin man in baggy blue coveralls came out and asked if he needed any help. "Not unless you got a transmission you can put in this thing," Arvin said.

"She went out on ye, huh?"

"It's shot," Arvin said.

"Where you headed?"

"Michigan."

"You welcome to use the phone if you want to call someone," the man said.

"Ain't no one to call." As soon as he said it, Arvin realized how true that statement really was. He thought for a minute. Though he hated the thought of giving the Bel Air up, he had to keep moving. He was going to have to make a sacrifice. He turned to the man and tried to smile. "How much would you give me for her?" he asked.

The man glanced at the car and shook his head. "I got no use for it."

"The engine's good. I just changed the points and plugs a couple days ago."

The man began walking the Chevy, kicking the tires, checking for putty. "I don't know," he said, rubbing the gray stubble on his chin.

"How about fifty bucks?" Arvin said.

"It ain't hot, is it?"

"The title's in my name."

"I'll give you thirty."

"Is that the best you can do?"

"Sonny, I got five kids at home," the man said.

"Okay, it's yours," Arvin said. "Just let me get my stuff." He watched the man go back inside the station. He took his bag out of the trunk and then sat down in the car one last time. The day he'd bought it, he and Earskell had burned up a whole tank of gas riding around, drove clear over to Beckley and back. He had a sudden feeling that he was going to lose a lot more before this was over. Reaching under the dash, he got the Luger, stuck it in his waistband. Then he took the title and a box of shells from the glove compartment. When he went inside, the man laid the thirty dollars on the counter. Arvin signed the title and dated it, then put the money in his wallet. He bought a Zagnut and a bottle of RC Cola. It was the first he'd eaten or drunk since the coffee that morning in his grandmother's kitchen. He looked out the window at the endless stream of cars going by on the highway while he chewed on the candy bar. "You ever hitchhike?" he asked the man.

39

ROY FINISHED PICKING ORANGES THAT DAY around five o'clock and collected his pay, which was thirteen dollars. He went to the store at the intersection and bought half a pound of pickle loaf and half a pound of cheese and a loaf of rye bread and two packs of Chesterfields and three fifths of White Port. It was nice getting paid every day. He felt like a rich man walking back to the spot where he and Theodore were camping. The boss was the best one he'd ever had, and Roy had been picking steady for three weeks. The man had told him today that there was maybe only another four or five days of work left. Theodore would be glad to hear that. He wanted to get back to the ocean awful bad. They had put away almost a hundred dollars in the last month, more money than they had had in a long, long time. Their plan was to buy some decent clothes and start preaching again. Roy thought they could find a couple of suits at the Goodwill for maybe ten or twelve bucks. Theodore couldn't play the guitar like he used to, but they could get along all right.

Roy crossed a drainage ditch and headed for their campsite under a small stand of stunted magnolia trees. He saw Theodore asleep on the ground next to his wheelchair, his guitar lying beside him. Roy shook his head and pulled out one of the bottles of wine and a pack of the smokes. He sat down on a stump and took a drink before he lit a cigarette. He had killed half the fifth before he finally noticed that the cripple's face was crawling with ants. Rushing to his side, Roy rolled him over on his back. "Theodore? Hey, come on, buddy, wake up," Roy pleaded, shaking him and slapping at the bugs. "Theodore?"

As soon as he tried to lift the man, Roy knew that he was dead, but he still struggled for fifteen minutes to get him back up in the wheelchair. He began pushing him through the sandy soil toward the highway, but went only a few feet before he stopped. The authorities would ask a lot of questions, he thought, as he watched a fancy car pass by in the distance. He looked around at the campsite. Maybe it would be better just to stay here. Theodore loved the ocean, but he liked the shade, too. And this grove of trees was as much a home as anything they'd had since their days with Bradford Amusements.

Roy sat down on the ground beside the wheelchair. They had done a lot of bad things over the years, and he spent the next several hours praying for the cripple's soul. He hoped someone would do the same for him when it came his time. Around sundown, he finally got up and fixed himself a sandwich. He ate part of it and tossed the rest in the weeds. Halfway through another cigarette, it dawned on him that he didn't have to run anymore. He could go back home now, turn himself in. They could do whatever they wanted to, as long as he got to see Lenora one more time. Theodore had never been able to understand that, how Roy could miss somebody he didn't really know. It was true that he could barely recall what his daughter's face had looked like, but even so, he had wondered a thousand times how her life had turned out. By the time he finished the smoke, he was already rehearsing some words he would say to her.

That night, he got drunk with his old friend one last time. He built a fire and talked to Theodore like he was still alive, told the same stories over again, the ones about Flapjack, and the Flamingo Lady, and the Zit-Eater, and all those other lost souls they had run into on the road. Several times he caught himself waiting on Theodore to laugh or add something that he'd forgotten. After a few hours, there were no more tales to tell, and Roy felt lonelier than he had ever felt in his life. "Hell of a long way from Coal Creek, ain't it, boy?" was the last thing he said before he lay down on his blanket.

He woke right before dawn. He wet a rag with some water from the gallon jug they always kept tied to the back of the wheelchair. He wiped the grime off Theodore's face and combed his hair, pressed his eyes shut with his thumb. There was a splash of wine left in the last bottle and he set it in the cripple's lap, placed his ragged straw hat on his head. Then Roy wrapped his few belongings in a blanket and stood with his hand on the dead man's shoulder. He closed his eyes and said a few more words. He realized that he would never preach again, but that was all right. He'd never been much good at it anyway. Most people just wanted to hear the cripple play. "I wish you was going with me, Theodore," Roy said. By the time he managed to catch a ride, he was already two miles down the road.

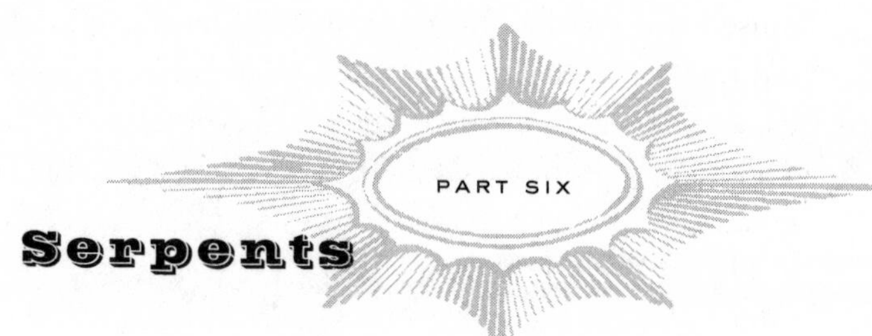

PART SIX

Serpents

40

THANK GOD, JULY WAS COMING TO AN END. Carl could hardly wait to get out on the road again. He hauled the two jars filled with Sandy's tips to the bank and turned it into paper money, then spent the next few days leading up to the vacation buying supplies—two new outfits and some frilly underwear from JC Penney for Sandy, a gallon of motor oil, spare spark plugs, a hacksaw he found on sale and bought on a whim, fifty feet of rope, a set of road maps of the southern states from the AAA office, two cartons of Salem, and a dozen dog dicks. By the time he finished shopping and had a mechanic put a set of brake pads on the car, they were down to $134, but that would take them far. Hell, he thought, as he sat at the kitchen table and counted again, they could live like kings for a week on this much money. He recalled the summer two years ago, when they had left Meade with $40. It was potted meat and stale chips and siphoned gas and sleeping in the sweltering car the whole way, but they had managed to stay out sixteen days with the money they scrounged off the models. Compared to that, they were in fine shape this time.

Still, there was something bothering him. He'd been looking through his photos one evening, trying to get pumped up for the hunt, when he came across one of Sandy holding on to last summer's army boy. He'd been vaguely aware that she hadn't acted quite the same since he had killed that one, like he had taken something precious from her that night. But in the picture he held in his hand was a look of disgust and disappointment in her face that he hadn't noticed before. As he sat there staring at it, he began to wish that he'd never bought her that gun. There was also the business with the waitress at the White Cow. Sandy had started asking him where he went in the evenings while she was at work, and though she had never come right out and accused him of anything, he was beginning to wonder if she might have heard something. The waitress didn't act as friendly as she used to, either. He was probably just being paranoid, but it was hard enough handling the models without having to worry about the bait turning on him, too. The next day, he paid a visit to the hardware store in Central Center. That night after she went to bed, he unloaded her pistol—she'd started carrying it in her purse—and replaced the hollow points with blanks. The more he thought about it, the less he could imagine a situation in which she would have to fire it anyway.

One of the last things he did in preparation for the trip was make a new print of his favorite photograph. He folded it and put it in his wallet. Sandy didn't know, but he always carried a copy when they went back out. It was a picture of her cradling the head of a model in her lap, one they had worked with on their first hunt, the summer after they killed the sex fiend in Colorado. It wasn't one of his best, but it was good for someone who was still learning. It reminded Carl of one of those paintings of Mary with the baby Jesus, the way Sandy was looking down at the model with a sweet, innocent look on her face, a look that he'd been able to occasionally catch that first year or two, but then was gone forever. And the boy? The way he remembered it, they had gone five days without a single hitcher. They were broke and arguing with each other, Sandy wanting to go home and him insisting that they keep on. Then they came around a bend on some potholed two-lane just below Chicago and there he was with his thumb out, like a gift straight out of heaven. He was a big cutup, that boy, full of fun and dumb jokes, and if Carl peered hard enough at the picture, he could still see that orneriness in his face. And every time he looked at it, he was also reminded that he could never find another girl to work with who would be as good as Sandy.

41

IT WAS A HOT SUNDAY MORNING, the first of August, and Carl's shirt was already soaked with sweat. He sat in the kitchen staring at the grimy woodwork and the coat of rancid grease on the wall behind the stove. He checked his watch, saw that it was noon. They should have been on the road four hours ago, but Sandy had come home stinking of booze last night, barging through the door with an ugly look on her red face and going on and on about this being the last trip for her. It had taken her all morning to get straightened up. When they walked outside to get in the car, she stopped and fumbled in her purse for her sunglasses. "Jesus Christ," she said. "I'm still sick."

"We got to stop and fill the gas can before we leave town," he said, ignoring her. He'd decided while waiting on her to get ready that he wasn't going to let her ruin the trip. If need be, he'd get rough with her once they got away from Ross County and that nosy fucking brother of hers.

"Shit, you had all week to do that," she said.

"I'm telling you, girl, you better watch it."

At the Texaco on Main Street, Carl got out and started filling the can. When the high, sharp sound of a siren cut through the air, he nearly jumped out in front of a Mustang leaving the pumps. Turning around, he saw Bodecker sitting in his cruiser behind the station wagon. The sheriff shut the siren off and got out of the car laughing. "Damn, Carl," he said, "I hope you didn't make a mess in your pants." He glanced in their car as he walked past, saw their stuff piled up in the back. "You all taking a trip?"

Sandy opened the door and stepped out. "Going on vacation," she said.

"Where to?" Bodecker asked.

"Virginia Beach," Carl said. He felt something wet and looked down, saw that he'd soaked one of his shoes with gasoline.

"I thought you went there last year," Bodecker said. He wondered if his sister had started up whoring again. If so, she was evidently being more careful about it. He hadn't heard any complaints about her since the woman's phone call last summer.

Carl glanced over at Sandy, then said, "Yeah, we like it there."

"I been thinking about taking me a little respite," Bodecker said. "So it's a good place to go, huh?"

"It's nice," Sandy said.

"What is it you like about it?"

She looked back toward Carl for help, but he was already bent over the can again, topping it off. His pants were hanging low, and she hoped Lee didn't notice the crack of his white ass showing. "It's just nice, that's all."

Bodecker pulled a toothpick out of his shirt pocket. "How long you gonna be gone?" he said.

Sandy crossed her arms in front of herself and gave him a dirty look. "Why all the fuckin' questions?" Her head was starting to pound again. She should have never mixed beer with the vodka.

"No reason, sis," he said. "Just curious."

She stared at him for a minute. She tried to imagine the

look on his smug face if she told him the truth. "About two weeks," she said.

They stood and watched Carl tighten the cap on the gas can. When he went inside the station to pay, Bodecker pulled the toothpick out of his mouth and snorted, "Vacation."

"Knock it off, Lee. What we do is our own business."

42

JAMIE JOHANSEN WAS THE FIRST OF HIS KIND that they ever picked up, hair down to his shoulders, a set of thin gold hoops hanging from his earlobes. That's what the woman told him as soon as he got in their filthy car, like it was the most exciting thing that had ever happened to her. Jamie had run away from home in Massachusetts the year before, which was also the last time he'd been to a barbershop. He didn't consider himself a hippie—the few whom he'd met on the streets acted retarded—but what the fuck? Let her think what she wanted. For the past six months, he'd been living with a family of transvestites in a run-down, cat-infested house in Philadelphia. He had finally split when two of the older sisters decided Jamie needed to share more of the money he was making in the bus station restroom over on Clark Street. Fuck these hags, Jamie figured. Just a bunch of losers in bad makeup and cheap wigs. He'd go to Miami and find himself a rich old fag who would be thrilled just to play with his long, beautiful hair and show him off on the beach. He looked out the car window at a sign that said something about Lexington. He couldn't even remember how he had ended up in Kentucky. Who the fuck goes to Kentucky?

And these two who just picked him up, another couple of losers. The woman seemed to think she was sexy or something, the way she kept smiling at him in the mirror and licking her lips, but just looking at her gave him the willies. There was a ripe, fishy smell coming from somewhere in the car, and he figured it had to be her. He could tell the fat man was dying to suck his dick, the way he kept turning around in the front seat and asking stupid questions so he could take another look at his crotch. They hadn't gone but five or six miles when Jamie decided that, if he got the chance, he was going to steal their car. Even this piece of junk would be better than hitchhiking. The man who picked him up last night, stiff black hat, long white fingers, had scared the shit out of him, talking about gangs of rabid rednecks and tribes of half-starved hoboes and the awful things they did to sweet, young waifs they caught out on the road. After relating a number of stories he had heard—boys buried alive, tamped down headfirst into tight holes like fence posts, others turned into a gooey mulligan stew seasoned with wild onions and windfall apples—the man had offered good money and a night in a nice motel for a special kind of party, one that involved a bag of cotton balls and a funnel in some way, but for the first time since he had left home, Jamie turned the good money down, could see the maid finding him the next morning hollowed out like a Beggar's Night pumpkin in the bathtub. These two here were like Ma and Pa Kettle compared to that crazy bastard.

Still, it surprised him when the woman turned off the highway and the man asked him straight out if he would be interested in fucking his wife while he took a few photographs. He hadn't seen that one coming, but he played it cool. Jamie wasn't really into women, especially ugly ones; but if he could talk the fat man into taking his clothes off too, stealing the car should be a piece of cake. He'd never had his own set of wheels before. He told the man, sure, he was interested, that is, if they were willing to pay for it. He looked past the man out the windshield smeared with the guts of dead insects. They were on a gravel road now. The woman had slowed down to a crawl and was evidently looking for a place to park.

"I thought your kind believed in that free love shit," the man said. "That's what Walter Cronkite said on the news the other night."

"A boy's still got to make a living, right?" Jamie said.

"I guess that's fair enough. How's twenty bucks sound?" The woman put the car in park and shut off the engine. They were sitting at the edge of a soybean field.

"Heck, I'll take you both on for twenty dollars," Jamie said with a smile.

"Both of us?" The fat man turned and looked at him with cold, gray eyes. "It sounds like you think I'm pretty." The woman gave a little giggle.

Jamie shrugged. He wondered if they would still be laughing when he drove away in their car. "I've had worse," he said.

"Oh, I doubt that," the man said, shoving his car door open.

43

"YOU ONLY BROUGHT THE ONE SHIRT?" Sandy asked him. They had been on the road six days, and had worked with two models, the kid with all the hair and a man with a harmonica who thought he was going to Nashville to become a country music star, that is, right up until a few minutes after they listened to him completely butcher Johnny Cash's "Ring of Fire," which happened to be Carl's favorite song that summer.

"Yeah," Carl said.

"Okay, we're gonna have to do some laundry," she said.

"Why?"

"You stink, that's why."

They came across a Laundromat in a small town in South Carolina a couple of hours later. Sandy made him take the shirt off. She carried a grocery bag of dirty clothes in and put them in a washer. He sat on a bench out front, watching the occasional car drive past and chewing on a cigar, his saggy tits nearly hanging to his fishy-white paunch. Sandy came out and sat on the other end of the bench and hid behind her sunglasses. Her blouse was plastered to her back with sweat. She rested her head against the building and shut her eyes.

"What we did was the best thing that could have happened to him," Carl said.

Jesus, Sandy thought, he's still talking about that fucker with the mouth harp. He had been yapping about him all morning. "I've already heard it," she said.

"I'm just saying, for one, he couldn't sing worth a shit. And he had, what, maybe three fucking teeth in his head? You ever look at them country music stars? Those people got expensive teeth. No, they would have laughed him right out of town, and then he would have went home and knocked up some damn ugly cow and been tied down by a bunch of screaming brats, and that would have been the end of it."

"The end of what?" Sandy said.

"The end of his dream, that's what. Maybe he couldn't see it last night, but I did that boy a big favor. He died with that dream still alive in his head."

"Jesus, Carl, what the hell's got into you?" She heard the washer stop and stood up, held out her hand. "Give me a quarter for the dryer."

He handed her some change, then bent down and untied his shoes, kicked them off. He wasn't wearing any socks. He was down to his trousers now. Taking his pocketknife out, he started cleaning his toenails. Two young boys, maybe nine or ten years old, came speeding around the corner on bicycles just as he smeared a gob of gray gunk on the seat of the bench. They both waved to him and smiled when he looked up. Just for a second, they made him wish, as they flew by pumping their legs and laughing as if they didn't have a care in the world, that he was somebody else.

44

ON THEIR TWELFTH DAY OUT, ONE GOT AWAY. That had never happened before. He was an ex-con named Danny Murdock, the fourth model they had picked up this trip. On his right forearm, he had a tattoo of two scaly serpents wrapped around a tombstone that Carl imagined doing something special with once they had him down. They had been riding around all afternoon drinking beer and sharing a jumbo bag of pork rinds and getting him relaxed. They found a spot to park along a long, narrow lake just a mile or so inside the Sumter National Forest. As soon as Sandy shut the engine off, Danny flung the door open and got out of the car. He stretched and yawned, then started ambling toward the water, shucking off his clothes as he went. "What are you doing?" Carl yelled.

Danny tossed his shirt on the ground and turned to look back at them. "Hey, I got no problem giving your old lady the cock, but let me get cleaned up first," he said, jerking his underwear down. "I'm warning you, though, ol' buddy, I get past the used part, she ain't gonna be happy with your ass no more."

"Boy, he's got a mouth on him, don't he?" Sandy said, as she walked around the front of the station wagon. She leaned against the fender and watched the man jump into the water.

Carl set the camera on the hood and smiled. "Not for long, he ain't." They shared another beer and watched him swim, arms pumping and feet kicking, out to the middle of the lake and then roll over on his back.

"I gotta say, that looks like fun," Sandy said. She kicked off her sandals and spread the blanket on the grass.

"Shit, hard to tell what's in that mud hole," Carl said. He opened another beer, tried to enjoy being out of the stinking car for a while. Eventually though, his patience with the swimmer wore thin. He had been out there playing over an hour. He went to the edge of the beach and started yelling and motioning for Danny to come in, and each time the man dove under and came back up whooping and splashing water like some schoolboy, Carl got a trifle more pissed. When Danny finally walked up out of the lake grinning with his dick hanging halfway to his knees and the evening sun sparkling all over his wet skin, Carl pulled the gun out of his pocket and said, "Are you clean enough yet?"

"What the hell?" the man said.

Carl motioned with the gun. "Goddamn it, get over there on that blanket like we talked about. Shit, we're losing the light here." He looked back at Sandy and nodded. She reached behind her head and started to undo her ponytail.

"Go fuck yourself!" Carl heard the man yell.

By the time he realized what was happening, Danny Murdock was already bolting into the woods on the other side of the road. Carl fired twice wildly and took after him. Slipping and stumbling, he went deep into the woods, until he was afraid he'd never find his way back to the car. He stopped and listened, but couldn't hear a thing except for the sound of his own raspy breathing. He was too fat and slow to be chasing anyone, let alone a long-legged prick who had bragged to them all afternoon about outrunning three squad cars on foot through downtown Spartanburg the week before. By then, it was near dusk, and he suddenly realized that the man might have circled back around to where Sandy was waiting at the car. But even with blanks in her gun, he should have heard a shot, that is, unless the fucker took her by surprise. God-damn that sneaking sonofabitch. He hated going back to the car empty-handed. Sandy would never let him hear the end of it. He hesitated a second, then pointed the pistol up in the air and fired twice.

She was standing by the open driver's door holding the .22 in her hands when he came crashing through the brush at the edge of the road, red-faced and panting. "We got to get out of here," he yelled. He grabbed the blanket they had spread on the ground behind the car and hurried over and scooped up the man's clothes and shoes out of the grass. He tossed them in the backseat and climbed in the front.

"Jesus, Carl, what happened?" she said as she started the car.

"Don't worry, I got the bastard," he said. "Put two through his stupid head."

She looked over at him. "You chased that fucker down?"

He heard the doubt in her voice. "Be quiet for a minute," he said. "I got to think." He pulled out a map and studied it for a minute or so, tracing his finger back and forth. "The way it looks we're maybe ten miles from the border. Just turn around and make a left where we came in, and we oughta run into the highway."

"I don't believe you," she said.

"What?"

"That guy took off like a deer. Ain't no way you caught up with him."

Carl took a couple of deep breaths. "He was hiding under a log. I damn near stepped on him."

"What's the hurry then?" she said. "Let's go back and take some pictures."

Carl laid the .38 on the dash and pulled his shirt up, wiped the sweat off his face. His heart was still beating like a hammer in his chest. "Sandy, just drive the goddamn car, okay?"

"He got away, didn't he?"

He looked out the passenger window into the darkening woods. "Yeah, the bastard got away."

She put the car in drive. "Don't lie to me no more, Carl," she said. "And another thing, while we're on the subject, if I hear about you messing around with that little twat at the White Cow again, you're gonna be sorry." Then she pressed her foot to the accelerator, and twenty minutes later, they crossed the state line into Georgia.

45

LATER THAT NIGHT, SANDY PARKED at the edge of a truck stop a few miles south of Atlanta. She ate a piece of beef jerky and crawled in the backseat to sleep. Around three AM, it began to rain. Carl sat in the front and listened to it beat on top of the car and thought about the ex-con. There's a lesson to be learned from this, he thought. He had just turned his back on the cowardly fucker for a second, but that had been long enough to screw everything up. He pulled the man's clothes from underneath the seat and started going through them. He found a broken switchblade and a Greenwood, South Carolina, address written inside a matchbook and eleven dollars in his wallet. Underneath the address were the words GOOD HEAD. He put the money in his pocket and rolled everything else up into a ball, then walked across the lot and tossed it in a trash barrel.

The rain was still coming down when she woke the next morning. Eating breakfast with Sandy at the truck stop, he wondered if any of the drivers sitting around them had ever killed a hitchhiker. It would be an excellent job for that sort of thing if a person was so inclined. As they started on their third cup of coffee, the rain let up and the sun popped out like a big, festering boil in the sky. By the time they paid the bill, wisps of steam were already rising up off the blacktopped parking lot. "About what happened yesterday," Carl said, as they walked back to the car, "I shouldn't have done that."

"Like I said," Sandy told him, "don't lie to me no more. We get caught, it's my ass in the sling just as much as yours."

Carl thought again about the blanks he'd stuck in her gun, but decided it would be better not to say anything about that. They would be home soon, and he could replace them without her ever knowing. "Ain't nobody gonna catch us," he said.

"Yeah, well, you probably didn't think one would ever get away, either."

"Don't worry," he said, "that won't ever happen again."

They drove around Atlanta and stopped in a place called Roswell for gas. They had twenty-four dollars and some change to get home on. Just as Carl was getting back in the station wagon after paying the cashier, a gaunt man in a worn black suit timidly approached. "You wouldn't be headin' north by any chance, would you?" he asked. Carl went ahead and picked his cigar up out of the ashtray before he turned to look the man over. The suit was several sizes too big. The cuffs of the pants were turned up several times to keep them from dragging on the ground. He could see a paper price tag still attached to the sleeve of the coat. The man was packing a flimsy bedroll; and though he could have easily passed for sixty, Carl figured the wayfarer at least a few years younger than that. For some reason, he reminded Carl of a preacher, one of the real ones that you seldom run into anymore: not one of those greedy, sweet-smelling bastards just out to take people's money and make a fat fucking living off God, but a man who truly believed in the teachings of Jesus. On second thought, that was probably taking things a bit too far; the old boy was probably just another bum.

"Might be," Carl said. He looked over at Sandy for some indication that she was on board, but she just shrugged and put her sunglasses back on. "Where you going?"

"Coal Creek, West Virginia."

Carl thought about the one who got away last night. That big-dicked sonofabitch was going to leave a bad taste in his mouth for a long time. "Aw, hell, why not?" he told the man. "Get in the back."

Once they pulled out on the highway, the man said, "Mister, I do appreciate this. My poor feet are 'bout wore out."

"Been having trouble getting rides, huh?"

"I've did more walking than riding, I can tell you that."

"Yeah," Carl said, "I don't understand people who won't pick up strangers. That should be a good thing, helping someone out."

"You sound like you a Christian," the man said.

Sandy choked back a laugh, but Carl ignored her. "In some ways, I suppose," he told the man. "But I have to admit, I don't follow it quite as close as I used to."

The man nodded and stared out the window. "It's hard to live a good life," he said. "It seems like the Devil don't ever let up."

"What's your name, honey?" Sandy asked. Carl glanced at her and smiled, then reached over and touched her leg. He'd been afraid, after the way he fucked up last night, that she was going to be a first-class bitch the rest of the trip.

"Roy," the man said, "Roy Laferty."

"So what's in West Virginia, Roy?" she said.

"Going home to see my daughter."

"That's nice," Sandy said. "When did you see her last?"

Roy thought for a minute. Lord, he'd never felt so tired. "It's been seventeen years almost." Riding in the car was making him sleepy. He hated to be impolite, but as hard as he tried, he couldn't keep his eyes open.

"What you been doing away from home that long?" Carl said. After waiting for a minute or so for the man to answer, he turned around and looked in the backseat. "Shit, he's passed out," he told Sandy.

"Just let him be for now," she said. "And as far as me actually fucking him, you can forget that. He smells worse than you do."

"All right, all right," Carl said, pulling the Georgia highway map out of the glove box. Thirty minutes later, he pointed at an exit ramp, told Sandy to take it. They drove two or three miles down a dusty clay road, eventually found a pull-off littered with party trash and a busted-up piano. "This is gonna have to do," Carl said, stepping out of the car. He opened the hitcher's door and shook his shoulder. "Hey there, buddy," he said, "come on, I want to show you something."

A couple of minutes later, Roy found himself in a stand of tall loblolly pines. The ground underneath them was carpeted with dry, brown needles. He couldn't recall exactly how long he had been traveling, maybe three days. He hadn't had much luck with rides, and he had walked until his feet were raw with blisters. Though he didn't think he could take another step, he didn't want to stop moving either. He wondered if the animals had gotten to Theodore yet. Then he saw that the woman was taking her clothes off, and that confused him. He looked around for the car he'd been riding in and saw the fat man pointing a pistol at him. There was a black camera hanging from his neck by a cord, an unlit cigar stuck between his thick lips. Maybe he was dreaming, Roy thought, but, damn, it seemed so real. He could smell the sap seeping from the trees in the heat. He saw the woman get down on a red plaid blanket, like the kind people might use for a picnic, and then the man said something that woke him up. "What?" Roy asked.

"I said I'm giving you a good thing here," Carl repeated. "She likes lanky ol' studs like you."

"What's going on here, mister?" Roy said.

Carl heaved a sigh. "Jesus Christ, man, pay attention. Like I said, you're gonna fuck my wife, and I'm going to take some pictures, that's all."

"Your wife?" Roy said. "I've never heard of such a thing. Here I thought you was a good feller."

"Just shut up and get that welfare suit off," Carl said.

Looking over at Sandy, Roy held his hands out. "Lady," he said, "I'm sorry, but I promised myself when Theodore died that I was gonna live right from now on, and I intend to stick to that."

"Oh, come on, sweetie," Sandy said. "We'll just take a few pictures and then the big dumb bastard will leave us alone."

"Woman, look at me. I been run through the wringer. Hell, I don't even know half the places I been. Do you really want these hands touching you?"

"You sonofabitch, you're going to do what I say," Carl said.

Roy shook his head. "No, mister. The last woman I was with was a bird, and that's the way it's going to stay. Theodore was afraid of her, so I didn't let on, but Priscilla, she really was a flamingo."

Carl laughed and threw his cigar down. Jesus Christ, what a mess. "Okay, looks like we got us a fruitcake."

Sandy stood up and started pulling her clothes back on. "Let's get the hell out of here," she said.

Just as Roy turned and watched her start to walk toward the car sitting out by the road, he felt the barrel of the gun press against the side of his head. "Don't even think about running," Carl told him.

"You don't have to worry about that," Roy said. "My runnin' days are over with." He raised his eyes and searched out a small patch of blue sky visible through the dense, green branches of the pines. A white wisp of a cloud drifted by. That's what dying will be like, he told himself. Just floating up in the air.

Nothing bad about that. He smiled a little. "I don't reckon you're gonna let me back in the car, are you?"

"You got that right," Carl said. He started to squeeze the trigger.

"Just one thing," Roy said, his voice filled with urgency.

"What's that?"

"Her name's Lenora."

"Who the fuck you talking about?"

"My little girl," Roy said.

46

IT WAS HARD TO BELIEVE, but the crazy bastard in the dirty suit was carrying almost a hundred dollars in his pocket. They ate barbecue and coleslaw at a pig shack in a colored section of Knoxville, and that night they stayed in a Holiday Inn in Johnson City, Tennessee. As usual, Sandy took her sweet time the next morning. By the time she announced that she was ready to go, Carl was sinking into a foul mood. Except for the photos of the boy in Kentucky, most of the others he had taken this time out were slop. Nothing had turned out right. He had sat up all night dwelling on it in a chair by the third-floor window, looking down on the parking lot and rolling a dog dick cigar between his fingers until it fell apart. He kept considering signs, maybe something he had missed. But nothing stood out, except for Sandy's mostly piss-poor attitude and the ex-con who got away. He swore he'd never hunt in the South again.

They entered southern West Virginia around noon. "Look, we still got the rest of today," he said. "If there's any fucking way possible, I want to shoot another roll of film before we get home, something good." They had pulled into a rest stop so he could check the oil in the car.

"Go ahead," Sandy said. "There's all kinds of pictures out there." She pointed out the window. "See, there's a bluebird just landed in that tree."

"Funny," he said. "You know what I mean."

She put the car into gear. "I don't care what you do, Carl, but I want to sleep in my own bed tonight."

"Good enough," he said.

Over the next four or five hours, they didn't come across a single hitchhiker. The closer they got to Ohio, the more agitated Carl became. He kept telling Sandy to slow down, made her stop and stretch her legs and drink coffee a couple of times just to keep his hopes alive a while longer. By the time they drove through Charleston and headed toward Point Pleasant, he was filled with disappointment and doubt. Maybe the ex-con really was a sign. If so, Carl thought, it could mean only one thing: they should quit while they were ahead. That's what he was thinking, as they approached the long line of traffic waiting to go over the silver metal bridge that would take them into Ohio. Then he saw the handsome, dark-haired boy with the gym bag standing on the walkway seven or eight car lengths up ahead. He leaned forward, breathed in the car exhaust and the stink from the river. The traffic moved a few feet, then stopped again. Somebody behind them in the line honked his horn. The boy turned and looked back toward the end of the line, his eyes squinting in the sun.

"Do you see that?" Carl said.

"But what about your fucking rules? Shit, we're heading back into Ohio."

Carl kept his eyes on the boy, prayed that nobody offered him a ride before they got close enough to pick him up. "Let's just see where's he's going. Hell, that can't hurt nothing, can it?"

Sandy took off her sunglasses, gave the boy a closer look. She knew Carl well enough to know that it wasn't going to stop with just giving him a ride, but from what she could see, he was maybe nicer than anything they'd ever come across before. And there certainly hadn't been any angels this trip. "I guess not," she said.

"But I need you to do some talking, okay? Give him that smile of yours, make him want it. I hate to point it out, but you been dropping the ball this trip. I can't do it alone."

"Sure, Carl," she said. "Anything you say. Hell, I'll offer to suck him off as soon as he plops his ass down in the backseat. That ought to do it."

"Jesus, you got a filthy mouth on you."

"Maybe so," she said. "But I just want to get this over with."

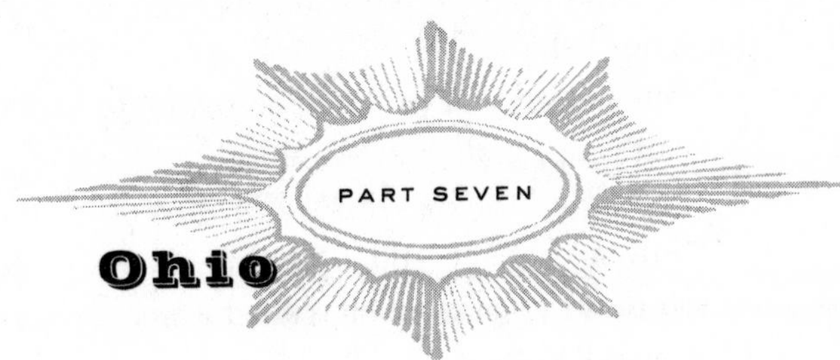

PART SEVEN

Ohio

47

IT SEEMED THAT THERE MUST BE a wreck up ahead, as slow as the traffic was moving. Arvin had just made up his mind to walk across the bridge when the car pulled up and the fat man asked him if he needed a ride. After selling the Bel Air, he'd walked out to the highway and caught a lift through Charleston with a fertilizer salesman—rumpled white shirt, gravy-stained tie, the stink of last night's alcohol seeping from his big pores—on his way to a feed and seed convention in Indianapolis. The salesman let him off on Route 35 at Nitro; and a few minutes later, he got another ride with a colored family in a pickup truck that took him to the edge of Point Pleasant. He sat in the back with a dozen baskets of tomatoes and green beans. The black man pointed the way to the bridge, and Arvin began walking. He could smell the Ohio River several blocks before he saw its greasy, blue-gray surface. A clock on a bank said 5:47. He could hardly believe that a person could travel so fast with just his thumb.

When he got in the black station wagon, the woman behind the wheel looked back at him and smiled. It seemed like she was almost happy to see him. Their names were Carl and Sandy, the fat man told him. "Where you going?" Carl asked.

"Meade, Ohio," Arvin said. "Ever hear of it?"

"We—" Sandy began to say.

"Sure," Carl interrupted. "If I'm not mistaken, I think it's a paper mill town." He took his cigar out of his mouth and looked over at the woman. "In fact, we're going right by there this trip, ain't we, babe?" This had to be a sign, Carl thought, picking up a fine-looking boy like this who was headed for Meade clear down here among the river rats.

"Yeah," she said. The traffic started moving again. The holdup was an accident on the Ohio side, two crumpled cars and a scattering of broken glass on the pavement. An ambulance turned its siren on and pulled out in front of them, barely avoiding a collision. A policeman blew a whistle, held his hand up for Sandy to stop.

"Jesus Christ, be careful," Carl said, shifting in his seat.

"Do you want to drive?" Sandy said, hitting the brakes too hard. They sat there for another few minutes while a man in coveralls hurriedly swept up glass. Sandy adjusted her rearview, took another look at the boy. She was so glad that she had gotten to take a bath this morning. She'd still be nice and clean for him. When she reached in her purse for a fresh pack of cigarettes, her hand brushed against the pistol. As she watched the man finish the cleanup, she fantasized about killing Carl and taking off with the boy. He was probably only six or seven years younger than she was. She could make something like that work. Maybe even have a kid or two. Then she closed the purse and started peeling the pack of Salems open. She'd never do it, of course, but it was still nice to think about.

"What's your name, honey?" she asked the boy, after the policeman waved them on through.

Arvin allowed himself a sigh of relief. He thought for sure the woman was going to get them pulled over. He looked at her again. She was rail thin and dirty-looking. Her face was caked with too much makeup, and her teeth were stained a dark yellow from too many years of cigarettes and neglect. A strong odor of sweat and filth was coming from the front seat, and he figured both of them were in bad need of a bath. "Billy Burns," he told her. That was the fertilizer salesman's name.

"That's a nice name," she said. "Where you coming from?"

"Tennessee."

"So what you going to Meade for?" Carl asked.

"Oh, just visiting, that's all."

"You got family there?"

"No," Arvin said. "But I used to live there a long time ago."

"Probably ain't changed much," Carl said. "Most of them little towns never do."

"Where is it you all live?" Arvin asked.

"We're from Fort Wayne. Been on vacation down in Florida. We like to meet new people, don't we, hon?"

"We sure do," Sandy said.

Just as they passed the sign that marked the Ross County line, Carl looked at his watch. They probably should have stopped before they got this far, but he knew a safe spot nearby where they could take the boy. He'd come across it last winter on one of his drives. Meade was just ten miles away now, and it was after six o'clock. That meant they had only another ninety or so minutes of decent light left. He had never broken any of the major rules before, but he'd already made up his mind. Tonight, he was going to kill a man in Ohio. Shit, if this worked out, he might even do away with that rule altogether. Maybe that's what this boy was all about, maybe not. There wasn't enough time to think about it. He shifted in his seat and said, "Billy, my bladder don't work like it used to. We're gonna pull over so I can take a leak, okay?"

"Yeah, sure. I just appreciate you givin' me a ride."

"There's a road up here to the right," Carl said to Sandy.

"How far?" Sandy asked.

"Maybe a mile."

Arvin leaned over and looked past Carl's head out the windshield. He didn't see any indication of a road, and he thought it a bit odd that the man knew there was one up ahead if he wasn't from around here. Maybe he's got a map, the boy told himself. He sat back in his seat again and watched the scenery going by. Except for the hills being smaller and more rounded off, it looked a lot like West Virginia. He wondered if anyone had found Teagardin's body yet.

Sandy turned off Route 35 onto a dirt and gravel road. She drove past a big farm that sat on the corner. After another mile or so, she slowed and asked Carl, "Here?"

"No, keep going," he said.

Arvin straightened up and looked around. They hadn't passed another house since the farm. The Luger was pressing against his groin, and he adjusted it a little.

"This looks like a good spot," Carl finally said, pointing at the vague remains of a driveway that led to a run-down house. It was obvious that the place had been empty for years. The few windows were busted out and the porch was caving in on one end. The front door was standing open, hanging crooked from one hinge. Across the road was a cornfield, the stalks withered and yellow from the hot, droughty weather. As soon as Sandy shut the engine off, Carl opened the glove compartment. He pulled out a fancy-looking camera, held it up for Arvin to see. "Bet you never would have guessed I'm a photographer, would you?" he said.

Arvin shrugged. "Probably not." He could hear the hum of insects outside the car in the dry weeds. Thousands of them.

"But look, I'm not one of them jackasses that shoot dumb pictures like you see in the newspaper, am I, Sandy?"

"No," she said, looking back at Arvin, "he's not. He's really good."

"You ever hear of Michelangelo or Leonardo . . . ? Oh, hell, I've done forgot his name. You know who I mean?"

"Yeah, I think so," Arvin said. He thought about the time Lenora showed him a painting called *Mona Lisa* in a book. She had asked him if he thought she looked anything like the pale woman in the picture, and he was glad he'd told her that she was prettier than that.

"Well, I like to think that someday people are gonna look at my photographs and think they're just as good as anything them guys ever made. The pictures I take, Billy, they're like art, like you see in a museum. You ever been to a museum?"

"No," Arvin said. "Can't say that I have."

"Well, maybe you will someday. So how about it?"

"How about what?" Arvin said.

"Why don't we get out here and you let me take some pictures of you with Sandy?"

"No, mister, I better not. It's been a long day for me, and I'd just as soon keep moving. I just want to get to Meade."

"Oh, come on, son, won't take but a few minutes. How about this? What if she got naked for you?"

Arvin reached for the door handle. "That's all right," he said. "I'm just gonna walk back up to the highway. You stay back here and take all the pictures you want."

"Now wait up, goddamn it," Carl said. "I didn't mean to get you all upset. But shit, wasn't no harm in me asking, was there?" He laid the camera down on the seat and sighed. "All right, just let me take my piss and we'll get on out of here."

Carl heaved his big body out of the car, walked around to the back. Sandy took a cigarette from her pack. Looking over, Arvin watched her hands tremble as she tried several times to strike a match. A feeling, one that he couldn't quite put a name on, suddenly twisted in his gut like a knife. He was already pulling the Luger from the waistband of his overalls when he heard Carl say, "Get out of the car, boy." The fat man was standing five feet away from the back door pointing a long-barreled pistol at him.

"If it's money you want," Arvin said, "I got a little bit." He eased the safety off the gun. "You can have it."

"Being nice now, huh?" Carl said. He spat in the grass. "I'll tell you what, you stuck-up cocksucker, you just hang on to that money for right now. Sandy and me will sort it out after we take my goddamn pictures."

"Better go ahead and do what he says, Billy," Sandy said. "He can get pretty excited if things don't go his way." When she glanced back at him and smiled with all her rotten teeth, Arvin nodded to himself and shoved his door open. Before it registered in Carl's mind what the boy held in his hand, the first blast had torn through his stomach. The force of the bullet started to spin him around. He staggered back three or four feet and caught himself. He tried to raise his gun and aim at the boy, but then another round hit him in the chest. He landed on his back in the weeds with a heavy thump. Though he could still feel the .38 in his hand, his fingers wouldn't work. Somewhere far off, he could hear Sandy's voice. It sounded like she was saying his name over and over again: Carl, Carl, Carl. He wanted to answer her, thought that if he just rested a minute, he could still straighten this mess out. Something cold began to crawl over him. He felt his body start to sink into a hole that seemed to be opening up beneath him in the ground, and it scared him, that feeling, the way it sucked the breath right out of him. Gritting his teeth, he fought to climb out before he sank in too deep. He felt himself rising. Yes, by God, he could still fix things, and then they would quit. He saw those two little boys on their bicycles riding by waving at him. No more pictures, he wanted to tell Sandy, but he was having trouble finding the air. Then something with huge black wings settled on top of him, pushing him down again, and even though he grabbed frantically at the grass and dirt with his left hand to keep from slipping, he couldn't stop himself this time.

When the woman started screaming the man's name, Arvin turned and saw her in the front seat digging something out of her purse. "Don't do that," he said, shaking his head. He stepped back from the car and pointed the Luger at her. "I'm begging you." Black streaks of mascara were running down her face. She cried the man's name one more time, and then stopped. Taking several deep breaths, she stared at the soles of Carl's shoes while she quieted down. One of them, she noticed, had a hole in it as big around as a fifty-cent piece. He hadn't mentioned it the whole trip. "Please, lady," Arvin said when he saw her smile.

"Fuck it," she said quietly, just before she drew a pistol up over the seat and fired. Though she aimed directly at the middle of the boy's body, he just stood there. Frantically, she pulled the hammer back again with her thumbs, but before she could get off the second round, Arvin shot her in the neck. The .22 dropped to the floorboards as the bullet knocked her against the driver's-side door. Pressing her hands against her throat, she tried to stop the red stream that was spurting from the wound. She began to choke, and coughed a gush of blood out on the seat. Her eyes settled on his face. They grew big for a few seconds and then slowly closed. Arvin listened to her take a few ragged breaths and then one last sticky heave. He couldn't believe that the woman had missed him. Jesus Christ, she was so close.

He sat down on the edge of the backseat and puked a little in the grass between his feet. A numbing despair began to settle over him, and he tried to shake it off. He stepped out into the dirt road and paced around in a circle. He put the Luger back in his pants and knelt down beside the man. He reached underneath him and pulled the wallet out of his back pocket and glanced through it quickly. He didn't see any driver's license, but he found a photograph behind some paper money. Suddenly he felt sick all over again. It was a picture of the woman cradling a dead man in her arms like a baby. She was wearing only a black bra and panties. There was what appeared to be a bullet hole above the man's right eye. She was looking down at him with a hint of sorrow on her face.

Arvin put the photograph in his shirt pocket and dropped the wallet on the fat man's chest. Then he opened the glove compartment, finding nothing but road maps and rolls of film. He listened again for any cars coming, wiped the sweat out of his eyes. "Think, goddamn it, think," he told himself. But the only thing he knew for sure was that he had to get out of this place fast. Picking up his gym bag, he took off walking west through the parched rows of corn. He was twenty yards out in the field when he stopped and turned around. He hurried back to the car and took two of the film canisters out of the glove box, stuck them in his pants pocket. Then he got a shirt out of his bag and wiped off everything that he might have touched. The insects resumed their humming.

48

HE DECIDED TO STAY OFF THE ROADS, and it was after midnight when Arvin finally walked into Meade. In the middle of town, right off Main Street, he found a squat brick motel called the Scioto Inn that still had its VACANCY sign on. He had never stayed in a motel before. The clerk, a boy not much older than himself, was gazing wearily at an old movie, *Abbott and Costello Meet the Mummy*, on a small black-and-white TV sitting in the corner. The room was five bucks a night. "We change the towels every other day," the clerk said.

In his room, Arvin stripped off his clothes and stood in the shower for a long time trying to get clean. Nervous and exhausted, he lay down on top of the bedspread and sipped a pint of whiskey. He was goddamn glad he'd remembered to bring it along. He noticed on the wall a small picture of Jesus hanging from the cross. When he got up to take a leak, he turned the picture over. It reminded him too much of the one in his grandmother's kitchen. By three o'clock in the morning, he was drunk enough to go to sleep.

He woke around ten the next morning after dreaming about the woman. In the dream, she fired the pistol at him just like she did yesterday afternoon, only this time she hit him squarely in the forehead, and he was the one who died instead of her. The other details were vague, but he thought maybe she took his picture. He almost wished that had happened as he went to the window and peeked out the curtain, half expecting the parking lot to be filled with police cruisers. He watched the traffic go by on Bridge Street while he smoked a cigarette, then he took another shower. After he got dressed, he went over to the office and asked if he could keep the room another day. The boy from last night was still on duty. He was half asleep, listlessly chewing a wad of pink bubble gum. "You must put in a lot of hours," Arvin said.

The boy yawned and nodded, rang up another night in the register. "Don't I know it," he said. "My old man owns the place, so I'm pretty much his slave when I'm not in college." He handed back the change from a twenty. "Better than getting shipped off to Vietnam, though."

"Yeah, I expect so," Arvin said. He put the loose bills in his wallet. "Used to be an eating place around here called the Wooden Spoon. Is it still in business?"

"Sure." The boy walked over to the door and pointed up the street. "Just walk over there to the light and turn left. You'll see it across from the bus station. They got good chili."

He stood outside the door of the Wooden Spoon a few minutes, looking across at the bus station trying to imagine his father getting off a Greyhound and seeing his mother for the first time, over twenty years ago. Once inside, he ordered ham and eggs and toast. Though he hadn't eaten anything since the candy bar yesterday afternoon, he found that he wasn't very hungry. Eventually the old, wrinkled waitress came over and picked up his plate without a word. She barely looked at him, but when he got up, he left her a dollar tip anyway.

Just as he walked outside, three cruisers sped past going east with their lights flashing and sirens blaring. His heart seemed to stop for a moment in his chest, and then began to race. He leaned against the side of the brick building and tried to light a cigarette, but his hands were shaking too much to strike a match, just like the woman yesterday evening. The sirens faded into the distance, and he calmed down enough to get it lit. A bus pulled into the alley beside the station just then. He watched a dozen or so people get out. A couple of them wore military uniforms. The bus driver, a heavy-jowled, sour-faced man in a gray shirt and black tie, leaned back in his seat and pulled his cap down over his eyes.

Arvin walked back over to his room and spent the rest of the day pacing the green, threadbare carpet. It was only a matter of time before the law figured out he was the one who killed Preston Teagardin. Taking off from Coal Creek so suddenly, he realized, was the dumbest damn thing he could have done. How much more obvious could he have been? The longer he walked the floor, the clearer it became that when he shot that preacher he had set something in motion that was going to follow him for the rest of his life. He knew in his gut that he should attempt to get out of Ohio immediately, but he couldn't bear the thought of leaving without seeing the old house and the prayer log one more time. No matter what else happened, he told himself, he had to try to set right those things about his father that still ate at his heart. Until then, he'd never be free anyway.

He wondered if he would ever feel clean again. There was no TV in the room, just a radio. The only station he could find without static was country and western. He let it play softly while he tried to go to sleep. Every once in a while, someone in the next room coughed, and the sound made him think of the woman choking on her blood. He was still thinking of her when morning came.

49

"I'M SORRY, LEE," HOWSER SAID as Bodecker approached. "This is all fucked up." He was standing next to Carl and Sandy's station wagon. It was Tuesday around noon. Bodecker had just arrived. A farmer had found the bodies approximately an hour ago, flagged down a Wonder Bread truck out along the highway. There were four cruisers lined up behind one another on the road, and men in gray uniforms standing around fanning themselves with their hats, waiting for orders. Howser was Bodecker's chief deputy, the only man he could depend on with anything beyond petty theft and writing speeding tickets. As far as the sheriff was concerned, the rest of them weren't fit to be crossing guards in front of a one-room schoolhouse.

He glanced down at Carl's body, and then looked in at his sister. The deputy had already told him on the radio that she was dead. "Jesus," he said, his voice nearly breaking. "Jesus Christ."

"I know," Howser said.

Bodecker took several deep gulps of air to steady himself and stuck his sunglasses in his pocket. "Give me a few minutes here alone with her."

"Sure," the deputy said. He walked over to where the other men were standing, said something to them in a low voice.

Squatting down beside the open passenger door, Bodecker studied Sandy closely, the lines in her face, the bad teeth, the faded bruises on her legs. She'd always been sort of fucked-up, but she was still his sister. He pulled his handkerchief out and wiped at his eyes. She was wearing a pair of skimpy shorts and a tight blouse. Still dressing like a whore, he thought. He climbed in the front seat, pulled her close, and looked over her shoulder. The bullet had gone through her neck and come out at the top of her back, just to the left of her spine, a couple of inches below the entry wound. It was buried in the padding of the driver's-side door. He used his penknife to dig out the slug. It looked like a 9 millimeter. He saw a .22 pistol lying near the brake pedal. "Was that back door open like that when you got here?" he called out to Howser.

The deputy left the men in the road and jogged back to the station wagon. "We ain't touched a thing, Lee."

"Where's the farmer that found 'em?"

"Said he had a sick heifer to tend to. But I questioned him pretty good before he left. He don't know nothing."

"You already take pictures?"

"Yeah, just got done when you pulled in."

He handed Howser the bullet, then leaned across the front seat again, picked up the .22 with his handkerchief. He sniffed the barrel, then released the cylinder, saw that it had been fired once. Pushing the extractor back, five shells fell out into his hand. The ends were crimped. "Hell, these are blanks."

"Blanks? Why the hell would a person do that, Lee?"

"I don't know, but it was a bad mistake, that's for certain." He set the gun on the seat next to the purse and the camera. Then he got out of the car and stepped over to where Carl lay. The dead man still had hold of the .38 in his right hand, some grass and dirt in the other. It looked like he had been clawing at the ground. Several flies crawled around his wounds and another rested on his lower lip. Bodecker checked the gun. "And this fucker, he didn't fire a shot."

"Either one of them holes he's got in him would account for that," Howser said.

"Wouldn't take much to put Carl down anyway," Bodecker said. He turned his head and spat. "He was about as worthless as they come." He picked up the wallet lying on top of the body and counted fifty-four dollars. He scratched his head. "Well, I guess it wasn't robbery, was it?"

"Any chance Tater Brown could have something to do with this?"

Bodecker's face reddened. "What the hell makes you think that?"

The deputy shrugged. "I don't know. I'm just throwing stuff out. I mean, who else does this kind of shit around here?"

Standing up, Bodecker shook his head. "No, this kind of thing's too out in the open for that slimy cocksucker. If he was the one done it, we wouldn't have come across them this easy. He'd have made sure the maggots got a few days alone with them."

"Yeah, I guess," the deputy said.

"What about the coroner?" Bodecker said.

"He's supposed to be on his way."

Bodecker nodded over at the other deputies. "Have them look around in that cornfield, see if they can find something, then you keep watch for that coroner." He wiped the sweat off his neck with his handkerchief. He waited until Howser walked away, then sat down in the passenger's seat of the station wagon. A camera was lying beside Sandy's purse. The dash was open. Underneath some wadded-up maps were several rolls of film, a box of .38 shells. Glancing around to make sure Howser was still talking to the deputies, Bodecker stuffed the film in his pants pocket, looked through the purse. He found a receipt from a Holiday Inn in Johnson City, Tennessee, dated two nights ago. He thought back to the day he'd seen them at the gas station. Sixteen days ago now, he figured. They had almost made it home.

Eventually he noticed what appeared to be dried vomit in the grass, ants crawling over it. He sat down on the backseat and placed his feet out on the ground, on both sides of the mess. He looked over where his brother-in-law lay in the grass. Whoever got sick was sitting right here in this seat when they did it, Bodecker said to himself. So Carl's standing outside with a gun and Sandy's in the front, and somebody else is in the back. He stared down at the puke for a few more seconds. Carl didn't even get a chance to fire before somebody got three shots off. And sometime in there, probably after the shooting was over, whoever it was got awful shook up. He thought back to the first time he'd killed a man for Tater. He'd nearly gotten sick himself that night. Chances are, then, he thought, whoever done this wasn't used to killing, but the fucker definitely knew how to handle a gun.

Bodecker watched the deputies cross the ditch and start moving slowly through the cornfield, the backs of their shirts dark with sweat. He heard a car coming, turned and saw Howser start walking up the road to meet the coroner. "Goddamn it, girl, what the hell were you doing out here?" he said to Sandy. Reaching across the seat, he hurriedly removed a couple of keys hanging on the same metal ring as the ignition key, put them in his shirt pocket. He heard Howser and the coroner behind him. The doctor stopped when he got close enough to see Sandy in the front seat. "Good Lord," he said.

"I don't think the Lord's got anything to do with this, Benny," Bodecker said. He looked over at the deputy. "Get Willis out here to help you dust for prints before we move the car. Go over that backseat real close."

"What you figure happened?" the coroner asked. He set his black bag on the hood of the car.

"The way it looks to me, Carl got shot by somebody sitting in the back. Then Sandy managed to get one round off with that .22, but, hell, she didn't have a chance. That fucking thing's loaded with blanks. And I think, judging from the place where the bullet came out her, whoever shot her was standing up by that time." He pointed at the ground a few feet from the back door. "Probably right here."

"Blanks?" the coroner said.

Bodecker ignored him. "How long you figure they been dead?"

The coroner got down on one knee and raised Carl's arm up, pressed on the mottled blue and gray skin with his fingers. "Oh, yesterday evening, I'd say. Thereabouts, anyway."

They all stood looking at Sandy silently for a minute or so, then Bodecker turned to the coroner. "You make sure she gets took good care of, okay?"

"Absolutely," Benny said.

"Have Webster's pick her up when you're done. Tell 'em I'll be over later to talk about the arrangements. I'm gonna head back to the office."

"What about the other one?" Benny asked, as Bodecker started to walk away.

The sheriff stopped and spit on the ground, looked over at the fat man. "However you got to work it, Benny, you make sure that one gets a pauper's grave. No marker, no name, no nothing."

50

"LEE," THE DISPATCHER SAID. "Had a call from a Sheriff Thompson in Lewisburg, West Virginia. He wants you to call him back soon as possible." He handed Bodecker a piece of paper with a number scrawled on it.

"Willis, is that a five or a six?"

The dispatcher looked at the paper. "No, that's a nine."

Bodecker shut the door of his office and sat down, opened a desk drawer, and took out a piece of hard candy. After seeing Sandy dead, the first thing he had thought about was a glass of whiskey. He stuck the candy in his mouth and dialed the number. "Sheriff Thompson? This is Lee Bodecker up in Ohio."

"Thanks for calling me back, Sheriff," the man said with a hillbilly drawl. "How you all doing up there?"

"I ain't bragging."

"The reason I called, well, it might not be nothing, but someone shot a man down here yesterday morning sometime, a preacher, and the boy we suspect might have been in on it used to live up in your parts."

"That right? How did he kill this man?"

"Shot him in the head while he was sitting in his car. Held the gun right up to the back of his skull. Made a hell of a mess, but at least he didn't suffer none."

"What kind of gun did he use?"

"Pistol, probably a Luger, one of them German guns. The boy was known to have one. His daddy brought it back from the war."

"That's a nine millimeter, ain't it?"

"That's right."

"What did you say his name is?"

"Didn't say, but the boy's name is Arvin Russell. Middle name's Eugene. His parents both died up around there the way I understand it. I think his daddy might have killed himself. He's been living with his grandmother down here in Coal Creek for maybe the past seven, eight years."

Bodecker frowned, stared across the room at the posters and flyers tacked on the wall. Russell. Russell? How did he know that name? "How old is he?" he asked Thompson.

"Arvin's eighteen. Listen, he ain't a bad sort, I've known him for a long time. And from what I've been hearing, this preacher might have deserved killing. Seems he was messing with young girls. But that still don't make it right, I guess."

"This boy driving?"

"He's got a blue Chevy Bel Air, a '54 model."

"What does he look like?"

"Oh, average build, dark hair, good-looking feller," Thompson said. "Arvin's quiet, but he ain't the type to take no shit, either. And, hell, he might not even be involved in this, but I can't find him right now, and he's the only good lead I got."

"You send us any information you got as far as the tags on the car or whatever, and we'll keep an eye out for him. And how about you letting me know if he shows up back down there, okay?"

"I'll do that."

"One more thing," Bodecker said. "You got a picture of him?"

"Not yet, I don't. I'm sure his grandmother's got some, but she ain't in the mood to cooperate right now. I get one, we'll make sure you get a copy."

By the time Bodecker hung up the phone, it was all coming back to him, the prayer log and those dead animals and that young kid had the pie juice smeared on his face. Arvin Eugene Russell. "I remember you now, boy." He walked over to a big map of the United States on the wall. He found Johnson City and Lewisburg, and traced his finger up through West Virginia and crossed over into Ohio on Route 35 at Point Pleasant. He stopped in the general spot off the highway where Carl and Sandy had been killed. So if it was this Russell boy, they must have met somewhere along in there. But Sandy had told him she was going to Virginia Beach. He studied the map some more. It didn't make sense, them staying in Johnson City. That was surely taking the long way around to get home. And besides that, what the fuck were they doing packing those guns?

He drove over to their apartment with the keys he'd taken from the ring. The smell of rotten garbage hit him when he opened the door. After raising a couple of windows, he looked through the rooms, but didn't find anything out of the ordinary. What the fuck am I looking for anyway? he thought. He sat down on the couch in the living room. Pulling out one of the canisters of film he had sneaked from the glove box, he rolled it around in his hand. He'd been sitting there maybe ten minutes when it finally occurred to him that something wasn't right about the apartment. Going through the rooms again, he couldn't find a single photograph. Why wouldn't Carl have any pictures hanging on the walls or at least lying around? That's all the shutterbug sonofabitch thought about. He started searching again, now in earnest, and soon found a shoe box under the bed, hidden behind some spare blankets.

Later, he sat on the couch staring numbly at a hole in the ceiling where the rain had leaked through. Chunks of plaster lay beneath it in a pile on the braided rug. He thought back to a day in the spring of 1960. By then, he'd been a deputy almost two years, and, because their mother had finally agreed with him to let her quit school, Sandy was working full-time at the Wooden Spoon. From what he could see, the job had done little to bring her out of her shell; she seemed as backward and forlorn as ever. But he'd heard stories about boys coming by at closing time and coaxing her into their cars for a quickie, then dumping her off in the sticks to find her own way home. Every time he stopped by the diner to check on her, he looked for her to announce a bastard on the way. And he guessed she did that day, just not the kind he was figuring on.

It was "All You Can Eat Fish" day. "Be right back," Sandy told him, as she hurried past with another plate piled high with perch for Doc Leedom. "I got something to tell you." The foot doctor came in every Friday and tried to kill himself with fried fish. It was the only time he ever stopped at the diner. All you could eat anything, he told his patients, was the dumbest idea a restaurant owner could ever come up with.

She grabbed the coffeepot, poured Bodecker a cup. "That fat ol' sonofabitch is running my legs off," she whispered.

Bodecker turned and watched the doctor cram a long piece of breaded fish into his mouth and swallow. "Heck, he don't even chew it, does he?"

"And he can do it all goddamn day," she said.

"So what's going on?"

She pushed back a loose lock of hair. "Well, I figured I should tell you before you hear it from someone else."

This was it, he thought, one in the oven, another worry to pour on his ulcer. Probably doesn't even know the daddy's name. "You ain't in trouble, are you?" he said.

"What? You mean pregnant?" She lit a cigarette. "Jesus, Lee. You never give me a break."

"Okay, what is it then?"

She blew a smoke ring over his head and winked. "I got myself engaged."

"You mean to be married?"

"Well, yeah," she said with a little laugh. "What other kind is there?"

"I'll be damned. What's his name?"

"Carl. Carl Henderson."

"Henderson," Bodecker repeated, as he poured some cream in his coffee from a tiny metal pitcher. "He one of them you went to school with? That bunch over off Plug Run?"

"Oh, shit, Lee," she said, "them boys are half retarded, you know that. Carl ain't even from around here. He grew up on the south side of Columbus."

"What's he do? For a living, I mean."

"He's a photographer."

"Oh, so he's got one of those studios?"

She stubbed out the cigarette in the ashtray and shook her head. "Not right now," she said. "A setup like that don't come cheap."

"Well, how does he make his money then?"

She rolled her eyes, let out a sigh. "Don't worry, he gets by."

"In other words, he ain't working."

"I seen his camera and everything."

"Shit, Sandy, Florence has got a camera, but I sure wouldn't call her a photographer." He looked back into the kitchen, where the grill cook was standing at an open refrigerator with his T-shirt pulled up, trying to get cooled off. He couldn't help but wonder if Henry had ever fucked her. People said he was hung like a Shetland pony. "Where in the hell did you meet this guy?"

"Right over there," Sandy said, pointing at a table in the corner.

"How long ago was that?"

"Last week," she said. "Don't worry, Lee. He's a nice guy." Within a month they were married.

Two hours later, he was back at the jail. He had a bottle of whiskey in a brown paper bag. The shoe box of photographs and the rolls of film were in the trunk of his cruiser. He locked the door to his office and poured himself a drink in a coffee cup. It was the first one he'd had in over a year, but he couldn't say that he enjoyed it. Florence called just as he was getting ready to have another. "I heard what happened," she said. "Why didn't you call me?"

"I know I should have."

"So it's true? Sandy's dead?"

"Her and that no-good sonofabitch both."

"My God, it's hard to believe. Weren't they on vacation?"

"I believe Carl was a lot worse than I ever gave him credit for."

"You don't sound right, Lee. Why don't you come on home?"

"I still got some work to do. Might be at it all night, the way things look."

"Any idea who did it?"

"No," he said, looking at the bottle sitting on the desk, "not really."

"Lee?"

"Yeah, Flo."

"You haven't been drinking, have you?"

51

ARVIN SAW THE NEWSPAPER IN THE RACK outside the doughnut shop when he went to get some coffee the next morning. He bought a copy and took it back to his room and read that the local sheriff's sister and husband had been found murdered. They were returning from a vacation in Virginia Beach. There was no mention of a suspect, but there was a photo of Sheriff Lee Bodecker alongside the story. Arvin recognized him as the same man who was on duty the night his father killed himself. Goddamn, he whispered. Hurriedly, he packed his stuff and started out the door. He stopped and went back inside. Taking the Calvary picture down off the wall, he wrapped it in the newspaper and stuck it in his bag.

Arvin began walking west on Main Street. At the edge of town, a logging truck headed for Bainbridge picked him up and dropped him off at the corner of Route 50 and Blaine Highway. On foot, he crossed Paint Creek at Schott's Bridge, and an hour later, he arrived at the edge of Knockemstiff. Except for a couple of new ranch-style houses standing in what had once been a cornfield, everything looked pretty much as he remembered it. He walked a bit farther, and then dropped over the small hill in the middle of the holler. Maude's store still sat on the corner, and behind it was the same camper that had been there eight years ago. He was glad to see it.

The storekeeper was sitting on a stool behind the candy

case when he went inside. It was still the same Hank, just older now, more frazzled around the edges. "Howdy," he said, looking down at Arvin's gym bag.

The boy nodded, set the bag on the concrete floor. He slid the door open on top of the pop case, searched out a bottle of root beer. He opened it and took a long drink.

Hank lit a cigarette and said, "You look like you been traveling."

"Yeah," Arvin said, leaning against the cooler.

"Where you headed?"

"Not sure exactly. There used to be a house on top of the hill behind here some lawyer owned. You know the one I'm talkin' about?"

"Sure, I do. Up on the Mitchell Flats."

"I used to live there." As soon as he said it, Arvin wished he could take it back.

Hank studied him for a moment, then said, "I'll be damned. You're that Russell boy, ain't you?"

"Yeah," Arvin said. "I thought I'd just stop and see the old place again."

"Son, I hate to tell you, but that house burned down four or five year ago. They think some kids did it. Wasn't nobody ever lived there after you and your folks. That lawyer's wife and her buck boyfriend went to prison for killing him, and as far as I know, it's been tied up in court ever since."

A wave of disappointment swept over Arvin. "Is there anything left of it at all?" he asked, trying to keep his voice steady.

"Just the foundation mostly. I think maybe the barn's still there, part of it anyway. Place is all growed up now."

Arvin stared out the big plate-glass window up toward the church while he finished the pop. He thought about the day his father ran the hunter down in the mud. After everything that had happened the last couple of days, it didn't seem like such a good memory now. He laid some saltines on the counter and asked for two slices of bologna and cheese. He bought a pack of Camels and a box of matches and another bottle of pop. "Well," he said, when the storekeeper finished putting the groceries in a sack, "I figure I'll walk on up there anyway. Heck, I come this far. Is it still okay to go up through the woods behind here?"

"Yeah, just cut across Clarence's pasture. He won't say nothing."

Arvin put the sack in his gym bag. From where he stood, he could see the green tin roof of the Wagners' old house. "There a girl named Janey Wagner still live around here?" he asked.

"Janey? No, she had to get married a couple year ago. Lives over in Massieville the last I heard."

The boy nodded and started for the door, then stopped. He turned back and looked at Hank. "I never did get to thank you for that night my dad died," he said. "You was awful good to me, and I want you to know I ain't forgot it."

Hank smiled. Two of his bottom teeth were missing. "You had that pie on your face. Damn Bodecker thought it was blood. Remember that?"

"Yeah, I remember everything about that night."

"I just heard on the radio where his sister got killed."

Arvin reached for the doorknob. "Is that right?"

"I didn't know her, but it probably should have been him instead. He's about as no-good as they come, and him the law in this county."

"Well," the boy said, pushing the door open. "Maybe I'll see you later."

"You come back this evening, we'll sit out by the camper and drink some beer."

"I'll do that."

"Hey, let me ask you something," Hank said. "You ever been to Cincinnati?"

The boy shook his head. "Not yet, but I've heard plenty about it."

52

A FEW MINUTES AFTER BODECKER got off the phone with his wife, Howser came in with a manila envelope that contained the slugs the coroner had dug out of Carl. They were both 9 millimeter. "Same as the one that hit Sandy," the deputy said.

"I figured as much. Just the one shooter."

"So, Willis told me some lawman down in West Virginia called you. Did it happen to have anything to do with this?"

Bodecker glanced over at the map on the wall. He thought about the photographs in the trunk of his car. He needed to get to that boy before anyone else did. "No. Just some bullshit about a preacher. To tell you the truth, I'm really not sure why he wanted to talk to us."

"Well."

"Get any prints off that car?"

Howser shook his head. "Looks like the back was wiped clean. All the others we found belonged to Carl and Sandy."

"Find anything else?"

"Not really. There was a gas receipt from Morehead, Kentucky, under the front seat. Shitload of maps in the glove box. Bunch of junk in the back, pillows, blankets, gas can, that kind of stuff."

Bodecker nodded and rubbed his eyes. "Go on home and get some rest. It looks like right now all we can do is hope that something pops up."

He finished off the fifth of whiskey in his office that night, and woke the next morning on the floor with dry pipes and a sick headache. He could remember that sometime during the night he had dreamed of walking in the woods with the Russell boy and coming upon all those decayed animals. He went into the restroom and washed up, then asked the dispatcher to bring him the newspaper and some coffee and a couple of aspirins. On his way out to the parking lot, Howser caught him and suggested they check the motels and the bus station. Bodecker thought for a moment. Though he wanted to take care of this problem himself, he couldn't be too obvious about it. "That's not a bad idea," Bodecker said. "Go ahead and send Taylor and Caldwell around."

"Who?" Howser said, a frown breaking out on his face.

"Taylor and Caldwell. Just make sure they understand this crazy sonofabitch would just as soon blow their heads off as look at them." He turned and went on out the door before the deputy could protest. As chickenshit as those two were, Bodecker didn't figure they would even get out of their cruiser after hearing that.

He drove to the liquor store, bought a pint of Jack Daniel's. Then he stopped at the White Cow to get a coffee to go. Everybody quit talking when he walked in. As he turned to leave, he thought maybe he should say something, about how they were doing everything possible to catch the killer, but he didn't. He poured some whiskey in his coffee and drove to the old dump on Reub Hill Road. Opening the trunk, he took the shoe box of photographs out and looked through them one more time. He counted twenty-six men. There were at least two hundred different shots, maybe more, bundled together with rubber bands. Setting the box on the ground, he tore a few stained and crinkled pages from a Frederick's of Hollywood catalog he found in the trash pile and stuffed them down in the box. Then he dropped the three film canisters on top and lit a match. Standing there in the hot sun, he drank the rest of his coffee and watched the pictures turn to ashes. When the last of them burned up, he took an Ithaca 37 from the trunk. He checked to make sure the shotgun was loaded and laid it on the backseat. He could smell last night's booze coming out of his skin. He ran a hand over his beard. It was the first morning he'd forgotten to shave since his army days.

When Hank saw the cruiser pull in the gravel lot, he folded the newspaper and set it on the counter. He watched Bodecker tip up a bottle. The last time Hank could recall seeing the sheriff in Knockemstiff was the evening he handed out wormy apples in front of the church to the kids on Halloween when he was running for election. He reached over and turned down his radio. The last few notes of Sonny James's "You're the Only World I Know" ended just as the sheriff came in the screen door. "I was hoping you'd still be around," he said to Hank.

"Why's that?" the storekeeper asked.

"You recall the time that crazy Russell bastard killed himself up in the woods behind here? You had his boy with you that night. Arvin was his name."

"I remember."

"That boy come through here maybe last night or this morning?"

Hank looked down at the counter. "I was sorry to hear about your sister."

"I asked you a question, goddamn it."

"What did he do? Get in some trouble?"

"You might say that," Bodecker said. He grabbed the newspaper off the counter, held the front page up in front of Hank's face.

The storekeeper's brow wrinkled as he read the black headlines once again. "He ain't the one done that, is he?"

Bodecker dropped the paper on the floor and pulled out his

revolver, pointed it at the storekeeper. "I ain't got time to fuck around, you dumb bastard. Have you seen him?"

Hank swallowed and turned his eyes toward the window, watched Talbert Johnson's hot rod slow down as it passed the store. "What you gonna do, shoot me?"

"Don't think I won't," Bodecker said. "After I splatter your thimbleful of brains all over the candy case, I'll put that butcher knife in your hand you got laying over there by your scroungy meat slicer. It'll be an easy self-defense. Judge, the crazy sonofabitch was trying to protect a killer." He cocked the gun. "Do yourself a favor. It's my sister we're talking about."

"Yeah, I seen him," Hank said reluctantly. "He was in here a little while ago. Bought a bottle of pop and some cigarettes."

"What was he driving?"

"I didn't see no car."

"So he was walking?"

"He might have been, I guess."

"Which way did he go when he left here?"

"I don't know," Hank said. "I wasn't paying attention."

"Don't lie to me. What did he have to say?"

Hank looked over at the pop case where the boy had stood and drank the root beer. "He mentioned something about the old house where he used to live, that's all."

Bodecker put the gun back in his holster. "See? That wasn't so hard, was it?" He started out the door. "You'll make a good little rat someday."

Hank watched him get in the cruiser and pull out onto Black Run Road. He placed both hands flat on the counter and bowed his head. Behind him, in a voice faint as a whisper, the radio announcer sent out another heartfelt request.

53

AT THE TOP OF THE FLATS, ARVIN STARTED SOUTH. The brush was thicker now along the edge of the woods, but it took him only a couple of minutes to find the deer path that he and his father had walked on their way to the prayer log. He could see the metal roof of the barn, and he hurried on. The house was gone, just like the storekeeper had said. He set his bag down and walked in where the back door used to be. He continued on through the kitchen and down the hall to the room where his mother had died. He kicked at black cinders and charred pieces of lumber, hoping to find some relic of hers or one of the little treasures he had kept in his bedroom window. But except for a rusty doorknob and his memories, there was nothing left. Some empty beer bottles were arranged in a neat row on one corner of the rock foundation where someone had sat and drank for an evening.

The barn was nothing now but a shell. All the wood siding had been torn off. The roof was rusted through in spots, the red paint faded and peeled away by the weather. Arvin stepped inside out of the sun, and there in a corner lay the feed bucket in which Willard had once carried his precious blood. He moved it over to a spot near the front and used it as a seat while he ate his lunch. He watched a red-tailed hawk make lazy circles in the sky. Then he took out the photograph of the woman with the dead man. Why would people do something like this? And how, he wondered again, did her bullet miss him when she wasn't more than five or six feet away? In the quiet, he could hear his father's voice: "There's a sign here, son. Better pay attention." He put the picture in his pocket and hid the bucket behind a bale of moldy straw. Then he started back across the field.

He found the deer path again and soon arrived at the clearing that Willard had worked so hard on. It was mostly grown over now with snakeroot and wild fern, but the prayer log was still there. Five of the crosses stood as well, streaked a dull red with rust from the nails. The other four lay on the ground, orange-flowered trumpet vines curled around them. His heart caught just for a second when he saw some of the remains of the dog still hanging from the first cross his father had ever raised. He leaned against a tree, thought about the days leading up to his mother's death, how Willard wanted so much for her to live. He would have done anything for her; fuck the blood and the stink and the insects and the heat. Anything, Arvin said to himself. And suddenly he realized, as he stood once again in his father's church, that Willard had needed to go wherever Charlotte went, so that he could keep on looking after her. All these years, Arvin had despised him for what he'd done, as if he didn't give a damn what happened to his boy after she died. Then he thought about the ride back from the cemetery, and Willard's talk about visiting Emma in Coal Creek. It had never occurred to him before, but that was as close as his father could get to telling him that he was leaving, too, and that he was sorry. "Maybe stay for a while," Willard had said that day. "You'll like it there."

He wiped some tears from his eyes and set his gym bag down on top of the log, then walked around and knelt at the dog's cross. He moved away some dead leaves. The skull was half buried in loam, the small hole from the .22 rifle still visible between the empty eye sockets. He found the moldy collar, a small clump of hair still stuck to the leather around the rusty metal buckle. "You were a good dog, Jack," he said. He gathered up all the remains he could find on the ground—the thin ribs, the hipbones, a single paw—and pulled off the brittle pieces still attached to the cross. He laid them gently in a small pile. With the sharp end of a tree branch and his hands, he dug a hole in the moist, black dirt at the foot of the cross. He went down a foot or so, arranged everything carefully in the bottom of the grave. Then he went over to his bag and got the painting of the crucifixion that he'd taken from the motel and hung it on one of the nails in the cross.

Going back to the other side of the log, he knelt down in the place where he had once prayed next to his father. He pulled the Luger out of his jeans and set it on top of the log. The air was thick and dead with the heat and humidity. He looked at Jesus hanging from the cross and closed his eyes. He tried his best to picture God, but his thoughts kept wandering. He finally gave up, found it easier to imagine his parents looking down on him instead. It seemed as if his entire life, everything he'd ever seen or said or done, had led up to this moment: alone at last with the ghosts of his childhood. He began to pray, the first time since his mother had died. "Tell me what to do," he whispered several times. After a minute or so, a sudden gust of wind came down off the hill behind him, and some of the bones still hanging in the trees began to knock together like wind chimes.

54

BODECKER TURNED ONTO THE DIRT LANE that led back to the house where the Russells used to live, his cruiser rocking gently in the ruts. He cocked his revolver and laid it on the seat. He eased slowly over flimsy saplings and tall clumps of horseweeds, coming to a stop about fifty yards from where the house had once stood. He could just make out the top of the rock foundation above the Johnson grass. The little that remained of the barn was another forty yards to the left. Maybe he would buy the property once this fucking mess was over with, he thought. He could build another house, plant an orchard. Let Matthews have the damn job of sheriff. Florence would like that. She was a worrier, that woman. He reached under the seat and got the pint, took a drink. He would have to do something about Tater, but that wouldn't be too difficult.

Then again, the Russell boy might be just the thing he needed to win another election. Someone who would kill a preacher for nailing some young pussy had to have a screw loose, no matter what that hick cop in West Virginia said. It would be easy to make the punk out to be a cold-blooded maniac; and people will vote for a hero every time. He took another hit off the pint and stuck it under the seat. "Better worry about that stuff later," Bodecker said out loud. Right now he had a job to do. Even if he didn't run for office again, he couldn't bear the thought of everyone knowing the truth about Sandy. He couldn't put it into words, what she'd been doing in some of those pictures.

Once out of the car, he holstered his revolver and reached in the rear for the shotgun. He tossed his hat in the front. His stomach was churning from the hangover, and he felt like shit. He flicked the safety off the shotgun and started walking slowly up the driveway. He stopped several times and listened, then moved on. It was quiet, just a few birds chirping. At the barn, he stood in the shade, looked out past the remains of the house. He licked his lips and wished he had another drink. A wasp flew about his head, and he smacked it down with his hand, crushed it with the heel of his boot. After a few minutes, he proceeded across the field, staying close to the tree line. He walked through patches of dry milkweed and nettles and burdock. He tried to recall how far he had followed the boy that night before they came to the path that led to where his daddy had bled out. He looked back toward the barn, but he couldn't remember. He should have brought Howser with him, he thought. That fucker loved to hunt.

He was just beginning to think he must have passed it by when he came upon some trampled-down weeds. His heart revved up just a little, and he wiped the sweat from his eyes. Bending down, he peered past the weeds and brush into the woods, saw the outline of the old deer path just a few feet in. He looked back over his shoulder and saw three black crows swoop low across the field cawing. He ducked under some blackberry brambles and took a few steps, and he was on the trail. Taking a deep breath, he started slowly down the hill, his shotgun at the ready. He could feel himself shaking inside with both fear and excitement, the same as when he'd killed those two men for Tater. He hoped this one would be as easy.

55

THE BREEZE DIED DOWN and the bones stopped tinkling. Arvin heard other things now, small, everyday sounds traveling upward from the holler: a screen door slamming, kids yelling, the drone of a lawn mower. Then the cicadas stopped their high-pitched buzzing just for a moment, and he opened his eyes. Turning his head slightly, he thought he heard a faint noise behind him, a dry leaf cracking under a foot, maybe a soft twig breaking. He couldn't be sure. When the cicadas began again, he grabbed the gun off the log. In a crouch, he made his way around a thicket of wild roses to the left of what remained of the clearing, and started up the hill. He had gone thirty or forty feet when he remembered his gym bag lying next to the prayer log. But by then, it was too late.

"Arvin Russell?" he heard a loud voice call out. He ducked behind a hickory tree and stood up slowly. Drawing in his breath, he glanced around the trunk and saw Bodecker, a shotgun in his hands. At first, he could just see part of the brown shirt and the boots. Then the lawman took a few more steps, and he could make out most of his red face. "Arvin? It's Sheriff Bodecker, son," the sheriff yelled. "Now I ain't here to hurt you, I promise. Just need to ask you some questions." Arvin watched him spit and wipe some sweat out of his eyes. Bodecker moved a few feet farther, and a wood grouse flew out of its hiding spot and across the clearing, its wings beating furiously. Jerking the shotgun up, Bodecker fired, then quickly jacked another shell into the chamber. "Damn, boy, I'm sorry about that," he called out. "Goddamn bird scared me. Come on out now so we can have us a talk." He crept on, stopped at the edge of the brushy clearing. He saw the gym bag on the ground, the framed Jesus hanging on the cross. Maybe this sonofabitch really is nuts, he thought. In the shadowy light of the woods, he could still make out some of the bones hanging from wires. "I figured this might be where you would come. Remember that night you brought me out here? That was an awful thing your daddy did."

Arvin eased the safety off on the Luger and picked up a chunk of dead wood at his feet. He tossed it high through an opening in the branches. When it bounced off a tree below the prayer log, Bodecker fired two more rounds in rapid succession. He jacked another shell into the chamber. Bits of leaf and bark floated through the air. "Goddamn, boy, don't fuck with me," he yelled. He swiveled around, looking wild-eyed in all directions, then moved closer to the log.

Arvin stepped out silently into the path behind him. "Better lay that gun down, Sheriff," the boy said. "I got one pointed right at you."

Bodecker froze in midstep, and then let his foot down slowly. Glancing down at the open gym bag, he saw a copy of this morning's *Meade Gazette*, lying on top of a pair of jeans. His picture on the front page stared back at him. From the sound of the voice, he judged the boy was directly behind him, maybe twenty feet away. He had two shells left in the scattergun. Against a pistol, that was pretty good odds. "Son, you know I can't do that. Hell, that's one of the first rules they teach you in law enforcement. You don't ever give up your weapon."

"I can't help it what they teach you," Arvin said. "Set it on the ground and step away." He could feel his heart pounding against his shirt. All the moisture suddenly seemed sucked out of the air.

"What? So you can kill me like you did my sister and that preacher down in West Virginia?"

Arvin's hand began to tremble when he heard the sheriff mention Teagardin. He thought for a second. "I got a snapshot in my pocket of her hugging on some dead guy. You turn loose of that gun, and I'll show it to you." He saw the lawman's back stiffen, and he tightened his grip on the Luger.

"You little sonofabitch," Bodecker said under his breath. He looked down at his likeness again in the newspaper. It had been taken right after he was elected. Sworn to uphold the law. He almost had to laugh. Then he raised the Ithaca and started to whirl around. The boy fired.

Bodecker's gun went off, the buckshot tearing a ragged hole in the wild roses to Arvin's right. The boy flinched and pulled the trigger again. The sheriff gave out a sharp cry as he dropped the shotgun and fell forward into the leaves. Arvin waited a minute or two, then cautiously approached. Bodecker was lying on his side looking at the ground. One bullet had shattered his wrist, and the other had gone in under his arm. From the looks of it, at least one of his lungs was pierced. With every heaving breath the man took, another spurt of bright red blood soaked the front of his shirt. When Bodecker saw the boy's worn boots step over the Ithaca, he attempted to pull his pistol out of his holster, but Arvin bent down and grabbed hold of it, tossed it a few feet away.

He set the Luger on top of the log and, as gently as he could, pushed Bodecker over onto his back. "I know she was your sister, but look here," Arvin said. He took the photograph out of his wallet and held it for the sheriff to see. "I didn't have no choice. I swear, I begged her to put the gun down." Bodecker looked up at the boy's face, then moved his eyes to Sandy and the dead man she held in her arms. He grimaced and tried to grab the picture with his good arm, but he was too weak to make anything but a halfhearted effort. Then he lay back and began to cough up blood, just like she had.

Though it seemed to Arvin as if hours went by while he listened to the sheriff fight to stay alive, it really took the man only a few minutes to die. There's no way to turn back now, he thought. But he couldn't go on like this, either. He imagined the door to a sad, empty room closing with a faint click, never to be opened again, and that calmed him a little. When he heard Bodecker expel his last, soggy breath, he made a decision. He picked the Luger up and walked around to the hole he had dug for Jack. Getting on his knees in the damp dirt, he rubbed his hand slowly over the gray metal barrel, thought about his father bringing the gun home all those years ago. Then he laid it in the hole alongside the animal's bones. He shoved all the dirt back in the hole with his hands and patted it down flat. With dead leaves and a few branches, he covered all traces of the grave. He took down the picture of the Savior and wrapped it and put it in his gym bag. Maybe someday he'd have a place to hang it. His father would have liked that. He stuck the photograph of Sandy and the two rolls of film in Bodecker's shirt pocket.

Arvin looked around one more time at the moss-covered log and the rotting gray crosses. He would never see this place again; probably never see Emma or Earskell either, for that matter. He turned and started up the deer path. When he came to the top of the hill, he brushed aside a spiderweb and stepped out of the dim woods. The cloudless sky was the deepest blue he'd ever seen, and the field seemed to be blazing with light. It looked as if it went on forever. He began walking north toward Paint Creek. If he hurried, he could be on Route 50 in an hour. If he was lucky, someone would give him a ride.

ACKNOWLEDGMENTS

I am extremely grateful to the following people and organizations, without which this book would not have been possible: Joan Bingham and PEN for the 2009 PEN/Robert Bingham Fellowship; the Ohio Arts Council for a 2010 Individual Excellence Award; Ohio State University for a 2008 Presidential Fellowship; my friend Mick Rothgeb for advice on firearms; Dr. John Gabis for answering my questions about blood; and James E. Talbert at the Greenbrier Historical Society for information about Lewisburg, West Virginia. I owe a special debt of gratitude to my agents and readers; Richard Pine and Nathaniel Jacks at Inkwell Management; and lastly, for his faith, patience, and guidance, I want to thank my editor, Gerry Howard, along with all the other wonderful people at Doubleday.

ALSO BY DONALD RAY POLLOCK

KNOCKEMSTIFF

In this unforgettable work of fiction, Donald Ray Pollock peers into the soul of a tough Midwestern town to reveal the sad, stunted but resilient lives of its residents. Spanning a period from the mid-sixties to the late nineties, the linked stories that comprise *Knockemstiff* feature a cast of recurring characters who are irresistibly, undeniably real. A father pumps his son full of steroids so he can vicariously relive his days as a perpetual runner-up body builder. A psychotic rural recluse comes upon two siblings committing incest and feels compelled to take action. Donald Ray Pollock presents his characters and the sordid goings-on with a stern intelligence, a bracing absence of value judgments, and a refreshingly dark sense of bottom-dog humor.

Fiction

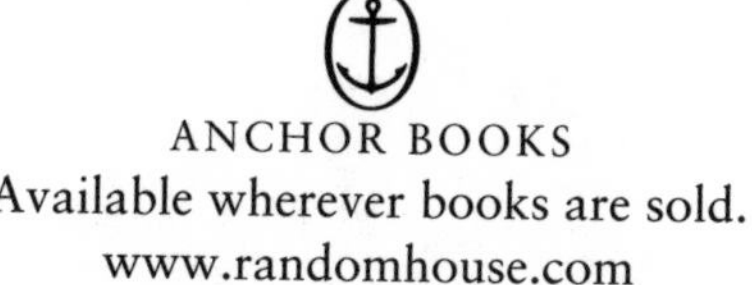

ANCHOR BOOKS
Available wherever books are sold.
www.randomhouse.com